Encyclopedia of Scientific Quantities and Units of Measurements

Volume 2

Dictionary of Scientific Units of Measurement

Including Summary Tables, 2400 entries and Types of Systems of Units

D.S. Dawoud

A.G. Batte

Contents

List of Tables

Preface

I. About the "Encyclopedia of Scientific Quantities and Units of Measurement

The authors are introducing to the reader an "Encyclopedia of Scientific Quantities and Units of Measurements". The encyclopedia consists of three volumes representing together the most comprehensive encyclopedia of Scientific and Engineering quantities and units of measurement. The three volumes of the encyclopedia are:

Volume I-   Dictionary of Scientific and Engineering Quantities.

Volume II -   Dictionary of Scientific Units of Measurements:

Volume III: Tables of Conversion

Volume I and Volume II are dictionaries that give definitions for the entities that form the dictionary. Some rules are considered while arranging the entities. The reader must be aware of the rules to be able to use the dictionary easily. We are going to start this general introduction by presenting such rules.

The "Dictionary of Scientific and Engineering Quantities" has about 1500 entries. The Dictionary of Units of Measurements has about 2500 entries.

II.   About this Volume: Dictionary of Units of Measurements

This dictionary gives the definition for 2504 units. The units include:

- all the units of the International System of Units (S.I.);
- many other units of the metric system used in everyday life or in science, either currently or recently;
- various non-metric scientific units such as the astronomical unit, the electronvolt, and the parsec;
- all the units of the traditional English systems;
- selected traditional units from cultures other than English; and

- Certain measurement terms and notations are not "units of measurement" in a strict sense but which are used much as if they were.

Each entry includes:

- Definition
- Symbol of the unit
- The system of units belongs to
- Conversion factors can be used to convert that unit into other units measuring the same concept.
- Cross references

The dictionary also includes a summary table for more than 1400 of the units. Each entry to the table includes the following:

- Measuring Unit
- Symbol
- System of units
- The physical quantity the unit is measuring
- Corresponding S.I. unit
- Conversion factor, to convert the unit to the corresponding S.I. unit

About The Authors

Bio: Professor Dawoud Shenouda Dawoud

Prof. Dawoud Shenouda Dawoud has a BSc (1965) and MSc (1969) from Cairo University in Communication Engineering. He completed his Ph.D. in Russia in 1973 in the field of Computer hardware, where he succeeded in owning 3 Patents in the field of designing new types of memory, which was the beginning of the FPGAs. In 1984, he was promoted to full Professor at the Egyptian Academy of Science and Technology, National Electronic Research Institute. During the period from 1973 to 1990, he supervised more than 5 PhDs and 15 MSc degrees, all of them focused in the fields of computer and embedded system designs. During the period from 1990-1999, he established the Faculty of Engineering at the University of Botswana. During this period, he supervised 3 PhDs and 7 MSc degrees. In the year 2000, he became Professor of Computer Engineering and Head of the Computer Engineering Department at the University of KwaZulu Natal, Durban, South Africa. For 10 years, he supervised research in the field of Security of Mobile Ad hoc Networks. He supervised 2 PhDs and many MSc degrees in this field and published more than 30 papers. During the same period, he was visiting the National University of Rwanda to run an MSc program in Communication. He supervised about 15 MSc students during these 4 years before moving to the National University of Rwanda in 2010 to become the Dean of the Faculty of Engineering.

In 2011 he moved to Uganda, where he became the Dean of the Faculty of Engineering at the International University of East Africa (IUEA), where he currently remains. During this time, he also served as the Vice Chancellor of IUEA for a period of 3 years.

Across his career, he has published over 200 Journal and Conference papers, as well as books in the fields of computer engineering, microcontroller system design, embedded system design and Security of Mobil Ad hoc Networks.

<h1 style="text-align:center">Bio of: Dr. A.G. Batte</h1>

Arthur Godfrey Batte, originally from Kampala, Uganda, began his educational journey by graduating from Makerere College School in 1998. He continued his academic pursuits by enrolling at Makerere University in 1999, where he successfully earned a B.Sc. in Geology in 2003, followed by an M.Sc. in Geology in 2006.

In 2007, he expanded his knowledge base by obtaining a Master's degree in Geoinformation Science and Earth Observations from the International Institute for Geoinformation Science and Earth Observations I.T.C. in the Netherlands. His quest for knowledge continued, leading him to complete a Ph.D. in Natural Sciences from the University of Frankfurt, Frankfurt am Main, Germany, in 2012.

Arthur Godfrey Batte embarked on a career in academia and research when he joined the Department of Geology and Petroleum Studies at Makerere University in 2008. Over the years, he has been actively involved in teaching various courses in Petroleum Geophysics, Reservoir Geophysics, Remote Sensing, and G.I.S., both at the undergraduate and postgraduate levels. His dedication and expertise in the field led to his progression from a lecturer and researcher at Makerere University from 2012 to 2018 to his current position as a Senior Lecturer and the Head of the Department.

Throughout his career, he has played a significant role in mentoring and supervising graduate students in the fields of geology, petroleum, and geophysics. Arthur Godfrey Batte has made substantial contributions to the scientific community, with a focus on Seismology and Hydrogeology. His research has primarily revolved around using seismic data to gain insights into the Earth's dynamics and internal structure. Additionally, he has actively participated in the review process for numerous peer-reviewed scientific journals and has been engaged in national university curriculum reviews.

Chapter 1

Introduction to Scientific Quantities and Units of Measurement

1.1 UNITS OF MEASUREMENTS

1. Name of the unit

1.1   Units: the names which consist of more than one word are entered with the most common word first. This is usually (but not always) the only substantive in the name.

1.2   Where the name of a unit is spelled in more than one way, the commonest spelling is preferred. A note draws your attention to the alternatives.

1.3   Some names are assigned to more than one unit. The names are separated either by a distinguishing comment in parentheses immediately after the name [e.g., second (of arc), second (of time)] or by numbering their usage.

1.4   Some units have more than one name, which is entered under each unit. A note draws your attention to the other names, and it is so worded that the preferred name is indicated.

1.5   Uppercase is used to write the names of the units. Foreign units (Asian, Russian, Latin American, Middle East, China, etc.) are written in lowercase and pronounced as in the related country.

2. Unit symbol

2.1   If there is only one unit symbol, it is placed immediately after the name of the unit. If there are two or more unit symbols, they are entered under a special subheading, and the order of preference is indicated.

2.2   An unqualified unit symbol conforms to a recommendation of the International Organisation for Standardisation (ISO). (B.S.) next to the unit symbol implies that it is recommended by the relevant British Standard but does not appear in an ISO recommendation. (O) next to the unit symbol implies that it is in common use but has not received formal recognition.

2.3   Alternative unit symbols are sometimes required because otherwise, two units with the same symbol may be used together.

3.   Quantity measured by the unit

3.1   This is entered under its own subheading. In some rare cases where the quantity is not included in Part I (Dictionary of Scientific and Engineering Quantities), an explanation is provided.

3.2   If the quantity measured has several different names, the basic name used as an entry in Part-I (Quantities) is provided: the other names are listed under this entry.

3.3   It should be noted that the term' volume' normally refers to length cubed [e.g., cubic meter, cubic foot] and 'capacity' to other measures [e.g., liter, gallon].

4.   System to which the unit belongs

4.1   This is mentioned directly after the quantity measured by the unit. The systems are summarized in Volume I and given in detail in Volume II. Conversion between the different systems of units is the subject of Volume III

4.2   Some units are characterized by the following descriptions:

     (a) Metric: derived from the S.I. and C.G.S. systems to the power of ten;

     (b) metric-derived: metric, but derived by a value that is not to the power of ten;

     (c) Imperial: derived from the F.P.S. (or a similar) system;

     (d) all

     (e) arbitrary

     (f) traditional

     (g) none

5.   Definition

5.1   A verbal definition is provided in every case except where the unit is a multiple or submultiple of a basic metric or imperial unit.

5.2   A defining equation is provided in all cases except where the verbal definition does not allow it.

5.3   The object of the defining equation of a metric or metric-derived unit is the unit size in terms of the corresponding S.I. (International System of Units) unit. In the former case, it is an exact conversion, whereas in the second case, the exact conversion may or may not be applicable.

5.4   Most of the other defining equations have more than one object. The first object is the unit size in terms of the basic unit of the same system and is, therefore, exact. It should therefore be characterised as a formal definition. The last object is the unit size in terms of the corresponding

S.I. unit, and it may or may not be an exact conversion.

5.5   The defining equation is immediately followed by a reciprocal defining equation. This gives the size of the corresponding S.I. unit in terms of the unit concerned. In many cases, this is not an exact conversion.

5.6   More definitions and equations are provided in Volume III.

5.7   The rule for the number of significant digits is as follows:

(a)   When the conversion is exact (i.e., it may be expressed by a terminating decimal), all the significant digits are included.

(b)   When the conversion is not exact (i.e., the decimal value involved is nonterminating), six significant digits are included.

(c)   When the value is based on a quantity experimentally measured to "x" significant digits, the conversion value is also given to "x" significant digits.

5.8   British Standards often provide full conversion tables [e.g., meter to inch, foot, mile, etc.; and reciprocal values]. Since the exclusive use of S.I. units is becoming very common in both scientific and non-scientific measurements, it is imperative to provide conversion values to and from the S.I. only.

5.9   An extensive table of unit relationships for the more common quantities are given in Table 4.1 of Volume III [e.g., 1 acre = 100 are = 10 square chains = 160 square rod = 0.4047 hectares; etc.],

5.10   Extensive tables of unit relationships based on physical phenomena are given in Volume III.

5.11   If the size of a unit used in the United Kingdom (U.K.) differs from the size of the corresponding unit used in the United States (U.S.), the name and unit symbols are modified by the addition of the letters U.K. and U.S.

5.12   Unit temperature and related temperature scales are included in the dictionary of units (Volume -II). Detailed explanations are provided in a separate section.

Units of paper sizes (A-size, B-size and C-size) have entries in the dictionary. Section 4.5 of Volume III discusses the subjects in more detail.

6.   Notes

6.1   These are numbered and entered under the final subheading.

6.2   A comment 'popularly' means that the usage is common, although it is not found in specialised or scientific works.

6.3   A comment that a unit 'has been called' by another name suggests that the alternative name is no longer used.

7.   Cross references

7.1   Units mentioned in the notes referring to other units are also entered in their correct alphabetical position.

7.2   Units with names that consist of two or more words are only entered under one word of the name (see 1.1) and not under each word

8.   U.S. variations

Although formerly, the sizes of many imperial units were differently defined in the United States from the definitions applied in the United Kingdom, these differences have now been eliminated in all cases except the following:

(a) Units of capacity. In the U.K., the gallon is defined as somewhat arbitrarily by the 1963 Weights and Measures Act. In the U.S., the gallon is defined in terms of the cubic inch.

(b) The hundredweight and the ton have different formal definitions. Where these variations exist, they are clearly pointed out.

9.   Lexicographic conventions

9.1 Unit names

The symbols for the S.I. units are intended to be identical, regardless of the language used, but unit names are ordinary nouns that apply the character set and follow the grammatical rules of the language concerned. Names of units follow the grammatical rules associated with nouns: in English and French, they begin with a lowercase letter (e.g., Newton, hertz, Pascal), even when the symbol for the unit begins with a capital letter. This also applies to "degrees Celsius" since "degree" is the unit. The official British and American spellings for certain S.I. units differ – British English, as well as Australian, Canadian, and New Zealand English, use the spelling *deca*, *metre*, and *litre*, whereas American English uses the spelling *Deka-*, *meter*, and *liter*, respectively.

9.2   Unit symbols and the values of quantities

Although the writing of unit names is language-specific, the writing of unit symbols and the values of quantities is consistent across all languages and therefore, the S.I. Brochure has specific rules in respect to writing them. The guideline produced by the National Institute of Standards and Technology (NIST) clarifies language-specific areas in respect of American English that were left open by the S.I. Brochure but are otherwise identical to the S.I. Brochure.

9.2.1 *General rules*

General rules for writing S.I. units and quantities apply to text that is either handwritten or produced using an automated process:

- The value of a quantity is written as a number followed by a space (representing a multiplication sign) and a unit symbol; e.g., 2.21 kg, 7.3×10^2 m^2, 22 K. This rule explicitly includes the percent sign (%) and the symbol for degrees Celsius (°C). Exceptions are symbols for plane angular degrees, minutes, and seconds (°, ′, and ″), which are placed immediately after the number with no intervening space.

- Symbols are mathematical entities and not abbreviations, and therefore, they do not have an appended period/full stop (.)unless the rules of grammar demand one for some reason, such as denoting the end of a sentence.

- A prefix is part of the unit, and its symbol is prepended to a unit symbol without a separator (e.g., k in km, M in MPa, G in GHz, μ in μg). Compound prefixes are unacceptable. A prefixed unit is atomic in expressions (e.g., km^2 is equivalent to (km)^2).

- Unit symbols are written using Roman (upright) type, regardless of the type used in the surrounding text.

- Symbols for derived units formed by multiplication are connected using a centre dot (·) or a non-breaking space, e.g., N·m or N m.

- Symbols for derived units formed by division are connected using a solidus (/)or given as a negative exponent. E.g., the "metre per second" can be written m/s, m s^{-1}, m·s^{-1}, or m/s. A solidus must not be used more than once in a given expression without parentheses to remove ambiguities; e.g., kg/(m·s^2) and kg·m^{-1}·s^{-2} are acceptable, but kg/m/s^2 is ambiguous and unacceptable.

The lowercase letters (neither "metres" nor "seconds" were named after individuals), the space between the value and the units, and the superscript "2" to denote "squared".

- The first letter of symbols for units derived from the name of a person is written in upper case; otherwise, they are written in lower case. E.g., the unit of pressure is named after Blaise Pascal and therefore, its symbol is written "Pa". However, the symbol for mole is written as "mol". "T" is the symbol for tesla, a measure of magnetic field strength, and "t" is the symbol for tonne, a measure of mass. Since 1979, the litre may exceptionally be written using either an uppercase "L" or a lowercase "l", a decision prompted by the similarity of the lowercase letter "l" to the numeral "1", especially with certain typefaces or English-style handwriting. The American NIST recommends that within the United States, "L" be used rather than "l".

- Symbols do not have a plural form, e.g., 25 kg and not 25 kg.

- Uppercase and lowercase prefixes are not interchangeable. E.g., the quantities 1 mW and 1 M.W. represent two different quantities (milliwatt and megawatt).

- The symbol for the decimal marker is either a point or a comma on the line. In practice, a decimal point is used in most English-speaking countries and most of Asia, and a comma is used in most of Latin America and in continental European countries.

- Spaces should be used as a thousand separator (1 000 000) in contrast to commas or periods (1,000,000 or 1.000.000) to reduce confusion resulting from the variation between these forms in different countries.

- Any line break inside a number, inside a compound unit, or between a number and a unit should be avoided. Where this is not possible, line breaks should coincide with thousand separators.

- Because the value of "billion" and "trillion" varies between languages, the dimensionless terms "ppb" (parts per billion) and "ppt" (parts per trillion) should be avoided. The SI Brochure does not suggest alternatives.

9.2.2 *Printing SI Symbols*

The rules covering the printing of quantities and units are part of ISO 80000-1:2009.

Further rules are specified in respect of the production of text using printing presses, word processors, typewriters, and the like.

1.2   QUANTITIES

10.   Name of the quantity

10.1   Quantities, the names of which consist of more than one word, are entered and preference is given to the most important word. This is usually (but not always) the only substantive in the name.

10.2   Some names are assigned to more than one quantity. The names are separated by numbering their usage.

10.3   Some quantities have more than one name, which is entered under each quantity.

A note draws attention to the other names and is so worded that the preferred name is indicated.

11. Symbol

11.1   If it is only one symbol, then it is placed immediately after the name of the quantity. If there are two or more symbols, then they are entered under a special subheading, and an order of preference is indicated.

11.2   An unqualified symbol conforms to a recommendation of the ISO. (B.S.) succeeding the symbol implies that it is recommended by the relevant British Standard but does not appear in an ISO recommendation. (O) succeeding the symbol implies that it is in common use but has not received formal recognition.

11.3   Alternative symbols are sometimes required because, otherwise, two quantities with the same symbol might appear in the same equation.

12. Definition

A verbal definition is provided, followed by a defining equation. Sometimes an alternative verbal definition and defining equation are also given.

13. Unit of measurement

This is entered first under the subheading 'unit'. For dimensional quantities, only the S.I. unit is given, except where its use has not been approved; then, the commonly used unit is given. For dimensionless quantities which possess units, the recommended unit is given, sometimes with an alternative. A full explanation of the unit is provided under the appropriate entry in Volume II (Measuring Units).

14. Dimensional forms

These are entered directly after the unit. The systems used are discussed in Chapter 1 of this book.

15.   Notes

15.1   These are numbered and entered under the final subheading.

15.2   In the case of an electrical quantity where the rationalised and unrationalised sizes are not equal, a special note marked (U/R) is included. Here, the first equation gives the connection between the two quantities; the second equation gives the definition of the unrationalised quantity (which is distinguished by an asterisk *) that corresponds to the formal definition of the rationalised quantity given previously. An absence of such a note automatically implies that the rationalised and unrationalised quantities are identical.

16. Cross-references

16.1   Quantities mentioned in the notes to other quantities are also entered in their correct alphabetical positions:

16.2   Quantities with names that consist of two or more words are only entered under one word of the name and not under each word.

Chapter 2

Introduction to Systems of Units

2.1 Introduction

Every fundamental formula of physical science can be placed in one of three categories.

Empirical laws

These are laws connecting certain quantities that appear, as a result of observations of the behaviour of the universe, to be true. They can be tested and shown to hold, often by laboratory experiment(s), but they cannot be validated absolutely from theoretical considerations. They are axioms from which it is possible to logically deduce the structure of the branch of science in which they are relevant. One example is Newton's second law of motion: the force F on a body is measured by the rate of change of momentum p it produces, and the change takes place in the direction of the force. This law is generally reduced to the equation.

$$F \propto \frac{dp}{dt}$$

(t = time).

Defining equations

These are equations set up for convenience to connect certain quantities in such a manner as to provide a useful new quantity. Thus, in order to state Newton's second law of motion in the form given above, we define momentum as the product of mass **m** and velocity v:

P $\propto$ mv

(a) Derived relationships

These are relationships between quantities deduced from the imposition of a set of conditions on a physical system. For example, the velocity achieved after a time t by a body that has moved with a uniform acceleration "**a**" **from** a state in which its velocity was u is given by:

$$v \propto u + at$$

The size of each of the *quantities* that occur in all three categories of the formula is expressed as a numerical value together with a *unit*. A *unit* is a particular amount of the physical quantity. For a given physical quantity, there are infinite possibilities for choosing its unit but all of them must be related by purely numerical factors. If the units are chosen in an arbitrary fashion, the constant of proportionality in each equation will take a value that depends on the units themselves, but if they are chosen in a systematic fashion, i.e., they belong to one of the recognized (or unrecognized but possible) systems of units, the constant takes a given fixed value that can be chosen at will. The units of the base physical quantities are called *base units*. The base units can be algebraically combined to form *derived units*. Some of the derived units are assigned special names and symbols. Out of the many possible systems of units, five are very popular: The International System of units (S.I.), the metric (natural) system of units (m, kg, s system), the English units, the U.S. customary systems of units (USCS) and the Gaussian system of units. It has been agreed that the International System of Units, or S.I., will replace all the other systems worldwide. The transition period will be long and complex, and the duality of units is expected to continue for at least a decade after the change is introduced.

After discussing the above mentioned five systems of units, many other systems are mentioned, especially the electrical and magnetic units.

2.2   Types of Systems

Every system can be described as either coherent or non-coherent, but some systems can be grouped under other headings.

2.2.1 Coherent: (or unitary, or 1:1) systems

A system is described as coherent if a quantity of unit size is derived from the combination of fundamental or previously derived units, each being of unit size.

In other words, a system of units is said to be coherent if all of its units are either base units or are derived from the base units without using any numerical factors other than one. The International System of Units (S.I.) is a coherent system. The American customary system of units is not coherent because, for example, the factor 550 is used in defining the unit of power, horsepower (550 foot-pounds per second).

[The SI is coherent. E.g., one unit of force (Newton) is the force experienced by one unit of mass (kilogramme) acted on by one unit of acceleration (meter per second squared).]

2.2.2 Non-coherent systems

A system that does not conform to the condition stated in 2.2(a) is non-coherent.

[The MkgfS system is non-coherent. E.g., one unit of force (kilogramme-force) is the force experienced by one unit of mass (kilogramme) acted on by 9.806 65 units of acceleration (metres per second squared).]

(c) 2.2.3 Gravitational systems

A system is described as gravitational if the size of one of its fundamental units (that of mass or force) depends on the size of g_n, the standard acceleration of free fall. It can be either coherent or non-coherent.

In other words, a system of units is said to be gravitational if its units for length, time, and force are base units that is not defined in terms of other units. Any measurements in mechanics can be expressed in such a system. Gravitational systems are mainly used by engineers.

Gravitational systems contrast with absolute systems. In a gravitational system, the unit of force is a base unit, and the unit of mass is derived from it. In an absolute system, the unit of mass is a base unit, and the unit of force is derived from it.

The system is called "gravitational" because the unit of force is often defined by the effect of gravity on a physical prototype. For example, in the old British gravitational system, the unit for force was the pound force, defined as the force exerted by the prototype pound at a place where the acceleration of gravity is the standard 32.174 feet per second per second. The unit of mass, the slug, was then derived from the pound-force by defining it as that mass that will accelerate at 1 foot per second per second when a 1 pound-force acts upon it.

[The F.S.S. system is a coherent gravitational system. The units of mass (slug) have a size of (g) pounds, where (g) is the numerical value of g_n, the latter being expressed in feet per second squared. The MkgfS system is a non-coherent gravitational system, as indicated in 2(b): = 9.806 65 metres per second squared.]

(d) 2.2.4 Technical systems

A system is described as technical if the definition of the unit of force involves an acceleration equal to that of the standard or local acceleration of free fall. Such a system is thus gravitational and non-coherent. The name must not be regarded as implying that the system is particularly recommended for technical purposes.

[The MkgfS system is a technical system: see 2(b), 2(c).]

(e) 2.2.5 Practical systems

A system is described as practical if all its units are used in practice for standard types of measurements. A practical system is incomplete in that it employs only a selection of units; however, every system has its practical collection of units.

[The term practical has usually been applied to the MKSf1 system whereby the units of basic electrical quantities were defined in terms of experimentally- measured quantities. The Hartree system is also a practical system.]

(f) 2.2.6 Natural systems

A system is described as natural if its units are of a convenient size for the measurement of quantities associated with the atom.
[The Hartree system is a natural system.)

(g) *2.2.7* Rationalised and unrationalised systems

A system is described as rationalised if the empirical laws and derived relationships that define its units are put in a logical, not irrational, form. Thus, relationships that are concerned with circular symmetry have a factor (coefficient) of 2π, and those concerned with spherical symmetry have a factor of 4π. Other relationships do not contain the factor π. A system that does not conform to this condition is termed unrationalised. All systems may be put in a rationalised or unrationalised form, but the problem of rationalisation is normally confined to electrical relationships.

[The SI is made rationalised; the C.G.S. system is normally unrationalised. In the former, the capacitance C of a parallel-plate condenser is given by

$$C = \varepsilon A/d$$

in the latter by

$$C = \varepsilon A/4\pi d$$

(ε = absolute permittivity of the medium between the plates, A = common area of the plates, d = separation of the plates, all the units in each case being those of the corresponding system).]

2.3   Types of Units

(a) *Fundamental (or basic) units*

The sizes of certain units in each system are given formal definitions based as far as possible on naturally occurring conditions and in such a manner as to be experimentally determined to an accuracy limited only by the apparatus and methods applied for their evaluation. These units are, where possible, totally unrelated to one another such that if it were found necessary to change the size or definition of one of the units (as has been done several times in the past), the sizes of the remaining units need not be altered. Such units are referred to as *fundamental.* One important aim is to produce a definitive system in which there are sufficient fundamental units to cover all possible relationships between quantities measured by the system.

The fundamental units normally employed in the various systems have been selected from those of the following quantities:

Length	
mass of force	Only by 2019, the size of the unit of mass has been defined in terms of naturally-occurring conditions.
Time	
Energy	Units of thermal and electrical energy have, in the past, been defined independently of those of mechanical energy.
electric current or resistance	Electric current is now preferred.
Temperature	
luminous	
molar value	The formal definition awaits international consideration.

The units of quantities other than length, mass, time and temperature are not fundamental in the sense that their sizes depend on the sizes of these four, but they are regarded as fundamental for reasons of convenience.

If, as in the case of mass, a certain standard has to be employed, the size of the standard need not be identical to the size of the fundamental unit of a given system.

[The mass standard is the International prototype kilogramme and the fundamental unit of mass in the C.G.S. system is the gramme. 1 gramme = 0.001 kilogramme.]

(b) *Supplementary units*

The sizes of some units can be specified in a totally theoretical manner because the quantities they measure are free from any physical nature (i.e., are dimensionless), being defined in terms of the ratio like physical quantities. These are described as supplementary units and are required in addition to the fundamental units to specify certain derived units. Being dimensionless, they are of identical size in every system. The two supplementary units required are those of plane angle and of solid angle.

(c) *Derived units*

Any unit, the size of which is determined directly or indirectly from the fundamental units of a system by means of an empirical law or defining equation, is described as a derived unit. Indirect determination implies that previously derived units or supplementary units are used instead of (or as well as) the fundamental units.

[The unit of momentum is a derived unit in most systems]

The names of derived units can be classified as follows:

(i)   Certain derived units have special names.

        [In the S.I., the unit of force is called the Newton.]

(ii)   Many derived units have names which are combinations of the fundamental units, the names being indicative of their definitions.

        [In the S.I., the unit of density, defined as mass divided by volume, is called the kilogramme per metre cubed.]

(iii)   Some derived units have names which are combinations of other derived units (if necessary, together with fundamental units).

        [In the S.I., the unit of torque is called the Newton metre; it could also be called the kilogramme metre squared per second squared.]

(d) *Absolute units*

A unit that belongs to a given system is described as absolute in that system if defined in a coherent and/or theoretical manner without reference to experimental determination.

[In the F.S.S. system, the unit of length (foot) is an absolute unit, whereas the unit of mass (slug) is not, since knowledge of its size can only be obtained through an experimental determination of the acceleration of free fall. A kilogramme is an absolute unit of mass in the S.I. but not in the C.G.S. system since, in the latter system, it is not coherent.]

(e) *Arbitrary units*

An arbitrary unit does not belong to any of the recognized systems of units. [The angstrom and the mile are arbitrary units of length. The calorie is an arbitrary unit of heat energy except in the somewhat artificial CGS-thermal system.]

(f) *International units*

A unit is described as international if it is defined with reference to experimental determination but belongs to a coherent system.

[The MKS Ω system originally possessed international units for electrical quantities and, through the unit of power, for non-electrical quantities.]

(g) *Metric and imperial units*

A unit is described as a metric if it belongs to or is derived from the units of the S.I. or C.G.S. (or similar) system, the constant of the defining equation being a multiple or sub-multiple of 10. A unit is described as imperial if it belongs to or is derived from the units of the F.P.S. (or a similar) system, the constant of the defining equation being an arbitrary but conventionally accepted number. A unit common to both systems (e.g., the second) and a supplementary unit (e.g., the radian) is not generally considered either metric or imperial. Other units (those of electricity, etc.) are regarded as metric if they are related in a system by multiples or submultiples of 10. A unit such as the grade (0.01 right angle) may be considered as metric, although it is strictly not part of the metric system.

2.4 Systems of Units

Out of the many possible systems of units (summarized in Table 1.1), five are very popular; The International System of Units SI, the Gaussian units, the Metric (Natural) system of units (m, kg, s system), the English units and the U.S. and the Customary Systems of Units (USCS)

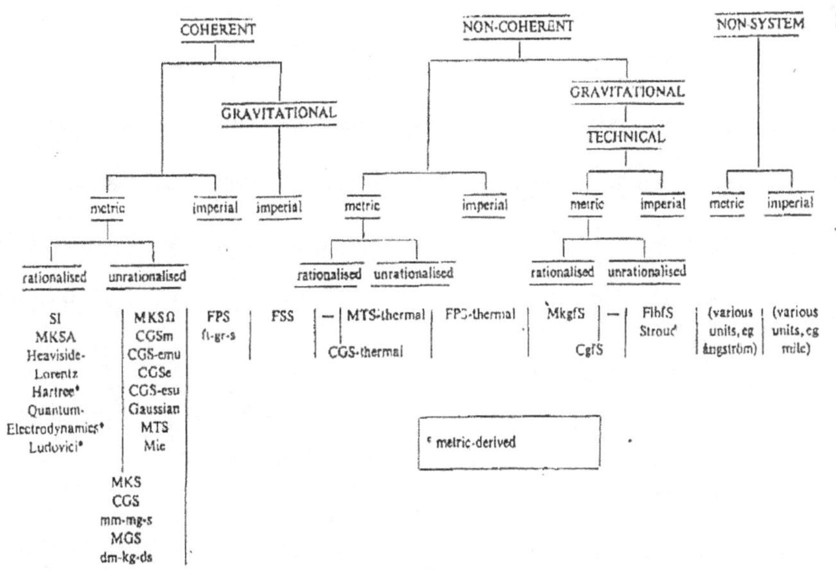

Table 2.1 Some of the Systems of Units

It has been agreed that the International System of Units, or S.I., will replace all the other systems worldwide. The transition period will be long and complex, and the duality of units is expected to continue for at least a decade after the change is introduced.

The SI system is the subject of Chapter 3. Section 2.8 of this chapter includes the summary of the rest of the units of systems.

2.5 Quantity, Unit, Measurement and Standard

2.5.1 Quantity and Units

Weights and measures were among the earliest tools invented by man. Primitive societies needed rudimentary measures for many tasks: constructing dwellings of an appropriate size and shape, fashioning clothing, or bartering food or raw materials.

Man, understandably, turned first to parts of the body and the natural surroundings for measuring instruments. Early Babylonian and Egyptian records and the Bible indicate that length was first measured with the forearm, hand, or finger and that time was measured by the periods of the sun, moon, and other heavenly bodies. When it was necessary to compare the capacities of containers such as gourds or clay, or metal vessels, they were filled with plant seeds which were then counted to measure the volumes. When means for weighing were invented, seeds and stones served as standards. For instance, the "carat," still used as a unit for gems, was derived from the carob seed. Our present knowledge of early weights and measures comes from many sources. Archaeologists have recovered some rather early standards and preserved them in museums. The comparison of the dimensions of buildings with the descriptions of contemporary writers is another source of information. An interesting example of this is the comparison of the dimensions of the Greek Parthenon with the description given by Plutarch, from which a fairly accurate idea of the size of the Attic foot is obtained. In some cases, we presented only plausible theories and sometimes, we selected an interpretation that could be tied to the evidence.

For example, does the fact that the length of the double-cubit of early Babylonia was equal (within two parts per thousand) to the length of the seconds' pendulum at Babylon suggest a scientific knowledge of the pendulum at a very early date, or is it merely a curious coincidence? By studying the evidence given by all available sources and correlating the relevant facts, we obtained some idea of the origin and development of the units. We observed that they have changed more or less gradually with the passing of time in a complex manner because of a great variety of modifying influences. We further observed that the units were modified and grouped into measurement systems: the Babylonian system, the Egyptian system, the Phileterian system of the Ptolemaic age, the Olympic system of Greece, the Roman system, and the British system, to mention only a few. Smith (1763) summarised the above discussions and showed the need for modern units in the following statement:

> *In like manner, there were natural measures of quantity, such as fathoms, cubits, inches, taken from the proportion of the human body, were once in use with every nation. But by a little observation, they found that one man's arm was longer or shorter than another's, and that one was not to be compared with the other, and therefore wise men who attended to these things would endeavor to fix upon some more accurate measure that equal quantities might be of equal values. Their method became absolutely necessary when people came to deal in many commodities, and in great quantities of them.*

Smith, 1763

Smith reports the cultural origin of the traditional units, which were more organic and less logical than the life needed. He/She highlights the need for modern units such as S.I. units.

Before discussing the history of the systems of units, it was imperative to present the statement of Flowers (2004) concerning units and quantities:

> To investigate any physical phenomena, measurements have to be made, communicated to others, and finally recorded in such a way that they will be understandable in the future. To do so, a system of quantities and units were required. Measurement is a comparison process in which the value of a quantity is expressed as the product of a value and a unit; that is,

$$\{quantity\} = \{numerical\ value\} \times \{unit\}$$

> Where the unit is an agreed-upon value of a quantity of the same type. The concept of a quantity such as a length is independent of the associated unit; the length is the same whether it is measured in feet or meters. A standard is a physical realization of the definition, with an agreed-upon value to be used as a reference.

(Flowers,—2004)

2.5.2 Units and Standards

Flowers used in his statement the two words "Units" and "Standard". Before proceeding any further, it is essential to establish the distinction between the terms "units" and "standards".

A unit is a special quantity in terms of which other quantities are expressed. In general, a unit is fixed by definition and is independent of such physical conditions as temperature. Examples: the meter, the litre, the gramme, the yard, the pound, and the gallon.

A standard is a physical realization or representation of a unit. In general, it is not entirely independent of physical conditions but rather a representation of the unit only under specified conditions. For example, a meter standard has a length of one meter when at some definite temperature and is supported in a certain manner. However, if supported in a different manner, it might have to be at a different temperature to have a length of one meter.

2.5.3 Some useful definitions

A **quantity, in the general sense,** is a property ascribed to phenomena, bodies, or substances that can be quantified for or assigned to a particular phenomenon, body, or substance. Examples are mass and electric charge.

A **quantity, in a particular sense,** is a quantifiable or assignable property ascribed to a particular phenomenon, body, or substance. Examples are the mass of the moon and the electric charge of the proton.

A **physical quantity** is a quantity that can be used in the mathematical equations of science and technology.

A **unit** is a particular physical quantity defined and adopted by convention, with which other particular quantities of the same kind are compared to express their value.

The **value of a physical quantity** is the quantitative expression of a particular physical quantity as the product of a number and a unit, the number being its numerical value. Thus, the numerical value of a particular physical quantity depends on the unit in which it is expressed.

For example, the value of the height h_W of the Washington Monument is $h_W = 169$ m $= 555$ ft. Here h_W is the physical quantity, its value expressed in the unit "Meter," unit symbol m, is 169 m, and its numerical value when expressed in meters is 169. However, the value of h_W expressed in the unit "foot," symbol ft, is 555 ft, and its numerical value, when expressed in feet, is 555.

2.6 Meaning of Measurement

Performing a measurement means comparing an unknown physical (or chemical or engineering) quantity with a quantity of the same type taken as a reference using an instrument.

A measurement necessarily involves a reference frame and, therefore, units. Hundreds of years ago, there were numerous numbers of units that had little in common with each other. The first coherent system of units only appeared during the French Revolution: the metric system. This system was internationally ratified by the Metre Convention on 20 May, 1875, a diplomatic treaty that set up the Bureau International des Poids et Mesures (BIPM).

In 1960, during the eleventh Conférence Générale des Poids et Mesures (CGPM), the International System of Units, the S.I., was developed. It now includes two classes of units:

- Base units;
- Derived units.

It suffices to say that once set up, this system may not be fixed. Progress made in science and technology, the new requirements from society, and the needs in terms of increased accuracy, will lead the LNE and all national metrology institutes to continuously improve the practical realisation of all S.I. units. This concern involves the references as well as the means to transfer to users in order to effectively allow the matching of these new needs. Definitions of units sometimes need to be changed and replaced by new definitions.

2.7   Dimensions, Units, Conversion Factors, and Significant Digits

- **Introduction**
  - There is a difference between dimensions and units. A ***dimension*** is a measure of a physical variable (without numerical values), while a ***unit*** is a way to assign a number or measurement to that dimension.
  - For example, length is a *dimension*, but it is measured in *units* of feet (ft) or meters (m).
  - There are three primary unit systems in use today:
    - the ***International System of Units*** (S.I. units, from *Le Systeme International d'Unites*, more commonly simply called ***metric units***)
    - the ***English Engineering System of Units*** (commonly called English units)
    - the ***British Gravitational System of Units*** (B.G.)
  - The latter two are similar, except for the choice of primary mass unit and use of the degree symbol, as discussed below.
  - Note: Besides the three primary units of systems, which will be discussed in detail throughout this book, many others will be introduced, e.g., the Gaussian system.

- **Primary dimensions and units**
  - In total, there are seven *primary dimensions*. Primary (sometimes called *basic*) dimensions are defined as independent or fundamental dimensions from which other dimensions can be derived.
  - The primary dimensions are mass, length, time, temperature, electric current, amount of light, and amount of matter. For most mechanical and thermal science analyses, however, only the first four of these are required. The others will not be of concern to most mechanical engineering applications.
  - In order to assign *numbers* to these primary dimensions, *primary units* must be assigned. These are listed in Table- 1.2 below for the three-unit systems:

Table-2.2   Primary Dimensions and Units

Primary Dimension	Symbol	SI unit	B.G. unit	English unit
Mass	m (sometimes M)	kg (kilogramme)	Slug	L.B.M. (pound-mass)
Length	L (sometimes l)	m (meter)	ft (foot)	ft (foot)
Time	t (sometimes T)	s (second)	s (second)	s (second)
Temperature	T (sometimes $\square$)	K (Kelvin)	^{o}R (degree Rankine)	R (Rankine)
electric current	I (sometimes I)	A (ampere)	A (ampere)	A (ampere)
amount of light (luminous intensity)	C (sometimes I)	c (candela)	c (candela)	c (candela)
amount of matter	n or N (sometimes μ)	mol (mole)	mol (mole)	mol (mole)

  - All other dimensions can be derived as combinations of these seven primary dimensions. These are called *secondary dimensions*, with their corresponding *secondary units*. A few examples are presented in Table- 1.3:

Table – 2.3 Secondary Dimensions and Units

Secondary Dimension	Symbol	SI unit	B.G. unit	English unit
Force	F (sometimes f)	N (Newton = kg·m/s^2)	lbf (pound-force)	lbf (pound-force)
Acceleration	A	m/s^2	ft/s^2	ft/s^2
Pressure	p or P	N/m^2, i.e., Pa (Pascal)	lbf/ft^2 (psf)	lbf/in^2 (psi) (note: 1 ft = 12 in)
Energy	E (sometimes e)	J (Joule = N·m)	ft·lbf (foot-pound)	ft·lbf (foot-pound)
Power	P	W (watt = J/s)	ft·lbf/s	ft·lbf/s

- o Note that there are several other units, both metric and English, in use today. For example, power is often expressed in units of Btu/hr, Btu/s, cal/s, ergs/s, or horsepower, in addition to the standard units of watt and ft·lbf/s. There are *conversion factors* listed in many textbooks to enable conversion from any of these units to any other.

  Note: The secondary dimensions and units will be addressed in detail later

- **Comment about the gravitational conversion constant, g_c**
  - o Some authors define the gravitational conversion constant, g_c, in Newton's second law of motion as **F** = m·**a**/g_c, instead of **F** = m·**a**. where g_c is defined using the English Engineering System of Units as

$$g_c = 32.174 \frac{1bm.ft}{1bf.s^2}$$

and in S.I. units as

$$g_c = 1 \frac{kg.m}{N.s^2}$$

  - o The present authors discourage the use of this constant since it leads to much confusion. Instead, Newton's law should remain in the fundamental form in which it was created, without an artificial constant inserted into the equation, simply for the unit's sake.

- o There has been much confusion (and numerical error!) because of the differences between lbf, lbm, and slug. In our opinion, the use of g_c has complicated and further confused the issue. The following is an attempt to clarify some of this confusion:

- **The relationship between force and mass units**
  - o The relationship between force, mass, and acceleration can be clearly understood using Newton's second law. The following is provided to avoid confusion, especially with English units.
  - o **S.I. units**:

Relationship   Newton's second law, $\mathbf{F} = m\,\mathbf{a}$. [Note: Bold notation indicates a vector.] By definition of the fundamental units, this yields $1\text{ N} = 1\text{ kg}\cdot\text{m/s}^2$.

Conversion

$$\left(\frac{N.s^2}{kg.m}\right)$$

Discussion   The above expression is dimensionless and has a value of 1. Thus, it is the conversion factor with which to multiply or divide any equation to simplify the units.

Example   How much force (in Newton's) is required to accelerate a mass of 13.3 kg at a constant acceleration of 1.20 m/s²?

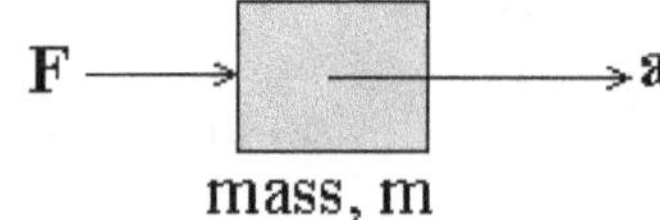

Solution:

$$F_x = m.a_x = (13.3\ kg)\left(1.20\frac{m}{s^2}\right)\left(\frac{N.s^2}{kg.m}\right) = 16.0\ N$$

F_x is the x-component of vector $\mathbf{F}$, and a_x is the x-component of acceleration vector $\mathbf{a}$.

Terminology   It is *not* proper to say that 1.00 kg *equals* 9.81 N, but it *is* proper to say that 1.00 kg *weighs* 9.81 N under standard earth gravity. This is obtained by utilizing Newton's second law with gravitational acceleration, i.e.

$$W = m \cdot g = (1.00 \; kg)\left(9.81 \; \frac{m}{s^2}\right)\left(\frac{N \cdot s^2}{kg \cdot m}\right) = 9.81 \; N$$

.

    o   **English units**:

Relationship	Newton's second law, F = m a. [Note: Bold notation indicates a vector.] By definition of the fundamental units, this yields 1 lbf = 1 slug□ ft/s², or 1 lbf = 32.174 lbm□ ft/s².
Conversion	$\left(\frac{1bf \cdot s^2}{slug \cdot ft}\right)$ or $\left(\frac{1bf \cdot s^2}{32.174 \; ibm \cdot ft}\right)$ or $\left(\frac{slug}{32.174 \; ibm}\right)$
Discussion	The above expressions are dimensionless and each has a value of 1. Thus, any of them can be considered a conversion factor with which to multiply or divide any equation to simplify the units.
Example	How much force (in lbf) is required to accelerate a mass of 13.3 lbm at a constant acceleration of 1.20 ft/s²? F ——→ ▭ ——→ a mass, m Solution: $$F_x = m \cdot a_x = (13.3 \; ibm)\left(1.20 \; \frac{m}{s^2}\right)\left(\frac{1bf \cdot s^2}{32.174 \; ibm \cdot ft}\right) = 0.496 \; ibf$$ F_x is the x-component of vector **F**, and a_x is the x-component of acceleration vector **a**.

<table>
<tr><td>Terminology</td><td>It is not proper to say that one lbm equals one lbf, but it is proper to say that one lbm weighs one lbf under standard earth gravity. This is obtained by utilizing Newton's second law with gravitational acceleration, i.e.,</td></tr>
</table>

$$W = m \cdot g = (1.00\ ibm)\left(32.174\ \frac{ft}{s^2}\right)\left(\frac{ibf \cdot s^2}{32.174\ ibm \cdot ft}\right) = 1.00\ ibf$$

- ***The Principle of Dimensional Homogeneity***

In any equation, each additive term *must* have the same dimensions. In simple terms, you cannot add apples and oranges.

- o Example - The area of a rectangle is the product of its width and its height, A = W. H. The dimensions of both terms in this equation are {length^2}. The equation A = H is clearly wrong, i.e., it is dimensionally inconsistent since the dimensions of the left term are {length^2} while those of the right term are {length}.
- o The Principle of Dimensional Homogeneity is sometimes useful when checking the algebra of a problem solution. Namely, dimensional inconsistency in an equation is a sure sign of an algebraic error!
- o The Principle of Dimensional Homogeneity also extends to *units*. The best way to avoid unit errors is to list the units along with any numbers in an equation. It is better to introduce conversion factors in the form of ratios. In the above example, suppose the width W of the rectangle is 48.0 inches, and the Height H is 2.0 feet. The area A is desired in square feet and is calculated correctly as follows:

A = W H = (48.0 in) (2.0 ft) (1 ft / 12 in) = 8.0 ft^2.

- ***Significant Digits***

Since the proliferation of calculators in the 1970s, the concept of significant digits has been largely ignored. As a result, many students and practicing engineers today present answers to five, six, or more significant digits, even when only two or three digits are significant. Many students, for example, will write out every digit (perhaps eight or ten) that is displayed on their calculators, not minding about how many of those digits are actually meaningful. The present authors encourage all students and engineers to consider significant digits in all written forms of communication - reports, papers, homework, exams, etc. Below is a discussion of the meaning and application of significant digits in engineering.

- o By default, an integer has an *infinite* number of significant digits. For example, the number 43 implies *exactly* 43, just like when counting the number of students in a classroom. Unfortunately, many authors do not follow this convention. It is unclear to the reader how many significant digits there are, especially when dealing with trailing zeroes.
- o The number of significant digits is determined by the overall accuracy of a measurement. For example, suppose the diameter of a pipe is measured to be 2.53 mm. By convention, the measurement is a better estimate when written to the least significant digit. Here, the micrometer is accurate to 0.01 mm, but the exact diameter may fall anywhere between 2.525 and 2.535 mm. In this example, the reading is a better estimate of three significant digits.
- o When considering the number of significant digits, leading zeroes for numbers below unity have no relevance, but zeroes within a value are considered. For example, 0.367 has three significant digits - the leading zero does not count. Note that this same value can be written in exponential notation as 3.67×10^{-1}, where the number of significant digits is more obvious. Consider the value 34.05. The zero here *does* count, so the value has four significant digits.
- o Trailing zeroes are more tricky, especially when not using exponential notation. For example, given a pressure reading of 101,300 Pascals, it is not obvious how many (if any) of the trailing zeroes are significant. Most likely, the pressure gauge is accurate to a hundred Pascals, and therefore, it is more appropriate to write this measurement as 101.3 kPa, avoiding the trailing zeroes altogether. The number of significant digits, in this case, is four. A reading of 101.30 kPa implies that the trailing zero *is* significant and the total number of significant digits is five.

o   If trailing zeroes are significant, there are two ways to indicate this: First, use exponential notation, which clearly indicates the accuracy. For example, if a reading of 1000 is accurate to all four digits, one would write it as 1.000×10^3. Second, one can write "1000." as a numerical value. The decimal point at the end of the number indicates that all three zeroes are significant. It is clear that "1000." represents four significant digits of accuracy. In this same example, if only three digits are significant, one would write the value as 1.00×10^3. If the exponential notation is not desired, but one still wishes to indicate the number of digits, one can write "1000 to three significant digits".

o   Here is an important rule to remember: ***When performing calculations or manipulations of several parameters, the final result is only as accurate as the least accurate parameter in the problem.*** For example, suppose A and B are multiplied to obtain C. If A = 2.3601 (five significant digits), and B = 0.34 (two significant digits), then C = 0.80 (only two digits are significant in the final result). Note that most students are tempted to write C = 0.802434, with six significant digits, since this is what is displayed on a calculator after multiplying these two digits. Let's analyze this simple example carefully. Suppose the exact value of B is 0.33501, which is read by the instrument as 0.34 and A is exactly 2.3601, as measured by a more accurate instrument, C which is equal to A Times B, is read as 0.79066 and written to five significant digits. Note that our first answer, C = 0.80, is off by one digit in the second decimal place. Likewise, if B is 0.34499, read by the instrument as 0.34, the product of A and B would be 0.81421 to five significant digits. Our original answer of 0.80 is again off by one digit in the second decimal place. The main point here is that 0.80 (to two significant digits) is the best we can expect from this multiplication since, to begin with, one of the values had only two significant digits. Another way of looking at this is to say that beyond the first two digits in the answer, the rest of the digits are meaningless or not significant. For example, if one reports what his/her calculator displays, i.e., 2.3601 times 0.34 equals 0.802434, the last four digits are meaningless. As shown above, the final result may fall between 0.79 and 0.81 - any digits beyond the two significant digits are not only meaningless but *misleading* since it implies more accuracy to the reader than is really there.

- o Most electronic instruments are prescribed to only three significant digits. When in doubt, for most engineering analyses, three digits are usually the maximum that can be expected.

- o When writing out intermediate results in a calculation, it is better to record more digits than the number which is significant, as this can avoid round-off errors in subsequent calculations. However, when displaying the final answer, the number of significant digits should be taken into consideration.

2.8   Summary of Some of the Systems of Units

2.8.1 British gravitational system of Units

A system of units used by engineers in the English-speaking world having the same relation to the foot - pound - second system as the meter — kilogramme-force — second system has to the meter - kilogramme - second system. Since engineers deal with forces instead of mass, it's convenient for them to use a system that has as its base units length, time, and force instead of length, time and mass. In the British gravitational system, the three base units are the foot, the second, and the pound-force.

2.8.2 centimeter-gram-second systems of units

The principal systems of units used in scientific work. In the United States, it was abbreviated cgs (no periods); in the rest of the world, C.G.S. The form cm-gm-sec is sometimes encountered.

A cgs system had been recommended by the great German physicist Wilhelm Weber. Its use was firmly established by the endorsement of a committee of the British Association for the Advancement of Science in *1872*, influenced by the equally great J. Clerk Maxwell.

Cgs systems were gradually superseded by meter-kilogramme-second-ampere (MKSA) systems and finally rendered obsolete in *1960* by the CGPM's adoption of S.I., which is an MKSA system. Many cgs units, however, are still in daily use; for example, in the controversy concerning the effect of electromagnetic fields on health, the field strengths have almost always been reported in milligauss.

The mechanical units are the same in all cgs systems. Length, mass, and time, however, are not sufficient to define electric and magnetic quantities; a fourth dimension must be included. The different cgs systems arose from differing choices of the additional dimension. (See: The cgs electrostatic system of units, The cgs electromagnetic system of units)

The cgs electric units were much too small for practical use in engineering, which led to the creation of the International System of Units (not to be confused with S.I.!), which is not a cgs system. All of these systems share certain names, such as volt and ampere, but with different meanings. To avoid confusion, the prefix "ab-" was often added to cgs electromagnetic units (especially by Americans) and "stat-" to cgs electrostatic system units. Many workers did not use the special names but simply referred to, for example, the "esu unit of charge" or the "emu unit of resistance."

Generalized cgs systems

During the transition from cgs to MKSA, it was often necessary to convert data expressed in units in a cgs system to units in MKSA. However, there is no easy way to do this, as the cgs systems are based on three fundamental quantities and the MKSA on four. If a cgs system could be created which had four dimensions and in which each unit in the cgs system corresponded to a unit in the four-dimensional cgs system, and physical quantities had the same numerical values, then values in this "generalized cgs system" could be converted to values in MKSA units by simple conversion factors.

At a meeting in Copenhagen in *1951*, the International Union of Pure and Applied Physics approved the introduction of two such generalized cgs systems (Resolution 5):

- centimeter-gram-second-franklin system of units (see next)
- centimeter-gram-second-biot system of units (see next)

2.8.3 centimeter-gram-second-biot system of units

A four-dimensional generalization of the cgs electromagnetic system of units, approved by the International Union of Pure and Applied Physics at a meeting in Copenhagen in *1951* (Resolution 5), adding to cgs as a fundamental unit what was later called the biot.

2.8.4 centimeter-gram-second electromagnetic system of units

Symbol, emu. The units in this system are formed in a manner similar to that of the cgs electrostatic system of units: the unit of electric current was defined using the law that describes the force between current-carrying wires. To do this, the permeability of free space (the magnetic constant relating the magnetic flux density in a vacuum to the strength of the external magnetic field) was set at 1.

To distinguish cgs electromagnetic units from units in the international system, they were sometimes given the prefix "ab-".

Abampere	Current
Abcoulomb	electric charge
Abfarad	Capacitance
Abhenry	Inductance
Abmho	electric conductance
Abohm	electric resistance
Abvolt	the electric potential difference, electromotive force
Gauss	magnetic flux density
Gilbert	the magnetic potential difference, magneto motive force
maxwell	magnetic flux
oersted	magnetic field strength
Stilb	Illuminance

Note: See the definitions in the dictionary

2.8.5 centimeter-gram-second-franklin system of units

A four-dimensional generalization of the cgs electrostatic system, approved by the International Union of Pure and Applied Physics at a meeting in Copenhagen in *1951* (Resolution 5), added to cgs as a fundamental unit that became known as the Franklin.

2.8.6 centimeter-gram-second Gaussian system of units

Sometimes called the symmetrical system, its only connection with Gauss is the name. The electric units come from the cgs electrostatic system and the magnetic units from the cgs electromagnetic system.

A characteristic of this system is that the velocity of light appears in many of the equations relating to electric and magnetic units. By Maxwell's equations, the product of the permittivity of free space and the permeability of free space is the reciprocal of the speed of light (c). As a result, taking the speed of light in centimeters per second, the ratio between a unit in the cgs electrostatic system and the corresponding unit in the cgs electromagnetic system is c, $\frac{1}{c}$, or some power of c.

2.8.7 centimeter-gram-second electrostatic system of units

Symbol, esu. In this system, an electric unit was provided by describing the size of a charge in terms of a force. If you have ever attracted or repelled with a comb rubbed against your clothing, you have observed a force acting between charged bodies.

Imagine two bodies with electric charges, Q_1 and Q_2, respectively. Coulomb's Inverse Square Law for electrostatic charges describes the force between them:

$$F \propto \frac{Q_1 Q_2}{\varepsilon r^2}$$

Where F is the force, r is the distance (which has to be considerably larger than the bodies themselves), and ε (epsilon) is what is called the permittivity of the medium between the charges.

In the cgs system, force is in dynes. The dyne has the base units.

$$\frac{\text{grams} \times \text{centimeters}}{\text{seconds}^2}$$

So let r be in centimeters. To define the unit of charge in the cgs electrostatic system of units, ε is disposed of by defining its value as equal to 1 for a vacuum. Inserting the other dimensions into Coulomb's law, the base units of the unit of charge are seen to be:

$$\frac{\sqrt{\text{grams} \times \text{centimeters}^3 \times \text{unit of } \varepsilon}}{\text{seconds}}$$

This unit is called the esu unit of charge, the electrostatic unit of charge, or the stat coulomb. All the other esu units are defined in terms of the esu unit of charge and the centimeter, gramme and second. To distinguish cgs electrostatic units from units in the international system, they were sometimes given the prefix "stat-".

Unit	Properties
Statampere	Current
Statvolt	the electric potential difference, electromotive force
Stattesla	magnetic flux density
Statohm	Resistance
Statweber	magnetic flux
Statfarad	Capacitance
Stathenry	Inductance
Statmho	conductance, admittance, susceptance

See the definitions in the dictionary.

In the revision of the S.I. system in *2019,* the CGPM adopted a fixed value for the elementary unit of charge, *e*, and let the value of the magnetic permeability of the vacuum, previously fixed, be determined experimentally. In the cgs electrostatic system, *e* is determined experimentally, and the vacuum magnetic permeability is fixed, which is how it used to be in S.I. The changes made the conversion factors previously used for converting units in the electrostatic cgs system to S.I. units obsolete.

2.8.8 foot-pound-second system of units

A coherent, absolute system of units based on the customary units in English. Major scientific work was done in this system in the *19th century*, but it was gradually eclipsed by various versions of the "metric system."

In this system, a pound is a unit of mass, not weight (weight is a force). The unit of force is the poundal.

Between *1893* and *1959*, in the United States, the foot and pound were defined by reference to the prototypes of the meter and the kilogramme. In the United Kingdom, the foot and pound were based on the British prototype yard and pound and so differed slightly from the American units. The foot-pound-second system employing the values of the British prototypes is also known as the British absolute system of units.

2.8.9 International System of Electrical and Magnetic Units

Note: This system is NOT the current "metric system," known as S.I., the Système International, or the International System of Units.

A practical system of electrical units was defined by the International Electrical Congress in Chicago in *1893*. A "practical" system is one whose units have magnitudes convenient for the purposes for which they are used, which often leads to their being much bigger than the absolute units on which they are ultimately based.

The absolute units on which the International System was based are those of the cgs electromagnetic system. The international ohm is 1,000,000,000 times the size of the cgs unit of resistance, its volt is 100,000,000 times the cgs unit of potential, its farad is $^{1}/_{1,000,000,000}$th of the cgs unit of capacitance, and so on. These multipliers were the same as those of the practical systems that preceded it, and the units were roughly the same size, all tracing their ancestry back to the British Assn. Committee of *1861*.

The International System was, nonetheless, a new system. Since *1884* the ohm (the legal ohm) was the resistance of a column of mercury with a cross sectional area of 1 square centimeter and a length of 106.0 cm, which was—not incidentally—about 1,000,000,000 cgs units of resistance. The *1893* Congress said the international ohm was 1,000,000,000 units of resistance of the cgs electromagnetic system and that it could be represented for practical purposes by a column of mercury 106.3 cm long. The change from 106.0 to 106.3, about a quarter of a percent, was the result of another 9 years of increasingly more sophisticated measurements of the value of the cgs unit of resistance, which enabled the new standard to come within 0.1% of 1,000,000,000 cgs units of resistance. The change in the ohm alone was enough to alter the values of all the other electric units, hence the need for a new name for the system.

The International System was modified by the London Electrical Conference in *1908* and discarded by the CGPM in *1948*. The following units are defined in the dictionary: international ampere, international coulomb and international ohm

2.8.10   meter—kilogramme-force—second systems of units

A metric system is used by engineers, who are much more concerned with force than with mass as such, and so prefer to work in a system with base units of length, **force** and time instead of length, **mass** and time. Abbreviation, m-kgf-s. It has the same relation to the meter-kilogramme-second system as the British Engineering system of units has to the foot-pound-second system. Such systems are often called technical or gravitational systems, and this system is often called the metric technical system.

The unit of force is the kilogramme-force. In Germany and Eastern Europe, it is sometimes called the kilopond.

The unit of mass in the m-kgf-s system is somewhat confused. It was once called the hyl, but unfortunately, that term has been used in two senses:

1) a mass such that a gram-force acting on it will accelerate it 1 meter per second per second, about $9.806\ 65 \times 10^{-3}$ kilogrammes; or

2) a mass such that a kilogramme-force acting on it will accelerate it 1 meter per second per second, about $9.806\ 65$ kilogrammes (the term kilohyle always applies to this second sense).

To avoid confusion, it is best to use the term metric-technical unit of mass (symbol, T.M.E.), which always has the second meaning. It has also been called the metric slug, alluding to the unit of mass in the British gravitational system.

2.8.11 meter-kilogramme-ohm-second system of units

A system of units proposed in *1940* by G. E. M. Jauncey and A. S. Langsdorf was formed by adding the ohm to the M.K.S. system. The reason for the choice of the ohm as the fourth fundamental unit is best described by the proposers themselves:

The problem now is to decide which electric or magnetic unit shall be chosen as the fourth fundamental unit. The practical electric units–the ampere, volt, etc.–are more commonly used than the magnetic units–the Oersted, Gilbert, etc.–and so our choice is limited to the ampere, volt, ohm, coulomb, farad and Henry.

As pointed out in Chapter I, it is desirable in selecting a set of fundamental units that each standard be of such character that it can be deposited in a suitable place for safe keeping and that, no matter what may have been the original specifications for the standard, the standard when once deposited should from then on become the accepted unit. Since it is difficult to think of a coulomb, ampere, or volt being deposited at Sèvres, France, or at the United States Bureau of Standards, our choice is limited to the ohm, farad, and Henry; and of these three, we definitely favor the ohm because when embodied in a resistor it is less destructible and less liable to change than either of the others. A mechanical shock could easily change the inductance of an inductor or the capacitance of a capacitor.

2.8.12   meter-kilogramme-second systems of units

Systems of units that take the meter, kilogramme, and second as their units of length, mass, and time. S.I. is such a system. Units for these three properties are enough to do Newtonian mechanics, a branch (some would say the trunk) of physics. In the United States, abbreviated as mks (no periods); in most of the world M.K.S.

The rise, rationalization, and replacement of M.K.S.

In the *last half of the 19th century*, when the "metric system" was beginning to gain worldwide acceptance, most of the scientific community decided to use a system of units based on the centimeter and gram (see centimeter-gram-second systems). During the same period, because the cgs electric units were much too small for everyday use, a separate system of much larger practical electric units arose. (See International System of Electric and Magnetic Units.)

Shortcomings of the cgs systems

The cgs systems' electric and magnetic units were their undoing. An agreement was never reached on a satisfactory way of reconciling the electric and magnetic units with each other or with the practical units, which made life difficult for anyone who needed to use both electric and magnetic units in the same problem. Further, because some of the units had been defined more than once, by different parties at different times (unit electric flux, for example, or the gauss), there was some confusion about what certain terms meant. Many wanted units that would be numerically equivalent to the practical units, and many objected to the fact that, in their usual form, the cgs systems were not rationalized.

The Giorgi System

One of the critics of the cgs systems was an Italian physicist, Giovanni Giorgi (*1871—1950*), who, as early as *1895,* condemned cgs in a letter to the English magazine *Electrician* (*April 1896*). In *October 1901*, in a talk given before the Italian Electrical Engineering Assn. Giorgi proposed a system that resolved most of the failings of the cgs systems. It used the meter, kilogramme, and second, and in a slightly later revised form, set the permeability of free space at 10^{-7} henry per meter (for the significance of permeability, see centimeter-gram-second systems of units). This choice gave the ampere the same value that it had as a practical unit, and in fact, the value for the permeability of free space is realized through the definition of the ampere. The Giorgi, or MKSA, system gradually caught on over the following decades.

A plenary session of the IEC at Scheveningen-Brussels in *1935* formally and unanimously adopted the Giorgi system, without rationalization, "for fear of producing dissension detrimental to the general acceptance of this system if a vote were taken upon the matter at that time" (from the minutes). It also left to the IPU (what is now the International Union of Pure and Applied Physics) and CIPM the question of what the fourth unit should be.

An insider writing in *1935* described the debate:

"In the E.M.M.U. Committee [the Committee on Electrical and magnetic magnitudes and Units of the International Electrotechnical Commission], a small majority has been in favor of rationalization; in the S.U.N. committee [the Committee on Symbols, units and nomenclature of the International Union for Pure and Applied Physics], a majority has been more definitely against it. It is clear that any attempt to force a decision one way or the other at the present time would divide the mks adherents into two opposing camps, the rationalists and the nonrationalists. It seems desirable, therefore, to avoid the issue and leave each writer free to follow his own choice, until experience may have crystallized opinion in the different countries."

A meeting of Advisory Committee #24 in Torquay in *June 1938* again deferred the rationalization question for future consideration, and voted to name the system "the Giorgi (MKS) system."

In *1950* the IEC decided to increase the value for the permeability of free space by a factor of 4π (the surface area of a sphere of radius 1), thus rationalizing the system. Expressions concerning spheres would contain "4π"; those concerning coils, "2π"; and those dealing with straight wires would not contain π at all. The resulting "rationalized MKSA system," was the direct ancestor of SI. The fourth unit was permeability of free space, originally set at 10^{-7} henry per meter (compare cgs electromagnetic system of units).

Chapter 3

Physical Quantities and SI Units

3.1   Overview

The *International System of Units* (abbreviated as *SI Units* from its French name, Système International d'unités) is an internationally agreed metric system of units of measurement that has been in existence since 1960. The history of the meter and the kilogramme, two of the fundamental units upon which this system is based, is traced back to the French Revolution. The system itself is based on the concept of seven fundamental base units of quantity, from which all other units of quantity can be derived. Following the end of the Second World War, it became increasingly apparent that a worldwide system of measurement was needed to replace the numerous and diverse systems of measurements in use at that time. In 1954, the *10th General Conference on Weights and Measures*, acting on the findings of an earlier study, proposed a system based on six base quantities. The quantities recommended were the *meter, kilogramme, second, ampere, kelvin* and *candela.*

The *General Conference on Weights and Measures* (abbreviated as CGPM from its French title, *Conférence Générale des Poids et Mesures*), which initially took place in 1889, has taken place every few years since 1897 in Sèvres, near Paris. After the 1954 proposals, the conference of 1960 (the 11th CGPM) introduced the new system to the world.

A seventh base unit, the *mole*, was introduced following the 14th CGPM, which took place in 1971. An official description of the system called the *SI Brochure*, first published in 1970 and currently (as of 2019) in its ninth edition, can be downloaded free of charge from the website of the *Bureau International des Poids et Mesures* (BIPM). The brochure is written and maintained by a subcommittee of the *International Committee for Weights and Measures* (abbreviated as CIPM from its French name - *Comité International des Poids et Mesures*). The relevant international standard is *ISO/IEC 80000.*

The role of the BIPM includes the establishment of standards for the principal physical quantities, and the maintenance of international prototypes. It is also responsible for *metrological research* (metrology is the science of measurement), making comparisons of international prototypes for verification purposes, and the calibration of standards. The overall functions of the BIPM are regulated by the CIPM. CIPM is governed by CGPM. The General Conference meets every four years to confirm new standards and resolutions, and to agree on financial, organisational and developmental issues.

3.2   SI base quantities and units

As discussed in section 1.4.1, the value of a physical quantity is usually expressed as the product of a *number* and a *unit*. In the past (and in some cases up until very recently), the *unit* represented a specific example or prototype of the quantity concerned, which was used as a point of reference. The *number* represents the ratio of the value of the quantity to the unit.

As of 2019, all of the base units are now defined with reference to seven "defining" physical constants that include fundamental constants of nature, such as the Planck constant and the speed of light. The most recent changes have been published in the ninth edition of the SI brochure in 2019. Four base units - the *kilogramme, ampere, kelvin* and *mole* were redefined using physical constants. The *second, meter*, and *candela*, that are already defined using physical constants, were subject to corrections.

For example, the *kilogramme* was previously defined with reference to a prototype. The prototype in question was a platinum-iridium cylinder held under tightly controlled conditions in a vault at the BIPM. Identical copies of the prototype are kept under identical conditions located all over the world. A quantity of *two kilogrammes* (2 kg) would have been defined as exactly twice the mass of the prototype or one of its copies. Currently, the SI Brochure of 2019 describes a kilogramme as:

"The kilogramme, symbol kg, is the SI unit of mass. It is defined by taking the fixed numerical value of the Planck constant h to be 6.626 070 15 $\times$ 10^{-34} when expressed in the unit J s. This is equal to kg m^2 s^{-1}, where the meter and the second are defined in terms of c and Δv_{Cs}."

According to the SI Brochure 2019 edition, the seven defining physical constants used to define the SI units:

" . . . are chosen in such a way that any unit of the SI can be written either through a defining constant itself or through products or quotients of defining constants."

The seven defining constants used to define the SI units are:

The unperturbed ground state hyperfine transition frequency of the caesium
133 atom, Δv_{Cs}**, is**   9 192 631 770 Hz
The speed of light in vacuum, c**, is** 299 792 458 m/s
The Planck constant h **is** $6.626\ 070\ 15 \times 10^{-34}$ J s
The elementary charge e **is** $1.602\ 176\ 634 \times 10^{-19}$ C
The Boltzmann constant k **is** $1.380\ 649 \times 10^{-23}$ J/K
The Avogadro constant N_A **is** $6.022\ 140\ 76 \times 10^{23}$ mol^{-1}
The luminous efficacy of monochromatic radiation of frequency 540×10^{12} **Hz,**
K_{cd}**, is** 683 lm/W

Where, according to the SI Brochure, the *hertz, joule, coulomb, lumen,* and *watt,* with unit symbols Hz, J, C, lm, and W, respectively, are related to the units *second, meter, kilogramme, ampere, kelvin, mole,* and *candela,* and with unit symbols s, m, kg, A, K, mol, and cd, respectively, according to Hz = s^{-1}, J = kg m^2 s^{-2}, C = A s, lm = cd m^2 m^{-2} = cd sr, and W = kg m^2 s^{-3}.

There are seven base quantities used in the International System of Units. The seven base quantities and their corresponding units are listed below:

- time (second)

- length (meter)

- mass (kilogramme)

- electric current (ampere)

- thermodynamic temperature (kelvin)

- amount of substance (mole)

- luminous intensity (candela)

These base quantities are assumed to be *independent* of one another. In other words, no base quantity is supposed to be defined in terms of any other base quantity (or quantities). Note, however, that although the base quantities themselves are considered to be independent, their respective *base units* are, in some cases, dependent on one another. The *meter,* for example, is defined as the length of the path travelled by light in a vacuum in a time interval of 1/(299 792 458) of a *second.*

Table 3.1 summarises the base quantities and their units. You may have noticed that an anomaly arises with respect to the *kilogramme* (the unit of *mass*). The kilogramme is the only SI base unit whose name and symbol include a prefix. You should be aware that multiples and submultiples of the kilogramme unit are formed by attaching the appropriate prefix name to the unit name *gram*, and the appropriate prefix symbol to the unit symbol *g (See "SI Prefix latter".* For example, one millionth of a kilogramme is one *milligram* (1 mg), and not one *micro kilogram* (1 μkg).

Table -3.1 SI Base Units

Qty	Sym.	Unit	Unit Sym.	Unit Definition
Time	T	second	S	The duration of 9, 192, 631, 770 periods of radiation corresponding to the transition between the two hyperfine levels of the ground state of the caesium 133 atom
Length	L	meter	M	The length of the path travelled by light in a vacuum during a time interval with a duration of 1/299, 792,458 of a second
Mass	M	kilogramme	Kg	The kilogramme is defined by taking the fixed numerical value of the Planck constant h to be 6.626 070 15 $\times$ 10^{-34} when expressed in the unit J s, which is equal to kg m2 s^{-1}, where the meter and the second are defined in terms of c and Δv_{Cs}. An earlier proposed definition, equivalent to the one above, describes the kilogramme as the mass of a body at rest whose equivalent energy equals the energy of a collection of photons whose frequencies sum to [1.356392489652 $\times$ 10^{50}] hertz.

electric current	*I*	ampere	A	The electric current corresponding to the flow of $1/(1.602\ 176\ 634 \times 10^{-19})$ elementary charges per second
thermodynamic temperature	*T*	kelvin	K	The change of thermodynamic temperature that results in a change of thermal energy kT by $1.380\ 649 \times 10^{-23}$ J
amount of substance	*N*	Mole	Mol	The amount of substance in a system that contains $6.022\ 140\ 76 \times 10^{23}$ specified elementary entities (elementary entities may be atoms, molecules, ions, electrons, other particles or specified groups of such particles)
luminous intensity	I_v	candela	Cd	The luminous intensity, in a given direction, of a source that emits monochromatic radiation of frequency 540×10^{12} hertz and has a radiant intensity in that direction of 1/683 watts per steradian

3.2.1 Dimensions of quantities

As mentioned earlier, each of the derived units of quantity identified by the International System of Units is defined as the product of powers of base units. Each base quantity is considered as having its own *dimension*, which is represented using an uppercase character printed in a sans serif roman font. Derived quantities are considered to have dimensions that can be expressed as products of powers of the dimensions of the base quantities from which they are derived. The dimension of any quantity Q is thus written as:

$$\dim Q = L^{\alpha}\ M^{\beta}\ T^{\lambda}\ I^{\delta}\ \Theta^{\varepsilon}\ N^{\zeta}\ J^{\eta}$$

The uppercase characters L, M, T, I, Θ, N and J (Θ is the upper-case Greek character *Theta*) represent the dimensions of the base quantities *length, mass, time, electric current, thermodynamic temperature, amount of substance* and *luminous intensity* respectively. The superscripted characters are the first seven lowercase characters from the Greek alphabet (*alpha, beta, lambda, delta, epsilon, zeta* and *eta*), which represent integer values called *dimensional exponents*. The dimensional exponents values can be positive, negative or zero. The dimension of a derived quantity essentially conveys the same information about the relationship between derived quantities and base quantities from which they are derived as the SI unit symbol for the derived quantity.

In some cases, all of the dimensional exponents are zero (as is the case where a quantity is defined as the ratio of two quantities of the same kind). Such quantities are known to be *dimensionless*, or of *dimension one*. The coherent derived unit for such a quantity (i.e., the ratio of two identical units) is the number *one*. The same principle applies to quantities that cannot be expressed in terms of base units, such as the *number of molecules*, which is essentially the result of a count. These quantities are also regarded as being dimensionless, or of dimension one. Most dimensionless quantities are simply expressed as numbers. Exceptions include the *radian* and the *steradian*, used to express values of plane angles and solid angles, respectively. Another notable exception is the *decibel*, which is described latter.

3.3   Derived units

The *derived units* of quantity identified by the International System of Units are all defined as *products of powers* of base units. A derived quantity can therefore be expressed in terms of one or more base quantities in the form of an algebraic expression. The derived units, which are products of powers of base units (i.e., those that include no numerical factor other than *one*), are known to be *coherent derived units*. This means that they are purely derived using products or quotients of integer powers of base quantities, and that no numerical factor other than one is involved.

The seven base units and twenty-two coherent derived units of the SI form a *coherent set* of twenty-nine units which are referred to as a *set of coherent SI units*. All other SI units are combinations of some of these twenty-nine units. The word "coherent" in this context means that equations between the numerical values of quantities are exactly in the same form as the corresponding equations between the quantities themselves.

The twenty-two coherent derived units have special names and symbols. Often, the name chosen acknowledges the contribution of a particular scientist. The unit of *force* (the *newton*) is named after *Sir Isaac Newton*, one of the greatest contributors to the field of classical mechanics. The unit of *pressure* (the *pascal*) is named after *Blaise Pascal* for his work in the fields of hydrodynamics and hydrostatics. Table-3.2. below lists some of the coherent derived units. Note that each unit named in the table has its own symbol, but can be defined in terms of other derived units or in terms of the SI base units, as shown in the last two columns. Table-3.2 is rearranged according to the scientific field in which the unit belongs, as shown in Table- 3.3

Table – 3.2 SI Units with Special Names and Symbols

Quantity	Unit	Unit Symbol	Base Units	Other Units
plane angle	Radian	Rad	m/m	-
solid angle	steradian	Sr	m^2/m^2	-
Frequency	Hertz	Hz	s^{-1}	-
Force	Newton	N	$kg\ m\ s^{-2}$	-
pressure, stress	Pascal	Pa	$kg\ m^{-1}\ s^{-2}$	-
energy, work, amount of heat	Joule	J	$kg\ m^2\ s^{-2}$	N m
power, radiant flux	Watt	W	$kg\ m^2\ s^{-3}$	J/s
electric charge, amount of electricity	coulomb	C	A s	-
electric potential difference, electromotive force	Volt	V	$kg\ m^2\ s^{-3}\ A^{-1}$	W/A
Capacitance	Farad	F	$kg^{-1}\ m^{-2}\ s^4\ A^2$	C/V
electric resistance	Ohm	Ω	$kg\ m^2\ s^{-3}\ A^{-2}$	V/A
electric conductance	siemens	S	$kg^{-1}\ m^{-2}\ s^3\ A^2$	A/V
magnetic flux	Weber	Wb	$kg\ m^2\ s^{-2}\ A^{-1}$	V s

magnetic flux density	Tesla	T	kg s^{-2} A^{-1}	Wb/m^2
Inductance	Henry	H	kg m^2 s^{-2} A^{-2}	Wb/A
Celsius temperature	degree Celsius	°C	K	-
luminous flux	Lumen	Lm	cd sr	cd sr
Illuminance	Lux	Lx	cd sr m^{-2}	lm/m^2
activity referred to a radio nuclide	becquerel	Bq	s^{-1}	-
absorbed dose, specific energy (imparted), kerma	Gray	Gy	m^2 s^{-2}	J/kg
dose equivalent, ambient dose equivalent, directional dose equivalent, personal dose equivalent	Sievert	Sv	m^2 s^{-2}	J/kg
catalytic activity	Katal	Kat	mol s^{-1}	-

Table-3.3 SI Units with Special Names divided per category

Quantity	Unit	Symbol	Equals	Definition / Note
Space and time:				
Plane angle	**radian**	**rad**		The plane angle which, when centered in a circle, cuts off an arc whose length is equal to the circle radius.
Solid angle	**steradian**	**sr**		The solid angle which, when centered in a sphere, cuts off a cap whose surface equals that of a square having the radius as a side.
Frequency	**hertz**	**Hz**	1 s^{-1}	[number of events or cycles]/[time].
Mechanics:				
Force	**newton**	**N**	1 kg.m.s^{-2}	[mass].[acceleration].
Pressure	**pascal**	**Pa**	1 N.m^{-2}	[force]/[area]. Also: stress.
Energy	**joule**	**J**	1 N.m	[force].[length]. Also: Work, Heat
Power	**watt**	**W**	1 J.s^{-1}	[energy]/[time]. Also: Radiant flux

Thermodynamics:				
Temperature	**celsius**	^oC	1 K	T [^oC] = T [K] -273.15 (the offset is exact!).
Electromagnetism:				
Charge	**coulomb**	**C**	1 A.s	[current].[time].
Potential	**volt**	**V**	1 W.A^{-1}	[power]/[current]. Only differences are measurable!
Resistance	**ohm**	**Ω**	1 V.A^{-1}	[Δpotential]/[current].
Conductance	**siemens**	**S**	1 A.V^{-1}	[current]/[Δpotential].
Capacitance	**farad**	**F**	1 C.V^{-1}	[charge]/[Δpotential].
Inductance	**henry**	**H**	1 V.s.A^{-1}	[Δpotential]/[rate of change of current].
Magnetic flux	**weber**	**Wb**	1 J.A^{-1}	[energy]/[current].
Magnetic flux density	**tesla**	**T**	1 Wb.m^{-2}	[magnetic flux]/[area]. Also, **magnetic induction**.
Optics:				
Luminous flux	**lumen**	**lm**	1 cd. sr	[luminosity]. [solid angle].
Illuminance	**lux**	**lx**	1 lm.m^{-2}	[luminous flux]/[area].
Convergence	**dioptry**	**dioptry**	1 m^{-1}	Inverse of focal length.
Radioactivity and radiation:				
Activity	**becquerel**	**Bq**	1 s^{-1}	[number of decay events]/[time].
Absorbed dose	**gray**	**Gy**	1 J.kg^{-1}	[energy]/[mass].
Dose equivalent	**sievert**	**Sv**	1 J.kg^{-1}	[energy]/[mass]. Absorbed dose re-normalized by biological effects.
Chemistry:				
Katalytic activity	**katal**	**kat**	1 mol.s^{-1}	[quantity of substance]/[time].

Note that the units for *plane angle* and *solid angle* (the *radian* and *steradian,* respectively) are both derived as the quotient of two identical SI base units. They are thus known to have the unit *one* (1) and are therefore described as *dimensionless units* or *units of dimension one* (the concept of dimension was described above).

Note that the temperature difference of *one degree Celsius* has exactly the same value as the temperature difference of *one kelvin*. The Celsius temperature scale tends to be used for day-to-day non-scientific purposes such as reporting the weather or specifying the temperature at which foodstuffs and medicines should be stored. In this kind of context, it is somewhat more meaningful to a member of the public than the Kelvin temperature scale.

The units in the coherent set can be combined to express the units of other derived quantities. Since this allows a potentially unlimited number of combinations, it was not possible to list all of them here. Table-3.4 lists some examples of derived quantities, together with the corresponding coherent derived units expressed in terms of base units.

Table- 3.4 Coherent Derived Units expressed in terms of Base Units

Qty	Sym.	Unit	Unit Sym.
Area	A	square meter	m^2
Volume	V	cubic meter	m^3
speed, velocity	V	meter per second	$m\ s^{-1}$
Acceleration	A	meter per second squared	$m\ s^{-2}$
Wavenumber	Σ	reciprocal meter	m^{-1}
density, mass density	P	kilogramme per cubic meter	$kg\ m^{-3}$
surface density	ρ_A	kilogramme per square meter	$kg\ m^{-2}$
specific volume	V	cubic meter per kilogramme	$m^3\ kg^{-1}$
current density	J	ampere per square meter	$A\ m^{-2}$
magnetic field strength	H	ampere per meter	$A\ m^{-1}$
amount of substance concentration	C	mole per cubic meter	$mol\ m^{-3}$
mass concentration	ρ, γ	kilogramme per cubic meter	$kg\ m^{-3}$
Luminance	L_v	candela per square meter	$cd\ m^{-2}$

Examples of coherent SI derived units shown in the Table-3.5 are based on a combination of derived units with special names and SI base units. The names and symbols for these units reflect the hybrid nature of these units. As with the units in the previous table, each unit has its own symbol but can be defined in terms of SI base units, as shown in the fourth column of Table- 3.5. The significance of being able to use both special and hybrid symbols in equations can be appreciated when considering the length of some of the base unit expressions.

Table-3.5 SI Derived Units with hybrid Names

Qty	Unit	Unit Symbol	Base Units
dynamic viscosity	pascal second	Pa s	$kg\ m^{-1}\ s^{-1}$
moment of force	newton meter	N m	$kg\ m^2\ s^{-2}$
surface tension	newton per meter	$N\ m^{-1}$	$kg\ s^{-2}$
angular velocity, angular frequency	radian per second	$rad\ s^{-1}$	s^{-1}
angular acceleration	radian per second squared	rad/s^2	s^{-2}
heat flux density, irradiance	watt per square meter	W/m^2	$kg\ s^{-3}$
heat capacity, entropy	joule per kelvin	$J\ K^{-1}$	$kg\ m^2\ s^{-2}\ K^{-1}$
Specific heat capacity, specific entropy	joule per kilogramme kelvin	$J\ K^{-1}\ kg^{-1}$	$m^2\ s^{-2}\ K^{-1}$
specific energy	joule per kilogramme	$J\ kg^{-1}$	$m^2\ s^{-2}$
thermal conductivity	watt per meter kelvin	$W\ m^{-1}\ K^{-1}$	$kg\ m\ s^{-3}\ K^{-1}$
energy density	joule per cubic meter	$J\ m^{-3}$	$kg\ m^{-1}\ s^{-2}$
electric field strength	volt per meter	$V\ m^{-1}$	$kg\ m\ s^{-3}\ A^{-1}$
electric charge density	coulomb per cubic meter	$C\ m^{-3}$	$A\ s\ m^{-3}$
surface charge density	coulomb per square meter	$C\ m^{-2}$	$A\ s\ m^{-2}$
electric flux density, electric displacement	coulomb per square meter	$C\ m^{-2}$	$A\ s\ m^{-2}$
Permittivity	farad per meter	$F\ m^{-1}$	$kg^{-1}\ m^{-3}\ s^4\ A^2$
Permeability	henry per meter	$H\ m^{-1}$	$kg\ m\ s^{-2}\ A^{-2}$
molar energy	joule per mole	$J\ mol^{-1}$	$kg\ m^2\ s^{-2}\ mol^{-1}$

molar entropy, molar heat capacity	joule per mole kelvin	$J\ K^{-1}\ mol^{-1}$	$kg\ m^2\ s^{-2}\ mol^{-1}\ K^{-1}$
exposure (x- and γ-rays)	coulomb per kilogramme	$C\ kg^{-1}$	$A\ s\ kg^{-1}$
absorbed dose rate	gray per second	$Gy\ s^{-1}$	$m^2\ s^{-3}$
radiant intensity	watt per steradian	$W\ sr^{-1}$	$kg\ m^2\ s^{-3}$
Radiance	watt per square meter steradian	$W\ sr^{-1}\ m^{-2}$	$kg\ s^{-3}$
catalytic activity concentration	katal per cubic meter	$kat\ m^{-3}$	$mol\ s^{-1}\ m^{-3}$

3.3.1   Other Derived units used in Mechanics:

In Table-3.6, we listed the SI derived units per category. Apart from the derived units used in Mechanics given in the table, there are other units used in mechanics, called **derived units**, which are expressed in terms of the base units of meter, second, and kilogram. The next table shows such derived units in mechanics.

Table – 3.6 Principal Units used in Mechanics

Quantity	International System (SI)			U.S. Customary System (USCS)		
	Unit	Symbol	Formula	Unit	Symbol	Formula
Acceleration (angular)	radian per second squared		rad/s^2	radian per second squared		rad/s^2
Acceleration (linear)	meter per second squared		m/s^2	foot per second squared		ft/s^2
Area	square meter		m^2	square foot		ft^2
Density (mass) (Specific mass)	kilogramme per cubic meter		kg/m^3	slug per cubic foot		$slug/ft^3$

Quantity						
Density (weight) (Specific weight)	newton per cubic meter		N/m^3	pound per cubic foot	pcf	lb/ft^3
Energy; work	Joule	J	N.m	foot-pound		ft-lb
Force	Newton	N	$kg.m/s^2$	Pound	lb	(base unit)
Force per unit length (Intensity of force)	newton per meter		N/m	pound per foot		lb/ft
Frequency	Hertz	Hz	s^{-1}	Hertz	Hz	s1
Length	Meter	m	(base unit)	Foot	ft	(base unit)
Mass	Kilogramme	Kg	(base unit)	Slug		$lb\text{-}s^2/ft$
Moment of a force; torque	newton meter		N.m	pound-foot		lb-ft
Moment of inertia (area)	meter to fourth power		m^4	inch to fourth power		$in.^4$
Moment of inertia (mass)	kilogramme meter squared		$kg.m^2$	slug foot squared		$slug\text{-}ft^2$
Power	Watt	W	J/s (N.m/s)	foot-pound per second		ft-lb/s
Pressure	Pascal	Pa	N/m^2	pound per square foot	psf	lb/ft^2
Section modulus	meter to third power		m^3	inch to third power		$in.^3$
Stress	Pascal	Pa	N/m^2	pound per square inch	psi	$lb/in.^2$

Time	Second	S	(base unit)	Second	s	(base unit)
Velocity (angular)	radian per second		rad/s	radian per second		rad/s
Velocity (linear)	meter per second		m/s	foot per second	fps	ft/s
Volume (liquids)	Liter	L	$10^{-3}m^3$	Gallon	gal.	231 in.^{3}
Volume (solids)	cubic meter		m^3	cubic foot	cf	ft^3

Notes: 1 joule (J) = 1 newton meter (N.m) = 1 watt second (Ws)

1 hertz (Hz) = 1 cycle per second (cps) or 1 revolution per second (rev/s)

1 watt (W) = 1 joule per second (J/s) = 1 newton meter per second (Nm/s)

1 pascal (Pa) = 1 newton per meter squared (N/m^2)

1 liter (L) = 0.001 cubic meter (m^3) = 1000 cubic centimeters (cm^3)

3.3.2   Derived Units per Category

- ## ELECTRICITY AND MAGNETISM

  Current intensity: The ampere (A)

the potential difference, U:	**volt (V = W/A)**
electrical capacitance, C:	farad (F = C/V)
Electrical resistance, R:	ohm (Ω = V/A)
inductance, L:	henri (H = Wb/A)
quantity of electricity, Q:	coulomb (C = A.s)
power, P:	watt (W = J/s)
Energy, W:	joule (J = N.m)
Magnetic induction, B:	tesla (T = Wb/m2)
Electric field, E:	volt per meter (V/m)
Magnetic field strength, H:	ampère per meter (A/m)

Electric conductance, G:	siemens (S = A/V)
Attenuation, η:	decibel (dB)

- **MASS AND RELATED QUANTITIES**

The mass: the kilogramme (kg)

density: ρ	**kg.m^{-3}**
volume: V	m^3
force: F	newton (N)
torque: M	N.m
pressure: p	pascal (Pa)
dynamic viscosity: η	Pa.s
kinematic viscosity: υ	m^2.s^{-1}
acoustic pressure: p	pascal (Pa)
dynamic volume: v	m^3
mass flow-rate: qm	kg.s^{-1}
volume flow-rate: qv	m^3.s^{-1}
air flow-rate: V	m.s^{-1}

- **LENGTH AND DIMENSIONAL QUANTITIES**

Length: the meter (m)

wavelength: λ	**meter (m)**
length of material standards: L	meter (m)
plane angle: α	radian (rad)
form measurement:	meter (m)

- **RADIOMETRY – PHOTOMETRY**

Photometry

Luminous intensity: the candela (cd) (m)

luminous flux: Φ	**lumen (lm)**
illuminance: E	lux (lx)
luminance: L	cd.m^{-2}

Radiometry of detectors

spectral responsivity: $S(\lambda)$	A.W^{-1}

Radiometry of sources

energy flow: Φ_e	**watt (W)**
radiance: L_e	W.m^{-2}.sr^{-1}
irradiance: E_e	W.m^{-2}
laser source power: P	watt (W)
laser source energy: Q	joule (J)

Radiometry of materials

regular spectral transmittance: $t(\Phi)$	flux ratio
diffuse spectral reflectance: $R(\lambda)$	flux ratio

Fibre optics

energy flow: P	**watt (W)**
wavelength: λ	meter (m)
propagation time: t	second (s)
fibre length	meter (m)
linear attenuation factor:	dB.m^{-1}

Reflectance	dB
detector (or fibre) passband	hertz (Hz) (ou Hz.m^{-1})

• TEMPERATURE AND THERMAL QUANTITIES

Thermometry and radiation thermometry

temperature in the ITS-90 or in the PLTS-2000: T	kelvin (K)
or t	degree Celsius (°C)

Metrology of thermal quantities

thermal conductivity: $\lambda = \alpha.\rho.C_p$	(ρ = density)	W.m^{-1}.K^{-1}
thermal diffusivity: $\alpha = \lambda/\rho.C_p$	(ρ = density)	m^2.s^{-1}
specific heat capacity: $C_p = (\partial H/\partial T)_p$	(H = enthalpy)	J.kg^{-1}.K^{-1}
spectral directional emissivity: ε_λ		dimensionless ratio
normal spectral emissivity: ε_λ		dimensionless ratio
total hemispherical emissivity: ε_λ		dimensionless ratio

Hygrometry

Temperature	dew point: T_d frost point: T_f	degree Celsius (°C)
l'humidité relative	with respect to water: U_w with respect to ice: U_i	percentage (%)

• AMOUNT OF SUBSTANCE - CHEMICAL ANALYSIS

The two main SI units used to express the amount of substance are the mole and the kilogramme. From the definition of the mole (amount of substance of a system which contains as many elementary entities as there are atoms in 0,012 kilogramme of carbon 12), there is a ratio between these two main SI units and consequently, they are both used. More precisely, the measurement of an amount of substance is expressed either in a mole or in kilogramme, or as concentrations (ratio of two quantities: mass/mass, mole/mole, mole /mass, etc.).

- **IONIZING RADIATION**

Radioactivity

activity: A	**Bq**
activity per mass unit: A_m	Bq.kg^{-1}
activity per volume unit: A_v	Bq.m^{-3}
emission rate: $\dot{N}$	s^{-1}
Emission rate per solid angle unit:	s^{-1}.sr^{-1}
neutron fluence rate: $\dot{\phi}$	m^{-2}.s^{-1}
with Bq: Becquerel	

Dosimetry: (photons, electrons, protons)

air kerma normal: $\dot{k}_n$	**Gy.m^2**
air kerma rate: $\dot{K}_{air}$	Gy.s^{-1}
absorbed dose rate to water: $\dot{D}_{water}$	Gy.s^{-1}
absorbed dose rate to graphite: $\dot{D}_g$	Gy.s^{-1}
absorbed dose rate to tissure: $\dot{D}_{tissus}$	Gy.s^{-1}
directional dose equivalent rate: $\dot{H}'(0,07 ; \alpha)$	Sv.s^{-1}
ambient dose equivalent rate: $\dot{H}^*(10)$	Sv.s^{-1}
with: Gy = gray, Sv = Sievert	

- **NEUTRON DOSIMETRY**

neutron fluence rate: $\dot{\phi}$	**m^2.s^{-1}**
kerma rate to tissue: $\dot{K}_{tissus}$	Gy.s^{-1}

ambient dose equivalent rate: $\dot{H}^{*}(10)$	Sv.s^{-1}
individual dose equivalent rate: $\dot{H}_{\mathrm{p}}(d)$	Sv.s^{-1}

- ## TIME AND FREQUENCY

Time: the second (s)

frequency: υ	**hertz (Hz)**
time interval:	second (s)
phase fluctuation spectral density:	(dBc/Hz)
rotation speed	(tr/min)

- ## DIMENSIONLESS DERIVED UNITS

Plane angle	**radian (rad) = m·m^{-1}**
Solid steradian angle	stéradian (sr) = m^{2}·m^{-2}

3.4 Non-SI units accepted for use with the SI units

The units detailed in the next tables are accepted for use as an International System of Units for a variety of reasons. Many are still in use. Some are required for the interpretation of scientific texts of historical importance, whereas some are used in specialised areas like medicine. The *hectare*, for example, is still commonly used to express land area. The use of the equivalent SI units is preferred for modern scientific texts. Wherever references are made to non-SI units, they should be cross referenced with their equivalent SI units. For each of the units listed in Table -3.7, an equivalent definition in terms of SI units is also given. Most of the units listed are commonly used and are likely to be so in the foreseeable future.

Note that in most cases, it is recommended that fractional values for plane angles expressed in degrees should be expressed using decimal fractions rather than minutes and seconds. Exceptions include navigation and surveying (due to the fact that one minute of latitude on the Earth's surface corresponds to approximately one nautical mile) and astronomy. In the field of astronomy, very small angles are significant due to the enormous distances involved. It is, therefore, convenient for astronomers to use a unit of measurement that can represent very small differences in angle in a meaningful way. Very small angles can be represented in terms of *arcseconds, microarcseconds* and *picoarcseconds*.

Table – 3.7 Non-SI Units still in widespread use

Qty	Unit	Unit Symbol	SI Units
Time	Minute	Min	1 min = 60 s
Time	Hour	H	1 h = 60 min = 3600 s
Time	Day	D	1 d = 24 h = 86 400 s
Length	astronomical unit	Ua	1 ua = 1.495 978 706 91 (6) × 10^{11} m
plane and phase angle	Degree	°	1° = (π/180) rad
plane and phase angle	Minute	′	1′ = (1/60)° = (π/10 800) rad
plane and phase angle	Second	″	1″ = (1/60)′ = (π/648 000) rad
Area	Hectare	Ha	1 ha = 1 hm^2 = 10^4 m^2
Volume	Litre	L or l	1L = 1 dm^3 = 10^3 cm^3 = 10^{-3} m^3
Mass	Tonne	T	1 t = 10^3 kg
Mass	Dalton	Da	1 Da = 1.660 539 040 (20) × 10^{-27} kg
Energy	Electron volt	eV	1 eV = 1.602 176 634 × 10^{-19} J
logarithmic ratio	Neper	Np	-
logarithmic ratio	Bel	B	-
logarithmic ratio	Decibel	dB	-

Table-3.8 Accepted non-SI units with experimental values.

Note: For the most recent values of these constantly improving units, see Constants of Physics.

Unit	Of	Symbol	Equals	Note
Electron volt	energy	**eV**	$1.60217733(49).10^{-19}$ J	Energy to move an electron across a potential difference of 1 V.
Astronomical unit	length	**au, AU, ua**	$1.49597870(30).10^{+11}$ m	Mean Earth-to-Sun distance. Also denoted as **ua**.
Atomic mass unit	mass	**u**	$1.6605402(10).10^{-27}$ kg	1/12 of the rest mass of an unbound ^{12}C atom in ground state.

Table-3.9. Units deprecated by the SI which are currently still in use in most countries

Unit	Of	Symbol	Equals	Note
Nautical mile	length	**mile**	1852 m	
Knot	velocity	**knot**	1 mile.h^{-1}	A nautical unit.
Are	area	**are**	100 m^2	
Hectare	area	**ha**	100 are	10000 m^2
Bar	pressure	**bar**	100000 Pa	Almost 1 atm = 101325 Pa (an obsolete unit)
Calory	energy	**cal**	4.1868 J	Note: the conversion factor is fixed by convention.
Ångström	length	**Å**	10^{-10} m	Used in atomic and molecular physics.
Barn	area	**b**	10^{-28} m^2	Used in particle physics (collision cross-sections).
Radioactivity and radiation:				
Curie	Radioactivity	**b**	$3.7*10^{+10}$ Bq	Note: the conversion factor is fixed by convention.

Röntgen	Radiation dose	**R**	0.000258 Ci.kg^{-1}	Note: the conversion factor is fixed by convention.
Rad	Radiation dose	**rad**	0.01 Gy	
Rem	Equivalent dose	**rem**	0.01 Sv	

Table -3.10 Additional Units commonly used

SI and Metric Units	
1 gal = 1 centimeter per second squared (cm/s^2) for example, g = 981 gals)	1 centimeter (cm) = 10^{-2} meters (m)
1 are (a) = 100 square meters (m^2)	1 cubic centimeter (cm^3) = 1 milliliter (mL)
1 hectare (ha) = 10,000 square meters (m^2)	1 micron = 1 micrometer (μm)= 10^{-6} meters (m)
1 erg = 10^{-7} joules (J)	1 gram (g) = 10^{-3} kilogrammes (kg)
1 kilowatt-hour (kWh) = 3.6 megajoules (MJ)	1 metric ton (t) = 1 megagram (Mg) = 1000 kilogrammes (kg)
1 dyne = 10^{-5} newtons (N)	1 watt (W) = 10^7 ergs per second (erg/s)
1 kilogram-force (kgf) = 1 kilopond (kp) = 9.80665 newtons (N)	1 dyne per square centimeter (dyne/cm^2) = 10^{-1} pascals (Pa)
	1 bar = 10^5 pascals (Pa)
	1 stere = 1 cubic meter (m^3)
USCS and Imperial Units	
1 kilowatt-hour (kWh) = 2,655,220 foot-pounds (ft-lb)	1 kilowatt (kW) =
1 British thermal unit (Btu) = 778.171 foot-pounds (ft-lb)	= 737.562 foot-pounds per second (ft-lb/s)
	= 1.34102 horsepower (hp)
1 kip (k) = 1000 pounds (lb)	1 pound per square inch (psi)
1 ounce (oz) = 1/16 pound (lb)	= 144 pounds per square foot (psf)
1 ton = 2000 pounds (lb)	1 revolution per minute (rpm)
	= 2π/60 radians per second (rad/s)

1 Imperial ton (or long ton) = 2240 pounds (lb)	1 mile per hour (mph)
1 poundal (pdl) = 0.0310810 pounds (lb)	= 22/15 feet per second (fps)
= 0.138255 newtons (N)	1 gallon (gal.) = 231 cubic inches (in.^{3})
1 inch (in.) = 1/12 foot (ft)	1 quart (qt) = 2 pints = 1/4 gallon (gal.)
1 mil = 0.001 inch (in.)	1 cubic foot (cf) = 576/77 gallons = 7.48052 gallons (gal.)
1 yard (yd) = 3 feet (ft)	1 Imperial gallon = 277.420 cubic inches (in.^{3})
1 mile = 5280 feet (ft)	
1 horsepower (hp) = 550 foot-pounds per second (ft-lb/s)	

Notes: 1.   In Chapter 3, a list of over 1600 units is given

     2.   Definitions for these units are provided in Chapter -4, Dictionary of Scientific Units.

3.5   Relationships between SI derived units with special names and symbols and SI base units

Figure 3.1 shows how the twenty-two (22) SI derived units with special names and symbols are related to the seven SI base units. In the first column, the symbols of the SI base units are shown in rectangles, together with the name of the unit shown at the upper left corner of the rectangle. The name of the associated base quantity is written in italics below the rectangle. In the third column, the symbols of the derived units with special names are shown in solid circles, together with the name of the unit shown at the upper left of the circle. The name of the associated derived quantity is written in italics below the circle, and an expression for the derived unit in terms of other units is shown in parenthesis at the upper right. In the second column are those derived units without special names [the cubic meter (m^3) accepted] that are used in the derivation of the derived units with special names. In the figure, the derivation of each derived unit is indicated by arrows that bring in units in the numerator (solid lines) and units in the denominator (broken lines), as appropriate.

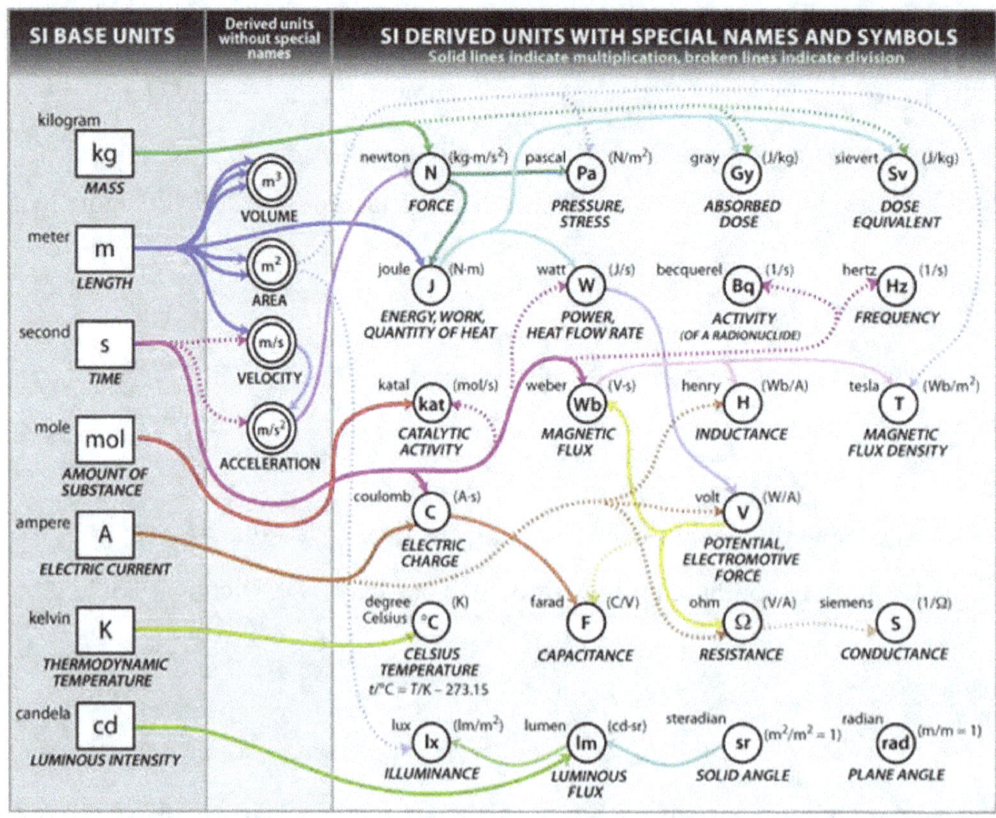

Figure 3.1: Relationships between SI derived units with special names and symbols and SI base units.

(Source: NIST, National Institute of Science and Technology, USA)

Two SI derived units with special names and symbols, i.e., the radian (symbol rad) and the steradian (symbol sr) (bottom of the third column of the figure), are drawn without any relationships to SI base units -- either direct or through other SI-derived units. This is because, in the SI, the quantities plane angle and solid angle are defined in such a way that their dimension is 1 -- they are the so-called dimensionless quantities. This means that the coherent SI derived unit for each of these quantities is the number 1. Plane angle is expressed as the ratio of two lengths, and solid angle as the ratio of area and the square of a length. The SI derived unit for plane angle is m/m = 1, and the SI derived unit for solid angle is $m^2/m^2 = 1$. To aid our understanding, the special name radian with the symbol rad is assigned the number 1 for use in expressing values of plane angle. Similarly, the special name steradian with the symbol sr is given to the number 1 for use in expressing values of solid angle. However, one has the option of using or not using these names and symbols in expressions for other SI derived units, as is convenient.

The unit "degree Celsius," which is equal in magnitude to the unit "kelvin," is used to express Celsius temperature t, defined by the quantity equation $t = T - T_0$, where $T_0 = 273.15$ K, the ice point. This equivalent is indicated in Figure 2.1 by the symbol K in parenthesis at the upper right of the °C circle. The numerical value of a Celsius temperature t expressed in degrees Celsius is given by the equation below the °C circle. A difference or interval of temperature may be expressed in kelvins or in degrees Celsius.

3.6 Presentational conventions

There are a number of widely accepted conventions for the expression of quantities in hand-written or printed documents and texts. These conventions have been in place with relatively little modification since the General Conference on Weights and Measures first introduced the System of International Units in 1960. They are primarily intended to ensure a uniform approach to the presentation of hand written or printed information and to ensure the readability of scientific journals, textbooks, academic papers, data sheets, reports, and other related documents. The presentational requirements will vary to some extent according to the norms of the language in which the work is written. We are concerned here only with the conventions as they apply to the English language. The following list represents some of the more important requirements.

- *Unit symbols* - these appear in roman (upright) type. They are printed in lowercase letters unless derived from a proper name, in which case, the first letter is capitalized (e.g., "Pa" for pascal). The exception to the rule is the symbol for the litre, which may be written either as "l" or "L". The latter is preferred in order to distinguish the symbol used for litre from the number one (1). Any multiple or sub-multiple prefix is considered to be part of the unit symbol, on which it is prepended without an intervening space (e.g., "km" for a kilometer, "mm" for millimeter, or "μm" for a micrometer).
- *Unit names* - these appear in roman (upright) type. All unit names are printed in lowercase characters, including the first letter, regardless of whether or not they are named after a

person, or whether or not the unit symbol begins with an uppercase character (i.e., "newton", not "Newton"). If a prefix is used with the unit name, it becomes part of the unit name and is formed as a single word (e.g., "micropascal", not "micro pascal" or "micro-pascal"). If a derived unit is a product of two or more separate units, either a space or a hyphen can be used to separate the names (e.g., "Newton meter" or "Newton-meter"). For units raised to a power, an appropriate modifier may precede or follow the unit name (e.g., "square meter" or "meter cubed").

- ***Compound units*** - units expressed as the product or quotient of other units are written in the same way as standard algebraic expressions. Multiplication is represented either by a space, or by the use of the *dot operator* (also called a *middle dot*). For example, the symbol for "Newton meter" is written as "N m" or "N·m". The division is represented by a *solidus* (forward stroke) or using negative exponents. The symbol for "newton per meter" is written either as "N/m" or as "N m^{-1}").

- ***Variables*** - unknown quantities in equations are usually represented using a single character in an italic font, e.g., "m" for mass or "I" for electric current. The quantity symbol may further be qualified, typically by using a subscripted number or label, e.g., "R_{LOAD}" for an unknown load resistance, or "I_1" for the unknown current in a specific branch of an electrical circuit (note, incidentally, that although serif fonts are often used for equations, this is not specifically mandated by the BIPM).

- ***Quantities*** - a quantity of known value is expressed as a number, followed by a space, and then the unit symbol. The space represents the multiplication operator. Exception to this rule is for a plane angle expressed in degrees, minutes and seconds. The degree, minute and second symbols always succeed in their respective numbers without an intervening space. For example, a value of thirty-five degrees is written as "35°". Numbers always appear as roman (upright) text.

- ***Combining units*** - different units should only be combined when expressing a quantity using non-SI units that is either a time or an angle. For example, time is commonly expressed in hours, minutes, and seconds. In fields such as navigation or astronomy, it is still customary to express plane angles in terms of degrees, minutes, and seconds. Note, however, that in other applications, angles given in degrees may alternatively be written as decimal fractions, e.g., "21.255°" rather than "21° 15′ 18″".

- ***Decimal markers*** - for any number that has a fractional part, the *decimal marker* (sometimes called the *decimal point*) is the symbol that separates the integral part of the number from its fractional part. This is usually either a period or a comma. For values of between *minus one* and *one*, the decimal marker is preceded by a zero, e.g., "0.123".

- ***The thousand separator*** - numbers consisting of long sequences of digits are often split into groups of three digits to make them easier to read. The preferred method of separating these groups is to use a space, since the use of dots or commas can be interpreted in different ways in different parts of the world. For example, the speed of light is expressed as "299 792 458 m/s". Note that if there are only four digits before or after the decimal marker, the separator becomes insignificant.

- ***Multiplication and division*** - various methods can be used to indicate multiplication. The names of the variables to be multiplied might be *juxtaposed* (placed next to one another), e.g., "xy". They may be enclosed within brackets, e.g., "$(x)(y)$". The multiplication sign can be used to indicate multiplication by placing the sign between the variables to be multiplied, e.g., "$x \times y$". Note that the multiplication sign should always be used where only numbers are being multiplied together, but should be avoided if variables names are involved (in order to avoid confusion with the common variable name x). Use of the middle dot ("·") is discouraged. Division is indicated using a *solidus*, e.g., "x/y" or negative index, e.g., "$x\,y^{-1}$".

3.7   Multiples and submultiples of SI units: SI Prefixes

Multiples and submultiples of SI units (both base units and derived units) are written by attaching prefixes to the units (see **Table 3.11** for a list of prefixes). The use of a prefix unusually suppresses the writing of large or small numbers. The general rule is that prefixes should be used to keep numbers within the range of 0.1 and 1000.

All of the recommended prefixes change the size of the quantity by a multiple or submultiple of three. Similarly, when powers of 10 are used as multipliers, the exponents of 10 should be multiples of three (for example, 40×10^3 N is satisfactory but 400×10^2 N is not). The exponent on a unit with a prefix refers to the entire unit; for instance, the symbol mm^2 means $(mm)^2$ and not $m(m)^2$.

Prefixes are printed as roman (upright) characters prepended to the unit symbol with no intervening space. Most *unit multiple* prefixes are upper case characters (the exceptions are *deca* (da), *hecto* (h) and *kilo* (k). All *unit submultiple* prefixes are lower case characters. Prefix names are always printed in lower case characters, except where they appear at the beginning of a sentence, and prefixed units appear as single words (e.g., *millimeter, micropascal* etc.). All multiples and submultiples are *integer powers of ten*. Above *one hundred* (or *one hundredth*) multiples and submultiples are *integer powers of one thousand,* although they are still expressed as powers of ten. Table - 3.11 lists the most commonly used multiple and submultiple prefixes. Table 3.12 lists the Binary prefixes for Bytes.

Table 3.11 SI Units prefixes together with examples of their correct usage.

Prefix	Symbol	Factor	Examples of usage	Origin
Yotta	**Y**	10^{24}	0.2 YW, 1.23Y [W]	Greek 'octo' (eight, 1000^8)
Zetta	**Z**	10^{21}	3.33 Zs, 3.33Z [s]	French 'sept' (seven, 1000^7)
Exa	**E**	10^{18}	1.23 Ekg, 1.23E [kg]	Greek 'six' (1000^6)
Peta	**P**	10^{15}	7.5 Ps, 7.5P [s]	Greek 'five' (1000^5)
Tera	**T**	10^{12}	0.5 Tm, 0.5T [m]	Greek 'teras' = monster
Giga	**G**	10^{9}	1.2 GΩ, 1.2G [Ω]	Greek 'gigas' = giant
Mega	**M**	10^{6}	7 MW, 7M [W]	Greek 'megas' = large
Kilo	**K, k**	10^{3}	33 km, 33K [m]	Greek 'kilioi' = thousand
hecto	**h**	100	**Deprecated by SI**	Greek 'hekaton' = hundred
Deca	**da**	10	**Deprecated by SI**	Greek 'deka' = ten
deci	**d**	0.1	**Deprecated by SI**	Latin 'decima pars' = one tenth
centi	**c**	0.01	**Deprecated by SI**	Latin 'centesima pars' = one hundredth
milli	**m, k**	10^{-3}	22 mm, 1.2m [m]	Latin 'millesima pars' = one thousandth
micro	**μ, u**	10^{-6}	2.7 uJ, 2.7μ [J]	Greek 'mikros' = small
nano	**n**	10^{-9}	2.2 nF, 2.2n [F]	Latin 'nanus' = dwarf
pico	**p**	10^{-12}	1.5 pA, 1.5p [A]	Spanish 'pico' = minimal measure

femto	**f**	10^{-15}	4.8 fs, 4.8f [s]	Danish and Norvegian 'femten' = fifteen (10^{-15})
Atto	**a**	10^{-18}	1.2 ag, 1.2a [g]	Danish and Norvegian 'atten' = eighteen (10^{-18})
zepto	**z**	10^{-21}	0.2 zm, 1.2z [m]	French 'sept' (seven, 1000^{-7})
yocto	**y**	10^{-24}	1 ys, 1y [s]	Greek 'octo' (eight, 1000^{-8})

Table 3.12. Binary prefixes for Bytes which are not a part of SI but are in common use in informatics

Prefix	Symbol	Factor	Value	Examples
Kilo	**KB**	2^{10}	1024	12345 KB = 12 641 280 bytes
Mega	**MB**	2^{20}	1 048 576	420 MB fits in my PC's dynamic RAM
Giga	**GB**	2^{30}	1 073 741 824	16 GB flash-memory pen drive costs $20
Tera	**TB**	2^{40}	1 099 511 627 776	3.9 TB hard disks are a reality
Peta	**PB**	2^{50}	1 125 899 906 842 624	13.5 PB is the CIA total memory capacity
Exa	**EB**	2^{60}	1 152 921 504 606 846 976	1 EB is still a bit out of reach (AD 2010)
Zetta	**ZB**	2^{70}	1 180 591 620 717 411 303 424	How many ZB to hard-copy a human being?
Yotta	**YB**	2^{80}	1 208 925 819 614 629 174 706 176	1 YYB is still nothing compared with the Universe

Pronunciation of SI Prefixes and Units

A guide to the pronunciation of a few SI names that are sometimes mispronounced is shown in **Table -3.13**. For example, a kilometer is pronounced *kill-oh-meter*, not *kil-om-enter*. The only prefix that generates arguments is giga—the official pronunciation is *jig-uh,* but many people say *gig-uh.*

Table -3.13 Pronunciation of SI Prefixes and Units

Prefix	Pronunciation
Tera	same as *terra*, as in *terra firma*
Giga	pronounced *jig-uh*; with *a* pronounced as in *about* (Alternate pronunciation: *gig-uh*)
Mega	same as *mega* in *megaphone*
Kilo	pronounced *kill-oh*; rhymes with *pillow*
Milli	pronounced *mill-eh*, as in *military*
Micro	same as *micro* in *microphone*
Nano	pronounced *nan-oh*; rhymes with *man-oh*
Pico	pronounced *pea-ko* *Note:* The first syllable of every prefix is accented.
Unit	**Pronunciation**
Joule	pronounced *jool*; rhymes with *cool* and *pool*
Kilogram	pronounced *kill-oh-gram*

Kilometer	pronounced *kill-oh-meter*
Pascal	pronounced *pas-kal*, with the accent on *kal*

References of the chapter

- *The International System of Units (SI)*, Bureau International des Poids et Measures (**BIPM**), **7th** Edition, 1998. Better known as the **SI brochure**, this document is publicly available from the BIPM site.
- Taylor B.N, *The International System of Units (SI)*, NIST Special Publication **330**, 2001 Edition (supersedes the 1991 Edition).
- *Metric System of Measurement: Interpretation of the International System of Units for the United States,* Federal Register **63**, No.144, July 28, 1998.

Web links

- BIPM. The home page of the SI System of Units.
- NIST Units of Measurements page.
- Tables of SI Units and Prefixes. URL of this document.
- Si dimensions of over 200 physical quantities.
- NIST Links to official on-line publications about the SI system.

Chapter 4

Summary of Measuring Units

This chapter gives a table that represents a summary of many of the measuring units defined in the dictionary. Each entry of the table gives the following information:

- Unit name,
- Unite Symbol,
- System of units it belongs to,
- the physical quantity that the unit measure,
- the corresponding SI unit and
- its SI equivalent

4.1   Summary of Measuring Units listed in Alphabetic order

Summary of some of the scientific units

UNIT	Symbol	System of Units	Quantity	Corresponding SI Unit	To Convert to SI, multiply it by
Abampere abA	abA	CGS-emu	Current	Ampere (A)	10
Abampere centimeter	$abA.cm^2$	CGS-emu	Electromagnetic moment	Ampere meter squared	10^{-3}
Abampere per square centimeter	abA/cm^2	CGS-emu	Current density	Ampere per square meter	10^5
Abampere -turns	abA-t	CGS-emu	Magnetomotive force	Ampere turn (At)	10
Abbe	Abbe	SI	Spatial frequency	Hertz per meter (Hz/m)	1
Abcoulomb	abC	CGS-emu	Charge, electric	Coulomb (C)	10

Abcoulomb centimeter	abC.cm	CGS-emu	Electric dipole	Coulomb meter (C.m)	10^{-1}
Abcoulomb per cubic centimeter	abC/cm^3	CGS-emu	Volume density of charge	Coulomb per cubic meter (C/m^3)	10^7
Abcoulomb per square centimeter	abC/cm^2	CGS-emu	Electric Polarization	Coulomb per square meter (C/m^2)	10^5
Abfarad	abF	CGS-emu	Capacitance	Farad (F)	10^9
Abhenry	abH	CGS-emu	Inductance	Henry (H)	10^{-9}
Abohm	ab Ω	CGS-emu	Resistance	Ohm (Ω)	10^{-9}
Abohm centimeter	ab Ω cm	CGS-emu	Resistivity	Ohm meter	10^{-11}
Absiemens	AbS	CGS-emu	Conductance	Siemens (S)	10^9
Absiemens per centimeter	aS/cm	CGS-emu	Conductivity	Siemens per meter (S/m)	10^{11}
Abtesla	AbT	CGS-emu	Magnetic flux density	Tesla (T)	10^{-4}

Summary of some of the scientific units (Cont.)

UNIT	Symbol	System of Units	Quantity	Corresponding SI Unit	To Convert to SI, multiply it by
Abvolt	AbV	CGS-emu	Potential	Volt (V)	10^{-8}
Abvolt per centimeter	abV/cm	CGS-emu	Electric field intensity	Volt per meter (V/m)	10^{-6}
Abweber	abWb	CGS-emu	Magnetic flux	Weber (W)	10^{-8}
Absorption unit (total)	Total	FPS	Equivalent absorption area	Square meter (m^2)	0.092 903 04
Acoustic ohm	acoustic ohm or dyn.s/cm^4	CGS	Acoustic impedance	Pascal second per cubic meter (Pa.s/m^3)	10^5
Acre	Acre	US and UK Imperial	Area	Square meter (m^2)	4.046856 4224 x10^3
Acre-foot	acre-ft	US unit	Volume	Cubic meter (m^3)	1.233 481 8 x10^3
Acre-foot per day	acre.ft/d	US unit	Volume flow rate	Cubic meter per second (m^3/s)	1.427 64x10^{-2}
Acre-foot per hour	acre. ft/h	US unit	Volume flow rate	Cubic meter per second (m^3/s)	1.233 48 x10^3
Acre-inch `	acre.in	US unit	Volume	Cubic meter (m^3)	1.027 90x10^2
Acre per pound	acre/Ib	US and UK unit	Specific surface	Square meter per kilogramme (m^2/kg)	8.921 69x10^3
Admiralty mile	admiralty mile	UK unit	Length	Meter (m)	1.853 184x10^3
Air mile	air mile	Non	Length	Meter (m)	1852

Summary of some of the scientific units (Cont.)

UNIT	Symbol	System of Units	Quantity	Corresponding SI Unit	To Convert to SI, multiply it by
Amagat Density unit	Amagat density unit	Arbitrary	Density of a gas	Mole per cubic meter (mol/m^3)	44.615 8
Amagat volume unit	Amagat volume unit	Arbitrary	Volume of a gas	Cubic meter (m^3)	0.022 413 6
American run	American run	US unit	Length per unit mass (yarn count)	Meter per kilogramme (m/kg)	$3.225\ 453\ 712\ x10^3$
Ampere	A, formerly amp	SI	Electric current	SI	SI
Ampere-hour	A.h	with SI	Electric charge	Coulomb (C)	$3.6x10^3$
Ampere x circular mil	A x circular mil	US and UK unit	Electromagnetic Moment	Ampere meter squared	$5.067\ 07x10^{-10}$
Ampere meter squared	$A.m^2$	SI	Electromagnetic moment, Bohr magneton and nuclear magneton	SI	SI
Ampere minute	A.min	with SI	Electric charge	Ampere second (A-s)	60
Ampere per inch	A/in	UK and US unit	Magnetic field strength	Ampere per meter (A/m)	$3.397\ 01x10$
Ampere per kilogramme	A/kg	SI	Exposure rate	Coulomb per kilogramme second (C/kg.s)	1
Ampere per meter	A/m	SI, MKS	Surface current density	SI	SI
Ampere per square meter	A/m^2	SI	Volume current density	SI	SI

Summary of some of the scientific units (Cont.)

UNIT	Symbol	System of Units	Quantity	Corresponding SI Unit	To Convert to SI, multiply it by
Ampere per square inch	A/in^2	Arbitrary	Current density	Ampere per square meter (A/m^2)	$1.550\ 0031 \times 10^3$
Ampere per square meter	A/m^2	SI	Current density	SI	SI
Ampere per square mil	A/mil^2	UK unit	Current density	Ampere per square meter	$1.550\ 003\ 1 \times 10^9$
Ampere per square meter kelvin	$A/(m^2 . K^2)$	SI	Richardson constant	SI	SI
Ampere square meter per joule second	$A.m^2/(J.s)$	SI	Gyromagnetic coefficient	SI	SI
Ampere, thermal	thermal ampere	SI	Thermal current	SI	SI
Ampere-turn	At and/or AT	SI	Magnetomotive Force	Magnetomotive Force	SI
Ampere-turn per weber	AT/Wb	SI	Reluctance	SI	SI
Angle at a point	Pla	Non	Plane angle	Radian (rad)	2π
Angstrom	A	Metric	Length	Meter (m)	10^{-10}
Anker	Anker	US unit	Capacity (volume)	Cubic meter (m^3)	37.854×10^{-3}
Apostilb	Asb	Metric	Luminance	Candela per square meter (cd/m^2)	$1/\pi$
Arcmin	'	All systems	Plane angle	Radian (rad)	$\pi/10800$
Are	A	Metric	Area	Square meter (m^2)	100
Artillery point	—	Arbitrary	Plane angle	Radian (rad)	$\pi/3200$
Assay ton (UK)	assay ton (UK)	UK unit	Mass	Kilogramme (kg)	$0.326\ 667 \times 10^{-1}$

Summary of some of the scientific units (Cont.)

UNIT	Symbol	System of Units	Quantity	Corresponding SI Unit	To Convert to SI, multiply it by
Assay ton (US)	assay ton (US)	US unit	Mass	Kilogramme (kg)	$0.291\ 667 \times 10^{-1}$
Astronomical unit	au or AU	with SI	Length	Meter (m)	$1.495\ 97870 \times 10^{11}$
Ata	Ata	Metric technical	Pressure (absolute)	Pascal (Pa)	$0.098\ 665 \times 10^{6}$
Atmo-meter	atmo-m	Arbitrary	Depth of equivalent atmosphere	molecules per square meter	2.68699×10^{25}
Atmosphere	Atm	Metric	Pressure	Pascal (Pa)	$1.013\ 250 \times 10^{5}$
Atmosphere, technical	At	Metric	Pressure	Pascal (Pa)	$9.8066\ 50 \times 10^{4}$
Atomic mass unit (unified)	amu or u	Arbitrary	Mass	Kilogramme (kg)	1.66024×10^{-27}
Atomic unit of charge	atomic unit of charge	Hartree system (base unit)	Electric charge	Coulomb (C)	1.60210×10^{-19}
Atomic unit of energy	atomic unit of energy	Hartree system (derived)	Energy	Joule (J)	4.8505×10^{-18}
Atomic unit of length	atomic unit of length	Hartree system (derived)	Length	Meter (m)	5.29167×10^{-11}
Atomic unit of mass	atomic unit of mass	Hartree (base unit)	Mass	Kilogramme (kg)	9.1084×10^{-31}
Atomic unit of time	atomic unit of time	Hartree system (derived)	Time	Second (s)	2.41884×10^{-17}
Atomic weight unit	awu	Arbitrary	Mass	Kilogramme (kg)	1.66026×10^{-27}
Bag	bag	UK unit	Volume	Cubic meter (m^3)	1.091061×10^{-1}

Summary of some of the scientific units (Cont.)

UNIT	Symbol	System of Units	Quantity	Corresponding SI Unit	To Convert to SI, multiply it by
Balmer	balmer	CGS	Reciprocal length	Per meter (/m)	100
Bar	bar	Metric	Pressure	Pascal (Pa)	10^5
Barad	barad	CGS	Pressure	Pascal (Pa)	0.1
Barge	barge	UK unit	Mass	Kilogramme (kg)	20.32093816×10^3
Barleycorn	barleycorn	UK unit	Length	Meter (m)	8.466 666
Barn	B	Metric	Area	Square meter (m^2)	10^{-28}
Barn per electron volt	b/eV	Arbitrary	Spectral cross section	Meter square per joule (m^2/J)	$0.624\ 146 \times 10^9$
Barn per erg	b/erg	Arbitrary	Spectral cross section	Meter square per joule (m^2/J)	10^{-21}
Barn per steradian	b/sr	Arbitrary	Angular cross section	Meter square per steradian (m^2/sr)	10^{-28}
Barn per steradian electronvolt	b/(sr.eV)	Arbitrary	Spectral angular cross section	Meter square per steradian joule (m^2/sr.J)	$0.624\ 146 \times 10^{-9}$
barn per steradian erg	b/(sr.erg)	Arbitrary	Spectral angular cross section	Meter square per steradian joule (m^2/sr.J)	10^{-21}
Barony	barony	UK unit	Area	Square meter (m^2)	$16.187\ 425\ 6 \times 10^6$
Barrel	Bbl	Arbitrary	Capacity, volume	Cubic meter (m^3)	0.1636591
Barrel (petroleum US)	USbbl petroleum	Imperial	Capacity, volume	Cubic meter (m^3)	0.158 987 3
Barrel (US, dry)	USbbl dry	Imperial	Capacity, volume	Cubic meter (m^3)	0.11562712

Summary of some of the scientific units (Cont.)

UNIT	Symbol	System of Units	Quantity	Corresponding SI Unit	To Convert to SI, multiply it by
Barrel (US, liquid)	USbbl liq	Imperial	Capacity, volume	Cubic meter (m^3)	0.11924047
Barrique	barrique	Metric	Capacity, volume	Cubic meter (m^3)	0.225
Barye	Barye	CGS	Pressure	Pascal (Pa)	0.1
Base box	base box	Imperial	Area	Square meter (m^2)	20.2322176
Baud	baud, also Bd	All	Information or signaling rate	All	All
B-Dose	B-dose	Arbitrary	Radiation dose	See definition	See definition
Becquerel	Bq	SI	Radioactivity	SI	SI
Becquerel per cubic meter	Bq/m^3	**SI**	Volume activity of radionuclide	SI	**SI**
Becquerel per kilogramme	Bq/kg	SI	Specific activity of a radionuclide	SI	SI
Becquerel per meter	Bq/m	SI	Linear activity of radionuclide	SI	SI
Becquerel per mole	Bq/mol	SI	Molar activity of radionuclide	SI	SI
Bel	B	All	Intensity level	All	(= 10 dB)
Benz	Benz	SI	Velocity	Meter per second (m/s)	1
Bes	Bes	CGS	Mass	Kilogramme (kg)	0.001
BeV	BeV	US unit	Energy	Joule (J)	$1.602\ 10 \times 10^{-10}$
Bicron	bicorn	Metric	Length	Meter (m)	**10^{-12}**
Biot	Bi	**CGSB**	Current	Ampere (A)	**10**

Summary of some of the scientific units (Cont.)

UNIT	Symbol	System of Units	Quantity	Corresponding SI Unit	To Convert to SI, multiply it by
Biot centimeter squared	$Bi.cm^2$	CGSB	Electromagnetic moment	Ampere meter square $(A.m^2)$	10^{-3}
Biot per centimeter	Bi/cm	CGSB	Magnetic field strength	Ampere per meter (A/m)	$7.957\ 75x10$
Biot per second	Bi.s	CGSB	Electric charge	Coulomb	10
Bit	Bit	None	Information for digital computer	None	None
Bit per second	bit/s	None	Bit rate or data signaling rate	None	None
Bit per square meter	$bit\ /m^2$	None	Surface bit density	None	None
Bit per meter	bit/m	None	Linear bit density	None	None
Blindwatt	bW or BW	German unit	Reactive power	Var	1
Blink	Blink	Arbitrary	Time	Second (s)	10^{-5} day = 0.864 s
Blondel	Blondel	Metric	Luminance	Candela per square meter (cd/m^2)	$1/\pi = 3.183$ $10x10^{-1}$
Board foot	board foot	Arbitrary	Volume (timber only)	Cubic meter (m^3)	$2.359\ 737x10^{-3}$
Board of Trade Unit	Board of Trade unit	Metric	Energy (electric)	Joule (J)	$3.6\ x10^6$
Bohar radius	Bohar	Arbitrary	Length	Meter	$53x10^{-12}$
Bole	Bole	CGS	Momentum	Kilogramme meter per second (kg.m/s)	10^{-5}
Boll	Boll	Arbitrary	Mass	Kilogramme (kg)	63.502 931 8
Bolts of cloth	bolts of	Arbitrary	Length	Meter (m)	36.576
Bottle	Bottle	Arbitrary	Mass	Kilogramme (kg)	39.008 943 82

Summary of some of the scientific units (Cont.)

UNIT	Symbol	System of Units	Quantity	Corresponding SI Unit	To Convert to SI, multiply it by
Bouge decimale	Bd	All	Luminous intensity	Cadela (cdj)	See: Candle, decimal
Brake horse-power	brake hp	Arbitrary	Power	Watt (W)	See definition
Brewster	B	Metric	Reciprocal stress, stress optical coefficient	Per pascal (/Pa)	10^{-12}
Brieze	Breeze	CGS	Mass	Kilogramme (kg)	10^{-3}
Brig	Brig	All	Logarithmic value	Neper or Octave	2.30259 Np 3.32193 octave
Bril	Bril	None	Luminance level	See definition	See definition
Brilliant, printer	Brilliant	None	Length	Meter (m)	1.230 109 3 $\times 10^{-3}$
British thermal unit (International Table)	Btu_{IT}	Imperial	Heat energy	Joule (J)	$1.05505585262 \times 10^3$
British thermal unit (mean)	Btu mean	Arbitrary	Heat energy	Joule (J)	1.05587×10^3
British thermal unit	Btu	Arbitrary	Heat energy	Joule (J)	1.054350×10^3
British Thermal unit (39°F)	Btu_{39}	Arbitrary	Heat energy	Joule (J)	1.05967×10^3
British thermal unit (59°F)	Btu_{59}	Arbitrary	Heat energy	Joule (J)	1.05480×10^3
British thermal unit (60° F)	Btu_{60}	Arbitrary	Heat energy	Joule (J)	1.05468×10^3
Btu (IT) foot per square foot hour degree Fahrenheit	$BtU_{IT}.ft/(h.ft^2.°F)$	Imperial	Thermal conductivity	Watt per meter kelvin (W/m.K)	1.730735
Btu foot per square foot hour degree Fahrenheit	$Btu ,ft/(h.ft^2.°F)$	Arbitrary	Thermal conductivity	Watt per meter kelvin (W/m.K)	1.729577

Summary of some of the scientific units (Cont.)

UNIT	Symbol	System of Units	Quantity	Corresponding SI Unit	To Convert to SI, multiply it by
Btu (IT) inch per square foot hour degree Fahrenheit	$Btu_{IT}.in/(h.ft^2.°F)$	Imperial	Thermal conductivity	Watt per meter kelvin (W/m.K)	1.442279×10^{-1}
Btu (therm) inch per square foot hour degree Fahrenheit	$Btu.in (h.ft^2.°F)$	Arbitrary	Thermal conductivity	Watt per meter kelvin (W/m.K)	1.441314×10^{-1}
Btu (IT) inch per square foot second degree Fahrenheit	$Btu_{IT}.in/ (s.ft^2.°F)$	Imperial	Thermal conductivity	Watt per meter kelvin (W/m.K)	5.192204×10^{2}
Btu (therm) inch per square foot second degree Fahrenheit	$Btu. in/ (s.ft^2.°F)$	Arbitrary	Thermal conductivity	Watt per meter kelvin (W/m.K)	5.188732×10^{2}
Btu (IT) per hour	Btu_{IT}/h	Arbitrary	Heat flow rate	Watt (W)	2.930711×10^{-1}
Btu (IT) per second	Btu_{IT}/s	Arbitrary	Heat flow rate	Watt (W)	1.055056×10^{3}
Btu (thermochemical) per hour	Btu/h	Arbitrary	Heat flow rate	Watt (W)	2.928751×10^{-1}
Btu (thermo) per Minute	Btu/min	Arbitrary	Heat flow rate	Watt (W)	1.757250×10
Btu (thermo) per Second	Btu/s	Arbitrary	Heat flow rate	Watt (W)	1.054350×10^{3}
Btu (IT) per square foot	Btu_{IT}/ft^2	Arbitrary	Flat density	Joule per square meter (J/m^2)	1.135653×10^{4}
Btu (thermo) per square foot	Btu/ft^2	Arbitrary	Heat density	Joule per square meter (J/m^2)	1.134893×10^{4}

Summary of some of the scientific units (Cont.)

UNIT	Symbol	System of Units	Quantity	Corresponding SI Unit	To Convert to SI, multiply it by
Btu (IT) per square foot second	$Btu_{IT}/(ft^2.s)$	Arbitrary	Density of heat flow	Watt per square meter (W/m^2)	1.135653×10^4
Btu (IT) per square foot hour	$Btu_{IT}/(ft^2.h)$	Arbitrary	Density of heat flow	Watt per square meter (W/m^2)	3.154591
Btu (thermo) per square foot hour	$Btu/(ft^2.h)$	Arbitrary	Density of heat flow	Watt per square meter (W/m^2)	3.152481
Btu (thermo) per square foot minute	$Btu/(ft^2.min)$	Arbitrary	Density of heat flow	Watt per square meter (W/m^2)	1.891489×10^2
Btu (thermo) per square foot second	$Btu/(ft^2.s)$	Arbitrary	Density of heat flow	Watt per square meter (W/m^2)	1.134893×10^4
Btu (thermo) per square inch second	$Btu/(in^2.s)$	Arbitrary	Density of heat flow	Watt per square meter (W/m^2)	1.634246×10^6
Btu (IT) per square foot hour degree Fahrenheit	$Btu_{IT}/(h.ft^2.°F)$	Arbitrary	Coefficient of heat transfer	Watt per meter squared kelvin ($W/m^2.K$)	$5.678\ 26$
Btu (thermo) per square foot hour degree Fahrenheit	$Btu/(h.ft^2.°F)$	Arbitrary	Coefficient of heat transfer	Watt per meter squared kelvin ($W/m^2.K$)	$5.674\ 66//$
Btu (IT) per square foot second degree Fahrenheit	$Btu_{IT}(s.ft^2.°F)$	Arbitrary	Coefficient of heat transfer	Watt per meter squared kelvin ($W/m^2.K$)	2.044175×10^4
Btu (thermo) per square foot second degree Fahrenheit	$Btu/(s.ft^2\ °F)$	Arbitrary	Coefficient of heat transfer	Watt per meter squared kelvin ($W/m^2.K$)	2.042868×10^4

Summary of some of the scientific units (Cont.)

UNIT	Symbol	System of Units	Quantity	Corresponding SI Unit	To Convert to SI, multiply it by
Btu (IT) per pound	Btu_{IT}/Ib	Arbitrary	Specific internal energy and calorific value (mass basis)	Joule per kilogramme (J/kg)	**2.326×10^3**
Btu (thermo) per pound	Btu/Ib	Arbitrary	Specific internal energy and calorific value (mass basis)	Joule per kilogramme (J/kg)	2.324444×10^3
Btu (IT) per pound degree Fahrenheit	$Btu_{IT}/(Ib.°F)$	Arbitrary	Specific heat capacity	Joule per kilogramme Kelvin (J/kg.K)	4.1868×10^3
Btu (thermo) per pound degree Fahrenheit	$Btu/(Ib.°F)$	Arbitrary	Specific heat capacity	Joule per kilogramme Kelvin (J/kg.K)	4.184×10^3
Btu (IT) per cubic feet	Btu_{1T}/ft^3	Arbitrary	Calorific value (volume basis)	Joule per cubic meter (J/m^3)	3.725895×10^4
Btu (thermo) per cubic feet	Btu/ft^3	Arbitrary	Calorific value (volume basis)	Joule per cubic meter (J/m^3)	3.723402×10^4
British Technical Unit of mass	British technical unit of mass	FIbfS	Mass	Kilogramme (kg)	14.593 9
Brix	**Brix**	**None**	Percentage of sugar by weight in solution	See definition	See definition
Bucket	Bucket		Volume, capacity	Cubic meter (m^3)	1.818435×10^{-2}
B-size	B-size	Metric	Paper size	See definition	See definition
Bushel UK	UK bu	UK unit	Capacity, volume	Cubic meter (m^3)	0.03636870
Bushel US	US bu	US unit	Capacity, volume	Cubic meter (m^3)	0.035239070166
Butt	Butt	Arbitrary	Capacity, volume	Cubic meter (m^3)	0.4769619
Byte	Byte	None	Information for digital computer	None	None
Cable (length)	cable length	Imperial	Length (particularly for marine use)	Meter (m)	219.456

Summary of some of the scientific units (Cont.)

UNIT	Symbol	System of Units	Quantity	Corresponding SI Unit	To Convert to SI, multiply it by
Calorie (International Table)	cal_{IT}	Metric derived	Heat energy	Joule (J)	4.186 8
Calorie (mean)	Crimean	Arbitrary	Heat energy	Joule (J)	4.190 02
Calorie (thermochemical)	cal_{tc}	Metric-derived		Joule (J)	4.184
Calorie (15°C)	cal15	Arbitrary	Heat energy	Joule (J)	4.185 80
Calorie (20°C)	cal_{20}	Arbitrary	Heat energy	Joule (J)	4.181 90
Caiorie (kilogram, IT)	$cali_{IT.kg}$	Metric-derived	Heat energy	Joule (J)	4.186 8
Calorie (kilogram, mean)	$Cal_{mean,kg}$	Arbitrary	Heat energy	Joule (J)	4.190 02
Calorie (kilogram, thermo.)	$^{C}altc,kg$	Metric-derived	Heat energy	Joule (J)	4.184×10^3
Calorie (thermo.) per square centimeter	cal_{tc}/cm^2	Metric-derived	Density of heat energy	Joule per square meter (J/m²)	4.184×10^3

Summary of some of the scientific units (Cont.)

UNIT	Symbol	System of Units	Quantity	Corresponding SI Unit	To Convert to SI, multiply it by
Calorie (IT) per gramme	cal_{IT}/g	Metric-derived	Specific internal energy	Joule per kilogramme (J/kg)	4.1868×10^3
Calorie(thermo.) per gramme	cal_{tc}/g	Metric-derived	Specific internal energy	Joule per kilogramme W	4.184×10^4
Calorie (IT) per gramme degree Celsius (or Kelvin)	$Cal_{IT}/(g.°C)$ or $cal_{IT}/(g.K)$	Metric-derived	Specific heat capacity and specific entropy	Joule per kilogramme kelvin (J/kg.K)	4.1868×10^3
Calorie (thermo.) per gramme degree Celsius	$cal_{tc}/(g.°C)$	Metric-derived	Specific heat capacity and specific entropy	Joule per kilogramme kelvin (J/kg.K)	4.184×10^3
Calorie(thermo.) per minute	cal_{tc}/min	Metric-derived	Heat flow rate	Watt (W)	6.973333×10^{-2}
Calorie (thermo.) per second	cal_{tc}/s	Metric-derived	Heat flow rate	Watt (W)	**4.184**
Calorie (thermo.) per centimeter squared second	$cal_{tc}/(cm^2.s)$	Metric-derived	Density of heat flow rate	Watt per square meter (W/m^2)	**4.184x10^4**
Calorie (thermo.) per centimeter squared minute	$cal_{tc}/(cm^2.min)$	Metric-derived	Density of heat flow rate	Watt per square meter (W/m^2)	6.973333×10^2
Calorie (thermo.) per centimeter squared second	$cal_{tc}/(cm^2.s)$	Metric-derived	Density of heat flow rate	Watt per square meter (W/m^2)	**4.184x10^4**

Summary of some of the scientific units (Cont.)

UNIT	Symbol	System of Units	Quantity	Corresponding SI Unit	To Convert to SI, multiply it by
Calorie (thermo.) per second centimeter degree Celsius (or Kelvin)	$cal_{tc}/(cm.s.°C)$	Metric-derived	Thermal conductivity	Watt per meter kelvin (W/m.K)	**4.184 x10²**
Candela	Cd	SI	Luminous intensity	SI	SI
Candle, decimal	Dc	All	Luminous intensity	See: Bouge Decimale	See: Bouge decimale
Candle-foot	Fc	FPS	Intensity of illumination	Lux (lux)	10.7639
Candle, International Standard	international candle	All	Luminous intensity	Candela (cd)	60
Candle, new	Cd	All	Luminous intensity	Candela (cd)	1
Candela per square centimeter	cd/cm^2	Arbitrary	Luminance	Candela per square meter (cd/m^2)	**10^4**
Candela per square foot	cd/ft^2	Arbitrary	Luminance	Candela per square meter (cd/m^2)	1.076 39x10
Candela per square inch	cd/in^2	US unit	Luminance	Candela per square meter (cd/m^2)	1.550 000x10³
Candela per square meter	cd/m^2	SI	Luminance	SI	SI
Cape foot	cape foot	Arbitrary	Length	Meter	0.314 858 4

Summary of some of the scientific units (Cont.)

UNIT	Symbol	System of Units	Quantity	Corresponding SI Unit	To Convert to SI, multiply it by
Carat	Carat	Imperial	Mass	Kilogramme (kg)	2.5919564×10^{-4}
Carat, metric	metric carat	Metric	Mass	Kilogramme (kg)	2×10^{-4}
Carcel	Carcel	All	Luminous intensity	Candela (cd)	576.6
Carton	Carton	Arbitrary	Mass	Kilogramm (kg)	4.082 331 33
Cascade unit	cascade unit	Arbitrary	Length	Meter (m)	See definition
CE'	ce'	Arbitrary	Time	Second (s)	864
Celo	Celo	FPS	Acceleration	Meter per second square (m/s^2)	0.304 8
Celsius degree	Deg	SI	Temperature interval	Kelvin (K)	1
Cent	Cent	All	Pitch interval	Octave *	$6.333\ 33 \times 10^{-4}$
Cent	Cent	All	Reactivity	Dollar *	10^{-2}
Cental	Ctl	UK unit	Mass	Kilogramme (kg)	45.359 237
Centesimal minute	$..^{cg}$	Arbitrary	Plane angle	Radian (rad)	$1.570\ 80 \times 10^{-4}$
Centesimal second	$..^{cc}$	Arbitrary	Plane angle	Radian (rad)	1.570809×10^{-6}
Centiare	Ca	with SI	Area	Square meter (m^2)	1
Centibar	Centibar	Arbitrary	Pressure	Pascal (Pa)	**1000**
Centigrade	$...^{cg}$	Arbitrary	Plane angle	Radian (rad)	1.57080×10^{-4}
Centigrade heat unit	CHU	Arbitrary	Heat energy	Joule (J)	1.89910049×10^{3}
Centigrade Heat Unit, mean	CHU_{mean}	Arbitrary	Heat energy	Joule (J)	1.90044×10^{s}
Centigramme	Eg	CGS	Mass	Kilogramme (kg)	$\mathbf{10^{5}}$
Centihg	Centihg	Metric	Pressure	Pascal (Pa)	1.33322387415
Centilitre	cl or cL	Metric	Capacity, volume	Cubic meter (m^3)	10^{5}
Centimeter	Cm	CGS, Mie	Length	Meter (m)	$\mathbf{10^{-2}}$

. **Summary of some of the scientific units (Cont.)**

UNIT	Symbol	System of Units	Quantity	Corresponding SI Unit	To Convert to SI, multiply it by
Centimeter	Cm	CGS-esu	Capacitance	Farad (F)	1.11265×10^{-12}
Centimeter	**Cm**	CGS-emu	Induction	Henry (H)	10^{-9}
Centimeter-candle	cm-c	CGS	Illumination intensity	Lux (lux)	10^4
Centimeter of mercury (conv.)	cmHg	Metric	Pressure	Pascal (Pa)	$1.33322387415 \times 10^3$
Centimeter of Water (4°C)	cmH_2O	Metric	Pressure	Pascal (Pa)	9.80638×10
Centimeter per second squared	cm/s^2	CGS	Acceleration (linear)	Meter per second square (m/s^2)	10^{-2}
Centimeter second degree Celsius per calorie (IT)	$cm.s°C/cal_{IT}$	CGS	Thermal resistivity	Meter kelvin per watt (mK/W)	$2.388\ 46 \times 10^{-3}$
Centimeter to the fourth power	cm^4	CGS	Second moment of area	Meter to the fourth power (m^4)	**10^{-8}**
Centipoise	cP	CGS	Viscosity, dynamic	Pascal second (Pa.s)	1.0×10^{-3}
Centistokes	cSt	CGS	Viscosity, kinematic	Meter square per second (m^2/s)	**1.0×10^{-6}**
Centner	Center	Imperial	Mass	Kilogramme (kg)	45.359237
Centner, metric	metric center	Metric	Mass	Kilogramme (kg)	**50**
Centrad	Centrad	All	Plane angle	Radian (rad)	**0.01**
CGSesu unit of magnetic field	-	CGS-esu	Magnetic field strength	Ampere per meter (A/m)	$2.654\ 42 \times 10^{-9}$
CGSesu unit of magnetic flux	-	CGS-esu	Magnetic flux	Weber (Wb)	$2.997\ 92 \times 10^2$
CGSesu unit of magnetic flux density	--	CGS-esu	Magnetic flux density	Tesla (T)	$2.997\ 92 \times 10^6$
CGSesu unit of magnetic polarization	-	CGS-esu	Magnetic polarization	Tesla (T)	$3.767\ 30 \times 10^7$
CGSesu of mnetization	-	CGS-esu	Magnetization	Ampere per meter (A/m)	$2.997\ 92 \times 10^7$
CGSesu unit of reluctance	-	CGS-esu	Reluctance	Per Henry (H^{-1})	$8.854\ 19 \times 10^{-14}$

Summary of some of the scientific units (Cont.)

UNIT	Symbol	System of Units	Quantity	Corresponding SI Unit	To Convert to SI, multiply it by
CGSemu unit of magnetic field strength	(=Oersted)	CGS-emu	Magnetic field strength	Ampere per meter (A/m)	7.95775x10
CGSemu unit of magnetic flux	(=Maxwell)	CGS-emu	Magnetic flux	Weber (Wb)	10^{-3}
CGSemu unit of magnetic		CGS-emu	Magnetic polarization	Tesla (T)	1.25664×10^{-3}
CGSemu unit of magnetization	-	CGS-emu	Magnetization	Ampere per meter (A/m)	10^{-3}
CGSemu unit of reluctance	-	CGS-emu	Reluctance	Per Henry(H^{-1})	7.95775×10^{7}
CGS technical unit of mass	CGS technical unit of mass	CgfS	Mass	Kilogramme (kg)	**0.980 665**
Chad	Chad	Metric	Neutron flux	See definition	See definition
Chain (also known as square chain)	Chain	US and UK	Area	Square meter (m^2)	404.68564224
Chain	Ch	US and UK	Length	Meter (m)	**20.116 84**
Chain, Engineer's	engineer's	US and UK	Length	Meter (m)	30.48
Chain, nautical	nautical chain	US and UK	Length	Meter (m)	4.572
Chaldron UK	UK chaldron	Arbitrary	Capacity, volume	Cubic meter (m^3)	1.30927
Chaldron US	US chaldron	Imperial	Capacity, volume	Cubic meter (m^3)	1.26860652600768
Charriere	charriere or Fr	French unit	Length	Meter (m)	$(1/3) \times 10^{-3}$

Summary of some of the scientific units (Cont.)

UNIT	Symbol	System of Units	Quantity	Corresponding SI Unit	To Convert to SI, multiply it by
Chemical mass unit	chemical mass unit	Arbitrary	Mass	Kilogramme (kg)	1.066026×10^{-27}
Chest	Chest	Arbitrary	Capacity, volume	Cubic meter (m^3)	0.568 245
Cheval-vapeur	Ch	Metric	Power	Watt (W)	735.49875
Cheval-vapeur-Heure	ch h	Metric	Energy	Joule (J)	2647795
Circle	Circle	All	Plane angle	Radian (rad)	2π
Circular inch	c.in	UK and US	Area	Square meter (m^2)	5.0670748×10^{-4}
Circular millimeter	c.mm	Arbitrary	Area	Square meter (m^2)	7.8539816×10^{-7}
Circular mil	c.mil	UK and US	Area	Square meter (m^2)	$5.067\ 074\ 8 \times 10^{-10}$
Circumference	Circumference	All	Plane angle	Radian (rad)	6.2831853
Clausius	Clausius	Arbitrary	Entropy	Joule per kelvin (J/K)	**$4.186\ 8 \times 10^3$**
Clo	Clo	Arbitrary	Thermal insulation of clothing	Meter kelvin per watt (m.K/W)	0.505566
Clo	Clo	US unit		Kelvin square meter per watt (K.m^2/W)	2.003712×10^{-1}
Clusec	Clusec	Metric-derived	Leak rate, power	Watt (W)	1.33322×10^{-6}
Comfort Index, Acoustical	ACI	None	Noise inside an aircraft cabin	See definition	See definition
Continental Horsepower	cont hp	Metric	Power	Watt (W)	$7.354\ 99 \times 10^2$
Comb	Comb	UK unit	Capacity, volume	Cubic meter (m^3)	0.145 474 8

Summary of some of the scientific units (Cont.)

UNIT	Symbol	System of Units	Quantity	Corresponding SI Unit	To Convert to SI, multiply it by
Cord	Cord	Arbitrary	Capacity, volume (for timber only)	Cubic meter (m^3)	3.624 573 4
Cord-feet	cord-ft	Arbitrary	Capacity, volume	Cubic meter	0.453 071 675
Coulomb	C	SI	Electric charge	SI	SI
Coulomb meter	C.m	SI	Electric dipole moment	SI	SI
Coulomb meter squared per kilogramme	$C.m^2/kg$	SI	Specific gamma ray constant	SI	SI
Coulomb meter squared per volt	$C.m^2/V$	SI	Polarizability of molecule	SI	SI
Coulomb per cubic meter	C/m^3 meter	SI	Volume charge density	SI	SI
Coulomb per Kilogramme	C/kg	SI	Exposure	SI	SI
Coulomb per kilogramme	C/(kg.s)	SI	Exposure rate	SI	SI
Coulomb per mole	C/mol	SI	Faraday constant	SI	SI
Coulomb per square meter	C/m^2	SI	Unit of surface charge density and polarization	SI	SI
Coulomb, thermal	thermal coulomb (or J/K)	SI	Thermal energy	**SI**	SI
Crinal	Crinal	Metric	Force	| Newton (N)	0.1
Crith	Crith	Arbitrary	Mass (particularly of gas)	Kilogramme (kg)	8.9885×10^{-5}
Crocodile	Crocodile	Metric	Electric potential	Volt (V)	$\mathbf{10^6}$
Cron	Cron	Arbitrary	Time	Second (s)	3.156×10^3

Summary of some of the scientific units (Cont.)

UNIT	Symbol	System of Units	Quantity	Corresponding SI Unit	To Convert to SI, multiply it by
C-Size		Metric	Paper size	See definition	See definition
Cubic centimeter	cm^3	CGS and mSI	Volume	Cubic meter (m^3)	10^6
Cubic centimeter per gramme	cm^3/g	CGS and mSI	Specific volume	Cubic meter per kilogramme (m^3/kg)	10^{-3}
Cubic centimeter per kilogramme	cm^3/kg	mSI	Specific volume	Cubic meter per kilogramme (m^3/kg)	**10^{-6}**
Cubic decimeter	dm^3	mSI	Volume	Cubic meter (m^3)	**1.0×10^{-3}**
Cubic decimeter per kilogramme	dm^3/kg	mSI	Specific volume	Cubic meter per kilogramme m^3/kg)	**10^{-3}**
Cubic foot	ft^3	US and UK	Volume	Cubic meter (m^3)	$2.831\ 68 \times 10^{-2}$
Cubic foot per pound	ft^3/lb	FPS	Specific volume	Cubic meter per kilogramme (m^3/kg)	$6.242\ 80 \times 10^{-2}$
Cubic foot per second	ft^3/s	FPS	Volume flow rate	Cubic meter per second (m^3/s)	$2.8316846592 \times 10^{-2}$
Cubic foot per ton (UK)	ft^3/UK ton	UK unit	Specific volume	Cubic meter per kilogramme (m^3/kg)	$2.786\ 96 \times 10^{-5}$
Cubic inch	in^3	US and UK unit	Volume	Cubic meter (m^3)	$1.638\ 706 \times 10^{-5}$
Cubic inch per pound	in^3/Ib	Arbitrary	Specific volume	Cubic meter per kilogramme (m^3/kg)	$3.612\ 73 \times 10^{-5}$
ubic meter	m^3	SI	Volume	SI	SI

Summary of some of the scientific units (Cont.)

UNIT	Symbol	System of Units	Quantity	Corresponding SI Unit	To Convert to SI, multiply it by
Cubic meter per coulomb	m^3/C	SI	Hall coefficient	SI	SI
Cubic meter per hour	m^3/h	with SI	Volume flow rate	Cubic meter per second (m^3/s)	$2.777\ 78 \times 10^{-4}$
Cubic meter per kilogramme	m^3/kg	SI	Specific volume	SI	SI
Cubic meter per mole	m^3/mol	SI	Molar volume	SI	SI
Cubic meter per second	m^3/s	SI	Volume flow rate	SI	SI
Cubic yard	yd^3	US and UK unit	Volume	Cubic meter (m^3)	$7.645\ 55 \times 10^{-1}$
Cubit	Cubit	Arbitrary	Length	Meter (m)	0.4572

Summary of some of the scientific units (Cont.)

UNIT	Symbol	System of Units	Quantity	Corresponding SI Unit	To Convert to SI, multiply it by
Cumec	cumec (m^3/s)	SI	Volume flow	SI	SI
Cup	Cup	Non	Volume, capacity	Cubic meter (m^3)	2.365882x10^{-4}
Curie	Ci	Arbitrary	Radioactive disintegration rate	Becquerel (Bq)	**3.7x10^{10}**
Curie megaelectron volt	Ci.MeV	Non	Power (nuclear)	Watt (W)	5.93x 10^{-3}
Curie per cubic meter	Ci/m^3	Arbitrary	Volume activity	Becquerel per cubic meter (Bq/m^3)	**3.7x10^{10}**
Curie per kilogramme	Ci/kg	Arbitrary	Specific activity	Becquerel per kilogramme (Bq/kg)	3.7 x 10^{10}
Cusec	Cusec (ft^3/s)	FPS	Volume flow rate	Cubic meter per second (m^3/s)	2.8316846592 x 10^{-2}
Cut	Cut	Imperial	Length	Meter (m)	274.32
Cycle per second	c/s	All	Frequency	Hertz (Hz)	1
Dalton	Dalton	Arbitrary	Mass	Kilogramme (kg)	1.66033x 10^{-27}
Daniel	Daniel	Arbitrary	Potential difference	Volt (V)	1.042
Daraf	Daraf	SI	Reciprocal capacitance	SI	SI
Darcy	D	CGS	Permeability of porous medium	Square meter (m^2)	9.869233 x 10^{-13}
Darwin	Darwin	None	Evolutionary rate of change	See definition	See definition
Day	D	Arbitrary	Time	Second (s)	86400
Day (sidereal)	-	Arbitrary	Time	Second (s)	8.616 409x10^4
Debye	D	Metric	Electric dipole moment	Coulomb meter (C.m)	3.33564x10^{-30}

Summary of some of the scientific units (Cont.)

UNIT	Symbol	System of Units	Quantity	Corresponding SI Unit	To Convert to SI multiply it by
Decibel	dB	All	Unit of dimensionless quantities e.g., power level difference	See definition	See definition
Decibel, Perceived	PNdB	All	Perceived noise level	See definition	See definition
Decibel above 1 femtowatt	dBf	All	Power level	See definition	See definition
Decibel above 1 kilowatt	dBkW	All	Power level	See definition	See definition
Decibel above 1 milliwatt	dBm	All	Power level	See definition	See definition
Decibel above 1	dBp	All	Power level	See definition	See definition
Decibel above 1 volt	dBV	All	Power level	See definition	See definition
Decibel above 1 watt	dbW	All	Power level	See definition	See definition
Decibel above reference coupling	dBx	All	Measure the coupling between two circuits	See definition	See definition
Decibel above reference noise	dBrn	All	Interfering effect of noise	See definition	See definition
Decilit	Decilit	All	Intensity level	Decibel (dB)	**1 dB**
Decilog	Decilog	All	Intensity level	Decibel (dB)	**1 dB**
Decilu	Decilu	All	Intensity level	Decibel (dB)	**1 dB**
Decimeter	**Dm**	with SI	Length	Meter (m)	0.1
Decimilligrade	....^{cc}	Arbitrary	Plane angle	Radian (rad)	$1.570\ 809 \times 10^{-6}$
Decistere	Dst	SI	Volume, capacity	Cubic meter (m^3)	0.1
Decomlog	Decomlog	All	Intensity level	Decibel (dB)	**1 dB**
Degree (of arc)	°	with SI	Plane angle	Radian (rad)	$\pi\,/180$
Degree (of hardness)	°Clark, ppm	Arbitrary	Hardness of water	See definition	See definition
Degree (of time)	Degree	Arbitrary	Time	Second (s)	**864**
Degree absolute	K	SI	Temperature	Kelvin (K)	1

Summary of some of the scientific units (Cont.)

UNIT	Symbol	System of Units	Quantity	Corresponding SI Unit	To Convert to SI, multiply it by
Degree American	degree API	None	Relative density	See definition	See definition
Degree Baume	degree Baume'	None	Relative density	See definition	See definition
Degree Celsius	°C	Metric, SI	Customary temperature	Kelvin (K)	1
Degree centigrade	°C	Metric, SI	Customary temperature	Kelvin (K)	**1**
Degree Clark	°Clark	Arbitrary	Water hardness	See definition	See definition
Degree Fahrenheit	°F	Arbitrary	Customary temperature	Kelvin (K)	See definition
Degree Kelvin	K	SI	Thermodynamic temperature	SI	SI
Degree per second	°/s	Arbitrary	Angular velocity	Radian per second (rad/s)	$1.745\ 33 \times 10^{-2}$
Degree per second squared.	°/s^2	Arbitrary	Angular acceleration	Radian per second squared (rad/s^2)	$1.745\ 33 \times 10^{-2}$
Degree Rankine	°R	Arbitrary	Thermodynamic Temperature	Kelvin (SI)	See definition
Degree Reaumur	°r	Arbitrary	Customary Temperature	Kelvin (K)	See definition
Degree Siks	degree Sikes	Arbitrary	Concentration	See definition	See definition
Degree, square	square degree	All	Solid angle	Steradian (sr)	$(\pi/180)^2$ $=3.04617 \times 10^{-4}$
Degree Twaddell	degree Twaddell	None	Relative density	See definition	See definition

Summary of some of the scientific units (Cont.)

UNIT	Symbol	System of Units	Quantity	Corresponding SI Unit	To Convert to SI, multiply it by
Demal	Demal	Metric-derived	Concentration	Kilogramme-equivalent per cubic meter (m^3)	1
Denier	Denier	Metric	Line density	Kilogramme per meter (kg/m)	$(1/9x10^6) =$ 1.1111 $1x10^{-7}$
Dex	Dex	All	Logarithmic value	Decibel (dB)	**10**
Dezitonne	Dt	German unit	Mass	Kilogramme (kg)	**100**
Dioptre	Dioptre	SI	Reciprocal length (power of lens)	Per meter (1/m)	**1**
Dollar	Dollar	All	Reactivity	See definition	See definition
Donkey	donkey	Metric	Power	Watt (W)	250
Drachm (UK)	Drachm	UK unit	Mass	Kilogramme (kg)	3.887 934 6 $x10^{-3}$
Drachm, fluid UK	UK fl dr	UK unit	Capacity, volume	Cubic meter (m^3)	$3.55163x10^{-6}$
Drachm, fluid US	US fl dr	US unit	Capacity, volume	Cubic meter (m^3)	3.696 716 2 $x10^{-6}$
Dram	Dr	Imperial	Mass	Kilogramme (kg)	0.00177185
Dram (US)	dram ap	Imperial	Mass	Kilogramme (kg)	3.8879346 x 10^{-3}
Drex	Drex	Metric (US and Canadian unit)	Line density	Kilogramme per meter (kg/m)	**10^7**
Dry barrel	dry bl	US unit	Volume, Capacity	Cubic meter (m^3)	1.15627 x 10^{-1}
Dry pint	dry pt	US unit	Volume, Capacity	Cubic meter (m^3)	$5.50610x10^{-4}$
Dry quart (US)	dry qt	US unit	Volume, Capacity	Cubic meter (m^3)	$1.0122x10^{-3}$
D-Unit	D-Unit D-unit	Arbitrary	Radiation dose	See definition	See definition
Duffieux	Duffieux	SI	Angular spatial frequency	Hertz per meter (Hz/m)	1
Duty	Duty	FIbfS	Energy	Joule (J)	1.35581794833140
Dyne	Dyne	CGS	Force	Newton (N)	**10^{-5}**
Dyne, large	SI	Force	Newton (N)	SI (= 1 N)

Summary of some of the scientific units (Cont.)

UNIT	Symbol	System of Units	Quantity	Corresponding SI Unit	To Convert to SI multiply it by
Dyne centimeter	dyn. Cm	CGS	Moment of force	Newton meter (N.m)	10^{-7}
Dyne centimeter per biot	Dyn. cm/Bi	CGSB	Magnetic flux	Weber (Wb)	10^{-8}
Dyne centimeter per second	dyn.cm/s	CGS	Moment of momentum	Kilogramme meter square per second $(kg.m^2/s)$	10^{-7}
Dyne per biot centimeter	dyn/(Bi.cm)	CGSB	Magnetic flux density and magnetic polarization	Tesla (T) Tesla (T)	10^{-4} $1.256\ 64 \times 10^{-3}$
Dyne per biot squared	dyn/Bi^2	CGSB	Permeability	Henry per meter (H/m)	$1.256\ 64 \times 10^{-6}$

Summary of some of the scientific units (Cont.)

UNIT	Symbol	System of Units	Quantity	Corresponding SI Unit	To Convert to SI. multiply it by
Dyne per centimeter	dyn/cm	CGS	Surface tension	Newton per meter (N/m)	10^{-3}
Dyne per cubic centimeter	dyn/cm^3	CGS	Specific weight	Newton per cubic meter (N/m^3)	10
Dyne per franklin	dyn/Fr	CGSF	Electric field strength	Volt per meter (V/m)	$2.997\ 92 \times 10^4$
Dyne per square centimeter	dyn/cm^2	CGS	Pressure	Pascal (Pa)	10^1
Dyne second	dyn.s	CGS	Momentum	Kilogramme meter per second (kg.m/s)	10^{-5}
Dyne second per centimeter	dyn.s/cm	CGS	Mechanical Impedance	Newton second per meter (N.s/m)	10^{-3}
Dyne second per centimeter cubed	$dyn.s/cm^3$	CGS	Specific acoustic impedance	Pascal second per meter (Pa.s/m)	10
Dyne second per centimeter to the fifth power	$dyn.s/cm^5$	CGS	Acoustic impedance	Pascal second per cubic meter ($Pa.s/m^3$)	10^5
Dyne second per square centimeter	$dyn.s/cm^2$	CGS	Viscosity (dynamic)	Pascal's second (Pa.s)	10^{-1}
Einstein Unit	Einstein unit	Arbitrary	Photoenergy	See definition	See definition
Electronvolt	eV	with SI	Energy	Joule (J)	$1.602189\ 2_{\times10^{-19}}$
Electronvolt per meter	eV/m	with SI	Linear stopping power and linear energy transfere	Joule per meter (J/m)	$1.602_{19}9 \times 10^{-}$
Electronvolt per square meter	eV/m^2	with SI	Energy fluence	Joule per square meter (J/m^2)	$1.602_{19}9 \times 10^{-}$
Electronvolt per square meter second	$eV/(m^2.s)$	with SI	Energy fluence rate	Watt per square meter (W/m^2)	$1.602_{19}9 \times 10^{-19}$
Electronvolt square meter	$eV.m^2$	with SI	Atomic stopping power	Joule square meter ($J.m^2$)	$1.602_{19}9 \times 10^{-19}$
Electronvolt square meter per kilogramme	$eV.m^2/kg$	with SI	Mass stopping power	Joule square meter per kilogramme ($J.m^2/kg$)	$1\ 602_{19}9 \times 10^{-19}$
Ell	Ell	UK unit	Length	Meter (m)	**1.143**

Summary of some of the scientific units (Cont.)

UNIT	Symbol	System of Units	Quantity	Corresponding SI Unit	To Convert to SI, multiply it by
Eman	Eman	Arbitrary	Radioactive Concentration	Becquerel (Bq)	3.7×10^3
Emerald, printer	Emerald	Arbitrary	Length	Meter (m)	$2.284\ 488\ 7 \times 10^{-3}$
EMU of capacitance	-	CGS – emu	Capacitance	Farad (F)	1×10^9
EMU of current	-	CGS-emu	Current, electric	Ampere (A)	10
EMU of electric potential	-	CGS-emu	Electric potential	Volt (V)	1×10^{-8}
EMU of inductance	-	CGS-emu	Inductance	Henry (H)	1×10^{-9}
EMU of resistance	-	CGS-emu	Resistance	Ohm (Q)	1×10^{-9}
Energy unit	energy unit	Arbitrary	Radiation dose	Joule per kilogramme	0.0093
Eon	Eon	Arbitrary	Time	Second (s)	10^9 year
Eotvos	E	Metric	Horizontal gradient of gravitational acceleration	Meter per second squared horizontal meter	10^{-9}
Engineer's chain	engineer's chain	US and UK	Length	Meter (m)	30.48
Erg	Erg	CGS	Energy	Joule (J)	10^{-7}
Erg per biot	erg/Bi	CGSB	Magnetic flux	Weber (Wb)	10^{-8}
Erg per biot squared	erg/Bi^2	CGSB	Inductance and mutual inductance	Henry (H)	10^{-9}
Erg per centimeter	erg/cm	CGS	Linear stopping power and linear energy transfer	Joule per meter (J/m)	10^{-5}
Erg per cubic centimeter	erg/cm^3	CGS	Energy density and calorific value (volume basis)	Joule per cubic meter (J/m^3)	10^{-1}
Erg per cubic centimeter degree Celsius	erg/(cm^3.°C)	CGS	Heat capacity per unit volume	Joule per cubic meter kelvin (J/m^3.K)	10^{-1}
Erg per cubic centimeter second	erg/(cm^3.s)	CGS	Heat release rate	Watt per cubic meter (W/m^3)	10^{-1}
Erg per centimeter second degree Celsius	erg/(cm.s.°C)	CGS	Thermal Conductivity	Watt per meter kelvin (W/m.K)	10^{-5}

Summary of some of the scientific units (Cont.)

UNIT	Symbol	System of Units	Quantity	Corresponding SI Unit	To Convert to SI multiply it by
Erg per degree Celsius	erg/°C	CGS	Heat capacity and entropy	Joule per kelvin(J/K)	10^{-7}
Erg per franklin	erg/Fr	CGSF	Electric potential	Volt (V)	$2.997\ 92 \times 10^{2}$
Erg per gramme	erg/g	CGS	Specific heat capacity and kerma	Joule per kilogramme (J/kg)	10^{-4}
Erg per gramme degree Celsius	erg/(g.°C)	CGS	Specific heat capacity	Joule per kilogramme kelvin (J/kg.K)	10^{-4}
Erg per gramme second	erg/(g.s)	CGS	Absorbed dose rate and kerma rate	Watt per kilogramme (W/kg)	10^{-4}
Erg per kelvin	erg/K	CGS	Heat capacity and entropy	Joule per kelvin (J/K)	10^{-7}
Erg per mole degree Celsius	erg/(mole.°C)	CGS	Molar gas constant	Joule per mole kelvin (J/mol.K)	10^{-7}
Erg per second	erg/s	CGS	Power and sound energy flux	Watt (W)	10^{-7}
Erg per second, steradian	erg/(s.sr)	CGS	Radiant density	Watt per steradian (W/sr)	10^{-7}
Erg per second steradian square	erg/(s.sr.cm^2)	CGS	Radiance	Watt per second square meter (W/s.m^2)	10^{-3}
Erg per square centimeter	erg/cm^2	CGS	Surface tension	Newton per meter (N/m)	10^{-3}
Erg per square centimeter second	erg/(cm^2.s)	CGS	Energy fluence rate	Watt per square meter (W/m^2)	10^{3}
Erg per square centimeter second degree Celsius	erg/(cm^2.s.°C)	CGS	Coefficient of heat transfer	Watt per meter squared second kelvin (W/m^2.s.K)	10^{-3}
Erg per square centimeter second kelvin to the fourth power	erg/(cm^2.s.K^4)	CGS	Stefan-Boltzmann Constant	Watt per square meter kelvin to fourth power (W/m^2.K^4)	10^{-3}

Summary of some of the scientific units (Cont.)

UNIT	Symbol	System of Units	Quantity	Corresponding SI Unit	To Convert to SI multiply it by
Erg second	erg.s	CGS	Planck constant	Joule second (J.S)	10^{-7}
Erg square centimeter	$erg.cm^2$	CGS	Atomic stopping power	Joule square meter $(J.m^2)$	10^{-11}
Erg square centimeter per gramme	$erg.cm^2/g$	CGS	Mass stopping power	Joule square meter per kilogramme $(J.m^2/kg)$	10^{-8}
Erg square centimeter per second	$erg.cm^2/s$	CGS	First radiation constant	Watt square meter $(W.m^2)$	10^{11}
Ergon	Ergons	Arbitrary	Energy associated with electromagnetic radiation	See definition	See definition
Erlang	E	Any	Telephone traffic intensity	See definition	See definition
ESU of capacitance	-	CGS-esu	Capacitance	Farad (F)	1.112 $650x10^{-12}$
ESU of current	-	CGS-esu	Current, electric	Ampere (A)	$3.335\ 6x10^{-10}$
ESU of electric potential	-	CGS-esu	Electric potential	Volt (V)	$2.997\ 9x10^2$
ESU of inductance	-	CGS-esu	Inductance	Henry (H)	$8.987\ 554$ $x10^{11}$
ESU of resistance	-	CGS-esu	Resistance	Ohm (Ω)	8.987 $554x10^{11}$
e-Unit	e-unit	Arbitrary	Radiation dose	Roentgen	7
E-Unit	E-unit	Arbitrary	Radiation dose rate	Roentgen per second	1
Fahrenheit degree	degF or ^oF	Arbitrary	Temperature interval	See definition	See definition
Farad	F	SI	Electric capacitance	SI	SI
Farad, thermal	thermal farad	SI	Thermal capacitance	Joule per square kelvin (J/K^2)	SI

Summary of some of the scientific units (Cont.)

UNIT	Symbol	System of Units	Quantity	Corresponding SI Unit	To Convert to SI, multiply it by
Farad per meter	F/m	**SI**	Permittivity	SI	SI
Faraday (based on carbon-12)	Faraday	Arbitrary	Charge	Coulomb (C)	9.64870×10^4
Faraday (Chemical)	faraday (chem.)	Arbitrary	Charge	Coulomb (C)	$9.649\ 57. \times 10^4$
Faraday (physical)	Faraday (phys.)	Arbitrary	Charge	Coulomb (C)	$9.652\ 19 \times 10^4$
Fathom	Fathom	Imperial	Length	Meter (m)	1.828 8
Fermi	Fermi	Metric	Length	Meter (m)	10^{-15}
Finsen unit	FU	Metric	Intensity of ultraviolet radiation	Watt per square meter (W/m^2)	10^s
Firkin (US)	Firkin	US unit	Capacity, volume	Cubic meter (m^3)	$34.067\ 75 \times 10^3$
Firkin (Brit.)	Firkin	UK unit	Capacity, volume	Cubic meter (m^3)	$40.913\ 64 \times 10^{-3}$
Fluid drachm (UK)	UK fl dr	UK unit	Capacity, volume	Cubic meter (m^3)	$3.5\ 5163 \times 10^{-5}$
Fluid dram (US)	US fl dr	US unit	Capacity, volume	Cubic meter (m^3)	$3.696\ 716\ 2 \times 10^6$
Fluid ounce (UK)	UK fl oz	UK unit	Capacity, volume	Cubic meter (m^3)	$2.841\ 31 \times 10^{-5}$
Fluid ounce (US)	US liq oz	US unit	Capacity, volume	Cubic meter (m^3)	$2.957\ 353 \times 10^{-5}$
Flux unit	Fu	Metric	Flux density of radio -astronomical source	Watt per square meter (W/m^2)	10^{-26}
Foot	Ft	FBS, FSS, FIbfS	Length	Meter (m)	**0.3048**
Foot-candle	ft. c	FBS	Intensity of illumination	Lux (lux)	10.76391
Foot-Candle, equivalent	equivalent foot-candle	Imperial	Luminance	Nit (nit)	3.426 25
Foot, Cape	Cape foot	Imperial	Length	Meter (m)	0.314 858 4
Foot-Lambert	ft-L	Imperial	Luminance	Nit (nit)	3.426 259
Foot, survey (US)	US survey foot	Arbitrary	Length	Meter (m)	0.304 800 6

Summary of some of the scientific units (Cont.)

UNIT	Symbol	System of Units	Quantity	Corresponding SI Unit	To Convert to SI multiply it by
Foot hour degree Fahrenheit per Btu	ft.h.°F/Btu	Arbitrary	Thermal resistivity	Meter kelvin per watt (m.K/W)	$5.777\ 89 \times 10^{-1}$
Foot of water	ft H_2O	Arbitrary	Pressure	Pascal (Pa)	$2.989\ 07 \times 10^{3}$
Foot per minute	ft/min	Arbitrary	Velocity	Meter per second (m/s)	5.08×10^{-3}
Foot per pound	ft/Ib	FPS	Specific length	Meter per kilogramme (m/kg)	$6.719\ 69 \times 10^{-1}$
Foot per second	| ft/s	FPS	Velocity	Meter per second (m/s)	3.048×10^{-1}
Foot per second squared	ft/s²	FPS	Acceleration	Meter per second squared (m/s²)	3.048×10^{-1}
Foot pound	ft lb	FPS	Work, torque	Joule (J)	1.355 82
Foot-poundal	ft pdl	FPS	Work, torque	Joule (J)	0.042 140 11
Foot poundal per second	ft.pdl/s	FPS	Power	Watt (W)	$4.214\ 01 \times 10^{-2}$
Foot pound-force	ft.Ibf	FIbfS	Work	Joule (J)	1.355 82
Foot pound-force per pound	ft.Ibf/Ib	Arbitrary	Specific internal energy and specific latent heat	Joule per kilogramme (J/kg)	2.989 07
Foot pound-force per pound degree Fahrenheit	ft.Ibf/(Ib.°F)	Arbitrary	Specific heat capacity	Joule per kilogramme kelvin (J/kg.K)	5.380 32
Foot pound-force per second	ft.Ibf/s	FIbfS	Power	Watt (W)	1.355 82
Foot squared per hour	ft²/h	Arbitrary	Kinematic viscosity	Meter squared per second (m²/s)	$2.580\ 64 \times 10^{-5}$
Foot squared per second	ft²s	FPS	Kinematic viscosity	Meter squared per second (m²/s)	$9.290\ 30 \times 10^{-2}$
Foot to the fourth power	ft⁴	FPS	Second moment of area	Meter to the fourth power (m⁴)	$8.630\ 97 \times 10^{-3}$
Fors	F	Metric	Acceleration	Meter per second square (m/s²)	9.80665
Fors	F	Metric	Force	Newton (N)	$g \times 10^{-3}$

Summary of some of the scientific units (Cont.)

UNIT	Symbol	System of Units	Quantity	Corresponding SI Unit	To Convert to SI, multiply it by
Fourier	Fourier	SI	Thermal resistance	Kelvin square per watt (K^2/W)	SI
Franklin	Fr	CGSF	Charge	Coulomb (C)	3.33564×10^{-10}
Franklin centimeter	Fr.cm	CGSF	Electric dipole moment	Coulomb meter (C.m)	$3.335\ 64 \times 10^{-12}$
Franklin per second	Fr/s	CGSF	Electric current	Ampere (A)	$3.335\ 64 \times 10^{-10}$
Franklin per square centimeter	Fr/cm^2	CGSF	Electric polarization	Coulomb per meter square (Cm^2)	$3.335\ 64 \times 1\ 0^{-6}$
Franklin squared per erg	Fr^2/erg	CGSF	Capacitance	Farad (F)	$1.112\ 65 \times 10^{-12}$
Franklin squared per erg	$Fr^2/(erg.cm)$	CGSF	Permittivity	Farad per meter (F/m)	$8.854\ 19 \times 10^{-12}$
Fraunhofer	F	All	Reduced width of a spectrum line	See definition	See definition
Freight ton	freight ton	Arbitrary	Volume (of ship cargo)	Cubic meter (m^3)	1.132 674
French	French	French unit	Length (diameter)	Meter (m)	**$(l/3) \times l0^{-3}$**
Fresnel	Fresnel	All	Frequency	Hertz (Hz)	**10^{12}**
Frigorie	Fg	Arbitrary	Fleat energy	Joule (J)	$4.1855 \times l0^3$
Frigorie per hour	fg/h	Arbitrary	Refrigeration Capacity	Watt (W)	1.162 64
Funal	Funal	MTS	Force	Newton (N)	**1000**
Furlong	Fur	Imperial	Length	Meter (m)	**201.168**
g, standard free fall	G	Metric	Acceleration	Meter per second squared (m/s^2)	**9.806 650**
G	G	Metric, Imperial	Acceleration	Meter per second square (m/s^2)	1
Gal	Gal	CGS	Acceleration	Meter per second square (m/s^2)	**10^{-2}**

Summary of some of the scientific units (Cont.)

UNIT	Symbol	System of Units	Quantity	Corresponding SI Unit	To Convert to SI, multiply by
Galileo	GAL or Gal	CGS	Acceleration	Meter per second square (m/s^2)	**10^{-2}**
Gallon (Canadian	gal (Canadian)	Canadian unit	Capacity, volume (liquid)	Cubic meter (m^3)	4.546 090 x10^{-3}
Gallon (UK)	UKgal	Arbitrary, Imperial	Capacity, volume	Cubic meter (m^3)	**4.546 09x10^{-3}**
Gallon (UK) per hour	UKgal/h	UK unit	Volume flow rate	Cubic meter per second (m^3/s)	1.262 80x10^{-6}
Gallon (UK) per mile	UKgal/mile	UK unit	Fuel consumption	Litres per kilometer (L/km)	2.824 81
Gallon (UK) per minute	UKgal/min	UK unit	Volume flow rate	Cubic meter per second (m^3/s)	7.576 82x10^{-5}
Gallon (UK) per pound	UKgal/Ib	UK unit	Specific volume	Cubic meter per kilogramme (m^3/kg)	1.002 24x10^{-2}
Gallon (UK) per second	UKgal/s	UK unit	Volume flow rate	Cubic meter per second (m^3/s)	4.546 09x10^{-3}
Gallon (US, dry)	Usgal (dry)	US unit	Capacity, volume JM	Cubic meter (m^3)	4.404 884 x10^{-3}
Gallon (US, liquid)	USgal	Arbitrary, Imperial	Capacity, volume (liquid)	Cubic meter (m^J)	**3.785 411 784 xl0^{-3}**
Gallon (US) per hour	USgal/h	US unit	Volumr flow rate	Cubic meter per second (m^3/s)	1.051 50x10^{-6}
Gallon (US) per mile	USgal/mile	US unit	Fuel consumption	Litres per kilometer (L/km)	2.352 15
Gallon (US) per minute	USgal/min	US unit	Volume flow rate	Cubic meter per second (m^3/s)	6.309 02x10^{-5}
Gallon (US liquid) per horsepower hour	USgal/(hp.h)	US unit	Specific fuel consumption	Cubic meter per joule (m^3/J)	1.410 089 x10^{-9}
Gallon (US) per pound	USgal/Ib	US unit	Specific volume	Cubic meter per kilogramme (m^3/kg)	8.345 40x10^{-3}
Gallon (US) per second	USgal/s	US unit	Volume flow rate	Cubic meter per second (m^3/s)	3.785 41x10^{-3}
Galvat	Galvat	MKSA	Current	Ampere (A)	0.999 835
Gamma	γ	Metric	Magnetic field strength	|Tesla (T)	10^{-9}

Summary of some of the scientific units (Cont.)

UNIT	Symbol	System of Units	Quantity	Corresponding SI Unit	To Convert to SI, multiply it by
Gamma	γ	Metric	Mass	Kilogramme (kg)	10^{-9}
Gammil	Gammil	Metric	Concentration	Kilogramme per cubic meter kg/m^3	1×10^{-3}
Gauss	G in physics, Gs in Engineering	CGS-emu	Magnetic flux density	Tesla (T)	10^{-4}
Gee pound	gee pound	FSS (FIbfS)	Mass	Kilogramme (kg)	1.459 39x10
Gemmho	Gemmho	Metric	Conductance	Siemens (S)	10^{-6}
Gibbs	Gibbs	Metric	Absorption (surface concentration)	Mole per square meter (mol/m^2)	10^{-6}
Gilbert	Gb	CGS-emu	Magnetomotive Force	Ampere (A)	7.957 75x10^{-}1
Gilbert per centimeter	Gb/cm	CGS-emu	Magnetic field strength	Ampere per meter (A/m)	7.957 75x10
Gilbert per Maxwell	Gb/Mx	Reluctance	CGS-emu	Per henry (H-1)	7.957 75x10^7
Gill (UK)	Gill	UK unit	Capacity, volume	Cubic meter (m3)	1.420 65x10^{-4}
Gill (US)	Gi	US unit	Capacity, volume (liquid)	Cubic meter (m3)	1.182 94x10^{-4}
Glug	Glug	CgfS	Mass	Kilogramme (kg)	0.980 665
Gon	........g	All	Plane angle	Radian (rad)	1.570 796x10^{-2}
Grade	........g	All	Plane angle	Radian (rad)	1.570 796x10^{-2}
Grade per second	g/s	All	Angular velocity	Radian per second (rad/s)	1.570 80x10^{-2}
Grade per second square	g/s2	All	Angular acceleration	Radian per second square (rad/s2)	1.570 80x10^{-2}

Summary of some of the scientific units (Cont.)

UNIT	Symbol	System of Units	Quantity	Corresponding SI Unit	To Convert to SI, multiply it by
Grain	gr (or grain)	UK and US	Mass	kilogramme (kg)	$6.479\ 891 \times 10^{-5}$
Grain, metric	metric grain	Metric	Mass	kilogramme (kg)	5×10^{-5}
Grain per cubic foot	gr/ft^3	Arbitrary	Mass density and concentration	Kilogramme per cubic meter (kg/m^3)	$2.288\ 35 \times 10^{-3}$
Grain per UK gallon	gr/UKgal	UK unit	Mass density and concentration	Kilogramme per cubic meter i (kg/m^3)	$1.425\ 38 \times 10^{-2}$
Grain per US gallon	gr/USgal	US unit	Mass density and concentration	Kilogramme per cubic meter (kg/m^3)	$1.711\ 81 \times 10^{-2}$
Gramme	g	CGS	Mass	Kilogramme (kg)	10^{-3}
Gramme-Calorie	cal-g	Arbitrary	Heat energy	Joule (J)	4.1855
Gramme centimeter per second	g.cm/s	CGS	Momentum	Kilogramme meter per second (kg.m/s)	10^{-5}
Gramme centimeter squared	g.cm^2	CGS	Moment of inertia	Kilogramme meter squared (kg.m^2)	10^{-7}
Gramme centimeter squared per second	g.cm^2/s	CGS	Moment of momentum	Kilogramme meter squared per second (kg.m^2/s)	10^{-7}
Gramme-equivalent	g-eq	Metric – derived	Mass	See definition	See definition
Gramme-force	Gf	CgfS	Force	Newton (N)	$9.806\ 65 \times 10^{-3}$

Summary of some of the scientific units (Cont.)

UNIT	Symbol	System of Units	| Quantity	Corresponding SI Unit	To Convert to SI, multiply it by
Gramme-molecule	g mol	Metric	Amount of substance	See definition	See definition
Gramme per cubic centimeter	g/cm^3	CGS	Mass density	kilogramme per cubic	10^3
Gramme per litre	g/L	Arbitrary	Mass density	kilogramme per cubic meter (kg/m^3)	1
Gramme per millilitre	g/mL	Arbitrary	Mass density	Kilogramme per cubic meter (kg/m^3)	10^3
Gramme per square meter	g/m^2	with SI	Surface density and grammage of paper or paperboard	Kilogramme per square meter (kg/m^2)	10^{-3}
Gramme per square meter day	$g/(m^2.d)$	with SI	Water vapour transmission rate	with SI	**with SI**
Gramme-rad	gramme-rad	Metric	Integral absorbed ionising radiation dose	Joule (J)	10^5
Gramme-Rontgen	gramme-rontgen	Arbitrary	Absorbed radioactive energy	Joule (J)	8.69×10^{-6}
Gramme-weight	Gwt	Metric	Force	See definition	See definition
Grav	G	Metric	Acceleration	Meter per second square (m/s^2)	9.806 65
Grave	Grave	Metric	Mass	kilogramme (kg)	1.000028×10^{-3}
Gray	Gy	SI	Absorbed dose, kerma	Joule per kilogramme	SI
Gray per second	Gy/s	SI	Absorbed dose rate and kerma rate	SI	SI
Gregorian year	-	Calendar year	Time	Second (s)	$3.155\ 695\ 2 \times 10^7$
Hand	Hand	None	Length	Meter (m)	**1.016×10^{-1}**
Hardness	-	-	Hardness	See definition	See definition

Summary of some of the scientific units (Cont.)

UNIT	Symbol	System of Units		Quantity	Corresponding SI Unit	To Convert to SI, multiply it by
Hartley	Hartley	None	Information	See definition	See definition
Hartree	Hartree	Hartree	Energy	Joule (J)	4.360×10^{-18}
Hectare	Ha	Arbitrary	Area	Square meter (m^2)	10^4
Hectogramme	**Hg**	Arbitrary	Mass	Kilogramme (kg)	10^{-1}
Hectolitre	**Hl**	Arbitrary	Capacity, volume	Cubic meter (m3)	10^{-1}
Hectopieze	**Hpz**	French unit	Pressure	Pascal (Pa)	10^5
Hefner candle	**hefiner**	All	Luminous intensity	Candela (cd)	**0.903**
Hefner-kerze	**HK**	German unit	Luminous intensity	Candela (cd)	**0.918**
Hehner	**Hehner**	Arbitrary	Concentration of	See definition	**See definition**
Helmholtz	**Helmholtz**	Metric	Dipole moment per unit area	Coulomb per meter (C/m)	**3.335 64x10⁻¹⁰**
Hemisphere	**Hemisphere**	Arbitrary	Solid angle	Steradian	**1 6.283 185 307**
Henry	**H**	SI	Electric inductance	SI	**SI**
Henry, thermal	**thermal henry**	SI	Thermal inductance	SI	**SI**
Henry per meter	**H/m**	SI	Permeability	SI	**SI**
Herschel	**Herschel**	Metric	Radiance	Watt per meter squared steradian	π
Hertz	**Hz**	All	Frequency	SI	**SI**
Hogshead	**Hhd**	Arbitrary	Volume, capacity	Cubic meter (nr)	**0.238 480 94**
Horsepower (550 ft.Ibf/s)	**mechanical horsepower**	Imperial (UK and US)	Power	Watt (W)	**$7.456\ 99 \times 10^2$**
Horsepower, boiler			Power	Watt (W)	**$9.809\ 50 \times 10^3$**
Horsepower, brake	**brake horsepower**	Arbitrary	Power	Watt	**See definition**
Horsepower,	**Electric**	Metric	Power	Watt (W)	**746**

Summary of some of the scientific units (Cont.)

UNIT	Symbol	System of Units	| Quantity	Corresponding SI Unit	To Convert to SI, multiply it by
Horsepower, indicated	Indicated horsepower	Arbitrary	Power	Watt (W)	See definition
Horsepower, metric	ch, PS and metric horsepower	Metric	Power	Watt (W)	7.354 99x10^2
Horsepower, water	Water horsepower	Arbitrary	Power	Watt (W)	7.460 43x10^2
Horsepower, UK		Imperial	Power	Watt (W)	7.457 0 x10^2
Horsepower hour (metric)	ch h, Psh, or horsepower hour metric	Metric	Work	Joule (J)	2.647 80x10^6
Horsepower hour	hp. H	US and UK	Energy	Joule (J)	2.684 52x10^5
Hour	H	Arbitrary	Time	Second (s)	**3600**
Hour angle	Ω	Arbitrary	Daily motion of the sun	See definition	See definition
Hour, sidereal		Arbitrary	Time	Second (s)	3.590 170x10^3
Hubble	Hubble	Arbitrary	Length	Light year	10^9
Hundredweight	Cwt	UK unit	Mass	Kilogramme (kg)	5.080 235x10
Hundredweight,	sh cwt	Imperial	Mass	Kilogramme (kg)	4.535 924x10
Hundredweight	cwt tr	UK unit	Mass	Kilogramme (kg)	3.732 417 217 xl0
Hyl	Hyl	Metric-technical	Mass	kilogramme (kg)	**9.806 65xl0^3**
Hydron	Hydron	Non	Acidity	See definition	See definition
Inch	In	Imperial	Length	Meter (m)	**2.54**
Inch, Circular	circular inch	Imperial	Area	Square meter (m^2)	5.067 08x10^{-4}
Inch of mercury (32°F)	inHg (32°F)	Arbitrary	Pressure	Pascal (Pa)	3.386 38xl0^3
Inch of mercury (60°F)	inHg (60°F)	Arbitrary	Pressure	Pascal (Pa)	3.376 85xl0^3

Summary of some of the scientific units (Cont.)

UNIT	Symbol	System of Units	Quantity	Corresponding SI Unit	To Convert to SI, multiply it by
Inch of water (39.2°F)	inH_2O (39.2°F)	Arbitrary	Pressure	Pascal (Pa)	$2.490\ 82 \times 10^2$
Inch of water (60°F)	inH_2O (60°F)	Arbitrary	Pressure	Pascal (Pa)	$2.488\ 4 \times 10^2$
Inch cubic	in^3		Volume, section modulus	Cubic meter (m^3)	**$1.638\ 706\ 4 \times 10^5$**
Inch per minute	in/min		Velocity	Meter per second (m/s)	$4.233\ 33. \times 10^{-4}$
Inch per second	in/s		Velocity	Meter per second (m/s)	**2.54×10^{-2}**
Inch squared per hour	in^2/h		Kinematic viscosity	Meter squared per second (m^2/s)	$1.7921 1 \times 10^{-7}$
Inch squared per second	in^2/s		Kinematic viscosity	Meter squared per second (m^2/s)	**$6.451\ 6 \times 10^{-4}$**
Inch to the fourth power	in^4		Second moment of area	Meter to the fourth power (ra^4)	$4.\ 162\ 31 \times 10^{-7}$
Inferno	Inferno	Arbitrary	Temperature	Kelvin (K)	**10^9**
Inhour	In	Arbitrary derived	Reactivity	See definition	See definition
Instant	Instant	Arbitrary	Time	Second (s)	0.086 4
Iodine number	iodine number	Arbitrary	Percentage of absorbed iodine	See definition	See definition
Jansky	Jy	Arbitrary	Radiant flux density	Watt per meter squared hertz	10^{-26}
Jar	J_y	CGS-esu derived	Capacitance	Farad (F)	**$(1/9) \times 10^{-8}$**
Jerk	Jerk	FPS	Rate of change of acceleration	Meter per second cubed (m/s^3)	**0.3048**
Joule	J	SI	Energy	SI	SI
Joule per cubic meter	J/m^3	SI	Energy density	SI	SI
Joule per kelvin	J/K	SI	Heat capacity, entropy	SI	SI

Summary of some of the scientific units (Cont.)

UNIT	Symbol	System of Units	Quantity	Corresponding SI Unit	To Convert to SI, multiply it by
Joule per kilogramme	J/kg	SI	Specific energy, specific enthalpy	SI	SI
Joule per kilogramme kelvin	J/(kg.K)	SI	Specific heat capacity, specific entropy	SI	SI
Joule per meter	J/m	SI	Linear stopping power, linear energy transfer	SI	SI
Joule per meter to the fourth power	J/m^4	SI	Spectral concentration	SI	SI
Joule per mole	J/mol	SI	Molar internal energy	SI	SI
Joule per mole kelvin	J/(mol.K)	SI	Molar heat capacity and molar entropy	SI	SI
Joule per pound kelvin	J/(Ib.K)	Arbitrary	Specific heat capacity, specific entropy	Joule per kilogramme kelvin (J/kg.K)	2.204 62
Kilocalorie (I.T.) per meter hour	$Kcal_{IT}/(m.h.K)$	Arbitrary	Thermal conductivity	Watt per meter kelvin (W/m.K)	**1.163**
Kilocalorie (I.T.) per square meter	$kcal_{IT}/(m^2.h)$	Arbitrary	Density of heat flow j rate	Watt per meter square (W/m^2)	**1.163**
Kilocalorie (I.T.) per square meter	$kcal_{IT}/(m^2.h.K)$	Arbitrary	Coefficient of heat transfer	Watt per meter square kelvin $(W/m^2.K)$	**1.163**
Kilogramme	Kg	SI	Mass	SI	SI
Kilogramme-calorie	Kcal	Arbitrary	Heat energy	Joule (J)	4185.5
Kilogramme-equivalent	kg-eq	Metric - derived	Mass	See definition	See definition

Summary of some of the scientific units (Cont.)

UNIT	Symbol	System of Units	Quantity	Corresponding SI Unit	To Convert to SI, multiply it by
Kilogramme-force	Kgf	MkgfS	Force	Newton (N)	**9.806 65**
Kilogramme-force Meter	kgf.m	MkgfS	Moment of force, torque, work, energy	Newton meter (N.m), Joule (J)	**9.806 65**
Kilogramme-force meter per kilogramme	kgf.m/kg	MkgfS	Specific internal energy, specific latent heat	Joule per kilogramme (J/kg)	**9.806 65**
Kilogramme-force meter per kilogramme	kgf.m/(kg.°C)	MkgfS	Specific heat capacity	Joule per kilogramme kelvin (J/kg.K)	**9.806 65**
Kilogramme-force meter	kgf.m/s	MkgfS	Power	Watt (W)	**9.806 65**

Summary of some of the scientific units (Cont.)

UNIT	Symbol	System of Units	Quantity	Corresponding SI Unit	To Convert to SI, multiply it by
Kilogramme-force meter second	kgf.m.s	MkgfS	Action	Joule second (J.s)	**9.806 65**
Kilogramme-force meter second square	$kgf.m.s^2$	MkgfS	Moment of inertia	kilogramme square meter ($kg.m^2$)	**9.806 65**
Kilogramme-force per centimeter	kgf/cm	MkgfS	Surface tension	Newton per meter (N/m)	**9.806 65**
Kilogramme-force per cubic meter	kgf/m^3	MkgfS	Specific weight	Newton per cubic meter (N/m^3)	**9.806 65**
Kilogramme-force per meter	kgf/m	MkgfS	Surface tension	Newton per meter (N/m)	**9.806 65**
Kilogramme-force per meter second degree Celsius	kgf/(m.s.°C)	MkgfS	Coefficient of heat transfer	Watt per square meter kelvin ($W/m^2.K$)	**9.806 65**
Kilogramme-force per second degree Celsius	kgf/(s.°C)	MkgfS	Thermal conductivity	Watt per meter kelvin (W/m.K)	**9.806 65**
Kilogramme-force per square centimeter	kgf/cm^2	MkgfS	Pressure	Pascal (Pa)	**9.806 65 x10^4**
Kilogramme-force per square meter	kgf/m^2	MkgfS	Pressure	Pascal (Pa)	**9.806 65**
Kilogramme-force second	kgf.s	MkgfS	Momentum	Kilogramme meter per second (kg.m/s)	**9.806 65**
Kilogramme-force second per square meter	$kgf.s/m^2$	MkgfS	Viscosity (dynamic)	Pascal's second (Pa.s)	**9.806 65**

Summary of some of the scientific units (Cont.)

UNIT	Symbol	System of Units	Quantity	Corresponding SI Unit	To Convert to SI, multiply it by
Kilogramme-force second squared per meter.	$kgf.s^2/m$	MkgfS	Mass	Kilogramme (kg)	**9.806 65**
Kilogramme-force second squared per meter to fourth power.	$kgf.s^2/m^4$	MkgfS	Density	Kilogramme per cubic meter (kg/m^3)	**9.806 65**
Kilogramme-meter	kilogramme-meter	MkgfS	Energy	Joule (J)	**9.806 65**
Kilogramme meter squared	$kg.m^2$	SI	Moment of inertia	SI	SI
Kilogramme meter squared per second	$kg.m^2/s$	SI	Moment of momentum	SI	SI
Kilogramme of ice melted per hour	-	US unit	Refrigeration	Watt (W)	92.618 529 79
Kilogramme per cubic meter	kg/m^3	SI	Density (mass)	SI	SI
Kilogramme per cubic meter pascal	$kg/(m^3.Pa)$	SI	Unitary mass density	SI	SI
Kilogramme per hectare	kg/ha	Arbitrary	Surface density	Kilogramme per square meter (kg/m^2)	**10^{-4}**
Kilogramme per hour	kg/h	with SI	Mass flow rate	Kilogramme per second (kg/s)	$2.777\ 78 \times 10^{-4}$
Kilogramme per litre	kg/L or kg/1	with SI	Density (mass)	Kilogramme per cubic meter (kg/m^3)	10^3

Summary of some of the scientific units (Cont.)

UNIT	Symbol	System of Units	Quantity	Corresponding SI Unit	To Convert to SI, multiply it by
Kilogramme per meter	kg/m	SI	Linear density	SI	SI
Kilogramme per mole	kg/mol	SI	Molar mass	SI	SI
Kilogramme per pascal second meter	kg/(Pa.s.m)	SI	Water vapour permeance	SI	SI
Kilogramme per pascal second square meter	kg/(Pa.s.m^2)	SI	Water vapour permeability	SI	SI
Kilogramme per second	kg/s	SI	Mass flow rate	SI	SI
Kilogramme per square meter	kg/m^2	SI	Surface density	SI	SI
Kilogramme-Weight	Kgwt	Metric	Force	Newton (N)	g (see definition)
Kilogramme meter	Kilogramme meter	MkgfS	Energy	Joule (J)	9.806 65
Kilohyl	Khyl	MkgfS	Mass	Kilogramme (kg)	**9.806 65**
Kilohyl per cubic meter	khyl/m^3	MkgfS	Density	Kilogramme per cubic meter	**9.806 65**
Kiloline	Kiloline	CGS	Magnetic flux	Weber (Wb)	1×10^5
Kiloliter	kL	Arbitrary	Volume, capacity	Cubic meter (m^3)	1.000 028
Kilometer	Km	with SI	Length	Meter (m)	**10^3**
Kilometer per hour	km/h	with SI	Velocity	Meter per second (m/s)	2.777 777 78 x10^{-1}
Kilopond	Kp	MkpS	Force	Newton (N)	**9.806 65**
Kilovolt per centimeter	kV/cm	with SI	Electric field strength	Volt per meter (V/m)	**10^5**

Summary of some of the scientific units (Cont.)

UNIT	Symbol	System of Units	Quantity	Corresponding SI Unit	To Convert to SI, multiply it by
Kilowatt	kW	with SI	Power	Watt (W)	10^3
Kilowatt (International)	kW (Int.)	Arbitrary	Power	Watt (W)	$1.000\ 165 \times 10^3$
Kilowatt-hour	kWh	Metric, with SI	Energy	Joule (J)	3.6×10^6
Kilowatt-hour (International)	kW.h (Int.)	Arbitrary	Energy	Joule (J)	$3.600\ 594 \times 10^6$
Kilowatt-hour per gramme	kW.h/gm	with SI	Specific energy, specific enthalpy	Joule per kilogramme (J/kg)	3.6×10^9
Kine	Kine	CGS	Velocity	Meter per second (m/s)	10^{-2}
Kintal	Kintal	Imperial	Mass	Kilogramme (kg)	45.359 237
Kip	Kip	Imperial	Mass	Kilogramme (kg)	453.592 37
Kip	Kip	US unit	Force	Newton (N)	$4.448\ 222 \times 10^3$
Kip per square inch	Ksi	US unit	Pressure	Pascal (Pa)	$6.894\ 757 \times 10^6$
Knot	Kn	Metric	Velocity	Meter per second (m/s)	(1852/3600)
Knot (UK)	UK kn	UK unit	Velocity	Meter per second (m/s)	(1852/3600) x 1.00064
Lambda	λ	Metric	Volume	Cubic meter (m^3)	10^{-9}
Lambert	L	Metric	Luminance	Candela per square meter	$3.183\ 10 \times 10^3$
Langley	Langley	Arbitrary	Energy area density	Joule per meter square (J/m^2)	$4.186\ 8 \times 10^4$
Langley (US)	langley (US)	US unit	Energy area density	Joule per meter square (J/m^2)	4.184×10^4
Langley per minute	langley/min	Arbitrary	Irradiance	Watt per square meter (W/m^2)	6.978×10^2
Last	Last	UK unit	Volume, capacity	Cubic meter (m^3)	2.909 414
Lea	Lea	UK unit	Length	Meter (m)	109.728
League (statute)	League	Imperial	Length	Meter (m)	$4.828\ 032 \times 10^3$
League (nautical, UK)	league (nat. UK)	UK unit	Length	Meter (m)	$5.559\ 552 \times 10^3$
League (nautical, International)	league (nat. Int.)	Arbitrary	Length	Meter (m)	5.556×10^3
Lentor	Lentor	CGS	Viscosity, kinematic	Meter square per second (m^2/s)	10^{-4}

Summary of some of the scientific units (Cont.)

UNIT	Symbol	System of Units	Quantity	Corresponding SI Unit	To Convert to SI, multiply it by
Leo	Leo	Metric	Acceleration	Meter per second squared (m/s^2)	10
Light-Watt	light-watt	All, SI	Luminous	SI	SI
Light year	light year	Arbitrary	Length	Meter (m)	9.4607×10^{15}
Line	Line	Arbitrary	Length	Meter (m)	$2.116\ 666\ 666 \times 10^{-3}$
Line, metric	metric line	Metric	Length	Meter (m)	10^{-3}
Line (of electric force)	Line	CGS-emu	Electric flux	Coulomb (C)	$3.335\ 64 \times 10^{-10}$
Line (of magnetic force)	Line	CGS emu	Magnetic flux	Weber (Wb)	10^{8}
Link	Li	Imperial	Length	Meter (m)	0.201 168
Link (Ramden's)	link (Ram.)	Arbitrary	Length	Meter (m)	0.304 8
Liquid ounce (US)	US liq oz	US unit	Volume, capacity	Cubic meter (m^3)	$2.957\ 35 \times 10^{-5}$
Liquid pint (US)	US liq pt	US unit	Volume, capacity	Cubic meter (m^3)	$4.731\ 76 \times 10^{-4}$
Liquid quart (US)	US liq qt	US unit	Volume, capacity	Cubic meter (m^3)	$9.463\ 53 \times 10^{-4}$
Litre	1, L	Metric	Capacity, volume	Cubic meter (m^3)	10^{-3}
Litre (old)	1	Metric	Capacity, volume	Cubic meter (m^3)	$1.000\ 028 \times 10^{-3}$
Litre-atmosphere	L. atm	Metric	Energy	Joule (J)	$1.013\ 25 \times 10^{2}$
Litre per 100 kilometer	L/100km	with SI	Fuel consumption	SI	See definition
Litre per kilogramme	L/kg or 1/kg	with SI	Specific volume	Cubic meter per kilogramme (m/kg)	10^{-3}
Litre per mole	L/mol or 1/mol	with SI	Molar volume	Cubic meter per mole (m^3/mol)	10^{-3}
Litre per second	L/s or 1/s	with SI	Volume flow rate	Cubic meter per second (m^3/s)	10^{-3}
Livre	Livre	Metric	Mass	Kilogramme (kg)	0.5

Summary of some of the scientific units (Cont.)

UNIT	Symbol	System of Units	Quantity	Corresponding SI Unit	To Convert to SI, multiply it by
Link	link (Ram.)	Arbitrary	Length	Meter (m)	**0.304 8**
Liquid ounce (US)	US liq oz	US unit	Volume, capacity	Cubic meter (m^3)	$2.957\ 35 \times 10^{-5}$
Liquid pint (US)	US liq pt	US unit	Volume, capacity	Cubic meter (m^3)	$4.731\ 76 \times 10^{-4}$
Liquid quart (US)	US liq qt	US unit	Volume, capacity	Cubic meter (m^3)	$9.463\ 53 \times 10^{-4}$
Litre	1, L	Metric	Capacity, volume	Cubic meter (m^3)	10^{-3}
Litre (old)	1	Metric	Capacity, volume	Cubic meter (m^3)	$1.000\ 028 \times 10^{-3}$
Litre-	L. atm	Metric	Energy	Joule (J)	**$1.013\ 25 \times 10^2$**
Litre per 100 kilometer	L/100km	with SI	Fuel consumption	SI	See definition
Litre per kilogramme	L/kg or 1/kg	with SI	Specific volume	Cubic meter per kilogramme (m/kg)	**10^{-3}**
Litre per mole	L/mol or 1/mol	with SI	Molar volume	Cubic meter per mole (m^3/mol)	10^{-3}
Litre per second	L/s or 1/s	with SI	Volume flow rate	Cubic meter per second (m^3/s)	10^{-3}
Livre	Livre	Metric	Mass	Kilogramme (kg)	**0.5**
Logit	Logit	All	Intensity level	Decibel (dB)	1
Loranze unit	Loranze unit	Gaussian	Reciprocal length of magnetic flux	Per tesla meter (1/T.m)	46.689
Loudness unit	LU	All	Loudness	Sone	0.001
Lumberg	Lumber	CGS	Luminous energy	Lumen second (lm.s)	1
Lumen	Lm	All, SI	Luminous flux	SI	SI
Lumen (at 5550 Angstrom)	lm (5550 Angstrom)	Arbitrary	Power	Watt (W)	$1.470\ 588\ 2 \times 10^{-3}$
Lumen hour	Im.h	with SI	Quantity of light	Lumen second (lm/s)	**3.6×10^3**

Summary of some of the scientific units (Cont.)

UNIT	Symbol	System of Units	Quantity	Corresponding SI Unit	To Convert to SI, multiply it by
Lumen per square foot	lm/ift^2	Arbitrary	Illuminance	Lux (lx)	1.076 39
Lumen per square meter	lm/m^2 (also lx)	SI	Luminous exitance	SI	SI
Lumen per watt	lm/W	SI	Luminous efficacy, luminosity factor	SI	SI
Lumen second	lm.s	SI	Quantity of light	SI	SI
Lumerg	Lumerg	CGS	Luminous energy	Lumen second (lm.s)	1
Lusec	Lusec	Metric	Leak rate, power	Watt (W)	1.332 2x10^{-4}
Lux	Lx	SI	Intensity of illumination	SI	SI
Lux hour	lx. h	with SI	Light exposure	Lux second (lx.s)	**3.6x10^3**
Lux second	lx.s	SI	Light exposure	SI	SI
Luxon			Retinal illumination	See definition	See definition
Mache	Mache	Arbitrary	Radioactive concentration, volume activity	Becquerel per cubic meter (Bq/m3)	1.369.x 104
Mach number	Ma, M	None	Ratio of speed	See definition	See definition
Mach unit	mach unit	Arbitrary	Radioactivity	Becquerel (Bq)	1.332x10
Magn	Magn	SI	Absolute permeability	Henry per meter (H/m)	1
Magnetic ohm	magnetic ohm (or Gb/Mx)	CGSemu	Reluctance	Per henry (1/H)	7.957 75x107
Magneton	Magneton	Arbitrary	Magnetic moment of an atomic particle	See definition	See definition

Summary of some of the scientific units (Cont.)

UNIT	Symbol	System of Units	Quantity	Corresponding SI Unit	To Convert to SI, multiply by
Magnitude	Mag	All	Brightness of stars	See definition	See definition
Mast	mast mast	UK unit	Mass	Kilogramme (kg)	0.933 104 3
Maxwell	Mx	CGSemu	Magnetic flux	Weber (Wb)	10^{-8}
Maxwell (Int.)	Mx (Int.)	Arbitrary	Magnetic flux	Weber (Wb)	1.000330×10^{-8}
Maxwell per square centimeter	Mx/cm^2 or G or Gs	CGSemu	Magnetic flux	Tesla (T)	10^{-4}
Mayer	Mayer	Metric	Specific heat capacity	Joule per kilogramme kelvin (J/kg.K)	1000
McLeod	Mcleod	Arbitrary, derived	Pressure level	See definition	See definition
Measurement ton	measurement ton	None	Volume (ship cargo)	Cubic meter (m^3)	1.132 674
Mechanical ohm	mechanical ohm	CGS	Mechanical impedance	Newton second per meter (N.s/m)	10^{-3}
Megabits per second	Mbit/s	None	Data transmission	-	-
Megabyte	Mbyte	None	Storage capacity in computer technology	-	-
Megabyte per second	Mbyt/s	None	Data transmission	-	-
Megaelectronvolt-Curie	MeV Ci	Arbitrary	Radioactive power	Watt (W)	$5.927\ 77 \times 10^{-3}$
Megagramme	Mg	with SI	Mass	Kilogramme (kg)	**10^3**
Megaton	Megaton	None	Magnitude of an explosion	See definition	See definition
Megawatt year of electricity	MWYE	Arbitrary	Energy	Joule (J)	$3.155\ 7 \times 10^{13}$

Summary of some of the scientific units (Cont.)

UNIT	Symbol	System of Units	Quantity	Corresponding SI Unit	To Convert to SI, multiply by
Mel	Mel	All	Subjective pitch	See definition	See definition
Meter	M	SI	Length	SI	SI
Meter-atmosphere	m-atm	Arbitrary	Depth of equivalent atmosphere	See definition	See definition
Meter-candle	m.c	SI	Intensity of illumination	Lumen per meter squared (lm/m^2)	1
Meter cubed	m^3	SI	Section modulus	SI	SI
Meter hour degree Celsius per kilocalorie (IT)	m.h.°C/kcal$_{IT}$	Arbitrary	Thermal resistivity	Meter kelvin per watt (m.K/W)	$8.598\ 45 \times 10^{-1}$
Meter kelvin	m.K	SI	Radiation constant	SI	SI
Meter kelvin per watt	m.K/W	SI	Thermal resistivity	SI	SI
Meter of water (conventional)	mH_2O	Arbitrary	Pressure	Pascal (Pa)	**$9.806\ 65 \times 10^3$**
Meter per kilogramme	m/kg	SI	Specific length	SI	SI
Meter per second	m/s	SI	Velocity, speed	SI	SI
Meter per second cubed	m/s^3	SI	Jerk	SI	SI
Meter per second squared	m/s^2	**SI**	Acceleration	SI	SI
Meter squared	m^2	SI	Area, slowing-down area, diffusion area, magnetic area	SI	SI
Meter squared per hour	m^2h	with SI	Kinematic viscosity	Meter squared per second (m^2/s)	$2.777\ 777\ 778 \times 10^{-4}$
Meter squared per second	m^2/s	SI	Kinematic viscosity	SI	SI
Meter to the fourth power	m^4	SI	Second moment of the area	SI	SI

Summary of some of the scientific units (Cont.)

UNIT	Symbol	System of Units	Quantity	Corresponding SI Unit	To Convert to SI, multiply by
Metric carat	metric carat	Metric, with SI	Mass	Kilogramme (kg)	2×10^{-4}
Metric slug	metric slug	MkgfS	Mass	Kilogramme (kg)	9.806 65
Metric technical unit of mass	metric technical unit of mass	MkgfS	Mass	Kilogramme (kg)	9.806 65
Mho	Mho	SI	Conductance, admittance, susceptance	SI	SI
Mic	Mic	Metric	Inductance	Henry (H)	10^{-6}
Micri-erg	micri-erg	Metric	Energy	Joule (J)	10^{-21}
Micril	Micril	Metric	Concentration	Kilogramme per meter cubed (kg/m)	1×10^{-3}
Micobar	μbar	Arbitrary	Pressure	Pascal (Pa)	10^{-1}
Micro-inch	μin	Arbitrary	Length	Meter (m)	2.54×10^{-8}
Microkatal	μkat	None	Enzyme activity	Micromole per second (mol/s)	1
Micrometer	μm	with SI	Length	Meter (m)	10^{-6}
Micrometer of mercury (convent.)	μmHg	Arbitrary	Pressure (fluid)	Pascal (Pa)	$1.333\ 22 \times 10^{-1}$
Micron	μm	Metric	Length	Meter (m)	10^{-6}
Micron	μHg	Metric	Pressure	Pascal (Pa)	$1.333\ 22 \times 10^{-1}$
Microtorr	μTorr	Arbitrary	Pressure (fluid)	Pascal (Pa)	$1.333\ 22 \times 10^{-4}$
Mil	Ml	Metric	Capacity, volume	Cubic meter (m^3)	10^{-6}
Mil (length)	Mil	Imperial	Length	Meter (m)	2.540×10^{-5}
Mil, angular	angular mil	All	Plane angle	Radian (rad)	1×10^{-3}
Mil, circular	circular mil	Imperial	Area	Meter square (m^2)	$5.067\ 07 \times 10^{'10}$
Mile	mi or mile	US and UK	Length	Meter (m)	$1.609\ 344 \times 10^3$

Summary of some of the scientific units (Cont.)

UNIT	Symbol	System of Units	Quantity	Corresponding SI Unit	To Convert to SI,
Mile, geographical	geographical mile	Imperial	Length		
Mile, nautical	n mi, n mile, sm	Metric, Imperial	Length	Meter (m)	**1.852×10^3**
Mile, nautical (UK)	UK nautical mile	UK unit	Length	Meter (m)	**$1.853\ 184 \times 10^3$**
Mile, sea	sea mile	Imperial	Length		
Mile, telegraph nautical	telegraph nautical mile	Imperial	Length	Meter (m)	$1.855\ 317\ 6 \times 10^3$
Mile (US statute)	mile (US, stat.)	US unit	Length	Meter (m)	$1.609\ 347 \times 10^3$
Mile per gallon (UK)	mile/UKgal	UK unit	Reciprocal fuel consumption	Kilometer per litre (km/L)	$3.540\ 06 \times 10^{-1}$
Mile per gallon (US)	mile/USgal		Reciprocal fuel	Kilometer per litre (km/L)	$4.251\ 44 \times 10^{-1}$
Mile per hour	mile/h	US unit UK and US UK and US	Velocity, speed	Meter per second (m/s)	**$4.470\ 4 \times 10^{-1}$**
Mile Square	mi^2	Arbitrary	Area	Square meter (m^2)	$2.589\ 988\ 11 \times 10^6$
Mile Square (US statute)	mi^2 (US, statute)	US unit	Area	Square meter (m^2)	$2.589\ 998 \times 10^6$
Milliampere-second	mA s	Metric	Radiation dose	Ampere second (A.s)	1×10^{-3}
Millibar	mbar or mb	Arbitrary	Pressure	Pascal (Pa)	**10^2**
Millicurie-	Mcd	Arbitrary	Radiation dose	See definition	See definition
Millicurie-of- intensity-hour	Imch	Arbitrary	Radiation dose	Coulomb per kilogramme	$2.162\ 04 \times 10^{-3}$

Summary of some of the scientific units (Cont.)

UNIT	Symbol	System of Units	Quantity	Corresponding SI Unit	To Convert to SI, multiply by
Millier	Millier	MTS	Mass	Kilogramme (kg)	1×10^3
Milligal	mGal	Arbitrary	Acceleration	Meter per second square (m/s^2)	10^{-5}
Milligrade	.....mg	Arbitrary	Plane angle	Radian (rad)	$1.570\ 80 \times 10^{-3}$
Milligramme-hour	mg h	Arbitrary	Radiation dose	See definition	See definition
Milligramme per litre	mg/1 or mg/L	with SI	Density, concentration	Kilogramme per cubic meter (kg/m^3)	10^{-3}
Millihg	Millihg	Metric	Pressure	Pascal (Pa)	$1.333\ 223\ 874 \times 10^2$
Millilitre	ml or mL	with SI	Volume	Cubic meter (m^3)	10^{-6}
Millimass unit	Mmu	Arbitrary	Mass	Kilogramme (kg)	$1.037\ 3\ 8 \times 10^{'31}$
Millimeter	Mm	with SI	Length	Meter (m)	10^{-3}
Millimeter of mercury	mmHg	Metric	Pressure	Pascal (Pa)	$1.333\ 22 \times 10^2$
Millimeter of	mmH$_2$0	Metric	Pressure	Pascal (Pa)	$9.806\ 65$
Minim (UK)	UKmin	UK unit	Volume, capacity	Cubic meter (m^3)	$5.919\ 39 \times 10^{-8}$
Minim (US)	USmin	US unit	Capacity, volume	Cubic meter (m^3)	$6.161\ 15 \times 10^{-8}$
Minute (of arc)	'	All	Plane angle	Radian (rad)	$2.908\ 88 \times 10^{-4}$
Minute (of time)	Min	Arbitrary	Time	Second (s)	60
Minute, centesimal	.....^{cc}	None	Plane angle	Radian (rad)	$1.570\ 809 \times 10^{-6}$
Mired	mired	Metric	Reciprocal of colour	Per kelvin (1/K)	10^6
Mite	Mite	Imperial	Mass	Kilogramme (kg)	$3.239\ 945\ 5 \times 10^{-6}$
Mohm	mohm	CGS	Mechanical mobility	Meter per newton second (m/N.s)	1000
Mohr cubic centimeter	Mohr cm^3	Arbitrary	Volume	Cubic meter (m^3)	1.00013×10^{-6}
Mole	Mol	SI	Amount of substance	SI	SI

Mole per cubic meter	mol/m^3	SI	Concentration	SI	SI
Mole per cubic meter second	$mol/m^3.s$	SI	Rate of concentration, rate of reaction	SI	SI
Mole per kilogramme	mol/kg	SI	Molality, ionic strength	SI	SI

Summary of some of the scientific units (Cont.)

UNIT	Symbol	System of Units	Quantity	Corresponding SI Unit	To Convert to S.I.,
Mole per litre	mol/1 or	with S.I.	Concentration	Mole per cubic	10^3
Mole per second	mol/s	S.I.	Molar flow rate	SI	SI
Mole per square	mol/m^2	S.I.	Surface	SI	SI
Mon	Mon	None	Flatness of rolled steel plates	See definition	See definition
Month	month	Arbitrary	Time	Second (s)	See definition
Morgan	morgan	Arbitrary	Genetic map distance	Metre (m)	$3x10^{-4}$
Moszkowski unit	moszkowski unit	None	Transition probability of nuclei	See definition	See definition
Motvos	E	Metric	Horizontal gradient of gravitational acceleration	Per second square $(1/s^2)$	10^{-9}
Mounce	mounce	Metric	Mass	Kilogramme (kg)	0.025
Mug	mug	Metric-technical	Mass	Kilogramme (kg)	9.806 65
Myriagramme	myriagramme	Arbitrary, with S.I.	Mass	Kilogramme (kg)	10
Myriametre	myriametre	Arbitrary, with S.I.	Length	Metre (m)	10^4
Nail	nail	U.K. unit	Length	Metre (m)	$5.715x10^{-2}$
Nanogramme per pascal second square metre	$ng/(Pa.s.m^2)$	with S.I.	Moisture transport in buildings	Kilogramme per pascal second square metre $(kg/Pa.s.m^2)$	10^{12}

| Nanon | nanon | Arbitrary | Length | Metre (m) | 10^{-9} |
| Nautical mile | n mile | Arbitrary | Length | Metre (m) | **1.852×10^3** |

Summary of some of the scientific units (Cont.)

UNIT	Symbol	System of Units	Quantity	Corresponding SI Unit	To Convert to SI, multiply it by
Nautical mile (U.K.)	nautical mile (U.K.)	U.K. unit	Length	Metre (m)	**1.853 184x10³**
Nautical point	nautical point	Arbitrary	Plane angle	Radian (rad)	0.196 349 54
Neper	Np	All	Amplitude level	Decibel (dB)	8.685 89
Neper per second	Np/s	All	Damping coefficient	Per second (1/s)	1
Nepit	Nepits	None	Quantity of information	See definition	See definition
Net ton	net ton	US unit	Mass	Kilogramme (kg)	9.071 847x10²
Neutron Roentgen	Neutron roentgen	Arbitrary	Radiation dose	See definition	See definition
New candle	Cd	SI	Luminous intensity	Candela (cd)	**1**
Newton	N	SI	Force	SI	SI
Newton metre	N.m	SI	Moment of force, torque	SI	SI
Newton per cubic metre	N/m³	SI	Specific weight	SI	SI
Newton per metre	N/m	SI	Surface tension, surface pressure	SI	SI
Newton second per metre	N.s/m	SI	Mechanical impedance	SI	SI
Newton square metre per kilogramme squared	M.m²/kg²	SI	Gravitational Constant	SI	SI
Nile	nile	All	Reactivity	See definition	See definition

Summary of some of the scientific units (Cont.)

UNIT	Symbol	System of Units	Quantity	Corresponding SI Unit	To Convert to SI, multiply it
Nit	Nt	SI	Luminance	Candela per square metre (cd/m^2)	SI
Nit	Nit	None	Quantity of information	See definition	See definition
Noggin	noggin	U.K. unit	Volume	Cubic metre (m^3)	1.420 652 3 x10^{-4}
Normkubikemeter	Nm^3	German unit	Volume (specially gas)	Cubic metre (m^3)	1
Normliter	In	German unit	Volume (specially gas)	Cubic metre (m^3)	10^{-3}
Nox	nox	Metric	Intensity of illumination	Lux (lx)	10^{-3}
Noy	noy	All	Noisiness	See definition	See definition
n-Unit	n-unit	Arbitrary	Radiation dose	See definition	See definition
Octant	octant	All	Plane angle	Radian (rad)	$\pi/4$
Octave	octave	All	Pitch interval	See definition	See definition
Octet	octet	None	Information	None	= 1 byte
Oersted	Oe	CGS-emu	Magnetic field strength	Ampere per metre (A/m)	7.957 75x10
Oersted (International)	Oe_{int}		Magnetic field strength	Ampere per metre (A/m)	7.956 437x10
Ohm	Ω	SI	Resistance, reactance, impedance	SI	SI
Ohm (International)	Ω_{int}		Resistance, reactance,	Ohm (Ω)	1.000 495

Summary of some of the scientific units (Cont.)

UNIT	Symbol	System of Units	Quantity	Corresponding SI Unit	To Convert to SI,
Ohm, acoustical	Ω_a	CGS	Acoustic resistance	Pascal second per metre cubed $(Pa.s/m^3)$	$Ix10^5$
Ohm, mechanical	Ω_m	CGS	Mechanical Resistance	Newton second per metre (N.s/m)	$1x10^{-3}$
Ohm, reciprocal	Ω^{-1}	SI	Conductance, admittance, susceptance	SI	SI
Ohm, specific acoustical	Ω_s	CGS	Specific acoustical resistance, reactance and impedance	Pascal second per metre (Pa.s/m)	10
Ohm, thermal	thermal ohm	S.I.	Thermal resistance	SI	SI
Ohm circular mil per foot	$\Omega.circ.mil/ft$	Arbitrary	Resistivity	Ohm metre (Ω m)	$1.662\ 426\ x10^{-9}$
Ohm metre	Ω m	S.I.	Resistivity	SI	SI
Ohm square millimetre per metre	Ω mm2/m	with S.I.	Resistivity	Ohm metre (Ωm)	10^{-6}
Ohma	ohma	MKSA	Electric potential	Volt (V)	1.000 34
Ohmad	ohmad	MKSA	Resistance	Ohm (Ω)	1.00049
Open window unit	Owu	FPS	Equivalent absorption area	Square metre (m^2)	$9.290\ 304x10^{-2}$
.Osmole	osm	None	Osmolality, osmolarity	See definition	See definition

Summary of some of the scientific units (Cont.)

UNIT	Symbol	System of	Quantity	Corresponding SI	To Convert to SI,
Ounce	Oz	Imperial	Mass	|Kilogramme (kg)	$2.834\ 95\text{x}10^{-2}$
Ounce, Apothecaries	oz apoth; oz ap	U.K. and U.S. unit	Mass	Kilogramme (kg)	$3.110\ 347685\ \text{x}10^{-2}$
Ounce,	Oz	Imperial	Mass	Kilogramme (kg)	$2.8\ 349\ 5\text{x}10^{-2}$
Ounce, troy	oz tr	Imperial	Mass	Kilogramme (kg)	| $3.11034768\text{x}10^{-2}$
Ounce, fluid (U.K.)	U.K. fl oz	Arbitrary	Capacity, volume	Cubic metre (cm^3)	$2.841307\text{x}10^{-5}$
Ounce, fluid (U.S.)	U.S. fl oz	Imperial	Capacity, volume	Cubic metre (m^3)	2.95735295625 $\text{X}10^{-5}$
Ounce, metric	metric	Metric	Mass	Kilogramme	0.025
Ounce inch square	oz.in^2	Arbitrary	Moment of inertia	Kilogramme metre squared kg.m^2)	$1.829\ 00\text{x}10^{'5}$
Ounce per cubic inch	oz/in^3	Arbitrary	Density	Kilogramme per cubic metre (kg/m^3)	$1.729\ 99\text{x}10^{3}$
Ounce per foot	oz/ft	Arbitrary	Linear density	Kilogramme per metre (kg/m)	$9.301\ 02\text{x}10^{4}$
Ounce per gallon (U.K.)	oz/UKgal	UK unit	Density, Concentration	Kilogramme per cubic metre .(kg/m^3)	6.236 021
Ounce per gallon (U.S.)	oz/USgal	US unit	Density, Concentration	Kilogramme per cubic metre (kg/m^3)	7.489 152
Ounce per inch	oz/in	Arbitrary	Linear density	Kilogramme per metre (kg/m)	1.116 12
Ounce per square foot	oz/ft^2	Arbitrary	Surface density	Kilogramme per square metre (kg/m^2)	$3.051\ 517\text{x}10^{-1}$
Ounce per square yard	oz/yd^2	Arbitrary	Surface density	Kilogramme per square metre (kg/m^2)	$3.390\ 575\text{x}10^{-2}$

Summary of some of the scientific units (Cont.)

UNIT	Symbol	System of Units	Quantity	Corresponding SI Unit	To Convert to SI, multiply it by
Ounce per yard	oz/yd	Arbitrary	Linear density	Kilogramme per metre (kg/m)	3.10034×10^{-2}
Ounce-force	Ozf	Arbitrary	Force	Newton (N)	$2.780\ 139 \times 10^{-1}$
Ounce-force inch	ozf in	Arbitrary	Moment of force, torque	Newton metre (N.m)	$7.061\ 5\ 52 \times 10^{-3}$
Ounce-force per square inch	ozf/in^2	Arbitrary	Pressure	Pascal (Pa)	$4.309\ 22 \times 10^2$
Ouncedal	ouncedal	Arbitrary Imperial	Force	Newton (N)	$8.6409346485 \times 10^{-3}$
Pace	Pace	Arbitrary	Length	Metre (m)	0.762
Pack	Pack	Arbitrary	Mass	Kilogramme(kg)	108.862 168 8
Packet	packet	None	Data	See definition	See definition
Page	Page	None	Information, memory	See definition	See definition
Palm	Palm	Arbitrary	Length	Metre (m)	7.62×10^{-2}
Par	Par	Metric-technical	Mass	Kilogramme (kg)	9.80665
Parker	Parker	Arbitrary	Absorbed	See definition	See definition
Parsec	P.C.	Arbitrary, with S.I.	Length	Metre (m)	3.08572×10^{16}
Part per million	part/million	Arbitrary	Density (mass),	Kilogramme per cubic metre	10^{-3}
Pascal	Pa	SI	Pressure	SI	SI
Pastille dose	pastille dose	Arbitrary	Radiation	See definition	See definition

Summary of some of the scientific units (Cont.)

UNIT	Symbol	System of Units	Quantity	Corresponding SI Unit	To Convert to SI, multiply it by
Peck (U.K.)	UKpk	Arbitrary	Capacity, volume	Cubic metre (m^3) (m^3)	**9.09218×10^{-3}**
Peck (U.S.)	USpk	Imperial	Capacity, volume	Cubic metre (m^3)	8.80976754172 $\times 10^3$
Pennyweight	dwt or pwt	Imperial	Mass	Kilogramme	1.55517384
Pentane candle	pentane candle	Arbitrary	Luminous intensity	Candela (cd)	≈ 1
Perch	P	Imperial	Area	Metre square	25.29285264
Perch	Perch	Imperial	Length	Metre (m)	5.0292
Perch, masonry)	perch (masonry)	Arbitrary	Volume	Cubic metre (m^3)	0.700 841 963
Perceived noise decibel	P.N. dB	Arbitrary	Sound pressure	See definition	See definition
Permicron	Permicron	Metric	Reciprocal length	Per metre (1/m)	10^6
Period	Period	Arbitrary	Geological time	See definition	See definition
Perm	Perm	U.S. unit	Water vapour permeability	Kilogramme per pascal second square metre ($kg/Pa.s.m^2$)	$57.213\ 5 \times 10^{-12}$ (at °C), $57.452\ 5 \times 10^{-12}$ (at 23°C)
Perm-inch	perm-in	U.S. unit	Water vapour permeance	Kilogramme per pascal second metre (kg/Pa.s.m)	$1.453\ 22 \times 1\ O^{-12}$ (at °C), $1.459\ 29 \times 10^{-12}$ (at 23°C)

Summary of some of the scientific units (Cont.)

UNIT	Symbol	System of Units	Quantity	Corresponding SI Unit	To Convert to SI, multiply it by
Permicron	Permicron	Metric	Reciprocal length	Per metre (1/m)	10^6
Petrograd standard	Petrograd standard	Arbitrary	Volume (only timber)	Cubic metre (m^3)	4.762 28
Phon	Phon	All	Equivalent loudness	See definition	See definition
Phot	Phot	CGS	Intensity of illumination	Lux (lx)	10^4
Phot-second	ph.s or phot-s	CGS	Exposure	Lux second	**10^4**
Photon	Photon	Arbitrary	Energy associated with electro-magnetic radiation	Joule (J)	See definition
Photon	Photon	Metric	Retinal illumination	See definition	See definition
Pica	Pica	Arbitrary	Length (used by printer's)	Metre (m)	4.217 517 6 x10^3
Pieze	Pz	MTS	Pressure	Pascal (Pa)	10^3
Pin (U.K.)	pin (U.K.)	U.K. unit	Capacity, volume (for ale and beer)	Cubic metre (m^3)	**20.457 405**
Pin (U.S.)	pin (U.S.)	U.S. unit 1	Capacity, volume (for ale and beer)	Cubic metre (m^3)	7.034 353 03
Pint (U.K.)	UKpt	Arbitrary	Capacity, volume	Cubic metre (m^3)	5.68261x10^{-4}

Summary of some of the scientific units (Cont.)

UNIT	Symbol	System of Units	Quantity	Corresponding SI Unit	To Convert to SI, multiply it by
Pint (U.S. liquid)	Us liq pt	Imperial	Capacity, volume	Cubic metre	$4.73176473\ 1\ \text{x}10^{-4}$
Pint (U.S. dry)	U.S. dry pt	Imperial	Capacity, volume	Cubic metre (m^3)	$5.50610\text{x}10^{-4}$
Planck	Planck	SI	Action	SI	SI
Pli	Pli	Imperial	Line density	Kilogramme per metre (kg/m)	17.8580
Point	Point	Metric	Mass	Kilogramme	$2\text{ x }10^{-6}$
Point, printer's	point (printer's)	Arbitrary	Length	Metre (m)	$3.514\ 598\text{x}10^{-4}$
Points of the compass	point of the compass	Arbitrary	Plane angle	Radian (rad)	0.196 349 54
Poise	P	CGS	Viscosity, dynamic	Newton second | per square metre (N.s/m^2)	0.1
Poiseuille	PI	SI	Viscosity, dynamic	SI	SI
Pole	Pole	Imperial	Area	Square metre	25.29285264
Pole	Pole	Imperial	Length	Metre (m)	5.0292
Poncelet	Poncelet	Metric-derived	Power	Watt (W)	**980.665**
Pond	. p	MkpS	Force	Newton (N)	**$9.806\ 65\text{x}10^{-3}$**
Pottle	Pottle	UK unit	Volume, capacity	Cubic metre (m^3)	$2.272\ 980\text{x}10^{-7}$
Poumar	Poumar	Imperial	Line density	Kilogramme per metre (kg/m)	$4.96055\text{x}10^{-7}$
Pound	Lb	FSS, FlbfS	Force	Newton (N)	4.4482216152605
Pound, avoirdupois	Lb	FPS	Mass	Kilogramme ..(kg) .	0.45359237
Pound, avoird. US	US lb advp	Imperial	Mass	Kilogramme (kg)	0.4535294277

Summary of some of the scientific units (Cont.)

UNIT	Symbol	System of Units	Quantity	Corresponding SI Unit	To Convert to SI, multiply it by
Pound, troy	Ibtr	Imperial	Mass	Kilogramme	0.3732417216
Poundal	Pdl	FPS	Force	Newton (N)	0.138254954376
Pound-force	Ibf	FSS, FlbfS	Force	Newton (N)	4.4482216152605
Pound-weight	Ibwt	Imperial	Force	Newton (N)	0.138254954376
Pour cent mille	Pcm	Arbitrary	Reactivity	See definition	See definition
Pragilbert	praGb	S.I. international	Magnetomotive force	Ampere-turn (A-t)	4π
Praoersted	praOe	S.I. international	Magnetic field strength	Ampere turn per metre (At/m)	4π
Preece	Preece	Metric	Electric resistivity	Ohm metre (Q.m)	10^{13}
Prism dioptre	prism dioptre	None	Deviating power of a prism	See definition	See definition
Promaxwell	promaxwell	CGS	Magnetic	Weber (Wb)	1
Prout	Prout	Arbitrary	Nuclear	Joule (J)	2.9714×10^{-14}
Psi	Psi	Imperial	Pressure	Pascal (Pa)	$6.894\,76 \times 10^{3}$
Puff	Puff	Metric	Capacitance	Farad (F)	10^{-12}
Pulsatance	Pulsatance	Arbitrary	Angular	See definition	See definition
Puncheon	Puncheon	U.K. unit	Volume, capacity	Cubic metre (m^3)	0.317 975 10
Pyron	Pyron	Arbitrary	Power area-density	Watt per square metre	697.8
Quad	Quad	Imperial	Energy	Joule (J)	$1.055055\,8526 \times 10^{18}$
Quadrant	Quadrant	All	Plane angle	Radian (rad)	2π

Summary of some of the scientific units (Cont.)

UNIT	Symbol	System of Units	Quantity	Corresponding SI Unit	To Convert to SI, multiply it by
Quadrant	Quadrant	MKSA	Inductance	Henry (H)	1.00049
Quadrant	Quadrant	Metric	Length	Metre (m)	10^7
Quantum	Quanta	Arbitrary	Energy associated	See definition	See definition
Quart (U.K.)	U.K. quart	Arbitrary	Capacity,	Cubic metre (m3)	1.136522×10^{-3}
Quart, reputed	reputed	U.K. unit	Volume,	Cubic metre	7.61×16^{-4}
Quart, U.S.	U.S. liq	Imperial	Capacity,	Cubic metre	0.946352946
Quart, U.S. dry	U.S. dry	Imperial	Capacity,	Cubic metre (m3)	$1.101\ 220\ 9 \times 10^3$
Quarter	Quarter	Arbitrary	Capacity,	Cubic metre	0.290950
Quarter, U.K.	Qr	Imperial	Mass	Kilogramme	12.70058636
Quarter, U.S.	Quarter	Imperial	Mass	Kilogramme	226.796185
Quarter, troy	qr tr	Imperial	Mass	Kilogramme	| 9.33104304
Quartern, U.K.	U.K. dry	U.K. unit	| Volume,	Cubic metre	$2.273\ 044 \times 10^3$
Quartern, U.K. liquid	U.K. liquid	U.K. unit	Volume,	Cubic metre	$0.142\ 065\ 2 \times 10^3$
Quintal	Q	Imperial	Mass	Kilogramme	45.359237
Quintal	Q	Metric	Mass	Kilogramme (kg)	100
Q-unit	Q	Arbitrary	Potential heat energy of fuel reserves	Joule (J)	10^{21}
Rad	rad, also rd	Arbitrary	Absorbed ionising radiation	Joule per kilogramme	0.01
Radian	Rad	SI, All	Plane angle	SI	SI

Summary of some of the scientific units (Cont.)

UNIT	Symbol	System of Units	Quantity	Corresponding SI Unit	To Convert to S.I., multiply it by
Radiation length (Radiation unit)	radiation length, or ru	Arbitrary	Length in cosmic-ray studies	See definition	0.693147 shower unit
Ram	Ram	CGS	Acoustical resistance	Pascal second per metre cubic (Pa s/m^3)	10^5
Ram	Ram	CGS	Mechanical resistance	Newton second | per metre (N s/m)	10^{-3}
Rankine degree	degR	Arbitrary	Temperature	See definition	See definition
Ra-size	Ra-size	Arbitrary	Size of untrimmed ...Bper	See definition	See definition
Ray	Ray	CGS	Acoustical or mechanical	Pascal second per metre cubic (Pa s/m^3)	10^5
Ray	Ray	CGS	Mechanical resistance	Newton second per metre (N s/m)	10^3
Rayl	Rayl	CGS	Specific acoustical resistance	Pascal second per metre (Pas/m)	10
Rayleigh	R	Arbitrary	Brightness	Watt per metre squared steradian (W/m^2 sr)	$(5.2720 \times 10^{25}) xf$
Reaumur degree	deg r	Arbitrary	Temperature interval	See definition	See definition
Reciprocal cubic metre	m^{-3}	S.I.	Number density	SI	SI

Summary of some of the scientific units (Cont.)

UNIT	Symbol	System of Units	Quantity	Corresponding SI Unit	To Convert to SI, multiply it by
Redwood no. 1	redwood no. 1	U.K. unit	Kinematic viscosity		See definition
Register ton	register ton	Arbitrary	Volume (internal capacity of a vessel)	Cubic metre (m^3)	2.831 685
Rem	Rem	Arbitrary	Absorbed ionising radiation dose	See definition	See definition
Rep	Rep	Arbitrary	Absorbed ionising radiation dose	See definition	See definition
Revolution	r, also rev	All	Plane angle	Radian (rad)	2π
Revolution per minute	r/min (also rpm)	All	Rotational frequency	Radian per second (rad/s)	0.104 720
Revolution per second	r/s (also rps)	All	Rotational frequency	Radian per second (rad/s)	2π
Reyn	Reyn	FBS	Viscosity, dynamic	Newton second per square metre $(N\ s/m^2)$	1.48816
Rhe (Dynamic)	Rhe	Metric	Fluidity, reciprocal viscosity	Metre square per newton second (m^2/N)	10^5
Rhe (kinematic)	Rhe	Metric	Fluidity, reciprocal viscosity	Second per square metre (s/m^2)	10^6
Rhm	Rhm	Arbitrary	Effective strength of gamma ray source	See definition	See definition
Richter magnitude	Richter, also M	No system	Intensity of earthquakes	See definition	See definition

Summary of some of the scientific units (Cont.)

UNIT	Symbol	System of Units	Quantity	Corresponding SI Unit	To Convert to SI, multiply it by
Right angle		All	Plane angle	Radian (rad)	$\pi/2$
Roc	Roc	CGS	Electrical	Siemens per	**100**
Rod	Rod	Imperial	Area	Square metre	25.29285264
Rod	Rod	Imperial	Length	Metre (m)	**5.0292**
Rod	Rod	Imperial	Volume	Cubic metre	28.316 847
Roentgen	R	Arbitrary	Radioactive dose	Coulomb per kilogramme	2.58×10^{-4}
Roentgen, equivalent biological	EBR	Arbitrary	Absorbed ionising radiation dose (for organic matter)	See definition	See definition
Roentgen-equivalent man	Rem	Arbitrary	Absorbed ionising radiation dose	See definition	See definition
Roentgen-	Rep	Arbitrary	Absorbed ionising	See definition	See definition
Roentgen-per-hour-at-one-metre	Rhm	Arbitrary	Radiation dose rate	See definition	See definition
Roentgen, tissue	roentgen tissue	Arbitrary	Absorbed ionising radiation dose	See definition	See definition
Rom	Rom	MKS	Electrical	Siemens per	1
Rood	Rood	Imperial	Area	Metre square (m^2)	$1.011\ 7141056 \times 10^3$
Room	Room	Imperial	Mass	Kilogramme (kg)	7.112 328 356
Rope	Rope	Imperial	Length	Metre (m)	6.096
Rowland	Rowland	Arbitrary	Wavelength	Metre (m)	9.9987×10^{-11}
Rum	Rum	CGS	Pressure	Pascal (Pa)	0.1

Summary of some of the scientific units (Cont.)

UNIT	Symbol	System of Units	Quantity	Corresponding SI Unit	To Convert to S.I., multiply it by
R-unit, Solomon	Solomon R-unit	Arbitrary	Radiation dose rate	Roentgen per hour	2100
R-unit, German	German R-unit	Germa unit	Radiation dose rate	Roentgen per hour	5250
Rutherford	Rd	Metric	Radioactive disintegration rate	Becqerel (Bq)	10^5
Rydberg	Rydberg	Hartree	Energy	Joule (J)	2.4252×10^{-18}
Rydberg	Rydberg	CGS	Reciprocal length	Per metre (1/m)	100
Sabin	Sabin	FPS	Equivalent absorption area	Metre square (m^2)	0.09290304
Samson	Samson	metre-gramme-wink	Force	Newton	9×10^{13}
Sauder's theatre cushion	Saunder's theatre cushion	None	Absorption of surface	See definition	See definition
Savart	S	All	Pitch interval	Octave	$3.321\ 93 \times 10^{-3}$
Savart modified	modified savart	All	Pitch interval	See definition	See definition
Saybolt universal second	SUS	US practical unit	Kinematic viscosity	See definition	See definition
Scruple	Scruple	Imperial	Mass	Kilogramme (kg)	1.295 978 2
Seam	Seam	U.K. unit	Capacity, volume	Cubic metre (m^3)	0.290 950

Summary of some of the scientific units (Cont.)

UNIT	Symbol	System of Units	Quantity	Corresponding SI Unit	To Convert to SI, multiply it by
Seam	Seam	U.K. unit	Mass	Kilogramme (kg)	54.431 084 4
Secohm	Secohm	MKSA	Inductance	Henry (H)	1.00049
Second (arc)	"	All	Plane angle	Radian (rad)	$(\pi/648000)$
Second	S	ALL, SI	Time	SI	SI
Second, centesimal	Cc	None	Plane angle	Radian (rad)	**$(\pi/2) \times 10^{-6}$**
Second, sidereal	second sidereal ary		Time	Second (s)	0.997 270
Sensation unit	sensation unit Arbitrary	Arbitrary	Loudness	See definition	See definition
Sextant	Sextant	All	Plane angle	Radian (rad)	**$\pi/3$**
Shackle	shackle Arbitrary	Arbitrary	Length	Metre (m)	27.432 06
Shake	Shake	Arbitrary	Time	second (s)	10^{-8}
Shed	Shed	Metric	Area (cross-section area of an atomic nucleus)	Metre Square (m^2)	10^{-52}
Shipload	Shipload	Arbitrary	Mass	Kilogramme	$2.458\ 833\ 52 \times 10^5$
Shipping ton	shipping ton	Arbitrary	Volume (of	Cubic metre	1.132 674
Short	sh cwt	U.S. unit	Mass	Kilogramme(kg)	$4.535\ 924 \times 10$
Short ton	sh tn ,	U.S. unit	Mass	Kilogramme	$9.071\ 847\ 4 \times 10^2$
Shower unit	S	Arbitrary	Length	Metre (m)	See definition
S.I. unit of	S.I. unit	S.I.	Exposure	Roentgen (R)	3.876×10^3
Sidereal year	sidereal year	Arbitrary	Time	Second (s)	$3.155\ 814\ 998 \times 10^7$
Siegbahn unit	X or XU	Arbitrary	Length	Metre (m)	1.00202×10^{-13}
Siemens	S	SI	Conductance	SI	SI

Summary of some of the scientific units (Cont.)

UNIT	Symbol	System of Units	Quantity	Corresponding SI Unit	To Convert to S.I., multiply it by
Sievert	Sv	SI	Dose equivalent	SI	SI
Sign	Sign	All	Plane angle	Radian (rad)	$\pi/6$ rad
Simon	Simon	metre-gramme-	Resistance	Ohm (Ω))	30
Siriometre	siriometre	Arbitrary	Length	Metre (m)	1.49600×10^{17}
Siriusweit	siriusweit	Arbitrary	Length	Metre (m)	$1.542\,86 \times 16^{17}$
Skein	Skein	Arbitrary	Length	Metre (m)	$097\,28 \times 10^2$
Skin	SED	Arbitrary	Radioactive dose	Roentgen (R)	10^3 (for y-ray)
Skot	Skot	Metric	Luminance	Candela per square metre (cd/m^2)	$(10^{-3}/\pi)$
Slug	Slug	FSS	Mass	Kilogramme (kg)	14.5939
Slug, metric	metric slug	Metric-technical	Mass	Kilogramme (kg)	9.80665
Snellen	Snellen	None	Visual power of the eye	See definition	See definition
Sol	Sol	Arbitrary	Time	Second (s)	8.8560×10^4
Solar day, mean	solar day	Arbitrary	Time	Second (s)	$8.663\,655\,5 \times 10^4$
Sone	Sone	Arbitrary	Loudness	See definition	See definition
Space (entire)	space (entire)	Arbitrary	Solid angle	Steradian (sr)	12.566 370 61

Summary of some of the scientific units (Cont.)

UNIT	Symbol	System of Units	Quantity	Corresponding SI Unit	To Convert to S.I., multiply it by
Span	Span	Arbitrary	Length	Metre (m)	**0.228 6**
Spat	S	Metric	Length	Metre (m)	10^{12}
Spat	Sp	Arbitrary	Solid angle	Steradian (sr)	12.566 4
Spherical right angle	spherical right angle	Arbitrary	Solid angle	Steradian (sr)	1.570 796 3
Square (of flooring)	Square	Arbitrary	Area	Square metre (m^2)	9.290 304
Square degree	$[]^0$ or $(^0)^2$	Arbitrary	Solid angle	Steradian (sr)	$(\pi/180)^2$
Square grade	$(g)^2$	Arbitrary	Solid angle	Steradian (sr)	$(\pi/200)^2$
Square inch	in^2	U.K. and	Area	Square metre	**0.645 16x10^{-3}**
Square inch per	$in^2/tonf$	U.K. unit	Compressibil	Per pascal (1/Pa)	64.749 Ox10^{-9}
Square metre	m^2	SI	Area	SI	SI
Square metre kelvin per watt	m^2 K/W	SI	Thermal insulation	SI	SI
Square metre per joule	m^2/J	SI	Spectral cross section	SI	SI

Summary of some of the scientific units (Cont.)

UNIT	Symbol	System of Units	Quantity	Corresponding SI Unit	To Convert to S.I., multiply it by
Square metre per kilogramme	m^2/kg	S.I.	Mass attenuation coefficient, mass absorption coefficient	SI	SI
Square metre per kilogramme-force second	$m^2/kgf.s$	MKFS	Fluidity	Per pascal second (1/Pa.s)	0.101 972
Square metre per mole	m^2/mol	S.I.	Molar absorption coefficient, molar attenuation coefficient	SI	SI
Square metre per second	m^2/s	S.I.	Diffusion coefficient, thermal diffusivity	SI	SI
Square metre per steradian	m^2/sr	S.I.	Angular cross section	SI	SI
Square metre per steradian joule	$m^2/sr.J$	SI	Spectral angular cross section	SI	SI
Square metre per volt second	$m^2/V.s$	S.I.	Mobility	SI	SI
Square mile	$mile^2$	U.K. and U.S.	Area	Square metre (m^2)	**2.589 988 11 x10^6**
Square mile per ton	$mile^2/UKton$	U.K. unit	Specific surface	Square metre per kilogramme (m^2/kg)	$2.549\ 08 \times 10^3$
Square yard	yd^2	U.K. and U.S.	Area	Square metre (m^2)	**0.836 127 36**

Summary of some of the scientific units (Cont.)

UNIT	Symbol	System of Units	Quantity	Corresponding SI Unit	To Convert to S.I., multiply it by
Square yard per ton	yd^2/UKton	U.K. unit	Specific surface	Square metre per kilogramme (m^2/kg)	$0.822\,922 \times 10^{-3}$
Stab	Stab	SI	Length	Metre	SI (=1 m)
Stack	Stack	Arbitrary	Volume, capacity	Cubic metre (m^3)	3.058 219 476
Stadia	Stadia	Ancient Egyptian unit	Length	Metre (m)	185
Standard	Standard	Arbitrary	Volume (only timber)	Cubic metre	4.762 28
Standard atmosphere	Standard Atmosphere	Arbitrary	Pressure	Pascal (Pa)	**$0.101\,325 \times 10^{6}$**
Standard cable	standard cable	None	Attenuation	See definition See definition	See definition
Standard cubic foot	SCF	Arbitrary	Volume (of gas)	See definition	See definition

<h2 align="center">Summary of some of the scientific units (Cont.)</h2>

UNIT	Symbol	System of Units	Quantity	Corresponding SI Unit	To Convert to S.I., multiply it by
Standard gravity	standard gravity	Arbitrary	Acceleration due to gravity	Metre per square second (m/s^2)	9.812 60
Standard volume	Standard Volume	Arbitrary	Volume (of gas)	Cubic metre (m^3)	22.414
Stat	St	Arbitrary	Radioactive disintegration rate	Becqerel (Bq)	**13.431xl0^{-17}**
Stathm	Stathm	CGS	Mass	Kilogramme (kg)	10^{-3}
Steradian	Sr	SI, All	Solid angle	SI	SI
Stere	St	SI	Volume	Cubic metre (m^3)	SI (= 1 m^3)
Sthene	Sn	MTS	Force	Newton (N)	10^3
Stigma	σ	Metric	Length	Metre (m)	10^{-12}
Stilb	Sb	CGS	Luminance	Candela per square metre (cd/m^2)	10^4
Stokes	St	CGS	Viscosity, kinematic	Metre square per second (m2/s)	10^4
Stone	Stone	UK Imperial	Mass	Kilogramme (kg)	6.35029318
Strich	Strich	Arbitrary	Length	Metre (m)	10^3
Strontium unit	S.U.	Arbitrary	Concentration of strontium-90	See definition	See definition
Sturgeon	Sturgeon	MKSA	Magnetic reluctance	Per henry (1/H)	0.999510

Summary of some of the scientific units (Cont.)

UNIT	Symbol	System of Units	Quantity	Corresponding SI Unit	To Convert to S.I., multiply it by
Sumner unit	Sumner unit	None	Enzyme activity	See definition	See definition
Sunshine unit	S.U.	Arbitrary	Concentration of strontium-90	See definition	See definition
Survey foot	U.S. survey	U.S. unit	Length	Metre (m)	0.304 800 6
Svedberg	S	All	Time, Sedimentation coefficient	Second (s)	10^{-13}
Sverdrup	Sverdrup	Arbitrary	Rate of flow (mainly ocean current)	Cubic metre per second (m3/s)	10^6
Talbot	Talbot	SI, All	Luminous energy	Lumen second (lm.s)	SI (= 1 lm s)
Techma	techma, TME (German)	MkgfS	Mass	Kilogramme (kg)	9.806 65
Technical atmosphere	At	Arbitrary	Pressure	Pascal (Pa)	9.806 65x104
Technical unit of mass, British					
Technical unit of mass, CGS					
Technical unit of mass, Metric (S.I.)					
Telegraph nautical mile	telegraph nautical mile	Arbitrary	Length	Metre (m)	$1.855\ 32 \times 10^3$
Tenthmetre	Tenthmetre	Metric	Length	Metre (m)	10^{-10}

<h1 style="text-align:center">Summary of some of the scientific units (Cont.)</h1>

UNIT	Symbol	System of Units	Quantity	Corresponding SI Unit	To Convert to S.I., multiply it by
Tesla	T	SI	Magnetic flux density	Weber per metre square (Wb/m^2)	SI·
Tex	Tex	Metric	Line density	Kilogramme per metre (kg/m)	10^{-6}
Therm	Therm	U.K. unit	Heat energy	Joule (J)	$1.05505585262 \times 10^8$
Therm (European	Therm (European	European Community	Heat energy	Joule (J)	$1.055\ 06 \times 10^8$
Therm (U.S.)	therm (U.S.)	U.S. unit	Heat energy	Joule (J)	**$1.054\ 804 \times 10^8$**
Therm per gallon	therm/UKga	UK unit	Calorific	Joule per cubic	$2.320\ 80 \times 10^8$
Thermal ampere	thermal	SI	Thermal	SI	SI
Thermal coulomb	Thermal Coulomb	SI	Thermal charge	Joule per kelvin (J/K)	SI
Thermal Farad	thermal farad	SI	Thermal capacitance	Joule per square kelvin (J/K^2)	SI
Thermal henry	thermal henry	SI	Thermal inductance	Joule square kelvin per square watt (JK^2/W^2)	SI
Thermal ohm	thermal ohm	SI	Thermal resistance	Kelvin square per watt (K^2/W)	SI

Summary of some of the scientific units (Cont.)

UNIT	Symbol	System of Units	Quantity	Corresponding SI Unit	To Convert to S.I., multiply it by
Thermal volt	thermal volt	SI	Thermal potential	Kelvin (K)	SI
Thermie	Th	Arbitrary	Heat energy	Joule (J)	4.1855×10^6
Thou	Thou	Imperial	Length	Metre (m)	2.54×10^{-5}
Thousandth mass unit	TMU	Arbitrary	Energy	Joule (J)	49176×10^{-13}
Thread	Thread	Arbitrary	Length	Metre (m)	1.371 6

Summary of some of the scientific units (Cont.)

UNIT	Symbol	System of Units	Quantity	Corresponding SI Unit	To Convert to S.I., multiply it by
360° year	360° year	Arbitrary	Time	Second (s)	$3.155\ 804\ 839 \times 10^7$
TME	TME	MkgfS	Mass	Kilogramme	**9.806 65**
Tod	Tod	Arbitrary	Mass	Kilogramme	12.700 586 36
Tog	Tog	Arbitrary	Insulation of clothing	kelvin metre square per watt (km^2/W)	0.1
Toise	Toise	Arbitrary	Length	Metre (m)	1.949
Tolerance unit	-	None	Engineering tolerance	See definition	See definition
Ton (of TNT)	Ton	Arbitrary	Explosive power	Joule (J)	5×10^5
Ton, avoirdupois	Ton	Imperial	Mass	Kilogramme (kg)	$1.016\ 046\ 908\ 8 \times 10^3$
Ton, assay U.K.	U.K. assay ton	Metric	Mass	Kilogramme (kg)	0.0326667
Ton, assay US	US assay ton	Metric	Mass	Kilogramme (kg)	0.0291667
Ton, fluid	fluid ton	Arbitrary	Volume, capacity	Cubic metre (m^3)	$9.061\ 4 \times 10^{-2}$
Ton, freight	freight ton	Arbitrary	Volume (of ship carge)	Cubic metre (m^3)	1.132 674
Ton, gross	Ton	Imperial	Mass	Kilogramme (kg)	$1.016\ 046\ 9088 \times 10^3$

Summary of some of the scientific units (Cont.)

UNIT	Symbol	System of Units	Quantity	Corresponding SI Unit	To Convert to S.I., multiply it by
Ton, long	Ton	Imperial	Mass	Kilogramme (kg)	$1.016\ 046\ 908\ 8 \times 10^3$
Ton, measurement	measurement ton	Arbitrary	Volume, capacity	Cubic metre (m^3)	1.132 674
Ton, metric	T	MTS	Mass	kilogramme (kg)	**10^3**
Ton, net	net ton or sh ton	Imperial	Mass	Kilogramme (kg)	907.184 74
Ton, register	register ton	Arbitrary	Volume	Cubic metre (m^3)	2.831 685
Ton, shipping	shipping ton	Arbitrary	Volume	Cubic metre	1.132 674
Ton, short	sh ton	Imperial	Mass	Kilogramme (kg).	907.184 74
Ton, troy	ton tr	Imperial	Mass	Kilogramme (kg)	746.4832
Ton-force	Tonf	Imperial	Force	Newton (N)	9964.0164181835
Ton-weight	Tonwt	Imperial	Force	Newton (N)	309.691097802
Ton mile	ton mile	UK unit	Traffic factor	Tonne kilometre (t/km)	1.635 17

Summary of some of the scientific units (Cont.)

UNIT	Symbol	System of Units	Quantity	Corresponding SI Unit	To Convert to S.I., multiply it by
Ton mile per gallon (U.K.)	ton mile/UKgal	UK unit	Traffic factor	Tonne kilometre per litre (t.km/L)	0.T359 687
Ton of refrigeration	ton of refrigeration	Imperial	Power	Watt (W)	3516.85
Tondal	Tondal	Imperial	Force	Newton (N)	309.69109780224
Tonne	T	MTS	Mass	Kilogramme (kg)	10^3
Tonne per cubic metre	t/m^3	with SI	Density (mass)	Kilogramme per cubic metre (kg/m^3)	10^3
Tor	Tor	SI	Pressure	Newton per square metre (N/m^2)	SI
Torr	Torr	Metric	Pressure	Pascal (Pa)	133.332
Torr litre per second	torr.L/s	Arbitrary	Leak rate	Pascal cubic metre per second (Pa m^3/s)	$1.333\ 22 \times 10^{-1}$
Tother	Tother	Arbitrary	Mass	Kilogramme (kg)	$1.088\ 621\ 688 \times 10^3$
Township (U.S.)	township (U.S.)	U.S. unit	Area	Square metre (m^2)	$93.239\ 571 \times 10^6$
Townsend	Townsend	CGS	Electrical breakdown in a gas	Volt per square metre (V/m^2)	10^{-13}

Summary of some of the scientific units (Cont.)

UNIT	Symbol	System of Units	Quantity	Corresponding SI Unit	To Convert to S.I., multiply it by
Transmission unit	T.U.	All	Intensity level	Decibel (dB)	1
Troland	Troland	Metric	Retinal illumination	See definition	See definition
Tropical year	a, a_{trop}	Arbitrary	Time	Second (s)	$3.155692\ 59747 \times 10^7$
TSI	Tsi	Imperial	Pressure	Pascal (Pa)	$1.54443.\text{x } 10^7$
Tub	Tub	Arbitrary	Mass	Kilogramme (kg)	38.101 759 08
Tun	Tun	Arbitrary	Volume, capacity	Cubic metre (m^3)	0.953 923 73
Turn	T	All	Plane angle	Radian (rad)	2π
Typp	Typp	Imperial	Reciprocal line density	Metre per kilogramme (m/kg)	$2.015\ 91 \times 10^3$
Unified atomic mass unit	U	with S.I.	Mass	Kilogramme (kg)	$1.660\ 565\ 5 \times 10^{-27}$
Unit pole	unit pole	CGS	Magnetic	Weber (Wb)	$0.125\ 663\ 7 \times 10^{-6}$
Vac	Vac	Metric	Pressure	Pascal (Pa)	100
VAR	Var	SI	Reactive	SI	SI (= 1 V.A.)
Verber	Verber	Arbitrary	Charge (electric)	Coulomb	1
Vibration	Vib	All	Frequency	Per second (1/s)	1

Summary of some of the scientific units (Cont.)

UNIT	Symbol	System of Units	Quantity	Corresponding SI Unit	To Convert to S.I., multiply it by
Violle	Violle	Metric	Luminous intensity	Candela (cd)	20.17
Voegtlin	Voegtlin	None	Activity for pituitary extract	See definition	See definition
Volt	V	SI	Electric potential	SI	SI
Volt-ampere	VA	SI	Energy	SI	SI
Volt, thermal	thermal volt	All	Thermal potential difference	Kelvin (K)	1
Volt per kelvin	V/K	SI	Seebeck coefficient and Thomson coefficient	SI	SI
Volt per metre	V/m	SI	Electric field strength	SI	SI
Volt squared per kelvin squared	V^2/K^2	SI	Lorenz coefficient	SI	SI

Summary of some of the scientific units (Cont.)

UNIT	Symbol	System of Units	Quantity	Corresponding SI Unit	To Convert to S.I., multiply it by
Volume unit	volume unit	All	Magnitude of a complex electric wave	See definition	See definition
Watt	W	SI	Power	(Joule per second	SI
Watt per hour	W/h	with S.I.	Energy	Joule (J)	3.6×10^3
Watt per cubic metre	W/m^3	SI	Heat release rate	SI	SI
Watt per kelvin	W/K	SI	Thermal	SI	SI
Watt per kilogramme	W/kg	SI	Absorbed dose rate,	SI	Watt per kilogramme
Watt per metre	W/m.K	SI	Thermal	**SI**	**SI**
Watt per square metre	W/m^2	SI	Density of heat flow	**SI**	**SI**
Watt per square metre kelvin	$W/m^2.K$	SI	Coefficient of heat transfer	**SI**	SI
Watt per square metre kelvin to the fourth power	$W/m^2.K^4$	SI	Stefan-Boltzmann Constant	SI	SI
Watt per steradian	W/sr	SI	Radiant intensity	**SI**	**SI**
Watt per steradian	$W/sr.m^2$	SI	Radiance	SI	SI

Summary of some of the scientific units (Cont.)

UNIT	Symbol	System of Units	Quantity	Corresponding SI Unit	To Convert to S.I., multiply it by
Watt square	$W.m^2$	SI	First	SI	SI
Wave number	wave number	CGS	Reciprocal length	Per metre	102
Weber	Wb	SI	Magnetic	SI	SI
Weber (pole strength)	Wb	CGS-emu	Magnetic pole strength	See definition	See definition

Summary of some of the scientific units (Cont.)

UNIT	Symbol	System of Units	Quantity	Corresponding SI Unit	To Convert to S.I., multiply it by
Weber metre	W.m	SI	Magnetic dipole	SI	SI
Week (mean	Week	Arbitrary	Time	Second (s)	$6.048\ 00 \times 10^5$
Weisskope unit	weisskope unit	None	The transition probability of nuclei	See definition	See definition
Wey	Wey	UK unit	Mass	kilogramme (kg)	$1.143\ 052\ 772\ \times 10^2$
Wink	Wink	Metre-Gramme-Wink	Time	Second (s)	**$(1/3000)\ x10^{-6}$**
X-unit	X, also XU	Arbitrary	Length	Metre (m)	$1.002\ 02 \times 10^{13}$
Yard	Yd	Imperial	Length	Metre (m)	**0.914 4**
Yard of land	yard of land	Arbitrary	Area	Square metre (m^2)	**121.405 692 672**
Year,	y or a	All	Time	Second (s)	$3.155\ 8433012 \times 10^7$
Year, Eclipse	y or a	All	Time	Second (s)	$2.994\ 797\ 07 \times 10^7$
Year, Gaussian	y or a	All	Time	Second (s)	$3.155\ 819\ 58 \times 10^7$
Year,	y or a	All	Time	Second (s)	$3.155\ 695\ 2 \times 10^7$
Year, Julian	y or a	All	Time	Second (s)	$3.155\ 76 \times 10^7$
Year, sidereal	y or a	All	Time	Second (s)	$3.155\ 814\ 998\ 4$
Year, Tropical	y or a	All	Time	Second (s)	$3.155692\ 59747$
Year, 360°	y or a	All	Time	Second (s)	$3.155\ 804\ 839 \times 10^7$

4.2 Summary of Measuring Units categorized by field of application

In the above table we listed the measuring units alphabetically. In this section we are categorizing the measuring unuts according to the field of aplication

Units of Measurement Categorized by the field of application

This dictionary has about 2400 entries each representing one of the measuring units. The entries are arranged alphabetically.

The units are covering about 75 different scientific, engineering, and physical application areas. Each entry of the dictionary gives the definition of the unit, symbol, systems of units, and in the majority of the cases, it gives the field of application.

Categorizing the units based on the field of application is an important matter especially when we look for the conversion between the units: It is possible only to convert between units from the same application category.

This section introduces the reader to the different application categories and the units belong to each category

List with the scientific units of measurement categorized according to the application field

1. Category: Measurement Units for Length

Category: Measurement Units for Length			
meter	light year	pole	barleycom
exameter	astronomical unit	fathom	Russian archin
petameter	MIL	fathom (based on US survey	Roman actus
terameter	nautical league (international)	foot)	cloth nail
gigameter	nautical league (UK)	yard	cloth span
megameter	league (US)	foot	vara de tarea
kilometer	nautical mile (UK)	foot (US survey)	vara conuquera
hectometer	nautical mile (international)	link	vara castellana
dekameter	mile	link (based on US survey	cubit (Greek)
decimeter	mile (based on US survey	foot)	long reed (Biblical)
centimeter	foot)	hand	reed (Biblical)
millimeter	mile (Roman)	nail	cubit (Biblical)
micrometer	kiloyard	inch	long cubit (Biblical)
nanometer	furlong	mil	span (Biblical)
picometer	furlong (based on US survey foot)	microinch	handbreadth (Biblical)
femtometer	chain	angstrom	fingerbreadth (Biblical)
attometer	chain (based on US survey foot)	X-unit	Planck length
megaparsec	rod	fermi	Electron radius (classical)
kiloparsec	rod (based on US survey foot)	arpent	Bohr radius
parsec		pica	Earth's equatorial radius
		point	Earth's polar radius
		twip	Earth's distance from sun
		aln	Sun's radius
		famn	

	perch	caliber ken	

2. Category: Measurement Unis of Angle

Category: Measurement Unis of Angle			
radian degree grad gon	minute. second sign mil	revolution circle turn quadrant	right　　　angle sextant

3. Category: Measurement Units of Area

Category: Measurement Units of Area			
$meter^2$ $kilometer^2$ $hectometer^2$ $dekameter^2$ $decimeter^2$ $centimeter^2$ $millimeter^2$ $micrometer^2$ $nanometer^2$ hectare are	barn $mile^2$ $mile^2$ (based on US survey foot) $yard^2$ $foot^2$ $inch^2$ circular　　　inch township section acre	acre (based on US survey foot) rood $chain^2$ rod^2 rod^2 (based on US survey foot) $perch^2$ $pole^2$ mil^2 circular mil	homestead sabin arpent cuerda plaza varas　castellanas　cuad varas　conuqueras　cuad Electron cross section

4. Category: Volume

Category: Volume			
$meter^3$ $kilometer^3$ $centimeter^3$ $millimeter^3$ liter exaliter petaliter teraliter gigaliter megaliter kiloliter hectoliter dekaliter deciliter centiliter milliliter microliter nanoliter tablespoon (US)	picoliter femtoliter attoliter cc drop barrel　　(petroleum) barrel　　　　(US) barrel　　　　(UK) gallon　　　　(US) gallon　　　　(UK) quart　　　　(US) quart　　　　(UK) pint　　　　(US) pint　　　　(UK) cup　　　　(US) cup　　　　(metric) cup　　　　(UK) fluid　ounce　(US) fluid　ounce　(UK)	tablespoon　(metric) tablespoon　(UK) dessertspoon　(US) dessertspoon　(UK) teaspoon　(US) teaspoon　(metric) teaspoon　(UK) gill　　　(US) gill　　　(UK) minim　　(US) minim　　(UK) $mile^3$ $yard^3$ $foot^3$ $inch^3$ ton　　register ccf $hundred\text{-}foot^3$ acre-foot	acre-foot (based on US survey foot) acre-inch dekastere stere decistere cord tun hogshead board　　　foot dram cor　　(Biblical) homer　　(Biblical) bath　　(Biblical) hin　　(Biblical) cab　　(Biblical) log　　(Biblical) Taza　　(Spanish) Earth's volume

5. Category: Dry Volume:

Category: Dry Volume			
liter barrel　dry　(US) pint　dry　(US)	peck　　(US) peck　　(UK) bushel　　(US)	cor　　(Biblical) homer　　(Biblical) ephah　　(Biblical)	omer　　(Biblical) cab　　(Biblical) log (Biblical)

quart dry (US)	bushel (UK)	seah (Biblical)	

6. Category: Time

Category: Time			
second	day	minute	decade
millisecond	week	hour	century
microsecond	month	year (sidereal)	millennium
nanosecond	month (synodic)	day (sidereal)	septennial
picosecond	year	hour (sidereal)	octennial
femtosecond	year (Julian)	minute (sidereal)	novennial
attosecond	year (leap)	second (sidereal)	quindecennial
shake	year (tropical)	fortnight	quinquennial
			Planck time

7. Category : Velocity

Category : Velocity			
meter/second		mile/hour	Cosmic velocity - third
meter/hour	millimeter/hour	mile/minute	Earth's velocity
meter/minute	millimeter/minute	mile/second	Velocity of sound in pure water
kilometer/hour	millimeter/second	knot	Velocity of sound in sea water
kilometer/minute	foot/hour	knot (UK)	(20 °C, 10 meter deep)
kilometer/second	foot/minute	Velocity of light in vacuum	Mach (20 °C, 1 atm)
centimeter/hour	foot/second	Cosmic velocity - first	Mach (SI standard)
centimeter/minute	yard/hour	Cosmic velocity - second	
centimeter/second	yard/minute		
	yard/second		

8. Category: Acceleration

Category: Acceleration			
meter/second^2	centimeter/second^2	femtometer/second^2	yard/second^2
kilometer/second^2	millimeter/second^2	attometer/second^2	foot/second^2
hectometer/second^2	micrometer/second^2	gal	inch/second^2
dekameter/second^2	nanometer/second^2	galileo	Acceleration of gravity
decimeter/second^2	picometer/second^2	mile/second^2	

9. Category: Velocity – Angular

Category: Velocity – Angular			
radian/second	radian/minute	degree/minute	revolution/hour
radian/day	degree/day	degree/second	revolution/minute
radian/hour	degree/hour	revolution/day	revolution/second

10. Category Acceleration – Angular

Acceleration – Angular			
radian/second^2	radian/minute	revolution/second^2	revolution/minute/second revolution/minute^2

11. Category: Mass

Category: Mass

kilogram	dalt	hundredweight (UK)	didrachma (Biblical Greek)
gram	kilopound	quarter (US)	drachma (Biblical Greek)
exagram	kip		bekan (Biblical Hebrew)
petagram	slug	hundredweight (US)	gerah (Biblical Hebrew)
teragram	pound-force second^2/foot	quarter (UK)	talent (Biblical Greek)
gigagram	pound	stone (US)	mina (Biblical Greek)
megagram	pound (troy or apothecary)	stone (UK)	tetradrachma (Biblical Greek)
hectogram	ounce	tonne	denarius (Biblical Roman)
dekagram	ounce (troy or apothecary)	pennyweight	assarion (Biblical Roman)
decigram	poundal	scruple (apothecary)	quadrans (Biblical Roman)
centigram	ton (short)	carat	lepton (Biblical Roman)
milligram	ton (long)	grain	Planck mass
microgram	ton (assay) (US)	gamma	Atomic mass unit
nanogram	ton (assay) (UK)	talent (Biblical Hebrew)	Electron mass (rest)
picogram	ton (metric)	mina (Biblical Hebrew)	Muon mass
femtogram	kiloton (metric)	shekel (Biblical Hebrew)	Proton mass
attogram	quintal (metric)		Neutron mass
on			Deuteron mass
kilogram-force second^2/meter			Earth's mass
			Sun's mass

12. Category: Density

Category: Density

kilogram/meter^3	teragram/liter	microgram/liter	ounce/inch^3
kilogram/centimeter^3	gigagram/liter	nanogram/liter	ounce/foot^3
gram/meter^3	megagram/liter	picogram/liter	ounce/gallon (US)
gram/centimeter^3	kilogram/liter	femtogram/liter	ounce/gallon (UK)
gram/millimeter^3	hectogram/liter	attogram/liter	grain/gallon (US)
milligram/meter^3	dekagram/liter	pound/inch^3	grain/gallon (UK)
milligram/centimeter^3	gram/liter	pound/foot^3	grain/foot^3
milligram/millimeter^3	decigram/liter	pound/yard^3	ton (short)/yard^3
exagram/liter	centigram/liter	pound/gallon (US)	ton (long)/yard^3
petagram/liter	milligram/liter	pound/gallon (UK)	slug/foot^3
			psi/1000 feet
			Earth's density (mean)

13. Category: Specific Volume

Category: Specific Volume

meter^3/kilogramm	liter/kilogram	foot^3/kilogram	gallon (US)/pound
centimeter^3/gram	liter/gram	foot^3/pound	gallon (UK)/pound

14. Category: Force

Category: Force

newton	dekanewton	attonewton	ton-force (metric)
exanewton	decinewton	dyne	kip-force
petanewton	centinewton	joule/meter	kilopound-force
teranewton	millinewton	joule/centimeter	pound-force
giganewton	micronewton	gram-force	ounce-force
meganewton	nanonewton	kilogram-force	poundal
kilonewton	piconewton	ton-force (short)	pound foot/second^2
hectonewton	femtonewton	ton-force (long)	pond
			kilopond

15. Category: Pressure

Category: Pressure

pascal	nanopascal	kilogram-force/centimeter^2	torr
exapascal	picopascal	kilogram-force/millimeter^2	centimeter mercury (0 °C)
petapascal	femtopascal	gram-force/centimeter^2	millimeter mercury (0 °C)
terapascal	attopascal	ton-force (short)/foot^2	inch mercury (32 °F)
gigapascal	newton/meter^2	ton-force (short)/inch^2	inch mercury (60 °F)
megapascal	newton/centimeter^2	ton-force (long)/foot^2	centimeter water (4 °C)
kilopascal	newton/millimeter^2	ton-force (long)/inch^2	millimeter water (4 °C)
hectopascal	kilonewton/meter^2	kip-force/inch^2	inch water (4 °C)
dekapascal	bar	ksi	foot water (4 °C)
decipascal	millibar	pound-force/foot^2	inch water (60 °F)
centipascal	microbar	pound-force/inch^2	foot water (60 °F)
millipascal	dyne/centimeter^2	psi	atmosphere technical
micropascal	kilogram-force/meter^2	poundal/foot^2	Standard atmosphere

16. Category: Moment of Inertia

Category: Moment of Inertia

kilogram meter^2	gram millimeter^2	centimeter second^2	pound-force foot second^2
kilogram centimeter^2	kilogram-force meter	ounce inch^2	pound inch^2
kilogram millimeter^2	second^2	ounce-force inch second^2	pound-force inch second^2
gram centimeter^2	kilogram-force	pound foot^2	slug foot^2

17. Category: Moment of Force

Category: Moment of Force

newton meter	micronewton meter	ton-force (metric) meter	pound-force foot
kilonewton meter	ton-force (short) meter	kilogram-force meter	poundal foot
millinewton meter	ton-force (long) meter	gram-force centimeter	poundal inch

18. Category: Torque

Category: Torque

newton meter	dyne meter	kilogram-force centimeter	gram-force millimeter
newton centimeter	dyne centimeter	kilogram-force millimeter	ounce-force foot
newton millimeter	dyne millimeter	gram-force meter	ounce-force inch
kilonewton meter	kilogram-force meter	gram-force centimeter	pound-force foot
			pound-force inch

19. Category: Energy

Category: Energy

joule	kilowatt-hour	mega Btu (IT)	kilogram-force meter
gigajoule	kilowatt-second	ton-hour (refrigeration)	kilopond meter
megajoule	watt-hour	fuel oil equivalent @kiloliter	pound-force foot
kilojoule	watt-second	fuel oil equivalent @barrel (US)	pound-force inch
millijoule	newton meter	gigaton	ounce-force inch
microjoule	horsepower hour	megaton	foot-pound
nanojoule	horsepower (metric) hour	kiloton	inch-pound
attojoule	kilocalorie (IT)	ton (explosives)	inch-ounce
megaelectron-volt	kilocalorie (th)	dyne centimeter	poundal foot
kiloelectron-volt	calorie (IT)	gram-force meter	therm
electron-volt	calorie (th)	gram-force centimeter	therm (EC)
erg	calorie (nutritional)	kilogram-force centimeter	therm (US)
gigawatt-hour	Btu (IT)		Hartree energy
megawatt-hour	Btu (th)		Rydberg constant

20. Category: Fuel Consumption

<table>
<tr><td colspan="4" align="center">Category: Fuel Consumption</td></tr>
<tr>
<td>meter/liter
exameter/liter
petameter/liter
terameter/liter
gigameter/liter
megameter/liter
kilometer/liter
hectometer/liter
dekameter/liter</td>
<td>centimeter/liter
mile (US)/liter
nautical mile/liter
nautical mile/gallon (US)
kilometer/gallon (US)
meter/gallon (US)
meter/gallon (UK)
mile/gallon (US)</td>
<td>mile/gallon (UK)
meter/meter^3
meter/centimeter^3
meter/yard^3
meter/foot^3
meter/inch^3
meter/quart (US)
meter/quart (UK)
meter/pint (US)
meter/pint (UK)</td>
<td>meter/cup (US)
meter/cup (UK)
meter/fluid ounce (US)
meter/fluid ounce (UK)
liter/meter
liter/100 km
gallon (US)/mile
gallon (US)/100 mi
gallon (UK)/mile
gallon (UK)/100 mi</td>
</tr>
</table>

21. Category: Fuel Efficiency - Mass

<table>
<tr><td colspan="4" align="center">Category: Fuel Efficiency – Mass</td></tr>
<tr>
<td>joule/kilogram
kilojoule/kilogram
calorie (IT)/gram
calorie (th)/gram</td>
<td>Btu (IT)/pound
Btu (th)/pound
kilogram/joule
kilogram/kilojoule</td>
<td>gram/calorie (IT)
gram/calorie (th)
pound/Btu (IT)
pound/Btu (th)</td>
<td>pound/horsepower/hour
gram/horsepower (metric)/hour
gram/kilowatt/hour</td>
</tr>
</table>

22. Category: Fuel Efficiency – Volume

<table>
<tr><td colspan="5" align="center">Category: Fuel Efficiency – Volume</td></tr>
<tr>
<td>joule/meter^3
joule/liter
megajoule/meter^3
kilojoule/meter^3</td>
<td>kilocalorie (IT)/meter^3
calorie (IT)/centimeter^3
therm/foot^3
therm/gallon (UK)</td>
<td>Btu (IT)/foot^3
Btu (th)/foot^3
CHU/foot^3
meter^3/joule</td>
<td>liter/joule
gallon (US)/horsepower
gallon (US)/horsepower (metric)</td>
</tr>
</table>

23. Category: Power

<table>
<tr><td colspan="4" align="center">Category: Power</td></tr>
<tr>
<td>watt
exawatt
petawatt
terawatt
gigawatt
megawatt
kilowatt
hectowatt
dekawatt
deciwatt
centiwatt
milliwatt
microwatt
nanowatt
picowatt
femtowatt
attowatt
horsepower, horsepower (UK), horsepower (550 ft*lbf/s)</td>
<td>horsepower (metric)
horsepower (boiler)
horsepower (electric)
horsepower (water)
pferdestarke (ps)
Btu (IT)/hour
Btu (IT)/minute
Btu (IT)/second
Btu (th)/hour
Btu (th)/minute
Btu (th)/second
MBtu (IT)/hour
MBH
ton (refrigeration)
kilocalorie (IT)/hour
kilocalorie (IT)/minute
kilocalorie (IT)/second
kilocalorie (th)/hour
kilocalorie (th)/minute
kilocalorie (th)/second</td>
<td>calorie (IT)/hour
calorie (IT)/minute
calorie (IT)/second
calorie (th)/hour
calorie (th)/minute
calorie (th)/second
foot pound-force/hour
foot pound-force/minute
foot pound-force/second
pound-foot/hour
pound-foot/minute
pound-foot/second
erg/second
kilovolt ampere
volt ampere
newton meter/second
joule/second
exajoule/second</td>
<td>petajoule/second
terajoule/second
gigajoule/second
megajoule/second
kilojoule/second
hectojoule/second
dekajoule/second
decijoule/second
centijoule/second
millijoule/second
microjoule/second
nanojoule/second
picojoule/second
femtojoule/second
attojoule/second
joule/hour
joule/minute
kilojoule/hour
kilojoule/minute</td>
</tr>
</table>

24. Category: Temperature

<table>
<tr><td align="center">Category: Temperature</td></tr>
</table>

| kelvin | degree Fahrenheit | degree Reaumur | |
| degree Celsius | degree Rankine | Triple point of water | |

25. Category: Temperature Interval

Category: Temperature Interval			
kelvin	degree centigrade	degree Rankine	
degree Celsius	degree Fahrenheit	degree Reaumur	

26. Category: Thermal Expansion

Category: Thermal Expansion		
length/lenght/kelvin	length/lenght/degree Fahrenheit	length/lenght/degree Reaumur
length/lenght/degree Celsius	length/lenght/degree Rankine	

27. Category: Thermal Resistance

Category: Thermal Resistance			
kelvin/watt	degree Fahrenheit hour/Btu (th)	degree Fahrenheit second/Btu (th)	degree Fahrenheit second/Btu (IT)
degree Fahrenheit hour/Btu (IT)			

28. Category: Thermal Conductivity

Category: Thermal Conductivity			
watt/meter/K	calorie (th)/second/centimeter/°C	Btu (th) inch/second/foot²/ °F	Btu (IT) inch/hour/foot²/ °F
watt/centimeter/°C	kilocalorie (IT)/hour/meter/ °C	Btu (IT) foot/hour/foot²/ °F	Btu (th) inch/hour/foot²/ °F
kilowatt/meter/K	kilocalorie (th)/hour/meter/ °C	Btu (th) foot/hour/foot²/ °F	
calorie (IT)/second/centimeter/°C	Btu (IT) inch/second/foot²/ °F		

29. Category: Specific Heat Capacity

Category: Specific Heat Capacity			
joule/kilogram/K	calorie (th)/gram/ °C	Btu (IT)/pound/ °F	Btu (th)/pound/ °R
joule/kilogram/ °C	kilocalorie (IT)/kilogram/ °C	Btu (th)/pound/ °F	Btu (IT)/pound/ °C
joule/gram/ °C	kilocalorie (th)/kilogram/ °C	Btu (IT)/pound/ °R	CHU/pound/ °C
kilojoule/kilogram/K	kilocalorie (IT)/kilogram/K	kilogram-force meter/kilogram/K	
kilojoule/kilogram/ °C	kilocalorie (th)/kilogram/K		
calorie (IT)/gram/ C	pound-force foot/pound/ °R		
calorie (IT)/gram/ °F			

30. Category: Heat Density

Category: Heat Density			
joule/meter²	calorie (th)/centimeter²	langley	Btu (th)/foot²
			Btu (IT)/foot²

31. Category: Heat Flux Density

Category: Heat Flux Density			
watt/meter²	kilocalorie (IT)/hour/foot²	pound/minute/foot²	Btu (IT)/minute/foot²
kilowatt/meter²	calorie (IT)/second/centimeter²	horsepower/foot²	Btu (IT)/hour/foot²
watt/centimeter²	calorie (IT)/minute/centimeter²	horsepower (metric)/foot²	Btu (th)/second/inch²
watt/inch²	calorie (IT)/hour/centimeter²	Btu (IT)/second/foot²	Btu (th)/second/foot²
joule/second/meter²	calorie (th)/second/centimeter²		Btu (th)/minute/foot²
kilocalorie (IT)/hour/meter²	calorie (th)/minute/centimeter²		
	calorie (th)/hour/centimeter²		

		Btu (th)/hour/foot^2
dyne/hour/centimeter		
erg/hour/millimeter^2 foot		CHU/hour/foot^2

32. Category: Heat Transfer Coefficient

Category: Heat Transfer Coefficient		
watt/meter^2/K watt/meter^2/ °C joule/second/meter^2/K	calorie (IT)/second/centimeter^2/ °C kilocalorie (IT)/hour/meter^2/ °C kilocalorie (IT)/hour/foot^2/ °C Btu (IT)/second/foot^2/ °F	Btu (th)/second/foot^2/ °F Btu (IT)/hour/foot^2/ °F Btu (th)/hour/foot^2/ °F CHU/hour/foot^2/ °C

33. Category: Flow

Category: Flow			
meter^3/second	gallon (US)/day	hundred-foot^3/day	inch^3/minute
meter^3/day	gallon (US)/hour	hundred-foot^3/hour	inch^3/second
meter^3/hour	gallon (US)/minute	hundred-foot^3/minute	pound/second (Gasoline at 15.5 °C)
meter^3/minute	gallon (US)/second	ounce/hour	pound/minute (Gasoline at 15.5 °C)
centimeter^3/day	gallon (UK)/day	ounce/minute	pound/hour (Gasoline at 15.5 °C)
centimeter^3/hour	gallon (UK)/hour	ounce/second	pound/day (Gasoline at 15.5 °C)
centimeter^3/minute	gallon (UK)/minute	ounce (UK)/hour	kilogram/second (Gasoline at 15.5 °C)
centimeter^3/second	gallon (UK)/second	ounce (UK)/minute	kilogram/minute (Gasoline at 15.5 °C)
liter/day	kilobarrel (US)/day	ounce (UK)/second	kilogram/hour (Gasoline at 15.5 °C)
liter/hour	barrel (US)/day	yard^3/hour	kilogram/day (Gasoline at 15.5 °C)
liter/minute	barrel (US)/hour	yard^3/minute	
liter/second	barrel (US)/minute	yard^3/second	
milliliter/day	barrel (US)/second	foot^3/hour	
milliliter/hour	acre-foot/year	foot^3/minute	
milliliter/minute	acre-foot/day	foot^3/second	
milliliter/second	acre-foot/hour	inch^3/hour	

34. Category: Flow – Mass

Category: Flow – Mass			
kilogram/second	kilogram/minute	hectogram/second	ton (metric)/hour
gram/second	kilogram/hour	dekagram/second	ton (metric)/day
gram/minute	kilogram/day	decigram/second	ton (short)/hour
gram/hour	exagram/second	centigram/second	pound/second
gram/day	petagram/second	milligram/second	pound/minute
milligram/minute	teragram/second	microgram/second	pound/hour
milligram/hour	gigagram/second	ton (metric)/second	pound/day
milligram/day	megagram/second	ton (metric)/minute	

35. Category: Flow – Molar

Category: Flow – Molar			
mol/second	hectomol/second	picomol/second	millimol/minute
examol/second	dekamol/second	femtomol/second	millimol/hour
petamol/second	decimol/second	attomol/second	millimol/day
teramol/second	centimol/second	mol/minute	kilomol/minute
gigamol/second	millimol/second	mol/hour	kilomol/hour
megamol/second	micromol/second	mol/day	kilomol/day
kilomol/second	nanomol/second		

36. Category: Mass Flux Density

Category: Mass Flux Density			
gram/second/meter^2 kilogram/hour/meter^2	kilogram/hour/foot^2 kilogram/second/meter^2	gram/second/centimeter^2 pound/hour/foot^2	pound/second/foot^2

37. Category: Concentration – Molar

Category: Concentration – Molar			
mol/meter^3 mol/liter mol/centimeter^3	mol/millimeter^3 kilomol/meter^3 kilomol/liter	kilomol/centimeter^3 kilomol/millimeter^3 millimol/meter^3	millimol/liter millimol/centimeter^3 millimol/millimeter^3

38. Category: Concentration – Solution

Category: Concentration – Solution			
kilogram/liter gram/liter milligram/liter	part/million (ppm) grain/gallon (US) grain/gallon (UK)	pound/gallon (US) pound/gallon (UK) pound/million gallon (US)	pound/million gallon (UK) pound/foot^3

39. Viscosity – Dynamic

Viscosity – Dynamic			
pascal second kilogram-force second/meter^2 newton second/meter^2 millinewton second/meter^2 dyne second/centimeter^2 poise exapoise	petapoise terapoise gigapoise megapoise kilopoise hectopoise dekapoise decipoise	centipoise millipoise micropoise nanopoise picopoise femtopoise attopoise	pound-force second/inch^2 pound-force second/foot^2 poundal second/foot^2 gram/centimeter/second slug/foot/second pound/foot/second pound/foot/hour

40. Category: Viscosity – Kinematic

Category: Viscosity – Kinematic			
meter^2/second meter^2/hour centimeter^2/second millimeter^2/second foot^2/second foot^2/hour	inch^2/second stokes exastokes petastokes terastokes gigastokes	megastokes kilostokes hectostokes dekastokes decistokes centistokes	millistokes microstokes nanostokes picostokes femtostokes attostokes

41. Category: Surface Tension

Category: Surface Tension			
newton/meter millinewnon/meter	gram-force/centimeter dyne/centimeter	erg/centimeter^2 erg/millimeter^2	poundal/inch pound-force/inch

42. Category: Permeability

Category: Permeability		
kilogram/pascal/second/meter^2 permeability (0 °C)	permeability (23 °C) permeability inches (0 °C)	permeability inches (23 °C)

43. Category - Sound

Category: Sound		
Bel	decibel	neper

44. Category - Luminance

Category: Luminance		
candela/meter^2	lumen/meter^2/steradian	lambert
candela/centimeter^2	lumen/centimeter^2/steradian	millilambert
candela/foot^2	lumen/foot^2/steradian	foot-lambert
candela/inch^2	watt/centimeter^2/steradian (at 555 nm)	apostilb
kilocandela/meter^2	nit	blondel
stilb	millinit	bril
		skot

45. Category - Luminous Intensity

Category: Luminous Intensity				
candle (international)	decimal candle	hefner candle	bougie decimal	
candle (German)	candle (pentane)	carcel unit	lumen/steradian	
candle (UK)	pentane candle (10 candle power)			

46. Category - Illumination

Category: Illumination		
lux	flame	lumen/meter^2
meter-candle	phot	lumen/centimeter^2
centimeter-candle	nox	lumen/foot^2
foot-candle	candela steradian/meter^2	watt/centimeter^2 (at 555 nm)

47. Category - Digital Image Resolution

Category: Digital Image Resolution			
dot/meter	dot/millimeter	dot/inch	pixel/inch

48. Category - Frequency Wavelength

Category: Frequency Wavelength			
hertz	megahertz	centihertz	cycle/second
exahertz	kilohertz	millihertz	wavelength in exametres
petahertz	hectohertz	microhertz	wavelength in petametres
terahertz	dekahertz	nanohertz	Electron Compton wavelength
gigahertz	decihertz	picohertz	Proton Compton wavelength
	attohertz	femtohertz	Neutron Compton wavelength

49. Category - Charge

Category: Charge			
coulomb	microcoulomb	EMU of charge	ampere-minute
megacoulomb	nanocoulomb	statcoulomb	ampere-second
		ESU of charge	faraday (based on carbon 12)

kilocoulomb millicoulomb	picocoulomb abcoulomb	franklin\ ampere-hour	Elementary charge

50. Category: Linear Charge Density

Category: Linear Charge Density		
coulomb/meter coulomb/centimeter	coulomb/inch abcoulomb/meter	abcoulomb/centimeter abcoulomb/inch

51. Category: Surface Charge Density

Category: Surface Charge Density		
coulomb/meter^2 coulomb/centimeter^2	coulomb/inch^2 abcoulomb/meter^2	abcoulomb/centimeter^2 abcoulomb/inch^2

52. Category: Volume Charge Density

Category: Volume Charge Density		
coulomb/meter^3 coulomb/centimeter^3	coulomb/inch^3 abcoulomb/meter^3	abcoulomb/centimeter^3 abcoulomb/inch^3

53. Category Current

Category: Current (Electric)		
ampere kiloampere milliampere biot	abampere EMU of current statampere	ESU of current CGS e.m. unit CGS e.s. unit

54. Category: Current Density

Category: Current Density		
ampere/meter ampere/centimeter ampere/inch	abampere/meter abampere/centimeter abampere/inch	oersted gilbert/centimeter

55. Surface Current Density

Category: Surface Current Density		
ampere/meter^2 ampere/centimeter^2	ampere/inch^2 ampere/mil^2	ampere/cicular mil abampere/centimeter^2

56. Electric Field Strength

Category: Electric Field Strength		
volt/meter kilovolt/meter kilovolt/centimeter volt/centimeter millivolt/meter	microvolt/meter kilovolt/inch volt/inch volt/mil abvolt/centimeter	statvolt/centimeter statvolt/inch newton/coulomb

57. Electric Potential

Category: Electric Potential

volt	abvolt	statvolt
watt/ampere	EMU of electric potential	ESU of electric potential

58. Electric Resistance

Category: Electric Resistance		
ohm	volt/ampere	EMU of resistance
megohm	reciprocal siemens	statohm
microhm	abohm	ESU of resistance
		Quantized Hall resistance

59. Electric Resistivity

Category: Electric Resistivity		
ohm meter	microhm centimeter	statohm centimeter
ohm centimeter	microhm inch	circular mil ohm/foot
ohm inch	abohm centimeter	

60. Electric Conductance

Category: Electric Conductance		
siemens	microsiemens	micromho
megasiemens	ampere/volt	abmho
kilosiemens	mho	statmho
millisiemens	gemmho	Quantized Hall conductance

61. Electric Conductivity

Category: Electric Conductivity		
siemens/meter	mho/centimeter	statmho/meter
picosiemens/meter	abmho/meter	statmho/centimeter
mho/meter	abmho/centimeter	

62. Electrostatic Capacitance

Category: Electrostatic Capacitance		
farad	hectofarad	picofarad
exafarad	dekafarad	femtofarad
petafarad	decifarad	attofarad
terafarad	centifarad	coulomb/volt
gigafarad	millifarad	abfarad
megafarad	microfarad	EMU of capacitance
kilofarad	nanofarad	statfarad
		ESU of capacitance

62. Inductance

Category: Inductance		
henry	hectohenry	picohenry
exahenry	dekahenry	femtohenry
petahenry	decihenry	attohenry
terahenry	centihenry	weber/ampere

gigahenry	millihenry	abhenry
megahenry	microhenry	EMU of inductance
kilohenry	nanohenry	stathenry
		ESU of inductance

63. Magnetomotive Force

Category: Magnetomotive Force			
ampere turn	milliampere turn	Gilbert	
kiloampere turn	abampere turn		

64. Magnetic Field Strength

Category: Magnetic Field Strength			
ampere/meter	ampere turn/meter	kiloampere/meter	Oersted

65. Magnetic Flux

Category: Magnetic Flux			
weber	unit pole	tesla meter^2	Magnetic flux quantum
milliweber	megaline	tesla centimeter^2	maxwell
microweber	kiloline	gauss centimeter^2	
volt second	line		

66. Magnetic Flux Density

Category: Magnetic Flux Density			
tesla	weber/inch^2	maxwell/inch^2	line/inch^2
weber/meter^2	maxwell/meter^2	gauss	gamma
weber/centimeter^2	maxwell/centimeter^2	line/centimeter^2	

67. Radiation

Category: Radiation			
gray/second	kilogray/second	microgray/second	joule/kilogram/second
exagray/second	hectogray/second	nanogray/second	watt/kilogram
petagray/second	dekagray/second	picogray/second	sievert/second
teragray/second	decigray/second	femtogray/second	rem/second
gigagray/second	centigray/second	attogray/second	
megagray/second	milligray/second	rad/second	

68. Radiation – Activity

Category: Activity			
Becquerel	kilobecquerel	millicurie	rutherford
terabecquerel	millibecquerel	microcurie	one/second
gigabecquerel	curie	nanocurie	disintegrations/second
megabecquerel	kilocurie	picocurie	disintegrations/minute

69. Radiation – Exposure

Category: Exposure			
coulomb/kilogram	microcoulomb/kilogram	tissue roentgen	rep
millicoulomb/kilogram	roentgen	parker	

70. Radiation - Absorbed Dose

Category: Radiation - Absorbed Dose			
rad	gray	kilogray	microgray
millirad	exagray	hectogray	nanogray
joule/kilogram	petagray	dekagray	picogray
joule/gram	teragray	decigray	femtogray
joule/centigram	gigagray	centigray	attogray
joule/milligram	megagray	milligray	

71. Numbers

Category : Numbers			
binary	base-8	base-19	base-30
octal	base-9	base-20	base-31
decimal	base-10	base-21	
hexadecimal	base-11	base-22	base-32
Roman numeral	base-12	base-23	base-33
base-2	base-13	base-24	
base-3	base-14	base-25	base-34
base-4	base-15	base-26	base-35
base-5	base-16	base-27	
base-6	base-17	base-28	base-36
base-7	base-18	base-29	

72. Category: Typography

Category: Typography			
twip	character (X)	inch	point (computer)
meter	character (Y)	pica (computer)	point (printer's)
centimeter	pixel (X)	pica (printer's)	en
millimeter	pixel (Y)	PostScript point	

73. Data Storage

Category: Data Storage			
bit	kilobyte (10^3 bytes)	petabit	Zip 100
nibble	megabit	petabyte	Zip 250
byte	megabyte	petabyte (10^{15} bytes)	Jaz 1GB
character	megabyte (10^6 bytes)	exabit	Jaz 2GB
word	gigabit	exabyte	CD (74 minute)
MAPM-word	gigabyte	exabyte (10^{18} bytes)	CD (80 minute)
quadruple-word	gigabyte (10^9 bytes)	floppy disk (3.5", DD)	DVD (1 layer, 1 side)
block	terabit	floppy disk (3.5", HD)	DVD (2 layer, 1 side)

kilobit	terabyte	floppy disk (3.5", ED)	DVD (1 layer, 2 side)
kilobyte	terabyte (10^{12} bytes)	floppy disk (5.25", DD)	DVD (2 layer, 2 side)
		floppy disk (5.25", HD)	

74. Data Transfer

Category - Data Transfer			
bit/second	ISDN (single channel)	IDE (DMA mode 0)	STS1 (signal)
byte/second	ISDN (dual channel)	IDE (DMA mode 1)	STS1 (payload)
kilobit/second (SI def.)	modem (110)	IDE (DMA mode 2)	STS3 (signal)
kilobyte/second (SI def.)	modem (300)	IDE (UDMA mode 0)	STS3 (payload)
kilobit/second	modem (1200)	IDE (UDMA mode 1)	STS3c (signal)
kilobyte/second	modem (2400)	IDE (UDMA mode 2)	STS3c (payload)
megabit/second (SI def.)	modem (9600)	IDE (UDMA mode 3)	STS12 (signal)
megabyte/second (SI def.)	modem (14.4k)	IDE (UDMA mode 4)	STS24 (signal)
megabit/second	modem (28.8k)	IDE (UDMA-33)	STS48 (signal)
megabyte/second	modem (33.6k)	IDE (UDMA-66)	STS192 (signal)
gigabit/second (SI def.)	modem (56k)	T0 (payload)	STM-1 (signal)
gigabyte/second (SI def.)	SCSI (Async)	T0 (B8ZS payload)	STM-4 (signal)
gigabit/second	SCSI (Sync)	T1 (signal)	STM-16 (signal)
gigabyte/second	SCSI (Fast)	T1 (payload)	STM-64 (signal)
terabit/second (SI def.)	SCSI (Fast Ultra)	T1Z (payload)	H0
terabyte/second (SI def.)	SCSI (Fast Wide)	T1C (signal)	H11
terabit/second	SCSI (Fast Ultra Wide)	T1C (payload)	H12
terabyte/second	SCSI (Ultra-2)	T2 (signal)	Virtual Tributary 1 (signal)
ethernet	SCSI (Ultra-3)	T3 (signal)	Virtual Tributary 1 (payload)
ethernet (fast)	SCSI (LVD Ultra80)	T3 (payload)	Virtual Tributary 2 (signal)
ethernet (gigabit)	SCSI (LVD Ultra160)	T3Z (payload)	Virtual Tributary 2 (payload)
OC1	USB	T4 (signal)	Virtual Tributary 6 (signal)
OC3	firewire (IEEE-1394)	E.P.T.A. 1 (signal)	Virtual Tributary 6 (payload)
OC12	IDE (PIO mode 0)	E.P.T.A. 1 (payload)	
OC24	IDE (PIO mode 1)	E.P.T.A. 2 (signal)	
OC48	IDE (PIO mode 2)	E.P.T.A. 2 (payload)	
OC192	IDE (PIO mode 3)	E.P.T.A. 3 (signal)	
OC768	IDE (PIO mode 4)	E.P.T.A. 3 (payload)	

Dictionary of Scientific Measuring Unites

A

a

An international symbol for year, adopted from the Latin word *annus*. Although English-speaking countries continue to use the traditional symbol *yr* for most purposes, scientists use the "*a*" symbol in papers and textbooks. This symbol often appear in combinations like Ma (million years) or Ga (billion years).

a (atto)

S.I. prefix $= 10^{-18}$

a

Abbreviations of the unit of area of land "are"

See; "are"

a or A

Shortened version of "am" or "AM" in a statement of time.

See, "time".

A

A symbol for international standard paper sizes, followed by the size number, as in A4 for a standard business- letter sheet. A table of sizes is provided.

"A" is also the S.I. symbol for the ampere

See "ampere".

A*

See "*angstrom star*".

ab...

A prefix denoting an unrationalized electrical or magnetical CGS-emu unit used mainly in U.S., "ab" is an abbreviation of "absolute electromagnetic". It represents a system of units different from absolute units. The following list shows the S.I. equivalents for each of the "ab" units:

Electric current: 1 **abampere** = 10 amperes

Electric charge: 1 **abcoulomb** = 10 coulombs

Capacitance: 1 **abfarad** = 10^9 farads = 1 gigafarad

Inductance: 1 **abhenry** = 10^{-9} ehnry = 1 nanohenry

Resistance: 1 **abohm** = 10^{-9} ohm = 1 nanoohm

Conductance: 1 **abmho** = 10^9 siemens

Magnetic flux density: 1 **abtesla** = 10^{-4} tesla = 1 gauss

Potential: 1 **abvolt** = 10^{-8} volt = 10 nanovolts

Power: 1 **abwatt** = 10^{-7} watt = 0.1 microwatt

Magnetic flux: 1 **abweber** = 10^{-8} weber = 1 maxwell.

The following table shows some of the units of this system.

CGS-emu unit	Unit Symbol	Quantity measured	Corresponding CGSm unit of equal size	Corresponding S.I. unit	To convert CGS- emu to S.I. unit, multiply by:
Abampere	abA	Current	Biot (Bi)	Ampere (A)	10
abampere centimeter square	abA cm^2	Electromagnetic moment	Bi cm^2	**Ampere square meter (A m^2)**	10^3
abampere per square centimeter	abA cm^{-2}	Current density	Bi/cm^2	Ampere per square meter (A/m^2)	10^5
Abcoulomb	abC	Charge	Biot second (Bi s)	Coulomb (C)	10
abcoulomb centimeter	abC cm	Electric Dipole moment	Bi s cm	Coulomb meter (C m)	10
abcoulomb per cubic centimeter	abC cm^{-3}	Volume density of charge	Bi s /cm^3	Coulomb per cubic meter (C/m^3)	10^7

abcoulomb per square centimeter	abC cm^{-2}	Electric polarization, and Electric flux density	Bi s/cm^2	Coulomb per square meter (C/m^2)	10^3 (for polarization), 7.95775xl0^3 (for flux density)
Abfarad	abF	Capacitance	Bi^{2}s^2/erg	Farad (F)	10^9
Abhenry	abH	Inductance	erg /Bi^2	Henry (H)	10^{-9}
Abohm	abΩ	Resistance; Impedance; Reactance	erg/Bi^2 s	Ohm (Ω)	10^{-9}
abohm centimeter	abΩcm	Resistivity	erg cm/Bi^{2}s	Ohm meter (Qm)	10^{-11}
ab siemens	abS	Conductance; Admittance; Susceptance	Bi^2 s/erg	Siemens (S)	10^9
absiemens per centimeter	abS cm^{-1}	Conductivity	Bi^{2}s/erg cm	Siemens per meter (S/m)	10^{-11}
ab tesla	abT	Magnetic flux density	erg/Bi cm^2	Tesla (T)	10^{-4}
Abvolt	abV	Potential; Electromotive force	erg/Bi s	Volt (V)	10^{-6}
abvolt per centimeter	abV cm^{-1}	Electric field strength	erg/Bi s cm	Volt per meter	10^{-6}
Abweber	abWb	Magnetic flux	erg/Bi	Weber (Wb)	10^{-8}

abbe

S.I. unit of linear spatial frequency.

1 abbe = 1 hertz per meter.

Note: 1. The unit is replacing the hertz per meter.

2. The name was suggested for the first time in 1973. The name of the unit was adopted from a German physicist Ernst Abbe (1840-1905)

See also *"duffieux"*.

absolute...

Deprecated adjective used when international units were in use before 1948, to distinguish them from the corresponding MKSA (= S.I.) units. The adjective absolute was used to indicate that the unit is a theoretically defined unit. These units are not the same as the absolute electromagnetic units (ab- units). The relationships between the international and absolute units of electromotive force (volt) and resistance (ohm) were formally defined during the CIPM of 1946. Accordingly, the relationships between the other units are defined as follows.

Unit	Unit Symbol		To convert from absolute to International, multiply by
	Absolute	Interna-Tional	
Ampere	A_{abs}	A_{int}	1.00015
Coulom	C_{abs}	C_{int}	1.00015
Farad	F_{abs}	F_{int}	1.00049
Henry	H_{abs}	H_{int}	0.999510
Joule	J_{abs}	J_{int}	0.999810
Mho			1.00049

Unit	Unit Symbol		To convert from absolute to international multiply by
	Absolute	Interna-Tional	
Ohm	Ω_{abs}	Ω_{int}	0.999510
Siemens	S_{abs}	S_{int}	1.00049
Tesla	T_{abs}	T_{int}	0.999660
Volt	V_{abs}	V_{int}	0.999660
Watt	W_{abs}	W_{int}	0.999810
Weber	Wb_{abs}	Wb_{int}	0.999660

See also "absolute unit" *and* "*absolute* units of electricity".

absolute degree

Unit of temperature.

See "kelvin".

absolute unit

If a quantity y is uniquely defined in terms of quantities $x_1, x_2, ...$ by the relation:

$$y = f(x_1, x_2, ...)$$

the unit of U_y can be obtained from the units $U_{x1}, U_{x2},...$ of $x_1, x_2,...$ from the equation:

$$Uy \propto f(U_{x1}, U_{x2},...).$$

An absolute unit is one where the constant of proportionality is unity. All S.I. units are absolute.

See also *"absolute"*.

absolute units of electricity

A system of units based on the three fundamental mechanical standards, i.e., the kilogram, meter and second. The fourth dimensional unit is the permeability of free space, which is assigned an arbitrary value of $4\pi x10^{-7}$ Newtons per square ampere.

Although the size of the absolute units of resistance and current depend on the value assigned to μ_0, the product is independent of μ_0 and the absolute electrical watt is thus equivalent to the mechanical joule per second.

See also *"absolute"*.

absorption unit (total)

FPS unit of the equivalent absorption area of a surface to a sound. One absorption unit (total) is equivalent to one square foot of a surface with a reverberation absorption coefficient of unity, which would absorb sound energy of a given frequency at the same rate as the surface under investigation.

1 (total) absorption unit = 1 square foot = 0.092 903 04 square meters.

Note: This unit is known as sabin. It has also been referred to as the open window unit.

See *"sabin"* and *"open window unit"*.

absorbance unit (A.U.)

A logarithmic unit is used to measure optical density. It communicates a value of the absorbance of light transmitted through a partially absorbing substance.

If T is the percentage of light transmitted, then the absorbance is defined to be $-\log_{10} T$ absorbance units. An increase in absorbance of 1.0 A.U. corresponds to a reduction in transmittance by a factor of 10. If the absorbance is 1.0 A.U., then 10% of the light is transmitted. At 2.0 A.U., only 1% of the light is transmitted, and so on. Note that A.U. is also used in astronomy as a symbol for the astronomical unit.

See *"astronomical unit"*.

abstat.

Deprecated prefix denoting a CGSe unit.

ab- *and* **stat-**

Prefixes used, primarily in the United States, to distinguish electric and magnetic units in the centimeter-gram-second electromagnetic system of units from the corresponding units in the centimeter-gram-second electrostatic system of units. The names of the CGS electromagnetic units began with "ab-"; the names of the electrostatic units with "stat-".

abv, abw

Symbols for alcohol by volume and alcohol by weight. 1% abv = 1% v/v and 1% abw = 1% w/v.

academic year

a unit of time in U.S. schools, generally equivalent to 9 months, commencing in August or September.

accm, acfm, acfh, acfd, acim (etc.)

symbols for "actual cubic centimeters per minute", "actual cubic feet per minute", "actual cubic feet per hour", "actual cubic feet per day", and "actual cubic inches per minute." Many similar abbreviations are used. These are units of the flow rate of gases.
See "sccm"

ACI

a symbol for the "anatomical Chinese inch" or t'sun.

acoustical comfort index (ACI)

Arbitrary unit for the noise inside an aircraft cabin. It is a value on an arbitrarily designed scale on which;
- +100 corresponds to zero noise
- 0 corresponds to conditions that are just tolerable
- -100 corresponds to intolerable conditions.

acoustical ohm (Ωa)

CGS unit of acoustical resistance, reactance and impedance. It is defined as the ratio of the sound pressure level of one dyne per square centimeter to a source sound strength of one cubic centimeter per second.

1 acoustical ohm = 10^5 pascals second per meter cubed

Note; 1. It is a name, which is sometimes equivalent to dyne second per centimeter to fifth power.

2. The names ram and rayl have been proposed as alternatives for this unit, but their used has never been enforced.

3. The idea of applying Kirchhoff's electrical circuit procedures to solve acoustical problems was suggested by Webster as early as 1919, but the acoustic ohm was first used by Stewart in 1926.

See "ram" *and* "rayl".

acre (ac or A)

An imperial (U.K. and U.S.) unit of area. One acre is equivalent to **4840** square yards.

1 acre = **4046. 856 422 4** square meters.

Note: 1. The unit is used for agrarian measurements.

2. The unit was first defined in England (1272-1307) during the reign of Edward I and is reputed to be the area which a yoke of oxen could plow in a day.

3. "Acre", an Old English word meaning a field, which is derived from the Latin *ager* and Greek *agros*, also meaning a field.

4. The acre was originally defined as the area, which could be plowed in a day by a yoke of oxen.

5. It was used in England at least as early as the eighth century and by the end of the ninth century, it was generally understood to be the area of a field that is one furlong (40 rods or 10 chains) long by 4 rods (or 1 chain) wide. Thus, an acre is 10 square chains, 160 square rods, 43 560 square feet or 4840 square yards.

6. There are exactly 640 acres in a square mile.

7. In metric countries, the unit corresponding to the acre is the hectare. The hectare is

equivalent to 10,000 square meters (the area of a square 100 meters on each side). One acre is equivalent to 0.404 687 3 hectares. Among traditional European land area units, the acre is typically defined as a day's work rather than the area of a square.

8. Similar units include the French journal, north German and Dutch morgen, south German and Swiss juchart, Austrian joch, and Czech jitro.

9. The following are the relationships between the acre and some other area units.

acre = 4046.8564224 meters squared

acre = 0.40468564224 hectares

acre = 4 roods

acre = 43560 sabins

acre = 40.468564224 are

acre = 4.0468564224E+31 barns

acre = 0.408163265306122 Japanese cho

acre = 0.37037037037037 Russian desyatina

acre = 4.34027777777778E-05 townships

acre = 0.0015625 sections of land

acre = 7986573.29788758 circular inches

acre = 7986573297887.58 circular mil

acre = 0.00625 homesteads

See also *"furlong, chain, rod, and hectare."*

acre (used as a unit of length)

various historical references mention "acre" as a unit of length, but there has never been any formal definition of such a unit. In older works, especially in Britain, an **acre of length** is a furlong and an **acre of breadth** is 4 rods, since these were the historic dimensions of an acre. In the U.S. and Canada, the acre was the area of a square about 208.710 feet (roughly 208 feet 8.5 inches or 63.615 meters). This length was known as an acre or the **side of an acre**. In contrast, the original area unit was sometimes called the **square acre**. All these usages are now obsolete.

acre per pound (acre lb^{-1} or acre /lb)

U.K. and U.S. imperial unit of specific surface.

1 acre per pound = 8.921 69 x 10^{-1} hectares per kilogram = 8.921 69 x 10^3 m^2/kg.

acre -foot (ac ft or af)

U.S. imperial unit of volume.

One acre-foot is a volume, one foot deep, occupying an area of one acre. Thus, an acre-foot contains exactly 43 560 cubic feet

1 acre-foot = 1.233 481 8 x 10^3 cubic meters.

Note: 1. Used in irrigation engineering. It is defined as the volume of water that is required to cover one acre to a depth of one foot.

2. The unit is used in U.S. for measuring irrigation water, runoff volume and reservoir capacity.

3. One acre-foot is about 325 851.4 U.S. gallons, or about 1233.482 cubic meters (0.123 348 hectare meters).

4. The symbol af is widely used in reservoir management in the U.S., often combined with symbols such as kaf (1000 acre feet) or maf (million acre feet; this symbol should be Maf).

acre-foot per day (ac ft d^{-1} or ac.ft/d)

U.S. imperial unit of volume flow rate.

1 acre-foot per day = 1.427 64 x 10^{-2} meters cubed per second.

acre-inch (ac.in)

U.S. imperial unit of volume. It is equivalent to one-twelfth of one acre-foot or 3630 cubic feet.

1 acre-inch = 1.027 90 x 10^{-2} cubic meters.

Note: The unit is used in the U.S. to measure water flow.

actus (Roman actus)

A Roman unit of length.

> Roman actus = 35.47872 meters
>
> Roman actus = 116.4 feett
>
> Roman actus = 349.2 hands
>
> Roman actus = 1596.34285714286 fingers
>
> Roman actus = 19555.2 typography agates
>
> Roman actus = 1.76363636363636 surveyor's chains

actus quadratus

Roman unit of area. It is a square of 120 pedes on a side = 14 400 square pedes, which is approximately equivalent to 126 square meters.
A.D.

Abbreviation for the Latin *anno domini,* "year of the Lord", the traditional designation for years of the common or Christian era. This abbreviation is often supplanted by C.E. (common era), especially in countries where Christianity is not the dominant religion.

-ad

A suffix is added to a number to create a unit of quantity equal to that number: for example, a 24ad is a unit of quantity equal to 24. Units of quantity equal to 1 through to 8 are known as: the monad, dyad, triad, tetrad, pentad, hexad, heptad, and octad, respectively. The terms are coined by adding -ad to the Greek numbers 1-8.

adila

An Islamic unit of mass, = ½ himl, approximately 125-150 kilograms.
See "himl"

admiralty mile

An obsolete name equivalent to the U.K. nautical mile.
See *"nautical mile".*

AEBI (Aebi)

A unit for the standardization of phosphates [Biology]

aeon

A unit of time equivalent to one billion years (1 Ga). Proposed in 1957 for use in geology, the aeon is not approved by the S.I. and has not gained much favor.

AFUE

An abbreviation for <u>A</u>nnual <u>F</u>uel <u>U</u>tilization <u>E</u>fficiency which is a measure of the efficiency of a gas furnace. The rating is designed to represent the percentage of fuel energy delivered as heat energy, averaged over the course of a typical heating season. The actual calculation is quite complex and considers many properties of the furnace. Older furnaces have ratings of 60% AFUE or even lower. The latest high-efficiency furnaces are rated between 90%-95% AFUE. The U.S. Department of Energy requires new furnaces to operate at 78% AFUE or better.

agate, agate line

A traditional unit of distance used in printing and advertising. The agate line is equivalent to 1/14 inch (1.814 millimeters).

Its name originates from the traditional type size known as agate, which sets approximately 14 lines to the inch.

    typography agate = 1.81428571428571E-03 meters

    typography agate = 7.14285714285714E-02 inches

    typography agate = 9.01875901875902E-05 surveyor's chains

    typography agate = 1.12734487734488E-06 miles

    typography agate = 0.857142857142857 lines

A.H.

Abbreviation for the Latin *anno hegirae,* which is traditionally used in the West to designate years of the Islamic calendar. The Islamic calendar is lunar, taking into account twelve lunar months to the year. Therefore, its years are shorter than ordinary solar years. Years are counted from the day of the Hijri (Hegira in Latin), the flight of Mohammed from Mecca to Medina, which is fixed at 16 July 622 AD according to the Julian calendar. The Islamic year AH 1427 began at sunset of 30 January 2006 in the current (Gregorian) calendar.

air mass

A unit used in astronomy in measuring the absorption of light from the stars by the atmosphere.

One air mass is the amount of absorption of light from a star directly overhead (at the *zenith)*. The absorption of light from other stars is greater, because their light must travel obliquely through the atmosphere. If Z is the *zenithal angle* (the angle between the star and the zenith), then the absorption of its light is estimated to be sec Z air masses, with "sec" being the secant trigonometric function.

air mile (air mile)

A unit of length.

1 air mile = 1 international nautical mile = 1852 meters.

Note: 1. It is used in air navigation.

2. The application of the above definition started in 1954.

3. The unit is also known as the aeronautical mile.

air watt

An engineering unit used to express the effective cleaning power of a vacuum cleaner or central vacuum system. The air watt is practically equivalent to the ordinary watt. Measurements of vacuum power, however, are computed from English units using the following formula established by the American Society for Testing and Materials (ASTM).

Power in air watts equals 0.117354-F-S, or close to F-S/8.5, where F is the air flow in the system in cubic feet per minute (CFM), and S is the suction pressure in inches of water column (in W.C.). This definition qualifies the air watt to be equal to 0.9983 watts.

ale gallon

A traditional unit of liquid volume in Britain and the U.S. The ale gallon is equivalent to 282 cubic inches (4.6212 liters) or about 1.2208 U.S. liquid gallons (1.0165 British imperial gallons). Standardized in the sixteenth century under Queen Elizabeth I, the ale gallon remained in use until the nineteenth century, but today, it is obsolete.
It is also known as the beer.

alexinic unit

A unit (biology) for standardization of blood serum.

See also *"Amboceptor unit"*.

allen-doisy unit

A unit (biology) for standardization of estrogens.

allergy unit (A.U.)

A measure of the potency of the compounds used by physicians in skin testing for allergies. The units are calibrated for each compound and the strength of the solutions is stated in allergy units per millimeter (A.U./ml).

almquist unit

A unit (biology) for standardization of vitamin K.
See also "Ansbacher unit".

almude

A traditional unit of volume in Spain and Portugal. The two countries used the name for units of quite different sizes.

The Spanish almude is comparable to the British gallon. It holds about 4.625 liters, which is equivalent to 1.017 imperial gallons or 1.222 U.S. liquid gallons.

The Portuguese almude is much larger. It holds about 16.7 liters, which is equivalent to 3.67 imperial gallons or 4.41 U.S. liquid gallons.

alpha T.E.

An abbreviation for "alpha tocopherol equivalent". It is a measure of vitamin E used in nutrition. Vitamin E is a group of related chemical compounds called tocopherols. The activity or potency of vitamin E in a food or food supplement is measured by the quantity (in milligrams) of alpha tocopherol (the most active of the forms of the vitamin), which is equivalent to the compounds present in the food or supplement. One milligram alpha T.E. is equivalent to 1.5 international units (I.U.).

alqueire

1. A traditional unit of volume for dry goods in Portugal and Brazil, equivalent to 1/4 fanga

(the Portuguese equivalent of the Spanish fanega). This is about 13.8 liters or 12.5 U.S. dry quarts.

2. A traditional unit of land area in Portugal and Brazil. Still commonly used to measure farmland in Brazil. The unit varies considerably from region to region.

One alqueire is equivalent to 2.42 hectares (5.980 acres) in Sao Paulo, 4.84 hectares (11.960 acres) in Rio de Janeiro, Minas Gerais, and Goias, 9.68 hectares (23.920 acres) in Bahia, and 2.7225 hectares (6.728 acres) in the northern part of the country of Bahia. In Portugal, this unit is considered obsolete. It was much smaller, approximately 0.14 hectare (0.35 acres).

alt h

Traditional abbreviation in pharmacy for *alternis horis* (every other hour). It is a unit of frequency sometimes used in medical prescriptions.

AM or am

Abbreviation for the Latin *ante meridiem* (before noon). It is used after a time to indicate that the time is before 12:00 (noon). The notations "AM" and "PM" are used extensively in the United States, where time is usually not stated on a 24-hour basis. Note: the ambiguous notation "12:00 am" should not be used, since it may be taken to mean either noon or midnight. Today, 12:00 am is commonly used to mean midnight.

AM

Abbreviation for the Latin *anno mundi*, "year of the world". This abbreviation is traditionally used to designate years in the Jewish calendar, which counts years from the creation of the world as described in the Hebrew scriptures. The Jewish calendar is lunisolar i.e., its years correspond to ordinary solar years. The first day of AM 1 is equivalent to 6 October 3761 BCE in the Julian calendar. AM 5766 began at sunset of 4 October 2005 in the current (Gregorian) calendar.

Link: Wikipedia provides a better description of the Jewish calendar together with its history.

amagat

Two units used in the study of gases at high pressures. The units are related reciprocally; which one is meant is evident from the context. Symbol, "amg" and more recently "am"[2].

The amagats are named for the French physicist Émile Hilaire Amagat (*1841– 1915*), who spent years studying gases under pressure and used the unit of volume in his publications, without, however, calling it an "amagat". It was subsequently taken up by Kammerlinne Onnes and other Dutch physicists. Currently, it is used, for example, in studying the atmospheres of planets.

amagat density unit

The standard unit of the gas molecular density in the Amagat unit system. One Amagat density unit is the density of a gas whereby, one mole occupies a volume of one Amagat volume unit.

1 Amagat density unit = 1 mole/Amagat volume unit = 44.615 8 moles per cubic meter.

Note: The unit is used in the study of the behavior of gases under pressure.

See *"Amagat system"* and *"Amagat volume unit."*

amagat system

A unit system where the unit of pressure is the atmosphere and the unit of volume is the gram-molecular volume. This system is used when studying the behavior of gases under pressure.

Note: 1. The system is named after E.H. Amagat (1841-1915), who studied the effect of high pressures on gases.

2. The Amagat system has been extensively used in Holland since the time of J.D. van der Waals (1837-1923), a renown Dutch theoretical physicist, but was not used in England until 1939.

See *"Amagat density unit"* and *"Amagat volume unit"*.

amagat volume unit

Unit of volume of a gas in the Amagat unit system. One Amagat volume unit is the volume occupied by one mole of a gas at standard temperature and pressure. The experimentally determined value is:

$$1 \text{ Amagat volume unit} = (0.022\ 413\ 6 \pm 0.000\ 003\ 0) \text{ cubic meters.}$$

Note: The Amagat volume unit has a size numerically equivalent to the reciprocal of the Amagat density unit.

See *"Amagat density unit"* and *"Amagat system."*

amber

An old English unit of volume used for both liquids and dry goods. The amber was equal equivalent to about 4 bushels or roughly 140 liters.

amboceptor unit

A unit (biology) for standardization of blood serum.

See also *"Alexinic unit"*.

American scale

A scale used in the 19th century to describe the size of coins, medallions, and similar flat round objects, adopted by the Numismatic Society of Philadelphia in *1858*. The interval of the scale is one-sixteenth of an inch of diameter. The scale numbers increase as the size of the coin increases. Thus, a number 16 coins is one inch in diameter.

american run

A U.S. unit used in the textile industry for describing the length per unit mass of a yam. One American run is the line density of a thread which has a length of 100 yards and a mass of one ounce.

1 American run = 100 yards per ounce

Note: This unit is used in the textile industry as a measure of yarn count. For example, if 1400 yards weight 1 ounce, then this would be equivalent to a 14-run yarns.

See also *"denier"* and *"drex"*, and *"tex"*.

ampere (A)

Base S.I. unit of electric current and S.I. unit of current linkage, magnetic potential difference and magnetomotive force. It is the constant current, which, if maintained in two straight parallel conductors of infinite length and of negligible circular cross-section, placed in a vacuum one meter apart, will produce a force of 2×10^{-7} Newtons per meter length between the two parallel conductors.

Note: 1. This unit was formerly known as the absolute ampere (A_{abs}), which differs from the international ampere.

2. The standard ampere has been experimentally determined down to an accuracy of 4 ppm at the National Physical Laboratory using an Ayrton-Jones current balance.

ampere x circular mil (A x circular mil)

U.K. and U.S. unit of electromagnetic moment. It communicates the value of the electromagnetic moment due to the passage of an unvarying current of one ampere through a conductor of one circular mil cross-section.

1 ampere x circular mil $= 5.067\ 07 \times 10^{-10}$ amperes meter squared.

ampere-hour (A h):

The S.I. unit of the quantity of electricity. The quantity of electricity conveyed across any cross-section of a conductor when an unvarying current of one ampere flows across the conductor for one hour.

1 Ampere- hour = 3,600 coulombs.

Note: The term is employed in stating the capacity of accumulator.

ampere meter squared (A.m^2)

S.I. unit of electromagnetic moment.

See also *"ampere square meter"*.

ampere-minute (A.min)

A unit of electric charge. It is equivalent to the charge transported in 1 minute by a current of 1 ampere.

1 ampere-minute = 60 coulombs.

ampere per meter (A.m^{-1})

S.I. unit of magnetic field strength, magnetization and linear current density. The unit is equivalent to Newton per Weber (N Wb^{-1})

One ampere per meter is equivalent to $\pi/250$ oersteds (12.566 371 millioersteds) in CGS units. The ampere per meter is also known as the S.I. unit of "magnetization" in the sense of magnetic dipole moment per unit volume; in this context, 1 A/m = 0.001 emu per cubic centimeter

ampere per square meter (Am^{-2} or A/m^2)

S.I. unit of electric current density.

ampere per square meter kelvin squared (Am^{-2} K^{-2} or A/m^2 K^2)

S.I. unit of Richardson constant.

ampere square meter (A.m^2)

S.I. unit of magnetic moment of a particle, Bohar magneton and nuclear magneton. See also *"ampere meter squared"*.

ampere square meter per joule per second (Am^{-2} J^{-1} s^{-1} or A m^2/J s)

S.I. unit of magnetogyric coefficient (gyromagnetic coefficient).

Note: The coulomb per kilogram (C kg^{-1}) can also be used; Am^2 J^{-1} s^{-1} = C kg^{-1}.

ampere, thermal

The S.I. unit of thermal current. One thermal ampere corresponds to an entropy flow of one watt per kelvin (W K^{-1}). Previously, it was defined as the heat flow rate of one watt.

ampere-turn (At or AT)

The S.I. unit of magnetomotive force. It conveys the value of the magnetomotive force resulting from the passage of a current of one ampere through one turn of a coil.

Note: The unit is used also to describe the electrical circuits of electro-magnets.

One ampere-turn is equivalent to $4\pi/10$ = 1.256 637 gilberts (Gb).

amphora

A historic unit of volume.

An amphora is the volume of an urn or jar of the same name. The urn was tall, with both handles close to the top on both sides (the word amphora comes from two Greek words meaning "on both sides" and "carry").

Amphoras were the containers of choice for shipping wine and many other commodities in the ancient world. Archaeologists report that the Greek amphora held about 38.8 liters (10.25 U.S. liquid gallons, or 8.54 British imperial gallons). The Roman amphora was smaller, about 25.5 liters (6.74 U.S. gallons or 5.61 British imperial gallons).

Note: The following are some relations between "Greek Amphora" and other volume units:

Greek amphora = 10.3 gallons

Greek amphora = 1.50584795321637 Roman amphoras

Greek amphora = 38.9897413752 liters

Greek amphora = 8.57654410167859 Canadian gallons

Greek amphora = 8.57654356967401 British gallons

Greek amphora = 1318.4 fluid ounces

Greek amphora = 10547.2 fluid drams

Greek amphora = 0.326984126984127 barrels

Greek amphora = 10.3 gallons

Greek amphora = 9.83497797329514 Israeli omers

Greek amphora = 878.933333333334 jiggers

Greek amphora = 0.276608755498926 coombs

angle at a point (pla)

Unit of plane angle. One angle at a point equivalent to 360°.

1 angle at a point (pla) = 360° = 2π radians.

Note: The symbol of the unit pla, is based on the Greek word "plenus angulus", which means complete angle.

angstrom (Å)

Metric unit of length, especially the wavelength of visible and near visible electromagnetic radiation.

1 Å=10^{-10} meters.

Note: 1. The angstrom is sometimes called the tenthmetre.

The angstrom was formerly defined as:

> 1 angstrom = 1/6438.469 6 of the wavelength of the red cadmium line in dry air at standard atmospheric pressure, 15°C and 0.03% by volume carbon dioxide.

This is now known as the international angstrom (1Å) and equivalent to 1.000 000 2 Å.

angstrom star (Å* or A*)

A unit used to measure the wavelength of X-rays. It is easier to measure the ratio between two X-ray wavelengths than to measure the wavelengths themselves. The wavelengths are usually stated as multiples of a standard wavelength. The X unit and the angstrom star are the units used for this purpose. Å* was defined by J.A. Bearden in 1965 to provide a unit approximately equal to the angstrom (10^{-10} meter or 0.1 nanometer). Later measurements have shown that A* is equivalent to approximately $1.000\ 0015 \times 10^{-10}$ meters or 100.000 15 picometers.

animal unit (A.U.)

A unit of feed consumption used in U.S. dairying and ranching.

One animal unit is the feed or grazing requirement of a mature cow weighing 1000 pounds (453.59 kilograms). This is approximately 26 pounds (11.8 kg) of dry forage. Total feed requirements are often expressed by the animal unit month (AUM), which is the feed required to sustain one animal unit of livestock for one month (780 pounds or 354 kg).

anker (anker)

U.S. unit of capacity (volume) equivalent to 10 U.S. gallon.

1 anker = 10 U.S. gallons = 37.854 liters.

Note: This unit is used to measure the capacity of liquids, especially honey, oil, vinegar, spirits and wine.

anna

A unit of land area in South Asia. In Pakistan, the anna is equivalent to 20.17 square yards or 16.86 square meters. In Nepal, the anna is almost twice the size observed in Pakistan:

31.8 square meters, 342 square feet, or 38 square yards.

annual percentage rate (% APR)

A unit used in the U.S. for stating interest rates and rates of return on an investment. By federal regulation, these rates can be stated in any way a financial institution wishes. The interest rates must be stated in % APR such that consumers can compare rates of different loans and investment opportunities. Mathematically, the natural rate r of return on money is the "instantaneous" rate. This is the rate that allows for compounding of interest continuously. The APR is the percentage growth rate a of the money over a period of one year, if the interest was compounded annually. The two rates are related by the formulas $a = e^r-1$ and $r=$In $(1 + a)$, where e^r is the natural exponential function and In is the natural logarithmic function

anomalistic month

Unit of time representing the average period of revolution of the Moon from perigee-to-perigee.

1 anomalistic month = 27 days, 13 hours, 18 minutes and 33.2 seconds.

Note: In the above definition, perigee means the nearest point to the Earth in the orbit of the Moon (or, in general, the orbit of an artificial satellite). At perigee, the Moon is 5% closer to Earth than its mean distance.

See also *"anomalistic period*

anomalistic period

The interval between two successive perigee passages of a satellite in orbit about a primary. Also known as perigee-to-perigee period.

Also defined as "The anomalistic period is **the time that elapses between two passages of an object at its periapsis** (in the case of the planets in the Solar System, called the perihelion), the point of its closest approach to the attracting body.

See also *"anomalistic month"*.

anomalistic year

Unit of time. The period of one revolution of the Earth about the sun from perihelion to perihelion.

1 anomalistic year = 365 days 6 hours 13 minutes 53.0 seconds in year 1900, increasing at the rate of 0.26 seconds per century.

Note: Perihelion is the point where the path of an object (i.e., the Earth) through space is closest to the sun. See also *"year"*.

ansbacher unit

A unit (biology) for standardization of vitamin K.

One Ansbacher unit = the least amount of vitamin K when injected into vitamin-K-deficient chicks weighing 70 to 100 grams, will result into a prothrombin time (a standardized test[1] of the time it takes the chick's blood to clot) of less than 6 minutes within 6 hours of the injection.

One Ansbacher unit = 0.0008 milligrams menadione. This is about 20 Dam units, or about the amount of vitamin K in 67 milligrams of dried alfalfa.

It is named after a renowned biochemist Stefan Ansbacher (*1905 – 1995*).
See also "Almquist unit" *and* "Dam Unit".

anson unit

- A unit (biology) for standardization of trypsin and proteinases.

- An old measure of the activity of a proteinase. It was based upon the extent to which a sample containing a particular proteinase can digest denatured hemoglobin, under standard conditions.

- A unit of enzyme concentration which is defined as the amount of enzyme that can digest urea-denatured hemoglobin at the same initial rate as one milliequivalent of tyrosine at standard conditions (25C and pH 7.50).

apgarscore

A numerical measure of the health of a newborn baby. One minute after birth (and at regular intervals thereafter through the first moments of life), newborns are rated either 0, or 1, or 2 on five indicators of health (respiratory effort, heart rate, skin color, muscle tone, and reflexive response to smell). Possible scores, therefore, range from 0 to 10. The unit is named after a renowned American anesthetist, Virginia Apgar (1909-1974).

API gravity (AMERICAN PETROLEUM INSTITUTE GRAVITY)

An arbitrary scale based on the formula: degree API = [141.5/ (specific gravity)] - 131.5] where the relative density measurement is estimated at 60°F. Its application enables a linear scale to be used on the stem of a density-measuring device, e.g., a hydrometre.

apostilb (asb)

Metric unit of luminance. It is defined as the luminance of a uniform diffuser emitting one lumen per meter squared. The S.I. unit candela per square meter is preferred.

$$1 \text{ asb} = (1/\pi) \text{ candelas per meter square.}$$

Note: 1. Formerly known as blondel.

2. The use of the unit was commissioned in 1935, but has not gained recommendation for scientific work.

3. The name of the unit is pseudo-Greek for luminance. It combines the ancient Greek *stilbein*, to "glitter" or "shine," with the prefix *apo-*, "away from."

apothecaries measure

A system of units of volume usually for liquid drugs, where 16 fluid ounces is equivalent to 1 pint.

apothecaries weight (or apothecaries units)

A system of units of mass, usually for drugs, where 1 pound is equivalent to 5760 grains or 1 troy pound. The system includes:

1 apothecaries ounce = **24** scruples

1 drachm (in U.K.), or 1 dram (dr) (in U.S.) = **3** scruples

1 scruple = 20 grains

1 grain = **1/480** apothecaries ounce

1 apothecary dram = 0.0038879346 kilograms

1 apothecary dram = 1.04166666666667E-02 apothecary pound

1 apothecary dram = 60 apothecary grains

1 apothecary dram = 3 apothecary scruples

1 apothecary dram = 0.125 apothecary ounces

1 apothecary dram = 0.125 troy ounces

1 apothecary dram = 1.04166666666667E-02 troy pounds

1 apothecary dram = 1.14285714285714E-05 cotton bale Egypt

1 apothecary grain = 1.73611111111111E-04 apothecary pounds

1 apothecary grain = 1.66666666666667E-02 apothecary dram

1 apothecary grain = 2.08333333333333E-03 apothecary ounces

1 apothecary grain = 0.05 apothecary scruples

1 apothecary grain = 0.00006479891 kilograms

1 apothecary grain = 1.66666666666667E-02 troy drams

1 apothecary grain = 1.73611111111111E-04 troy pounds

1 apothecary pound = 5760 apothecary grains

1 apothecary pound = 12 apothecary ounces

1 apothecary pound = 96 apothecary drams

1 apothecary pound = 288 apothecary scruples

1 apothecary pound = 1 troy pounds

1 apothecary pound = 5760 avoirdupois grains

1 apothecary pound = 373.2417216 grams

1 apothecary pound = 3.12078409700437E-02 Mexican arrobas

1 apothecary pound = 0.3732417216 kilograms

1 apothecary scruple = 3.47222222222222E-03 apothecary pounds

1 apothecary scruple = 0.333333333333333 apothecary drams

1 apothecary scruple = 20 apothecary grains

1 apothecary scruple = 4.16666666666667E-02 apothecary ounces

1 apothecary scruple = 1.2959782 grams

1 apothecary ounce = 24 apothecary scruples

1 apothecary ounce = 8 apothecary drams

1 apothecary ounce = 8.33333333333333E-02 apothecary pounds

1 apothecary ounce = 480 apothecary grains

1 apothecary ounce = 0.0311034768 kilograms

1 kilogram = 257.205972549024 apothecary drams

1 kilogram = 15432.3583529414 apothecary grains

1 kilogram = 32.150746568628 apothecary ounces

1 kilogram = 2.679228880719 apothecary pounds

1 kilogram = 771.617917647071 apothecary scruples

Note: The legalization of these units was recorded in the Medical Education Acts of 1858 and 1862. The weights are now obsolete and have been omitted from recent editions of the British Pharmacopoeia.

arcmin (')

Unit of geometrical plane angle. One arcmin is one sixtieth of the degree.

$1' = 1/60$ degree $= \pi /10\ 800$ radians

Note: This unit is known as the minute (of arc).

archin

A traditional Russian unit of distance.

Peter the Great standardized the arshin at exactly 28 English inches, or 71.12 centimeters, during the early 1700s.

The arshin was also used in several other countries neighboring Russia.

The arshin is also used as a unit of area equivalent to one square arshin, which would equate to 5.4445 square feet or 0.5058 square meters.

Russian archin = 0.7112 meters

Russian archin = 3.53535353535354E-02 surveyor's chains

Russian archin = 2.33333333333333E-02 engineer's chains

Russian archin = 4.41919191919192E-04 miles

Russian archin = 392 typography agates

Russian archin = 2.00458190148912E-02 Roman actus

Russian archin = 1.53677277716795 Greek cubits

Russian archin = 0.384193194291987 Greek fathoms

Russian archin = 3.07354555433589 Greek spans

ardeb

An arbitrary unit of dray capacity used in the Middle East.

1 ardeb = 198 liters (about 5.62 U.S. bushels).

1 "standard ardeb" = 195 liters.

In Egypt, 1 *ardeb* of certain commodities represented a defined weight instead of a volume, and in the case of some commodities, the definition differed for present purchase (the "spot" market) or for future delivery, see next table.

Commodity	Spot market	Future delivery
beans	327 *rotls*	320 rotls
wheat or maize	310 *rotls*	300 rotls
barley	250 *rotls*	240 rotls
lentils	330 *rotls*	330 rotls
cottonseed	270 *rotls*	270 rotls

are (a)

It is the metric derived unit of area. It is the area of a square of side length ten meters.

1 are = 100 square meters

Note: 1. This unit was approved by the CIPM in 1879 and is used in agrarian applications. The hectare is more widely use in practice than the are. Hectare = 100 ares

2. Recently, the CGPM has been discouraging the use of the hectare in favor of expressing all areas in square meters.

3. According to the current national standard in the United States, the are is not to be used. Square meters should be used instead.

Ref. IEEE/ASTM S.I. 10™-2002.American National Standard for use of the International System of Units (S.I.):

The Modern Metric System. New York: IEEE, *30 December 2002.*

armour unit

A unit (biology) for the standardization of adrenal cortical hormones and trypsin.

arm's-length

In English, the term "arm's-length" is used figuratively to mean "a distance discouraging familiarity or conflict." In many cultures, the length of a human arm is standardized as a unit of distance equivalent to about 70 centimeters or 28 inches. Examples include the Italian braccio, the Russian sadzhen, and the Turkish pik.

arpent

[1] A traditional unit of distance in French-speaking countries. The arpent is equivalent to 30 toises or 10 perches. This is about 191.8 feet or 58.47 meters. The unit was used to measure land. In fact, *arpentage* is the French word for surveying. In Canada, the arpent has an official definition of 191.835 English feet (58.471 308 meters).

[2] A traditional unit of area in French North America (Quebec and Louisiana), equal to one square arpent . The arpent of area is equivalent to 900 square toises, 100 (square) perches, approximately 0.8445 acres or 0.3419 hectares. By the official Canadian definition, the arpent of area contains 36 800.667 23 English square feet or about 0.844 827 acres (0.341 889 hectares).

arroba (@)

A traditional unit of weight in Spain and Portugal, equivalent to 1/4 quintal. The Spanish and Portuguese quintals exist in different sizes.

In Spain, the arroba is equivalent to 25.36 pounds (11.50 kilograms); arrobas of very similar sizes were established in the Spanish speaking countries of Latin America.

In Portugal and Brazil, the arroba is traditionally equivalent to 32.38 pounds (14.69 kilograms, but recently, this has been "metricized" to be exactly 15 kilograms).

In Mexico, the Mexican arroba = 11.95987001979 kilograms

The arroba has also been used as a metric unit equivalent to 15 kilograms. The name of the unit originates from *ar rub;* Arabic for "the quarter." The @ character has been used in Spanish as a symbol for the arroba since the sixteenth century.

The Mexican arroba is related to some other units as follows:

Mexican arroba = 3076.15 troy drams

Mexican arroba = 0.01195987001979 metric tons

Mexican arroba = 0.0131835 short tons

Mexican arroba = 410.048000129941 assay tons

Mexican arroba = 25.9773399014778 Mexican libras

Mexican arroba = 26.367 pounds

arroba oil (SPANISH)

Unit of volume

Spanish oil arroba = 0.01256756712288 meters cubed

It is related to some other volume units by:

Spanish oil arroba =2.76447812148716 British gallons

Spanish oil arroba = 22.1158249718972 British pints

Spanish oil arroba = 424.96 fluid ounces

Spanish oil arroba = 16.5868756346541 wine bottles

Spanish oil arroba = 849.92 tablespoons

Spanish oil arroba = 0.356637308060751 dry bushels

arroba wine, SPANISH

Unit of volume

Spanish wine arroba = 0.0162772706712 meters cubed

It is related to some other unit of volume by:

Spanish wine arroba = 0.461909766464226 dry bushels

Spanish wine arroba = 550.4 fluid ounces

Spanish wine arroba = 3.58049877180565 British gallons

Spanish wine arroba = 28.6439901744452 British pints

Spanish wine arroba = 21.4830015750038 wine bottles

Spanish wine arroba = 0.115477441616056 coombs

artaba

A historic unit of volume used for both liquid and dry measurement throughout the Middle East. In ancient times, the artaba varied in size between 35 and 55 liters. In recent centuries, the Arab artaba, which is equivalent to about 66 liters, was a common unit in both Arab and non-Arab regions.

artillery point (—)

Unit of plane angle. One artillery point is equivalent to 1/1600 of the right angle.

$$1^- = \frac{1\ RIGHT\ ANGLE}{1600} = \frac{\pi}{3200}\ \text{rad} = 0^0\ 3'\ 22.5''$$

as, ass, or aas

A traditional unit of mass of gold and silver used in most of northern Europe except in England. The unit varies in size from 48 to 58 milligrams (0.75 to 0.90 English grains).

ASA number

For many years, the initials of the American Standards Association appeared on film packages in the United States as a measure of the speed of the photographic emulsion (the material on a film that "develops" to form a picture).

The scale is arbitrary, but the speed at which the image registers itself on the film is proportional to the ASA number. Thus ASA 400 film registers an image twice as fast as ASA 200 film and four times as fast as ASA 100 film. The ASA number is now combined with the European DIN rating as a composite ISO rating. For example, ASA 400 film is now marked ISO 400/27° because 27 is the DIN rating corresponding to ASA 400.

A-size

Metric unit used to define the size of which (trimmed) paper and boards are manufactured.

assay pound

A weight, which varies from time to time (usually 0.5 grams), used by assayers to proportionately represent a pound.

assay ton (AT or assay ton)

Metric unit of mass.

1. U.K. assay ton: One U.K. assay ton contains as many milligrams as a long ton contains troy ounces.

1 U.K. assay ton = (2240x7000)/480 milligrams = 0.0326667 kilograms.

2. U.S. assay ton: One U.S. assay ton equally contains as many milligrams as a short ton contains troy ounces. It is sometimes referred to as the short assay ton.

1 U.S. assay ton = (2000x7000)/480 milligrams = 0.0291667 kilograms

astronomical unit (A.U.):

Unit of length used within the S.I. system, whose value is obtained experimentally. The astronomical unit is the radius of the unperturbed circular orbit of a body of negligible mass orbiting the sun with a sidereal angular velocity of 0.017202098950 radians per day of 86400 ephemeris seconds.

1 A.U. = 1.495 978 70 x 10^{11} meters.

Note: 1. The given value of the astronomical unit was adopted in 1979.

2. The astronomical unit does not have an international symbol. A.U. is customarily used in English, U.A. in French.

3. This unit is used for astronomical measurements of distances, normally confined to the solar system.

4. The astronomical unit is one of the four units used in the S.I. system, whose values are obtained experimentally. The other three units are: "electron volt", "unified atomic mass unit", and "parsec".

5. The official symbol for the unit is ua, but the symbol au is common in English-speaking countries.

6. Note that A.U. is also used as the symbol for the absorbance unit (see above).

ata (ata)

A metric technical unit of absolute pressure.

1 ata = 1 technical atmosphere.

See *"atmosphere, technical."*

atmo-meter (atmo-m)

Arbitrary unit of depth of equivalent atmosphere. It is defined as: x atom-m of gas. X is the depth in meter that an atmosphere would have if gas A was the only constituent in the same amount that it exists in the atmosphere, reduced to standard temperature and pressure. The number of molecules in a unit volume of gas at standard temperature and pressure expressed by the ratio of Avogadro's number to one Amagat volume unit.

1 atmo-meter = 2.686 99 x 10^{25} molecules per cubic meter.

Note: 1. This unit is known as the meter-atmosphere.

   2. This unit is based on Dalton's law of partial pressures.

atmosphere (atm)

The metric unit of the pressure. It is usually used when indicating extremely high pressure. Consequently, it is not widely used in some fields, such as refrigeration or air conditioning. It is defined as the pressure resulting from a column of mercury of height 760 millimeters. The 10CGPM of 1954 formally adopted the new definition of the atmosphere to be: 1 atm = **101325** pascals.

*Note:*1. The name of this unit is more correctly referred to as the standard atmosphere. It has was incorrectly referred to as the normal atmosphere.

   2. The unit should not be confused with the technical atmosphere.

See *"atmosphere, technical"*.

atmosphere, technical (at):

Metric unit for the pressure. It is the pressure resulting from a one kilogram-force acting uniformly over an area of one square centimeter.

1 at = 1 kgf/cm^2 = 98066.5 Pascals.

Note: The unit must not be confused with the (standard) atmosphere (atm). It is related to other units as follows:

1 at = 0.967841 atm and 1 atm = 1.03323 at.

See *"atmosphere"*.

atomic mass unit, chemical scale (amu chemical)

Unit of atomic mass ("weight"). One atomic mass (chemical) is equivalent to one-sixteenth of the weighted average mass of the three naturally occurring neutral isotopes of oxygen. The isotopes are $^{16}_{8}O$, $^{17}_{8}O$ and $^{18}_{8}O$, which exist in the ratio of 506: 0.24: 1. The experimentally derived value is :

1 amu (chemical) = (1.660 26 ± 000 05) x 10^{-27} kilograms.

Note: This unit is also known as the chemical mass unit. It was formerly known as the atomic weight unit.

See also "atomic weight unit", "*atomic mass unit, unified*" and "*atomic mass unit, physical*".

atomic mass unit, Physical scale (amu physical)

Unit of atomic mass ("weight"). One atomic mass unit (physical) is equivalent to one-sixteenth of the mass of a neutral oxygen-16 atom.

$$1 \text{ amu (physical)} = (1.659\ 81 \pm 0.000\ 05) \times 10^{-27} \text{ kilograms.}$$

See also "*atomic mass unit, chemical*" and "*atomic mass unit, unified*".

atomic mass unit (unified) (u)

Unit of mass used in addition to S.I. unit as the unit of (unified) atomic mass constant. One atomic mass unit (modified) is equivalent to one-twelfth of the remaining mass of a neutral carbon-12 atom.

$$1 \text{ u} = 1.660\ 565\ 5 \times 10^{-27} \text{ kilograms.}$$

Note: 1. This unit is also a unit of (rest) mass of particles, mass excess and mass defect.

2. This unit is also known as the atomic mass unit (international scale) or the Dalton.

3. Atomic mass unit (unified) is one of four units used within the S.I. system, whose values are obtained experimentally. The other three are: "electron volt ", astronomical unit", and "parsec.

4. Use of old atomic mass unit (amu), defined by reference to oxygen, is deprecated.

atomic second

Unit of time. It was defined in 1967 as the duration of 9,192,631,770 periods of the radiation corresponding to the two hyperfine levels of the fundamental state of the atom of cesium-133.

See also "*atomic time*".

atomic system of units

System of units suggested by Hartree in 1927 used to reduce the numerical work in problems involving the atom. The fundamental units in the system are the atomic unit of charge *(e,* the charge on the electron), the atomic unit of mass *m,* (the rest mass of an electron), atomic unit of action ($h/2\pi$, where h is Planck's constant) and the electric constant (e_0). The derived units are, the atomic unit of length (a, radius of the first Bohr orbit in the hydrogen atom), atomic unit of energy (also known as Hartree) (e^2/a^2) and the atomic unit of time (π, the reciprocal of the angular frequency $1/4\pi Rc$, where R is Rydberg's constant and c is speed of light).

Note: 1. The system is also known as the Hartree system of unit.

2. The system is one of two systems of unit from the Natural Systems of Units. The other system is the Quantum-Electrodynamics System which is often used in the study of radiation).

See *"atomic unit of charge"*, *"atomic unit of energy"*, *"atomic unit of length"*, *"atomic unit of mass"*, and *"atomic unit of time"*.

atomic time

Any time system standardized with reference to atomic resonance, such as the international standard cesium-133 transition.

See *"atomic second"*.

atomic unit of charge

Fundamental unit of the Hartree system of units. It is equivalent to the charge on an electron. The experimentally derived value of the unit is:

1 atomic unit of charge = $(1.6210 \pm 0.000\ 07) \times 10^{-19}$ coulombs.

atomic unit of energy

Derived unit of energy of the Hartree system of units. It is defined as:

1. The potential energy of an electron in the first orbit in Bohr's theory of the hydrogen atom. It is expressed as:

$$1 \text{ Atomic unit of energy} = e^2/a_0,$$

where, e is the electron's charge and a_0 the atomic unit of length.

$$1 \text{ Atomic unit of energy} = 27.190 \text{ electronvolts} = 4.8505 \times 10^{-18} \text{ joules}.$$

Note: This unit is also known as *"Hartree"*.

See *"Hartree"*.

2. The atomic unit of energy is sometimes defined as one half of the above value. In this

case, it is the ionization potential of the hydrogen atom.

$$1 \text{ Atomic unit of energy} = e^2 Ha_0 = 2.4252 \times 10^{-18} \text{ joules.}$$

Note: The unit, according to this definition, is also known as "rydberg".

See *"atomic unit of length"* and *"rydberg."*

atomic unit of length

Derived unit of length of the Hartree system of units. The radius of the first orbit of Bohr's theory of the hydrogen atom. The experimentally derived value is:

$$1 \text{ Atomic unit of length} = 5.29167 \times 10^{-11} \text{ meters.}$$

atomic unit of mass

Fundamental unit of mass of the Hartree system of units. One atomic unit of mass is equivalent to the rest mass of the electron. The experimentally derived value is:

$$1 \text{ Atomic unit of mass} = 9.1084 \times 10^{-31} \text{ kilograms.}$$

Note: It should not be confused with the atomic mass unit.

See *"atomic mass unit".*

atomic unit of time

Fundamental unit of time of the Hartree system of units. It is the period of the first orbit of the Bohr's theory of the hydrogen atom. The experimentally derived value is:

$$1 \text{ Atomic unit of time} = 2.41884 \times 10^{-17} \text{ seconds.}$$

atomic weight unit (awu)

Arbitrary unit of mass. It is equivalent to one-sixteenth of the weighted average mass of the three naturally occurring neutral isotopes of oxygen. The isotopes are, $^{16}_{8}O$, $^{17}_{8}O$ and $^{18}_{8}O$, which exists in the ratio of 506: 0.24 :

1. The experimentally derived value is:

$$1 \text{ Atomic weight unit} = 1.66026 \times 10^{-27} \text{ kilograms.}$$

Note: 1. The unit is commonly referred to as the atomic mass unit (chemical scale). It is also known as the *"chemical mass unit".*

2. The atomic mass unit (international) is preferred to the atomic weight unit.

See *"chemical mass unit".*

atmo-meter

Unit of depth of equivalent atmosphere. Also known as meter-atmosphere.
See "*meter-atmosphere*

atta (A)

Deprecated prefix denoting x 10^{18}. The S.I. prefix exa is currently used.
See *"exa"*.

atto (a)

S.I. prefix denoting x 10^{-18}. Examples: attocoulomb (aC), attojoule (aJ), attometre (am).

atu

The metric technical unit of pressure below atmospheric pressure.

1 atu = 1 technical atmosphere.

atu

The metric technical unit of overpressure or gauge pressure.

1 atu = 1 technical atmosphere.

A*unit

Unit of length. It is used as an atomic standard unit of length based on the tungsten K- line.
It has a value of 10^{-13} meters approximately.
Note: The unit is used for measurement of X-ray wavelengths and crystal dimensions.

aught (/0)

A unit used by jewelers and craftsmen to measure the size of small beads (often called seed beads). The measurement scale is inverted such that, larger numbers of aughts correspond to smaller beads. Beads of size 11/0 are a common size, with an average a little less than 2 millimeters in diameter. Other sizes are more or less inversely proportional.

It is the number of beads that could comfortably be strung on one inch of cord. With present sizes, a string of *n* beads of size *n*/0 occupies about 0.8 inches (20 mm).

The word *aught*, meaning zero, is a fairly recent corruption of the old English word *naught*, meaning nothing. Apparently, the phrase *a naught*, meaning a zero, came to be misspelled as *an aught*

aume

An old English wine measure equivalent to about 40 gallons (roughly 150 liters). The aume is the English version of a German unit, the ohm.

Avogadro s number, Avogadro constant (N_A)

A unit of relative quantity equivalent to the number of atoms or molecules per mole of a substance. The currently accepted value is 6.022 141 99 x 10^{23} per mole with an uncertainty of 0.000 000 47 x 10^{23} per mole (about 80 parts per billion).

The atomic mass unit (see above), in grams, is equivalent to one divided by this number.

The unit is named after the Italian chemist and physicist Amedeo Avogadro (1776-1856). Avogadro, using Dalton's atomic theory, concluded that equal volumes of gases (at the same temperature and pressure) must contain the equal number of molecules.

Avoirdupois units

Units of mass used in U.K. and U.S. The system has been used for measurement of mass of any substance except precious stones, precious metals, and drugs. It includes the following.

1 ton (ton) = 2240 pounds (lb)

1 hundredweight (cwt) = 112 pounds (lb)

1 cental (ctl) 1 quarter (qr)	= 100 pounds (lb)
1 stone (stone) 1 pound (lb)	= 28 pounds (lb)
1 ounce (oz)	= 14 pounds (lb)
1 dram (dr) 1 grain (gr)	= 0.453 592 37 kilograms = 1/16 pound (lb)

= 1/16 ounce (oz)

= 1/7000 pound (lb)

Note: 1. In the U.S., the first two units are known as long ton/gross ton, and long hundredweight. These units are rarely used. The following units are, however, used:

1 short ton = **2000** pounds (lb)

1 short hundredweight= **100** pounds (lb).

2. The grain has no officially approved symbol in the U.S.

B

B

Informal abbreviation for "billion" generally means the American billion 10^9. This abbreviation is nonmetric. The metric abbreviation for 10^9 is G, referring to the prefix giga-. The B form has been used in units such as Bcf (billion cubic feet) and BeV (billion electron volts).

B

A symbol for international standard paper sizes, succeeded by the size number, e.g., B4. A table of paper sizes is provided in volume III.

bag

British unit of volume, i.e., capacity. The bag is three bushels.
1 bag = 3 imperial bushel = 0.109 106 1 cubic metres.
See *"bushel, UK"*.

bag

An old English unit of weight, varying in the contents of the bag, generally weighing between 2-4 hundredweight (100-200 kilogrammes).

bag

A unit for weight of cement. Traditionally, a bag of Portland cement weighs 94 pounds (42.6 kilogrammes) in the U.S. and 87.5 pounds (39.7 kilogrammes) in Canada. However, cement is now being sold in metric-sized bags of 50 kilogrammes (110.2 pounds) by many suppliers.

Note: Bags for particular commodities often have conventional or even legal capacities. In the United States, for example, a bag of cement contains 1 cubic foot and weighs 94 pounds. Bags of feed, flour, etc., typically weigh 100 pounds

bag

1. In Burma, the unit of dry capacity = 3 *thamardi tinn* = 27 imperial gallons, approximately 122.74 liters.

2. In Sierra Leone, the unit of dry capacity is approximately 80 liters.

baht

A traditional weight unit in Thailand equivalent to 15 grams or 1/40 catty (0.5291 ounces). The baht, originally the weight of a silver coin of the same name, is used to measure the weight of precious metals. The unit is pronounced *hot*.
See: "catty", "ounce."

baker's dozen

An informal unit of quantity, equivalent to 13. Bakers often throw in an extra item for each dozen bought, to make a total of 13. This is a very old custom, dating back to the thirteenth century, when the weights and prices of loaves of bread were strictly regulated by royal proclamations called *assizes*. Bakers could be jailed if they failed to provide fair weights for the listed prices.

bale (bl) [1]

A bundle of merchandise, usually pressed and bound in some way. The word "bale" has been used in many ways to describe standard packages of various commodities. For example, in paper trade, a bale of paper is traditionally equivalent to 10 reams.

1 bale of paper = 5 bundles = 10 reams = 200 quires.

When the quire is 25 sheets, a bale contains 5000 sheets.

In agriculture, a bale of hay is a large round bundle of material left in the field until needed. These bales can weigh up to 1500 pounds (700 kilogrammes). In U.S. garden shops, a bale of straw is typically 3 cubic feet (0.085 cubic meter).

Note: In Belgium and the Netherlands, a unit of mass = ½ *charge* = 2 *cent* (each of 100 pounds) = 1 950 000 Dutch, which is approximately 93.732 kilogrammes.

bale (bl) [2]

A commercial unit of weight used for shipments of cotton. In the United States, one bale of cotton, formerly equivalent to 500 pounds (226.80 kg), is now equivalent to 480 pounds (217.72 kg). The British used the Egyptian bale, formerly equivalent to 750 pounds (340.19 kg), but now, it is equivalent to 720 pounds (326.59 kg). Other countries use a variety of cotton bale weight.

ball [1]

A unit for measuring the degree of ice coverage of polar seas. One ball equals 10% coverage. The unit was invented by the Russian naval officer N. N. Zhubov (1895-1960).

ball [2]

1. In Germany, a unit for the count of sheets of paper. Before 1877, it was 4800 sheets of writing paper or 5000 sheets of printing paper. After 1877, it became 10000 sheets of paper.

2. In some German-speaking areas, it is a quantity of cloth, 10 - 12 pieces of 32 ells. See source below.

Balmer

CGS unit of reciprocal length and wavenumber.

A unit of wavenumber, proposed in 1951. It is equivalent to the number of waves in a centimeter.

Note: 1. This unit is known as kayser. It is also known as the rydberg.

 2. The Balmer was named after a renown spectroscopist J. J. Balmer (1825-1898), from which the Balmer lines were named.

See "*kayser*" and "*rydberg* (1)".

balthazar

A large wine bottle containing about 12 liters, 16 times the volume of a regular bottle.

banana equivalent dose (BED)

This is an informal unit often used in informal discussions of naturally occurring radiation sources.

One banana equivalent dose is the radiation dose carried by a single banana. Obviously, it depends on the size of the banana. One BED is usually considered to be 0.1 microsievert (μSv).

Note: Since bananas are rich in potassium, they contain a small amount of the naturally occurring radioisotope potassium 40 as well as trace amounts of carbon 14.

bar (bar)

Metric unit for the pressure (of fluid).

1 bar = 10^5 pascals.

Note: 1. The unit was previously defined as 1 bar = 1 dyn/cm^2 (CGS unit). This is also known as a barye.

2. The millibar (millibar = 0.001 bar) is more commonly used.

3. 1000 millibars are sometimes regarded by meteorologists as the standard atmosphere, although this could be 1013.25 millibars.

See *"barye"* and *"barad"*.

barad

CGS unit of pressure. It is the pressure resulting from a force of one dyne acting uniformly over an area of one square centimetre.

1 barad = 1 dyn/cm^2 = 0.1 pascal.

Note: The barad is the former name of the barye. It is also called rum.

See *"barye"* and *"rum"*.

Barcol hardness (BH)

A measure of hardness, primarily for plastics and soft metals, made with a Barcol Impressor. Measurements on the Barcol scale are typically between 30 and 90. There is no precise conversion between these readings and other hardness scales. The manufacturer, however, provides a data bulletin with tables for approximate conversion to Rockwell, Brinell, and Vickers hardness numbers.

barge

Imperial unit of mass, equivalent to 21.2 tonnes.

1 barge = 21.2 ton = 20.320 938 16 x 10^3 kilogrammes *Note:* 1. The unit is also called keel.

2. The unit is used mainly for measuring coal.

See *"ton", "keel."*

barleycorn

Imperial (UK) unit of length equivalent to ⅓ inch.

1 barleycorn = ⅓ inch = 8.466 666 666 x 10^{-3} metres.

Note: In Anglo-Saxon England, where barley was a basic crop, barleycorns played this traditional role.

The weight of a barleycorn, later renamed the grain, is the original basis of all English weight systems, including the older troy system and the later, the avoirdupois system. As a length unit, 3 barleycorns were equal to the Saxon *ynce* (inch). The English foot was defined as 12 *ynces,* i.e., 36 barleycorns.

bar liter

A metric unit of energy used to measure the potential energy of gases under pressure. The energy is computed by multiplying the volume of gas in liters by the pressure in bars. One bar liter is equivalent to exactly 100 joules or approximately 73.7562 foot pounds. This unit is not acceptable in the SI system.

barn (b)

Metric unit for the cross-sectional area. It is used especially with the cross-sectional area of an atomic nucleus.

1 b = 10^{-28} metre square.

Note: 1. The unit gives a measure of the probability of a particular nuclear process occurring when nuclear projectiles pass through matter by giving the effective target area of the bombarded nucleus for that particular area. (When atoms are bombarded with smaller particles such as electrons, the electrons are scattered as if the nucleus of the atom was a tiny solid object.)

2. In July 1976, the Council of Ministers of the EEC proposed the abolition of the bam. This unit has been supplanted by 100 square femtometer (fm^2) i.e., 1 barn = 100 fm^2.

3. The following units are related to the barn.

	Unit Symbol	Quantity Measured	Corresponding SI unit	To convert to SI, multiply it by:
r electron volt	b/eV	Unit of spectral cross section	metre square per joule (m^2/J)	$6.241\ 46 \times 10^{10}$
r erg	b/erg	Unit of spectral cross section	metre square per joule (m^2/J)	10^{-21}
r steradian	b/sr	Unit of angular cross section	metre square per steradian (m^2/sr)	10^{-28}
per steradian electronvolt	b/(sr.eV)	Unit of spectral angular cross section	metre square per steradian joule (m^2/ sr.J)	$6.241\ 46 \times 10^{-10}$
r steradian erg	b/(sr.erg)	Unit of spectral angular cross section	metre square per steradian joule (m^2/sr J)	10^{-21}

baromil

CGS unit of length used in graduating a mercury barometer.

BARONY (barony)

Imperial (UK) unit of area, equivalent to 4000 acres.

1 barony = **4000** acres = $16.187\ 425\ 6 \times 10^6$ square metres.

Note: The unit is used for land measurement.

See *"acre"*

barrel

U.S. unit of volume (capacity) for petroleum.

1 barrel = 0.158 982 84 cubic metres.

Note: 1. The above definition is used for petroleum. For other liquids, the barrel (U.S., liq.) is used, which is defined as:

1 barrel (U.S., liq.) = 0.119 237 13 cubic metres.

2.	By international standards, a barrel of petroleum is equivalent to 42 U.S. gallon, which is approximately 158.987 liters.

3.The symbol bo (barrel of oil) is used for the barrel in the petroleum industry.

4.The petroleum barrel emerged from the Pennsylvania oilfields (the first commercial oilfields) in the late nineteenth century. Apparently, 40-gallon barrels were increased to 42 gallons to provide insurance against any spillage or under filling.

5.Coincidentally, this unit has the same size as the traditional tierce, i.e., the wine barrel.

barrel (U.K)

British unit of volume (capacity).

1 barrel (Brit.) = 0.163 654 6 cubic metres.

Note: The above definition is used for liquids and dry substances, i.e.

Barrel (Brit., liq.) = Barrel (Brit., dry)

See *"barrel"* and *"barrel, US dry"*.

barrel, U.S. dry (bbl)

U.S. unit of volume (capacity) for dry measure.

1 bbl = 0.115 627 123 584 cubic metres.

Note: 1. This is the standard barrel used for fruits, vegetables and dry commodities.

2.	There is no corresponding U.K. unit.

3.	The U.S. dry barrel, established during a Congress in 1912, is 105 dry quarts, which is approximately 4.083 cubic feet or 115.63 liters. (This is the only case in the United States customary system where a dry volume is less than the corresponding fluid volume)

4.	For certain commodities, other sizes are traditional in the U.S. For example, a barrel of sugar was traditionally 5 cubic feet (about 141.58 liters). In Newfoundland, a barrel of herring held 32 Imperial gallons (145.47 liters), but a barrel of sand was only 18 Imperial gallons (81.83 liters).

barrel (bbl or brl or bl) [1]

A commercial unit of volume is used to measure liquids such as beer and wine. The official U.S. definition of the barrel is 31.5 gallons, which is approximately 4.211 cubic feet or

119.24 liters. This unit is equivalent to the traditional British wine barrel.

1.   In Britain, the barrel is now known to be 36 imperial gallons, which is substantially larger, i.e., about 5.780 cubic feet or 163.66 liters.

This unit is slightly smaller than the traditional British beer and ale barrel that holds 5.875 cubic feet or 166.36 liters.

2.   There are other official barrels, known in some U.S. states, most of which fall between the general range of 30 - 40 gallons. A barrel of beer in the U.S., for example, is 31 U.S. gallons (117.35 liters).

3.   The origin of the standard symbol bbl is not clear. The "b" may have originally been doubled to indicate the plural (1 bl, 2 bbl), or possibly, it was doubled to eliminate any confusion with the symbol bl that is used for the bale (see above).

Note: Some websites claim that "bbl" was initially a symbol for "blue barrels" delivered by Standard Oil in its early days. This claim is false because there were citations of this symbol as early as the late 1700s before Standard Oil was founded.

barrel (bbl) [2]

A commercial unit of weight, varying with the commodity being measured. In the U.S., for example, a barrel of flour traditionally holds 196 pounds (88.90 kg) and a barrel of beef, fish, or pork 200 pounds (90.72 kg). A barrel of cement is traditionally equivalent to 4 bags, which is 376 pounds (170.55 kg) in the U.S. and 350 pounds (158.76 kg) in Canada. In old England, a barrel of herrings was 32 pounds (14.51 kg) and a barrel of soap was 256 pounds (116.12 kg).

barrel bulk

A commercial unit of volume equivalent to 5 cubic feet or 0.141 584 cubic meters. There are approximately 8 barrels bulk in a freight ton and 20 barrels bulk in a register ton.

barrels per calendar day (BCD)

A unit measuring the average rate of oil processing in petroleum refinery, with allowances for downtime over a period of time.

barrels per day (BD or bpd)

A unit measuring the rate at which petroleum is produced at the refinery.

barrels per stream day (BSD)

A measurement used to denote rate of oil or oil-product flow while a fluid-processing unit is in continuous operation.

Barrer or barrer

A CGS unit of gas permeability for membranes, contact lenses, and similar thin materials. Permeability in this context is defined as the gas flow rate multiplied by the thickness of the material, divided by the area and by the pressure difference across the material. To measure this quantity, the barrer is the permeability represented by a flow rate of 10^{-10} cubic centimeters per second (volume at standard temperature and pressure, i.e., 0 °C and 1 atmosphere, respectively), multiplied by 1 centimeter of thickness, per square centimeter of area and centimeter of mercury difference in pressure. That is:

1 barrer = 10^{-10} cm^2.s^{-1}.cm Hg^{-1}, or, in SI units, 7.5005 x 10^{-18} m^2.s^{-1}.Pa^{-1}.

The unit was named after a renown New Zealand chemist Richard M. Barrer (1910-1996), who was a researcher in the field of diffusion of gases.

barrique

Metric unit of capacity (volume) equivalent to 225 litres.

1 barrique = 225 litres = 0.225 cubic metres.

Note: Used mainly to measure calret wine.

barye (barye or ba)

CGS unit of pressure. It is the pressure resulting from a force of one dyne acting uniformly over an area of one square centimetre.

1 barye = 1 dyne per centimetre squared (dyn/cm^2) = 0.1 pascals.

Note: 1. It is more common to refer to this unit as the microbar or dyn/cm^2.

2. The unit was formerly known as the "barad" or "rum

3. The unit was at one time equated to dyn/cm^2 by the relation, 1 barye = 10^6 dyn/cm^2. It

is now referred to as the bar.

See "barad", "rum," and bar".

base box (base box)

Imperial unit of area. One base box is the area formed by 112 plates. Each plate of dimensions 20 inches x 14 inches equates to 31360 square inches.

1 base box = 31 360 square inches = 20.232 217 6 square metres.

Note: 1. This unit is used in metal plating.

2. Sometimes, the value of the unit is taken as the area when painting the two sides of the plates. In this case, 1 base box = 62 720 square inches.

basic module (M)

a unit of length equivalent to 100 mm (1 decimeter) or about 3.937 inches, used in the construction industry.

Note: The international standard ISO 2848 Building Construction - Modular Coordination introduced the decimeter unit and provided rules and principles for its implementation. The idea was that important building dimensions and modular dimensions should be multiples of the basic module.

The symbol M is used in the standard instead of the equivalent metric symbols (for example, 85M rather than 8.5 m).

basis point (bp)

A unit of proportion equivalent to 0.01% or 10^{-4}. The basis point is used in finance to measure small fluctuations in interest rates and the rates of return on investments. Prior to the introduction of the basis point, these fluctuations were measured awkwardly in 64ths of a percent.

basis weight

A unit used in the paper industry to express the weight (really, the thickness) of paper. The basis weight is the weight in pounds of one ream (500 sheets) of a basic size sheet.

See also *"pound weight"* and *"ream."*

baud (baud or Bd)

Arbitrary unit for signaling rate for digital communications. One baud is equivalent to one change of state per second. When there are two possible states (e.g., two tone frequencies), 1 baud = 1 bit per second.

However, when there are 2^n possible states (e.g., four possible phase shifts in a sinusoidal wave), 1 baud = n bit per second.

Note: 1. For low-speed transmission, where modems with frequency- shift keying (FSK) are used, the terms *baud* and *bit per second (bit/s)* can be used interchangeably otherwise, the two terms are not interchangeable.

 2. This unit was named after the French engineer J.M. Baudot (1845-1903), the inventor of the Baudot code for telegraphy.

 3. The unit was proposed at the International Telegraph Conference in 1927.

See also *"bit"*.

baume degree

A unit of specific gravity on a Baume scale, which is a hydrometer scale for sugar solution specifying the percentage by weight of sugar in the solution at a specific temperature.

Note: 1. Frequently used to express the sugar level in wine.

 2. Named after Baume.

 3. Balling degree and Brix degree are also used for getting sugar contents.

See *"Brix"* and also *"Sikes degree"*.

BB

A common shot pellet size in the U.S. The diameter of BB shot is sometimes informally referred to as a distance unit. The BB shot has a diameter of 0.180 inches (4.572 mm).

BC, BCE

Abbreviations for "before Christ" and "before common era," respectively. These are standard designations for years before the beginning of the common or Christian era.

Apparently, there is no year designated as 0 in the common system for numbering years. The year 1 CE (or 1 AD) was preceded by 1 BCE (or 1 BC). The absence of a year 0 implies that the number of years elapsing between the year n BCE and the year m CE (or n BC and m AD) is n + m-1

Bcfe

A symbol used in the natural gas industry representing 1 billion cubic feet of gas equivalent (cfe). This is an energy unit equivalent to 1.091 petajoules (PJ).

bcm [1]

A symbol for "billion cubic microns per square inch", used in flexographic printing. In this process, a roller engraved with a large number of tiny cells is used to transfer ink to the printing plate. The unit measures the total volume of these cells per unit area of the roller. One billion (10^9) cubic microns per square inch is equivalent to one cubic millimeter per square inch (mm^3/in^2) or one microliter per square inch ($\mu L/in^2$). The appropriate SI unit for volume per area measure is the micrometer or micron (μm). 1 bcm is equivalent to 1.5500 pm.

bcm [2]

Abbreviation for "bank cubic meter" (see above).

B/D

Symbol for barrels of oil per day (see barrel above), used in the energy industry to measure the rate at which oil is pumped from a well.

B-dose (B-dose)

Arbitrary unit for radiation dose. One B-dose is the dose of radiation required to change the colour of a barium platinocyanide pastille from a specified apple-green colour (tint 'A') to a specified red -brown (tint 'B'). It is equivalent to 500 roentgens.

Note: This unit is obsolete and the pastille dose is currently recommended unit.

beat

A unit of time equivalent to 0.001 days or 86.4 seconds.

"Metric time," meaning decimalized time, dating back at least to the French Revolution of the 1790's. In most metric time proposals, a day is divided into 10 **metric hours**, with each metric hour containing 100 metric minutes (or beats) and each metric minute containing 100 **metric seconds** (sometimes called **blinks**). In 1998, the Swatch Corporation repackaged the metric time as **Internet time.** In their proposal, time is counted in beats from midnight Central European Standard (winter) time (2300 Universal Time of the previous day, or 6:00 pm U.S. Eastern Standard Time of the previous day). The time at n beats is recorded as @n. beat. Thus, midnight U.S. Eastern Standard Time is @250.beat.

beat [2]

a musical unit representing a single rhythmic stress. In most musical compositions, beats are organized into measures, with each measure containing a set number of beats, with each set carrying a primary or accented stress. At the same time, the tempo of the music is expressed by setting a number of beats equal to a whole note. If there are m beats in a measure and n beats in a whole note, then the fraction m/n is known as the time signature of the composition. For example, a waltz has a time signature of ¾ (3 beats per measure and 4 beats per whole note), while a march has a time signature of 4/4.

beat [3]

a unit of relative time in acting, representing a short, silent pause for dramatic effect. In the script, playwrights may specify a pause of one, two, or more beats. The unit does not have a definite length, but the director and the actors usually have an intuitive sense of how long a beat should be at a specific point in the action.

Beaufort scale

A wind-speed scale relating to visual observation of the effect of wind on sea (see Table). It is also used for the effect of wind on vegetation, e.g., scale 7 implies moderate gale, with a wave height of 4-6m containing streaks of foam.

Note: 1. The scale was introduced by Admiral F. Beaufort in 1806. The Board of Trade have utilized it since 1862.

2.   The number on the Beaufort scale (the first column in the Table) is sometimes called Beaufort number (B). It is related to the wind velocity (V) expressed in miles per hour by the empirical formula: $V \times 1.87 \times B^{15}$.

3.   The Beaufort scale is represented on weather maps by a wind arrow. The direction of the arrow indicates the direction of the wind. Each feather on the arrow indicates two points on the Beaufort scale.

Beaufort		Wind speed at 6 metre height			
Scale	Description	km/h	m/s	Mph	knots
0	Calm	0-1	0-0.3	0-1	0-1
1	Light air	1-5	0.3-1.5	1-3	1-3
2	Light breeze	6-11	1.6-3.1	4-7	4-6
3	Gentle breeze	12-19	3.2-5.4	8-12	7-10
4	Moderate breeze	20-28	5.5-7.9	13-18	11-16
5	Fresh breeze	29-38	8.0-10	19-24	17-21
6	Strong breeze	39-49	11-13	25-31	22-27
7	Moderate gale	50-61	14-17	32-38	28-33
8	Fresh gale	62-74	18-20	39-46	34-40
9	Strong gale	75-88	21-24	47-54	41-47
10	Whole gale	89-102	25-28	55-63	48-55
11	Storm	103-117	29-32	64-75	56-65
12	Hurricane	118-	33-	76-	66-

becquerel (Bq):

The SI derived unit of radioactivity. The becquerel is the activity of a radionuclide, decaying at the rate of one spontaneous nuclear transition per second.

$1 \text{ Bq} = 1 \text{ s}^{-1}$

Note: 1. The unit was named after the French physicist A.H. Becquerel (1852-1908).

2. The unit was approved by the 15th CGPM in May 1975.

Note: both the becquerel and the hertz are basically defined as one event per second, yet they measure different items. The hertz is used to measure the rates of events that happen periodically in a fixed and definite cycle. The becquerel is used to measure the rates of events that happen sporadically and unpredictably, not in a definite cycle.

becquerel per cubic metre (Bq m^{-3})

SI unit of volume activity (of radionuclide).

Note: Bq m^{-3} = m^{-3} s^{-1}.

becquerel per kilogramme (Bq m^{3})

SI unit of specific activity (of radionuclide)

Note: Bq kg^{-1} = kg^{-1} s^{-1}.

becquerel per metre (Bq m^{-1})

SI unit of linear activity (of radionuclide)

Note: Bq m^{-1} = m^{-1} s^{-1}.

becquerel per mole (Bq mol^{-1})

SI unit of molar activity (of radionuclide)

Note: Bq mol^{-1} = s^{-1} mol^{-1}.

bee space

An informal unit of distance used in beekeeping. In a hive, bees seal up an opening smaller than a bee space, and they fill a larger opening with new honeycomb. If an opening is equal to a bee space, then the bees leave it open as a passageway. A hive can be disassembled to remove the honey if the individual comb frames are carefully spaced, one bee space apart. This discovery was made by the British beekeeper Lorenzo Longstroth in 1852. This unit is crucial in modern beekeeping. The exact size of the bee space varies somewhat with the strain of bees being raised, but it is generally about ¼ inch or 6.5 millimeters.

bel (B or b)

Unit of intensity level. One bel is the intensity level, which corresponds to a power ratio *(P₁/P₂)* of 10. In general, the intensity level N in bels is equivalent to the two powers P_1

and P_2, expressed in the same units, by the formula: N (in bels) = $log\ (P_1/P_2)$.

Note: 1. This basic unit is not used in practice. However, its submultiple decibel (dB or db) is instead used.

1 dB = 0.1 bels.

2. The names **decilit, decilog, decilu, decomlog, log it** and **transmission unit (TU)** have been used at various times for the decibel.

bell

A traditional unit of time.

On ships at sea, a practical measure of time is the watch, which is a period of 4 hours. The watch is divided into 8 bells. Therefore, one bell is equivalent to ½ hour or 30 minutes. Every 30 minutes, the ship's bell sounds the number of bells elapsed since the start of the watch.

benz

SI unit for velocity. This unit has been proposed by Germany, but has not been formerly recognized.

1 benz = 1 metre per second.

bes

CGS unit of mass. It is equivalent to one gramme.

1 bes = 1 gramme.

Note: This name, like other names, was proposed as an alternative to the gramme, but was never used. In Italy, it has been proposed as an alternative for the kilogramme.

See also, *"stathm"* and *"brieze"*.

BeV

U.S. unit of energy.

1 BeV = 1 billion electronvolt = 10^9 eV = 1.602 10x10^{-10} Joules

Note: The international unit is GeV (giga electron volt), which has the same value as the BeV.

bhp

Abbreviation for brake horsepower. The brake horsepower of an engine is the effective power output, sometimes measured as the resistance an engine provides to a brake attached to the output shaft.

See also *"horsepower"*.

bi-

A common English prefix meaning *"two"*. In statements of frequency, *bi-* and *semi-* have been used interchangeably. It is not always clear what the word, for example, "bimonthly" means. In adverbs of frequency, bi- means "every two." For example, a **biweekly** payroll is paid once every two weeks, a **bimonthly** magazine is published once every two months, the U.S. House of representatives are elected **biennially** (every two years). For an event that happens twice per time unit, semi- is used.

biannually

A confusing expression of frequency. The word is used for both twice a year and once every two years. Therefore, it should be avoided. Twice a year is *semiannually* and once every two years is *biennially.*

bicron

Metric unit of length.

1 bicron = 10^{-12} metres

Note: This unit is also known as the stigma.

See *"stigma"*.

BID or b.i.d.

Abbreviation for the Latin phrase *bis in die* (twice a day). A unit of frequency traditionally used by doctors in writing medical prescriptions.

biennium

A unit of time equivalent to two years. Many U.S. states, including North Carolina, elect legislators every two years and adopt budgets for this two-year period, called a biennium.

bigha

A traditional unit of land area in South Asia.

The bigha varies in size from region to region. In India, for example, it is generally less than an acre (0.4 hectares). In Bengal (both in Bangladesh and in West Bengal, India), the bigha was standardized under British colonial rule at 1600 square yards (0.1338 hectares or 0.3306 acres). This is often interpreted as being 1/3 acre.

In central India, bighas were standardized at 3025 square yards or 5/8 acres (0.2529 hectares).

In Nepal, the bigha is equivalent to 0.677 hectares (1.67 acres).

The bigha was divided into 20 katthas, and each kattha contains 20 dhurs.

See also *"kattha", "acre", hectare."*

billennia

a new word meaning "billions of years, "billennia has appeared informally in several scientific writing phrases such as "countless billennia" or "the billennia of evolutionary time". The word billennium was, however, coined for a different purpose. It is a registered trademark of the billennium® organizing committee, used in the words of a committee spokesperson to describe the positive spirit of the millennium, which is an ongoing and enduring movement.

billiard

A unit of quantity equivalent to 10^{15}. it is one quadrillion in American terminology or 1000 billion in traditional British terminology.

The name is coined to parallel milliard, which has long been a name to refer to 1000 million.

billion

In European countries like the U.K., a billion means 10^{12} (corresponding to tera in SI system), and in U.S. and Canada, its value is $\mathbf{10^9}$ (corresponding to giga in SI system).

Note: The U.S. value has increasingly gained recognition in some fields such as economy and finance.

biot (Bi)

CGSB (CGS Biot) unit of electric current. One biot is the constant current, which, if maintained between two rectilinear parallel conductors of infinite length and of negligible cross section, and placed at a distance of one centimetre apart in a vacuum, would produce a force equivalent to two dynes per centimetre of length.

1 Bi = **10** Amperes.

Note: 1. The unit was named after the French physicist J.B. Biot (1774-1862).

2 The CGS-emu equivalent of the biot is the abampere:

1 Bi = 1 abampere.

3. In optics, the Biot is also used as a unit of rotational strength in substances exhibiting circular dichroism. It is equivalent to 10^{-40} times the corresponding CGS unit.

4. The following units are related to the biot in the CGSB system:

Unit	Unit Symbol	Quantity Measured	Corresponding SI unit	To convert to SI, multiply it by:
Biot centimetre squared	Bi cm^2	Electromagnetic Moment	Ampere metre square	10^{-3}
Biot per centimeter	Bi/cm	Magnetic field strength	Ampere per metre	79.577 5
Biot second	Bi s	Electric charge	Coulomb	10

bit (bit)

Unit of information in computer technology, where information is coded as the physical state of two valued systems (usually 0 and 1). It is a contraction of the "binary digit".

1 bit = 1 binary digit.

Note:

1. This unit is often called the bit because if the message is a bit string and all strings are equally likely to be received, then the information content is equal to the number of bits.

2. The bit can also be defined as: A dimensionless unit of storage capacity specifying that the capacity of a storage device can be expressed by the logarithm to the base 2 of the number of states of the device.

3. In information and communications theory, if a message has a probability p of being received, then its information content is $-\log_2 p$ shannons.

4. The unit has also been called the *baud or "shannon"*

5. The bit is also the basic unit of the amount of data.

6. Somewhat more generally, the bit is used as a logarithmic unit of data storage capacity, equal to the base-2 logarithm of the number of possible states of the storage device or location. For example, if a storage location stores one letter, then it has 26 possible states, and its storage capacity is $\log_2 26 = 4.7004$ bits.

bits per second (bit/s or bps)

Unit of measure for data transmission, i.e., the instantaneous speed at which a device or channel transmits data. Often mistakenly confused with the baud.

See *"baud"*.

bits per unit area (e.g., bit/mm^2, bit/cm^2)

Unit of (surface) bit density. It is used as a unit of information density or storage density, for example, on hard disks.

bits per unit length (e.g., bit/mm, bit/cm)

Unit of (linear) bit density. It is used as unit of information density or storage density, for example, on track of a disk or on a tape.

blind watt (bW or BW)

Unit of reactive power. It has the same value as the SI unit var.

1 blindwatt = 1 var

Note: This is a deprecated German name.

blink

Arbitrary unit of time. One blink is equivalent to 10^{-5} day.

1 blink = $\mathbf{10^{-5}}$ days = 0.864 seconds

This unit is also known as the metric second. In most metric time proposals, the day is divided into 10 hours, each hour into 100 minutes (called beats in "Internet time": see "beat" above), and each minute into 100 seconds or blinks. An eye blink takes less than half as much time as this unit.

block

[1} An informal unit of distance popular in the U.S. A block is the average distance between street intersections in the rectangular street grids. It is common in most American cities. The length of a block varies from about 1/20 mile (80 meters) in New York to about 1/16 mile (100 meters) in many Midwestern cities to about 1/10 mile (160 meters) in cities of the South and West. (In New York and some other cities, streets running on one direction are closer together than streets running perpendicular. In these cities, people often speak of "short blocks" or "long blocks.")

[2] A "unit" used in describing the distance between two locations in a city using the number of intersections encountered between these two locations. e.g., "12 blocks" implies that the traveler will cross 12 street intersections before reaching the destination.

[3] An informal unit of area equivalent to one square block [1]. A typical block has an area of roughly 2-5 acres or 1-2 hectares.

blondel (blondel)

Metric unit for luminance. It is defined as the luminance of a uniform diffuser emitting one lumen per metre squared.

1 blondel = $(1/\pi)$ cd m^{-2}

Note: It is recommended to call this unit the apostilb.

See *"apostilb"*

blood alcohol level (BAL)

A legal measurement of alcohol concentration in the bloodstream, determining whether a person is considered legally impaired or intoxicated.

The blood alcohol level is usually stated as a percentage, such as 0.10%. In most U.S. states, this is a measurement of "weight by volume" (w/v). 0.10% w/v is equivalent to 100 milligrams of alcohol per deciliter (100 milliliters) of blood, which is the same as 1 gram per liter (g/L). In a few states, the measurement is the percentage mass concentration (w/w, or milligrams of alcohol per milligram of blood). 0.10% w/v is the same alcohol concentration as 0.1055% w/v or 1.055 g/L. Internationally, blood alcohol levels are often stated in millimoles per liter (mmol/L). 1 millimole per liter is equivalent to 4.61 mg/dL or 0.00461% w/v. Each 0.01% w/v is equivalent to about 2.169 mmol/L. See also *"mole."*

board foot (board foot, bd ft, fbm, or BF))

Unit of volume used for timber only. It is the volume of a board of an area of one square foot and one inch thick.

1 board foot = **144** cubic inches = 2.359 74 x $10^{|3}$ cubic metres.

Note: If lumber is stacked neatly, the number of board feet from the dimensions of the stack can be computed, no matter how wide or thick the boards are. For example, a stack of two-by-fours 4 ft high, 4 ft wide, and 8 ft long contains 4 x 4 x 8 = 128 cubic feet, equivalent to 128 x 12 = 1536 board feet. The symbol fbm is an abbreviation for "foot, board measure."

Board Of Trade Unit (BOTU)

Metric unit for electric energy. One Board of Trade unit is the energy expended when a power of one kilowatt is available for one hour.

1 Board of Trade Unit = 1 kW h.

Note: It is better to call this unit the kilowatt-hour.

body inch

an English name for the sun, the basic distance measurement used in acupuncture.

body mass index (BMI)

A measure of ''fatness" used in medicine and health.

The BMI is equal to a person's mass ("weight") M (in kilogrammes) divided by the square of his or her height H (in meters):

$BMI = M/H^2$.

If measurements are made in traditional English units, the equivalent formula is $BMI = 703.07.M/H^2$, where M is measured in pounds and H in inches.

In the U.S., a person with a BMI less than 20 is considered underweight, a person with a BMI of 25 or more is considered overweight, and a person with a BMI of 30 or more is considered obese.

boe

Abbreviation for "barrel of oil equivalent," a commercial unit of energy. One boe is equivalent to about 6.119 gigajoules (GJ) or 5.800 million Btu.

See *"Btu"*

bohr or bohr radius (a_0)
Unit of length. Equal to the radius of the first Bohar orbit of the hydrogen atom.

1 Bohar radius = 53 x 10^{-12} metres.

Note: This unit was proposed by Hartree in 1928.

boiler horsepower

A traditional unit measuring the power delivered by a boiler. The boiler horsepower is defined as the power required to convert 30 pounds (13.61 kilogrammes) per hour of water at 100 °F (37.78 °C) to saturated steam at a pressure of 70 pounds per square inch gauge (482.6 kilopascals gauge). This power, which is about 33 471 Btu per hour or 9.8095 kilowatts, is 13 times greater than the usual mechanical definition of the horsepower, taken to be sufficient to run an engine producing one horsepower of mechanical power.

See *"horsepower, watt, and joule."*

bole

CGS unit of momentum. It is the momentum possessed by a mass of one gramme moving at a velocity of one centimetre per second.

1 bole = 1 gramme centimetre per second = 10^5 kilogramme metre per second.

Note: The name was proposed by the British Association in 1886 but has never been used.

boll

Arbitrary unit of mass equivalent to 140 pounds.

1 boll = 140 pounds = 63.502 931 8 kilogrammes.

Note: Used mainly to measure flour.

bolt of cloth (bolt of cloth)

Unit of length, specially for cloths. It is equivalent to 120 feet.

1 bolt of cloth = 36.576 metres.

Note: Sometimes, one bolt represents a strip of cloth 100 yards (91.44 meters) long, but the width varies

according to the fabric. Cotton bolts are traditionally 42 inches (1.067 meters) wide and wool bolts are usually 60 inches (1.524 meters) wide. Thus, a bolt of cotton is 116.667 square yards (97.566 m^2) and a bolt of wool is 166.667 square yards (139.355 m^2).

bone-dry unit (bdu)

A unit used in the forest products industry to measure bulk products such as wood chips. One bone-dry unit is the volume of wood chips (or whatever), which would weigh 2400 pounds (1.0886 metric ton) if all the moisture content were removed.

The bone-dry ton (bdt) is a similar unit, but it is based on a weight of 2000 pounds (0.9072 metric ton). The bone-dry metric ton (bdmt) is based on the weight of one ton (2204.623 pounds).

bottle

[1] Arbitrary unit of mass, equivalent to 86 pounds.

1 bottle = 86 pounds = 39.008 943 82 kilogrammes.

Note: Used mainly to measure mercury.

[2] A unit of volume. This unit varies according to the nature of the contents. For a long time in the U.S., a bottle of milk has been 1 quart (1/4 gallon or 946.36 milliliters), a bottle of whiskey is 1 fifth (1/5 gallon or 757.1 milliliters), and a bottle of champagne is 2/3 quart (1/6 gallon or 630.91 milliliters). In the British Empire, a common bottle size is 2/3 Imperial quart (1/6 gallon or 757.68 milliliters), a unit known as the reputed quart. Today

wine is customarily sold in bottles containing 750 milliliters (about 25.3605 U.S. fluid ounces or 26.3963 British Imperial fluid ounces). Other countries have traditional units of about this same size. For example, the Russian boutylka contains 768.95 milliliters. See also *"gallon, quart, and fluid ounce."*

bougie decimale (bd)

Unit of luminous intensity. The International Electrical Congress of 1889 defined this unit as: "One bougie decimale is such that the luminance of one square centimetre of the surface of molten platinum at its temperature of solidification is 20 bougie decimales.

The above definition was legalized in France by the decree of 1919.

Note: The bougie decimal was replaced by the candela.

See *"candela"*.

bougie nouvelle

Name of a unit of luminous intensity changed at 9th CGPM in 1948 to **candela**.

See *"candela"*.

bovate

An old English unit of land area equivalent to ⅛ hide. This was roughly 15 acres or 6 hectares. The word originates from the Latin word *bovis,* (an ox). The bovate was an area that could be farmed with the help of one ox.

box

A unit of volume, usually informal but standardized in certain industries. In the U.S., a box of citrus fruit contains 1.6 bushels (56.383 liters).

BP

Abbreviation for "years before present", a unit of time used in anthropology, geology, and paleontology. By international convention, the year 1950 CE (or AD) represents the present. Therefore, years "BP" are really years before 1950.

BP unit

A unit used in Britain to measure the potency of a vitamin or a drug, i.e., its expected biological effects.

For each substance where this unit applies, the British Pharmacopoeia Commission has determined the biological effect associated with a dose of 1 BP unit. Other quantities of the substance can be expressed in terms of this standard unit. In many cases, the BP unit is equivalent to the international unit (IU). Since the British Pharmacopoeia includes the standards of the European Pharmacopoeia, BP units are equivalent to "Ph Eur" units for those substances using both sets of standards.

bpd

Abbreviation for barrels per day, a unit of production used in the petroleum industry.

bpm

Abbreviation for beats per minute, the common unit of tempo in music. The symbol is also applied in medicine for heart rates and respiration rates (breaths per minute). Technically, 1 bpm is equivalent to 1/60 hertz.
See *"hertz"*

braccio

A traditional Italian unit of distance. The word braccio implies "arm". It is the length of a man's arm, which is about 27 or 28 inches (68-71 centimeters). In modern times, the braccio has become an informal metric unit of exactly 70 centimeters (about 27.56 inches).

brace

Another name for a pair. The word is used mostly by hunters, who may speak of a brace of partridges or a brace of shotguns. Derived from the Latin word *bracchia* for both arms. It literally means "one for each arm".

brake horsepower (bhp)

The effective power output of an engine, sometimes measured as the resistance the engine provides to a brake attached to the output shaft.
See also *"horsepower"*.

brasse

a traditional unit of distance in France, comparable to the English fathom. The brasse is equivalent to 5 pieds (French feet). Using the *pied de roi* as the standard for the pied, this is about 1.624 meters or 5.328 English feet, slightly shorter than the Spanish braza (next entry). Note that the French have another fathom-size unit, known as the toise, which is equivalent to 6 pieds (about 1.949 meters or 6.395 English feet). The brasse was commonly used at sea and the toise on land. The name of the unit is related to *bras* (arm) and *brassée* (armful), recalling the traditional definition of the fathom as a man's arm span.

braza

A traditional unit of distance in Spain and Latin America.

The braza is comparable to the English fathom. In Spain, it is equivalent to 2 varas, 8 palmos, or about 1.67 meters (5.48 feet or 65.75 inches). In Latin America, the braza is larger than the fathom. The Argentine braza is 1.73 meters (5.68 feet or 68.16 inches). Using the Texas definition of the vara, the braza is 1.693 meters (5.556 feet or 66.67 inches). The Portuguese braca is equivalent to 10 palmos or about 2.20 meters (7.22 feet or 86.6 inches).

breadth

Another name for a span (9 inches or 22.86 centimeters). This unit is traditionally used to measure the dimensions of flags.

See also *"span."*

breakfast cup

A unit of liquid volume, used in food recipes in Britain.

The breakfast cup corresponds to the cup used by American cooks. It is based on British Imperial units.

1 breakfast cup = ½ Imperial pint

This is equivalent to 10 Imperial fluid ounces, 17.339 cubic inches, 1.20 U.S. cup, or about 284 milliliters. This unit is also known as a **tumblerful**.

See also *"pint, fluid ounce, and milliliter."*

breve

The standard unit of relative time in music equivalent to the time length of 2 whole notes. Although this is the longest interval in musical notation. The word originates from the Latin word *brevis,* meaning brief.

The breve is equivalent to 2 semibreves, 4 minims, 8 crotchets, or 16 quavers.

brewster (B):

The metric unit of the stress optical coefficient of a material (the reciprocal stress). The stress optical coefficient C in brewsters is related to the tensile strength σ (expressed in bars), which produces a relative retardation *s* (expressed in angstroms), when light passes through a material of thickness *t* (expressed in millimetres) in a direction perpendicular to the stress. This is given by the formula:

$C = s/\sigma t.$

It is equally defined as: one brewster is equivalent to the stress optical coefficient where a stress of 1 bar produces a relative retardation between the components of a linearly polarized light beam of 1 angstrom, when the light passes through a thickness of 1 millimetre, in a direction perpendicular to the stress.

$1B = 10^{-12}/Pa.$

The brewster has dimensions reciprocal to those of stress. One brewster is also defined to be equal

10^{-12} square meters per newton (m^2/N) or 10^{-13} square centimeters per dyne (cm^2/dyn). The unit is named for the British physicist David Brewster (1781-1868), who discovered stress-induced birefringence in 1816.

brieze

CGS unit of mass. It is equivalent to one gramme.

1 brieze = 1 gramme.

Note: This name, just like other names, was proposed in 1951 by Povani as an alternative for the gramme, but was never used

See also, *"stathm"* and *"bes"*.

brig

Unit of logarithmic value. For a value of 10^x, the size of this value is given as x brig. The brig is related to units such as the decibel, the neper and the octave by the relations:

1 brig = 10 dB,

1 brig = In 10 neper $\approx$2.302 59 neper,

1 brig = (1/log 2) octave $\approx$3.321 93 octave.

Note: 1. This unit is also called **dex**.

2. The unit is analogous to the bel, but the latter is restricted to power ratios.

See *"dex"* and *"bel"*.

bright, brightness

A unit describing surface brightness, or reflectivity, especially of paper. The fraction of light reflected by a surface is called its *albedo*, and its brightness is the albedo expressed as a percentage. Thus "88 bright" paper reflects 0.88, or 88%, of the light falling shining on the paper.

bril

A unit used to express the "brilliance" or subjective brightness of a source of light. The scale used is logarithmic. An increase of 1 bril implies doubling the luminance (and, thus, the actual amount of light energy) emitted by the source.

A luminance of 1 lambert is defined to have a brilliance of 100 brils. Mathematically, the brilliance in brils is equivalent to (log L)/log 2 + 100, where L is the luminance in lamberts.

See *"lambert"*.

brilliant, printers'

Unit of length used by printers to measure type size. One brilliant is equivalent to 3.5 points.

1 brilliant = 3.5 point = 0.123 010 93 centimetre.

See *"point"* and also *"emerald"*, *"printers"*, and *"pica."*

Brinell hardbess (HB or BHN)

A measure of the hardness of a metal introduced by J. A. Brinell in 1900. In the Brinell test (generally used for metals of uniform hardness), a hard object, such as a steel ball, is pressed into the material being tested. The ball is of a specified diameter, usually 1 centimeter. The Brinell hardness is the amount of force applied to the ball divided by the area of the indentation the ball makes on the material. The result is measured in kilogrammes of force per square millimeter, but should be stated as an empirical reading, without units. For readings up to about HB 500, Brinell hardness is about 0.96 times the Vickers hardness.

British absolute system of unit

A measurement system based on the foot, the second, and the pound mass. The force unit is the poundal.

The system is also known as foot - pound - second (FPS) system of unit.

British engineering system of units

See *"British gravitational system of units"*.

British gravitational system of units

A measurement system of units based on the foot, the second, and the slug mass.

The system is also known as British engineering system of units or engineer's system unit.

Note: 1 slug weighs 32.174 pounds at sea level and at 45° latitude. It is also equivalent to 14.594 kilogramme.

British horsepower (Bhp)

the traditional horsepower, equivalent to 745.7 watts, as opposed to the metric horsepower, which is equivalent to 735.5 watts. Note that in the symbol bhp, with the lower case "b" is used for brake horsepower.

See "horsepower"

British shipping ton

See: "ton, shipping."

British thermal unit (Btu)

Unit of heat energy. It is the heat energy required to raise the temperature of one pound of water through one degree Fahrenheit. Since this depends upon the temperature of the water, it is common to indicate the temperature range that a particular Btu refers to. Some of the values are:

1. International table British Thermal Unit (Btu_{IT}):

The 5th International Conference on the Properties of Steam (ICPS), July 1956, adopted the value of this unit in such a way that both the values of the specific heat capacity in international table kilocalories per kilogramme kelvin ($kcal_{IT}/kg\ K$) and international table British thermal units per pound degree Fahrenheit ($Btu_{IT}\ /lb\ degF$) are equal in size. Considering the following relations:

$1\ Kcal_{IT} = 4\ 186.8$ joule and 1 kelvin $= (9/5)$ degree Fahrenheit, this implies that:

$1\ BtU_{IT}$ per pound $= 2.326$ joules per kilogramme. Accordingly,

$1\ Btu_{IT} = 1055.055\ 852\ 62$ joule.

2. Sixty degrees Fahrenheit British Thermal Unit ($Btu_{60/61}$):

Is defined as the quantity of heat required to raise the temperature of one pound of air-free water from 60°F to 61°F at a constant pressure of one standard atmosphere. The experimentally derived value of the unit is:

$1\ Btu_{60/61} = 1.054.5$ joule

3. Mean British Thermal Unit (Btu_{mean}):

Is defined as (1/180) of the quantity of heat required to raise the temperature of one pound of air-free water from 32°F to 212°F at a constant pressure of one standard atmosphere. The experimentally derived value of the unit is:

$1\ Btu_{mean} = 1055.8$ joule.

4. Thirty-nine degrees Fahrenheit British Thermal Unit ($Btu_{39/40}$):

Is defined as the quantity of heat required to raise the temperature of one pound of air-free water from 39°F to 40°F at a constant pressure of one standard atmosphere. The experimentally derived value of the unit is:

$1\ Btu_{60/61} = 1.059.52$ joule

Note: The following units are related to the British Thermal Unit. (The Btu_{IT} is used throughout the table).

Unit	Unit symbol	Quantity Measured	Corresponding SI unit	To convert to SI, multiply it by:
Btu foot per square foot hour degree Fahrenheit	Btu. ft/ft^2.h.°F)	Unite of thermal conductivity	Watt per metre kelvin (W/m.K)	1.730 73
Btu per cubic foot	Btu/ft^3	Unit of calorific value,	Joule per metre	3.725 89
Btu per cubic foot hour	Btu/ft^3.h	Unit of heat release rate	Watt per cubic metre	1.034 97 x 10
Btu per hoot hour degree Fahrenheit	Btu/ft.h.°F	Unit of thermal conductivity	Watt per metre kelvin (W/m.K)	1.730 73
Btu per foot second degree Fahrenheit	Btu/ft.s.°F	Unit of thermal conductivity	Watt per metre kelvin (W/m.K)	6.230 64x10^3
Btu per hour	Btu/h	Unit of heat flow rate	Watt (W)	2.930 71x10^{-1}
Btu per pound	Btu/Ib	Unit of specific internal energy and calorific value (mass basis)	Joule per kilogramme (J/kg)	2.326x10^3
Btu per pound degree Fahrenheit	Btu/Ib.°F	Unit of specific heat capacity	Joule per kilogramme kelvin (J/kg.K)	4.1868x10^3
Btu per square foot hour	Btu/ft^2.h	Unit of density of heat flow	Watt per square metre (W/m^2)	3.154 59
Btu per square foot second degree Fahrenheit	Btu/ft^2.s.°F	Unit of coefficient of heat transfer	Watt per metre square kelvin (W/m^{2}K)	2.04417x10^4

B-SIZE

Metric unit used to define the size of which (trimmed) paper and boards are manufactured.
See "Volume- III"

British technical unit of mass

FIbfS unit of mass. One British technical unit of mass is the mass that acquires an acceleration of one foot per second square under the influence of a one pound-force.

1 British technical unit of mass = 9.806 65/0.304 8 pound = 14.593 9 kilogramme.

Note: The unit is known as **slug.**

See *"slug"*

brix (or brix degree, °Bx)

A unit used as a standard measure for the specific gravity using the Brix scale. The Brix scale is a hydrometer scale that indicates the percentage of sugar by weight in a solution at a specific temperature.

Note: 1. Frequently used to express the sugar level in wine.

2. Named after the German scientist A.F.W. Brix.

3. Bailling degree and Baume degree are also used for getting acquiring the sugar content.

4. The unit was named after the Austrian scientist Adolf Brix (d. 1870), who invented a hydrometer, which reads directly the percentage of sugar in the juice, provided the reading is taken at a specified temperature.

5. In winemaking, the alcohol concentration in the finished wine is estimated to be 0.55 times the sugar concentration in the brix of the unfermented juice. In the U.S. citrus fruit industry, juice concentrate is generally required to contain at least 42 brix of soluble solids (sugars and acids).

See *"Baume degree"* and also *"Sikes degree"*.

bucket

A unit of volume generally informal. In the U.S., many commodities (both wet and dry) are sold in plastic buckets holding 5 U.S. liquid gallon (about 18.927 liters). In Britain, a bucket is often 4 gallons, or 18.182 liters, based on the British Imperial gallon.

bunder

A traditional Dutch unit of land area. Since the adoption of the metric system in the Netherlands in 1809, the bunder has been considered to be equivalent to the hectare (2.471 acres). Historically, the unit varied with locality, generally in the range of 0.85-1.3 hectare. In Belgium, the unit is known as the **bonnier,** which is used in French- speaking provinces.

bundle (bdl)

[1]   A unit of quantity for paper, equivalent to 2 reams or 40 quires. This would be 960 sheets using the old definition of 24 sheets per quire, or 1000 sheets using the latest quire of 25 sheets.

[2]   A traditional unit of length for yam, equivalent to 20 hanks. For cotton yam, a bundle contains 16 800 yards (about 15.362 kilometers). For wool, a bundle contains 11 200 yards (10.241 kilometers).

[3]   In construction trades, a bundle is a package of shingles. Shingles are usually packed such that exactly 3, 4, or 5 bundles are needed to cover a square (100 square feet or 9.29 square meters). Asphalt shingles are often sold in bundles of 27, with 3 bundles per square, but the heavier cedar shingles generally require 5 bundles per square.

bushel, UK (UK bu)

UK unit of volume, i.e., capacity. One bushel is equivalent to 8 gallons
1 UK bu = 8 gallons = 0.036 368 7 cubic metres.
Note: 1. This unit is used in UK for the measurement of solid and liquid substances.
2. The unit was originally defined in Magna Carta (1216) as the volume occupied by a quarter (500 pounds) of water.
3. This unit dates back to the early fourteenth century. King Edward, I defined the bushel to be 8 gallons in 1303.
4. In the United States, the customary bushel is based on an old British unit known as the **Winchester bushel.**
5. The origin of the word "bushel" is unclear. Some scholars speculate that it was derived from an ancient Celtic unit, but most argue that it is of medieval French origin, probably a slang name for a wooden crate (the French word for wood is *bois).*

6. There are also other bushels.

See *"bag"* and also *"bushel, US"*.

bushel, US (USbu)

US unit of volume, i.e., capacity. Is defined as:

1 USbu = 0.035 239 070 166 88 cubic metres.

Note: 1. This unit is used in US for the measurement of solid substances. This unit is also known as stricken or struck bushel. A heaped bushel of apples of 2747.715 cubic inches was established by the US court of Customs Appeals in February 15, 1912.

2. There exist other bushels.

See also *"bushel, UK"*.

business day

a unit of time equivalent to one day during which a business is open. Phrases such as "8-10 business days" are common. They refer to a period of time containing that number of business days plus the number of days the business is not open during the period. Therefore, "8 business days" implies 10-12 actual days, or even longer if holidays intervene.

butcher

A unit of volume for beer in South Australia. A butcher of beer is a glass that can hold 200 milliliters (about 7 imperial fluid ounces). This is known as a glass or a seven in other parts of Australia.

butt

Arbitrary British unit of volume (capacity). One butt is equivalent to 126 gallons (US).

1 butt = 0.476 961 9 cubic metres.

button measure

A unit of distance equivalent to 1/40 inch (0.635 millimeters) used for measuring the thickness of buttons.

This unit is also known as the line. This is a contradicting idea since a line is generally equivalent to 1/12 inch.

Bya or bya

A common abbreviation (in English speaking countries) for "billion years ago."

byte

Unit of information for digital computers. A group of 8 bits representing any of 256 values. A byte may represent a single binary number, 8 bits of a longer binary number, two decimal digits (binary coded decimal BCD system), one decimal digit with a plus or minus sign, or a graphical character (e.g., a letter, a number or any symbol).

Note: 1. The term byte was introduced by IBM in 1964, with the introduction of the System 360 series

of mainframe computers.

 2. The generic term, used by CCITT and similar organizations, is *octet.*

See *"octet".*

C

c

a symbol for the speed of light. One of the fundamental principles of physics is that light always travels at the same speed in a vacuum, exactly 299 792 458 meters per second or about 670 617 300 miles per hour. Another fundamental principle is that no object can travel faster than light. At speeds that are large fractions of the speed of light, the theory of relativity predicts a variety of strange physical effects. In calculations involving relativity, speeds are customarily expressed as fractions of the speed of light, such as $0.95\ c$.

C [1]

the Roman numeral 100, sometimes used as a unit of quantity or as a prefix meaning 100, as in Cwt (hundredweight) or CCF (100 cubic feet).

C [2]

a symbol for international standard paper sizes, followed by the size number, as in C4. The C series of sizes is used primarily for envelopes. Wikipedia has a description of this scale.

C [3]

a unit of relative current for batteries. For a particular battery, a current of 1C is a current in amperes numerically equal to the rated capacity of the battery in ampere hours. In other words, a 1C current will completely charge or discharge the battery in one hour.

CA, CCA

abbreviations for "cranking amps" and "cold cranking amps," respectively. These units are often seen on motor vehicle batteries in the U.S. The amps involved are ordinary amperes of electric current. "Cranking amps" measure the current supplied by the battery when starting the vehicle at a temperature of 32 °F (0 °C), while "cold cranking amps" measure the current supplied at 0 °F (-17.8 °C).

caballeria

A traditional unit of land area in Spanish speaking countries.

1.   In Spain and Peru, the caballeria is equal to 60 fanegas, which is roughly 40 hectares (100 acres).

2.   In Central America, it equals 60 manzanas, which is roughly 45 hectares (110 acres).

3.   In Cuba, the caballeria is a smaller unit equal to 33.162 acres or 13.420 hectares, but in the Dominican Republic, it is a larger unit equal to 1200 tareas or about 75.4 hectares (186.5 acres).

4.   In Puerto Rico, the caballeria was equal to 200 cuerdas (see below) which is about 78.6 hectares (194.0 acres).

See also "fanegas", "manzanas," and "tareas".

cable (length) (cable length)

Imperial unit of length, particularly for marine use. The following definitions are given to the unit:

1.   1 cable length = 120 fathoms = 720 feet = 0.1185 nautical mile =219.456 metre.

2.   1 cable length = 100 fathoms = 182.88 metre.

3.   1 cable length = (1/10) UK nautical mile = 608 feet = 185.318 metre.

4.   Some navies are now using a metric cable equal to exactly 200 meters (about 656.17 ft).

Note: Originally, the unit was equal to the length of a ship's anchor cable.

See: *"fathom", "nautical mile", "metre", "feet."*

cabot

A traditional unit of volume in Jersey (Channel Islands), used for both liquid and dry commodities in trade.

The cabot equals 10 pots, which is 17.375 Imperial quarts or about 19.747 liters.

For dry commodities, the cabot is roughly comparable to 1/2 bushel.

See also "bushel", "pot", and "quart."

cade

An old name for a cask, sometimes used as a unit of measure for fish.

A cade of herring, for example, was 720 fish.

calendar year (cal yr)

A civil unit of time, equal to 365 days or (in leap years) 366 days.

Note: In archaeology, climatology, and other sciences studying the earth over the last 40 000 years or so, a careful distinction must be made between calendar years (cal yr) and radiocarbon years (^{14}C yr).

See also "year."

caliber (cal) [1]

A unit used to express the bore of a gun. (The bore is the inside diameter of the gun barrel.) Traditionally, the diameter was stated in inches, so that ".22 caliber" referred to a pistol having a bore of 0.22 inches (5.588 mm). This usage is declining because the bore diameters of many guns are now stated directly in millimeters. "Caliber" is the American spelling; elsewhere, the unit is often spelled "calibre."

caliber (cal) [2]

A measure of the relative length of a gun barrel, defined as the length divided by the diameter of the bore. Thus a 50-caliber gun on a warship has a barrel 50 times longer than its bore. Confining the shell within the barrel for a longer time increases the velocity, so guns with a higher caliber usually have a longer range.

caliper

The thickness of a sheet of paper or card stock.

Traditionally measured in points (thousandths of an inch), caliper is now measured in microns (micrometers).

The word "caliper" is sometimes used in place of the proper unit, as in ".004 caliper" (.004 inch or 4 points) or "120 caliper" (120 microns).

call second (cs)

A unit of telecommunications traffic equal to one or more calls or other communications having an aggregate duration of one second.

The **call minute (Cmin)** and **call hour (Ch)** are defined similarly.

callipic cycle

A unit of time equal to 76 years or 4 Metonic cycles.

Formerly used in astronomy in predicting the phases of the Moon. After the passage of one Callipic cycle, the phases of the Moon repeat essentially on the same calendar dates as in the preceding cycle.

The cycle is named for the Greek astronomer Callipus, who discovered it in 330 BCE.

calorie, Fifteen-Degree (cal_{15}):

An arbitrary unit of heat energy. It is defined as the quantity of heat required to raise the temperature of one gramme of air-free water from 14.5°C to 15.5°C at a constant pressure of one standard atmosphere. The CIMP in 1950 adopted the experimentally- derived value of this unit:

1 cal_{IT} = 4.1855 ± 0.0005 joule

Note: 1. This unit is also called "**gramme calorie (cal-gm)**

2. The "large calorie" or the "kilogramme calorie" is defined as.

  1 kilogramme-calorie = 1000 cal_{15}

3. The deprecated value of 4.185 8 joule was given by NBS at 1939 to this unit.

4. These are the "calories" that joggers are trying to get rid of, the ones we gain by eating.

calorie (International Table) (cal_{IT}):

Unit of quantity of heat energy. The Fifth International Conference on the Properties of Steam of 1956 adopted the following formal definition for the international table calorie:

1 cal_{IT} = 4.186 8 joule (J)

  The 9th "Conference Generale des Poids et Mesures (9CGPM)" of 1948 adopted the joule as the unit of heat, avoiding the use of the calorie as far as possible.

Note: When the name calorie or symbol cal are used unspecified after July 1956, they refer to the international table calorie.

calorie, (Thermochemical) (cal_{tc}):

This is metric derived unit for heat energy. By formal adoption,

1 cal_{CT} =4.184 J.

Note: 1. This unit has been used in thermochemistry, in preference to the others defined calories.

2. Former units include:

- The **"four-degree calorie (cal$_4$)"**. This is defined as the quantity of heat required to raise the temperature of one gramme of air-free water from 3.5°C to 4.5°C at a constant pressure of one standard atmosphere. The experimentally derived value of this unit is: 1 cal$_4$ - 4.2045 J.

- The " **mean calorie (cal$_{mean}$)** This unit is defined as one-hundredth of the quantity of heat required to rise the temperature of one gramme of air-free water from 0°C to 100°C at a constant pressure of one standard atmosphere. The experimentally-derived value is 1 cal$_{mean}$=4.1897 J.

3. The 9CGPM of 1948 adopted the joule as the unit of measurement of heat energy and recommended that the calorie be avoided.

calorie (I.T.) per centimetre second kelvin or degree Celsius (cal$_{IT}$ cm^{-1} s^{-1} K^{-1})

Unit of thermal conductivity.

1 cal$_{IT}$ cm^{-1} s^{-1} K^{-1} = **4.186 8 x10^2** watt per metre kelvin.

calorie (I.T.) per gramme (cal$_{IT}$ g^{-1})

Unit of specific internal energy. The internal energy per gramme.

1 cal$_{IT}$ g^{-1} = **4.186 8 x 10^3** joule per kilogramme.

calorie (I.T.) per gramme kelvin or degree celsius (cal$_{IT}$ g^{-1} K^{-1})

Unit of specific heat capacity and specific entropy.

1 cal$_{IT}$ g^{-1} K^{-1} = 4.186 8 x 10^3 joule per kilogramme kelvin.

calorie (I.T.) per kelvin or degree celsius

Unit of heat capacity.

1 cal$_{IT}$ = 4.186 8 joule per kelvin.

calorie (I.T.) per second (cal$_{IT}$ s^{-1})

Unit of heat flow rate.

1 cal$_{IT}$ s^{-1} = 4.186 8 watt

calorie (I.T.) per second centimetre kelvin or degree celsius

(cal$_{IT}$ s^{-1} cm^{-1} K^{-1})

Unit of thermal conductivity

1 cal$_{IT}$ s^{-1} cm^{-1} K^{-1} = **4.186 8 x10^2** watt per metre kelvin.

calorie(I.T.) persecondsquare centimetre kelvin or degree celsius (cal$_{IT}$ s^{-1} cm^{-2} K^{-1})

Unit of coefficient of heat transfer.

1 cal$_{IT}$ s^{-1} cm^{-2} K^{-1} = 4.186 8 x 10^4 watt per square metre kelvin

calorie (I.T.) per square centimetre second (cal$_{IT}$ cm^{-2} s^{-1})

Unit of density of heat flow rate.

1 cal$_{IT}$ cm^{-2} s^{-1} = **4.186 8 x10^4** watt per square metre.

calorie(i.t.) per square centimetre second kelvin or degree celsius (cal$_{it}$ cm^2 s^{-1} k^{-1})

Unit of coefficient of heat transfer.

1 cal$_{IT}$ cm^{-2} s^{-1} K^{-1} = **4.186 8** watt per square metre kelvin.

caña, canna, canne

Traditional units of distance in Spain, Italy, and southern France, respectively. The caña varied in size, but it was most often defined as 8 palmos, which makes it the Mediterranean version of the fathom, equal to roughly 2 meters (6.5 feet). In Italy, a measuring stick is still called a *canna metrica*. The unit is sometimes translated as "rod" in English, but "fathom" is the proper choice.

See: *"fathom", and "palmos."*

candela (cd)

Base SI unit of luminous intensity. It is the luminous intensity, in the perpendicular direction, of a surface of

$1/600,000$ m^{-2} of a full radiator at the temperature of freezing platinum under a pressure of 101,325 Newton m^{-2}.'

The translation of the official French definition given at the 9CGPM of 1948 is: The magnitude of the candela is such that the luminance of a full radiator at the temperature of solidification of platinum (2045K) is 60 candelas per square centimetre.

Note: 1. It is acceptable to call this basic SI unit the **"new candle"**

2. This unit is occasionally referred to as a **violle,** a name after **Violle,** who proposed it for the first time in 1884.

3. There is some suggestions to redefine the candela to be "the luminous intensity of a source emitting only monochromatic radiation of frequency 540.0154×10^{12} hertz in a direction for which the radiant intensity is $1/683$ watt per sterdian".

4. In order to produce 1 candela of single-frequency light of wavelength *l*, a lamp would have to radiate $1/(683\ V(l))$ watts per steradian, where $V(l)$ is the relative sensitivity of the eye at wavelength *l*.

Note: Values of V(*l*), defined by the International Commission on Illumination (CIE), are available online from the Color and Vision Research Laboratories of the University of California at San Diego and the University of Tubingen, Germany.

See *"candle, new"*.

candela per square centimetre (cd cm^{-2})

Multiple of the SI unit of luminance.

1 candela per square centimetre = **10^4** candela per square metre.

Note: This unit is also called "stilb".

See *"stilb"*.

candela per square foot (cd ft^{-2})

Unit of luminance

1 candela per square foot = **1.076 39 x10** candela per square metre.

candela per square inch (cd in^{-2})

Unit of luminance.

1 candela per square inch = **1.550 00 x 10^3** candela per square metre.

candela per square metre (cd m^{-2})

SI unit of luminance.

Note: Formerly called nit

See *"nif"*

candle (cd)

An older name of the candela, or of the candlepower.

See: "candela", "candlepower."

candle, decimal

See *"bougie decimale".*

candle, international standard (international standard candle)

Unit of luminous intensity. It is equal to the average luminous intensity of the candle standards of the UK, the US and France. The average measured value of this unit is:

1 international standard candle = 58.9 $\pm$ 0.2 candles = 60 candela.

This unit had previously different definitions:

1. Before 1800 the definition was" the mean intensity of the British standard candle. The British standard candle was made of spermaceti wax, weighed one-sixth of a pound, and burned at a rate of 120 grains per hour.

2. At 1800 it was defined as" one-tenth of the intensity of the Carcel lamp.

3. At 1877 it was defined as approximately the intensity of Vernon Harcourt pentane

vapour lamp.

See " *carcel"*.

candle, new (cd)

Unit of luminous intensity. The official definition of this basic SI unit, given at the 9CGPM, is: The magnitude of the new candle is such that the luminance of a full radiator at the temperature of solidification of platinum (2045K) is 60 new candles per square centimetre.

Note: 1. The name of the unit is now the candela.

2. The name new candle was adopted by the CIE in 1937 for the CGS and MKS of light intensity.

See *"candela "* and *"bougie nouvelle"*.

candlepower (cp)

A unit formerly used for measuring the light-radiating capacity of a lamp or other light source. One candlepower represents the radiating capacity of a light with the intensity of one ''international candle,'' or about 0.981 candela as now defined.

Since 1948 the candela has been the official SI unit of light intensity, and the term "candlepower" now means a measurement of light intensity in candelas, just as "voltage" means a measurement of electric potential in volts.

candy

A traditional weight unit of South Asia.

The candy was quite variable, generally within the range of 500 to 800 pounds (225 to 365 kilogrammes).

In the international cotton trade, the candy was generally equal to exactly 7 (British) hundredweight, which is 784 ponds or 355.62 kilogrammes.

See also *"hundredweight."*

can sizes

Food cans are identified by their nominal dimensions, diameter x height. (The ''nominal'' dimensions are somewhat

larger than the actual dimensions, as is the case for lumber and some other products.)

In the metric world, the dimensions are 2- or 3-digit numbers representing dimensions in millimeters.

In traditional U.S. nomenclature, the dimensions are stated as 3-digit numbers, with the first digit representing inches and the remaining two digits representing 16ths of an inch. A common can for fruits and vegetables, for example, is designated 83 x 116 in metric terminology, or 307 x 409 (3-7/16 x 4-9/16) in traditional terminology. If only one number is mentioned, it is the diameter; thus, a "404" can has a nominal diameter of 4-4/16 = 4.25 inches and a "65" can has a nominal diameter of 65 millimeters.

cantar

An English spelling for the Arab form of the quintal.

In recent years, the cantar has been interpreted as a metric unit equal to 50 kilogrammes (110.23 pounds); traditional cantars tended to be a few percent larger than this.

canvas

In rowing, a "canvas" is the distance between the bowman and the bow, or between the coxswain and the stem. These areas were once covered by canvas. Winning by a canvas in rowing is analogous to winning by a head in a horse race.

cape foot

Unit of length. One cape foot equal 1.033 foot.

1 cape foot = 1.033 foot = 0.314 858 4 metre.

1. This is a traditional unit of distance in South Africa.

2. This unit is not the traditional Dutch foot, but it is similar in length to the "Rhine foot" of northern Germany.

3. The Cape foot was widely used for land measurement and appears on many deeds in South Africa. Europeans often referred to South Africa as "The Cape," meaning the Cape of Good Hope.

carat

Imperial unit of mass, which is equal to 4 grains.

1 carat = 4 grains = **2.591 956 4 x 10^{-4}** kilogramme

Note:

1. This is an obsolete unit of troy measure, now replaced by metric carat.

2. Originally spelled **karat,** the word comes from the Greek *Iteration,* a carob bean; carob beans were used as standards of weight and length in ancient Greece in much the same way barleycorns were used in old England.

3. Traditionally, the carat was equal to 4 grains. The definition of the grain differed from one country to another, but typically it was about 50 milligrams and thus, the carat was about 200 milligrams.

4. In the U. S. and Britain, the diamond carat was formerly defined by law to be 3.2 troy grains, which is about 207 milligrams. Jewelers everywhere now use a **metric carat,** defined in 1907 to be exactly 200 milligrams.

See *"carat, metric*

carat (2)

The fineness of gold expressed in parts by weight of gold per 24 parts of the alloy. Thus 22 carat gold is 22/24 pure gold by weight.

Note: In US, the purity of gold is spelt karat, but the mass of precious stones is expressed in carats.

carat, metric (metric carat):

Metric unit for mass, especially precious stones.

1 metric carat = 200 milligramme = 2×10^{-4} kg.

Note: The 4CGPM of 1907 adopted the metric carat for commercial transactions in diamonds, pearls and other precious stones.

cars [1]

An informal unit used in the treatment of diabetes, equal to 15 grams of carbohydrates. This unit is known under various names, including **carbo, carb unit, choice,** or **exchange.** The significance of 15 grams is that, in a very rough way, that quantity of carbohydrate requires about 1 unit of injected insulin for patients with Type I diabetes (the actual ratio between carbohydrate and insulin varies considerably from patient to patient and is usually much lower for patients with Type II diabetes).

carb [2]

An informal unit equal to 1 gram of carbohydrate commonly used in describing low-carbohydrate diets such as the Atkins diet. This newer usage of the term "carb" conflicts with the traditional use by diabetics (previous entry).

carcel (carcel)

Unit of luminous intensity (Former French unit).

1 carcel = 9.61 international standard candles.

Note: The unit was defined as the intensity of a standard Carcel lamp, which burnt colza oil in a precisely defined way.

carga

A traditional unit in Spanish and Portuguese speaking countries.

The word means "load". It was often used as a unit of mass or weight equal to 3 quintals or as a unit of volume equal to the volume holding 3 quintals of the commodity being shipped.

carnegie unit

A unit of academic credit used in college admissions decisions in the U.S.

The unit was introduced by the Carnegie Foundation for the Advancement of Teaching in 1914 to provide colleges with a standard measure of students' course work in high schools. A Carnegie unit represents the equivalent of one academic year of study in a subject in a class meeting 4 or 5 times a week for 40 to 60 minutes per meeting, a minimum of 120 hours of total class time.

carreau

A traditional unit of land area in Haiti equal to approximately 1.29 hectares (3.18 acres).

The unit originated as the area of a square 100 pas (Haitian paces) on a side, with the pas being equal to 3.5 pieds (French feet).

Foreigners are not allowed to own more than 1 carreau of urban land or 5 carreaux of rural land in Haiti.

cart

A unit of volume, generally informal, equal to the capacity of a small cart.

In Newfoundland, a cart of salt traditionally equaled 6 tubs or 108 Imperial gallons (490.98 liters).

carton (carton)

Arbitrary unit of mass, equal 9 pound.

1 carton = 9 pound = 4.082 331 33 kilogramme

Note: 1. Used mainly to measure plums.

2. The size of a carton is usually not standardized, but certain sizes are customary. In the U.S. citrus fruit industry, a standard carton is equal to 1/2 box or 0.8 bushel (28.191 liters).

cascade unit (cascade unit)

Arbitrary unit of length used in cosmic-ray studies.

1 cascade unit = In 2 shower units.

Note: 1. This unit is also called the radiation length or radiation unit.

2. The cascade unit is an individual unit of length, i.e., its size depends on the conditions of a given set of circumstances.

case

A conventional unit of sales for many items, varying with the item and over time.

A case of wine, for example, is traditionally twelve 750-milliliter bottles.

The word comes from the Latin *capsa*, a chest.

castellation

A unit of angle measure equal to 1/6 turn or 60°, used in mechanical engineering. A castellated nut is a locknut having a raised rim with a number of equally spaced slots, usually 6.

A cotter pin fits into one of the slots and into a hole bored in the bolt, holding the nut in place with a precise degree of torque, or "tightness". To turn the nut, one castellation is to turn it from one slot to the next, that is, by 1/6 turn.

catty

A weight unit of the colonial period in East and Southeast Asia, originating as the *kati* in Malaya.

The catty varied a little from market to market. Typically it was equal to about 4/3 pound avoirdupois (604.79 grams), and it is still equal to that weight in Malaysia.

In Thailand, the catty is used now as a metric unit equal to exactly 600 grams (1.3228 pounds).

In China, the catty was identified with the jin, a traditional Chinese unit.

cawny or caney

A traditional unit of land area in southern India, equal to about 4/3 acre (0.54 hectare).

The name is an English transliteration of a Tamil word for the unit.

CE' (ce')

Arbitrary unit of time.

1 ce' = 0.01day = 864 second.

Note: 1. This unit has also been called degree.

2. The ce' was divided into dedice' (=1/10 ce') and millice' (= 1/1000 ce') to give periods of time analogous to the minute and the second.

See also *"degree (of time)*

CE

Abbreviation for "common era." This abbreviation is a non-religious designation used in place of the traditional AD for years of the common or Christian era. Years of the common era are supposed to be counted from the birth of Jesus of Nazareth, the founder of the Christian religion. However, the year-numbering system was not established until more than 500 years later. It is based on calculations of the priest and scholar Dionysius Exiguus, placing Jesus's birth in the Roman year 753 AUC. Dionysius knew he had incomplete information, and there is evidence that he picked this particular date to simplify the calculation of the date of Easter. According to the Biblical account, Jesus was born several years before the death of Herod the Great, who died, we now know, in 750 AUC (4 BC). Thus the calculation of the common era is off by 6 or 7 years at least. In the conventional use of the common era system, there is no year 0 and the year prior to 1 CE is designated 1 BCE (or 1 BC). In astronomy, however, it simplifies calculations to define the year 0 CE = 1 BC and to apply negative numbers to earlier years. Thus Herod died in -3 CE, and, in general, $-n$ CE is the year more commonly called $n+1$ BC.

celo

FBS unit of acceleration. It is the acceleration of a body, the velocity of which changes by one foot per second in one second.

1 celo = 1 foot per square second = 0.304 8 metre per square second.

celsius degree (deg):

The SI unit of the temperature interval or temperature difference. The Celsius degree is one-hundredth of the interval between the freezing and boiling points of pure air-free water, both under a pressure of one (standard) atmosphere. (1deg = 1kelvin).

Note: The unit symbol was formerly degC.

cent

1.   **IN SOUND**

Unit for (pitch) interval. The interval equals two 1/1200 of the interval of two frequencies $f_1 f_2$ *(f₁> f₂)* having the ratio 2:1, viz. the octave. The pitch interval I_C between any two tones, f and A, in cents, is:

$7_c = (1200/\log_{10}2) \log (f_1/f_2)$

Note: 1. Algebraic addition of the number of cents in two different intervals, e.g., f_1 to f_2 and f_2 to f_3,

gives the number of cents in the interval f_1 to f_3

2. From the definition, 7_C (in cents) is related to the corresponding pitch interval I_0 in octaves by the relation: $I_C = 1200\ I_0$.

3.   **IN NUCLEAR PHYSICS**

Unit of reactivity, i.e., for the departure of a nuclear reactor from its critical condition. The cent is one hundredth of the dollar.

1 cent = 0.01 dollars.

Note:

1. Cent is also an old English unit of quantity, usually equal to 100 but sometimes 120 (the **great** or **long hundred)** or some other figure of similar size. The Latin number 100, **centum,** is also used in English works for this quantity.

2. Cent is also an informal name for 1/100 of almost any unit, for example, a centiliter (0.01 liter). Phrases such as "15 cents of an inch" were formerly common in English.

See *"dollar"* and also *"octave".*

cental (ctl)

Imperial (UK) unit of mass. It is equal to one hundred pounds.

1 cental = **100** pound = 45.359237 kilogramme

Note: This is the UK name of the unit; the US name is the **short hundred weight,** or just the **hundredweight.** It is also known as the **centner** and the **quintal.**

See *"hundredweight", "centner",* and *"quintal".*

centesimal minute (...^{cg})

Unit of plane angle, It is equal to one hundredth of a grade.

1 centesimal minute = 10^{-2} grade = **1.57080 x 10^{-4}** rad.

Note: The unit is also known as centigrade.

See *"centigrade".*

centesimal second (...^{cc})

Unit of plane angle. It is equal to one hundredth of the centigrade.

1 centesimal second = 10^{-2} centigrade = 10^{-4} grade = **1.57080 x 10^{-6}** rad.

Note: The unit is also known as one hundredth of a centigrade.

See *"centigrade, one hundredth of* a."

centi (c)

SI prefix denoting x10^{-2}. It should be avoided as far as possible and used only where well established in practice. Examples are: centigrade (...^{cg}), centigramme (e.g.), centilitre (cl, cL), centimetre (cm), centipoise (cP) and centistokes (cSt).

centiare (ca)

Unit of area. It is equal to one square metre.

1 ca = 1 metre square.

Note: Also spelled **centare.**

centibar

Unit of pressure.

1 centibar = 0.01 bar = 1000 pascal.

= 7.5006 torr, or 0.1450 pounds per square inch (lbf/in^2 or psi).

The centibar is traditionally used in agriculture as a unit of soil water tension (the water pressure on the roots of plants) as measured by devices called tensiometers.

centigon (cgon)

A unit of angle measure.

1 cenrigon = 0.01 gon = 0.01 grad, or 0.0001 right angle; this is equivalent to 0.009°, 0.54 areminute, or exactly 32.4 arcseconds.

The centigon is useful in navigation (potentially, at least) because 1 centigon of latitude is equivalent to 1 kilometer on the earth's surface, in the same way, that 1 nautical mile is equivalent to 1 minute of latitude in traditional navigation.

centigrade (...^{cg})

Unit of plane angle. It is equal to one-hundredth of the grade.

$1^{cg} = 10^{-2}$ grade = **1.57080 x 10^{-4} rad.**

Note: The unit is also known as centesimal minute.

centigrade, one hundredth of a (...^{cc})

Unit of plane angle.

One hundredth of a centigrade = 10^{-4} grade = 1.57080 x 10^{-6} rad.

Note: The unit is also known as centesimal second.

See *"centesimal second*

centigrade degree

See *"Celsius degree*

centigrade heat unit (CHU)

Arbitrary unit of heat energy. It is the quantity of heat required to raise the temperature of 1 pound of air free water through 1 °C at a constant pressure of one standard atmosphere.

1 CHU = (9/5) British thermal unit.

Note: The unit is known as **pound-Calorie.**

centigrade heat unit, means (CHU$_{mean}$)

Arbitrary unit of heat energy. It is one-hundredth of the quantity of heat required to raise the temperature of one pound of air-free water from 0°C to 100°C at a constant pressure of one standard atmosphere.

1 CHU$_{mean}$ $=$ (9/5) mean British thermal unit (Btu$_{mean}$) $=$ 1900.44 joule.

Note: The unit is also known as the mean pound Celsius heat unit.

centigramme

Unit of mass.

1 centigramme = **0.01** gramme = **10^{-5}** kilogramme

centilitre

Unit of volume.

1 centilitre = 0.01 litre = 10^{-5} cubic metre.

centihg (centigh)

Metric unit for pressure. It is defined as the pressure that would support a column of mercury of length one centimetre and density 13595.1 kilogrammes per cubic metre under the standard acceleration of free fall (g_n).

1 centihg= 133.22387415 pascal.

Note: 1. It is recommended to call this unit the "(conventional) centimetre of mercury".

2. This unit equals in size to the "decatorr" to one part in seven million.

See *"centimetre of mercury.*

centimetre (cm) (electrostatic)

CGS-esu unit of capacitance. It is the capacitance of a condenser having a charge of one statcoulomb, across the plates of which the potential difference of one statvolt.

1 centimetre = (1 statecoulomb) / (1 statvolt)

$= 10^5 /(c^2)$ Farad $= 1.11265 \times 10^{-12}$ Farad

Note: 1. In the above equation, c is the velocity of electromagnetic radiation in vacuo.

2. The alternative name of the unit is **"statfarad"**.

centimetre (cm) (electromagnetic)

CGS-emu unit of inductance. It is the inductance of a coil in a closed circuit that gives rise to a magnetic flux of one maxwell per abampere.

1 centimetre = 1 Maxwell per abampere $= 10^{-9}$ henry.

Note: The alternative name of this unit is "abhenry".

centimetre (cm)

CGS unit of length. It is equal to one hundredth of the metre.

1 centimetre $= 10^{-2}$ metre.

centimetre -candle (cm-c)

CGS unit of intensity of illumination. It is equal to the illumination of one lumen uniformly over an area of one square centimetre.

1 centimetre-candle = 1 lumen per square centimetre $= 10^4$ lux.

Note: The name centimetre-candle is deprecated name. The new name " **phot"** should be used.

See *"phot"*.

centimetre of mercury (conventional) (cmHg):

Metric unit for pressure. The conventional centimetre of mercury is defined as the pressure that would support a column of mercury of length one centimetre and density 13595.1 kilogrammes per cubic metre under standard acceleration of free fall (gn).

1 cmHg = 1333.22387415 pascal.

Note: This unit is also called **"centihg"** and equals in size to the **"decatorr** " to one part in seven million.

See *"centigh"*.

centimeter of water (cmH₂O, cm WC, cm CE, cm WS)

a unit of pressure equal to the pressure exerted at the Earth's surface by a water column (WC) 1 centimeter high. This is about 98.067 pascals, 0.980 67 millibars, 0.3937 inch of water, or 2.04 pounds per square foot. The unit is used in respiratory medicine and elsewhere to measure air pressures. The French symbol is cm CE (*colonne d'eau*), and the German symbol is cm WS (*Wassersäule*).

centimetre per second squared (cms⁻²)

CGS unit of (linear) acceleration. It is the acceleration of a body, the velocity of which changes by one centimetre per second in one second.

1 centimetre per second square = 10^{-2} metre per second squared.

centimetre second degree per calorie (IT) (cm s°C/cal$_{IT}$)

Unit of thermal resistivity

1 cm s °C/cal$_{IT}$ = 2.38846 x 10^{-3} metre kelvin per watt (m K/W)

centimeter to the fourth power (cm⁴)

CGS of second moment of area.

1 centimetre to fourth power = 10^{-8} metre to the fourth power.

centimorgan

A unit of genetic separation used in genetics and biotechnology. If two locations on a chromosome have a 1% probability of being separated during recombination in a single generation, then the distance between those locations is one centimorgan. In humans, the centimorgan is approximately equal to one million base pairs. The unit honors the pioneering American geneticist Thomas Hunt Morgan (1866-1945), who received the 1933 Nobel Prize in Medicine for his discoveries concerning the role played by the chromosome in heredity.

centinewton (cN)

A metric unit of force equal to 0.01 newton.

This unit has some popularity in engineering as a substitute for the gram of force (gf), since it equals about 1.019 72 gf (about 0.0360 ounces of force in the English system). In the textile industry, the breaking strength of fibers is commonly expressed in centinewtons per tex.

centipoise (cP)

Unit of dynamic viscosity. It is equal to one hundredth of the poise.

1 centipoise = 10^{-2} poise = 10^{-3} pascal second.

Note: The dynamic viscosity of water at 20 °C (68 °F) is about 1 centipoise.

The correct symbol for the unit is cP, but cPs, cPo, and even cps are sometimes used.

See *"poise*

centiradian

a unit of angle measure equal to 0.01 radian or about 0.572958° (34' 22.65").

centisecond (cs or csec)

a unit of time equal to 0.01 second or 10 milliseconds. Centiseconds are frequently used in the study of human speech to measure precisely the length of sounds.

centistokes (cSt)

CGS unit of kinematic viscosity. It is equal to the kinematic viscosity of a fluid having a dynamic viscosity of 1 centipoise and a density of 1 gramme per cubic 277iopter277er.

1 centistokes = 10^{-2} stokes = 10^{-6} metre squared per second.

See *"stokes"* and *"poise*

centner

Imperial unit of mass. It is equal to one hundred pound.

1 centner =100 pound

= 45.359237 kilogramme.

Note: In the US, this unit is called the "short hundredweight", or just "hundredweight". It is also known as the quintal and the cental.

See "hundredweight", "cental", and "quintal".

centrad (centrad)

Unit of plane angle, used specially to specify angles of deviation of narrow angle prisms. The centrad is one hundredth of a radian.

1 centrad = 0.01 radian.

See also "prism 278iopter".

century [1]

A unit of quantity equal to 100. In ancient Rome, a "century" was originally a company of about 100 soldiers led by an officer called a centurion.

century [2]

A traditional unit of time equal to 100 years. In naming centuries, historians recall that there was no year 0 in the conventional year numbering system. Thus the First Century included the years 1-100 and the Twentieth Century included the years 1901-2000. (As an example, in the other direction, the Fifth Century BC included the years 500-401 BC.) With this convention, 2001 is the first year of the Twenty-first Century.

cetane number

A measure of the ability of diesel fuel to reduce engine knocking. The cetane number plays the same role in diesel engine technology that the octane number plays in conventional automobile engine technology.

It is the percentage by volume of cetane which must be added to methylnaphthalene to give the mixture the same resistance to knocking as the diesel fuel sample being tested.

Cetane is the name of a hydrocarbon compound whose molecules contain 16 carbon atoms and 34 hydrogen atoms, the 16 carbons being arranged in a long chain. Adding one oxygen atom to cetane produces cetyl alcohol, a waxy compound found in whale oil. The words "cetyl" and "cetane" are both derived from the Latin word *cetus* for a whale.

CGS-esu

Unit of the so-called electrostatic CGS system based on the permittivity of free space having unit size. Some of the units of this system are:

CGS esu Unit	The SI unit	To convert from CGSesu into SI, multiply by
CGSesu unit of magnetic field strength	Ampere per metre (A m$^{'1}$)	$2.654\ 42 \times 10^{-9}$
CGSesu unit of magnetic flux	Weber (Wb)	$2.997\ 92 \times 10^{2}$
CGSesu unit of magnetic flux density	Tesla (T)	$2.997\ 92 \times 10^{6}\ 3.767\ 30 \times 10^{7}$
CGSesu unit of magnetic polarization	Tesla (T)	$2.997\ 92 \times 10^{7}$
CGSesu unit of magnetization	Ampere per metre (Am$^{'1}$)	$2.998\ 8.954\ 19 \times 10^{-14}$
CGSesu unit of reluctance	Per Henry (H$^{'1}$)	

CGS-emu

Unit of the so-called electromagnetic CGS system based on the permeability of free space having unit size. Some of the units of this system are:

CGSemu Unit	The SI unit	To convert from CGSemu into SI, multiply by
CGSemu of magnetic field strength	Ampere per metre (Am^{-1})	$7.957\ 75 \times 10$
CGSemu unit of magnetic flux	Weber (Wb)	10^{s}
CGSemu unit of magnetic	Tesla (T)	$1.256\ 64 \times 10^{-3}$
CGSemu unit of magnetization	Ampere per metre (Am^{-1})	10^{-3}
CGSemu unit of reluctance	Per Henry (H^{-1})	$7.957\ 75 \times 10^{7}$

CGS technical unit of mass

CgfS unit of mass. One CGS technical unit of mass is the mass that acquires an acceleration of one centimetre per second squared under the influence of a force of one gramme-force.

1 CGS technical unit of mass = 980.665 gramme = 0.980 665 kilogramme.

Note: The unit is known as the glug.

See *"glug"*.

chad (chad):

Metric unit for neutron flux. This unit has two alternative definitions:

1.   One chad is a neutron flux of one neutron per square centimetre per second, i.e. 1 chad = 1 neutron/cm^2.

2.   One chad is a neutron flux of 10^{12} neutron per square centimetre per second, i.e. 1 chad = 10^{12} neutron/cm^2.

Note: This unit has rarely been used.

chain (chain)

Imperial unit of area.

1 chain = 484 square yards = 404.68564224 metre squared.

Note: This unit is more strictly called the **square chain.**

chain (ch)

Imperial unit of length. It is equal to length of 22 yards.

1 chain (ch) = 22 yards = 20.116 8 metre.

Note: This is the legally defined chain, commonly called "Gunter's chain," in the US. Also called imperial chain or surveyor's chain. It must be distinguished from the engineer's chain and the nautical chain.

See *"chain, engineer's"* and *"chain, nautical"*.

chain, engineer's (engineer's chain)

Imperial unit of length. It is equal to one hundred feet.

1 engineer's chain = 100 feet = 30.48 metre.

chain, nautical (nautical chain)

Imperial unit of length. It is equal to 15 feet.

1 nautical chain = 15 feet = 4.572 metre.

chaldron (chaldron)

1. UK arbitrary unit of capacity (volume). It is equal to 36 UK bushels.

1 UK chaldron = 36 UK bushels = 1.30927 cubic metre.

2. US imperial unit of capacity (volume). It is equal to 36 US bushels.

1 US chaldron = 36 US bushels = 1.26860652600768 cubic metre.

Note: The UK chaldron is used for the measurement of solid and liquid substance; the US chaldron is used only for the measurement of solid substance.

See *"bushel, UK"* and *"bushel, US"*.

3. UK arbitrary unit of mass and specially for coal equal to 25.5 hundredweight.

1 chaldron = 25.5 hundredweight = 1295.459 809 kilogramme.

See also *"room"* and *"shipload.'*

character (character)

Unit of information in computer technology. It is a group of n bits, usually representing one of 2^n possible graphic symbols and/or control functions (control characters). The value of n may be 8 bits (case of EBCDIC and extended ASCII code), 7 bits (ASCII code), 6 bits (BCD, BCDIC), 5 (Baudot, telegraph, code), 16 bits (case of ideographic characters, such as Chinese, Kanji, etc.), or any equipment-dependent number.

charka

A traditional Russian unit of volume contains about 123.0 milliliters, 4.159 U.S. fluid ounces or 4.329 imperial fluid ounces.

There are 6.25 charki in a biutylka (bottle) and 10 in a schtoff.

The word charka means a cup or glass.

charriere

French unit for grading the sizes (diameters) of catheters and probes.

1 charriere = (1/3) mm

Note: This unit is used within the range of (1/3) mm to 10 mm, determined on "Charriere filiere", hence the name.

The symbol Fr (for French scale) is sometimes used for this unit.

chemical mass unit (chemical mass unit)

Arbitrary unit of mass. It is equal to one-sixteenth of the weighted average mass of the three naturally occurring neutral isotopes of oxygen, the isotopes are, $^{16}_{8}O$, $^{17}_{8}O$ and $^{18}_{8}O$, which are found in the ratio of 506: 0.24: 1 and thus the experimentally derived value is:

1 chemical mass unit = (1.66026 $\pm$0.00005) x 10^{-27} kilogramme.

Note: 1. The unit is better called the atomic mass unit (chemical scale). It is called the atomic weight unit.

2. The atomic mass unit (international) is preferred to the chemical mass unit.

See *"atomic weight unit"*.

chest (chest)

Arbitrary unit of capacity (volume) equal 125 gallon.

1 chest = 125 gallon = 568.245 x 10^{-3} cubic metre *Note:* 1. The unit is used mainly to measure olive oil.

2. "chest" is also an arbitrary unit of mass. Its value depends on the commodity.

cheval vapeur

metric unit of power. The french name of the metric horsepower.

See *"horsepower, metric"*.

chiliad [1]

a unit of quantity equal to 1000. The word comes from the Greek numeral 1000, *chilioi*, which is also the origin of the metric prefix kilo-. Pronounced "killiad," the chiliad was once fairly common in learned writing, but it has nearly disappeared from use today.

chiliad [2]

another name for a millennium (1000 years).

chopine

a traditional French unit of volume.

The unit varied regionally, but by the 18th century, it was more or less standardized as 23.475 cubic pouces (465.7 milliliters).

The chopine is obsolete in France today, but the word survives (especially in Canada) as a French name for the English pint units.

choppin

a traditional Scottish unit of volume equal to 2 mutchkins or 1/2 scots pint.

The choppin is equivalent to about 52.1 cubic inches, 1.80 u.s. liquid pints, 1.50 British imperial pints, or 854 milliliters.

cicero (cc)

a unit of distance used by typesetters and printers in continental Europe, equal to 12 didot points. This is approximately 0.1780 inch or 4.52 millimeters.

The cicero corresponds to the British and American pica. Presumably, this unit got its name because a type of this size was used in printing the works of classical authors such as the Roman statesman and orator Marcus tullius cicero (106-43 bce).

cinque

an old English word for the number 5, pronounced "sink," and derived from the French number 5, *cinq.*

In English history, the original cinque ports were sandwich, Dover, Hythe, Romney and hastings. The word survives today as the name for a 5-spot showing in dice or for a 5-card in card games.

circle (circle)

unit of (geometrical) plane angle.

1 circle = 2 π radians = 360°.

note: it is also called the **turn** and also **circumference.**

Circular inch (circular inch)

U.K. and U.S. unit of area. It is the area of a circle of one inch in diametre.

1 circular inch = 7.85398 x10^{-1} inches squared = 5.06707 x10^{-4} meters squared.

Note: it is equal to 10^6 circular mils.

See *"circular mils"*.

circular mil (circular mil)

U.K. and us unit of area. It is the area of a circle one-thousandth of an inch in diametre.

1 circular mil = 7.85398 x 10^{-7} inches squared = 5.06707x10^{-10} meters squared.

Note: it is equal to **10^{-6}** circular inches.

See *"mil"* and *"circular inch"*.

civil year

a year as measured by the conventional (Gregorian) calendar, equal to 365 days in most years but 366 days in a leap year. See year]. This is the same unit as the calendar year (see above). Both names are often used to specify years beginning with January 1, as opposed to a fiscal year beginning on some other date.

Clausius (Clausius)

an arbitrary unit of entropy. It is the entropy associated with a temperature of one kelvin in which there is an increase in the heat of one thousand calories (i.t.)

1 clausius = **1000** calorie (i.t.) per kelvin = **4.186 8x10^3** joules per kelvin.

click

U.S. military slang for the kilometer (about 0.621 miles). also spelled **klick** or **klik.** This unit became popular during the Vietnam War, but it was invented by u.s. troops in Germany during the 1950s. Occasionally it was used as a non-metric unit equal to 1000 yards (0.9144 kilometers).

CLO (clo)

An arbitrary unit of thermal insulation of clothing. It is the amount of insulation necessary to maintain comfort and a mean skin temperature of 92°F in a room at 70°F with air movement not over 10 feet per minute, the humidity not over 50% with a metabolism of 50 kilocalories per square meter per hour. The unit is formally defined by:

1 clo = 0.875 feet hour degree Fahrenheit per international table British thermal unit.

= 0.505 566 meters kelvin per watt.

Note: 1. This U.S. unit was originally defined as the insulation required to maintain a stationary person at a comfortable temperature under indoor conditions.

2. The best clothing has a value of about 4 clo per inch of thickness.

clove

An old English unit of weight.

A clove is usually considered equal to 1/2 stone or 1/16 hundredweight; that's 7 pounds (3.175 kilograms) by the modem definition of the stone, but in the past, the clove varied from 6.25 to 8 pounds.

clusec (clusec):

Metric-derived unit for leak rate, i.e., for power. One clusec is a leak rate of one centiliter per second, at a pressure of one millitorr.

1 clusec = 1×10^{-5} torr/s = $1.333\ 22 \times 10^{-6}$ W.

Note: 1. This unit is used for the measurement of the power of evacuation of a vacuum pump

2. 1 clusec = 0.01 lusec

See "lusec".

CmA

A unit of relative electric current used especially in connection with nickel metal hydride (NiMH) storage batteries.

The symbol designates the current flow per hour, into or out of the battery, as a fraction of the battery's rated capacity. In other words, a current of 0.1 CmA would completely charge or discharge the battery in 10 hours. Put another way, if the rated capacity of the battery is 2 ampere hours or 2000 milliampere hours, then 0.1 CmA is a current flow of 200 milliamperes.

cmil

Symbol for the circular mil (see above). Note that this is *not* a centimil.

coffee measure

A flat-bottomed scoop or spoon used to measure coffee in U.S. homes. The coffee measure holds 2 U.S. tablespoons (about 29.57 milliliters).

coffee spoon

A unit of volume formerly used in U.S. food recipes. A coffee spoon is 1/2 teaspoon, 1/12 fluid ounce, or about 2.5 milliliters.

collothun

An ancient Persian unit of liquid volume, equal to 1/8 artaba or (in recent centuries) about 8.25 liters.

color redering index (CRI)

A scale used in engineering to measure the ability of an artificial lighting system to show the "true" colors of objects, that is, the colors those object display in natural daylight out of doors. The scale is from 0 to 100, with higher numbers representing a higher degree of fidelity of color. The test procedure, developed by the Illuminating Engineering Society of North America (IESNA), involves the comparison of eight test colors under both natural lighting and the artificial source being tested.

color temperature (CCT)

A measure of the overall "color" of a light source.

The measurement is obtained by comparing the spectrum, or mix of colors (wavelengths of length), produced by the light source to the spectrum of a "black body," a theoretical object that absorbs all radiation falling on it. (A blackbody is also a perfectly efficient radiator of energy, its spectrum depending only on its temperature.). The measurement is expressed in kelvins (K). Lower temperatures indicate more red and yellow light, and higher temperatures indicate more blue. Incandescent light bulbs are "cool" with a color temperature of about 2800 K, while daylight at noon is much "hotter" (bluer) at about 6000 K. Fluorescent lighting can be produced with a broad range of color temperatures, including everything between these two values. "CCT" stands for "correlated color temperature."

color units

Several systems have been devised to measure colors. For most of us not directly concerned with dyes, paints, or inks, the subject was academic until recently, but now computers require precise methods for describing the colors to be displayed or printed. These methods typically use three variables, reflecting the fact that the human eye has three types of color sensors. Computer monitors use the RGB system, which specifies colors with three variables measuring the intensity of the three primary colors red, blue, and green in color. Frequently each variable is specified by one byte and therefore takes values in the range 0 to 255. If all three are 0, the resulting color is black; if all three are 255, the resulting color is white. The RGB settings for the Carolina blue background of this page are R=153, G=204, and B=255. Since it is difficult to estimate the relative amounts of red, green, and blue needed to create a particular color, many graphics design programs use the HSV color system, which describes colors using three variables called **hue, saturation,** and **value.** Once again, all three variables are assigned values from 0 to 255. Hue, which is what we call "color" in ordinary language, is described on a circular scale. Hue values begin with red at 0 and run through yellow, green, blue, and purple before returning to red at 255. Saturation is the purity of the color, the extent to which it is not watered down with gray. The pure color has a saturation of 255. As saturation is reduced, the color becomes grayer, until at saturation 0, the color is replaced by a neutral gray of the same intensity as the original color. The value (or intensity) of the color is its brightness. The pure or most natural form of the color has value in the middle of the scale, at 127. As the value is increased, the color becomes brighter. In the opposite direction, the color becomes less bright, becoming black at value 0. This page's background has a hue of 140, a saturation of 240, and a value of 192 in the HSV system.

copla, colp, or collop

A traditional Irish unit.

The colpa was originally a unit of livestock equal to one cow or horse or to 6 sheep. Later it was used as a unit of pastureland equal to the pasturage supporting one colpa of livestock. This varied according to the quality of the land, but it was roughly equal to the Irish acre (0.6555 hectares).

"Collop" is an English version of the Irish word "colpa."

column inch (col in)

A unit of relative area used in journalism. A column inch is an area one column wide and one inch deep. The width of a column varies; a standard size in the U.S. is 2-1/16 inch. At this width, a column inch is 2.0625 square inches or about 13.31 square centimeters.

commercial acre

A unit of area used in U.S. real estate, equal to exactly 36 000 square feet or about 0.826 45 ordinary acres (0.334 45 hectares).

The unit was invented by commercial realtors to express the approximate portion of an acre of subdivided land that remains to be sold in the retail market after portions are set aside (dedicated) for necessary streets and other utilities. Buyer beware! It is legal to sell land by the commercial acre in many U.S. states, although most consumers are not aware of the smaller size of the unit.

cone, cone number

A measure of temperature used by potters.

Pyrometric cones are cone-shaped objects designed to soften and bend after absorbing a specific amount of heat. Potters place these cones in the kiln and observe them through peepholes; when the cone bends all the way over, the proper amount of heat has been delivered to the pottery being fired. Although cones bend within narrow temperature ranges, there is not a simple relationship between cone number and temperature. Technical tables are posted on the Internet by the Orton Ceramic Foundation.

cong

A metric unit of area used in Vietnam. One cong equals 1000 square meters, which is 0.1 hectares, 0.24177 acres, or 1196.00 square yards.

congius

A historic unit of liquid volume.

The Roman congius was equal to about 3.2 liters (3.4 U.S. quarts or 2.8 British Imperial quarts); it was divided into 6 sextarii (sixths), which corresponded closely to modern pints. In the nineteenth century, the congius was used in British medicine and pharmacology as a name for the British Imperial gallon (4.546 09 liters).

continental horsepower (cont hp)

Unit of power.

See *"horsepower, metric"*

coomb

U.K. unit of volume (capacity). One coomb equals 4 bushels or 16 U.K. pecks.

1 coomb = 16 U.K. pecks = 0.145 474 8 cubic meters See *"bushel, U.K."* and *"peck, U.K."*

COP

An abbreviation for the **coefficient of performance,** a measure of the efficiency of heat pumps, air conditioners, refrigerators, and freezers. The COP is the ratio of the useful energy output of the system divided by the electric energy input when the unit is operating in a steady-state test condition. Typical values are in the range 2-4. (The energy output exceeds the input, because the system takes advantage of the heat released or absorbed by the refrigerant when it condenses or evaporates.) A heat pump that delivers two units of cooling for each unit of electricity also rejects three units of heat; thus, it has a COP of 2.0 for cooling or 3.0 for heat. For air conditioners, the COP is considered to equal the energy efficiency ratio (EER) divided by 3.412.

cord (cord)

Unit of volume, for timber only. It is equal to 128 cubic feet.

1   cord = 128 cubic feet = 3.62456 cubic meters

Note:

1. Like most traditional units of trade, the cord has varied somewhat according to local custom.

In the United States, the cord is defined legally as the volume of a stack of firewood 4 feet wide, 8 feet long, and 4 feet high. (In Maryland, the law specifies that the wood be stacked "tight enough that a chipmunk cannot run through it." Presumably, it is up to the buyer to provide the chipmunk.) One cord is a volume of 128 cubic feet, about 3.6247 cubic meters, or 3.6247 steres. The name apparently comes from an old method of measuring a stack of firewood using a cord or string.

2. **Cord (cd)**: In the **U.S.** timber industry, the cord is also used as a unit of weight for pulpwood. The weight varies with tree species, ranging from about 5200 pounds (2.36 metric tons) for pine to about 5800 pounds (2.63 metric tons) for hardwood.

cord foot (cd ft)

A traditional unit of volume used to measure stacked firewood. A cord foot is the volume of a stack of firewood 4 feet wide, 1 foot long, and 4 feet high. Thus, the cord foot is 1/8 cord, or 16 cubic feet, or about 0.4531 cubic meters.

cordel [1]

A traditional unit of distance in Spain and Latin America. More specifically, the cordel is a rope used in land measurement.

In Mexico and the southwestern U.S., the cordel measured 50 varas or about 42.33 meters (138.9 feet), using the Texas standard of 33 1/3 inches for the vara. In Cuba, however, the cordel was only 24 varas or about 20.35 meters (66.8 feet). Longer cordels were used in some parts of South America.

cordel [2]

A unit of area equal to one square cordel: about 1792 square meters (2143 square yards or 0.433 acre) in Mexico and the southwestern U.S. or about 414.2 square meters (495.4 square yards).

Coulomb (C):

The SI unit of electric charge. It is also SI unit of electric flux and elementary charge. It is the quantity of electricity transported in one second by one ampere.

Note: This unit was formerly called *the absolute coulomb* (C_{abs}).

Coulomb meter (C m)

SI unit of electric dipole moment and transition dipole moment of a molecule.

1 Cm = 1m s A

coulomb meter squared (C m^2)

SI unit of quadrupole moment of a molecule and quadrupole moment of nucleus.

coulomb meter squared per kilogram (C m^2 kg^{-1})

SI unit of specific gamma ray constant.

Note: C m^2 kg^{-1} = m^2 kg^{-1} s A.

coulomb meter squared per volt (C m^2 V^{-1})

SI unit of electric polarizability of molecule.

Note: C m^2 V^1 = kg^{-1} s^4 A^2.

coulomb per cubic meter (Cm^{-3})

SI unit of volume density of charge.

Note: C m^{-3} = m^{-3} s A.

coulomb per kilogram (C kg^1)

SI unit of exposure and gyromagnetic coefficient.

Note: C kg^{-1} = kg^{-1} s A = A m^2 J^{-1} s^{-1} .

coulomb per kilogram second (C kg^{-1} s^{-1})

SI unit of exposure rate.

Note: C kg^{-1} s^{-1} = kg^{-1} A.

coulomb per mole (Cmol^{-1})

SI unit of Faraday constant.

coulomb per square meter (Cm^{-2})

SI unit of surface charge density, electric displacement, electric flux density and electric polarization.

Note: C m^{-2} = m^{-2} s A.

coulomb, thermal

The SI unit of the thermal charge. One thermal coulomb corresponds to an increase in entropy of one joule per kelvin (J/K).

Note: The former definition of this unit was such that it corresponded to a quantity of heat of one joule.

count (ct)

[1] A unit of quantity equal to 1. This unit is used in commerce to specify that the quantity stated represents a reliable count. For example, a carton marked "oranges 24 ct" contains exactly 24 oranges.

[2] A traditional unit measuring the texture of a fabric, equal to the number of threads per inch. A 100-count fabric has 39.37 threads per centimeter.

[3] An informal unit of volume in bartending, equal to 0.5 fluid ounce (14.8 milliliters). Bartenders usually fit bottles with pourers designed to restrict the flow to 0.5 fluid ounces per second. They can then measure a quantity of liquid by counting, "one thousand one, one thousand two, ..." while pouring. This is much faster than using a measuring glass and just about as accurate.

[4] A measure of size used in the U.S. for shrimp and similar items described by the number of items per pound. Thus "50 count" shrimp weigh an average of 1/50 pound each.

cousins

English, like most languages, has a procedure for stating the precise relationship between persons of common descent; a typical designation is "second cousins, once removed." First cousins are persons sharing a common grandparent; second cousins are persons sharing a common great-grandparent, and, generally, for $n > 1$, n-*th* cousins are persons sharing a common $(n - 1)$-times-great-grandparent. This means n-th cousins have $n + 1$ generations in each of their descents from the common ancestor. The "removed" phrase is used when the number of generations in the descent from the common ancestor is not the same for both cousins: "r times removed" means the difference in the number of generations is r. Thus, for yi-th cousins r times removed, the common ancestor is an $(n - 1)$-times-great-grandparent of one cousin and an $(n + r - 1)$-times-great-grandparent of the other cousin. (In the case of first cousins r times removed, the grandparent of one cousin is also an r-times-great- grandparent of the other cousin.) For /7-th cousins r times removed, there are $n + 1$ generations in the descent from a common ancestor for one cousin, and $n + r + 1$

generation for the other. The number of degrees of consanguinity between *n*-th cousins *r* times removed is *2n + r + 2*.

covado,covido

Portuguese and Arabic names, respectively, for the cubit (see below).

The Portuguese covado is equal to 3 palmos (66 centimeters, or 20.12 inches), while the Arabic covido is about 48 centimeters or 19 inches.

cover

A traditional Welsh unit of area, standardized in the British system to be exactly 2/3 acres (about 0.2698 hectares).

The word is an Anglicized version of the Welsh name *cyfair* for the unit.

cran (cran)

Arbitrary units in the herring fishing industry used to indicate the quantity of fish. One cran is the quantity of herring occupying a volume of 37.5 Imperial gallons.

Note: The cran was originally defined as the quantity of fish needed to fill a barrel.

crinal (crinal):

Metric unit for force.

1 crinal = 0.1 newtons.

Note: The name of the unit is derived from crinis meaning a hair, because it was considered that a force of one crinal might just break a hair.

crith (crith)

Arbitrary unit of mass, particularly the mass of gas. It is the mass of one liter of hydrogen at standard temperature and pressure. The experimentally derived value is: 1 crith = 8.9885 x 10^{-5} kilograms.

Note: The mass of one liter of any gas at standard temperature and pressure measured in criths is numerically equal to one-half of its relative molecular mass (molecular weight).

crocodile (crocodile):

Metric unit for electric potential, potential difference and electromotive force.

1 crocodile = 10^6 volts.

Note: This unit is employed at an informal level in a number of U.K. nuclear physics laboratories.

cron (cron)

Arbitrary unit of time. One cron equal to a million year.

1 cron = 10^6 years = 3.156 x 10^{13} seconds.

Note: The unit was suggested by J.S. Huxley in 1957 and since then has almost never been employed

crore

A traditional unit of quantity in India, equal to 10^7 or 10 million.

Large numbers are usually described in India using the crore and the lakh (10^5); for example, the number 25 600 000 is called 2 crore 56 lakh and written "2,56,00,000".

crotchet

A unit of relative time in music equal to 1/4 whole note or 1/8 breve. The word, pronounced *crotch-it,* comes from the old Norse word *krok* for a hook; in this context, it refers to the traditional hooked symbol for a quarter note.

crumb

A unit of information in computer science, equal to 2 bits. The unit is thought to have originated at IBM in the early 1980s. There are 2 crumbs in a nibble.

See also *"bit", "byte", and "nibble."*

C-size

Metric unit used to define the size to which (trimmed) paper and boards is manufactured. See "Section 3.5 of Chapter 5".

cuadra

[1] A traditional Latin American unit of distance. The cuadra is generally equal to 100 varas (about 84 meters or 275 feet) in Central America and northern South America. In Argentina and Chile, the cuadra is equal to 150 varas (roughly 130 meters or 410 feet).

[2]   A traditional Latin American unit of area equal to one square cuadra [1]. Except in Argentina and Chile, this is 10 000 square varas, generally in the range of 1.75-1.85 acres (0.71-0.75 hectares). In Argentina and Chile, the cuadra was 22 500 square varas (4.18 acres or 1.69 hectares).

cuartillo

A traditional Spanish unit of volume comparable to the liter or the English quart. The cuartillo equals 4 octavillos or 1/4 almude and contains 1.156 25 liters, which is about 1.222 U.S. liquid quarts or 1.017 British imperial quarts.

cubic meter (m^3)

SI unit of volume. Also, SI unit of section modulus.

cubic centimeter (cm^3)

Sub-multiple of the SI unit of volume also CGS unit of volume.
1 cubic centimeter = 10^{-6} cubic meters.

cubic centimeter per gram ($cm^3\ g^{-1}$)

Sub-multiple of the SI unit of specific volume and also CGS of specific volume. The volume in cubic centimeter of one gram of the substance.
1 cubic centimeter per gram = 10^{-3} cubic meters per kilogram.

cubic centimeter per kilogram ($cm^3\ kg^1$)

Sub-multiple of the SI unit of specific volume. The volume in cubic centimeter of one kilogram of the substance.
1 cubic centimeter per kilogram = 10^{-6} cubic meters per kilogram.

cubic decimeter (dm^3)

Sub-multiple of the SI unit of volume.
1 cubic decimeter = 1×10^{-3} cubic meters.
Note: This unit is equivalent to the liter.
See *"liter"*.

cubic foot (ft^3)

U.K. and U.S. unit of volume 1 cubic foot = 2.831 68 x 10^{-2} cubic meters.

cubic foot per pound (ft^3 lb-^{1})

FPS unit of specific volume. The volume in cubic foot of one pound of the substance.

1 cubic foot per pound = **6.242 80 x 10^{-2}** cubic meters per kilogram.

cubic foot per second (ft^3 s^{-1})

FPS unit of volume flow rate. It is the rate at which a volume of one cubic foot flows in one second.

1 cubic foot per second = **2.831 68 x 10^{-2}** cubic meters per second.

Note: This unit is also called " cusec."

See *"cusec"*.

cubic foot per uk ton (ft^3 Ukton^{-1})

U.K. unit of specific volume.

1 cubic foot per U.K. ton = 2.786 96 x 10^{-5} cubic meters per kilogram.

cubic inch (in^3)

U.K. and U.S. unit of volume.

1 cubic inch = 1.638 706 x 10^{-5} cubic meters.

cubic inch per pound (in^3 lb^{-1})

Unit of specific volume.

1 cubic inch per pound = 3.612 73 x 10^{-5} cubic meters per kilogram.

cubic meter (m^3)

SI unit of volume.

cubic meter per coulomb (m^3 C^{-1})

SI unit of Hall coefficient.

cubic meter per hour (m³ h⁻¹)

Unit for volume flow rate used with SI system. It is the rate at which a volume of one cubic meter flows in one hour.

1 cubic meter per hour = 2.77778 x 10^{-4} cubic meters per second.

cubic meter per kilogram (m³ kg⁻¹)

SI unit of specific volume.

cubic meter per mole (m³*mol⁻¹*)

SI unit of molar volume, molar magnetic susceptibility, molar refraction, second virial coefficient, and volume of activation.

cubic meter per mole second (m³ mol⁻¹ s⁻¹)

SI unit of collision frequency factor.

cubic meter per second (m³ s⁻¹)

SI unit of volume flow rate. The rate at which a volume of one cubic meter flows in one second.

Note: This unit is also called "cumec"

See *"cumec".*

cubic yard (yd³)

U.K. and U.S. unit of volume.

1 cubic yard = 7.645 55 x 10^{-1} cubic meters.

cubit (cubit)

Unit of length. It is equal to 18 inches.

1 cubit = 0.4572 meters.

Note: One of the oldest known units of length. It originated in Egypt in the Third Dynasty (2800-2300 B.C.). The word comes from the Latin *cubitum,* "elbow," because the unit represents the length of a man's forearm from his elbow to the tip of his outstretched middle finger. This distance tends to be about 18 inches or roughly 45 centimeters.

In ancient times, the cubit was usually defined as to equal 24 digits or 6 palms. The Egyptian royal or "long" cubit, however, was equal to 28 digits or 7 palms. In the English system, the digit is conventionally identified as 3/4 inch; this makes the ordinary cubit exactly 18 inches (45.72 centimeters). The Roman cubit was shorter, about 44.4 centimeters (17.5 inches). The ordinary Egyptian cubit was just under 45 centimeters, and most authorities estimate the royal cubit at about 52.35 centimeters (20.61 inches).

cuerda (cda)

[1] A traditional unit of land area in Puerto Rico. The cuerda is equal to about 3930 square meters, 4700 square yards, 0.393 hectares, or 0.971 acres. Because the cuerda and the acre are so close to being equal, they are often treated informally as being equal. Mainlanders sometimes call the unit the "Spanish acre."

[2] A traditional unit of distance in Guatemala equal to 25 varas or about 21 meters (roughly 69 feet). Since *cuerda* means a cord or rope in Spanish, this unit probably arose as the length of a measuring rope. The cuerda is also used as an area measure equal to 1 square cuerda or 625 square varas; this is about 440 square meters or 527 square yards.

[3] A traditional unit of volume for firewood in Cuba, analogous to the U.S. cord (see above). A cuerda of firewood is equal to 128 cubic pies, 2.87 cubic meters, or 0.79 cords.

cumec (cumec)

SI unit of volume flow rate. It is the rate at which a volume of one cubic meter flows in one second.

1 cumec = 1 cubic meter per second.

See *"cubic meter per second."*

cunit

A measure of wood volume used in forestry. One cunit (pronounced *cue-nit)* is a volume of timber containing 100 cubic feet (2.8317 cubic meters) of actual wood (excluding bark and air between the logs). The unit is used mostly for wood intended as pulpwood or firewood.

cup (cup)

U.S. unit of volume (capacity).

1 cup = 2.365 882 x 10^{-4} cubic meters.

Technically, one cup equals exactly 14.4375 cubic inches.

Note: 1. American cooks use the same size cup for measuring both liquid and dry substances. In Canada, a cup is equal to 8 Imperial fluid ounces (13.8710 cubic inches or 227.3 milliliters). In Britain, cooks sometimes used a similar but larger unit called the breakfast cup, equal to 10 Imperial fluid ounces.

2. The cup is also an informal metric unit of volume equal to 250 milliliters, commonly used in recipes in Australia.

3. The cup is also an informal unit of volume for coffee. The size of a cup of coffee varies according to local custom, but a typical size is about 5 fluid ounces or 150 milliliters.

curie (Ci)

Arbitrary unit of activity of radionuclide. It is the quantity of a radioactive nuclide required to produce 3.7 x 10^{10} disintegrating atoms per second, or, simply, 3.7 x 10^{10} disintegrations per second.

1 curie = *3.1 x 10^4* rutherfords = 3.7 x10^{10} becquerels.

Note: 1. The above definition was agreed at the Copenhagen meeting of the International Commission on Radiological Units in July 1953.

2. The original definition of the curie (adopted at a Radiography Conference in 1910) was the quantity of radon that is in radioactive equilibrium with one gram of radium. The quantity of radon involved is 0.66 cubic millimeters approximately at standard temperature and pressure, and this gives rise to 3.61x10^{10} disintegrating atoms per second approximately. The definition was later modified to: One curie is the quantity of a radioactive nuclide producing the same disintegration rate as one gram of random.

3. The unit is named after Pierre Curie.

curie megaelectronvolt (Ci MeV)

Unit of power (nuclear).

1 curie megaelectronvolt = 5.93 x 10^{-3} watts.

curie per cubic meter (Ci m^{-3})

Unit of volume activity.

1 curie per cubic meter = 3.7 x 10^{10} becquerels per cubic meter.

curie per kilogram (Ci kg^{-1})

Unit of specific activity of radionuclide.

1 curie per kilogram = 3.7 x 10^{10} becquerels per kilogram.

cusec (cusec)

FPS unit of volume flow rate. Is the rate at which a volume of one cubic foot flows in one second.

1 cusec = 1 cubic foot per second = 28.316846592 cubic meters per second.

Note: It is also called "cubic foot per second."

See *"cubic foot per second"*

cut (cut)

Imperial unit of length equal to 300 yards.

1 cut = 300 yards = 274.32 meters *Note:* The unit is used for linen yam.

cycle per second (c/s or cps)

Unit of frequency. One cycle per second is the frequency of a periodic occurrence that has a period of one second.

1 c/s = 1 hertz.

Note: This unit, sometimes (incorrectly) referred to in short as cycle, is better called hertz. It has also been called the vibration.

D

D- UNIT

Arbitrary unit of X-ray dosage

1 D unit = 10^2 rontegns.

daily value (DV)

a unit of nutrition used in the United States. The U.S. Food and Drug Administration establishes recommended daily amounts of various nutrients, both "good" ones like vitamins and "bad" ones like fat and sodium. These so-called daily values are based on a hypothetical person, male or female, who requires a diet of 2000 Calories per day. The results are approximate at best, since nutritional needs vary with age, sex, and other factors. Food packages generally carry nutritional lables specifying the amount of each nutrient contained in a standard serving, expressed as a percentage of the daily value (%DV). Wikipedia has a table of the official daily values.

See, "Calories"

daktylos

an ancient Greek unit of length (distance) equal to a finger width. Its value varied, as shown next table

Attic	1.8 cm
Olympic	2.0 cm
Pergamene	2.1 cm
Aeginetan	2.1 cm

There were 16 daktylos in the pous, the Greek foot, and 24 in a pechys (cubit). This unit was the Greek predecessor of the Roman digit (see below).

In modern Greece, two units of length, the daktylos = 1 inch and the royal daktylos = 1 centimeter.

See: *"pous," "cubit," "digit, Roman."*

dalton (Da or D)

Arbitrary unit of mass. It is equal to one-twelfth of the mass of a neutral carbon-12 atom. The experimentally derived value is:

1 dalton = (1.660 33 + 0.000 05) x 10^{-27} kilograms

Note: 1. This unit is also called **the atomic mass unit** (international). The SI accepts dalton as an alternate name for the unified atomic mass unit and specifies Da as its proper symbol.

2. The unit is named after the English chemist and physicist J. Dalton (1766- 1844), who proposed the atomic theory of matter in 1803

3. The dalton is often used in microbiology and biochemistry to state the masses of large organic molecules; these measurements are typically in kilodaltons (kDa).

See *"atomic mass unit"*.

Dam unit

A unit of quantity of vitamin K, ⅟₃₀₀th of the amount of vitamin K found in a gram of dried alfalfa, about ½₀ Ansbacher unit.

It is named for the Danish biochemist Carl Peter Henrik Dam (*1895 – 1976*), who discovered vitamin K.

dan

As unit of mass:

Dan is a traditional Chinese weight unit, previously spelled **tan** in many English works. The word means "shoulder pole", and also, as a measure, the load carried on a shoulder pole. It was also previously synonymous with the catty.

1.   During the European colonial era, the unit was equal to 100 catties or 133.333 pounds.

2.   In modern China, the dan is equal to 100 jins, which is exactly 50 kilograms (110.231 pounds). The dan is the Chinese equivalent of the European quintal or hundredweight.

3.   In China, *20th century*, a unit of mass, = 50 kilograms.

As unit of capacity:

In China, *20th century*, a unit of capacity = 10 *dou*, approximately 100 liters.

Note: The character for the *dan* has another pronunciation, *shi*, with the meaning "stone." The unit should not, however, be called a shi. Europeans often called this unit a pikul.

daniell (daniell)

Arbitrary unit of potential, potential difference and electromotive force.

1 daniell = 1.042 volts.

Note: 1. This unit was meant to be the electromotive force of a Daniell cell, although this is now known to have a value of 1.08 volts.

2. This unit is named after the English chemist and physicist J.F. Daniell (1790- 1845), the inventor of Daniell cell.

Danjon scale of lunar eclipse brightness

The Moon often remains visible during a lunar eclipse because the Earth's atmosphere bends sunlight passing through it. The light bent by the atmosphere is directed into the Earth's shadow, and thus lights the Moon. Dust in the air reddens this light (as it does on sunsets).

A scale devised by Andre Danjon (*1890–1967*) is used by observers of lunar eclipses to describe how bright the eclipsed Moon is.

L value	Description
0	Very dark eclipse, Moon almost invisible.
1	Dark eclipse. Gray or brownish coloration. Details distinguishable only with difficulty.
2	Deep red or rust-colored eclipse. Very dark central shadow, but outer edge of the umbra is brighter.
3	Brick-red eclipse. The umbral shadow usually has a bright or yellow rim.

4	Very bright copper-red or orange eclipse. Umbral shadow has a bluish, very bright rim.

daraf

The SI unit of elastance, i.e., reciprocal capacitance. One daraf is the elastance of a substance that has a capacitance of one farad (F). 1 daraf = 1/F.

Note: 1. The name of the unit is derived by writing Farad backward.

2. This unit is rarely employed: the reciprocal farad is used instead

3. Proposed by Vladimir Karapetoff in *1910*. A. E. Kennelly but not much used.

darcy (D)

CGS unit for measuring permeability of porous solids. A permeability if one darcy will permit a flow of 1 cubic centimeter per second (cm^3 s^{-1}) of fluid of 1 centipoize (cP) viscosity through an area of 1 square centimeter (cm^2) under a pressure gradient of 1 atmosphere per centimeter ($atm\ cm^{-1}$).

$1\ d = 9.869\ 233 \times 10^{-13}$ square meters

Note: 1. The permeability has the same units as the area; since there is no SI unit of permeability, square meters are used.

2. The name of the unit is derived after the French scientist H. Darcy (1803-1858), who investigated the flow of fluids in porous media.

3. The unit is sometimes spelled **darcie.**

4. In Petroleum Engineering, this unit is used as a measure of rock permeability; because a darcy is too large to characterize many oil-producing rocks, the **milidarcy** is used to express the permeabilities in the oil industry. Commercial gas and oil sands show permeabilities from a few millidarcies to several thousands.

dariba

In Egypt, a unit of dry capacity. Also romanized as Daribaj. The *20th-century* value for customs purposes = 1,584 liters (about 45.0 U.S. bushels).

darwin

Unit of evolutionary rate of change. Consider one dimension of part of an animal or plant or the whole animal or plant (e.g., its height). If, as a result of evolution, that dimension increases from S_o to S_t (expressed in the same units) in a time t years according to the formula

$$S_t = S_o \ e^{\ Et/1000000},$$

Its evolutionary rate of change is E and is measured in darwins.

Equally, one Darwin is the increase or decrease in any hereditary character multiplied by a factor of 2.7 million years.

Note: 1. The name of the unit is after Charles Darwin (1809-1882), who put the theory of evolution.

dash (ds)

In the United States, dash is an informal unit of volume used in food and drink recipes, mostly met in recipes for mixed drinks. Originally the dash was usually a liquid measure, small but indefinite in amount, roughly 1/8 teaspoon or a little less. More recently, it has been used as both a liquid and dry measure. Kitchen supply stores in the U.S. and other countries have begun selling sets of "minispoons" in which the dash spoon is designed to hold exactly 1/8 teaspoon, which is roughly 0.02 fluid ounces or 0.6 milliliter.

Note: the dash is usually taken as 1/8 teaspoon, but according to Trader Vic (Victor Bergeron), the famous saloonkeeper, in mixed drinks, a dash is 1/8 teaspoon when applied to bitters; otherwise (for sugar syrup, orgeat, grenadine, lemon juice, etc.) a dash is ¼ U.S. fluid ounce = 1½ teaspoons.

data mile

a unit of distance used in radar technology. The data mile equals exactly 6000 ft or 1828.8 meters; this is equivalent to about 1.137 statute (ordinary) miles or 0.9875 nautical miles. U.S. military radar equipment is often calibrated in data miles.

day (d)

Unit of time used with SI system.

1 day = **8.64 x10^4** seconds

Note: 1. The above definition is that of the mean solar day, the time interval between consecutive passages of the sun across the meridian, averaged over one year.

2. The symbol j formally used in France.

See also *"day, sidereal."*

day, sidereal (sidereal day)

Unit of time. It is the time for one complete rotation of the Earth on its axis. The experimentally observed value is:

1 sidereal day = 23 hours 56 minutes 4.098 92 seconds = 86 164.098 92 seconds.

deadweight ton (dwt)

a traditional unit of weight or mass used in the shipping industry. The deadweight tonnage of a ship is the difference between its weight when completely empty and its weight when fully loaded. This includes the weight of everything portable carried by the ship: the cargo, fuel, supplies, crew, and passengers. The deadweight ton is traditionally equal to the British ("long") ton of 2240 pounds (1016.047 kilograms). However, more and more often, it is being taken to equal the metric ton (exactly 1000 kilograms, or 2204.623 pounds).

debye (D)

Unit of electric dipole moment equal to 10^{-18} electrostatic units. Equal and opposite charges, each equal to the electronic charge (4.80×10^{-10} e.s.u), displaced 10^{-8} centimeters, produce a dipole moment of 4.8 debyes.

1 debye = $3.335\ 64 \times 10^{-30}$ coulomb meters.

Note: 1.   The unit name is after P. J. Deby (1884-1966), the pioneer authority on polar molecules.

2.   It is also the product of the electron charge and the radius of the first Bohr orbit of hydrogen, 2.54×10^{-18} esu cm

3.   Also, Product of the electron charge and 1 angstrom, 4.803×10^{-18} esu cm

dec (da)

SI prefix denoting x10. It is recommended to avoid its use as far as possible and to be used only where well established in practice. Examples are: decagramme (dag), decajoule (daJ), decanewton (daN).

See also *"deka-. "*

decade

A group of assembly of 10 units; for example, a decade counter counts 10 in one column, and a decade box inserts resistance quantities in multiples of power 10.

The interval between any two quantities having the ratio of 10:1.

In science, decade is a period of 10 years, especially a 10-year period beginning with 1 or 0, such as 1951 to 1960 or 1970 – 1979.

decay time [1]

a unit of relative time used in physics. Decay time is similar to <u>half-life</u>, but shorter and less familiar. It is the time required for an exponentially decaying process (such as radioactivity) to decrease to $1/e = 36.7879\%$ of its original value. The fraction of activity remaining at time T, if T is measured in decay time units, is simply e^{-T}. The decay time equals 0.693 147 half-life.

decay time [2]

a unit of relative time used in various engineering applications. In many cases, it is the time required for a decaying process to decrease to 10% of its original value. However, a variety of definitions are used in different fields.

deci (d)

SI prefix denoting $x\ 10^{-1}$. It is recommended to avoid its use as far as possible and to be used only where well established in practice. Examples are decibel (dB), decigram (dg), and decimeter (dm).

deciatina (or desiatina) [Russian word десятиннЬій.]

In Russia, a unit of land area, *15th–20th centuries*. Also romanized as *dèçïatina* and *dessiatine*.

Originally the *desiatina* was the area of a square whose sides were $^1/_{10}$th of a versta, which area was equal to 2 chetverti or 2,500 square sazheni (about 1.092 hectares, or about 2.7 acres).

A decree of *1753* defined the official *desiatina* as 2,400 square *sazheni* (about 1.0925 hectares or 2.7 acres, the length of the *sazhen* having changed). In addition to this official *desiatina*, a number of others were used, including:

Household *or* oblique desiatina	$80 \times 40 = 3{,}200$ square *sazheni*
household circle desiatina	$60 \times 60 = 3{,}600$ square *sazheni*
hundred desiatina	$100 \times 100 = 10{,}000$ square *sazheni*
melon field	$80 \times 100 = 800$ square *sazheni*

In the system of cossack land tenure established in the *19th century*, one of the last survivals of feudalism, each male cossack was entitled to 30 *desiatiny*, although in practice, it varied from 9 to 23.

After the adoption of the metric system, the use of the desiatina was limited by a decree of the Sovnarcom on *14 September 1918*, and it was finally abolished altogether, effective *1* September 1927.

decibel (db or dB)

The SI unit of acoustical or electrical power ratio, amplitude level difference, sound pressure lever, sound reduction index and sound intensity level. Although the **bel** is officially the unit, this is usually regarded as being too large, so decibel is preferred. The difference between the two power levels, P_1 and P_2, is given as follows: $10 \log_{10} (P_1/P_2)$ decibels and for amplitude difference Q_1 and Q_2:

$20 \log_{10} (Q_1/Q_2)$ decibels

Note: 1. In audio systems, the logarithmic scale is convenient since between the thresholds of audibility and feeling, the sound intensity increases in the ration of 1 to 10^{12}. One decibel represents an increase in the intensity of 26%, which is about the smallest change that the ear can detect. In using the decibel scale, the intensity with which a note is compared is usually the threshold in the intensity of a note of the same frequency; in this case, the relative magnitude of the note is called its sensation level.

2. Sometimes, the decibel is accompanied by one or more letters to indicate special usage, e.g., dB(A) for "A-weighted bB." It is preferred in such cases to add the distinguishing term to the name and the distinguishing letter as a subscript to the symbol, of the relevant quantity. For example, A-weighted sound pressure level L_{pA} = 80 dB rather than sound pressure level L_p = 80 dB (A). (See, also, decibel above 1 femtowatt, decibel above 1 kilowatt,..).

3. The following namex have been suggested in recent years for the decibel: logit (in 1952), decilog (in 1954), decomlog (in 1954), decilu (in 1954) and decilit (in 1955).

See *"logit," "decomlog", "decilu", "decilit"* and also *"perceived noise decibel"*.

decibel above 1 femtowatt (dBf)

A power level equal to 10 times the common logarithm of the ratio of the given power P in watts to femtowatt (1 femtowatt = 10^{-15} watts)

Power level in dBf = 10 log $_{10}$ ($P/10^{-15}$).

decibel above 1 kilowatt (dBk)

A measure of power equal to 10 times the common logarithm of the ratio of a given power P to 1000 watts.

Power in dBk = 10 log $_{10}$ ($P/1000$).

decibel above 1 milliwatt (dBm)

A measure of power equal to 10 times the common logarithm of the ratio of a given power P to 0.001 watts.

Power in dBm = 10 log $_{10}$ ($P/0.001$).

A negative value, such as -2.3 dBm, means decibels below 1 milliwatt.

decibel above 1 picowatt (dBp)

A measure of power equal to 10 times the common logarithm of the ratio of a given power P to 1 picowatt.

Power in dBp = 10 log $_{10}$ ($P/10^{-12}$).

decibel above 1 volt (dBV)

A measured power level equal to the ratio of voltage V at any point in a transmission system to a reference level of volt. Voltage in dBV is given by the formula:

Voltage in dBV = 20 log $_{10}$ (V/1).

Negative values mean decibels below 1 volt.

decibel above 1 watt (dBW)

A measure power level equal to the ratio of power at any point P in a transmission system to a reference level of 1 watt. The power level in dBW is given by the formula:

Power in dBW = 10 log $_{10}$ (P/1).

Negative values mean decibels below 1 watt.

decibel above reference coupling (Dbx)

A measure of the coupling between two circuits, expressed in relation to a reference value of coupling that gives a specified reading on a specified noise-measuring set when a test tone of 90 dBa is impressed on one circuit

decibel above reference noise (dBrn)

Units used to show the relationship between the interfering effect of a noise frequency, or band of noise frequencies, and a fixed amount of noise power commonly called reference noise; a 1000 hertz tone having a power level of -90 dBm was selected as the reference noise power: superseded by adjusted decibel unit.

See also *"perceived noise decibel."*

dB Z

a unit of radar reflectivity used in meteorology. The unit measures the amount of energy returned to a weather radar site as a function of the amount transmitted. The scale is logarithmic, with a difference of 10 dB Z, indicating a 10-fold increase in energy returned. For display purposes, dB Z values are grouped as follows:

(Level 1, 18-30 dBZ) - Light precipitation

(Level 2, 30-38 dBZ) - Light to moderate rain

(Level 3, 38-44 dBZ) - Moderate to heavy rain

(Level 4, 44-50 dBZ) - Heavy rain

(Level 5, 50-57 dBZ) - Very heavy rain; hail possible

(Level 6, >57 dBZ) - Very heavy rain and hail; large hail possible

The colorful "radar images" shown on television are actually plots of these levels.

decilit

Unit of intensity level, equal to the decibel.

1 decilit = 1 decibel

Note: 1. This was one of several names proposed as alternatives for the decibel, but almost never employed.

2. The name of the unit was proposed in 1955 by Bell Telephone Laboratories and it is from the ***decil**ogarithmic **unit.***

See also, *"decilog", "decilu" and "decomlog".*

decilog

Unit of intensity level, equal to the decibel.

1 decilog = 1 decibel

Note: 1. This was one of several names proposed as alternatives for the decibel, but almost never employed.

2. Decilog is used by Rose as a unit of his scale of pressure. In this scale, the decilog in pressure is analogous to the decibel in sound.

See also, *"decilit", "decilu" and "decomlog".*

decilu

Unit of intensity level, equal to the decibel.

1 decilu = 1 decibel

Note: 1. This was one of several names proposed as alternatives for the decibel, but almost never employed.

See also, *"decilit", "decilog" and "decomlog".*

decimal candle

An obsolete unit of luminous intensity was first defined on *21 May 1889* at the Second International Electrical Congress (Paris). Its value was set at $\frac{1}{20}^{\text{th}}$ of a violle, a choice which made it nominally equivalent to the British Parliamentary candle.

In *1896*, the International Electrotechnical Congress in Geneva redefined the decimal candle as equal to the output of a standard Hefner lamp. The Conference of Photometricians (Geneva) redefined it as equal to 1 hefner.

In *1906*, the Laboratoire Central de l'Electricitè (Paris) defined the decimal candle by saying the output of a Carcel lamp burning colza oil at a rate of 42 grams per hour was 9.6 decimal candles.

In *1909*, the Laboratoire Central de l'Electricitè (France), the National Physical Laboratory (Britain), the Bureau of Standards (United States) and the Physicalische Technische Reichanstalt (Germany) redefined the unit and renamed it the international candle.

decimilligrade (.. ^{cc})

Unit of plane angle. It is equal to 10^{-4} grades.

1 decimilligrade = 10^{-4} grades

Note: This unit should be called one hundredth of a centigrade; also called centesimal second.

See *"centigrade, one hundredth of a"* and *"centesimal second."*

deciliter (dl or dL)

a fairly common metric unit of volume equal to 0.1 liter or 100 cubic centimeters. A deciliter contains 6.10237 cubic inches, 3.38140 U.S. fluid ounces, or 3.519 British fluid ounces. The deciliter is similar in size to the gill, an old English unit of volume. The deciliter is commonly used in medicine to express blood volume in units of concentration, such as micrograms per deciliter (μg/dL).

decimal foot

an informal term sometimes used in surveying and construction in the United States. The decimal foot is the same as an ordinary foot, but it is divided decimally instead of being divided into 12 inches. 1 inch is equal to 1/12 = 0.0833333... ft.

decimeter (dm)

a fairly common metric unit of distance equal to 10 centimeters or 3.9370 inches. The decimeter is very close to the hand, a traditional English unit.

decimillimeter (dmm)

a metric unit of distance equal to 0.1 millimeters (10^{-4} meters) or about 3.937 <u>mils</u>. The unit is used in civil engineering for stating the results of penetration tests of asphalt concrete, in which a needle is pushed into the concrete under specified conditions.

Although this unit is allowed by some standards agencies, the use of compound prefixes such as decimilli- is not permitted in the SI.

decipascal second (dPa·s)

a unit of dynamic viscosity equal to 0.1 pascal seconds (Pa·s) or 1 poise. This rather clumsy SI unit is occasionally used because of its equivalence with the poise, an older unit not allowed in the SI.

decipol

an empirical unit of ventilation describing the rate at which polluted indoor air is mixed with outdoor air.

One decipol obtains when indoor air that is being polluted at a rate of 1 olf is diluted with 10 liters per second of unpolluted air. Also, it is defined, as one olf is defined as the indoor odor intensity produced by one "standard person," and one decipol is the perceived odor intensity level in a space having an odor source of strength one olf and ventilation at the rate of 10 liters/second with unpolluted air. Measurements are recorded by human observers using protocols laid out by Fanger and his colleagues.

It is introduced by the Danish environmental scientist P.O. Fanger in 1988.

decitex (dtex)

a common metric unit of yarn density equal to 0.1 tex, 0.9 denier (see below), or 0.1 milligrams per meter. This unit was previously called the **drex**.

decitonne (dt or dtn)

A metric unit of mass or weight equal to 100 kilograms (approximately 220.4623 pounds). This unit is becoming common in international trade; it is the same as the Russian centner, the German doppelzentner (see below), and the French metric quintal.

decomlog

Unit of intensity level, equal to the decibel.

1 decomlog = 1 decibel.

Note: This is one of several names proposed as alternatives for the decibel but almost never employed.

See *"decilit", "decilog" and "decilu"*.

deg

Deprecated abbreviation for degree when used as a unit of temperature interval or difference. If unspecified by the addition of another letter, it refers to degree Kelvin or degree Celsius, as degK = degC.

degC

Deprecated abbreviation for degree Celsius when used as a unit of temperature interval.

degF

Deprecated abbreviation for degree Fahrenheit when used as a unit of temperature interval. See *"Fahrenheit degree"*.

degK

Deprecated abbreviation for degree Kelvin when used as a unit of temperature interval.

degR

Deprecated abbreviation for degree Rankine when used as a unit of temperature interval.

degre'

Unit of time. Also called ce' or degree (of time).

See *"ce" and degree (of time)"*.

degree (deg)

Deprecated unit of temperature interval

See *"deg"*.

degree (...^{0})

Unit of the geometrical plane angle used with SI system. It is equal to (1/360) of a full rotation.

$1° = (1/360)$ of a full rotation $= 2\pi/320$ radians

Note: 1. The degree is usually subdivided into minutes and seconds. It can be subdivided decimally so that, e.g., 4° 7' 30" is written as 4.125°. The degree with its subdivision is recommended for use when radian is not suitable.

2. When using decimal fractions of a degree, the unit symbol (°) is placed after the figures, e.g., 4.125°. In astronomical work, it generally precedes the decimal point, e.g., 4°. 125.

3. When using the degree to describe latitude and longitude, it is required to have a reference. Degrees of latitude have been measured from an arbitrary zero at the terrestrial equator since the beginning of the sixteenth century. The zero for degrees of longitude varied from country to country until it was agreed at the Meridian Conference held at Washington in 1884 that longitude be measured from an arbitrary zero at Greenwich.

degree (of Hardness)

Unit of hardness of water.

1. <u>English degree or Clark degree (°Clark):</u>

Is defined as 1 part of calcium carbonate to 70 000 parts of water, alternatively, 1 grain of calcium carbonate to 1 gallon of water.

2. <u>French degree:</u>

Is defined as 1 part of calcium carbonate to 100 000 parts of water:

3. <u>German degree:</u>

Is defined as 1 part of calcium oxide to 100 000 parts of water.

The descriptive terms soft, slightly hard, moderately hard and very hard are usually used. The ranges of these terms are as follows:

	Hardness		
Descriptive term	In the U.K.		In the U.S.
	°Clark	ppm	ppm
Soft	0	0	0
Slightly hard	5	70	55
Moderately hard	10	140	100
Very hard	15	210	200
	>15	>210	.200

Note: ppm is the abbreviation of "part per million."

See *"degree Clark".*

degree (of Time)

Arbitrary unit of time.

1 degree = 0.01 days = **864** seconds

Note: This is a metric unit suggested for the measurement of time. It was suggested in 1900 to divide the day into 100 parts, each to be called a degree. The degree was subdivided into grades, namely decigrade, centigrade, milligrade and decimilligrade. This system has almost never been used. It is also called the ce'.

degree absolute

Deprecated name of Kelvin

See *"Kelvin"*.

degree of American petroleum industry (degree API)

Unit of relative density. It is defined as: the relative density d of a liquid in degrees API is related to the density relative to water S60/60, both liquids being at 60°F by the defining equation;

If S is the specific gravity of the petroleum at temperature of 60 °F (15.56 °C), the API degree rating is equal to d = (141.5/S) - 131.5 degrees.

See also *"degree Baume'" and "degree Twaddell."*

degree Baume' (°B)

Unit of relative density. The relative density d of a liquid in degrees Baume' is related to the density relative to water s15/15, both liquids being at 15°C by the defining equations:

1. For relative densities less than 1:

$$d = \frac{144.3}{S15/15} - 144.3$$

2. For relative densities greater than 1:

$$d = 144.3 - \frac{144.3}{S15/15}$$

See also *"degree AIP" and "degree Twaddell."*

degree CELSIUS (°C)

SI unit of Celsius temperature and temperature interval. It is defined as 1/100 of the interval between the freezing and boiling points of pure air-free water, both under pressure of one standard atmosphere.

It is related to the other temperature scales by the relations:

For temperatures:

$$T°C = (T + 273.15) \text{ K} = (1.8\,T + 32)\ °F = (1.8\,T + 491.67)\ °R$$

For temperature intervals:

$1\,^\circ C = 1\,K = 1.8\,^\circ F = 1.8\,^\circ R$

Note: 1. In the above expressions: K = Kelvin, °F = degree Fahrenheit, and °R = degree Reaumur.

2. The use of the word centigrade for the Celsius temperature scale was abandoned by the "Conference Generale des Poids et Mesures" in 1948.

3. The word centigrade is still employed by meteorologists in the U.K. The use of the term centigrade should be restricted to the unit 0.1 grade.

degree centigrade

See *"degree Celsius"*.

degree Clark (°Clark)

Arbitrary unit of water hardness. 1 °Clark represents 1 grain of calcium carbonate in one imperial gallon of water. Alternatively, it represents 1 part of calcium carbonate to 70,000 parts of water.

Note: 1. This unit is equivalent to the English degree.

2. It is tending to be displaced by the use of "parts per million (ppm)."

See also *"degree (of hardness)."*

degree -day

Any of the various units of measurement that represent one degree of variation from a given standard temperature on a given day; for example, cooling degree-day, heating degree-day, and growing degree-day; used in calculating air-conditioning, heating, and agricultural needs, respectively.

degree Fahrenheit (°F)

Unit of Fahrenheit temperature and temperature interval. It is related to the other temperature scales by the relations:

For temperatures:

For temperatures:

$T\,^\circ F = (5/9)\,[T + 459.67]\,K = (5/9)[T + 32]\,^\circ C = (T + 459.670)\,^\circ R$

For temperature intervals:

$1\,^\circ F = (5/9)\,K = (5/9)\,^\circ F = 1\,^\circ R$

Note: 1. In the above expressions: K = Kelvin, °C = degree Celsius, and °R = degree

Reaumur.

See "Appendix-3"

degree Kelvin (^{o}K)

Former SI unit of thermodynamic temperature. The name of this unit was changed at the 13th CGPM, 1967, to kelvin and its symbol to K.

See *"kelvin"* and "Appendix- 3".

degree square

Unit of solid angle.

1 square degree = $(\pi/180)^2$ steradians.

degree per second (^{0}s^{-1})

Unit of angular velocity.

1 degree per second = 1.745 33 x 10^{-2} radians per second.

degree per second squared (^{o}s^{-2})

Unit of angular acceleration. It is the angular acceleration of a body, the angular velocity of which changes by one degree per second in one second.

1 degree per second square = 1.745 33 x 10^{-2} radians per second square.

degree KMW (°KMW)

a unit used in Austria to measure the sugar content of must, the unfermented liquor from which wine is made. One degree KMW is roughly equivalent to 1% sugar by weight or 5° Oe; for the exact conversion, see below under degree Oeschle. KMW is an abbreviation for Klosterneuburger Mostwaage (Klosterneuburg Must Scale).

degree Lovibond (°L)

a unit used in the U.S. to measure the color (really the darkness) of beer and honey. The scale is open-ended, but most readings fall between 1 (a very light gold or yellow) and 25 (a very dark brown).

degree MacMichael (°McM)

a unit used to measure the viscosity, or thickness, of chocolate. Typical values range from around 60 °McM (very thin chocolates suitable for pouring into molds) to around 190

°McM (very thick chocolates suitable for hand dipping or forming around a center). A MacMichael viscometer is used to make the measurement.

degree Oechsle (°Oe)

a unit used in Germany and Switzerland to measure the sugar content of must, the unfermented liquor from which wine is made. One degree Oechsle (or Öchsle) is roughly equivalent to 0.2% sugar by weight. This unit is related legally to °KMW by the formula °Oe = °KMW * ([.022 * °KMW] + 4.54).

degree Plato (°P)

a unit measuring sugar content, especially of the wort, the unfermented liquor from which beer is made. Named for a German chemist, one degree Plato represents a sugar content equivalent to 1% sucrose by weight. Not all the sugar in a wort is sucrose; the unit standardizes the measurement to the sucrose equivalent. The reading is made with a device called a saccharometer. The **degree Balling** is a somewhat older unit equivalent (approximately) to the degree Plato. In Europe, beer is often taxed either by the degree Plato or by the actual alcohol content. There is no precise conversion between these quantities, but for tax purposes, it is often assumed that 1% alcohol (1 degree [6], see above) is equivalent to 2.5 degrees Plato; that is, 1 degree Plato is legally equivalent to 0.4% alcohol.

degree Quevenne (°Q)

a unit measuring the density of milk. 1 degree Quevenne represents a difference in specific gravity of 0.001, so, for example, 20 °Q milk has a specific density of 1.020.

degree Rankine (°R)

Unit of Rankine temperature (thermodynamic temperature) and temperature interval.

1. For temperature; The temperature T_R in degree Rankine is related to the corresponding temperature T_F in degree Fahrenheit and to that in kelvin T_K by the relations:

$$T_R = (5/9)\, T_K = T_F + 459.67$$

2. For temperature interval:

$$1\,°R = (5/9)\,K = (5/9)\,°C = 1\,°F$$

Note: 1. From the definition, 0°R = 0 K.

2. The freezing point of pure air-free water is 491.67°R (both under a pressure of one standard atmosphere).

See also *"Rankine degree"* and Appendix-3.

degree Reaumur (°r)

Arbitrary unit of customary temperature. The temperature in T_R degree Reaumur is related to the temperature T_C in degree Celsius by the formula.

$$T_r = (4/5) \, T_c$$

The temperature intervals on the two scales are related by the same formula.

Note: 1. The temperature T_r is related to the temperature T_K in kelvin by the formula:

$$T_r = (4/5) \, T_K - 218.52.$$

Accordingly, $0°r = 273.15 \text{ K}$.

2. The freezing point of pure air-free water is $0°r$ and its boiling point is $80°r$ (both under a pressure of one standard atmosphere).

See *"Reaumur degree"* and "Appendi- 3".

degree Sikes (degree sikes)

Arbitrary unit of concentration. This is an arbitrary measurement which, used in conjunction with a set of tables, gives the concentration of an alcohol/water mixture:

0   degree Sikes corresponds to   66.7 over proof

10   degree Sikes corresponds to   58.4 over proof

100   degree Sikes corresponds to   pure water

Note: Proof spirit is spirit (i.e., alcohol/water mixture) with a density 12/13 of that pure distilled water, both liquids at 51 °F. Its relative density (60°F/60°F) is 0.919 76, there being, at this temperature, 49.28% alcohol by mass (57.10% alcohol by volume). On dilution, 100 volumes of the spirit of strength P over proof yields (100 + P) volumes of proof spirit.

degree TWADDELL (°Tw)

Unit of relative density. The relative density d of a liquid in degrees Twaddell is related to the density relative to water S60/60, both liquids being at 60 °F, by the defining equation:

$$d = 200 \, (S60/60 - 1).$$

See *"degree API"* and *"degree Baume"*.

deka – or dek - (deka)

Metric prefix meaning "ten" as in dekaliter (10 liters), dekagramme (10 gram), 10 dekameter (10 meters) and dekapoize (10 poise).

See *"deca-"*.

dekagram or decagram (dag)

A common metric unit of mass, the dekagram is frequently used in European food recipes. One dekagram is equal to 10 grams, 0.01 kilograms, or 0.352 739 66 ounces. The symbol **dkg** sometimes used for this unit is incorrect.

dekaliter or decaliter (daL or dal)

a metric unit of volume equal to 10 liters and comparable to the English peck. The dekaliter is equal to about 2.641 72 U.S. liquid gallons, 1.135 10 U.S. pecks, or 2.199 69 British Imperial gallons (1.099 85 British pecks). The symbol **dkL,** sometimes used for this unit, is incorrect.

dekameter or decameter (dam)

A common metric unit of distance equal to 10 meters (about 32.8084 feet). The symbol **dkm,** sometimes used for this unit, is incorrect.

dekanewton or decanewton (daN)

a fairly common metric unit of force equal to 10 newtons. The dekanewton is equal to 1 megadyne, to 1.019 716 kilograms of force (kgf) or kiloponds (kp), to 2.248 09 pounds of force (lbf), and to 72.3301 poundals. In engineering, the dekanewton is a convenient substitute for the kilogram of force or kilopond, since it is nearly equal to those units.

dekan

a unit of angle measure equal to 10° or 1/36 circle. The ancient Egyptians divided the circle of the Zodiac into 36 divisions, which the Greeks called dekans. The unit is still used occasionally in astrology, where one dekan equals 1/3 sign.

dekare, dekar, or decare

A metric unit of area equal to 10 ares, that is, 1000 square meters or 0.1 hectare. In English units, the dekare equals approximately 10 763.91 square feet, 1195.99 square yards, or 0.247 105 acres. Various traditional units of land area have been identified with the dekare, including the Middle Eastern dunum (see below), the Norwegian mål, the Greek stremma, and the Vietnamese cong.

See also, "are", "hectare", "acre."

dekatherm or decatherm (DTH)

a unit of energy equal to 10 therms, 1 million-Btu, or about 1.055 057 gigajoules (GJ). This unit is used in the energy industry as a synonym for the million-Btu (MM Btu).

See also, "Btu," "Joul."

demal (D)

Metric- derived unit for concentration. It is defined as the concentration of one gram-equivalent of solute in one cubic decimeter of solvent.

1demal = 1 g-eq/dm^3 = 1 kilogram equivalent per cubic meter.

denier

Metric unit for the density. The denier is defined as the line density of a thread that has a mass of gram and a length of 9000 m.

1 denier = (1/9000) gram per meter.

Note: 1. This unit is used mainly in the textile industry as a measure of yarn count.

2. It is better to use the unit **"tex"** instead of denier.

See also *"tex"* and *"drex"* also *"yarn number."*

desiccant unit (DU)

a unit measuring the amount of a drying agent. One desiccant unit is the amount of the drying agent that can absorb 3 grams of water at a relative humidity of 20% and 6 grams at a relative humidity of 40% when the temperature is between 21 °C (69.8 °F) and 25 °C (77 °F). (Different industrial standards differ slightly in the temperature specification.)

dessertspoon or dessertspoonful (dsp or dssp)

a unit of volume sometimes used in food recipes. The dessertspoon is equal to 2 teaspoons; this is roughly equivalent to 10 milliliters in the U.S. In the metric world, a measuring spoon holding exactly 10 milliliters is often called a dessertspoon.

dessiatina

a traditional unit of land area in Russia equal to 2400 square sadzhens. By coincidence, this makes the dessiatina very nearly the same as a hectare: it equals about 1.0925 hectare or 2.6996 acres.

See also *"acre", "hectare" and "sadzhens."*

deuce

an old English word for two, derived from the old French *deus* (now spelled *deux*). The word survives as the name for a two-spot showing in dice or a two card in card games. In tennis, "deuce" describes a tie situation in which a player must win the next two points in order to win the game.

dex

Unit of logarithmic value. For a value of 10^x, the size of the value is given as x brig. The brig is related to the decibel, the neper and the octave by the relations:

1 brig = 10 dB

1 brig = In 10 neper ≈ 2.302 59 neper,

1 brig = (1/log 2) octave ≈ 3.321 93 octave

Note: 1. This unit is also called brig.

2. The name of the unit is derived from the words *d*ecimal *ex*ponent.

See also *"brig"*.

dezitonne

German unit of mass. It is equal to 100 kilograms.

1 denzitonne = **100** kilograms.

Note: it is the German name of the **quintal**

See also *"quintal"*.

dhur

a traditional unit of land area in South Asia, equal to 1/20 kattha or 1/400 bigha. Like the bigha, the dhur varied in size from one region to another. In Nepal, where the unit is still in use, the dhur equals about 16.9 square meters or 20.2 square yards.

See also *"kattha" and "bigha."*

dialogue unit (dlu)

a unit of relative distance used in computer graphics. Actually, there are two units: the horizontal dialogue unit equals 1/4 the average width of the font being used, and the vertical dialogue unit equals 1/8 the average height of the font. If the font's aspect ratio (the ratio of height to width) is 2:1, these two units will be the same. This is often the case. The unit is used particularly in the design of dialog boxes.

diastatic index

A unit that measures the activity of the enzyme diastase. Diastase was the first enzyme to be discovered and is actually the group of amylases, enzymes that convert starches to sugars. One diastase unit is the amount of enzyme which will convert 0.01 gram of starch to the prescribed end-point in 1 hour at 40°C. Symbol DN. The diastatic index is usually measured by the Schade method (now modified by White and Pairent and Hadorn and Zürcher), and the unit is also called the Schade unit or the Gothe unit.

The unit mainly occurs in tests of honey. To greatly oversimplify an exacting procedure, the honey is mixed with a starch solution and iodine added at intervals. As in the familiar school experiment, iodine turns the starch blue. Diastase converts the starch to sugar; the more starch converted to sugar, the less blue. The time needed for the solution to reach an absorbance of 0.235 (0.301 in the German standard) is noted. 300 divided by the time in minutes gives the DN number.

In recent years, the Schade test has been replaced by a method using Phadebas tablets, which gives more consistent results. The determinations are usually converted to Schade units.

A major use of the index is controlling the quality of honey. In Europe, for example, the minimum permitted DN for honey is 8 DN per gram. The *Codex Alimentarius* also recommends this level "for voluntary application by commercial partners," and since honeys from certain species of flower naturally have much lower levels of diastase, for those "not less than 3 Schade Units".

digit

a historic unit of distance equal to the width of a person's finger. Used in all the ancient civilizations of the Middle East and Mediterranean, the digit was equal to 0.75 inch or 19 millimeters with only the smallest variations. Typically, there were 4 digits in a palm, 16 in a foot, and 24 (sometimes 28) in a cubit. The word digit is from the Latin word for a finger or toe, *digitus*.

See also, "cubit", "palm," "foot."

digitus

An ancient Roman unit of length, about 18.48 millimeters

dimension (dim)

a mathematical unit measuring the number of independent directions in a set or space. Traditionally, a space has as many dimensions as there are mutually perpendicular directions at each point in the space: thus, a line has 1 dimensions, a plane has 2 dimensions, and the ordinary space we live in has 3 dimensions. The theory of relativity is set in a "space-time" having 4 dimensions, and higher dimensional spaces are frequently used in science and economics. In addition, mathematicians have developed several methods for assigning fractional dimensions to certain complex sets.

dioptre

SI unit for reciprocal length and it is used especially as a unit for the power of a lens. In general, one dioptre is the reciprocal of a distance which has a length of one meter. In particular, it is the power of a lens which has a focal length of one meter.

1dioptre = 1/m

Note: 1. It is also applicable to vergence and curvature, convergence bring regarded as positive.

2. The idea of defining the power of the lens as the reciprocal of its focal length was introduced for the first time by Nagel in 1868. The dioptre was adapted as a unit in 1875.

diraa

a traditional Egyptian unit of distance equal to about 58 centimeters (22.8 inches).

dish

In Derbyshire, England, *13ᵗʰ – 20ᵗʰ centuries*, a unit of capacity used for lead ore since *1851* was about 520.16 cubic inches.

A document of *1288* says the miner's measure is 14 Winchester pints. Taking each pint at about 33.75 cubic inches makes the dish about 472.5 cubic inches. In *1513,* a bronze prototype called the Wirksworth Dish was made, probably in the form of measures already used by the miners. From this standard, the miners made oak troughs for everyday use.

Two Wirksworth Dishes survive, one in the Science Museum in London and the other in the Derby Industrial Museum. Which is the prototype and which a copy is not certain. The Derby example has a capacity of 464.40 cubic inches and the London one has 487.2 cubic inches.

Sometime before *1820,* the size of the dish began to differ between the Low Peak district, where it was still 14 pints, and the High Peak District, where it was 16 pints.

The High Peak Mining Customs and Mineral Courts Act of *1851* (14 and 15 Victoria c 94) provided that the dish in the High Peak should contain 15 pints. These would be imperial pints, making the dish 520.16 cubic inches. An act of the following year said that if the prototype was ever lost, the Wirksworth local council was also to switch to the 15 imperial pints' standard.

Dobson unit (DU)

a unit used in geophysics to measure the ozone in the atmosphere. One Dobson unit represents the amount of atmospheric ozone that would form a uniform layer 0.01 millimeters (10 micrometers) thick at standard temperature (0 °C) and pressure (1 atmosphere or 1013.25 millibars). The Dobson unit equals 10^{-5} atmo-meters. Under normal conditions, the atmosphere contains about 300 Dobson units of ozone, but this falls to 100 Dobson units or less in the "ozone holes" over the Earth's poles. The unit is named for the British physicist G.M.B. Dobson; in 1920, he invented a spectrometer to measure ozone concentrations from the ground.

dog watch

a unit of time on ships at sea equal to 2 hours, one half the usual length of a watch.

dog year

an informal unit of time equal to 1/7 of a normal or "human" year. According to folklore, dogs age 7 times faster than humans.

dol

a unit proposed for the measurement of pain. James Hardy, Herbert Wolff, and Helen Goodell, all of Cornell University, proposed the unit based on their studies of pain during the 1940s and 1950s; they defined one dol to equal 2 "just noticeable differences" (jnd's) in pain. However, the unit did not come into widespread use and other methods are now used to assess the level of pain experienced by patients. The name of the unit is from the Latin word for pain, *dolor*.

dollar

Unit of reactivity, i.t. the departure of a nuclear reactor from its critical condition. It is the amount of reactivity equal to the delayed neutron fraction.

Alternatively, the amount of activity required to make a nuclear reactor critical using only prompt neutrons.

1 dollar = 100 cents.

Note: 1. The delayed neutron fraction is the ratio of the mean number of delayed neutrons per fission to the mean total number of neutrons per fission.

2. The unit was first suggested in the 1940s.

See *"cent"*.

donkey power

Metric unit for power.

1 donkey power = 250 watts.

Note: The unit was first proposed in 1884.

drachm (drachm in U.K., and dram ap in U.S.)

Imperial unit of mass. It is equal to 1/8 of the apothecaries' ounce.

1 drachm = (1/8) apothecaries' ounce = 3.8879346×10^{-3} kilograms.

Note: 1. In U.S., the unit is called dram.

2. The drachm is one of three imperial units used in the scale of drugs. The other two are the scruple and the **apothecaries ounce.**

See *"scruple"* and *"ounce apothecaries."*

double word or double word

a unit of information equal to 2 short words, 4 bytes or 32 bits. See also word [2].

douzième

a traditional unit of distance used in watchmaking. The word is French for "twelfth," and a douzième is equal to 1/12 Swiss ligne. This is about 188 micrometers (microns) or 7.4 mils.

dozen (doz or dz)

a familiar unit of quantity equal to 12. Division into units of 12 rather than 10 has the advantage that 12 can be evenly divided into halves, thirds, or quarters. For this reason, units of 12 have been common since the earliest civilizations of the Middle East. "Dozen" comes from an old French word *dozaine,* related to the Latin word *duodecem*, "twelve." One dozen (that is, 144) is called a gross, and one dozen gross is called a great gross.

dram (dr)

Imperial unit of mass. It is equal to one sixteenth of the avoirdupois ounce.

1dram = (1/16) ounce (avoirdupois) = 0.00177185 kilograms

Note: The unit is used in U.K. There is no corresponding U.S. unit. The U.S. unit called dram is the same as the U.K. unit called drachm.

See *"drachm"*.

dram, fluid (fl dr)

1. Arbitrary U.K. unit of volume used for measurement of liquid subsistence and occasionally of solid substance.

   1 U.K. fl dr = (1/8) U.K. fluid ounce = 3.355163×10^{-6} cubic meters.

2. Imperial U.S. unit of volume used for the measurement of liquid subsistence.

   1 U.S. fl dr = (1/8) U.S. fluid ounce = $3.6966911953 \times 10^{-6}$ kilograms.

Note: The unit is also known as *"fluid drahm"*.

dray barrel (bbl)

See *"barrel, dry"*.

dray pint (dry pt)

See *"pint, dry"*.

dray quart (U.S.) (dr qt)

See *"quart, dry"*.

drex

Metric unit of line density. It is defined as the line density of the thread, which has a mass of one gram and a length of ten kilometers.

1 drex = 0.1 g/km

Note: 1. The unit is used mainly in the textile industry as a measure of yarn count.

2. It is better to use the unit **"tex"** instead of denier.

See *"denier"* and *"tex"*.

drill sizes

Traditional drill sizes are numbers 1-80, with larger numbers indicating smaller drills. Number 1 has a diameter of 0.2280 inches and number 80 has a diameter of 0.0135 inches. Larger sizes are designated by letters or by specifying the diameter directly in 64ths of an inch. The metric drill size is the diameter in millimeters. EngineersEdge.com has a table showing the traditional sizes and metric equivalents.

drink

a unit measuring the alcohol content of beverages used in describing the medical effects of alcohol. U.S. physicians generally consider one drink equal to 0.5 U.S. fluid ounces of alcohol; the appropriate metric equivalent would be 15 milliliters. In U.S. fluid units, one drink corresponds to about 4 ounces of wine, 10-12 ounces of beer, or 1.25 ounces of whiskey.

In Australia, a legal unit, the quantity of any alcoholic beverage that contains 10 grams of ethanol (ethyl alcohol). A bottle's label must state the number of drinks it contains.

drap

a traditional unit of weight in Scotland, equal to 1/16 Scots ounce or about 1.9 grams. Sometimes spelled **drop**, this unit was the Scottish counterpart of the English dram [1].

drop (gtt) [1]

a unit of volume used in pharmacy. Traditionally, the drop was another name for a minim, a unit of volume equal to 1/60 fluid dram or 1/480 fluid ounce (about 0.0616 milliliter in the U.S., 0.0592 milliliters in Britain). Now that prescriptions are written in metric units, the pharmacist's drop is equal to exactly 0.05 milliliter (20 drops/ml). In hospitals, intravenous tubing is used to deliver medication in drops of various sizes ranging from 10 drops/ml to 60 drops/ml. The traditional abbreviation is from the Latin *gutta*, drop. Originally, **gt** was the symbol for a single drop, with **gtt** being the plural.

See also "fluid dram," and "fluid ounce."

drop [2]

an informal unit of volume used in recipes. According to some older kitchen references, 24 drops = 1/4 teaspoon; with U.S. definitions, this makes the drop equal to 1/576 fluid ounce or about 0.051 milliliters, comparable to the pharmacist's drop (previous entry).

See also, "teaspoon."

drought severity category (D)

a measure of drought severity developed by the U.S. National Drought Mitigation Center and used widely by other agencies in the U.S. Categories are denoted D0-D5, with higher numbers indicating more severe drought. The Center has a description of the scale.

DUFFIEUX

SI unit of angular spatial frequency.

Note: The name is after P.M. Duffieux and was suggested for the first time in 1973.

See also *"abbe"*.

duty (duty)

FIbfS unit of energy. It is defined as the work done when the point of application of a force of one pound-force (Ibf) is displaced through a distance of one foot in the direction of the force.

1 duty = 1 ft Ibf = 1.355 817 948 331 400 4 joules.

Note: 1. The unit was introduced by J. Watt (1738-1819)

3. It is better to use **foot pound-force** in place of this unit.

dyne (dyne)

CGS unit of force. It is the force which, when applied to a body of mass one gram, gives it an acceleration of one centimeter per second squared.

1 dyne = 10^{-5} Newton.

See also *"dyne, large"*.

Note: The following table shows some units related to the dyne.

Unit	Unit Symbol	Quantity measured	Corresponding SI unit	To convert to SI, multiply by:
Dyne centimeter	dyn. cm	CGS unit of moment of force	Newton meter (N.m)	10^{-7}
Dyne centimeter per biot	dyn. cm/Bi	CGSB unit of magnetic flux	Weber (Wb)	10^{-8}
Dyne centimeter per second	dyn.cm/s	CGS unit of momentum	Kilogram meter squared per second (kg. m^2/s)	10^{-7}
Dyne per biot centimeter	dyn/Bi.cm	CGSB unit of magnetic flux density; magnetic polarization	Tesla (T)	10^{-4} 1.256064 x 10^{-3}
Dyne per biot squared	dyn/Bi^2	CGSB unit of permeability	Henry per meter (H/m)	1.256 64x10^{-6}
Dyne per centimeter	dyn/cm	CGS unit of surface tension	Newton per meter (N/m)	10^{-3}
Dyne per cubic centimeter	dyn/Bi^3	CGS unit of specific weight	Newton per cubic meter (N/m^3)	10
Dyne per franklin	dyn/Fr	CGSF unit of electric field strength	Volt per meter	2.997 92x10^4
Dyne per square centimeter	dyn/cm^2	CGS unit of pressure	Pascal (Pa)	10^{-1}
Dyne second	dyn/s	CGS unit of momentum	Kilogram meter per second (kg.m/s)	10^{-5}
Dyne second per centimeter	dyn.s/cm	CGS unit of mechanical impedance	Newton second per meter (N.s/m)	10^{-3}

Dyne second per centimeter cubed	dyn.s/cm^3	CGS unit of specific acoustic impedance	Pascal second per meter (Pa.s/m)	**10**
Dyne seconder per centimeter to the fifth power	dyn.s/cm^5	CGS unit of specific acoustic impedance	Pascal second per meter cubic (Pa.s/ cm^3)	**10^5**
Dyne second per square centimeter	Dyn.s/cm^2 or Poise	CGS unit of dynamic viscosity	Pascal second (Pa.s)	**10^{-1}**

E

e [1]

a symbol for the electric charge on one electron. Since the charges on other particles in atomic physics are whole-number multiples of this charge, the symbol *e* is often used as a unit of measure. In November 2018, CGPM adopted a new definition of the ampere by specifying a fixed value of *e* is equal to approximately $1.602\ 176\ 634 \times 10^{-19}$ coulomb, or $160.217\ 663\ 4$ zeptocoulombs (zC).

See also "Coulomb."

e [2]

a mathematical unit used as the base of "natural" logarithms and exponentials. The real number *e* is irrational, which means that its decimal expansion is infinite and non-repeating. To 25 significant digits, *e* equals $2.718\ 281\ 828\ 459\ 045\ 235\ 360\ 287$. Of the many properties of this number, the most important is that the rate of change in the function e^x is equal to the value of the function itself: an example of the behavior we call "exponential growth." As a result, the larger the value of this function is, the faster the function grows. The Swiss mathematician Leonhard Euler (1707-1783) introduced the symbol *e*, probably because it is the first letter of the word "exponential." Other mathematicians continued to use the letter in his honor. It is sometimes called the Euler number.

e [3]

The estimated Symbol often seen following a measurement of quantity on packages of cosmetics and other products, primarily in the European Union (EU). The EU is an "average fill" jurisdiction: this means that the statement of quantity represents the average quantity in the package. (The U.S. is a "minimum fill" jurisdiction: the statement of quantity in the U.S. represents the minimum quantity in the package.) Manufacturers and suppliers using the Estimated Symbol are asserting that the product meets EU regulations, limiting the amount that the package contents can vary from the stated average.

earthquake intensity scales

One way of describing the size of an earthquake is by the amount of ground motion at a particular location. To measure ground motion requires a seismometer. Ground motion can be estimated from effects like damage to buildings or from events that people who experienced a quake typically remember, such as the ringing of church bells, or even whether they felt the earthquake at all (seated persons typically notice earthquakes that people moving around do not). A scale can be constructed whose steps are defined by the kinds of damage and events that typically occur together. With such a scale, scientists arriving at the scene of an earthquake can assign a number to the earthquake's intensity at that location by gathering witnesses' impressions.

A. Rossi-Forel Scale

In 1883, Michele Stefano de Rossi and François-Alphonse Forel published a 10-step intensity scale, which was widely used in the 19th and early 20th centuries. Measurements on this scale are prefixed with the initials "R.F.," followed by a Roman numeral. Its steps roughly correspond to those of the Mercalli Scale, except "R.F. X" lumps together steps 10 through 12 on the Mercalli scale.

B. Mercalli Scale

In 1902, Giuseppe Mercalli greatly improved the Rossi-Forel Scale by increasing the number of steps to 12 and the intensity scale has since been known as the Mercalli Scale. Further improvements were made by August Heinrich Sieberg in 1923, Harry Oscar Wood and Frank Neumann in 1931, and Charles Richter in 1956. These improvements made the descriptions less regional and more precise (instead of "buildings fall," the latest scales specified what kinds of buildings fall) and have refined the groupings to include events that occur together.

The initials "M.M." (for Modified Mercalli) are often written before the step number. Intensities on the Mercalli Scale are usually expressed in Roman numerals, a convention worth preserving because it aids in distinguishing intensity ratings from magnitude ratings.

The Modified Mercalli Scale can be used to specify the damage at some particular location but not the intensity of the earthquake in general. For example, the intensity depends a great deal on the nature of the ground. An earthquake's intensity will be much greater in a town built on a fill than in one built on granite. In 1985, for example, an earthquake 300km away caused catastrophic damage in Mexico City, but the impact was felt mainly in 15- to 25-story buildings. The buildings had a natural resonance at a period of around two seconds, and the geological conditions beneath the city picked up such waves from the quake and amplified them. If the size of the earthquake is to be described without reference to location, some other technique must be used.

Modified Mercalli Scale, 1956 version		
Intensity value	**Characteristics**	**Richter (note 1)**
I	Only detectable by seismographs. (note 2)	<3.5
II	Felt by persons at rest on upper floors or favorably placed.	3.5
III	Felt indoors. Hanging objects swing. Vibration like the passing of light trucks. Duration estimated. May not be recognized as an earthquake.	4.2
IV	Hanging objects swing. Vibration like passing of heavy trucks. Windows, dishes, and doors rattle. Parked cars rock. Glasses clink. Crockery clashes. In the upper range of IV, wooden walls and frames creak.	4.5
V	Felt outdoors; direction estimated. Sleepers awakened. Liquids disturbed, some spilled. Small unstable objects displaced or upset. Doors swing, close, open. Shutters, pictures, move. Pendulum clocks stop, start, change rate.	4.8
VI	Felt by all. Many frightened and run outdoors. Persons walk unsteadily. Windows, dishes, glassware broken. Knickknacks, books, etc., fall off shelves. Pictures fall off walls. Furniture moves or overturned. Weak plaster and masonry D cracked. Small bells ring (church, school). Trees bushes sway visibly or are heard to rustle.	5.4
VII	Difficult to stand. Noticed by drivers. Hanging objects quiver; furniture breaks; damage to masonry D, including cracks. Weak chimneys broken off at roof line. Fall of plaster, loose bricks, stones,	6.1

	tiles, cornices, unbraced parapets and architectural ornaments. Some cracks in masonry C. Waves on ponds, water turbid with mud. Small slides and caving in along sand and gravel banks. Large bells ring. Concrete irrigation ditches damaged.	
VIII	Steering of cars affected. Damage to masonry C and partial collapse; some damage to masonry B, none to masonry A. Fall of stucco and some masonry walls. Twisting, fall of chimneys, factory stacks, monuments, towers, elevated tanks. Frame houses moved on foundations if not bolted down; loose panel walls were thrown out. Decayed piling broken off. Branches broken from trees. Changes in flow or temperature of springs and wells. Cracks in wet ground and on steep slopes.	6.5
IX	General panic. Masonry D destroyed; masonry C heavily damaged, sometimes with complete collapse; masonry B seriously damaged. General damage to foundations. Frame structures, if not bolted down, shift off foundations. Frames racked. Serious damage to reservoirs. Underground pipes break. Conspicuous cracks in the ground. In alluviated areas, sand and mud ejected, earthquake fountains, sand craters.	6.9
X	Most masonry and frame structures destroyed with their foundations. Some well-built wooden structures and bridges destroyed. Serious damage to dams, dikes, and embankments. Large landslides. Water thrown on banks of canals, rivers, lakes, etc. Sand and mud shifted horizontally on beaches and flat land. Rails bent slightly.	7.3
XI	Rails bent greatly. Underground pipelines are completely out of service.	8.1
XII	Damage nearly total. Large rock masses displaced. Lines of sight and level distorted. Objects thrown into the air.	>8.1

Masonry A: shows good workmanship, mortar and design. Reinforced especially laterally, and bound together using steel, concrete, etc. It is designed to reduce lateral forces.

Masonry B: Good workmanship and mortar. Reinforced but not designed in detail to resist lateral forces.

Masonry C: Ordinary workmanship and mortar. No extreme weaknesses like failing to tie in at corners. Neither reinforced nor designed against horizontal forces.

Masonry D: Weak materials, such as adobe, poor mortar, and low standards of workmanship. Weak horizontally.

From: *Elementary Seismology*, by Charles Francis Richter. Copyright © 1958 by W. H. Freeman and Company. Reprinted with permission.

Notes

1. Any Richter scale, equivalent to a Mercalli intensity, is the best approximate since the two scales measure different things. The number given is an estimate of the Mercalli intensity experienced at or near the epicenter of the earthquake.

2. Intensity I is assigned to some quakes that were detected by people if they were very far from the epicenter and could feel the quake only because of exceptionally favorable circumstances. For example, in 1964, a few people in Seattle felt the Alaska earthquake because they were up in the Space Needle, and some people in Houston skyscrapers felt the 1985 Mexican earthquake.

earth-rate unit (eru)

A unit of angular velocity, equivalent to 15° per hour (one revolution per day), the rate at which the earth rotates on its axis. This unit is used to measure the drift rates of gyroscopes and various pointing devices in aerospace engineering.

EBHC

A unit of telecommunications traffic density, equivalent to 2 call minutes (120 call seconds) per hour, or $\frac{1}{30}$ Erlang (see below). EBHC stands for "equated busy-hour call."

eclipse year

Unit of time. The interval between two successive conjunctions of the sun with the same node of the moon's orbit. It is equivalent to 346.620 031 days in the year 1900 and increasing with 0.000032 days every century.

1 eclipse year = 346 days 14 hours 52 minutes 50.7 seconds = $2.994\ 797\ 07 \times 10^7$ seconds.

Note: It is also known as **nodical year** and also **draconic year.**

See *"year"*.

ecm

A unit of electric dipole moment used in physics. The moment of an electric dipole is the product of an electric charge and the distance of which the charge is displaced from the center of the charge. The ecm is the product of the charge e on an electron and a distance of 1 centimeter (cm). In SI units, 1 ecm = 1.602 178 x 10^{-21} coulomb meters (C·m). See also, "coulomb."

einstein unit

Arbitrary unit of photoenergy. It is equivalent to the Avogadro's number times the energy of one photon of light of the frequency in question. In other words, the photo energy E in Einstein units is related to the frequency f of the associated electromagnetic radiation in hertz by the formula:

$E = N_0\, h\, f,$

where N_0 = Avogadro's constant in atoms per mole and

h = Planck's constant in joule seconds.

Note: The unit was named after Albert Einstein (1879-1955) and it has been used since 1940.

el

The Dutch ell, a traditional unit of length, equivalent to about 68-70 centimeters (roughly 27 inches).

Note: 1. Before metrication, the *el* had several local values. The *Amsterdam el* was 687.81 millimeters. In Aksel, 750 millimeters. The *brugse el*, for raw cloth, is 70 centimeters. The *brabantse el* was 694.38 millimeters. In 1725, the latter length, under the name *Haagse el* (Hague *el*), was the official national el for everything measured in *els*.

2. In Indonesia and Surinam, el, is a unit of length, approximately 0.69 meters (approximately 27.1 inches), derived from the *haagse el* of the Netherlands.

electromagnetic units of electricity (CGSemu)

A CGS system of electric and magnetic units based on the centimeter, gram, and second in which the permeability of free space μ_0 is equated to unity. The unit magnetic pole is defined in this system as two units of the same sign, placed at a distance of 1 centimeter apart in free space, which will repel each other with the force of one dyne. The unit of current is defined as the current, which, if maintained in two straight parallel wires having infinite length and placed 1 centimeter apart in vacuum, would produce between these conductors a force of 2 dynes per centimeter length.

See also *"Practical Units of electricity"*.

electronvolt (eV)

Unit for energy used with the SI system, whose value is obtained experimentally. The electrovolt is the kinetic energy acquired by an electron passing through a potential difference of 1 volt in a vacuum.

1 eV = (1.602192 ± 0.000007) x 10^{-19} joules.

Note: 1. The electronvolt is one of four units used in the SI system, whose values are obtained experimentally. The other three units are: the *"unified atomic mass unit"*, *"astronomical unit,"* and *"parsec"*.

2. The unit electronvolt was originally known as the equivalent volt.

electronvolt per meter (eV m^{-1})

Unit for linear stopping power and linear energy transfer used in the SI system.

1 eV m^{-1} = 1.60219 x 10^{-19} Joules per meter.

electronvolt per square meter (eV m^{-2})

Unit for energy fluence used in the SI system.

1 eV m^{-2} = 1.60219 x 10^{-19} Joules per square meter.

electronvolt per square meter second (eV m^{-2} s^{-1})

Unit for energy fluence rate used in the SI system.

1 eV m^{-2} s^{-1} = 1.60219 x 10^{-19} Watts per square meter

electronvolt square meter (eV m^{2})

Unit for atomic stopping power used in the SI system.

1 eV m^{2} = 1.60219 x 10^{-19} Joules per square meter.

electronvolt square meter per kilogram (eV m^{2} kg^{-1})

Unit for mass stopping power used in the SI system.

1 eV m^{2} kg^{-1} = 1.60219 x 10^{-19} Joules per square meter per kilogram

electrostatic units of electricity (CGS-esu)

A CGS system of electric and magnetic units based on the centimeter, gram, second in which the permittivity of free space is given value, i.e., a pure number.

The unit charge in this system is defined as being two units of the same sign, placed at a distance of 1 centimeter apart in free space, repel each other with a force of 1 dyne.

The ratio of the electrostatic unit of charge to the electromagnetic unit is equivalent to $1/c$, where c = velocity of light in vacuum.

See also *"state…"* and *"electromagnetic units of electricity."*

ell

Unit of length. One ell is equivalent to 45 inches.

1 ell = 45 inches = 1.143 meters

In England, 1 ell = 20 nails = 5 quarters (of the yard) = 45 inches.

Note: In 1824, the use of the ell was prohibited by the act establishing imperial measures. It is a peculiarity of the English ell that it was never legally defined, even though since Elizabeth I, the Exchequer kept a standard (a bronze bar) and many statutes referred to it obliquely.

ell

A traditional unit of length used primarily for measuring cloth. In the English system, one ell is equivalent to 20 nails, 45 inches, or 1.25 yards (exactly 1.143 meters). This word originates from the Latin word *ulna*, which originally meant the elbow and is now the name of the bone of the forearm. The history of the unit is not clear. Some believe that the ell was originally a double forearm length, i.e., 2 cubits or 36 inches, the same length as a yard. The ell and the yard do seem to be used in some medieval documents, with *ulna* being used for both. In Scotland, the ell was equivalent to 37 Scots inches or 37.2 English inches (94.5 centimeters), only slightly longer than the yard (This Scottish length might also reflect an old practice of cloth merchants in giving an extra inch with each yard to allow for any irregular cutting at the ends of the piece). However, the English ell for cloth is definitely longer than the yard. Its length is measured from the shoulder to the fingers of the opposite hand. This reflects the practice of cloth merchants of holding the cloth at the shoulder with one hand and pulling the piece through with the opposite hand. A similar length of the cloth ell is used in France, where it was called the **aune**. The Dutch el and

German elle are a little more than half the English ell. They may represent "arm's-length" units like the Italian braccio, the Russian sadzhen, and the Turkish pik.

See also "inch", "yard", "cubit," "pik."

elle

A traditional unit of distance in German-speaking countries. The elle varied considerably but was always shorter than the English ell or French aune. A typical value in northern Germany was exactly 2 fuss (German feet), which would be close to 24 inches or 60 centimeters. In the south, the elle was usually longer, about 2.5 fuss. In Vienna, the elle was eventually standardized at 30.68 inches (77.93 centimeters). Although the German word *Elle* is often translated to "yard" in English, it is not a good equivalent.

em

A printer's unit of relative distance. One em is the height of the type size (in points) being used. If a 12-point type is set, then one em is 12 points, and so on. See *"point"*.

eman

Arbitrary unit of radioactive concentration. It is defined as a concentration of 10^{-7} curie of radioactive material in one meter of a medium

1 eman = 10^{-7} curies per cubic meter.

emerald, printers'

Unit of length used by printers to measure type size. One emerald is equivalent to 6.5 points

1 emerald = 6.5 points = 0.228 448 87 centimeters

See also *"point"* and also *"brilliant, printers' and pica."*

emu

A CGS unit of magnetic dipole moment, equivalent to 4pi micro-oersteds ($1.256\ 637 \times 10^{-5}$ Oe). In SI units, one emu is equivalent to 0.001 A·m^2.

See also, "oersted."

emu/cm^3 or emu/cc

A CGS unit of magnetization. In SI units, one emu/cm^3 can be interpreted either as $4\pi/10$ milliteslas (1.256 637 mT) as a unit of magnetic polarization or excess magnetic induction or as 1000 amperes per meter as a unit of magnetic dipole moment per unit volume.

en

A printer's unit of relative distance, equivalent to ½ em. If a 12-point type is being set, then one en is 6 points, and so on.

encablure

A traditional French unit of distance corresponding to the English cable. The encablure was equivalent to 120 brasses or 600 pieds. This is about 194.88 meters or 639.37 English feet. Most navies, including the French, now use a metric cable, equivalent to exactly 200 meters. In France, this metric unit is sometimes called the *encablure nouvelle* (new cable).

energy factor (EF)

A measure of the energy efficiency of an appliance. In the U.S., the Department of Energy has defined energy factors for a variety of appliances. For dishwashers, the energy factor is the number of cycles per kilowatt hour of power input. For cloth washers, it is the capacity of the washer in cubic feet divided by the number of kilowatt hours of power input per washing cycle. For cloth dryers, it is the number of pounds of clothes dried per kilowatt hour of power consumed.

engineer's chain

See "chain".

Engler degree

A unit of kinematic viscosity on an Engler viscometer. It is the time (in seconds) required for 200 milliliters of the liquid being tested to flow through the device. The conversion of Engler degrees to absolute units requires an appropriate table. For liquids having a viscosity of 100 centistokes or more, the Engler degree is roughly equivalent to 7.6 centistokes.

enhanced Fujita scale (EF)

The revised Fujita scale used for estimating the strength of tornados. It was implemented by the U.S. National Weather Service in 2007.

ennead

A unit of quantity, equivalent to 9, coined from the Greek word for nine, *ennea*.

enzyme unit (U or EU)

A unit used by biochemists to measure the activity of enzymes. Enzymes are proteins that are produced by living cells to facilitate the necessary chemical reactions within a cell. One enzyme unit is the quantity of enzymes needed to cause a reaction to process 1 micromole of substance per minute under specified conditions. Thus, one enzyme unit has a catalytic activity of $\frac{1}{60}$ microkatal (μkt) or 16.667 nanokatals (nkt).

See also, "mole," "katal."

energy unit (energy unit)

Arbitrary unit of radiation dose. It is defined as the dose of radiation, whose associated ionizing particles, the same energy is dissipated per gram of material as is dissipated from one rontgen of hard X- or radium gamma radiation in one gram of water. The experimentally derived value of this unit is:

1 energy unit = 0.0093 joules per kilogram.

Note: It is important to distinguish between this unit and the e-unit and the E-unit.

See also *"e-unit"* and *"E-unit."*

eon (eon)

Arbitrary unit of time. One eon is equivalent to 10^9 years.

I eon = 10^9 years

Note: This unit was suggested for the first time in 1968.

eötvös (E)

Metric unit of horizontal gradient of gravitational acceleration. One eötvös is a change in the gravitational acceleration of 10^{-9} galileo over a horizontal distance of one centimeter.

1 E = 10^{-9} Galileo per horizontal centimeter = 10^{-9} meters per second square per horizontal meter.

Note: 1. The changes in the earth's gravitational field are generally within the range of 5 to 50 eötvös.

2. The name of the unit is after Baron Ronald von Eötvös (1848-1919).

Eötvös unit (E)

A unit used in geophysics to measure the change in the acceleration of gravity with horizontal distance. One Eötvös unit is equivalent to 10^{-9} Gals per centimeter or 10^{-4} Gals per kilometer. In proper SI terms, the Eötvös unit is equivalent to 10^{-9} per second squared (s^{-2}). The unit honors the Hungarian physicist Roland von Eötvös (1848-1919).

ephah

An ancient unit of volume for grains and dry commodities used in the Bible. The ephah is equivalent to about 40.32 liters or 1.4239 cubic feet or about 1.144 U.S. bushels.

epoch [1]

A measure of time used in astronomy. In an epoch system, time is specified in years and/or fractions of years (such as epoch 1998.5). To set a starting point for a system, a specific epoch time must be fixed as a particular clock time of a particular date. In 1984, the International Astronomical Union agreed that epoch times should be fixed, i.e., epoch 2000.0 is equivalent to 12 hours Universal Time of the day 2000 January 1. Other epoch conventions were used in the past. See also Julian's epoch. The name originates from the Greek word "*epoche,*" meaning a stopping point or fixed point.

epoch [2]

A unit of time equivalent to 19 years used in predictions of the tides. In this context, an epoch is another name for a Metonic cycle. All possible alignments of the sun and moon occur in this 19-year cycle. Tidal heights and other tidal phenomena are averaged over this period.

equivalent or equivalent weight (Eq)

A unit of the relative amount of substance used in chemistry. One equivalent weight of an element, compound, or ion is the weight in grams of that substance, which would react with or replace one gram of hydrogen. Since one gram of hydrogen is equivalent to one mole and given that hydrogen has one electron free to react with other substances, then 1 Eq of a substance is effectively equivalent to one mole divided by the valence of the substance (the number of electrons the substance would engage in participating in the reaction). In practice, an Eq is a large unit and measurements are more likely to be in milliequivalents (mEq or meq).

ephemeris day

Unit of time used in SI system.

See *"day"*.

ephemeris second

The fundamental unit of time in the SI system of 1960, equivalent to 1/315 569 25.974 7 of the tropical year, defined by the mean motion of the sun in longitude at the epoch 1900 January 0 day 12 hours.

See also *"second (of time)"*.

equi-viscous temperature (EVT)

Unit of viscosity used in the tar industry. It is defined as the temperature in degrees Celsius, at which tar has a viscosity of 50 seconds when measured in a standard tax efflux viscometer.

Note: 1. This unit is widely used in Europe.

2. This unit was first suggested by H. Fuidge in 1930.

erg (erg)

CGS unit of work (energy). It is the work done when the point of application of a force of one dyne is displaced through a distance of one centimeter in the direction of the force.

1 erg = **10^{-7}** joules.

Note: The following units are equated to the erg. All units in the table are CGS units except; the "erg per franklin", which is the CGSF (cm-g-s-Franklin) unit, and the "erg per biot squared," which are CGSB (cm-g-s-Biot) units.

Unit	Unit Symbol	Quantity measured	Corresponding SI unit	To convert to SI, multiply by:
erg per biot	erg/Bi	Unit of magnetic flux	Weber (Wb)	10^{-8}
erg per biot squared	erg/bi^2	Self-inductance and mutual inductance	Henry (H)	10^{-9}
erg per centimeter	erg/cm	Linear stopping power and linear energy transfer	Joule per meter (J/m)	10^{-5}

erg per cubic meter	erg/ cm^3	Energy density and calorific value	Joule per cubic meter (J/ m^3)	10^{-1}
erg per cubic centimeter degree Celsius	erg/ cm^3· ^{o}C	Heat capacity per unit volume	Joule per cubic meter kelvin (J/ m^3 K)	10^{-1}
erg per cubic centimeter second	erg/ cm^3·s	Heat release rate	Watt per cubic meter (W/m$^{3)}$	10^{-1}
erg per centimeter second degree Celsius	erg/ cm^3·s. ^{o}C	Thermal conductivity	Watt per meter kelvin (W/m.K)	10^{-5}
erg per franklin	erg/Fr	Electric potential	Volt (V)	2.997 92x10^2
erg per gram	erg/g	Specific energy and kerma	Joule per kilogram (J/kg) or Gray (Gy)	10^{-4}
erg per gram degree Celsius	erg/g. ^{o}C	Specific heat capacity	Joule per kilogram (J/kg.K)	10^{-4}
erg per gram second	erg/g.s	Absorbed dose rate and kerma rate	Watt per kilogram (W/Kg) or Gray per second (Gy/s)	10^{-4}
erg per kelvin	erg/K	Heat capacity and entropy	Joule per kelvin (J/K)	10^{-7}
erg per mole degree Celsius	erg/mol.^{o}C	Molar gas constant	Joule per mole kelvin (J/mol.K)	10^{-7}
erg per second	erg/s	Power and sound energy flux	Watt (W)	10^{-7}
erg per second steradian	erg/s.sr	Radiant intensity	Watt per steradian (W/sr)	10^{-7}
Erg per second steradian square centimeter	erg/s.sr. cm^2	Radiance	Watt per steradian square meter(W/sr. m^2)	10^{-3}
erg per square centimeter second	erg/ cm^2·s	Energy fluence rate	Watt per meter square (W/m^2)	10^{-3}
erg per square centimeter second degree Celsius	erg/ cm^2·s. ^{o}C	Coefficient of heat transfer	Watt per square meter second kelvin(W/m^2 sK)	10^{-3}
erg per square centimeter second kelvin to the fourth power	erg/ cm^2·sk^4	Stefan-Boltzmann constant	Watt per square meter kelvin to the fourth power (W/m^{2}K^4)	10^{-3}
erg second	erg.s	Planck constant	Joule second (J.s)	10^{-7}
erg square centimeter	erg/ cm^2	Atomic stopping power	Joule square meter (J/m^2)	10^{-11}

erg square centimeter per gram	erg/ cm^2·g	Mass stopping power	Joule square meter per kilogram (J/m^2/kg)	10^{-8}
erg square centimeter per second	erg/ cm^2/s	First radiation constant	Watt square meter(W/m^2)	10^{-11}

ergon (ergon)

Arbitrary unit of energy associated with electromagnetic radiation. It is defined as the energy E (in ergons) that is related to the frequency f of the electromagnetic radiation in hertz by the formula:

$E = hf$

Where h = plank's constant in joule seconds.

Note: 1. The name of the unit was suggested by Partington in 1913.

2. This unit is also known as the **quantum** or **photon**

See also *"quantum"* and *"photon"*.

Erlang (E or Erl)

Unit of telephone traffic intensity. One Erlang is the telephone traffic intensity of a call rate of one call per hour.

The unit is dimensionless.

Note: 1. The telephone traffic industry is the product of the number of calls made in a given period of time and the average length of the calls measured in the same time unit.

2. In the traffic calculation, one Erlang implies a single resource in continuous use (or two channels at 50% use, and so on, pro rata). For example, if a bank has two tellers and they are both busy the whole time, this would represent two Erlangs of traffic.

3. The unit was named after a Danish engineer, Agner Krarup Erlang (1878-1929), the founder of the telephone traffic theory (the queuing theory).

4. Traffic measured in Erlangs is used to calculate the grade of service (GOS) or quality of service (QoS).

5. There are a range of different Erlang formulas, including Erlang B, Extended Erlang B, Erlang C and a related Engset formula to calculate GOS.

i. Erlang B

Calculates the blocking probability in a loss system. If a request is not served immediately when it tries to use a resource, then the request is aborted. These systems are, therefore, not queued. The formula assumes that the blocked traffic is immediately cleared.

Erlang B formula

$E_b\ (0,\ t) = 1$

$$E_b(r, t) = \frac{tE_b(r-1, t)}{r + tE_b(r-1, t)}$$

where,

E_b is the probability of blocking

r is the number of resources (e.g., Servers or circuits in a group).

T is the amount of traffic offered in Erlangs.

Erlang formula B works for loss systems. Thus, it applies to telephone systems, both for fixed and mobile networks, because of their real-time nature, where they simply do not (and are not intended to) provide traffic buffering.

ii. Erlang C

This formula is used to calculate the probability of queuing offered traffic. This formula assumes that blocked calls stay in the system until they can be handled. This formula can be applied in the designing of call center staffing arrangements because when calls cannot be immediately answered, they are placed in a queue. The formula is used to determine the number of agents or customer service representatives needed to staff a call center.

Erlang C formula

$$P(>0) = \dfrac{\dfrac{A^N}{N!}\dfrac{N}{N-A}}{\displaystyle\sum_{x=0}^{N-1}\dfrac{A}{x!} + \dfrac{A^N}{N!}\dfrac{N}{N-A}}$$

Where:

A is the total traffic units offered in Erlangs

N is the number of servers in a full availability environment

P (>0) is probability that delay is greater than 0

P is probability of loss –

Erlang C formula is used for queuing systems. It applies to *packet data networks* (such as the internet, etc.) because of their non *real-time nature*. Delay time, generally acceptable for packet transmission, allows the incorporation of data buffers along with routers. The buffer provides queuing for the data traffic.

6. Other frequently used units for traffic intensity are: Taraffic Unit (TU), Equated Busy-Hour Call (EBHC), Appels Resuits a'l'heure (ARHC), Cent Call Seconds (CCS) and unit call (UC).

Whereby:

1n Erl = 1 TU = 30 EBHC = 30 ARHC = 36 CCS = 36 UC.

estadio

A traditional unit of distance in Spain and Portugal. The estadio, like the stade and the English furlong, is equivalent to ⅛ mile. The Spanish estadio is equivalent to ⅛ milla or 625 pies. This is about 571 feet or 174 meters. The Portuguese unit is ⅛ milha, which is much longer, about 856 feet or 261 meters.

See: *"feet", "stad", "furlong."*

e-unit (e-unit)

Arbitrary unit of radiation dose due to X-rays.

1 e-unit = approximately 7 rontegens.

Note: 1. The unit was first used by W. Friedrich in 1916.

2. This unit must not be confused with the E-unit or the energy unit.

See also *"E-unit"* and *"energy unit"*.

E-unit (E-unit)

Arbitrary unit of radiation dose rate (intensity) due to X-rays.

1 E-unit = approximately 1 rontegen per second.

Note: 1. The unit was first used by W. Duane in 1914.

2. This unit must not be confused with the e-unit or the energy unit.

See also *"e-unit"* and *"energy unit"*.

exa (E)

SI prefix denoting x 10^{18}. Examples are exahertz (Ehz), exajoule (EJ) and exaohm (EΩ).
See also *"atta"*.

exabyte (EB)

A unit of information equivalent to 10^{18} (one U.S. quintillion) bytes. The petabyte is often used to mean 2^{60} = 1 152 921 504 606 846 976 bytes, which does not apply to the rules of the SI. The unit equivalent to 2^{60} bytes should be known as the **exbibyte** (see above).

exajoule (EJ)

A metric unit of energy. One exajoule is equivalent to 947.817 (U.S.) trillion Btu, 277.7778 petawatt hours, or about 9480 megatherms. The unit is often used in discussing global energy production, which is measured in hundreds of exajoules per year.
See also, "Btu"

exameter (Em)

A metric unit of distance equivalent to 10^{15} kilometers. This is equivalent to about 621.371 trillion miles, 105.7 light years, or 32.408 parsecs. One exameter is approximately the distance from the earth to the Hyades star cluster in Taurus.

exposure value (EV)

A unit used in photography to describe relative exposure. EV 0 is assigned to a specific combination of exposure time and lens aperture, such as 1 second at f/1. The difference between two exposure values is equal to the number of stops separating the two exposure settings. Different combinations of exposure time and lens aperture can have the same exposure value. The unit was invented to simplify the relationship. Regardless of camera settings, EV 6 is one stop "faster" than EV 5, i.e., an EV 6 setting records an image with half as much light as an EV 5 setting.

F

faggot

A traditional unit of volume for firewood. A faggot was 3 feet in length and 2 feet in circumference. This is a volume of about 0.955 cubic feet or 27 liters. There are about 134 faggots in a cord.

See also "cord."

fahrenheit degree (deg F)

Arbitrary unit of temperature interval or temperature difference. One Fahrenheit degree is ($\frac{1}{180}$) of the interval between the freezing and boiling points of pure air-free water, both under pressure of one standard atmosphere.

1 degF = (5/9) kelvin.

See *"degree Fahrenheit"* and *"degF"*.

Fahrenheit temperature scale

A temperature scale used in the English-speaking world and parts of Europe, having the melting point of ice at 32 degrees and the boiling point of water at 212 degrees.

The following equations are used for converting between degrees Celsius and Fahrenheit.

$$F = \frac{9}{5}C + 32 \qquad\qquad C = \frac{5}{9}(F - 32)$$

fall [1]

A traditional unit of distance, equivalent to 6 ells. The fall was used in land measurement, somewhat like the rod [1]. Measurements in rods were often made with an actual wood pole, while measurements in falls were often made with a rope 6 ells long. The distance falling under the rope was called a fall. The fall was used mostly in Scotland, where its traditional length was 6 Scots ells or about 18.6 English feet (5.67 meters). The **Scots furlong** was equivalent to 40 falls (226.8 meters) rather than 40 rods, and the **Scots mile** was equivalent to 320 falls (5952 English feet, 1.127 English miles or 1814.2 meters). After the unification of Scotland and England, the fall was reinterpreted to be equivalent to 6 English ells (22.5 feet or 6.858 meters).

See also "ell", "rod", "feet."

fall [2]

A traditional unit of area, equivalent to one square fall [1]. In the traditional Scots system of measurement, a fall of land is equivalent to about 346 square feet or 32.15 square meters. A traditional **Scots acre** was equivalent to 160 falls or about 6150 square English yards (1.27 English acres or 0.514 hectares). In the English system, a fall of land is 506.25 square feet, 56.25 square yards, or about 47.03 square meters.

fanega [1]

A Spanish unit of volume, mostly for dry goods. The word is derived from an Arabic word *faniqa,* meaning a large sack. The fanega is equivalent to 12 almudes or 48 cuartillos. This is about 55.50 liters or 1.960 cubic feet (1.575 U.S. bushels). Similar units have been used in Portugal and in most of the Latin American countries. In Chile and Argentina, however, a much larger fanega, roughly 2.5 U.S. bushels, was customary.

See also, "bushel", "almude."

fanega [2] or fanegada

A traditional unit of land area in Spain and in some Latin American countries. The unit was used to quantify the amount of land that could be planted with a fanega [1] of seed. It varied considerably from one area to another. In 1801, it was standardized in Spain as the area of a square, 96 varas (80.2 meters) on a side. This is equivalent to 0.643 hectares (1.59 acres). After the introduction of the metric system, it became customary to refer to an area 80 meters square as a fanega. This unit is informally used in some parts of Spain. The Central American manzana is a counterpart of this traditional Spanish unit.

See also, "hectare", "acre", "vara."

farad (F)

The SI unit of electric capacitance. It is the capacitance of a capacitor between the plates of which there appears a difference of potential of one volt when it is charged by one coulomb of electricity. Practical units are the microfarad (10^{-6} farads), the nanofarad (10^{-9} farads) and the picrofarad (10^{-12} farads).

Note: 1. The unit is named after an English scientist, Michael Faraday (1791-1867)

2. The unit was formerly known as the absolute farad (F_{abs}). It is crucial to distinguish it from the international farad (F_{int}).

3. The original definition of the farad gave it a size equivalent to 10^{-6} of the value given in the above definition. It was known as Latimer Clark farad.

farad, thermal (thermal farad)

The SI unit of thermal capacitance. One thermal farad is the thermal capacitance, when an amount of entropy of one joule per kelvin added to a body, raises its temperature by one kelvin.

1 thermal farad = 1 joule per square kelvin.

Formerly, the unit was defined as the thermal farad, corresponding to a quantity of heat of one joule, resulting in a temperature increase of one kelvin.

1 thermal farad = 1 joule per kelvin.

faraday (Fa)

Arbitrary unit of electric charge. It is the charge necessary to liberate one gram-equivalent of a substance in electrolysis. The experimentally derived value is:

1 faraday = 96 487.0 $\pm$ 1.6 coulombs.

Note: The unit is named after an English scientist, Michael Faraday (1791-1867)

farad per meter (F m^{-1} or F/m)

The SI unit of permittivity.

Fathom (fth or fath)

Imperial unit of length, particularly marine depth. It is equivalent to two yards (six feet)

1 fathom = **2** yards = **1.828 8** meters.

Note: The name fathom is derived, most probably, from the Anglo-Saxon faethm, *"to embrace"*, i.e., it is the distance between the hands when the arms are stretched out.

fatt

A traditional unit of volume of grain, generally equivalent to 9 bushels or ¼ chalder. This is about 317 liters based on the traditional grain bushel now used in the U.S. or about 327 liters based on the British Imperial bushel.

FAU

Abbreviation for **Formazin Attenuation Unit**, a unit used to quantify the water turbidity. This unit is used to express the turbidity measured by a nephelometer, which directly measures the fraction of light transmitted through a water sample as compared to the fraction transmitted through a standard preparation of formazin. The procedure is specified by standard ISO 7027 of the International Organization for Standardization.

FCC unit

A U.S. measure of purity and effectiveness for chemical substances added to foods. FCC stands for Food Chemical Codex, a code of standards prepared by the U.S. Institute of Medicine for the U.S. Food and Drug Administration. Perhaps most familiar to consumers is the FCC unit for the enzyme lactase, taken by those who are lactose intolerant. There is no definite conversion between FCC units and milligrams, because different manufacturers prepare their products in different ways. Instead, FCC units provide a way to judge the relative effectiveness of different preparations, no matter what their weights.

feddan

An Egyptian unit of land area formerly used throughout the Middle East and North Africa. The feddan is equivalent to about 0.42 hectares or 1.038 acres.

See also "hectare", "acre."

femto (f)

SI prefix denoting $\times 10^{-15}$. Examples: femtoampere (fA), femtometer (fm) and femtovolt (fV).

fermi (fm or f)

Metric unit for length, especially in nuclear physics.

1 fermi = 10^{-15} meters.

Note: 1. The name fathom is after an Italian physicist, Enrico Fermi (1901-1954).

2. The unit was first used in 1956, but it has become obsolete.

FEU

A unit of cargo capacity, especially for container ships. These ships carry cargo in standard metal boxes, called containers, that can be transferred easily to trains or trucks. FEU is an abbreviation for "forty-foot equivalent unit." One FEU represents the cargo capacity of a standard container 40 feet long, 8 feet wide, and (usually) a little over 8 feet high. One FEU roughly equivalent to 25 register tons (see ton [3]) or 72 cubic meters.

See also, "feet," "ton."

fibrin unit (FU)

A unit of potency for nattokinase, an enzyme that reduces the viscosity of blood and reduces its tendency to clot. The enzyme was discovered in natto, a traditional cheese-like Japanese food made from a fermented soybean mash. The unit is defined in terms of a specific test of a preparation's ability to dissolve fibrin, the protein found in clots. There is no standard equivalence to milligrams.

field box

A unit of volume in the U.S. citrus fruit industry is equivalent to 10 boxes or 16 bushels (0.5638 cubic meters).

fifth [1]

A traditional U.S. unit of liquid volume, equivalent to 4/5 quart, which is the same as ⅕ gallon, which contains exactly 46.2 cubic inches, or about 757.084 milliliters. This unit is an American version of the traditional bottle.

See also "gallon" "bottle."

fifth [2]

A unit used in music to describe the ratio in frequency between notes. Two notes differ by a fifth, if the higher note has a frequency exactly 3/2 times the frequency of the lower one. On the standard 12-tone scale, the perfect fifth is very closely approximated as 7 half steps, corresponding to a frequency ratio of $2^{7/12} = 1.4983$.

fillette

A half bottle of champagne (375 milliliters).

See also, "bottle."

fineness (fine)

A unit of proportion, equivalent to $\frac{1}{1000}$. This unit is used to express the purity of alloys of gold or other precious metals. A statement that a gold bar is "999 fine" means that the bar contains at most 0.1% other metals.

finger [1]

A traditional unit of distance, equivalent to 2 nails or 4.5 inches (11.43 centimeters). This unit represents the length of the middle finger, from the tip to the joint, where the finger is attached to the hand.

See also, "nail" "inch."

finger [2]

A name for the digit, a unit of distance, equivalent to ¾ inch (19.05 millimeters). The finger-width was a common unit of measurement in Anglo-Saxon England. After the 12-inch English foot became established, the finger existed as an informal measure.

See also, "digit."

Finsen unit (FU)

Metric unit for the intensity of ultraviolet radiation. It is defined as the intensity of ultraviolet radiation of a specified wavelength with an energy density of 100000 watts per square meter.

1 FU = 10^5 Watts per square meter.

Note: 1. The wavelength normally specified is 296.7 nanometres.

2. A ray of 2 FU will cause sunburn in 15 minutes.

3. The unit was named after a Danish-Faroese physician, Niels Ryberg Finsen (1860-1904).

firkin (fir)

U.S. and British units of volume. It is equivalent to nine gallons.

1. 1 firkin (U.S.) = 9 gallons (U.S., liquid) = 34.067 75 x 10^{-3} cubic meters.

2. 1 firkin (U.K.) = 9 gallons (U.K.) = 40.913 64 x 10^{-3} cubic meters.

firkin (fir) [2]

A traditional unit of weight of butter or soap, equivalent to 4 stones or 56 pounds (about 25.40 kilograms)

See also "stone" "pound."

fistmele

A traditional unit of distance, equivalent to the width of a clenched fist with the thumb extended. This is about 6.5 inches or 16.5 centimeters, making the fistmele equivalent to the Saxon shaftment. The unit is used in archery, where it measures the brace height of a bow (the distance from the center of the grip to the bowstring) and also in kayaking, where it measures various critical dimensions of the boat. In both cases, the intention is that if the fist of an archer or kayaker is used in establishing the unit, then the bow or the boat will fit that person precisely.

flat

An informal unit of angle measure equivalent to ⅙ turn or 60°. Hex nuts have 6 flat sides. To turn the nut "one flat" is to turn it ⅙ revolution.

flick (f) [1]

A unit of spectral radiance used in optical and communications engineering. Radiance is the power radiated per unit solid angle per unit of emitting surface. Radiance varies with wavelength, and to measure this variation, spectral radiance is defined as the radiance per unit of wavelength span. The flick is a short name for the spectral radiance of 1 watt per steradian per square centimeter of surface per micrometer of span in wavelength. This is mathematically equivalent to 10^{10} watts per steradian per cubic meter. In practice, spectral radiance is typically in microflicks.

see also "Watt", "Steradian."

flick (f) [2]

A proposed unit of time intended to help in coordinating the frame rates of various video display devices. The flick is defined to be $\frac{1}{705\ 600\ 000}$ seconds or about 1.417 234 nanoseconds.

flight level (FL)

In most countries, the assigned flight levels of aircraft are stated using the symbol FL succeeded by the assigned altitude in hectofeet (multiples of 100 feet). Thus, FL245 represents an assigned altitude of 24,500 feet. (These levels are nominal rather than precise since the altimeters of aircraft are actually barometers measuring air pressure. They are calibrated before and during flight to provide reasonable and consistent estimates of altitude. The assigned levels are always multiples of 500 feet.) Metric flight levels are used in China, Mongolia, Russia, and the former Soviet Republic of Central Asia.

flock

An old English unit of quantity, equivalent to 2 scores or 40

flops

A unit of computing power equivalent to one floating point operation per second. In computer science, there is a distinction between fixed point numbers (which have a fixed number of decimal places) and floating point numbers (which are stored with as many digits as the computer's design allows). A floating point operation is an addition or subtraction of two floating point numbers. The power of supercomputers is being measured in teraflops (Tflops): trillions of floating point operations per second.

fluid dram or fluidram (fl dr)

A unit of volume in the traditional apothecary system equivalent to ⅛ fluid ounce. This unit is usually called the fluid dram or fluidram to avoid confusion with the weight dram. The U.S. fluid dram contains about 0.225 586 cubic inches or 3.696 691 milliliters. In the British Imperial system, the fluid dram is about 0.216 734 cubic inches or 3.551 633 milliliters.

See also, "dram."

fluid ounce (fl oz)

A traditional unit of liquid volume called the fluid ounce to avoid it being confused with the weight ounce. In the U.S. customary system, there are 16 fluid ounces in a pint, so each fluid ounce represents 1.804 687 cubic inches or 29.573 531 milliliters. In the British Imperial system, there are 20 fluid ounces in an Imperial pint, so each fluid ounce represents about 1.733 871 cubic inches or 28.413 063 milliliters. A U.S. fluid ounce of water weighs just a bit more than one ounce avoirdupois. A British fluid ounce weighs exactly one ounce at a specified temperature and pressure.

See also, "ounce."

fluid scruple

A traditional British unit of liquid volume equivalent to ⅓ fluidram or about 1.1839 milliliters.

fluid drachm

See *"dram, fluid"*.

fluid dram

See *"dram, fluid"*.

fluid ton

A unit of volume (capacity). A fluid ton is equivalent to 32 cubic feet

1 fluid ton = 32 cubic feet = 0.0090614 cubic meters.

Note: The unit is used for many hydrometallurgical and other industrial purposes.

flux unit (fu)

Metric unit for flux density of radio-astronomical sources.

1 fu = 10^{-26} watt per meter squared hertz

foamines (fu)

CGS unit of time indicates foaminess. It is defined as the time required to produce unit volume of foam when passing unit volume of air through the liquid.

Note: The unit was first suggested in 1938.

foot (ft)

U.K. and U.S. unit and FPS and FlbfS base unit of length. It is ⅓ of a yard.

1 foot = (⅓) yard = **0.304 8** meters.

See *"yard" and also "survey foot"*.

Note: 1. The foot was defined in the Statue of Edward I as: "It is ordained that three grains of barley, dry and round, make an inch, twelve inches make a foot, three foot make an ulna….".

2. The units in the table below are related to the foot.

Unit	Unit Symbol	Quantity measured	Corresponding SI unit	To convert to SI, multiply by:
Foot cubed (cubic foot)	ft^3	Volume, modulus of section	Cubic meter (m^3)	2.831 68 x 10^2
Foot hour degree Fahrenheit per Btu	ft.h.^{o}F/Btu	Thermal resistivity	Meter kelvin per watt (m.K/W)	5.777 89 x 10^{-1}
Foot per minute	ft/min	Velocity	Meter per second (m/s)	**5.08 x 10^{-3}**
Foot per pound	ft/Ib	FPS unit of specific length	Meter per kilogram (m/kg)	6.719 69 x 10^{-1}
Foot per second	ft/s	FPS unit of velocity	Meter per second (m/s)	**3.048 x 10^{-1}**
Foot per second square	ft/s^2	FPS unit of acceleration	Meter per second squared (m/s^2)	**3.048 x 10^{-1}**
Foot poundal per second	ft.pdl/s	FPS unit of power	Watt (W)	4.214 01 x 10^{-2}
Foot pound-force	ft.Ibf	FIbfS unit of work	Joule (J)	1.355 82
Foot pound-force per pound	ft.Ibf/Ib	Specific internal energy and specific latent heat	Joule per kilogram (J/kg)	2.989 07
Foot pound-force per pound degree Fahrenheit	ft. ibf/(Ib.^{o}F)	Specific heat capacity	Joule per kilogram kelvin (J/kg.K)	5.380 32
Foot pound-force per second	ft. Ibf/s	FIbfS unit of power	Watt (W)	1.355 82
Foot squared per hour	ft^2/h	Kinematic viscosity	Meter squared per second (m^2/s)	**2.580 64 x 10^{-5}**
Foot squared per second	ft^2/s	FPS unit of kinematic viscosity	Meter squared per second (m^2/s)	9.290 30x 10^{-2}
Foot to the fourth power	ft^4	FPS unit of second moment of area	Meter to the fourth power Meter squared per second (m^4)	8.630 97 x 10^{-3}

football field [1]

A common informal unit of distance in the United States and Canada. It has not been quite agreed as to whether the unit is exactly 100 yards (91.44 meters), the distance between the goal lines on an American football field, or 120 yards (109.728 meters), the distance including the two end zones. Canadian football fields are 110 yards (100.58 meters) long between the goal lines and 150 yards (137.16 meters), including the end zones. As a distance equals to the length of an athletic field, this unit is analogous to the classical stade or *stadium*, although the stade is roughly twice as long as a football field.

football field [2]

An informal unit of area in the United States and Canada. Including the end zones, an American football field represents an area of about 1.3223 acres or 0.535 hectares, while the Canadian football field has an area of 2.0145 acres or 0.815 hectares.

See also "acre", "hectare."

foot, board (ft)

Unit of volume used in the U.K. for timber.
See *"board foot."*

foot-candle (fc)

FPS intensity of illumination. One foot-candle is the illumination of one lumen uniformly over an area of one square foot.
1 lumen = 1 lumen per square foot = 10.763 9 lux.

foot-candle, equivalent

Imperial unit of luminance. One equivalent foot-candle is the luminance of a uniform diffuser emitting one lumen per square foot.
1 equivalent foot-candle = $1/[(0.3048)^2\pi]$ nit $\approx$ 3.426 25 nits
Note: This unit is better referred to as foot-lambert.
See *"foot-lambert."*

foot, Cape (Cape foot)

Imperial derived unit of length.
1 Cape foot = 0.314 858 4 meters.

foot- lambert (ft-L)

Imperial unit of luminance. It is the luminance of a uniform diffuser emitting one lumen per square foot.
1 foot-lambert = $1/[(0.3048)^2\pi]$ nit $\approx$ 3.426 25 nits
Note: This unit is also known as **equivalent foot-candle.**

See *"foot-candle, equivalent"*.

foot of water (ftH$_2$O)

Unit of pressure.

1 ftH$_2$O = 2.989 07 x 10^3 Pascals.

foot pound (ft ib)

1. FPS unit of work. It is defined as the work done when a force of 1-pound weight is applied over a distance of 1 foot.

    1 ft Ib = 1.355 82 joules.

2. FPS unit of torque, equivalent to the torque produced by 1 pound of force acting as a perpendicular distance of 1 foot from an axis of rotation.

Note: 1. This unit and symbol are often incorrectly used for the FIbfS unit foot pound-force.

2. The unit is also known as **pound-foot**.

foot-pound-second (system of units)

A coherent, absolute system of units based on the customary units in English. Major scientific work was done in this system in the *19th century*, but it was gradually eclipsed by various versions of the "metric system."

In this system, the pound is a unit of mass, not weight (weight is a force). The unit of force is the poundal.

Between *1893* and *1959*, in the United States, the foot and pound were defined by reference to the prototypes of the meter and the kilogram. In the United Kingdom, the foot and pound were based on the British prototype yard and pound and so differed slightly from the American units. The foot-pound-second system employing the values of the British prototypes is also known as the British absolute system of units.

See also "poundal," "pound."

foot-pound per second (ft·lbf/s or ft·lb/s)

A traditional unit of power equivalent to about 1.355 818 watts or 0.001 818 horsepowers.

See also "watt" "horsepower."

foot poundal (ft pbl)

1. FPS unit of work. It is defined as the work done when a force of magnitude 1 poundal is applied over a distance of 1 foot.

   1 ft Ib = 0.042 140 11 joules.

2. FPS unit of torque that is equivalent to the torque produced by a force of magnitude 1 poundal acting as a perpendicular distance of 1 foot from an axis of rotation.

Note: 1. The unit is also known as **poundal-foot**

fors (f)

1. Metric unit of acceleration and specific force (i.e., force per unit mass). The fors is equivalent to the standard acceleration of free fall.

   1 fors = 9.806 65 meters per second square.

Note: This unit is better called the G. It is also called **grav.**

2. Metric unit of force. One fors is the force, which, when applied to a body of mass one gram, gives it an acceleration equal to the local value of the acceleration of free fall (g) expressed in centimeter per second squared.

   1 fors = g x 10^{-5} newtons.

Note: 1. This is an inconsistent unit, better known as the gram-weight. It is better to replace its use with the gram-force.

2. The unit and the name was suggested by the SUN Committee (International Committee for the Correlation of Scientific Symbols, Units and Nomenclature) in 195

fother

A traditional English unit of weight of lead. The fother, equivalent to 30 fotmals (next entry), was always a smaller unit than a (long) ton. The original version seems to have been equivalent to 2160 avoirdupois pounds, and the version that was used in the nineteenth century was equivalent to 19.5 hundredweights or 2184 pounds.

See also "ton," "pound," and "hundredweight."

fotmal

A traditional English unit of weight of lead. In medieval England, the fotmal was equivalent to 70 "mercantile" pounds, which is equivalent to 72 avoirdupois pounds.

See also, "pound."

fourth

A unit used in music to describe the ratio in frequency between notes. Two notes differ by a fourth if the higher note has a frequency exactly 4/3 times the frequency of the lower one. On the standard 12-tone scale, the perfect fourth is very closely approximated as 5 half steps, corresponding to a frequency ratio of $2^{5/12} = 1.3348$.

FOURIER (fourier)

The SI unit of thermal resistance. It is defined as the thermal resistance of which a temperature difference of one kelvin causes an entropy flow of one watt per kelvin.

1 fourier = 1 kelvin square per watt.

Note: 1. It is better to use the name thermal ohm for this unit.

2. The unit was named after the French scientist John Baptiste Joseph Fourier (1768-1830).

3. The name was suggested for the first time by Harper in 1928 as a metric unit of thermal conductivity.

FRANKLIN (Fr)

CGSF unit of electric charge and electric flux.

1. For electric charge:

One Franklin is that charge, which exerts on an equal charge at a distance of one centimeter in a vacuum, a force of one dyne.

1 franklin = 3.335 64 x 10^{-10} coulombs.

Note: 1. The above definition was adopted by the SUN Committee (International Committee for the Correlation of Scientific Symbols, Units and Nomenclature) in 1961.

2. The unit was named after Benjamin Franklin (1706-1790).

2. For electric flux:

1 franklin = 2.654 42 x 10^{-11} coulombs

Note: The following units are related to the Franklin. All the units are CGSF units.

Unit	Unit Symbol	Quantity measured	Corresponding SI unit	To convert to SI, multiply by:

Franklin centimeter	Fr.cm	Electric dipole moment	Coulomb meter (C/m)	3.335 64 x 10^{-12}
Franklin per second	Fr/s	Electric current	Ampere (A)	3.335 64 x 10^{-10}
Franklin per square centimeter	Fr/cm^2	Electric polarization and Electric flux density	Coulomb per square meter (C/m^2)	3.335 64 x 10^{-6} and 2.654 42 x 10^{-7}
Franklin squared per erg	Fr^2/erg	Capacitance	Farad (F)	1.112 65 x 10^{-12}
Franklin squared per erg centimeter	Fr^2/erg.cm	Permittivity	Farad per meter (F/m)	8.854 19 x 10^{-12}

FRAUNHOFER (F)

Unit of reduced width of spectrum line. The reduced width W of a spectrum line in frauhofers is related to its wavelength λ and equivalent width $\Delta\lambda$, both measures in the same units, by the relation:

$W = 10^6 \Delta\lambda/\lambda$.

Note: The unit was named after a German physicist Joseph Ritter von Fraunhofer (1787-1826)

freight ton (freight ton)

Unit of volume used for ship cargo. It represents a volume of forty cubic foot.

1 freight ton = 40 cubic feett = 1.132 674 cubic meters.

Note: The unit is called **measurement ton** or **shipping ton.**

french

A unit of length used mainly for small diameters and particularly that of fiber optic bundles. The unit is equivalent to ⅓ millimeters.

Fresnel (Fresnel)

Unit of frequency.

1 fresnel = 10^{12} hertz

Note: 1. The unit was initially used in 1930 as the product of the wave number in Kaysers by $10^{-10}\,c$, where c is the velocity of light in meter per second.

2. The unit was named after a French Civil Engineerer Augustin-Jean Fresnel (1788-1827).

See *"Kayser"*.

frigorie (fg)

Arbitrary unit of heat energy (for refrigeration). One frigorie corresponds to the extraction of one thousand calories (calorie 15° C of heat from the body to be cooled).

1 frigorie = 1000 Cal_{15} = 4,185.5 joules

Note: The name was coined from the calorie by supplanting the Latin *calor*, for heat, with *frigor*, for cold.

frigorie per hour (fg h $^{-1}$ or fg/h)

Unit of refrigeration capacity.

1 frigorie per hour = 1.162 64 watts.

fringe value

Unit of stress optical coefficient of material, i.e., reciprocal stress.

See *"brewster"*.

fuder

a traditional German unit of liquid volume. A "fuder" is a cartload. In most of the German states, the traditional fuder held about 9 hectoliters (roughly 238 U.S. gallons), making the fuder about the same size as the British tun or the French wine tonneau. In the Mosel wine region of Germany, a fuder is now a metric unit equal to 10 hectoliters (1 cubic meter, or 264.17 U.S. gallons). In Austria, the traditional fuder was equal to 18.11 hectoliters (478.42 U.S. gallons), twice the size of the German unit. In Belgium today, the fuder (or foudre) is a metric unit equal to 30 hectoliters (792.52 U.S. gallons).

Fujita scale (EF)

an empirical scale for estimating the wind speed of a tornado from the damage it causes. The scale, as developed by the American meteorologists Theodore Fujita and Allen

Pearson, ranged from F0 to F5. In 2007, the U.S. National Weather Service began using a revised version called the EF (Enhanced Fujita) scale; the designations in the new scale are EF0 to EF5.

funal (funal)

MTS unit of force. It is equivalent to the force, which, when applied to a body of mass one ton, gives it an acceleration of one meter per second square.

1 funal = 1 ton meter per second square = 1000 newtons.

Note: This unit is also known as **sthene**.

See *"sthene."*.

funt

A traditional Russian unit of weight or mass corresponding to the German pfund (which is pronounced "funt"). The funt is equivalent to about 0.9028 pounds avoirdupois or 409.5 grams.

The plural is **funte**.

furlong (fur)

Imperial unit of length.

1 fur = (⅛) mile = 660 feet = **201.168** meters.

Note: This is an obsolete unit but is still used in horse racing.

fuß or fuss

the German foot. The length of the fuß varied somewhat; the Viennese version was equal to 12.444 inches or 31.608 centimeters, while the **Rheinfuss** (Rhine foot), used in much of western and northern Germany, was equal to 12.357 inches or 31.387 centimeters. In Bavaria, a shorter fuß of about 29 centimeters was used. There's no change in the plural.

FY

a symbol for the fiscal year, in particular, the U.S. federal fiscal year ending on September 30.

G

g

Metric and Imperial unit of acceleration equal to standard acceleration of free fall:

1. As a metric unit:

One g is equivalent to the standard acceleration of free fall.

1 g = 9.806 65 metres per second squared

Note: This unit is sometimes used in aeronautical and astronautical applications.

It is also known as **grav** or **fors**.

See *"grav" and "fors"*.

2. As imperial unit:

One g is equal to the standard acceleration of free fall expressed in feet per second squared.

1 g = 32.2 feet per second squared (rounded to three significant figures), or

= 32.1740 feet per second square (rounded to six significant figures).

Notes:

1.   At latitude p, a conventional value of the acceleration of gravity at sea level is given by the **International Gravity Formula** below,

$$g(p) = \frac{9.7803267714(1 + 0.00193185138639\sin(p))}{\sqrt{1 - 0.0069437999013\sin^2(p)}}$$

The variation caused by the oblateness of the Earth and the acceleration we experience due to the rotation of the Earth is about half a percent, from 9.780 327 metres per second squared at the Equator to 9.833 421 metres per second squared at the poles.

2.   The symbol g was initially used as a unit in aeronautical and space engineering, where it is important to limit the accelerations experienced by the crew members of aircraft and spaceships, the "g forces" as they are called. This use became familiar through the

space programs and now, a variety of accelerations are measured in *g*'s. The names **"gee"** and **"grav"** are also used for this unit. Note that g is also the symbol for the gramme.

G [1]

An informal abbreviation used in computer science for $2^{30} = 1\ 073\ 741\ 824$. See also giga-[2] and gibi-.

G [2]

A symbol for grand, a slang term for 1000.

Ga

Symbol for one billion (10^9) years. The "*a*" stands for the Latin *annus*, year.

gal (Gal)

CGS unit for linear acceleration.

1 Gal = 10^{-2} metres per second squared.

Note: 1. The unit was formally known as Galileo.

2. The unit is commonly used in geodetic measurement.

3. The name of the unit is after an Italian astronomer, Galileo Galilei (1564-1642)

galactic year

the unit of time in which the Solar System makes one revolution around the center of the Milky Way galaxy. The galactic year is estimated to be about 225 million ordinary years. The age of the Solar System is about 20 galactic years.

galileo

CGS unit for acceleration. It is the former name for Gal.

Note: The unit, name Galileo, was proposed in 1972 for an SI unit of linear momentum, but it was never used.

See *"Gal"*.

gallon (U.K.) (UKgal)

Imperial unit of volume (capacity). According to the Weights and Measure Act (WMA) of 1963, one U.K. gallon is defined as the space occupied by ten pounds weight of distilled water of density 0.998 859 grammes per millimetre in an air of density 0.0001 217 grammes per milliliter against weights of density 8.136 grammes per milliliter.

1 UKgal= **4.546 09 x 10^{-3}** cubic metres.

Note: 1. The same value of the gallon is recognized in Canada and Australia.

2. The UMR, 1976 redefined the gallon as **4.546 09** cubic decimetres.

3. The National Physical Laboratory recognizes a value of:

1 UKgal = 277.420 cubic inches to six significant digits.

4. The U.K. gallon is used for the measurement of liquid and solid substances, although it is usually used for the former.

5. In the following table, some of the units related to the U.K. gallon are given. See *"gallon (U.S.)"*.

Unit	Unit Symbol	Quantity measured	Corresponding SI unit	To convert to SI, multiply by:
Gallon (U.K.) per hour	UKgal/hr	Volume flow rate	Cubic metre per second (m^3/s)	1.262 80 x 10^{-6}
Gallon (U.K.) per mile	UKgal/mile	Fuel consumption	Liters per kilometre	2.824 81
Gallon (U.K.) per minute	UKgal/min	Volume flow rate	Cubic metre per second (m^3/s)	7.576 82 x 10^{-5}
Gallon (U.K.) per pound	UKgal/Ib	Specific volume	Cubic metre per kilogramme (m^3/kg)	1.002 24 x 10^{-2}
Gallon (U.K.) per second	UKgal/s	Volume flow rate	Cubic metre per second (m^3/s)	4.546 09 x 10^{-3}

gallon (U.S.) (USgal)

U.S. unit of volume (capacity) for liquid measure. The U.S. gallon is equivalent to 231 cubic inches.

1 USgal = 231 cubic inches = 3.785 411 784 x 10^{-3} cubic metres.

Note: 1. The U.S. gallon is used only for the measurement of liquid substance.

2. In the following table, some of the units related to the U.S. gallon and the U.K. gallon are given.

Unit	Unit Symbol	Quantity measured	Corresponding SI unit	To convert to SI, multiply by:
Gallon (U.S.) per hour	USgal/hr	Volume flow rate	Cubic metre per second (m^3/s)	1.051 50 x 10^{-6}
Gallon (U.S.) per mile	USgal/mile	Fuel consumption	Liters per kilometre	2.352 15
Gallon (U.S.) per minute	USgal/min	Volume flow rate	Cubic metre per second (m^3/s)	6.309 02 x 10^{-5}
Gallon (U.S.) per pound	USgal/Ib	Specific volume	Cubic metre per kilogramme (m^3/kg)	8.345 40 x 10^{-3}
Gallon (U.S.) per second	USgal/s	Volume flow rate	Cubic metre per second (m^3/s)	3.785 41 x 10^{-3}

gallon of gasoline equivalent (GGE)

A unit of energy established by the U.S. Environmental Protection Agency to allow comparisons of energy efficiency between various energy sources for motor vehicles. The GGE is equivalent to 114,000 Btu or 33.41 kilowatt hours. This is a typical energy content for a gallon of gasoline. For each energy source, EPA has identified a quantity of that source that delivers one GGE of energy.

gallon per 100 miles (gal/100 mi)

A measure of fuel consumption rate for vehicles. In metric countries, fuel consumption is stated in liters per 100 kilometres (L/100km). This is the corresponding measure in traditional U.S. units. Since 2013, it has been stated on the window stickers of new vehicles in addition to the more familiar (to Americans) measure of miles per gallon. One gallon per 100 miles is equivalent to about 2.352 15 liters per 100 kilometres. A consumption rate of x gallons per 100 miles is equivalent to exactly $100/x$ miles per gallon.

galopin

A French name for a small glass of beer, typically 200 milliliters (about 6.76 U.S. fluid ounces).

galvat (galvat)

MKSA unit electric current. Another name for the international ampere.

1 galvat = 1 international ampere = 0.999 835 amperes.

Note: This name was proposed for the international unit of current but was never used.

gamma(γ)

Definition -1: Metric unit of magnetic flux density.

$1\gamma = 10^{-9}$ Teslas

Definition -2: Metric unit of mass.

$$1\gamma = 10^{-9} \text{ kilogrammes.}$$

gammil (gammil)

Metric unit for concentration. It is the concentration of one milligramme of solute in one liter of solvent.

1 gammil = 0.001 kilogrammes per cubic metre

Note: 1. Is also known as **the mircogammil** and **micril**.

2. The name of the unit was proposed for the first time in 1946.

See *"micril"*.

garnets

A traditional unit of liquid volume in Russia. The garnets is equivalent to approximately 3.28 liters. This is about 3.47 U.S. quarts or 2.89 British Imperial quarts.

gas permeation unit (GPU)

A CGS unit of gas permeance for membranes, contact lenses, and similar thin materials. Permeance is defined as the gas flow rate through the material per unit of area and per unit of pressure difference across the material. The unit is equivalent to 10^4 <u>barrers</u> per centimetre, or 10^{-6} cm·s^{-1}·cmHg^{-1}, or, in SI units, 7.5005×10^{-16} m·s^{-1}·Pa^{-1}.

gauge (ga) [1]

A traditional unit for measuring the interior diameter of a shotgun barrel. The gauge of a shotgun was the number of lead balls, each of a size just fitting inside the barrel, that were required to make up a pound. In other words, if a lead ball weighing $\frac{1}{12}$ pounds just fits in the barrel of a shotgun, then it was a 12-gauge shotgun. Today, the internal diameters for each gauge number are read from a table.

gauge (ga) [2]

A unit expressing the fineness of a knitted fabric, equivalent to the number of loops per 1.5 inches (38.1 millimetres). The same unit is also used to express the size of the knitting needles used to create a fabric of that fineness.

gauge (ga) [3]

A traditional unit for measuring the diameter (or the cross-sectional area) of a wire. Various wire gauge scales have been used in the U.S. and U.K. In traditional scales, larger gauge numbers represent thinner wires. (For very thick wires, repeated zeros are used instead of negative numbers, i.e., gauges 00, 000, and 0000 represent -1, -2, and -3, respectively.) In the **American Wire Gauge** (AWG) scale, 0000 gauge represents a wire having a diameter of 0.46 <u>inches</u> and 36 gauge represents a diameter of 0.005 inches (5 mils). Diameters for the other gauges are obtained by geometric interpolation, implying that the ratio between successive diameters is constant, except if rounding off is necessary. Thus, n gauge wire has a diameter of $.005 \cdot 92^{((36-n)/39)}$ inches. The **metric wire gauge** number is equivalent to the cross-sectional area of the wire in square millimetres. Wikipedia provides a table of wire gauge equivalents.

gauge (ga) [4]

A traditional unit for measuring the thickness of sheet metal. Larger gauge numbers represent thinner metal. 10 gauge represents a thickness of 0.1345 inches (3.416 millimetres) and an increase in the gauge number by 1 corresponds to a reduction of about 10% in the thickness. Wikipedia provides a table.

gauge (ga) [5]

A traditional unit for measuring the thickness of plastic film. In this concept, 1 gauge is equivalent to 0.01 mil [1] or 10^{-5} inches (0.254 micrometres).

gauge (ga) [6]

A traditional unit for measuring the thickness of tennis racquet strings. There are two systems in use. In the U.S. system, larger gauge numbers indicate thinner strings. In the European system, larger gauge numbers indicate thicker strings. Tennis-warehouse.com provides a table of U.S. sizes.

GAUSS (G; Gs)

CGS-emu unit of magnetic flux density. The gauss is the area-density of one Maxwell of magnetic flux per square centimetre.

1 gauss = 1 Maxwell/square centimetre = 10^{-4} Teslas.

Note: 1. The name of the unit was proposed at the Third International Electrical Congress in 1891 as the practical unit of magnetic flux density. However, the name international tesla is now currently used. It was proposed by the American Institute of Electrical Engineers in 1894 for the rationalized CGS-emu of magnetic flux density. It was also proposed during the 5th International Congress of 1900 as the CGS-emu of magnetic field strength as well as flux density. These two quantities were at that time regarded as dimensionally equivalent. The International Electrical Congress commissioned its present use in 1930.

2. The symbol G is used in physics and the symbol Gs in engineering.

3. The unit was named after a German mathematician Johann Carl Friedrich Gauss (1777-1855)

gaussian year

Unit of time. It is the time period from Kepler's laws, based on the earth-sun distance being one astronomical unit. It is equivalent to **365.256 898** days.

1 gaussian year = 356 days 6 hours 9 minutes 55.8 seconds = $3.155\ 819\ 58 \times 10^7$ seconds. See *"year"*.

GDU

A symbol for **gelatin digesting unit**, used for measuring dosage of bromelain, an enzyme used as a digestive aid. It is also used for the reduction of pain and inflammation. This unit cannot be converted to a weight unit because different preparations of the enzyme differ in activity. Bromelain is also measured in milk clotting units (MCU). 1 GDU is equivalent to approximately 1.5 MCU.

gear inch

A traditional unit for measuring the gears of bicycles. For low gears, the pedals are easy to turn but have to be turned very fast to achieve any speed. For high gears, the pedals are harder to turn but do not have to be turned fast to achieve high speed. The gear value is computed in gear inches as the diameter of the drive wheel times the size of the front sprocket divided by the size of the rear sprocket. All these measurements are expressed in inches. (This is the same as the diameter of the drive wheel times the number of gear teeth on the front sprocket, divided by the number of teeth on the rear sprocket). This is the diameter that the drive wheel would need to have to give the same pedal effort as if the pedals were attached directly to the wheel, just like on a child's tricycle. Values range from about 25 gear inches for the low gears on mountain bikes to more than 100 gear inches for the highest gears on racing bikes.

gee pound (gee pound)

FSS unit of mass. One gee pound is the mass that acquires an acceleration of one foot per second squared under the influence of a force of one pound-force.

1 gee pound = 9.806 65/0.304 8 pounds = 14.593 9 kilogrammes.

Note: This unit is also known as **slug**.

See *"slug"*.

gemmho (gemmho)

Metric unit for conductance. It is the conductance of a substance, which has a resistance of one megaohm.

1 gemmho = 10^{-6} siemens

generation (gen)

An informal unit of time. Roughly speaking, a generation is the average length of time between the birth of a parent and the birth of the child. This leaves a question, however:

should the father, or the mother, or both parents be included in the calculation? Various answers to this question, plus a lack of consistent data, have led to a range of estimates for the length of a generation, from about 25 to 35 years. Genealogists tend to use the higher figures, while anthropologists use the lower ones. There are some researches suggesting that the approximate length of the generation today is about 28 years.

German legal metre (Glm)

An obsolete unit of distance, longer than a metre by 13.5965 micrometres (less than 1 part in 70 000). This unit was used in surveying in Namibia, a former German colony.

geographical mile

Another name for the nautical mile, especially the Admiralty mile (6080 feet or 1853.184 metres). For a (different) German use of the term *geographische meile*, see meile.

GeV

The symbol for one billion (10^9) electronvolts. Thanks to Einstein's equation $E = mc^2$ equating mass with energy, the GeV can be regarded either as a unit of energy, equivalent to 160.217 646 2 picojoules, or as a unit of mass, equivalent to $1.782\ 662 \times 10^{-24}$ grammes or 1.073 544 atomic mass units.

gibbs (gibbs)

Metric unit for absorption, i.e., surface concentration. One gibbs is defined as the absorption of the micromole over one square metre.

1 gibbs = 10^{-6} moles per square metre

Note: The name of the unit was proposed by Dean in 1951, after an American scientist, Josiah Willard Gibbs (1838-1903).

giga (G)

SI prefix denoting $\times 10^9$. Examples are gigabecquerel (GBq), gigacalorie (Gcal), gigahertz (GHz), gigajoule (GJ), gigawatt (GW)

gigabits per second (Gbit/s)

Unit of measure for extremely high-speed data communication.

gigabyte (Gbyte)

Unit of storage capacity in digital computer technology.

For mainframe memory:

1 Gbyte = 2^{30} bytes = 1,703,741,824 bytes.

For external storage (e.g., mainframe-attached direct access storage, magnetic tape, etc.):

1 Gbyte = 10^9 bytes.

gigaparsec (Gpc)

a non-metric unit of distance equal to one billion parsecs, 3.2616 billion light years, or 30.856 78 zettameters (30.856 78 x 10^{21} kilometers). The unit is used in astronomy.

See also "parsecs," "light year."

gigapascal (GPa)

a metric unit of pressure. One gigapascal equals 10 kilobars or approximately 145 038 pounds (72.519 short tons) per square inch. Pressures in this range are common inside the earth and can be produced by various high-energy events.

gigatonne (Gt)

a metric unit of mass or weight equal to one billion metric tons (tonnes) or about 2.2046 trillion pounds. This very large unit is used, for example, in discussing the amounts of carbon added to the atmosphere by human activities.

Gilbert (Gb)

CGS-emu unit of magneto-motive force. One gilbert is the magnetomotive force around a closed path enclosing a surface through which flows a current of $(1/4\ \pi)$ abamperes.

1 Gb = $(10/\pi)$ ampere turn = 0.795 775 amper turn

Note: 1. The name gilbert was proposed by the American Institute of Electrical Engineering in 1894 for the rationalized CGS-emu unit of magneto-motive force. The International Electrical Congress (IEC) in 1930 commissioned its present use.

2. The unit was named after an English physicist, William Gilbert (1544-1603)

See *"ampere-turn."*

gilbert per maxwell (Gb/Mx)

CGS-emu unit of reluctance.

1 gilbert per maxwell = 7.957 75 x $10^7\ H^{-1}$.

gill (U.K.) (UK gill)

Arbitrary unit of volume (capacity). It is derived from the gallon and defined as one fourth of the U.K. pint.

1 UKgill = (¼) U.K. pint = 1.420 65 x 10^{-4} cubic metres.

Note: This unit is used for the measurement of liquid and solid substances.

See also *"noggin"*.

gill (US) (USgill and also gi)

Imperial U.S. unit of volume (capacity). It is equivalent to one fourth of the U.S. pint.

1 USgill = (¼) U.S. pint = 1.182 94 x 10^{-4} cubic metres.

Note: This unit is used for the measurement of liquids.

gillion

an informal alternate name for the number 10^9, called "billion" in America but often called "milliard" in France and "thousand million" in Britain. The reasoning here is that if mega- means a million and tera- a trillion, then giga- should mean a gillion!

glass [1]

A unit of time measured by an hourglass or sandglass. At sea, time was traditionally measured with half-hourglasses, making the glass a nautical unit of time, equivalent to ½ hour. In this context, the glass is another name for the bell.

glass [2]

Another name for the U.S. cup (236.6 milliliters). Doctors in the U.S. are fond of saying that everyone should drink 8 glasses of water a day, and this is the amount they have in mind for a glass.

glass [3]

An informal unit of volume used in Australian pubs. In several states of Australia, a glass of beer is usually 200 milliliters, but it is 235 milliliters in Queensland and 285 milliliters in Western Australia.

glug (glug)

CgfS unit of mass. The glug is the mass that acquires an acceleration of one centimetre per second squared under the influence of a force of one gramme-force.

1 glug = 980.665 grammes = 0.980655 kilogrammes

Note: 1. This unit is also known as the **CGS-technical unit of mass**.

2. The name has been in use since 1957.

glycemic index

A measure devised around *1981* to indicate how fast an ingested carbohydrate becomes glucose in the human bloodstream.[1] British spelling, glycaemic index. Symbol, GI. Persons with diabetes use the glycemic index in regulating their diet. Generally speaking, the more processed a food, the higher its glycemic index, although there are many exceptions.

gnat's eye

An idiomatic "unit" of distance. It is common to hear that something is "as small as a gnat's eye." In fact, the eyes of typical gnats tend to have diameters similar in size to a hair's breadth, roughly 100-150 micrometres (0.10-0.15 millimetres).

go

A traditional Japanese unit of liquid volume. One go is about 180.39 milliliters, 0.3812 U.S. pints, or 0.3174 British Imperial pints.

goad

A traditional unit of distance, sometimes used in measuring cloth. One goad is equivalent to 54 inches or 1.5 yards (1.3716 metres). A goad was originally a spear. Later, it was a pointed rod used for prodding animals to get a move on. The unit must have originated as the length of such an instrument.

gon (gon also ...^{g})

A unit of plane angle (German), equivalent to one-hundredth of a right angle.

1 gon = 0.01 right angle = 0.9°

Note: The unit is also known as **grade**.

See also *"grade"*.

googol

A name that means 10 to the power 100.

googolpex

A name that means 10 to the power googol.

See *"googol"*.

grade (…^{g})

Unit of plane angel, equivalent to one-hundredth of a right angle.

1 grade = 0.01 right angle = 0.9°.

Note: This unit has only been used in Europe. In Germany, it has also specifically been called the gon.

See also *"gon"* and *"minute, centesimal"*.

grad, grade [1], gradian, or **gon (^{g} or gr or grd)**

A unit of angle measurement, equivalent to $\frac{1}{400}$ circle, 0.01 right angle, 0.9°, or 54'. In the early years of the metric system, this unit was introduced in France, where it was known as the **grade**. The **grad** is its English equivalent that was introduced by engineers around 1900. The name **gon** represents this unit in German, Swedish, and other northern European languages. In these countries, the word *grad* means *degree*. Although many calculators will display angle measurements in grads as well as degrees or radians, it is difficult to find actual applications of the grad today.

grade [2]

A measure of the steepness of a slope, such as the slope of a road or a ramp. Usually stated as a percentage in the U.S. The grade is the same quantity known as the slope in mathematics. The amount of (vertical) change in elevation per unit distance horizontally ("rise over run"). Thus, a 5% grade has an elevation gain of 0.05 metres for each metre of horizontal distance or 0.05 feet for each foot of horizontal distance. Grades are also stated as ratios ($\frac{1}{20}$ grade or 1 in 20 grades) and, in some countries, as per mileage (50 °/oo grade). The angle of inclination, in grads or grades [1], is *not* equivalent to the percentage grade in this sense. For a 5% grade, the angle of inclination is about 2.86° or 3.18 grads.

grade [3]

A measure of quality for ball bearings. A bearing of grade g is required to be spherical to an accuracy of g parts per million (g 10^{-6}). Thus, lower-grade numbers represent better bearings. A 25-grade bearing is spherical to within 25 ppm, but a 1000-grade bearing is only spherical to within 1000 ppm, or 0.1%.

grade point (gp or GP)

A unit of academic recognition used in U.S. schools and colleges. To compute the number of grade points awarded to a student for a course, the student's grade (often assigned as a letter or a percentage) is converted to a standard scale (traditionally 0.0-4.0, with 4.0 being the highest score). This scale number is multiplied by the number of semester hours or quarter hours assigned to the course. Thus, a student who has a grade of A (4.0) for a course of 3 semester hours of credit receives 12 grade points.

grade point average (GPA)

An index of academic achievement used in U.S. schools and colleges. It is equal to the number of grade points received, divided by the number of semester hours or quarter hours of courses attempted by the student.

grain (gr)

Imperial unit of mass. The unit of weight of moisture of water vapor in air. 7000 grains is equivalent to a weight of 1Ib.

It is also used to denote the weight of dust particles in air.

1 gr = $\frac{1}{7000}$ Ib = 6.479 891 x 10^{-5} kilogrammes.

Note: The grain is an important unit common to and linking the avoirdupois, apothecaries' and troy systems.

grain metric (metric grain)

1 metric grain = 50 milligrammes = 5 x 10^{-5} kilogrammes.

Note: This unit is employed for commercial transactions in diamonds, pearls and other precious stones.

grain (gr) [1]

A traditional unit of weight. The grain, which is equivalent to $\frac{1}{480}$ troy ounce (see also pound [2]), or exactly 64.798 91 milligrammes, was the legal foundation of traditional English weight systems, with various pounds being defined as a specified number of grains (For example, 5760 grains in a troy pound and 7000 grains in an avoirdupois pound). In the version of the troy system used by jewelers, there are 24 grains in a pennyweight and 20 pennyweights in an ounce. In the version used by apothecaries, there are 20 grains in a scruple, 3 scruples in a dram, and 8 drams in an ounce. Originally, the grain was defined in England as the weight of a barleycorn. This made the English grain larger than the corresponding grain units of France and other nations of the Continent because those units were based on the weight of the smaller wheat grain.

grain (gr) [2]

A unit of weight formerly used by jewelers in measuring diamonds and other precious stones. The jeweler's grain is exactly ¼ carat. Now that the carat has been standardized at 200 milligrammes, the jeweler's grain is exactly 50 milligrammes, or approximately 0.7716 troy grains. This unit is widely used for measuring pearls, and therefore, it is sometimes known as the **pearl grain**.

grain (gr) [3]

A traditional French unit of weight, equivalent to 53.115 milligrammes.

grain per gallon (gr/gal or gpg)

A traditional unit measuring the hardness of water. Water is "hard" if it contains dissolved minerals such as calcium or magnesium salts. 1 gpg is equivalent to about 17.118 milligrammes per liter. This unit is also known as the **Clark degree**; see degree [4].

gramme (g)

CGS base unit of mass and sub-multiple of SI unit of mass.

1 g = 0.001 kilogrammes.

Note: 1. In the U.S., the name of this unit is spelled as a *gramme*. The spelling in the official translation of ISO Recommendations is always gramme.

2. The names **bes, brieze** and **stathm** have been proposed as alternatives for the gramme, but never used.

See also *"bes", "brieze"* and *"stathm"*.

gramme-atom (gramme-atom)

Unit of mass of an element. If the relative atomic mass of the element is n, then,

1 gramme-atom = n gramme

Note: This is an obsolete unit.

See also *"gramme-molecule"*.

gramme-calorie (cal)

Arbitrary unit of heat energy. It is the quantity of heat required to raise the temperature of one gramme of air-free water from 14.5°C at a constant pressure of one standard atmosphere. The experimentally derived size of this unit is:

1 cal = 4.1855 + 0.0005 joules

Note: This unit is known as a fifteen-degree calorie. It has also been known as the small calorie.

See *"calorie, fifteen degree"*.

gramme-equivalent (g-eq)

Metric-derived unit for mass. The gramme-equivalent is the mass of an element or radical in grammes equivalent to (i.e., that combines with or replaces) three grammes of tetravalent carbon-12.

gramme-force (gf)

Cgts unit of force. It is the force, which when applied to a body of mass one gramme, gives it an acceleration equal to the standard acceleration of free fall.

1 gf = 980.665 dynes = 0.00980665 newtons.

gramme-molecule (gmol)

Metric unit for the amount of substance. This is the former name of the mole.

1 gmol = 1 mole

Note: For a compound of relative molecular mass n, the gramme-molecule is defined as 1 gramme-molecule = n gramme.

gramme-rad (gramme-rad)

Metric unit for the integral absorbed ionizing radiation dose.

1 gramme rad = 10^{-5} joules

gramme-rontgen

Arbitrary unit of absorbed radioactive energy. It is equal to the energy absorbed when one rontgen is delivered to one gramme of air. The experimentally derived value of the unit is:

1 gramme-rontgen = 8.69 x 10^{-6} joules

gramme-weight (gwt)

Metric unit for the force. One gramme-weight is the force, which, when applied to a body of mass one gramme, gives it an acceleration equal to the local value of the acceleration of free fall (g) expressed in centimetres per second squared.

1 gwt = g dyne = g x 10^{-5}.

Note: 1. The definition shows the inconsistency of the unit. Its use is deprecated.

2. The unit is also known as the "**fors**".

3. It is preferred to use the "gramme-force" rather than the gramme-weight.

See "**fors**".

grav (G)

Metric unit for acceleration. One grav is equivalent to the standard acceleration of free fall.

1 G = 9.80665 metres per second squared.

Note: This unit is sometimes used in aeronautical and astronautical applications. It is usually called G and has also been known as the "fors."

grave (graves)

Metric unit for the mass. This unit is the original name of kilogramme. It is the mass of one.

(original) liter of pure air-free water.

1 grave = 1.000028×10^{-3} kilogrammes.

Note: This unit was proposed by the French government in 1792.

gray (Gy)

The SI unit of absorbed dose. The absorbed dose (D) produced by ionizing radiation is the quotient of the energy transferred to the material in a volume element by radiation and the mass of the volume unit of that material. The definition can be redefined as: The gray is the absorbed dose when the energy per unit mass imparted to matter by ionizing radiation is one joule per kilogramme.

1 Gy = Joule per kilogramme

Note: 1. The gray is also used for the ionizing radiation quantities: specific energy imparted, kerma, and absorbed dose index, which have the SI unit joule per kilogramme.

2. The unit was adopted by the 15th CGPM in 1975 and is named after a British physicist Louis Harold Gray (1905-1965)

gray per second (Gy s^{-1})

SI unit of absorbed dose rate and kerma rate. It is the absorbed dose in one second when the energy per unit mass imparted to matter by ionizing radiation is one joule per kilogramme.

1 Gy per second = 1 Watt per kilogramme

gregorian year

Unit of time. It is a calendar year with 97 intercalated days in every 400 years. It is equivalent to **365.242 5** days.

1 Gregorian year = 356 days 5 hours 49 minutes 12 seconds = 3.155 695 2 x 10^7 seconds. See *"year"*.

grit

A measure of fineness for abrasive materials such as sandpaper, sanding belts, or the finer materials used to polish optical surfaces. Originally, the grit number was the number of holes in a standard screen. If the screen had, say, 240 holes, then the particles that would pass through the screen were described as 240 grits. However, very fine abrasive particles (such as 500 to 1000 grits) are too small to be screened in this way. Therefore, the measure is defined by tables giving the average particle size in micrometres for each grit size. Currently, there are two grit size scales in use, the CAMI scale, originally created by the Coated Abrasive Manufacturers Institute and the FEPA scale, created by the Federation of European Producers of Abrasives and incorporated in the ISO 6344 standard. Wikipedia provides a table comparing these two scales.

gros

A traditional French weight unit is equivalent to 3 deniers (about 3.8242264 grammes).

gross (gro or gr)

A unit of quantity, equivalent to a dozen <u>dozen</u>, or 144. This commercial unit has been in use since at least the 1400s.

gross ton (GT)

The name "gross ton" is used in at least two ways. (1) as another name for the British Imperial or long ton of 2240 pounds (see ton [1]), and (2) as another name for the register ton, a unit of volume, equivalent to 100 cubic feet (see ton [3]), used for describing the entire interior volume of a ship as opposed to the cargo-carrying capacity. To avoid confusion, it is preferable to use "long ton" for use (1) and "gross register ton" for use (2).

ground

An informal unit of land area in India, especially southern India, equivalent to roughly 200-220 square metres or 2150-2400 square feet.

growler

A container of beer designed for carryout. In the U.S., a growler generally holds ½ gallon (about 1.89 liters).

gry

A proposed unit of distance in the English traditional system. The name was first used in June 1679 by the philosopher John Locke (1632-1704) as a unit equivalent to 0.001 feet, 0.01 inches, or 0.1 lines in a decimalized distance system. (Thomas Jefferson, who was very familiar with Locke's writings, later proposed a similar system in the U.S., but he referred to 0.001 foot to a point rather than a gry). In 1813, the gry was revived in another decimal measurement scheme in Britain. All these ideas failed, but the gry had some limited use in the nineteenth century as a unit, equivalent to 0.1 lines or $\frac{1}{120}$ inch (0.211 667 millimetres). Long forgotten, the gry recently bounced back into the limelight in connection with a trick question circulating on the internet, which asked for three common English words ending in -gry. The word "gry" is from the ancient Greek, where it meant "a trifling amount."

gsm

A common but non-standard symbol for grammes per square metre, the metric unit of density for paper and for fabric. Paper density measured using this unit is often known as the **grammage**.

gt, gtt

Traditional pharmicist's abbreviations for a drop. Originally, gt was the singular (1 gt) and gtt the plural. The symbol comes from the Latin word *gutta* for a drop.

g/t

Symbol for grammes per tonne (metric ton), a unit of proportion equivalent to 0.001 grammes per kilogramme or 1 part per million by mass. This unit is used, for example, in quantifying the concentration of gold, silver, or other minerals in ores.

Gunter's chain

The traditional surveyor's chain equivalent to 4 rods [1]; see chain.

Gurley unit

see porosity.

gutenberg

A unit of distance used in typography equivalent to $\frac{1}{7200}$ inch or 3.5278 micrometres. The gutenberg is 0.01 points [2], more or less, depending on how the point is defined. The unit is named for Johannes Gutenberg (ca. 1390-1468), a German inventor, printer, publisher and goldsmith.

H

h

Planck's constant, equivalent to approximately $0.0662\ 606\ 876 \times 10^{-33}$ joule seconds, a fundamental constant of physics also used as a unit of "action" or of angular momentum in particle physics. The unit was suggested by a German physicist Max Planck (1858-1947), who discovered in 1900 that at atomic and subatomic scales, energy occurs in discrete packets known as quanta. Each quantum has energy $h.f$, where f is the frequency of the radiation in hertz (see below).

hacienda

A large traditional unit of land area in Mexico and the southwestern U.S. This word also refers to a large estate, a ranch, or plantation. As a unit, it is equivalent to 5 square leguas or 125 million squares varas. Using the Taxas definition of the vara, this would be about 8960 hectares or 22 140 acres (34.59 square miles). Using the shorter Mexican vara, this would be about 8778 hectares or 21 690 acres.
See also *"vara", "leguas"*.

hair's breadth

A common informal unit of distance. Human hairs vary considerably in width, depending on age, color, genetics, and other factors. An average hair breadth ranges between 70 and 100 micrometres (μm) in diameter. As a rough standard, a hair's breadth is 100 μm or 0.1 millimetres (mm).

half

[1] A unit of proportion, equivalent to ½. The English word "half," like the German prefix "halb-" is often placed before the name of a unit to create a combination which functions as a new unit, equivalent to half the old one. **Half dozen, half hour** and **half gallon** are typical and common examples.
[2] An informal name for ½ of many units. For example, in Britain, a "half" often means a ½ pint glass of beer, cider, lemonade or whatever.

half life

A unit of relative time measuring the rate at which a radioactive substance decays or, more generally, the rate of decrease for any process that decreases exponentially. In the case of radioactivity, the half-life is the time required for the activity to be reduced by half. After a second half life, the activity is again reduced by half, so it is then ¼ the original activity. To reduce the activity to 0.1% of the original amount requires about 9.966 half-lives.

half-month

A formal unit of time used in astronomy to construct official designations for comets and provisional designations for newly discovered minor planets. The 24 half-months in the year are designated with letters A through Y (the letter I is not used). For example, the famous Comet Hale-Bopp has the official designation of C/1995 O1, indicating that it was the first comet discovered during the second half of July (letter O) in 1995. The minor planet "Utima Thule," visited by the New Horizons spacecraft in 2019, had a provisional designation of 2014 MU_{69}. The first term, 2014M, represents the second half of June 2014, when this minor planet was discovered. U_{69} is a code indicating that Ultima Thule was the 1745th minor planet reported during that half month, i.e., $1745 = 25 \cdot 69 + 20$ for the letter U. Ultima Thule has since received a permanent designation as minor planet 486958.

half step

A unit used in music to describe the ratio in frequency between notes. It is equivalent to $\frac{1}{12}$ octave. The half step measures the difference between adjacent notes in the standard 12-tone scale, as on a piano keyboard. Two notes differ in frequency by a half step if the higher one has frequency equivalent to 2 = 1.0595 times the frequency of the lower one.

hand

A traditional unit of distance, now used mostly to measure the height of horses. One hand is equivalent to 4 inches, ⅓ foot, or 10.16 centimetres.

handle

A traditional unit of volume for beer, used in pubs in the Northern Territory of Australia. A handle of beer is 285 milliliters (10 fluid ounces). Glasses of this size are called middies or pots in most Australian states and schooners in South Australia.

See *"middies"* and *"pots"*.

hank

A traditional measure of length for yarn. The length of yarn in a hank varies with the market and the materials. For example, a hank of cotton yarn traditionally included 840 yards (768 metres) of yarn, while a hank of wool yarn was 50 yards (512 metres). For both cotton and wool, these traditional hanks are equivalent to 7 leas or to 12 cuts. In the U.S., however, a hank of woolen yarn is generally 1600 yards (1463 metres). In retail trade, a hank is often equivalent to 6 or 7 skeins of varying size.

hardness

A measure of the hardness of a metal or mineral. Hardness is a property easy to appreciate but difficulty to quantify or measure. The Mohs hardness scale is used in geology to give a rough estimate of hardness by testing which minerals are able to scratch the sample. In metallurgy, samples are tested for hardness by machines, which indent the surface under a controlled pressure. The resulting measurement is often computed as the force applied divided by the surface area of the indentation. The Brinell, Vickers, Rockwell, and Knoop tests are among the techniques used. Plastics, rubber, and similar materials are tested with instruments called durometers and the resulting readings are often designated duro.

See also "Part II for hardness."

hardness number

See "Chapter 3"

hartley (Hartley also Hart)

Unit of information for digital computers.

1 hartley = $\log_2 10$ bits

Note: The Hartley is similar to the Shannon. If the probability of receiving a particular message is p, then the information content of the message is $-\log_{10} p$ hartleys. For example, if a message is a string of 5 letters or numerals, with all combinations being equally likely, then a particular message has probability $\frac{1}{365}$ and the information content of a message is $5(\log10_{10}36) = 7.7815$ hartleys. One Hartley is equivalent to $\log_2 10 = 3.321\ 928$ Shannons or $\log_e 10 = 2.302\ 585$ nats.

See also *"Shannon"*.

hartree (*Eh or* **Ha**)

Derived unit of energy of the Hartree system of units. It is used mainly in atomic studies. In CGS units, it is equivalent to $4\pi^4 me^4/h$, where e is the charge of an electron, m mass of an electron, and h Planck's constant.

1 hartree = 27.213 eV = 4.3597 x 10^{-18} Joules.

Note: 1. This unit is more often called the atomic unit of energy.

2. The unit is named after an English mathematician, Douglas Rayner Hartree (1897-1958), who proposed the atomic units in 1928.

See "*atomic unit of energy*" and "*hartree system of units*".

hartree system of units

System of units suggested by Hartree in 1927 to reduce the numerical work in problems involving the atom. The fundamental units in the system are the atomic unit of charge e (the charge on the electron), the atomic unit of mass m (the rest mass of an electron), atomic unit of action ($h/2\pi$, where h is Planck's constant*)* and the electric constant (ε_0). The derived units are the atomic unit of length a (radius of the first Bohr orbit in the hydrogen atom), the atomic unit of energy (also called hartree) (e^2/a^2) and the atomic unit of time π (the reciprocal of the angular frequency *1/4\pi Rc, where R* is Rydberg's constant and c speed of light).

Note: 1. The system is also known as the **Atomic System of Unit**.

2. The system is one of two systems of unit that form the National Systems of Units. The other system is the **Quantam-Electrodynamics System,** which is often employed in the study of radiation.

See "*atomic unit of charge,*" "*atomic unit of energy,*" "*atomic unit of length,*" "*atomic unit of mass,*" and "*atomic unit of time.*"

head (hd) [1]

An informal unit of length, equivalent to the approximate length of a horse's head. It is used in expressing the results of a horse race.

head (hd) [2]

A notation seen in measurements of water pressure. See foot of head.

head (hd) [3]

A unit of quantity for livestock, equivalent to one animal. No "s" is appended for its plural. One speaks of "35 head" of cattle and not "35 heads" of cattle.

heaped bushel

A traditional unit of volume in the U.S. The heaped bushel is just what its name implies. The volume of a bushel container filled to overflowing. Officially, the heaped bushel was supposed to be equivalent to 1.278 regular or "struck" bushes. This is a volume of 2748.237 cubic inches, 1.5904 cubic feet, or 45.036 liters. In practice, the heaped bushel was frequently interpreted as 1.25 bushels, which is equivalent to exactly 5 pecks, 2688.025 cubic inches, 1.5556 cubic feet, or 44.049 liters.

See *"bushel"*.

heat index (HI or HX)

A measure of the combined effect of heat and humidity on the human body. U.S. meteorologists compute the index from the temperature T (in °F) and the relative humidity H (as a fraction, i.e., H = 0.65 if the relative humidity is 65%). The formula used is:

$HI = -42.379 + 2.04901523\ T + 1014.333127H - 2.475541\ TH - 00683783\ T^2 - 548\ 1717\ H^2 + 0.122874\ T^2H + 8.5282\ TH^2 - 0.0199\ T^2\ H^2$.

heat unit, mean pound-centigrade

The mean pound-centigrade heat unit is the average value from 0°C to 100°C of the heat required to raise the temperature of one pound of water by one centigrade degree. This is one-hundredth of the heat required between freezing point and boiling point. It is nine-fifths of the mean British Thermal Unit (Btu)

hebdo- (hebdo)

An obsolete metric prefix denoting ten million (10^7). It was coined from the Greek *hebdomos*, seventh. A group of seven is sometimes referred to as a **hebdomad**, a word related to the French *hebdomadaire*, weekly.

hectare (ha)

Metric unit of area. The hector is equivalent to 100 ares.

1 hectare = 100 ares = 10^4 square metres.

Approximately 107 639.1 square feet, 11 959.9 square yards, or 2.471 054 acres.

Note: 1. The unit was adopted by the CIPM in 1879.

2. The unit used for agrarian measures only.

hectare metre (ha.m)

A unit of volume used to measure the capacity of reservoirs. It is equivalent to the volume of water, one metre deep, covering one hectare. The unit is used mostly in British Commonwealth countries, especially India, where it provides a metric unit comparable to the traditional English acre-foot. Reservoir capacities are often stated in millions of hectare metres (Mha·m or MHM). One hectare metre is equivalent to exactly 10,000 cubic metres or about 8.1071-acre feet.

hect- or hector- (h)

SI prefix denoting x 10^2. It is recommended not to use this unit and only be used when well established in practice. Examples include hectare (ha), hectoliter (hl or hL) and hectopieze (hpz).

hectobar (hbar)

A fairly common metric unit of pressure equivalent to 100 bars, 10 megapascals, or 1 dekanewton per square millimetre. This is approximately 1450.38 pounds per square inch or 208 855 pounds per square foot.

hectofoot (hft)

A unit of distance, equivalent to 100 feet. The only known use for this odd unit is in statements of the assigned flight level of an aircraft.

hectogramme (hg)

A common metric unit of mass, equivalent to 100 grammes or about 3.5274 ounces.

hectokilogramme (hkg)

A non-standard metric unit of mass equivalent to 100 kilogrammes or about 220.462 26 pounds. This unit was fairly common in the past, especially in agriculture, but since the SI now prohibits using more than one prefix on a metric unit, the hectokilogramme is now considered to be obsolete.

hectoliter (hl)

Unit of volume (capacity).

1 hectoliter = 10^{-1} cubic metres.

Note: The unit is used in the brewing industry.

hectometre (hm)

A metric unit of distance, equivalent to 100 metres, 328.084 feet, or 109.361 yards. This unit is not used much in everyday life in metric countries, but it appears in various scientific contexts.

hectopascal (hPa)

A metric unit of pressure equivalent to 100 pascals or 0.1 kilopascals (kPa). The hectopascal, used almost entirely in measurements of air pressure, is identical to the millibar (mb). The millibar has been used to measure air pressure for many years, but it is not an SI unit. Although meteorologists in various countries use the hectopascal as a kind of alias for the millibar, the natural SI unit for air pressure is the kilopascal.

hectopieze (hpz)

Unit of pressure. This unit is equivalent to 1 bar.

1 hectopieze = **1** bar = $\mathbf{10^5}$ pascals.

Note: The unit was formerly used in France.

heer

A traditional measure of length for linen and woolen yarn, equivalent to 2 cuts or ⅙ hank. This is equivalent to 80 yards (73.152 metres).

See also*"hank"*.

Hefner candle (HC) or Hefnerkerze (HK)

Unit of luminous intensity.

1 hefner candle = 0.903 candela.

Note: 1. This unit, until 1942, was used widely in Germany under the name **Hefner-Kerze**, symbol HK.

2. The unit is named after a German electrical engineer, Friedrich von Hefner-Altenack (1845-1904), who invented a laboratory light standard, the Hefner lamp, which burned isopentyl acetate to provide light of intensity 1 HK.

helek (hl)

A traditional Hebrew unit of time equivalent to $1/1080$ hour, $1/18$ minutes or 10/3 seconds. The plural is **halakim**. Halakim are used in formulas establishing the instant of a new moon, which marks the start of the month in the Jewish calendar. In English, the unit is often known as a **part** of an hour. The Jews inherited this unit from the Babylonians. It was widely used throughout the ancient Middle East.

hefnerkerze (HK)

Unit of luminous intensity used in Germany from 1893 to 1940.

1 hefnerkerze ≈ 0.9 international candles.

Hehner number

An arbitrary unit of concentration of fatty acids in oils. It is defined as a hehner number of x, corresponding to x kilogrammes of water-insoluble fatty acids in one hundred kilogrammes of an oil or fat.

Note: This unit is also known as the Hehner value or Hehner number.

helmholtz

Metric unit of dipole moment per unit area. One helmholtz is equivalent to one debye (D) per angstrom squared.

1 helmholtz = 1 D/angstrom = 0.01 franklins per centimetre = 3.33564×10^{-10} coulombs per metre.

Note: The unit was proposed by Guggenheim in 1940 and its name is after a German physicist, Herman Ludwig Ferdinand von Helmholtz (1821-1894).

hemisphere

Arbitrary unit of solid angle. One hemisphere is the solid angle of half the entire space surrounding the center of a sphere.

1 hemisphere = 0.5 space (entire) = 6.282 185 307 steradians.

henry (H)

The SI unit of electrical inductance, i.e., self-inductance, mutual inductance and permeance. The inductance of a closed circuit in which an electromotive force of one volt is produced when the electric current in the circuit varies uniformly at the rate of one ampere per second. Practical units are microhenry (10^{-6} henries) and the millihenry (10^{-3} henries).

Note: 1. The unit was formally known as the absolute henry (H_{abs}).

2. The size of the standard henry has been experimentally determined using the Campbell apparatus at the National Physical Laboratory down to an accuracy of 10 parts per million.

3. The name Henry was approved for the unit at the Chicago meeting of the IEC in 1893.

The unit was named after an American scientist, Joseph Henry (1797-1878).

henry, thermal

The SI unit of thermal inductance. It is the thermal inductance of which an entropy flow of one wall per kelvin is associated with a kinetic energy of one joule.

1 thermal henry =1 Joule Kelvin squared per watt squared.

The former definition of this unit was such that it corresponded to a heat flow rate of one watt associated with a kinetic energy of one joule. 1 thermal henry = 1 Joule per watt squared

henry per metre (H m^{-1})

The SI unit of permeability.

Note: This unit is also known as **"magn"**.

See *"magn"*.

herschel

Metric unit of radiance.

1 herschel = π watt per metre squared per steradian

Note: 1. The name was suggested by Moon in 1942. The name is after an English mathematician, John Frederick William Herschel (1792-1871).

2. This unit has never been used.

hertz (Hz)

The SI unit of frequency. It is the number of repetitions of a regular occurrence in one second. 1Hz = 1 per second.

Note: 1. This unit is also used in all the systems of units.

2. This unit is also known as the cycle (per second), but it is recommended to use hertz. It has also been known as the vibration.

3. The name of the unit is after a German physicist Heinrich Rudolf Hertz (1857-1894). It was adopted by the EMMU committee of the International Electro-technical Commission in October 1933.

hexit

A unit of information, equivalent to 4 bits or ½ byte. A string of 4 bits has 16 possible states (0-15). It is usually represented as a single base -16 or **hex**adecimal dig**it** (in the hexadecimal system, the letters A through F are used to represent the numbers 0 through 15, respectively). A hexit of data is also known as a **nibble** or a **quabit.**

See also *"bit"* and *"byte"*.

hide

A very old English unit of land area, dating from perhaps the seventh century. The hide was the amount of land that could be cultivated by a single plowman and, thus, the amount of land necessary to support a family. Depending on local conditions, this could be as little as 60 acres or as much as 180 acres (44-72 hectares). The hide was more or less standardized as 120 acres (48.6 hectares) after the Norman conquest of 1066. The hide continued to be used throughout medieval times, but it is now obsolete. The unit was also known as the **carucate**.

himle

An Islamic unit of mass, *at least as early as the 14ᵗʰ century*, conceptually the carrying capacity of a camel, about 250 kilogrammes. Also romanized as *haml* and *heml*. In literature himl = 300 *mann* = 600 *ratl*.

As *heml*, in the United Arab Republic, a unit of mass, approximately 249.6 kilograms.

hin

An ancient Hebrew unit of liquid capacity mentioned several times in the Bible. The unit varied in size over time, but typically, it was around 3.7 liters, a little smaller than the U.S. gallon.

hogshead

Arbitrary unit of volume (capacity). One hogshead is equivalent to a half butt (Brit.)

1 hogshead = 0.5 butts = 0.238 480 94 cubic metres.

See *"butt"*.

hold

One of two Hungarian units of land area. The traditional **Magyar hold** or Hungarian acre is equivalent to 1200 square öl (fathoms) or about 0.4314 hectares (1.066 acres). The official **kataszteri hold** or cadastral hold, used for land taxation, is 1600 square öl or about 0.5752 hectares (1.421 acres). This unit is equivalent to the Austrian joch.

homestead

A historical unit of area in the U.S., equivalent to 160 acres (64.75 hectares). Under the Homestead Act passed by Congress in 1862, settlers in the western states were allowed to take the title of a homestead of 160 acres of land by registering a claim, settling on the land and cultivating it. A homestead is equivalent to ¼ square mile or ¼ section in U.S. government technology.

hoppus foot, hoppus broad foot

Traditional units of volume in British forestry. In the 1736 manual practical calculation, the English surveyor Edward Hoppus advised foresters to estimate the volume of wood in a log of length L and girth (circumference) G as $L(G/4)^2$. Since the correct formula is $L.G^2/(4 \cdot pi)$, the resulting value, known as the hoppus volume, is smaller than the actual volume of the log. It seems like an error, but in fact, not all the wood in a log can be used. The hoppus volume is a fairly reasonable estimate of the usable volume of wood in the log. Volume measurements made using the hoppus formula are stated in **hoppus feet**. To this effect, this makes the hoppus foot a unit volume, equivalent to 4/pi = 1.273 cubic feet or 0.036 054 cubic metres. Similarly, the hoppus board foot is equivalent to $\frac{1}{12}$ hoppus foot or 1.273 board feet, which is almost exactly 3 liters (0.00300 cubic metres). The British forestry industry switched its unit of timber measurement from hoppus feet to cubic metres in 1971.

hoppus ton

A traditional unit of volume in British forestry. One hoppus is equivalent to 50 hoppus feet or 1.8027 cubic metres. Shipments of tropical hardwoods from Southeast Asia, especially shipments of teak from Myanmar (Burma), are still stated in hoppus tons.

horse

Slang for the horsepower, as in "200-horse engines".

horsepower (hp)

Imperial (British and U.S.) unit of power, defined as a rate of work equivalent to **33000** feet pound per minute.

1 hp = 7.457 x 10^2 watts.

Note: 1. This unit is sometimes known as the British horsepower to distinguish it from the metric horsepower.

2. This unit was named after a Scottish inventor, James Watt (1736-1819), in 1782 as a selling aid for his steam pumping engines.

The inventor of the steam engine who determined after careful measurements that a horse is typically capable of a power rate of 550 foot-pounds per second. This means that a horse, harnessed to an appropriate machine, can lift 550 pounds at the rate of 1 foot per second.

See also *"horsepower, brake," "horsepower, metric,"* and *"horsepower indicated."*

horsepower, brake

Name given to the effective or shaft horsepower of an engine, i.e., the derived power that can be measured by means of a brake or dynamometer. It must be distinguished from the indicated horsepower, which is the theoretical power available from the working substance, if there were no friction and fluid losses due to imperfection in the mechanism used for converting heat into work.

See also *"horsepower, indicated."*

horsepower indicated

The indicated and the nominal horsepower are theoretical values for the power available that is derived from the dimensions of the engine. In the case of a piston engine, the indicated horsepower is given by *ASPN*/33 000 and the nominal horsepower by $D^2N(S)^{1/3}/15.6$, where A is the area of the piston in square inches, S is the stroke in feet, N is the number of cylinders, P is the pressure on the piston in pounds per square inch and D is the cylinder diameter in inches.

In the USA, the indicated horsepower of an automobile is generally the brake horsepower developed when the engine is running at 4,000 revolutions per minute.

horsepower, metric (metric horsepower)

Metric unit of power. 1 metric horsepower = 75 kilogramme-force per second.

1 metric horsepower = 75 kilogramme-force per second = 753.49875 watts.

Note: This unit is known as "**cheval vapeur** (ch)" in franch and **Pferdestarke** (PS)" in Germany. It is also known as the **Continental horsepower** (cont. hp).

The following definitions have been or are widely used for the horsepower

Mechanical horsepower hp(I)	$\equiv 33{,}000$ ft·lbf/min $= 550$ ft·lbf/s $\approx 17{,}696$ lbm·ft²/s³ $= 745.69987$ W ≈ 76.04 kgf·m/s ≈ 76.04 kg · 9.80665 m/s² · 1 m/s
Metric horsepower hp(M) – also *PS, KM, cv, hk, pk, ks* or *ch*	$\equiv 75$ kgf·m/s $\equiv 75$ kg · 9.80665 m/s² · 1 m/s $\equiv 735.49875$ W ≈ 542.476038840742 ft·lbf/s
Electrical horsepower hp(E)	$\equiv 746$ W
Boiler horsepower hp(S)	$\equiv 33{,}475$ BTU/h $= 9{,}812.5$ W
Hydraulic horsepower	$=$ flow rate (US gal/min) × pressure (lbf/in²) × 7/12,000 or $=$ flow rate (US gal/min) × pressure (lbf/in²) / 1714

	= 550 ft·lbf/s = 745.69987 W
Air horsepower	=flow rate (cubic feet/minute) × pressure (inches water column) / 6,356 or = 550 ft·lbf/s = 745.69987 W

Hounsfield unit (HU)

A unit used in medical imaging (CT or MRI scanning) to describe the amount of x-ray attenuation of each "voxel" (volume element) in a three-dimensional image. The voxels are normally represented as 12-bit binary numbers and, therefore, have $2^{12} = 4096$ possible values. These values are arranged on a scaled from -1024 HU to +3071 HU, calibrated such that -1024 HU is the attenuation produced by air and 0 HU is the attenuation produced by water. Tissue and bone produce attenuations in the positive range. The reading in Hounsfield units is known as the **CT number**. The unit is named after a British engineer, Godfrey Hounsfield, who demonstrated the first CT scanner in 1972. For this invention, he received the Nobel Prize in medicine in 1979.

hour (h)

Arbitrary unit of time.

1 hour = **3600** seconds.

hour angel (ω)

An arbitrary unit that describes the daily motion of the sun relative to a solar collector. It is used mainly in solar collector analysis. The hour angle is expressed by the equation:

$\omega = 2\pi \, (12 - t_{zone}) - (\lambda - \lambda_{zone}) - C \, 24$

Where t_{zone} = local time in hours,

λ = longitude,

λ_{zone} = to longitude defining the local time zone and

C = a small correction factor associated with earth's motion to the sun.

hubble (hubble)

Unit of length. One hubble is an astronomical distance, equivalent to 10^9 light years.

1 hubble = 10^9 light years.

Note: In practice, most astronomers use the megaparsec for measuring such stupendous distances. The unit honors the American astronomer Edwin Hubble (1889-1953), who discovered the expansion of the universe later explained by the Big Bang theory.

hundredweight

Imperial unit of mass.

1. Avoirdupois measure; *symbol:* cwt.

   The hundredweight, equivalent to 112 pounds.

   1 cwt = 112 pounds = 50.802 345 44 kilogrammes.

Note: This is the U.K. name of the unit. In the U.S., it is known as the long hundredweight. The hundredweight in the U.K. known as the **cental**, the **centner** or the **quintal**.

2. Troy measure; *symbol:* cwt tr.

   The troy hundredweight equivalent to 100 troy pounds.

   1 cwt = 100 troy pounds = 37.324 172 16 kilogrammes.

hundredweight, short (sh cwt)

Imperial unit of mass. One short hundredweight is equivalent to 100 pounds.

1 sh cwt = 100 pounds = 45.359 237 kilogrammes.

Note: This unit is used in the U.S. In the U.K., however, it is known as the **centner**, the **cental** or the **quintal**.

hüvelyk

The Hungarian inch unit equivalent to $\frac{1}{12}$ lab or about 2.63 centimetres. As it is used in many languages, the inch unit also means "thumb."

hyl (hyl)

The m-kgf-s (metric – technical) unit of mass. The hyl is the mass that acquires an acceleration of one metre per second squared under the influence of a force of one kilogramme-force.

1 hyl = 9.80665 kilogrammes.

Note: This unit is not often used. It is generally referred to as the metric technical unit of mass. It is also known as the **"metric slug."** Alternative names proposed (but were never used) are the **"mug"** and the **"par."**

hydron

Unit of acidity

See "Chapter 3".

I

i

A mathematical number equivalent to the square root of -1. Although often called the **imaginary unit,** *i* is quite real in many applications. For example, in vector geometry, it is used to represent a counterclockwise rotation by 90°. The Swiss mathematician Leonhard Euler (1707-1783) introduced the symbol *i* for the imaginary unit in 1777.

imperial (imp.)

An adjective indicating a particular unit of the imperial units.

see *"imperial units"*.

imperial units

Are used in trade in the U.K. under the Weight and Measures Act 1963. The related Acts and Regulations are listed below:

1. *Units of Length*: Inch, Foot, Link, Yard, rod (pole or perch), Chain, Furlong, Mile.
2. *Units of Area*: Square inch, Square foot, Square rod (pole or perch), Square yard, rood, Acre, Square mile.
3. *Units of volume*: Cubic inch, Cubic foot, Cubic yard.
4. *Units of Capacity:* Fluid ounce, Gill, Pint, Quart, Gallon, Peck, Bushel, Chaldron.
5. *Units of mass*: Grain, Dram, Ounce, Pound, Atone, Quarter, Central, Hundredweight, Ton.

    In addition, there are units used in connection with the weight of precious metals and precious stones, e.g., Pennyweight and Ounce Troy.

    There are units used in the sale of drugs, the so-called apothecaries units. These are Scruple and Drachm.

Note: The imperial units must not be confused with the American units of the same name.

inch (in or sometimes ")

Imperial unit of length. The inch is equivalent to $\frac{1}{12}$ foot.

1 inch = $\frac{1}{12}$ foot = 2.54×10^{-2} metres.

Note: 1. The inch, as a unit of measure, dates back to the time of Edward I when it was defined as follows:

"It is established that three grains of barley, dry and round, make an inch, twelve inches make a foot, 3 feet make an ulna…".

2. The name inch is derived from the Anglo-Saxon *ynce,* which means twelfth part.

inch. circular (circular inch)

Imperial unit of area. One circular inch is the area of a circle of diameter one inch.

1circular inch = $\pi/4$ inch square = 5.067 08 x 10^{-4} square metres.

inch of mercury (in Hg)

A traditional unit of atmospheric pressure.

In the U.S., atmospheric pressure is customarily expressed as the height of a column of mercury, exerting the same pressure as the atmosphere. When a traditional mercury barometer is used, this height is read directly as the height of the mercury column. These readings must be corrected for temperature since mercury, like most liquids, tends to expand as it warms.

The conventional equivalent of an inch of mercury is 0.491 153 pounds per square inch or 3.386 38 kilopascals (33.8638 millibars). The Hg, which is the symbol used for the unit, is the chemical symbol for mercury. It originates from the Latin word *hydragyrum* ('water-silver") for liquid metal.

See also *"pascal".*

inch of water column (in WC)

A traditional unit of pressure used in plumbing to describe both water and gas pressures. The conventional equivalent of one inch of water is 249.0889 pascals, which is 2.490 889 millibars, and about 0.036 127 pounds per square inch (psi) or about 0.073 556 inches (1.868 32 millimetres) of mercury.

inch of water gauge (in wg or "wg)

Another common name for the inch of water column. The word "gauge" (or "gauge") after a pressure reading indicates that the pressure stated is actually the difference between the absolute, or total, pressure and the air pressure at the time of the reading.

inch. pound (in Ibf or in Ib)

A traditional unit for work or energy, equivalent to $\frac{1}{12}$ foot pound, about 0.112 985 joules or 1.0709×10^{-4} Btu.

See also *"Btu"* and *"Joule"*.

inferno (inferno)

Unit of temperature (stellar temperature).

1 inferno = 10^9 kelvins.

Note: The unit was suggested for the first time in 1968.

inhour (ih)

An arbitrary unit of reactivity (a measure of the departure of a nuclear reactor for its critical condition). The reactivity R of a nuclear reactor in inhour is related to the reactor period T in hours by the formula:

R = 1/T

Thus, 1 hour is the reactivity that corresponds to a period of 1 hour.

Note: 1. The unit was proposed in 1947 and used mainly in the U.S. The symbol of the unit is the abbreviation of *"inverse hour."*

2. The reactor period is the time required (under conditions in which the neutron flux is varying exponentially) for the neutron flux to change by a factor of e.

instant

Unit of time. The unit is proposed to be a subdivision of the degree'.

1 instant = 10^{-4} degre's = 10^{-6} days = 0.0864 seconds.

See *"degre' "* and *"degree (time)"*.

international...

The original definitions of electrical units were given in terms of experimentally determined quantities. They were originally designated practical units, and later international units, and the unit symbols were assigned the subscript int. The international units were abandoned at the 9CGPM of 1948 in favor of the (theoretically defined) absolute units. The relationships between the international and absolute units of electromotive force (the volt) and the resistance were formally defined at CIPM of 1946, and the relationships between other international and absolute units are derived from them. The relationships are provided in the following table.

Unit	Unit Symbol	Quantity measured	Corresponding SI unit	To convert to SI, multiply by:
International Ampere	A_{int}	Electric current	(absolute) Ampere	$9.998\ 5 \times 10^{-1}$
International Candle	IC	Luminous intensity	Candela	1.02
International Coulomb	C_{int}	Electric charge	(absolute) Coulomb	$9.998\ 5 \times 10^{-1}$
International Farad	F_{int}	Capacitance	(absolute) Farad	$9.995\ 1 \times 10^{-1}$
International Henry	H_{int}	Inductance	(absolute) Henry	1.000 49
International Joule	J_{int}	Work, energy and heat	(absolute) Joule	1.000 19
International Nautical mile	N mile	Length	Metre	1.852×10^{-3}
International ohm	Ω_{int}	Resistance	(absolute) ohm	1.000 49
International Siemens	S_{int}	Conductance	(absolute) Siemens	$9.995\ 1 \times 10^{-1}$
International Tesla	T_{int}	Magnetic flux density	(absolute) Tesla	1.000 34
International Volt	V_{int}	Electric potential	(absolute) Volt	1.000 34
International Watt	W_{int}	Power	(absolute) Watt	1.000 19
International Weber	Wb_{int}	Magnetic flux	(absolute) Weber	1.000 34

international atomic time (IAT, TAI in France)

The most precisely determined timescale now available. It was set up by the Bureau Internationale de l'Heure in Paris and adopted in 1972. Atomic time is measured using atomic clocks, the fundamental unit being the SI second. Civil timekeeping is based on IAT.

International Bitterness Unit (IBU or BU)

A unit used by brewers to describe the bitterness—in moderation, a valued quality—of beer. One International Bitterness Unit is equivalent to 1 milligram of iso-alpha acid per liter of beer.

Notes: 1. Measurements in IBU are useful in maintaining consistent quality in a brewery. 2. Almost all beers fall in the 1-100 IBU range. An upper limit is reached when the beer is saturated with iso-alpha acid, somewhere around 110 to 120 IBU.

3. A few examples of IBU measurements of familiar types of beer:

- Everyday American lagers, 8-15 IBU
- ordinary bitter, 25-35 IBU
- India Pale Ale (American versions), 40-70 IBU (the American "Imperial" or "double" IP ales go as high as 120 IBU)
- Russian Imperial Stout, up to 90 IBU

4. In Australia, beers with IBU values lower than four cannot be called beer.

5. In Germany, selling Pilsner beer with an IBU value below 20 constitutes fraud.

6. The unit is standardized through cooperation between the American Society of Brewing Chemists, the Europe Brewery Convention, the Institute & Guild of Brewing, and the Brewery Convention of Japan.

7. The International Bitterness Unit is NOT a measure of perceived bitterness but of the concentration of a certain class of chemical compounds from hops. Unlike, say, the Scoville unit for the heat of peppers, which was originally measured using human tasters, the IBU number for a beer has always been determined solely by objective chemical tests in a laboratory. No tasting is involved.

8. Brewers can estimate the bitterness using a formula based both on the quantity and quality of hops used and on the brewing technique (for example, how long the hops are boiled). One of the empirical formulas that can be used for estimating the bitterness is:

$$IBU = H \times \frac{A + \frac{B}{9}}{0.3}$$

where

- H is the concentration of hops in grams per liter.
- A is the concentration of alpha acids in the hops, expressed as a percentage.
- B is the concentration of beta acids in the hops, expressed as a percentage.

international candle

Unit of luminous intensity. The standardizing laboratories of France, Great Britain and the U.S. approved this unit in 1909 and was maintained by electric incandescent lamps. It was superseded in 1948 by the candela.

See *"candle," "international standard,"* and *"Candela"*.

international foot

The current foot unit of English-speaking countries equivalent to exactly 30.48 centimetres.

international practical temperature scale (IPTS)

A temperature scale based on the thermodynamic temperature, consisting of certain fixed points (physical properties of pure substances) at which temperatures are defined absolutely, together with experimental procedures for measuring temperature between these points. The original scale was introduced in 1927, and there have been several changes since then. The 1968 version (known as IPTS-68) had eleven fixed points defined in both Celsius and thermodynamic temperature scales. The most recent version was introduced in 1990 (IPTS-90) and has sixteen fixed points with temperatures as signed in kelvin as follows:

Triple point of hydrogen	13.803 3
Boiling point of hydrogen (33 321.3 Pa)	17.035
Boiling point of hydrogen (101 292 Pa)	20.27
Triple point of neon	24.556 1
Triple point of oxygen	54.358 4

Triple point of argon	83.805 8
Triple point of mercury	234.315 6
Triple point of water	273.16 (0.01°C)
Melting point of gallium	302.914 6
Freezing point of indium	429.748 5
Freezing point of tin	505.078
Freezing point of zinc	692.677
Freezing point of aluminum	933.473
Freezing point of silver	1234.93
Freezing point of gold	13337.33
Freezing point of copper	1357.77

At low temperatures (0-5 K), intermediate temperatures between fixed points are measured by vapor-pressure determinations of ^{3}He and ^{4}He. In the range of 3-24.56 1 K, a constant-volume gas thermometer is used. A platinum-resistance thermometer is used for temperatures above 13.803 3 K and at high temperatures (> 1234.93), radiation pyrometry is used. For particular temperature ranges, specified fixed points and equations are defined.

international nautical mile

A nautical mile, as currently defined by international agreement, equivalent to exactly 1852 metres or 6076.11549 feet. This unit is sometimes used to distinguish the current nautical mile from older units.

See also *"nautical mile"*.

international rubber hardness degree (IRHD)

A unit used to measure the hardness of rubber and similar materials (technically known as elastomers). Measurements are made using an IRHD durometer, and the results are usually similar but not identical to readings made with the older Shore "A" durometer. The International Organization for Standardization (ISO) and the American Society for Testing and Materials (ASTM), among other standards agencies, have published IRHD test procedures.

international units of electricity

A system of units based on two mechanical standards (metre and seconds) and two electrical standards (volt and ampere). The electrical standards are defined using silver electrolysis (ampere), standard cell (volt) or mercury resistance (ohm).

The international units and absolute electrical units are not equal. The relation between them is:

1 international volt = 1.000330 absolute volts,

1 international ampere = 0.999835 absolute amperes,

1 international ohm = 1.000495 absolute ohms.

See also *"international…"* and *"absolute…"*.

Internet time

a global decimal time system proposed by the Swatch Corporation.

iodine number

Arbitrary measure for the percentage of absorbed iodine. An iodine number of x corresponds to x kilogrammes of iodine absorbed by one hundred kilogrammes of a substance.

Note: The iodine number is used as a measure of the proportion of unsaturated linkages in a sample of oil or fat.

Irish acre

A traditional unit of land area in Ireland, equivalent to 160 square Irish perches (see next entry). This is equivalent in English units to 7840 square yards, 70 560 square feet, or about 1.6198 English acres (0.6555 hectares). The colpa, a traditional Irish unit of pasturage, is approximately equivalent to the Irish acre.

Irish mile

The traditional mile in Ireland is 6720 feet, which is 1.272 727 English miles or 2.048 256 kilometres. The discrepancy arose because the Irish or rod was standardized at 21 feet instead of the English figure of 16.5 feet. Just as in England, the Irish was equivalent to 4 perches (84 feet instead of 66 feet), the Irish was equivalent to 10 chains (840 feet instead of 660 feet) and the mile was equivalent to 8 furlongs.

iron

A traditional unit measuring the thickness of leather used in making shoes, especially the soles of the shoes. One iron is equivalent to ¼₈ inch (0.5292 millimetres), so a sole ¼ inch think is described as "12 iron". The origin of this unit is unclear.

Istanbul kilesi

Unit of capacity in Turkey

1 Istanbul kilesi = 37 liters.

itrw

An ancient Egyptian unit of distance

1 itrw = 20,000 *schesup*, about 10.46 kilometers (about 6.5 miles).

The word also meant "river," and in concept, an *itrw* was the distance a boat could be towed along the Nile River in one day. It was also used to describe distances over land, however.

izenbi

Informal unit of area used in Morocco

1 izenbi = 1,800 square meters.

J

jack

An English unit of capacity = ¼ cup.

In colonial America, a jack was a mug or pitcher made of leather and waterproofed with wax or tar, of no certain volume.

Jackson turbidity units

An obsolete unit used in measuring the clarity of water. The lower the value, the clearer the water. Symbol, JTU or Jtu, is also known as the **Jackson Candle unit**. Water containing 100 parts per million silica had a turbidity of 21.5 JTU. The scale was built around suspensions of silica, in the form of diatomaceous earth.

The test relied on the human eye. The flame of a standard candle was viewed through a vertical tube, which was gradually filled with the water to be measured until the flame was no longer distinct. The depth of water in the tube had a scale marked in JTU that indicated the turbidity.

Both the unit and the measuring technique are now obsolete. However, measurements using the units that substituted it (i.e., NTU and FTU) are numerically close to JTU measurements but with a much lower margin of error.

jacktam

A unit of length, used in West Africa in which, cloth was sold, 4 yards (about 3.658 metres).

Jacobi's unit

In the *19ᵗʰ century*, two units were used in the investigations of electricity. Both of these were suggested by a German physicist Moritz Hermann von Jacobi (*1801-1875*):

1. **Jacobi's unit of current** defines the strength of an electric current by the quantity of oxygen plus hydrogen gas generated by the electrolysis of water under specified conditions. One of Jacobi's units is that where the strength of an electric current in which 1 minute yields 1 cubic centimetre of mixed gas, measured at a temperature of 0°C and a pressure of 760 millimetres of mercury. It is approximately 0.09657 amperes.

   In Germany, this unit is called the *Jacobische Knallgaseinheit*. There is no simple English equivalent for the German word *Knallgas*, literally "explosion gas," an apt name for a 1:2 mixture of oxygen and hydrogen.

2. **Jacobi's unit of resistance** is the resistance of 1 metre of wire with a circular cross section, 1 millimetre in diameter, and made of a particular copper alloy. Jacobi sent lengths of wires representing this unit to numerous prominent scientists in *1848*. The measurement of Fleeming Jenkin was found to be about 0.6367 of a B.A. ohm.

Note: "B.A. unit" of resistance is an absolute unit based on a meter-gram-second system of units.

JANSKY (Jy)

A unit of radiant flux density that is used in astronomy throughout the spectral range, especially for radio and infrared measurements. It refers to a particular frequency.

1 jansky = 10^{-26} watts per metre squared per hertz

In measuring signal strength, it's necessary to take into account both the area of the receiving antenna and the width of the frequency band in which the signal occurs. Accordingly, one jansky equals a flux of 10^{-26} watts per square meter of receiving area per hertz of the frequency band (W/m^2Hz). Although it is not an SI unit, the jansky is approved by the International Astronomical Union and is widely used by astronomers. It honors Karl G. Jansky (1905-1950), the American electrical engineer who discovered radio waves from space in 1930. The jansky is sometimes called the **flux unit**.

jar (jar)

CGS-esu derived unit of capacitance.

1   jar = 10^3 state farads = (⅑) x 10^{-8} farads.

Note: The unit represented the approximate capacitance of a Layden jar.

jarra

Informal unit of liquid capacity. Its value depends on the country:

-   In Libya, a unit of liquid capacity approximately 14.13 liters.
-   In Mexico, a unit of liquid capacity approximately 8.2128 liters (about 2.17 U.S. gallons).
-   In Bolivia, it has different values depend on the measured commodity and the town. Examples are shown in the next table.

Department	Town	Volume in liters	Commodity
La Paz	Viacha	6	chicha
Chuquisaca	Yotala	0.5	milk
	Tarabuco	7.50	
Potosi	Arampampa	2.25	chicha
	Uyuni	1	chicha
Santa Cruz	Lagunillas	7.5	
	Santa Cruz	5	
	Valle Grande	7.5	
Tarija	Entre Rios	1	chicha
Cochabamba	Arani	1.5	
	Independencia	4.5	
	Sacaba	1.5	
	Quillacollo	6	

Source: [Bolivia] Ministerio de Agricultura, Ganaderia y Colonizacion. Dirección General de Economia Rural.

jarda

Informal unit of length. Its value varies from country to country:

- In the Cape Verde Islands, 1 jarda is approximately 0.88 meters.
- In Macau, 1 jarda is approximately 0.895 meters.
- In Malta , 1 jarda = 1 yard.

jareeb

Informal unit of measurement used in Pakistan. It is used as unit of length and as a unit of area:

- a unit of length = 22 yards, approximately 20.1168 meters.
- a unit of area = 484 square yards, approximately 404.7 square meters.

Jerib or djerib

A traditional unit of land area in the Middle East or Southwestern Asia. The jerib originally varied considerably from one area to another. In modern times, it has become identified with the hectare in many countries, including Turkey and Iran. In Afghanistan, however, it is usually equivalent to $\frac{1}{5}$ hectare (2000 square metres or 0.494 acres).

jerk (jerk)

FPS unit of rate of change of acceleration. One jerk is a rate of change of acceleration of one foot per second squared per second.

jerk = 1 foot per second cubed.

Note: 1. The unit has been used by engineers in U.K.

2. No name has been given to the corresponding unit in the metric systems, nor has the name 'jerk' been recognized by the ISO."

Jersey foot

A traditional unit of distance in Jersey, one of the Channel Islands. Also known as the *pied-perche*. The jersey foot is equivalent to 11 English inches or 0.9167 English feet.

The jersey foot is divided into 12 jersey inches, making 13.09 jersey inches equivalent to an English foot.

jiffy [1]

A unit of time used in computer engineering. A jiffy is the length of one cycle, or tick, of the computer's system clock. In the past, this was often equivalent to one period of the alternating current powering the computer. $\frac{1}{60}$ seconds in the U.S. and Canada, and usually $\frac{1}{50}$ second elsewhere. More recently, the jiffy has become standardized, more or less, as 0.01 seconds (10 milliseconds). The word jiffy, meaning the instant or very brief time, appeared in the English vocabulary during the eighteenth century, but its origin is unknown.

jiffy [2]

A unit of time used in chemistry and physics, equivalent to a "light centimetre." It is the time required for light to travel a distance of one centimetre. This is a very brief interval indeed, about 33.3564 picoseconds. This definition of the jiffy was proposed by the American physical chemist Gilbert Newton Lewis (1875-1946), who was one of the first scientist to apply the principles of quantum physics in chemistry.

jigger

A unit of volume of liquor, usually considered equivalent to 1.5 (U.S.) fluid ounces or 44.360 milliliters.

jin

A traditional unit of weight in China, comparable to the English pound. During the European colonial era, the jin was identified together with the catty, a Malay unit widely used in various forms throughout East and Southeast Asia. Like the catty, the jin was then equivalent to ⅓ pounds or 604.79 grammes. Traditionally, it was divided into 16 liang. In modern China, however, the jin is a metric unit, equivalent to exactly 500 grammes (1.1023 pounds) and divided into 10 liangs. The kilogramme itself is usually known as the **gongjin,** or "metric jin". The spellings **chin** and **gin** also have been used for the jin.

jitro

A traditional unit of land area in the Czech Republic, identical to the Austrian joch.
See also *"joch"*

Jo

An informal unit of area used in Japan to measure the size of rooms in houses and apartments. One jo is the area of a traditional tatami mat, 180 by 90 centimetres of 1.62 square metres, 1.94 square metres (1.94 square yards).
See also *"joch."*

joch

A traditional unit of area in German speaking countries, especially in Austria. One joch is the area of a square 40 klafters (about 83 yards) on a side, which is equivalent to 0.5755 hectares or about 1.422 acres. The plural is **joche.** Joch is also the word for a yoke in German. This unit represents an area that could be plowed in a day by a yoke of oxen. In what is now the Czech Republic, this unit was known as the **jitro**; in Croatia, it is known as the **jutro.**

jonnes

A unit of detectivity, i.e., the ability of an electronic device to detect radiant energy such as light waves or infrared radiation. In a 1959 article ("Quantum Efficiency of Human Vision," Journal of the Optical Society of America. 49(7): 645-653), Robert Clark Jones defined the "specific detectivity" of a device to be $D^* = $ [square root $(aw)]/N$, where a is the area of the detector, w is the frequency bandwidth and N is the power of the noise generated by the device. The quantity is measured in the complex unit cm. $Hz^{1/2}/W$, customarily known as the "Jones." In modern equipment, detectives are often quite large, between the range of 10^9 to 10^{12} Jones.

joule (J):

The SI unit of energy, including work and quantity of heat. It is the work done when a point of application of a force of one newton is displaced through a distance of one metre in the direction of the force.

1 J = 1 Newton metre.

Note: 1. The joule is also a unit of the Hamilton function, Language function, kinetic energy operator, Hamiltonian operator, Coulomb integral, Resonance integral, Ionization energy, Hartree energy, Electron affinity, Dissociation energy, Quadrupole interaction energy tensor, Level width, Disintegration energy, Work function, Gap energy, Fermi energy, Enthalpy, Helmholtz energy, Gibbs energy, Van der Waals constant, Van der Waals-Hamaker constant.

2. The unit was originally proposed by the British Association in 1888, who recommended that it be named after James Prescott Joule (1818-1889).

3. In 1948, the joule was adopted as the unit of heat by the International Conference on Weights and Measures, such that the specific heat of water at 15°C is 4185.5 joule (kg °C)$^{-1}$.

4. The former definition of the thermal coulomb made it equivalent to the joule.

See *"coulomb, thermal".*

joule per coulomb (J C^{-1}):

SI unit of electric potential. This unit is also known as the volt.

See *"volt"*.

joule per cubic metre (J m^{-3}):

SI unit of energy density, radiant energy density. The amount of energy in joules per unit volume.

Note: It is also a unit of calorific value (volume basis) and refrigerating capacity per unit volume.

joule per cubic metre hertz (J m^{-3} Hz^{-1}):

SI unit of spectral energy density in terms of frequency.

joule per kelvin (J K^{-1}):

SI unit of heat capacity and entropy.

Note: It is also known as the unit of Boltzmann constant, Massieu function and Planck function.

joule per kilogramme (J Kg^{-1}):

SI unit of specific energy and specific enthalpy.

Note: 1. It is also a unit of specific latent heat, calorific value (mass basis), specific energy and exergy.

2. The SI unit Gray (Gy) can be used instead of joule per kilogramme, especially for quantities such as absorbed dose and other ionizing radiation quantities, specific energy imparted, kerma, and absorbed dose index.

3. The SI unit Sievert (Sv) is preferred instead of joule per kilogramme as a unit for dose equivalent.

See *"Gray"* and *"Sievert"*.

joule per kilogramme kelvin (J kg^{-1} K^{-1}):

SI unit of specific heat capacity and specific entropy.

joule per metre (J m^{-1}):

SI unit of total linear stopping power and linear energy transfer.

joule per metre to the fourth power (J m^{-4}):

SI unit of spectral concentration of radiant energy density in terms of wavelength.

joule per mole (J mol^{-1}):

SI unit of molar internal energy.

Note: It is also a unit of chemical potential, standard reaction enthalpy, standard reaction Gibbs function, the affinity of reaction, standard partial molar enthalpy, the energy of activation, standard enthalpy of activation, standard Gibbs energy of activation and electrochemical potential.

joule per mole kelvin (J mol^{-1} K^{-1}):

SI unit of molar heat capacity and molar entropy.

Note: It is also a unit of unit molar gas constant, standard partial molar entropy, standard reaction entropy and standard entropy of activation.

joule per square metre (J m^{-2}):

SI unit of energy and radiation exposure.

Note: It is also a unit of surface tension, vibrational force constant and spectral radiant energy density in terms of wavenumber.

joule per square tesla (J T^{-2}):

SI unit of magnetizability of a molecule.

joule per tesla (J T^{-1}):

SI unit of magnetic dipole moment of a molecule.

Note: 1. It is also a unit of Bohar magneton and nuclear magneton.

2. The unit ampere metre square can be used instead of joule per tesla.

joule per second (J s^{-1}):

SI unit of Planck constant and angular momentum.

Note: It is also a unit of action. In this context, it is known as the "planck".

joule per square metre (J m^{-2}):

SI unit of total atomic stopping power.

joule per square metre per kilogramme (J m^{-2} kg^{-1}):

SI unit of total mass stopping power.

journal

A traditional unit of land area in France, equivalent to the area that could be plowed in a da (*jour* is the French word for day). The unit varied from one region to another, generally ranging between 0.3-0.45 hectares (0.75-1.1 acres). The juchart was a very similar unit used in Switzerland and southern Germany.

jow

Informal unit of length at In India.

1 jow = 0.25 inch (about 0.63 centimeter).

Also called a Jacob.

juchart or juchert

A traditional unit of land area used in southern Germany and German-speaking Switzerland. Like the Austrian joch and the French journal (see above), the juchart represents an area that could be plowed in a day by a yoke of oxen. The juchart varied considerably from place to place, but often, it was about 4000 square metres, very close to the size of the English acre. In Bavaria, the juchart was standardized early in the nineteenth century at 3407.27 square metres (0.8420 acres). In Switzerland, after the introduction of the metric system in the mid nineteenth century, the juchart was generally understood to be equivalent to 3600 square metres (0.8896 acres). The joch, the journal, and the juchart are ultimately derived from a Roman unit, the **jugerum,** which was very small, about 2500 square metres. The unit is also known as the tagwerk **("day's work").**

jug

An informal name of the Scots pint, a unit of volume equivalent to about 1.80 U.S. liquid quarts or 1.70 liters. Specifically, the **jug of Stirling** is the actual vessel (on display at the Stirling Museum), which was the legal standard for Scottish volume measurements prior to the introduction of the British Imperial units.

julian day (JD)

A continuous count of days beginning with January 1, 4713 BC (-4712 CE), which is the beginning of what is known as the Julian period. A French scholar, Joseph Justus Scaliger (1540-1609), introduced the Julian period in 1582 (the same year the Gregorian calendar was proclaimed) and defined it to be 7980 years, the product of a 28-year cycle of the Julian calendar (after which, the days of the week recur on the same dates), a 19-year Metonic cycle (after which, the phases of the Moon recur on the same dates), and a 15-year indication cycle (a unit of civil time in ancient Rome). It happens that 4713 BC is the last year in which all three cycles begun simultaneously. In 1849, the British astronomer John Herschel introduced the Julian day as a means of providing an exact date for astronomical events, independent of all calendars. The Julian day begins at noon Universal Time, and the exact times of observations are expressed using decimal fractions of the Julian day. The first moment of the year 2004 CE Universal Time was JD 2 453 005. 5.

julian epoch (J)

A measure of time used in astronomy. The word *epoch* originates from the Greek and means a fixed or standard instant of time. Other times are stated with reference to this fixed time using years and fractions of years. In 1984, astronomers agreed to fix the standard epoch at 12 hours University Time of 2000 January 1 (JD 2 451 545.0). This instant is designated J2000.0. Other times are specified with reference to this time using a year of length 365.25 days, the average length of the year in the Julian calendar. This implies that J2001.0, for example, is 18 hours Universal Time of 2001 January 1 (exactly 365.25 days after J2000.0).

julian period

A unit of time, equivalent to exactly 7980 years in the Julian calendar, i.e., exactly 2 914 695 days.

julian year

Unit of time. Calendar year with one intercalated day in every four years.

1 Julian year = **3.155 76 x 10^7** seconds = **8.766 x 10^3** hours = **365.25** days

See also *"year"*.

jungbo

A traditional unit of land area in North Korea.

1 jungbo = 1 hectare.

See also "hectare."

jupitar

A unit of mass currently used in astronomy to express the masses of new planets being discovered in orbit around various stars. It is equivalent to the mass of the planet Jupiter, estimated to be about 1.899 x 10^{24} metric tons, or 1.899 yottatonnes (Yt). By coincidence, this is approximately 0.001 Suns (0.000 955 Suns, to be more exact).

jutro

A traditional unit of land area in Croatia. The jutro is equivalent to 5754.64 square metres (1.422 acres), identical to the Austrian joch (see above) and Czech jitro. This is the area of a square, 40 hvati on a side.

This word means "morning," i.e., it represents the area that could be plowed in one morning. The plural is **jutra.**

K

K

Unit of reactivity, i.e., a measure of the departure of a nuclear reactor from its critical condition. It is defined as:

1 k is a charge in reactivity of unity.

Note: The name of the unit is itself the unit symbol.

K

An informal abbreviation for one thousand used in expressions where the unit is understood, such as "10K run" (10 kilometres) or "700K disk" (700 kilobytes or kibibytes). Note that "K" is also the symbol for the kelvin (see below) and is often used as a symbol for the karat. Also note that the symbol for the metric prefix kilo- (1000) is actually k-, not K-. In computer science, K often represents $2^{10} = 1024$.

kabiet

A unit of length in Thailand.

1 kabiet = 25/48 centimeters, about 5.2 millimeters (about 0.206 inch).

The unit is also romanized as *krabiat.*

In Laos, the *kabiet louang,* a unit of length 5 5/24 mm (about 5.208 mm)

Kad (Plural, *kadi.*)

In Russia, a unit of dry capacity for grain, commonly measured by mass, = 14 *pudy*, about 504 pounds.

kaf

A symbol for 1000 acre feet. This symbol is commonly used in reservoir management in the U.S. 1 kaf = about 1.2335 million cubic meters.

See "acre feet"

kafiz

An Arabic word which gave rise to numerous units, from Spain to India.

1.   In Iran, a unit of area = 100 square meters (0.027 acre).

2.   In India, a unit of mass and a unit of land area.

kaima

A unit of capacity used in Sweden. It is about 2.62 liters.

kairi

The Japanese name for the nautical mile.

kal

In the United States, a unit of power = one pound of water at 100°F evaporated into steam of 70 pounds per square inch, about 1110.2 Btu.

30 kals per hour = 1 commercial boiler horsepower.

Note: **In** Malay] **kal is a** measure of capacity; = ½ a chupak.

kala

In Morocco, a unit of length, = 50 centimeters.

kanal

A traditional unit of land area in Pakistan, equal to 20 marlas. Under British rule, the marla and kanal were standardized so that the kanal equals exactly 605 square yards or 1/8 acre; this is equivalent to about 505.857 square meters.

See also "acre," and "square meter."

kande

In Denmark, two units:

1. A unit of mass used for butter, = 2 *stobe* = 8 *skaalpund* = 16 *mark*.

Note: Before *1683*, the unit was about 3.96 kilogrammes. After *1683*, = 4 kilogrammes.

2.   A unit of capacity used for honey, = 2 *stobe* = 4 *potter*, about 3.872 liter.

kanne

Metric unit of capacity (i.e., volume).

1 kanne = 1 liter = 10^{-3} cubic metres.

Note: The name was proposed as an alternative to the liter, but was never used.

kantar

A widespread Arabic unit of mass, originally indicating 100 of some smaller unit. In Egypt, it is equivalent to 100 rotls, in Morocco, it is equivalent to 100 kilogrammes. Like the English word "century," it descends from the Latin word for hundred. It is also romanized as guntar and kanthar. Some values:

Cyprus		about 55.882 kilogrammes (about 123.2 pounds). = 44 okes
	Aleppo kantar	for carobs. About 228.6 kilogrammes (about 504.0 pounds). = 180 okes.
Egypt		Guillame says the customs kantar (or cantaro) = 100 rotls, 99.0492 pounds av., 45 kilogrammes of cotton, 44.5 kilogrammes of other produce.
Jordan	Nabulsi	about 228.5 kilogrammes (about 636.0 pounds). = 225 okka.
	Shami	about 256.4 kilogrammes (about 565.3 pounds). = 200 okka
Lebanon		about 256.4 kilogrammes (about 565.3 pounds). = 100 rottol
Libya	Cyrenaica	about 64.10 kilogrammes (about 141.3 pounds= 50 okes
	Tripolitania	about 51.28 kilogrammes (about 113.1 pounds). = 40 okes
Morocco		= 100 kilogrammes (about 220.5 pounds).
Saudi Arabia		about 51.347 kilogrammes (about 113.2 pounds).
		around 1920, 49.92 kilogrammes
Sudan		About 44.928 kilogrammes, about 99.05 pounds = 100 artal.

	Large kantar or **kantar of Alexandria**	at least as early as the 19th – 20th century, 141.523 kilogrammes (312 pounds). = 315 artal.
Syria	Aleppo and Homs	about 320.5 kilogrammes (about 706.6 pounds).
	Damascus	about 256.4 kilogrammes (about 565.3 pounds). = 200 oke
Tunis		the cartar, = 100 rottol, about 50.39 kilogrammes
Turkey		about 56.45 kilogrammes (about 124.5 pounds). = 44 okka. Under the 1881 decimalization law, the kantar was 128.3 kilogrammes, = 100 ock.
United Arab Republic		44.928 kilogrammes (99.05 pounds).

kappland

A traditional unit of land area in Sweden. The kappland is equivalent to $\frac{1}{32}$ tunnland or 1750 square Stockholm feet (*kvadratfot*). This is equivalent to 154.26775 square metres or about 184.50 square yards.

The *kappland* was originally a seed measure of land area, the amount of land that would be sown with a kappe of seed.

See also "yard."

kapp line (of magnetic force)

CGSemu derived unit of magnetic flux. One kapp line represents 6000 maxwells.

1 kapp line = 6000 maxwells = 6 x 10^{-5} weber.

Note: The unit was devised by a British electrical engineer, Gisbert Kapp (1852-1922), in 1886, who named the line after himself and was used only by him.

See also *"line (of magnetic force)."*

Katha

An obsolete unit of area.

A **katha** (also spelled **kattha** or **cottah**) is a unit of area mostly used for land measure in Eastern India, Nepal, and Bangladesh. After metrication in the mid-20th century by both countries, the unit became officially obsolete. But this unit is still used in much of Bangladesh, Eastern India and Nepal.

The measurement of katha varies significantly from place to place.

- In Gorakhpur state, 1 katha = **1361 square feet**. The length of the area should be 40 ft and the breath should be 34.025 feet and length × breath = 1361 **square feet.**

- In Bangladesh, one katha is standardized to 720 square feet (67 square metres), and 20 katha equals 1 bigha.

  The following relations are used:

  - 1 katha or Cottah = 720 **square feet** (approx) = 66.8902 **square feet** = approx. 1.65 decimals.

  - 1 bigha = 20 katha = 14,400 square feet = 1320 square meter (approx.)

  - 1 acre = 3.0245 bigha approx. = 1600 square yards

  - 1 hectare = 2.47 acre = 7.47494 bigha = 100 Ayer

- In Nepal, it is equivalent to 338.63 square metres (3,645 **square feet**).

- In the Indian state of Bihar, one katha may vary from 750 to 2000 **square feet**. This can also be 32 by 30 feet in length and breadth, respectively.

- In South Bihar and Patna,

  - 1 katha is generally equal to 1361 **square feet**.

  - 20 katha equals 1 bigha.

  - One katha is further subdivided into 20 dhur.

  - One dhur is further subdivided into 20 dhurki.

  - 1 hectare = 2.4712 acres or approx. 4 bigha.

- o   1 acre = 1.6 bigha or 32 katha; 1 bigha = 20 katha; 1 katha = 20 dhoor;

  - o   1 dhoor = 6.25 or 6.5 haath; 1 katha = 4 decimals.

- In Aurangabad and Gaya, 1 katha is generally equivalent to 1361.25 square feet. In Saran district, 1 katha is equivalent to 4 decimals (1 decimal in Bihar is equivalent to 435.56 square feet).

- In Assam, 1 katha is generally equivalent to 2880 square feet.

- In West Bengal, 1 katha is equivalent to 720 square feet.

The origin of the term and measurement unit was during the Pala Empire.

karat *or* carat

1. A unit of proportion indicating what part of an alloy is precious metal. Pure unalloyed gold is 24 karats. 12-karat gold is $^{12}/_{24}$, or 50% gold, and so on. In the United States, it is spelled with an initial "k" to distinguish it from the carat, a unit of mass, but in the rest of the world, it is spelled with a "c." The word originates from the Arabic *qirat*, which represents the ratio $^1/_{24}$, much as in English, the word "nail" used to represent $^1/_{16}$ of a larger unit, and sometimes $^1/_{16}$ of a yard or $^1/_{16}$ of a hundredweight. In Lebanon today, one kirat is $^1/_{24}{}^{th}$ of a drah.

Pure gold is quite soft and not suitable for objects like rings. A ring is made of 18-karat gold alloy to improve performance, not to save on the cost of materials. Alloys below 14 karats, however, are liable to crack.

Gold Alloys Permitted in England	
Period	**Legal Fineness in carats**
1477-1575	18
1575-1798	22
1798-1854	18, 22
1854-1932	9, 12, 15, 18, 22

1932	9, 14, 18, 22

2. In German-speaking Europe, the Karat of Cologne, a unit of mass used for gold and silver, = $^9/_{160}$ Quentchen, weighs about 205.5 milligrammes. In Frankfurt am Main, however, 1 Karat = $^1/_{1156}$ Mark, about 205.8 milligrammes. Article 4 of the law establishing the metric system in Austria specified that the *Wiener Karat* (Vienna karat) was equivalent to 205.969 grammes.

kartos

A unit of liquid capacity.

In Cyprus, approximately 4.5 imperial quarts (approximately 5.114 liters, or 5.40 U.S. liquid quarts).

kat

In SI, a derived unit of enzyme activity. The symbol, is "kat". One katal is that catalytic activity, which will raise the rate of reaction by one mole per second in a specified assay system. The katal was adopted by Resolution 12 of the 21st CGPM in *October 1999*, on the recommendation of the International Federation of Clinical Chemistry and Laboratory Medicine. In its resolution, the CGPM recommended that "when the katal is used, the measurand be specified by reference to the measurement procedure. The measurement procedure must identify the indicator reaction." The katal is not used to express a rate of reaction itself, which should be expressed in moles per second. Prior to the katal's adoption by the CGPM, researchers had been using a similar unit for approximately 30 years. The International Union of Biochemistry adopted a unit in *1964,* which was generally nameless (although sometimes known as an "international unit") but later acquired the symbol "U." That earlier enzyme unit used minutes rather than seconds as its unit of time, which was not in keeping with SI (minutes are not an SI unit) or with the usual way of expressing rate constants in chemical kinetics. In *1966,* the International Union of Pure and Applied Chemistry and the International Federation of Clinical Chemistry recommended adoption of the unit to be known as the **catal** (symbol, cat), such that 1 catal was equivalent to the catalytic amount of a system, which catalyses as many cycles per second of a stated reaction scheme as there are atoms in 0.012 kilogrammes of the pure nuclide ^{12}C. When the katal was first proposed, it was conceived as a unit of rate of reaction, but the 1978 recommendation distinguishes between catalytic activity and rate of reaction. The katal is too large for most purposes and it is usually encountered as the microkatal, nanokatal or picokatal. The CGPM is exceedingly reluctant to add new names for derived units to the SI since there is almost no end to the number of derived units that might be named. In the case of the katal, the argument that human safety required it carried the day:

"The case for its introduction was based on the need to introduce it from the viewpoint of human safety; for nurses particularly have been finding it difficult to compound and convey quantities involving combinations of three or more SI units. On this basis, the CCU forwarded a recommendation for its adoption to the CIPM."

kati

A traditional Malaysian unit of weight, usually spelled "catty" in English.

kattha or katta

A traditional unit of land area in South Asia, equivalent to 20 dhurs or $\frac{1}{20}$ bigha. Like the bigha, the kattha varied in size from one region to another. In Nepal, where the unit is still in use, the kattha is equivalent to about 338 square metres or 442 square yards.

See also "bigha" and "dhurs"

kayser (K)

CGS unit of the reciprocal length and wave number. One kayser is the reciprocal length of a distance, which has a length of one centimetre.

1 K = 1/cm = 100/metre.

Note: 1. The name of the unit was approved in 1952 to commemorate Johannes Hendrik Kayser (1853-1940).

2. The energy represented by 1 kayser is 123.976 6 x 10^{-6} electronvolts.

3. This unit is also known as the **balmer** or the **Rydberg.**

See *"balmer"* and *"Rydberg (1)"*.

kbp

A symbol for 1000 base pairs, used in biochemistry and genetics. As is well known, DNA has the form of a double helix, with bases on one strand paired with bases on the other strand. Thus, the length of a segment or fragment of DNA is measured by the number of base pairs.

kBtu

A symbol for 1000 British thermal units. This unit of energy is equivalent to about 1.055 megajoules (MJ) or 0.2931 kilowatt hours (kWh).

kcmil

A symbol for 1000 circular mils, a unit of area equivalent to about 0.5067 square millimetres commonly used in stating wire gauges.

keddah

A traditional Egyptian unit of liquid volume also used in other parts of the Middle East. The keddah is equivalent to about 2.0625 liters (about 2.18 U.S. liquid quarts or 1.815 British Imperial quarts).

keel (keel)

Imperial unit of mass, equivalent to 21.2 tons.

Keel was a unit used to measure coal in the northeast of England. This unit was used to express the quantity of coal carried by a keelboat on the Tyne and Wear rivers. In 1750, it was said to be equivalent to 8 Newcastle chaldrons (wagons), a measure of volume, or a weight of 21.2 long tons or 424 cwt (21.54 metric tons).

> 1 keel = 21,540.19446656 kilogrammes (47,488.0000000 pounds)

Note: 1. The unit is also known as the barge.

2. The unit is used mainly for measuring coal.

See *"ton" and "barge."*

keg [1]

A traditional unit of volume or quantity that varies with the item contained in the keg. A keg of herring, for example, contains 60 fish. A keg of wine is frequently 12 U.S. gallons (about 45.42 liters), and a keg of beer is ½ barrel or 15.5 U.S. gallons (about 58.67 liters). "Keg" comes from an old Norse word for a small barrel.

See also "gallon," barrel."

keg [2]

A traditional unit of weight for nails. A keg of nails weighs 100 pounds and, thus, has a mass of about 45.359 kilogrammes.

See also "kilogramme."

kela

In Saudi Arabia, a unit of mass approximately 3.2205 kilogrammes.
See also "keleh"

keleh *or* kilah

In Egypt, a unit of capacity 16.5 liters (about 0.468 bushels).

kelvin (kelvin)

Metric unit of energy, particularly electrical energy.
1 kelvin = 1 kilowatt-hour
Note: This is the old name of the kilowatt-hour. It was once known as the *"Board of Trade unit."*
See also *"board of trade unit"*.

kelvin (k)

Base SI unit of thermodynamic temperature (formerly known as degree Kelvin), having an SI unit of temperature interval (difference). It is the fraction, $\frac{1}{273.16}$, of the thermodynamic temperature of the triple point of water. The symbol K is now used with the symbol $^\circ$.

Note: 1. The above definition has been adopted from the decision made during the 10CGPM of 1954 to define the thermodynamic scale of temperature on which the triple point of water is a fixed fundamental point attributing to the temperature of 273.16 K.

2. Basing on this definition, the absolute zero is fixed at -273.16K.

3. The freezing point ("standard temperature") of pure air-free water under a pressure of one standard atmosphere is 273.15 K and its boiling point is 373.15K.

4. The unit is named after a British mathematician, William Thomson, 1st Baron Kelvin (1824-1907).

See also *"kelvin degree"*

kelvin degree (K, formerly degK)

The SI unit of temperature interval or difference. It is equivalent to $\frac{1}{273.16}$ of the interval between the absolute zero and the triple point of water. It was initially defined as one-hundredth of the interval between the freezing and boiling points of pure air-free water, both under a pressure of one standard atmosphere.

Note: The unit was formerly named the Kelvin degree. This name was supplanted with the Kelvin (K)

See also *"kelvin"* and *"degK"*

kelvin metre (K m)

The SI unit of the second radiation constant.

kelvin per pascal (K Pa^{-1})

The SI unit of Joint- Thomson coefficient.

kelvin per watt (K W^{-1})

The SI unit of thermal resistance.

ken

A traditional Japanese unit of length, comparable to the English fathom. The ken is equivalent to 6 shaku, which is about 1.818 metres (5.965 feet). The ken is the length of a traditional tatami mat. At sea, this unit is also known as the **hiro**.

See also "fathom," "feet."

kerat

A traditional Middle Eastern unit of length, equivalent to about 9/8 inch or 2.86 centimetres. The unit has the same Arabic root as the carat or karat.

See "carat"

KerMetric time

An informal unit of time.

KerMetric time is a concept that divides the day into 100 equal parts called Kermits. Each Kermit is equivalent to 14.4 minutes.

A more precise time can be counted by dividing by 1000 or even 10000.

The name Kermit originates from a combination of the surname of the president of the National Research Council in 1983 (Dr. Larkin Kerwin). The original working model of KerMetric time, as conceived by W. Thayer of NRC, was assembled by the designated Clock Construction Team of John Phillips, Ron Hawkins, Les Moore and Willie Thayer in 1983.

kilderkin

U.K. unit of volume (capacity). It is equivalent to 18 U.K. gallons.
1 kilderkin = 18 U.K. gallons = 0.081 829 57 cubic metres.
Note: The unit is used mainly for measuring ale and beer.

kilah or keleh

In Egypt, a unit of capacity 16.5 liters (about 0.468 bushels).
See also "kela."

Kile

The **kile** (Ottoman Turkish: كيله) was an Ottoman unit of volume, similar to a bushel. Like other dry measures, it is also often defined as a specific weight of a particular commodity. Its value varied widely by location, period, and commodity, from 8 to 132 oka. The 'standard' kile was 36 litres or 20 oka.

See also "bushel," "oka", "litre."

kilo (k)

SI prefix denoting x 10^3. Examples include: kiloampere (kA), kilobar (kbar), kilobecquerel (kBq), kilocalorie (kcal), kilocoulomb (kC), kilogramme (kg), etc.

Note: In case of computer (memory capacity) and information, the prefix denotes $2^{10}=$ 1024, e.g., kilobytes = 1024 bytes.

kilobits per second (kbit/s)

Unit of measure for high-speed data transmission. (e.g., 64 kilobits per second)

Kilofors (kf)

A unit suggested in *1957* by the SUN Commission as a renaming of the kilogram-force. The proposed symbol was kf.

See also "kilogramme -force. "

kilobyte (kbyte)

Unit of storage capacity in computer technology. For internal storage (inner memory):

1 kilobyte = 2^{10} bytes = 1024 bytes,

For external storage (e.g., magnetic disk, magnetic tape, etc.):

1 kilobyte = 10^3 bytes.

kilobytes per second (kbyte/s)

Unit of measure, commonly used for transfer rates to and from peripheral devices

kilogramme (kg)

Base SI unit of mass. It is also the SI unit of (rest) mass of particles, mass defect and mass excess. It is the mass of a particular cylinder of platinum iridium alloy, also known as the International Prototype Kilogramme, which is preserved in a vault at Sevres, France, by the International Bureau of Weights and Measures. This definition has been adopted by the 1CGPM of 1889 and the 3CGPM of 1901.

Note: 1. The prototype of the international kilogramme is cylinder with a height equal to its diameter. It is made from an alloy of 90% platinum and 10% iridium. The prototype is kept in the International Bureau of Weights and Measures at Sevres (near Paris), but there is a copy in the custody of the National Physical Laboratory in the U.K.

2. The initial definition of the kilogramme that was suggested by the Paris Academy of Sciences in 1791 is; The kilogramme is the mass of one cubic decimetre of water at the temperature of its maximum density. 1 kg of water at this temperature (3.98 °C) was subsequently found to occupy a volume of 1.000028 cubic decimetres, and this volume was known as the liter until its recent definition that mentioned above.

3. In the British Parliament during the 1962-1963 session, a weights and measures Bill was passed in which the Imperial pound was defined as follows; "the pound shall weigh exactly 0.453 92 37 kilogrammes. This Act passed in 1963, makes the kilogramme a fundamental unit of mass in both the metric and the foot pound second (FPS) systems of unit.

4. In the U.S., the name of this unit is spelled as "kilogramme." The official translation of ISO Recommendations is always the kilogramme.

kilogramme-calorie (kcal)

Arbitrary unit of heat energy. One kcal is the quantity of heat required to raise the temperature of one kilogramme of air-free water from 14.5°C to 15.5°C at a constant pressure of one standard atmosphere. The experimentally derived value is:

1 kcal = 4185.5 $\pm$ 0.5 joules.

Note: 1. The unit is better regarded as one thousand fifteen-degree calories.

2. The unit is also known as the large calorie.

See *"calorie, fifteen degrees."*

kilogramme-equivalent (kg-eq)

Metric-derived unit of mass. One kg-eq is the mass of an element or radical in kilogrammes equivalent to (i.e., that combines with or replaces) three kilogrammes of tetravalent carbon-12.

kilogramme metre per second (kg ms^{-1})

SI unit of momentum.

kilogramme metre squared (kg m^{2})

SI unit of moment of inertia and inertial effect.

kilogramme metre squared per second (kg m^2 s^{-1})

SI unit of moment of momentum

kilogramme -force (kgf)

MkgfS unit of force. It is defined as the force, which, when applied to a body of mass one kilogramme, gives it an acceleration equivalent to the standard acceleration of free fall.

1 kgf = 9.806 65 newtons.

Note: 1. In Germany and German-speaking countries, this unit is known as the **Kilopond (kp)**.

2. Some of the units which are related to the kilogramme-force unit I are provided in the table below.

All units are MkgfS units.

Unit	Unit Symbol	Quantity measured	Corresponding SI unit	To convert to SI, multiply by:
Kilogramme-force metre	Kgf m	Moment of force, torque, work and energy	Newton metre (N.m) or Joule (J)	**9.806 65**
Kilogramme-force metre per kilogramme	Kgf.m/kg	Specific internal energy, specific latent heat	Joule per kilogramme (J/kg)	**9.806 65**
Kilogramme-force metre per kilogramme degree Celsius	Kgf.m (kg. ^{o}C)	Specific heat capacity	Joule per kilogramme kelvin (J/kg.K)	**9.806 65**
Kilogramme-force metre per second	Kgf.m/s	Power	Watt (W)	**9 806 65**

Kilogramme-force metre per second	Kgf.m.s	Action	Joule Second (J.s)	**9.806 65**
Kilogramme-force metre second squared	Kgf.m.s^2	Moment of inertia	Kilogramme metre square (Kg/m^2)	**9.806 65**
Kilogramme-force per centimeter	Kgf/cm	Surface tension	Newton per metre (N/m)	**9.806 65**
Kilogramme-force per cubic metre	Kgf/m^3	Specific weight	Newton per cubic metre (N/m^3)	**9.806 65**
Kilogramme-force per metre	Kgf/m	Surface tension	Newton per metre (N/m)	**9.806 65**
Kilogramme-force per metre second degree Celsius	Kgf/(m.s.ºC)	Coefficient of heat transfer	Watt per metre squared kelvin (W/m^2 K)	**9.806 65**
Kilogramme-force per second degree Celsius	Kgf/(s.ºC)	Thermal conductivity	Watt per metre kelvin (W/m·K)	**9.806 65**
Kilogramme-force per square centimetre	Kgf/cm^2	Pressure	Pascal (Pa)	**9.806 65 x 10^4**
Kilogramme-force per square metre	Kgf/m^2	Pressure	Pascal (Pa)	**9.806 65**
Kilogramme-force second	Kgf/s	Momentum	Kilogramme metre per second (kg.m/s)	**9.806 65**
Kilogramme-force second per square metre	Kgf.s/m^2	Dynamic viscosity	Pascal second (Pa s)	**9.806 65**

Kilogramme-force second squared per metre	Kgf.s^2/m	Mass	Kilogramme (kg)	**9.806 65**
Kilogramme-force second squared per metre to the fourth power	Kgf.s^2/m^2	Density	kilogramme per cubic metre (kg/m^3)	**9.806 65**

kilogramme per cubic metre (kg m^{-3})

SI unit of density, mass density and mass concentration.

kilogramme per cubic metre pascal (kg m^{-3} Pa^{-1})

SI unit of unitary mass density.

kilogramme per metre (kg m^{-1})

SI unit of linear density.

kilogramme per mole (kg mol^{-1})

SI unit of molar mass.

kilogramme per pascal second metre (kg Pa^{-1} s^{-1} m^{-1})

SI unit of water vapor permeance.

kilogramme per pascal second square metre (kg Pa^{-1} s^{-1} m^{-2})

SI unit of water vapor permeability.

kilogramme per second (kg s^{-1})

SI unit of mass flow rate.

kilogramme per square metre (kg m^{-2})

SI unit of surface density.

Note: Used in agriculture, sheet metal and plating. It is also a unit of mean mass range.

kilogramme metre (kilogrammetre)

MkgfS unit of energy. It is defined as the work done when the point of application of a force of one kilogramme-force is displaced through a distance of one metre in the direction of the force.

1 kilogramme = 1 kgf m = 9.806 65 joules.

See *"kilogramme-force"*.

kilogramme-weight (kgwt)

Metric unit of force. It is defined as the force, which, when applied to a body of mass of one kilogramme, gives it an acceleration equivalent to the local value of the acceleration of free fall expressed in metres per second squared.

1 kgwt = g newton.

Note: The application of this unit is an inconsistent unit and its use has been deprecated. This unit has been replaced by the kilogramme-force.

kilocalorie (kcal)

Unit of heat.

1 kilocalorie (IT) = $4.186\ 8 \times 10^3$ joules.

Note: The physiologists, when discussing metabolism, express their findings in calories by they actually mean kilocalories. For example, saying that eating one gramme of butter is equivalent to …calories means that burning one gramme of butter in an atmosphere of pure oxygen in a bomb calorimeter, ….kilocalories of heat will be released.

kiloacrefoot (kaf)

A unit of volume used to measure the capacity of reservoirs. It is equivalent to 1000 acre feet. A kiloacrefoot contains exactly 43 560 000 cubic feet or about 1 233 482 cubic metres (123.3482 hectare metres).

See also "acre feet."

kiloampere (kA)

A unit of electric current equivalent to 1000 amperes.

See also "ampere"

kilobar (kbar or kb)

A metric unit of pressure, used particularly in industrial applications and in geology for measuring high pressures. The kilobar is equivalent to 1000 bars, 100 megapascals, or about 14 503 pounds per square inch. (Note: in the investment world, a kilobar is a bar of gold, silver, or platinum weighing 1 kilogramme.)

See also "bar," "pascal."

kilobase (kb)

A unit of genetic information equivalent to the information carried by 1000 pairs of the base units in the double-helix of DNA. It is also used as a unit of relative distance equal to the length of a strand of DNA containing 1000 base pairs.

kilobecquerel (kBq)

A unit of radioactivity equivalent to 1000 atomic disintegrations per second or 27.027 nanocuries (nCi).

kilobit (kbit or kb)

A unit of information, equivalent to 1000 bits, or in some cases, equivalent to 1024 bits or 128 bytes. The larger unit is now supposed to be called a **kibibit**.

See also "bit", "byte"

kilobit per second (kbps, kb/s)

A unit of data transmission rate equivalent to 1000 bits per second. The symbol kb/s is preferable to kbps for this unit.

kilogramme-molecule

A unit of quantity of substance; one kilogramme-molecule is a quantity such that the number of molecules it contains is equal to Avogadro's constant. A predecessor of the mole.

See also "mole"

kilohyl

The unit of mass in the meter—kilogram force—second system of units approximately 9.80665 kilogrammes.

Sometimes called the metric technical unit of mass (symbol, TME), the metric slug, the mug, or the par. It is also called the hyl.

The Russian physicist M. F. Malikov proposed it be called the "inerta," symbol i, but this name was never used.

kilopond (kp)

MkpS unit of force. It is defined as the force, which, when applied to a body of mass one kilogramme, give it an acceleration equivalent to the standard acceleration of free fall.

1 kp = 9.806 65 newtons

1 kilocalorie (IT) = 4.186 8 x 10^3 joules.

Note: 1. This unit is preferred in Germany and German-speaking countries instead of **kilogramme-force.**

2. It is better to use the kilogramme-force.

See *"kilogramme-force"*.

kilovolt-ampere (kVA)

1,000 volt-amperes.

kilowatt (kW)

1,000 watts

kilowatt - hour (kW h)

Unit for electric energy used in SI system, equivalent to the work done, when power of 1 kilowatt is expended for one hour.

1 kW h = 10^3 watt hour = 3.6 x 10^6 joules.

This unit is used for electric work.

Note: 1. The unit is also known as the Board of Trade unit or the Kelvin

2. It is the commercial unit with which electricity is sold to the consumer.

3. The original definition of the unit was "the energy contained in a current of one thousand amperes flowing under an electromotive force of one volt during one hour."

See *"Board of Trade unit"*.

kin

The Japanese version of the catty, a common weight unit of the Far East. The Japanese identified this unit as a traditional unit, equivalent to about 1.323 pounds or almost exactly 600 grammes; this is about 0.75% smaller than the Chinese catty.

See also "catty"

kine (kine)

CGS unit of velocity. One kine is the velocity of which, a distance of one centimetre is traversed in one second.

1 kine = 1 centimetre per second = 10^{-2} metres per second.

Note: This name was suggested by the British Association in 1888 as the name of the CGS unit of velocity.

King-Armstrong unit

An obsolete unit used to assay the enzyme phosphatase, particularly in blood serum. One King-Armstrong unit was originally the amount of phosphatase that, acting upon disodium phenylphosphate in excess for 30 minutes at 37.5°C, at pH 9.0, liberates 1 milligram of phenol. Sometimes simply called a "King". It was designed to yield numerical values equal to Jenner and Kay units.

kintal (kintal)

Imperial unit of mass. It is equivalent to 100 pounds.

1 kintal = 100 pounds = 45.359 237 kilogrammes.

Note: The unit is also known as **centner, cental and quital**.

See *"center", "cental"* and *"quital"*.

kintar

In Iraq (Baghdad) and some other Arab countries, a unit of mass approximately 274.27 kilogrammes.

kip (kip)

Imperial unit of mass. A kip is equivalent to 1000 pounds.

1 kip = 1000 pounds = 453.592 37 kilogrammes.

Note: 1. The name originates from combining the words "kilo" and "pound". Thus, 1000 pounds is known as a kilopound, or kip or sometimes, kIb.

2. This unit is used mainly by engineers for expressing the load on a structure.

3. The unit is also used in the U.S. as unit of force.

1 kip = 1000 pound-force = 4.448 22 x 10^3 newtons.

As a unit of force, it is sometimes known as the **kip-force** (symbol **kipf** or **kIbf)** to distinguish it from the unit of mass.

3. The kip is also the name of obsolete units of measure in historic England and Malaysia and also the currency of Laos.

kirat

See also "carat" and "karat."

In the Arab world, Kirat (or carat or Karat) is an informal unit of mass and length with value differs from place to place:

1. In Lebanon, *20ᵗʰ century*, two units of length,

    - one used in agriculture, approximately 3.16 centimeters.
    - the other for textiles, approximately 2.83… (i.e., 2 ⅚ centimeters.

2. In Sudan , a unit of weight, approximately 195 milligrams.

3. In the United Arab Republic, *20ᵗʰ century*, a unit of area, approximately 175.035 square meters.

4. In Egypt, *in the 20th century*, a unit of dry capacity was about 64.46 milliliters. In the *19ᵗʰ century*, about 59.7 milliliters were. Also Romanized as *qyrâṭ*.

5. In India, a unit of mass,

    Kirrát, A carat, the 24th part of an ounce.

kit

Has two meanings:

1. Unit of mass: In the fish trade in Great Britain, a unit of mass used at quayside. For white fish in Hull, Grimsby, Fleetwood and Lowestoft, = 10 stone = 140 pounds. Eight-stone (112 pounds) and 12-stone (168 pounds) kits were used for some species at Milford Haven.

2. Unit of liquid capacity: In the Dutch East Indies, a unit of liquid capacity used for oil = 10 kan. The kan was defined legally in 1873 as 1.5751 liters, which would make the kit 15.751 liters.

However, it is often given as 15.159 liters.

KLOC (kloc)

A computer programming expression, the K-LOC or KLOC, pronounced as *kay-lok*, standing for "kilo-lines of code", i.e., thousand lines of code. The unit was used, especially by IBM managers, to express the amount of work required to develop a piece of software. Given that estimates of 20 lines of functional code per day per programmer were often used, it is apparent that 1 K-LOC could take one programmer as long as 50 working days or 10 working weeks. This measure is no longer in widespread use because different computer languages require different numbers of lines to achieve the same result (occasionally, the measure "assembly equivalent lines of code" is used, with appropriate conversion factors from the language actually used to assembly language).

Error rates in programming are also measured in "Errors per K-LOC," which is known as the *defect density*. NASA's SATC is one of the few organizations that claim zero defects in a large (>500K-LOC) project, for the space shuttle software.

An alternative measurement was defined by Pegasus Mail author David Harris. The "WaP" is equivalent to 71,500 lines of program code because this number of lines is the length of one edition of Leo Tolstoy's *War and Peace*.

Knoop hardness (HK or KHN)

A measure of the hardness of a metal was introduced by Knoop in 1939. The Knoop test is similar to the Vickers test in that a diamond penetrator is used to indent the sample being tested, but it uses a rhombohedral diamond rather than a pyramidal diamond point. It is similar to the Rockwell test in that the hardness measure is the depth of the penetration rather than its area. The result is measured in kilogrammes of force per square millimetre, but should be stated as an empirical measurement, without units.

knot (kn or kt)

Metric and Imperial unit of velocity, especially in aviation and navigation.

1. As Metric Unit: *Symbol:* kn

It is defined as the velocity of which a distance of one nautical mile (n mil) is traversed in one hour.

1 kn = 1 nautical mile per hour = 1852/3600 metres per second.

Note: i. This unit is also known as the **international knot.**

ii. The U.S. adopted this unit (the international knot) in July 1954.

iii. [1913 Webster] defines the knot as a unit of length used in navigation. It is equivalent to the distance spanned by one minute of arc in latitude, i.e., 1,852 metres

2.   As Imperial Unit: *Symbol:* UKkn

One U.K. knot is defined as the velocity at which, a distance of one U.K. nautical mile (6080 feet) is traversed in one hour

1 UKkn = 6080/3600 feet per second = 0.514 773 metres per second.

kunitz unit

A unit used to describe the concentration or activity of the enzyme ribonuclease. One kunitz is the amount of ribonuclease required to cause a decrease of 100% per minute in the ultraviolet light (300 nanometres) absorbed at 25° by a 0.05% solution of yeast nucleic acid in a 0.05 molar acetate buffer solution (pH 5.0).

Note: The unit was proposed for the first time in 1946 by the Russian biochemist Moses Kunitz (1887 - 1978).

Koku

An old Japanese unit of volume

- The *koku* (石) is a Chinese-based Japanese unit of volume. 1 koku is equivalent to 10 *to* (斗) or approximately 180 litres (40 imperial gallons; 48 U.S. gallons), or about 150 kilogrammes (330 pounds).

- This unit is equivalent to 100 <u>shō</u> and 1000 <u>gō.</u> One *gō* is the volume of the plastic measuring cup that is supplied with commercial Japanese rice cookers.

- The *koku* in Japan was typically used as a dry measure. The amount of rice production measured in *koku* was the metric by which the magnitude of a feudal domain (<u>han</u>) was evaluated. A feudal lord was only considered *daimyō* class when his domain amounted to at least 10,000 *koku*. As a rule of thumb, one *koku* was considered a sufficient quantity of rice to feed one person for one year.

- The Chinese equivalent or cognate unit for capacity is the **shi** or **dan**. *shih, tan* also known as **hu** (斛; *hú*; *hu*), is now approximately 103 litres, but historically about 59.44 litres (13.07 imperial gallons; 15.70 U.S. gallons).

Krügerl or Krügel

A common unit of volume for beer in Austria, equivalent to ½ liter. The name of the unit is related to *Krug*, a jug or tankard.

ksf, ksi

A symbol for kips (kilopounds) per square foot or per square inch, which are traditional engineering units of pressure or stress. 1 ksf = 47.880 257 kilopascals (kPa) and 1 ksi = 6.894 757 megapascals (MPa). These units are often used to express the strength of materials (meaning the maximum pressure the material can resist).

ksym/s

A unit of radio transmission rate equivalent to 1000 symbols per second.

kulmet

A traditional Latvian unit of volume equal to about 10.93 liters (2.40 British imperial gallons or 2.89 U.S. liquid gallons). A similar Estonian unit, the **külimet**, is equivalent o about 11.48 liters (2.53 British Imperial gallons or 3.03 U.S. liquid gallons).

See also "gallon."

kunitz or Kunitz unit

A unit used in biochemistry to describe the concentration or activity of the enzyme ribonuclease, which attacks ribonucleic acid (RNA). The action of the enzyme causes an increase in the absorbance of ultraviolet light. One kunitz is the concentration of the enzyme, causing an increase in absorbance at a wavelength of 260 nanometres by 0.001 per milliliter of enzyme, when acting upon highly polymerized DNA at 25 °C and pH 5.0

under specified conditions. The unit's name recognizes the Russian-American biochemist Moses Kunitz (1887-1978), who proposed the standard test in 1946.

kvadrat-

Scandinavian prefix meaning "square". In particular, a **kvadratmeter** is a square meter. The prefix is common to Danish, Norwegian, and Swedish.

kwan

A traditional Japanese unit of weight equivalent to 6.25 kin (see above), which is about 8.27 pounds or 3.75 kilogrammes.

kya

A common abbreviation (in English speaking countries) for "thousand years ago". The "k" is the metric symbol for kilo- (1000).

kyu

A metric unit of distance, used in typography and graphic design. The kyu, originally written Q, is equivalent to exactly 0.25 millimetres, about 0.71 points, or about 14.173 twips. The spelling "kyu" seems to have been introduced by the software company Macromedia.

Kz

An improper symbol, is sometimes used mistakenly to express the kilohertz (kHz).

L

L

The Roman numeral 50.

L, l

Symbols for the liter. The lowercase l is the official symbol, but since it may be confused with the numeral 1, the SI permits the capital letter L to be used instead. Sometimes, a script version of the lowercase letter is used, but this is not approved by the SI.

labor

A traditional unit of area in Latin American countries. The labor is equivalent to the area of a square, 1000 varas on a side or 0.04 légua. Using the Texas standard for the vara (33⅓ inches), this is equivalent to 177.136 acres or 71.685 hectares. The word *labor* means work in Spanish, as it does in English. As a unit, it represents the area that could be cultivated by a single farmer, somewhat like the old English hide.

See also "varas", "acre", "hectare."

lachsa

A unit of mass in the Philippines. The unit is about 28.8 kilograms.

lachter

A traditional unit of length used in mining in Germany and other German speaking regions. A variation on the fathom, the unit varied regionally (and even from mine to mine), but it was usually close to 2 meters (about 78.74 inches). The lachter was divided into 8 spann or 80 lachterzoll.

A *lachter* was roughly equal to the amount which a man could contain within his outstretched arms. It was similar to the *klafter* (ca. 1.8 meters or 5.91 feet) but was usually rather larger.

The lachter was - with regional differences - subdivided into *Achtel* (also known as a *Spann, Gräpel* or *Gröbel*), *(Lachter)Zoll, Primen* (or *Prinen*) and *Sekunden*:

- 1 *lachter* = 8 *Spann* = 80 (*Lachter*)*Zoll* = 800 *Primen* = 8,000 *Sekunden*

In the 19th century, a decimal system of subdivision was established:

- 1 lachter = 10 Lachterfuß = 100 Lachterzoll = 1,000 Lachterlinien

Note: Like other units of measure, the *lachter* varied in length depending on the region, but there could also be differences in length within the same region. In addition, there could also be differences between various mining fields within a territory. The specification and use of conversion tables only make sense if it is known for certain where and at which times the values were valid.

See also, "decimal system" and "fathom."

lachterzoll

The "lachter inch", a traditional unit of length, is equivalent to $\frac{1}{80}$ lachter (previous entry). This was roughly 2.5 centimeters, about the same as the English unch, but a bit shorter than the standard German zoll. In the 1900s, a decimal lachterzoll, equivalent to $\frac{1}{100}$ lachter, was also used. This was about 2 centimeters (0.78 inches or 0.76 zoll).

lakh or lac

A traditional unit of count in India, equivalent to 10^5 or 100 000. In India, the lakh is commonly used instead of the million. Commas are used to isolate the number of lakhs. For example, the number 5 300 000 is equivalent to 53 lakh and written "53,00,000".
See also "crore".

lambda (λ)

Metric unit of volume.
1 λ = 1 microliter $=10^{-6}$ liters = 10^9 meters cubed.

lambert (L)

Metric unit of luminance (photometric brightness). It is the uniform luminance of a perfectly diffusing surface, emitting or reflecting the light of one lumen per square centimeter. It is equivalent to $1/\pi$ candela per square centimeter.

1 L = $(1/\pi)$ candela per square centimeter = $(1/\pi)$ stilb.

Note: The use of this unit is deprecated and was supplanted by the **stilb.**

Lambda

An uncommon metric unit of volume which discontinued with the introduction of the SI

Lambda (written λ, in lowercase) is a non-SI unit of volume equivalent to 10^{-9} cubic metres (m3), 1 cubic millimeter (mm^3) or 1 microliter (mL). Introduced by the BIPM in 1880, the lambda has been used in chemistry and in law for measuring volume, but its use is not recommended.

This use of λ parallels the pre-SI use of μ on its own for a micrometre and γ for a microgram. Although the use of λ is deprecated, some clinical laboratories continue to apply it. The standard abbreviation μL for a microliter has the disadvantage that it can be misread as mL (a unit 1000 times larger). In pharmaceutical use, no abbreviation for a microliter is considered safe. The recommended practice is to write "microliter" in full.

land mile

The ordinary statute mile, equivalent to 5280 feet or 1609.344 meters, is sometimes known as a "land mile" to distinguish it from the nautical mile. Similarly, a **land league** is equivalent to 3 statute miles (5280 yards or 4828.03 meters) as distinguished from 3 nautical miles.

See also, "mile", "nautical mile."

lane meter

A unit of deck area for "roll on/roll off" ships. Cargo vessels are designed so that containers or other cargo can be rolled on and off the decks of the ship. A lane is a strip of deck 2 meters wide. A lane meter is an area of the deck, one lane wide and one meter long, i.e., 2 square meters (21.528 square feet).

langley (Langley)

An arbitrary unit for energy per unit area (energy area-density) is commonly employed in radiation theory. One Langley is the energy area-density of one calorie (international) of heat energy over one square centimeter.

1 langley = 1 cal_{IT}/cm^2 = 4.1868 x 10^4 Joules per meter squared.

Note: The unit was formerly defined as 1 langley = 1 cal_{IT}/cm^2 minute, but this was later known as the pyron.

See also *"langley per minute"* and *"pyron"*.

langley per minute (langley/min)

Unit of irradiance.

1 langley/min = 1 cal$_{IT}$/ (cm^2.s) = 6.978 x 10^2 watts per square meter.

Note: The unit is used mainly as a unit of **insolation** (= **in**coming **so**lar radia**tion**).

langmuir (L)

A unit of exposure used in high-vacuum physics in the study of the adsorption of gases by a surface such as a crystal. The langmuir measures the product of the gas pressure and the time of exposure. One langmuir is defined to be 10^{-6} Torr·sec or, in SI units, about 0.133 322 millipascal second (mPa·s). The unit is named for the American chemist and physicist Irving Langmuir (118-1957).

lap

An informal unit of distance used in athletic competitions. In athletics ("track"), a lap is the length of one trip around a running track. This may vary from track to track, but at the level of serious competition, most tracks have a standard length. In English speaking countries, this was formerly ¼ mile (1320 feet or 402.336 meters). Tracks used in most competitions today have a length of exactly 400 meters (1312.34 feet). In swimming, a lap is one tour of the pool, i.e., twice the length of the pool, a distance of exactly 100 meters (328.08 feet) in Olympic-size pools but only 50 meters (164.04 feet) in many recreational and "short-course" pools.

See also "mile" and "feet."

last (last)

U.K. unit of volume (capacity), equivalent to 80 U.K. bushels.

1 last = **80** U.K. bushels = 2.909 414 x 10^3 liters.

See *"bushel, U.K."*.

lb, lbf, lbm

lb is the traditional symbol in English, Spanish, and Italian for the pound. It is derived from the Latin word *libra* for the Roman version of the same unit. The symbols lbf and lbm are used to distinguish between pounds of force and pounds of mass, respectively.

See also "pound."

lea (lea)

Imperial (U.K.) unit of length, equivalent to 120 yards.

1 lea = **120** yards = **109.728** meters.

Note: The unit is used mainly with the cotton yarn.

league (league)

Imperial unit of length. One league is equivalent to three miles.

1 league = 3 miles = 4 828.032 meters.

Note: This unit was widely used throughout Europe as an inherent unit of distance.

It is derived from an ancient Celtic unit and adopted by the Romans as the *leuga*. The league became a common unit of measurement throughout Western Europe. It was intended to represent roughly, the distance a person could walk in an hour. The Celtic unit seems to have been rather short (about 1.5 Roman miles, which is roughly 1.4 statute miles or 2275 meters), but the unit grew longer over time. In many cases, it was equivalent to 3 miles, using whatever version of the mile was current. At sea, the league was most often equivalent to 3 nautical miles, which is $\frac{1}{20}$ degree, 3.45 statute miles, or exactly 5556 meters. In the U.S. and Britain, the standard practice is to define the league as 3 statute miles (about 4828.03 meters) on land or 3 nautical miles at sea.

leap

A traditional Welsh unit of distance equivalent to 6 feet 9 inches or 2.0574 meters.

leap second

An extra second is added at the end of a day (June 30 or December 31) to realign timekeeping with the Earth's rate of rotation. See *"day"* for details.

leap year

A unit of civil time equal to 366 days. See year [2]. Normally, the day of the week on which a specific date falls advances by one day from year to year. For example, August 1 falls on Tuesday in 2006 and on Wednesday in 2007. But following the addition of an extra day on February 29, a date "leaps" over a day of the week: in 2008, a leap year, August 1 leaps over Thursday to fall on Friday. A leap year is sometimes called a bissextile year.

légua [1]

The Spanish league. The traditional légua is equivalent to 5000 varas, which is close to 2.6 miles or 4.2 kilometers. Using the Texas definition of the vara, the légua is 2.6305 miles, 13889 feet, or 4233.4 meters. Using the traditional Spanish definition, it would be 2.597 miles, 13712 feet, or 4179.4 meters. Technically, this unit was abolished by Philip II in 1568, but it remained widely used, especially in the Americas. During the late 18th and early 19th centuries, a league of 8000 varas (4.15 miles or 6680 meters) was legal in Spain. At sea, Spanish sailors used the usual marine league (3 nautical miles or 5556 meters) or Philip V's "geographical" league of $\frac{1}{17.5}$ degree (3.429 nautical miles or 6350.5 meters). At present, the légua is used informally in Argentina and in other Spanish-speaking countries as a metric unit equivalent to exactly 5 kilometers (3.107 miles).

See also "vara", "mile", "feet", and "nautical mile."

légua [2]

A traditional Spanish unit of area equivalent to one square légua [1]. In Spanish-speaking Latin America and the southwestern states of the U.S., land was customarily measured in leguas, with 1 légua equivalent to 25 labors (see above) or 25 million square varas. Using the Texas definition of the vara as the starting point, the légua is 4428.4 acres, 6.919 square miles, 1792 hectares, or 17.92 square kilometers. A slightly larger figure of 4439 acres (1796 hectares) is used in California. Larger sizes, between 1800 and 1900 hectares, were formerly used in some parts of South America. In Mexico and Texas, this unit is often called a **sitio**.

See also "acre", "hectare."

légua or legoa

The Portuguese league is equivalent to 3 milhas (Portuguese miles). This is equal to about 3.836 statute miles or 6174.1 meters.

See also "mile."

Lenat

Non-conventional unit that measures Bogosity.

The unit of **bogosity**, i.e., how bogus a person, claim, or proceeding is. It is derived from the fictional field of Quantum bogodynamics, is the Lenat. The Lenat is seldom used, as it is understood that it is too large for normal conversation. Its most common form is the microLenat.

lentor (lentor)

CGS unit of kinematic viscosity. One lentor is the kinematic viscosity of a fluid with a dynamic viscosity of one poise and a density of one gram per centimeter cubed.

1 lentor = 1 poise centimeter cubed per gram = 10^{-4} meters square per second.

Note: This unit is also known as **stokes.**

See *"stokes"*.

leo (leo)

Metric unit of acceleration. One leo represents an acceleration of one decimeter per second squared.

1 leo = 10 meters per second squared.

Note: The unit has rarely been used.

lenz

A proposed special name for a unit of magnetic field strength in SI, with dimensions of amperes per meter. It was rejected at the first meeting of the Comité Consultatif des Unités in 1966.

Lessa also known as Lecha

An obsolete unit of area.

A **lessa** was a customary unit of area used in the Indian state of Manipur and neighboring regions. After metrication in the mid-20th century, the unit became obsolete.

lest

Used in Norway as unit of capacity, unit of mass, and unit of count:

1.	As a unit of Capacity, its value varies by commodity:
    o	For grain, = 12 *tønner,* about 1650 liters.

o For coal and salt, = 18 *tønner*, about 2502 liters.

o for ore, = 16 *tønner*, about 3952 liters.

2.   As a unit of mass, varying by commodity:

o For flax and hemp = 6 *skippund*, about 960 kilograms.

o For wool, = 12 *skippund*, about 1920 kg.

o For grain, = 16 *skippund*, about 2560 kg.

3. A unit of count:

- = 12 sekker (sacks) of wool.
- = 144 hides or skins.
- = 12 barrel = 14,400 herring.

lethal dose (LD)

A measure used in pharmacology to express the percentage of a population killed by a dose of the substance being studied. The measurement is often given as a subscript. For example, the potency of a drug or pesticide is commonly expressed by stating the size of the LD_{50} dose and the amount of the substance that kills 50% of the test population.

lǐ or li

A traditional unit of distance in China. A Confucian proverb widely misquoted in the West as "a journey of a thousand miles begins with a single step" actually means "a journey of a thousand li begins with a single step." Although the traditional li was approximately ⅓ mile or 500 meters, the late imperial governments of China used a li of 1800 ch'ih, which is 2115 feet, about 0.401 miles, or 644.65 meters. In modern China, the li is equivalent to exactly 0.5 kilometers or 500 meters. In Chinese, the kilometer itself is often known as a gongli or "metric li." See also "gong."

liang

A traditional Chinese unit of weight. During the European colonial period, the liang was equal to ¹⁄₁₆ catty, ¹⁄₁₂ pound, or about 37.8 grams. This made it similar to a tael. In modern China, the liang is equivalent to ¹⁄₁₀ jin or 10 qian. This is exactly 50 grams (1.7637 ounces).

libra (also libbra)

Units of mass and capacity used in many countries worldwide. It was used during ancient times.

A traditional unit of weight in Italian, Spanish, and Portuguese speaking countries. The libra was the Roman unit from which the English pound is descended; the symbol "lb" for the pound comes from this unit. The Roman libra contained only 12 unciae (ounces) and was about 0.722 English pounds. The traditional Italian libbra was often of similar size, but a wide variety of libbras were used in Italian markets over the centuries. The Spanish and Portuguese units are larger, generally in the range from 1.011 to 1.016 English pounds (very close to 460 grams). The Spanish libra equals 16 onzas, and the Portuguese libra equals 16 onças. The word "libra" is sometimes used now for the kilogram, a much larger unit.

1. In Rome and the Roman Empire, it is a unit of mass from the *mid-19th century,* taken to be about 327.45 grams.

2. In Spain, it is a unit of mass varying locally. The *libra* most commonly used was the Castillian libra (*libra de Castilla*), which is about 460.093 grams, (approximately 1.014 pounds' avoirdupois). This is the origin of the value of the *libra*in Chile, Cuba, Ecuador, El Salvador, Guatemala, Honduras, Mexico, Nicaragua, and Peru.

    Even within the same district, the value differed. For example, according to Doursther, there were four *libra* used in Valencia:

    *   The *libra sutil*, *libra menor*, or *libreta*, which, according to one determination, are equivalent to 355.3 grams and, according to another determination, are equivalent to exactly 356 grams. This was the everyday *libra* of commerce. It was subdivided into 12 *onzas*, like the Roman *libra*.

    *   The *libbra gruesa* or *libra mayor*, of 18 *onzas*, used for salted fish, calfskin, leather for the soles of shoes, and so on, is about 532.5 grams (taking the *libra sutil* as 355 grams).

    *   A *libra* for saffron and other spices, of 16 *onzas*, is about 473.3 grams.

    *   A *libra* of 36 *onzas* for bread and other foodstuffs is about 1065 grams.

3. In Colombia, a unit of mass is equivalent to 16 onzas or 500 grams (approximately 1.1012 pounds). An example of seeking round values in the course of metrication.

4. In the Dominican Republic and El Salvador, it is equivalent to 1 pound avoirdupois (approximately 453.592 grams). An example of the name of an old unit inheriting a value from a new trading system.

5. In Portugal, a unit of mass is approximately 459 grams (approximately 1.012 pounds avoirdupois). Also known as an arratel.
From Portugal, the unit was extended to Brazil and lasted till the *20th century* in the Cape Verde Islands and Paraguay.

6. In Argentina, a unit of mass is equivalent to 16 *onza*, which is about 459.35 grams (or about 1.0127 pounds avoirdupois). On *18 December 1835*, the city of Buenos Aires defined the *libra* as the weight of 33 cubic *pulgadas* of distilled water at its maximum density.
The *libra de boticario* was, however, different and according to the Treasury Ministry in *1879*, it was equivalent to 344.55 grams, which is 12 of the standard *onza* of Buenos Aires.

7. In Patras in the Peloponnese, Greece (during the *19ᵗʰ century*), it was a unit of capacity, determined by mass, used for oil and honey. A nineteenth of a barile is about 3.064 kilograms (6.775 pounds avoidupois).

8. In Costa Rica, it is equivalent to 460.0627 grams and divided into 16 *onzas*. (In apothecary's weight, however, the *libra* was 345.04704 grams and divided into 12 *onzas*. Apothecary's weight was already out of use in Costa Rica in the *19th century*.) In modern times, it is equivalent to 460 grams.

9. In Chile, a unit of mass, is about 460 grams.

10. In Cuba and El Salvador, a unit of mass equivalent to 16 *onzas* or 460.00 grams.

11. In Ecuador, a unit of mass equivalent to 460.00 grams.

12. In the province of Alicante, Spain, a unit of liquid capacity for oil, equivalent to 600 milliliters. In concept, this amount of oil would weigh 1 *libra*.
In the province of Huesca, two units of liquid capacity, one for oil, about 370 milliliters, and one for spirits, about 360 milliliters. In Navarra, 410 milliliters.

13. In ancient Rome, a unit of capacity for oil.

lieue

The French league. A variety of lieue units were used for land measurement in France, but generally, these units were around 2.4-2.5 statute miles in length. In the 18th century, the legal unit was the *lieue de poste*, defined to be equivalent to 2000 toises or 2 *milles* (2.4221 miles or 3898 meters). In metric France, the lieue is now considered to equal exactly 4 kilometers (2.4855 miles). See league (above). At sea, the lieue was often taken to be equivalent to $\frac{1}{25}$ degrees or 2.4 nautical miles (4445 meters or 2.7619 miles). This unit was gradually replaced by the internationally recognized 3 nautical miles (5556 meters or 3.452 miles). In the classic Jules Verne novel *Vingt Mille Lieues sous les Mers* (*Twenty Thousand Leagues under the Sea*), the unit in the title is the metric *lieue* of exactly 4000 meters.

See also "mile", "degree", and "nautical mile."

light-watt (light-watt)

SI unit (also for all systems of units) of luminous power, equivalent to the luminous power of light of a single wave λ length, whose radiant power is $1/V_\lambda$ watts, where V_λ is the value of the luminosity function at λ.

1 light-watt = 1 talbot per second = 1 lumberg per second.

See *"talbot"* and *"lumber"*.

light-year (ly)

A unit of distance employed particularly in popular works on astronomy. It is the distance traveled by light (electromagnetic wave) in vacuo in one year.

1 light-year = 9.4607 x 10^{15} meters = 0.307 parsecs.

Note: 1. In general, the size of the light year depends on the type of the year chosen and, the experimentally determined sizes of the year and the velocity of electromagnetic waves in vacuo.

2. The unit was used for the first time in 1888.

Ligne

The French unit of length is roughly equivalent to 2.25 millimeters (0.089 inches), or 9 points.

The ***ligne*** (pronounced [liɲ]), or **line** or **Paris line**, is a historic unit of length used in France and elsewhere prior to the adoption of the metric system in the late 18th century and used in various sciences after that time. The *loi du 19 frimaire a VIII* (Law of 10 December 1799) states that one meter is equivalent to exactly 443.296 French lines.

It is vestigially retained today by French and Swiss watchmakers to measure the size of watch movements in button making and in ribbon manufacture.

ligula

A Roman unit of liquid volume is equivalent to $\frac{1}{48}$ sextarius or about 11.07 milliliters. The word literally means "a lick."

line (li)

Unit of length, equivalent to $\frac{1}{12}$ inch.

1 line = $\frac{1}{12}$ inch.

Note: The unit is used mainly by botanists in describing the size of plants.

The line was not recognized by any statute of the English Parliament, but was usually understood as $\frac{1}{4}$ of a barleycorn, which itself was recognized by statute as $\frac{1}{3}$ of an inch but often reckoned as $\frac{1}{4}$ of an inch instead. The line was eventually decimalized as $\frac{1}{10}$ of an inch without recourse to barleycorns. The button trade used the term, redefined as $\frac{1}{40}$ of an inch.

Other similar small units known as lines include:

- The Russian *liniya* (ли́ния), $\frac{1}{10}$ of the *diuym,* which had been set precisely equivalent to an English inch that was suggested by Peter the Great
- The French *ligne* or Paris line, $\frac{1}{12}$ of the French inch (*pouce*) and about 1.06 liters.
- The Portuguese *linha*, $\frac{1}{12}$ of the Portuguese inch or 12 "points" (*pontos*) or 2.29 millimetres.
- The German *linie* was usually $\frac{1}{12}$ of the German inch, but sometimes also $\frac{1}{10}$ German inch.
- The Vienna line, is $\frac{1}{12}$ of a Vienna inch.

See also, "inch."

line, metric (metric line)

Metric unit of length.

1 metric line = 1 millimeter = 10^{-3} meters.

line (of electric force)

CGSesu unit of electric flux. One line (of electric force) is the electric flux associated with an electric charge of one franklin.

1 line (of electric force) = 1 franklin = 3.335 64 x 10^{-10} coulombs.

See *"franklin"*.

line (of magnetic force)

CGSesu unit of magnetic flux. One line (of magnetic flux) is the magnetic flux, after linking a circuit of one turn, produces in it an electromagnetic force of one abvolt as it decays to zero at a uniform rate in one second.

1 line (of magnetic force) = 1 abvolt second = 10^{-8} webers.

Note: The unit is better known as the **Maxwell**. A flux of 6000 maxwells is known as a **kappline.**

See *"**kappline**"*.

line-turn

A unit of linkage of magnetic flux. Also known as a Maxwell-turn.

Note: Linkage of magnetic flux is a measure of the flux and the number of turns of the coil or circuit with which it links. Quantitatively, it is the product of the number of liens of magnetic flux and the number of turns of the coil or circuit through which they pass.

linear foot (or "lineal" foot) (ft or lf)

Terms used loosely to describe a one-foot length of any long, narrow object. The correct term is **linear foot**. The word "lineal" refers to a line of ancestry, not to length. Boards, pipes, and fencing are typical objects measured and sold by the linear foot. In the moving industry, a linear foot is a one-foot length of a moving van, usually a volume of about 72 cubic feet (roughly 2 cubic meters). Occasionally, the term "linear foot" is used as an alternate name for the board foot, but this is appropriate only if the board is 12 inches wide.

Terms such as **linear meter** and **linear yard** are used in a similar way to indicate one-meter or one-yard lengths.

link (li)

Imperial unit of length. The link is one hundredth of the chain.

1 link = **0.01** chains = **0.201 168** meters.

Note: The unit is also known as **Gunter's link or surveyor's link**.

See *"chain"*.

Lipmann unit

A unit of quantity of coenzyme A, for the formation of which pantothenic acid is required. One Lipmann unit = 2.4 micrograms of pure coenzyme A (corresponding to 0.7 micrograms of pantothenic acid).

liquid ounce (U.S.) (U.S. liq oz)

U.S. unit of volume (capacity) for liquid measure.

1 liquid ounce (U.S.) = 2.957 35 x 10^{-5} cubic meters.

Note: The unit is also known as a fluid ounce.

liquid pint (U.S.) (U.S. liq pt)

U.S. unit of volume (capacity) for liquid measure. The liquid pint (U.S.) is equivalent to 28.875 cubic inches.

1 liquid pint (U.S.) = **28.875** cubic inches = 4.731 76 x 10^{-4} cubic meters.

liquid quart (U.S.) (U.S. liq qt)

U.S. unit of volume (capacity) for liquid measure.

1 liquid quart (U.S.) = 9.463 53 x 10^{-4} cubic meters.

liter (l or L)

Metric unit capacity, i.e., volume.

(1) In 1795, the liter was intended to be identical to the cubic decimeter.

(2) The first official definition was suggested by the 3CGPM of 1901. The 3CGPM decided to associate the liter with the kilogram and defined the liter as follows: one liter is the volume occupied by a mass of one kilogram of pure air-free water at the temperature of its maximum density under a pressure of one (standard) atmosphere.

(3) At the 1950 CIPM, the original definition was formalized as:

1 liter – 1.000028 x 10^{-3} cubic meters.

(4) In 1964, the 12CGPM withdrew the above definition of the liter and declared that the word "liter" was a special name for the cubic decimeter. Thus, its use is permitted in SI but discouraged since it creates two units for the same quantity, and its use in precision measurements might conflict with measurements recorded under the old definition.

1 liter = 1 decimeter cubed = 0.001 cubic meters.

Note: 1. It was agreed that the third definition above should reflect a special meaning of the word liter and that it should not be used to express the results of accurate measurement. However, the third definition has now been replaced by the second definition for scientific purposes. In the U.K., the Weights and Measures Act of 1963 still adheres to the second definition of the liter, although for practical purposes, the third is likely to be used. In the French law, the third definition replaced the second definition.

2. The CGPM in October 1979 approved L and l as alternative symbols for liter. Since the letter symbol l can easily be confused with the number 1, the symbol L is recommended for use in the U.S.

3. When the unit was first introduced in 1793, it was known as the pinte, but the name was replaced by liter in 1975.

4. The liter was recognized as a unit of volume in England by the Order in Council dated 19 May 1890.

liter- atmosphere (l.atm)

Metric unit of energy. The one liter-atmosphere is defined as the work done on a piston by a fluid under the pressure of one (standard) atmosphere, when the volume swept out by the piston is one liter.

1 liter-atmosphere = **101325** x 10^{-3} joules.

liter per 100 kilometers (l/100km or L/100km)

Unit which can be used in addition to SI units for fuel consumption.

2	liter per 100 kilometers = 3.540 06 x 10^{-3} U.K. gallons per mile.

livre (livre)

Metric unit of mass.

1 livre = 0.5 kilograms.

= 1.10232 pounds.

Note: In French, the word livre means pound. The Italian equivalent is the **libbra**, and the German equivalent is the **Pfund.**

LLD Unit

A unit of quantity of vitamin B_{12} based on biological activity. 11,000 LLD Units = 1 microgram vitamin B_{12} =1 USP Unit (liver extract). LLD is an abbreviation of *Lactobacillus lactis* Dorner.

load

A traditional but generally informal unit of volume.

- In U.S. landscaping and some construction trades, a load often means a cubic yard (0.764555 cubic meters).
- In ordinary language within the U.S., a load often means a volume of a pickup truck, that means the unit is a varying unit.
- In Britain, prior to modern times, a load was sometimes a standardized unit, but it varied with the commodity being carried. A typical size was 40 bushels (roughly 1.4 cubic meters).
- In Cyprus, a unit of liquid capacity = exactly 36 imperial gallons, approximately 163.659 liters.
- In Gambia, Ghana, Nigeria and Sierra Leone, a unit of mass used for cocoa = exactly 60 pounds av.
- In the lead mining districts of Derbyshire, England, a unit of capacity for lead ore. In the High Peak, after *1851*, 16â…ž imperial gallons, or in mass about 500 pounds.

log

A traditional unit of distance in forestry equivalent to 16 feet. The unit is defined this way since 16 feet is the standard length of logs being transported to the sawmill. Foresters have techniques for estimating the height of the "marketable" section of a standing tree in logs.

logit (logit)

Unit of intensity level. One logit is equivalent to one decibel

1 logit = 1 decibel.

Note: This name was proposed for the first time in 1952 for the decibel. Many other names were also proposed as alternatives for the decibel.

long dozen

Another name for the baker's dozen, equivalent to 13.

long hundredweight

The British hundredweight equivalent to 112 pounds.

long ton

The traditional British ton, equivalent to 2240 pounds.

longword

A unit of information, generally equivalent to 2 words.

London quarter

- The **quarter** (lit. "one-fourth") is used as the name of several distinct English units based on ¼ sizes of some base units.

- The "**quarter of London**", mentioned by the *Magna Carta* as the national standard measure for wine, ale, and grain, was ¼ ton or tun. It continued to be used, e.g., to regulate the prices of bread. This quarter was a unit of 8 bushels of 8 gallons each, understood at the time as a measure of both weight and volume. The grain gallon or half-peck was composed of 76,800 (Tower) grains weight. The ale gallon was composed of the ale filling an equivalent container and the wine gallon was composed of the wine weighing an equivalent amount to a full gallon of grain.

See also "ale", "grain", "gallon", "peck", "bushel."

lorentz unit

Gaussian unit of reciprocal length used to measure the difference in wave-numbers between a (zero-field) spectrum line and its Zeeman components. It is equivalent to $e/4\pi$ mc, where m is the rest mass of the electron, e is the charge on the electron and c is the speed of electromagnetic radiation in vacuo.

1 lorentz unit = 46.689 per tesla meter.

Note: 1. The unit is used for the reciprocal length per magnetic flux density.

2. The unit is equivalent to the Bohar magneton expressed in wave-numbers.

3. The name of the unit is after a Dutch physicist, Hendrik Antoon Lorentz (1853-1928).

Lot

- A **lot** is an old unit of weight used in many European countries from the Middle Ages until the beginning of the 20th century. Most often, it was defined as either $\frac{1}{30}$ or $\frac{1}{32}$ of a pound (or, more precisely, of whatever mass value one local pound had at the time). Recorded values range from 10 to 50 grammes.

- In the Imperial and U.S. customary systems of measurement, a lot is $\frac{1}{32}$ of a pound, or $\frac{1}{2}$ an ounce, making it exactly 14.174 761 562 5 grams if derived from the international pound.

See also "gram", "ounce", and "pound."

loundness unit (LU)

Unit of loudness, equivalent to the loudness of sound having 0 phon. It is also equivalent to loudness of 0.001.

1 LU = 0.001 sones = 0 phon.

Note: 1. The unit was proposed for the first time in 1937 and adopted by the American Standards Association in 1942.

2. The **sone** is the preferred unit of loudness.

See *"sone"* and *"phon"*.

Lovelace (LI)

Non-conventional unit that measures Quality

The Lovelace (Ll) is the unit of the lack of quality of an operating system, i.e., a measure of system administrators' opinions about how badly implemented it is. The unit has been coined by members of the system administrator profession, who hold a basic tenet that "software that does not suck does not exist". According to the Usenet alt. sysadmin. recovery FAQ, one Lovelace is considered a rather large quantity. Similar to other large units like the Farad and the Henry, SI prefixes are commonly used to denote practical quantities

See also "Farad" and "Henry."

lpi

Abbreviation for lines per inch, a unit used to state the resolution of display devices (such as television or computer monitor screens) or to state the line spacing of printed pages.

lug [1]

An old English name for a rod (5.5 yards or 5.0292 meters). In some parts of England, this unit represented a longer rod of 7 yards (6.4008 meters), a unit also known as the **great lug**.

lug [2]

A shallow box or crate for produce, such as cherries, grapes, or peaches. The size of a lug varies with the item it contains. Typical lugs hold about 16-28 pounds (7-13 kilograms) of produce in a volume of roughly ⅓ bushel (about 12 liters). This unit seems to be particularly common in produce markets in the midwestern U.S.

lumberg (lumberg)

CGS, which belongs to all systems, is a unit of luminous energy. It is equivalent to the luminous energy, corresponding to a radiant energy of $1/K$ ergs, were K is the luminous efficiency in lumens (lm) per watt. Alternatively, it is the energy radiated per second in unit solid angle by a standard point source of one candle, with all the components of the light having their mechanical values weighted accordingly to their luminosity values.

1 lumberg = 1 lumen-second

Note: This unit was formerly known as **"lumerg"**. It is equivalent in size to the **"Talbot"**.

See *"talbot" and "lumen-second."*

lumen (lm)

The SI unit of luminous flux. It is the luminous flux emitted in a solid angle of one steradian (sr) by a uniform point source having an intensity of one candela (cd).

1 lumen-minute = 1 candela per steradian.

Alternatively, it is equivalent to the luminous flux received on a unit surface, all points of which are at a unit distance from such a source.

See *"lumen-minute"*.

lumen-hour (lm h)

Unit for quantity of light used in SI system. It is the quantity of light radiated or received for 1 hour by a flux of lumen.

Note: The unit was adopted in 1920 by the Illuminating Engineering Society of New York and the American Engineering Standards Committee.

See *"lumen-second"*.

lumen per square meter (lm m^{-2})

SI unit of luminous existence.

Note: The SI unit "lux" is used instead of lumen per square meter for the case of illuminance.

lumen per watt (lm W^{-1})

SI unit of luminous efficacy and luminosity factor.

lumen second (lm s)

SI unit of quantity of light. It is the quantity of light radiated or received for a period of 1 second by a flux of 1 lumen.

Note: It is used, for example, in the measurement of light flashes.

lumerg (lumerg)

CGS unit of luminous intensity. An early name for the lumber.

See *"lumberg"*.

lunar day

The time interval between two successive crossings of the meridian by the Moon.

lunar month

The period of revolution of the Moon about the Earth, especially a syndical month.

lusec (lusec)

Metric unit of leak rate, i.e., power. One lusec is a leak rate of one liter per second at a pressure of one millitorr.

1 lusec = 0.001 1 torrs per second = 1.3322 x 10^{-4} watts.

Note: 1. This unit is used for the measurement of the power of evacuation of a vacuum pump.

2. 1 lusec = 100 clusecs.

See *"clusec"*.

lux (lx)

The SI unit of illuminance of a surface. It is the illumination of one lumen uniformly over an area of one square meter.

1 lx = 1 lumen per square meter.

Note: The unit was introduced in Germany in 1897 and it was associated with the meter-hefner.

lux second (lx s)

The SI unit of exposure.

luxon

Metric unit of retinal illumination. One luxon is defined as the retinal illumination produced by a surface having a luminance of one nit when the area of the pupil of the eye is one square millimeter.

Note: This unit was originally proposed in 1916 by an American physicist, Leonard Thompson Troland (1899-1932), who called it **"photon"**. However, the unit **"troland" is** preferred.

See also *"photon"* and *"troland"*.

M

M [1]

An informal abbreviation for million in expressions such as "$500M" for 500 million dollars or "Unemployment Reaches 4M" in a newspaper headline. In binary contexts such as computer memory, M often represents $2^{20} = 1\ 048\ 576$.

M [2]

The Roman numeral 1000 is sometimes used in symbols to indicate a thousand, as in **Mcf**, a traditional symbol for 1000 cubic feet. Given the widespread use of M to mean one million, the older use of M to imply one thousand is very confusing and should be scrapped.

M [3]

The symbol for "molar" in chemistry.

Ma

A symbol for one million years, often used in astronomy and geology. The "a" stands for the Latin *annum*.

ma

1.   A unit of length in Hong Kong. The unit is approximately 0.89155 meters. Sometimes referred to as "Chinese yard."
2.   In India, a land measure, the twentieth of a *Veli*.

mab

Symbol for "meters above the bottom" (bottom of the sea), a unit used in oceanography.

mace

A traditional Chinese unit for weighing precious metals, especially silver. In the European colonial period, the mace was considered equivalent to 0.1 taels or liang. This would be 2/15 ounces or about 3.78 grams.

Macedonian cubit

The **Macedonian cubit** was a unit of measurement used in ancient Macedonia. It was approximately 14 inches long, making it somewhat shorter than other cubit measurements used in the ancient world.

See also "cubit."

Mach number (Ma; M)

Mach number is the ratio *(v/c)* of the velocity *(v)* of an object or fluid to the velocity of *sound (c)* in the same medium and under the same conditions used. E.g., to express the velocity of an aircraft, M1 = the velocity of sound, M2 = twice the velocity of sound etc. The velocity of sound in dry air at 0°C is about 331.46 meters per second = 1193.3 kilometers per hour.

Note: 1. The number was used for the first time in 1887 by the Austrian scientist Ernst Mach (1838-1916) and it was named after him.

2. The Mach number is used in aerodynamics, ballistics and in heat transfer work.

Mache or mache

Arbitrary unit of radioactive concentration. One mache is a concentration of 3.7×10^{-7} curies of radioactive material in one cubic meter of a medium.

1 mache = 3.7×10^{-7} curies per cubic meter.

See also *"mache unit"*.

mache unit

Arbitrary unit of radioactivity. The quantity of radioactive emanation, which sets up a saturation current, equivalent to 10^{-3} stats units of current.

1 mache unit = 3.6×10^{-10} curies.

Note: The unit was defined by the International Radium Standards Committee in 1930. It is named after an Austrian physicist, Heinrich Mache (1876-1954).

See also *"mache"*.

maf or Maf

A symbol for one million acre-feet. This symbol, which is commonly used in reservoir management in the U.S., should be written **Maf**. 1 Maf = about 1.2335 billion (10^9) cubic meters.

See also "acre feet"

magn

The SI unit of absolute permeability. This unit has been proposed by the USSR but has not received general acceptance.

1 magn = 1 henry per meter

magnitude (mag)

Unit used in all systems of units for the brightness of stars and other astronomical bodies. The magnitude M of two stars relates the intensities I_1 *and* I_2 of their light outputs (expressed in the same units) by the formula $M = 2.5$ logs (I_1, I_2). Thus, 1 mag is the magnitude difference that corresponds to an intensity ratio of $10^{-0.4}$.

Magnitude can be one of:

- absolute magnitude
- bolometric magnitude
- integrated magnitude
- photographic magnitude
- stellar magnitude
- magnitudes, visual

magnitude, absolute (of heavenly bodies)

A star's absolute magnitude is the apparent magnitude it would have if it were 10 parsecs away (an arbitrarily chosen distance) and there were no intervening gas or dust. Symbol, M (in contrast to the lowercase "m" for apparent magnitude).

magnitude, bolometric

Bolometric magnitude takes into account all the radiation emitted by the star, whatever its wavelength. (There are even stars that shine entirely in the infrared, outside the band of visible light.) Because the Earth's atmosphere blocks some wavelengths, determining bolometric magnitudes is extremely difficult, and they have been found for only a few stars.

magnitude, integrated

To assign a magnitude to astronomical objects that are not point sources, such as galaxies and nebulas, astronomers treat them as if all the light from such an object to the telescope came from a point. So the Orion nebula, whose integrated magnitude is 6, doesn't look as bright as a magnitude 6 star.

If light from all the stars (excluding the Sun) were combined in a single star, it would have an apparent magnitude of -6.7, much less than the full Moon.

The range of brightness of everything seen in the sky before the *1990s* can be summed up in two gigantic leaps of apparent magnitude: the Sun is about 25 magnitudes (10^{10}) brighter than the brightest star, Sirius, and Sirius is 25 magnitudes brighter than the faintest star that can be photographed by the 200-inch telescope on Mt. Palomar.

magnitudes, photographic (photographic magnitudes of stars)

In *July 1850*, W. C. Bond took what is believed to be the first astronomical photograph on a wet collodion plate. Photography extended the range of observable magnitudes far beyond that of the eye, because, in a time exposure, a photographic plate can soak up light for hours on end, which the eye cannot.

Only a few stars are near enough, and big enough, that a telescope can image them as a disk.[1] Most are so far away that they appear as points with no diameter, but on a photographic plate, the brighter the star, the bigger the image. Bond was also the first to notice that the diameters of the stars' images appeared to be proportional to the logarithm of their brightness. Later, workers have refined the relationship.

$$\log (d + a) = e \log (b + k \log E)$$

where

d = diameter of disk in image

E = exposure of the plate

a, b, k, e = constants

Equation	a	e	b	k
Greenwich	0	2	*	*
Ross	*	2	*	*
Scheiner	0	1	*	*

* determined empirically. See the discussion of the Greenwich, Ross and Scheiner formulas in the sources

So, magnitudes can be determined by measuring the diameters of star images on a photographic plate. Magnitudes that have been determined in this way are called photographic magnitudes. Most astronomical photographs are taken on types of film that are not equally sensitive to light of all colors. **Blue magnitude** or **photovisual magnitude** refers to a photographic magnitude that has been measured using photographic plates whose sensitivity to various colors is similar to that of the human eye.

(sources: Wikipedia and

(Frank Elmore Ross.

The Physics of the Developed Photographic Image.

Monographs on the Theory of Photography, no. 5.

New York: D. Van Nostrand; Rochester, NY: Eastman Kodak Co., *1924*.)

magnitude (mag) [1]

A unit traditionally used in astronomy to express the apparent brightness of stars, planets, and other objects in the sky. For centuries, the brightest stars were said to be of the "first magnitude," and fainter ones of the "second magnitude," and so on, down to "sixth magnitude" for the faintest stars visible to the unaided eye. When it became possible to measure stellar brightness precisely, it was discovered that stars of a given traditional magnitude were roughly 2.5 times brighter than stars of the next magnitude. Astronomers agreed to define the magnitude scale such that a difference of exactly 5.0 mags corresponds to a brightness difference of exactly 100 times. A difference of 1.0 mag then corresponds to a brightness difference of the fifth root of 100 or about 2.512 times. The scale is upside down, i.e., brighter stars have lower, not higher, magnitudes, in keeping with the historical origin of the scale. The zero point (0.0 mag) is set arbitrarily, such that the stars historically listed as "first magnitude" have magnitude measurements of 1.5 mags or brighter. The brightest stars and planets have negative magnitudes on this scale. Note, however, that the scale is commonly used to describe the *apparent magnitude* of objects as we view them on Earth, but astronomers also use it for *absolute magnitude*, which is the magnitude the object would have if it were placed at a standard distance of 10 parsecs (32.61 light years) from Earth.

magnitude (mag) [2]

A unit used in Earth science to measure the intensity of earthquakes. Geologists use several scales to measure earthquake intensity, but the most popular one is the Richter magnitude scale, developed in 1935 by an American seismologist, Charles Francis Richter (1900-1985) of the California Institute of Technology. The Richter magnitude is computed from the measured amplitude and frequency of the earthquake's shock waves received by a seismograph and adjusted to account for the distance between the observing station and the epicenter of the earthquake. An increase of 1.0 in the Richter magnitude corresponds to an increase of 10 times in the amplitude of the waves and to an increase of about 31 times more energy released by the quake. The most powerful earthquakes recorded so far had magnitudes of about 8.5. The Richter magnitude measures the intensity of the earthquake but not the intensity of the earthquake's effects. The effects also depend on the depth of the earthquake, the geology of the area around the epicenter, and many other factors. Earthquake effects are rated using the Mercalli scale (see Earthquake scale).

magnetic ohm

CGS unit of reluctance. The magnetic ohm is the name sometimes used for gilbert per Maxwell.

1 magnetic ohm = 1 gilbert per Maxwell = 7.957 75 x 10^7 per henry

magneton

A unit of magnetic moment used for atomic, molecular, or nuclear magnets, such as the Bohr magneton, Wiess magneton, or nuclear magneton.

1. **Bohr Magneton**

    The magneton was first calculated by Bohr for the intrinsic magnetic moment of an electron. It is defined as:

    Bohr magneton = $eh/4\pi m$,

    Where e is the charge on the electron, m is the rest mass of the electron and h is the Planck's constant.

    1 Bohr magneton = 9.274 0780 x 10^{-24} ampere meter squared (or Joule per Tesla)

    Note: According to the wave mechanics of Dirac, the magnetic moment associated with the spin of the electron would be exactly one Bohr magneton, but quantum electrodynamics shows that there is a small difference.

2. **Nuclear Magneton**

    The nuclear magneton is equivalent to $(m/m_p).\beta$, where m_p is the mass of the proton. The value of the nuclear magneton is:

    1 nuclear magneton = 5.0508240 x 10^{-24} ampere meter squared (or Joule per Tesla)

    Note: The magnetic moment of a proton is equivalent to 2.792 85 nuclear magnetons.

3. **Weiss Magneton**

    Is a unit of magnetic moment, equivalent to 1.853 x 10^{-21} ergs per Oersted, or about one-fifth of Bohr magneton. It is an experimentally derived unit. The magnetic moments of certain molecules being close to integral multiples of the quantity.

magnum

A traditional unit of volume for wine generally equivalent to 2 bottles. This is now exactly 1.5 liters (about 2.114 U.S. quarts).

man hour

A common unit of labor, equivalent to the work of one person for one hour. The name **person hour** is commonly used for this unit.

manpower

An informal unit of power, equivalent to 0.1 horsepowers or about 74.57 watts. The unit seems to have been invented by American engineers.

manzana

A traditional unit of land area in Central America. The manzana is the area of a square of 100 <u>varas</u> on a side. Thus, it varies according to the length of the vara. The Costa Rican manzana is equivalent to 0.698 896 hectares or about 1.727 acres. Very similar units are used in Guatemala, Honduras, and Nicaragua. The word *manzana* means an apple, but the unit is probably related to *manzanar* orchard.

Marabba

A **marabba** is an obsolete unit of area in India and Pakistan approximately equivalent to 25 acres (10.117 hectares). After metrification by both countries in the 20th century, the unit became obsolete.

marathon

A traditional unit of distance used in athletics. The length of a marathon is exactly 42 195 meters (about half an inch longer than 26 miles or 385 yards). Invented for the first modern Olympic Games in Athens in 1896. The marathon recalls a run made in 490 BC by a Greek soldier (possibly Pheidippides) to bring to Athens the news of the Greek victory over the Persians at the Battle of Marathon. However, the actual distance from Marathon to Athens is only about 36.75 kilometers. The 1896 run was exactly 40 kilometers from the Marathon Bridge to the Olympic Stadium. At the 1908 Olympics in London, a course of 26 miles, i.e., 385 yards, brought runners from Windsor Castle to White City Stadium (the story is that exactly 26 miles was intended, but Queen Alexandra insisted that the finish line be moved in front of the royal box). The marathons at the Olympic Games varied in length until the 1924 Olympics in Paris when the International Olympic Committee adopted the 1908 London distance as official.

marc, marco, or mark

Traditional units of weight in various countries of Western Europe. In each country, the unit is equivalent to ½ the unit corresponding to the English pound. Thus, the French **marc** is equivalent to ½ livre, 8 ounces or about 244.75 grams. The Spanish **marco** is equivalent to ½ libra or about 230 grams. The German mark is equivalent to ½ pfund or about 280.5 grams and the English mark is equivalent to 8 ounces or 226.8 grams. The English unit was used almost entirely for measuring precious metals.

Like the German systems, the French poids de marc weight system considered one "Marc" equivalent to half a pound (8 ounces).

Just as the pound of 12 troy ounces (373 grams) lent its name to the pound unit of currency, the mark lent its name to the mark unit of currency.

See also "ounce", "pound", "gram."

Mars year (MY)

A unit of time, equivalent to the length of time for Mars to complete one orbit around the Sun. The Mars year is equivalent to about 686.98 Earth solar days, or 668.5991 sols (Martian days). Scientists have agreed that a Mars year begins at the spring equinox in the northern hemisphere of the planet. To provide a numbering system for Mars years, it is agreed that Mars year 0 (MY0) began on 24 May 1953. The Planetary Society provides a table listing the spring equinox dates for MY01 through MY40.

mast

Imperial (U.K.) unit of mass, equivalent to 2.5 troy pounds.

1 mast = 2.5 pounds (troy) = 0.933 104 3 kilograms.

The unit is used for amber, coral, and gold and silver.

maxwell (Mx)

CGS unit of magnetic flux. One Maxwell is the magnetic flux, after linking a circuit of one turn, produces in it an electromotive force of one abvolt as it decays to zero at a uniform rate in one second.

1 maxwell = 1 abvolt second = 10^{-8} webers.

Note: 1. The name of the unit is after a Scottish mathematician, James Clerk Maxwell (1831-1879)

2. The unit is also known as the **abweber** or **line** (of magnetic force).

See *"line (of magnetic force)"*.

mayer (mayer)

Metric unit of specific heat capacity. One meyer is equivalent to the quantity of heat in joules required to raise the temperature of one gram of substance by one kelvin.

1 mayer = 1 joule per gram kelvin = 1000 joules per kilogram kelvin.

Note: The unit was named after a German physician, Julius Robert von Mayer (1814-1878)

MBF or MBM

Traditional symbols for 1000 (not one million) board feet. A unit of volume for timber, equivalent to 250/3 = 83.333 cubic feet or 2.360 cubic meters. "BM" stands for "board measure."

See also "board feet."

mbsl

A common symbol for "meters below sea level" used in geology and oceanography.

MBH, MBtuh

Symbols for 1000 (not one million) Btu (British thermal units) per hour. A unit traditionally used in the U.S. heating and air conditioning industry to state rates of heating or cooling. One MBH is equivalent to about 0.293 071 kilowatts.

See also " Btu" and "watt."

McLEOD

Unit of pressure level (i.e., pressure on a logarithmic scale). Pressure P in McLeods is related to the pressure p in millimeters of mercury by the relation:

$$P = -\log_{10}P$$

Thus, one Mcleod is the pressure level corresponding to the pressure of one tenth of millimeters of mercury.

Note: This unit is also known as the **freight ton**.

mechanical ohm

Arbitrary unit of mechanical impedance. It is also referred to as dyne second per centimeter.

1 mechanical ohm = 1 dyn second per centimeter = 10^{-3} Newton seconds per meter.

Note: The mechanical ohm was proposed at first by Firestone in 1933 and he assigned the unit dyne per kine to the dimensions of the unit. The kine is the name given to the CGS unit of velocity.

See *"kine"*

mega (M)

SI prefix denoting x 10^6. Examples are megaampere (MA), megabecquerel (Mbq), megacoulomb (MC), megagray (MGy), megahertz (MHz), etc.

Note: When referring to memory capacity or information rate, the prefix mega denotes $2^{20}=1048576$, e.g., megabyte (Mbyte) = 2^{20} bytes.

megabits per second (Mbit/s)

Unit of measure for high-speed data transmission. For example, 16 Mbit/s for Token Ring and 10 megabit per second for Ethernet.

megabyte (Mbyte)

Unit of storage in computer technology.

For internal computer storage (inner memory):

1 Mbyte = 2^{20} bytes = 1 048 576 bytes.

For external storage (direct-access storage, tape etc.):

1 Mbyte = 10^6 bytes.

megabyte per second (Mbyte/s)

Unit of measure commonly used in measuring information.

megaelectronvolt-curie (Me V Ci)

Arbitrary unit of radioactive power. One megaelectronvolt-curie is the power, equivalent to that generated by one curie emitting a mean energy of megaelectronvolt per disintegration.

1 Me V Ci = 0.005 927 77 watts.

megaton

A unit used to define the magnitude of an explosion. One megaton is equivalent to the detonation of a million tons of TNT.

Note: This unit was used at first in 1950 to describe the force of explosion of a hydrogen bomb.

megawatt year of electricity (MWYE)

A unit of electric energy, equivalent to the energy delivered by a power of 1,000,000 watts over a period of one tropical year

1 MWYE = 3.1557 x 10^{13} joules

measure

A musical unit representing a series of beats [2] (rhythmic stresses) with one primary or accented stress. A measure is also known as a **bar** because the end of a measure is represented in musical notation by a vertical bar.

measurement ton (MTON or MT)

A unit of volume used for measuring the cargo of a ship, truck, train, or other freight carrier. It is equivalent to exactly 40 cubic feet, or approximately 1.1326 cubic meters. This unit was traditionally known as a freight ton (see ton [5]), but that term now means a metric ton of freight in most international usage. However, the confusion seems impossible to dispel. Some shippers are now using "measurement ton" to mean a metric ton of freight. (The way out of this dilemma is simple. Measure volume in cubic meters and weight in metric tons.)

mebi- (Mi-)

A binary prefix meaning 2^{20} = 1 048 576. This prefix, which was adopted by the International Electrotechnical Commission in 1998, is intended to replace mega- for binary applications in computer science. In particular, a **mebibyte (MiB)** is 2^{20} = 1 048 576 bytes. The prefix is a contraction of "megabinary."

mebibyte

A unit of information, equivalent to 2^{20} = 1 048 576 bytes.

MED

A common symbol for "minimum erythemal dose" is the smallest amount of ultraviolet radiation that produces observable reddening (erythema) of the skin (Skin is sensitive to reddening by radiation in only a narrow band of wavelengths around 300 nanometres). The MED obviously varies from one person to another. Doctors and tanning salon operators typically use a value of 200 jouls per square meter (J/m^2), which represents the MED of a highly sensitive individual. Persons with dark skin have MEDs' in the range of 1000 joules per square meter. Regulatory agencies are adapting to the use of the standard erythemal dose (SED), a unit equivalent to exactly 100 joules per square meter. In tanning, a dose rate of one MED per hour is equivalent to 55.55 milliwatts per square meter of the skin surface.

See also "joul."

meg

Informal contraction of "megabyte", used in computer science.

mega- (M-) [1]

A metric prefix meaning 10^6, or one million. (The form meg- is often used before a vowel, as in *megohm* for one million ohms). The prefix is also common in ordinary language, meaning "very large," as in *megabucks* or *megadose*. The prefix is derived from the Greek word for large *megas*.

mega- (M-) [2]

In measuring the storage capacity of a computer, the prefix mega- often means $2^{20} = 1\ 048\ 576$ instead of an even one million. As agreed during the 1998 resolution of the International Electrotechnical Commission, the new prefix mebi- (Mi-) was to replace mega- for 2^{20}.

megabar (Mbar)

A metric unit of pressure. The megabar, is equivalent to one million bars, 100 gigapascals (GPa) or about 14.503 million pounds per square inch. Such intense pressures are found within the Earth or in various advanced scientific experiments.

See also "Pascal" "bar."

megabarrel (Mbbl, Mbo, MMb, or Mb)

A unit of volume used in the energy industry. It is equivalent to one million barrels of oil. One megabarrel is equivalent to 42 million U.S. gallons, which is about 158.987 megaliters (ML).

See also "barrel" and "gallon."

megabase (Mb)

A unit of genetic information, equivalent to the information carried by 1 million pairs of the base units in the double-helix of DNA. It is also used as a unit of relative distance, equivalent to the length of a strand of DNA containing 1 million base pairs. In humans, one megabase corresponds to approximately a gene separation of one centimorgan.

megabecquerel (MBq)

A unit of radioactivity, equivalent to one million atomic disintegrations per second or 27.027 microcuries.

megabits per second (Mbit/s, Mb/s, or Mbps)

A unit of data transmission speed commonly used to measure the speed of Internet connections. One megabit per second is equivalent to one million bits per second. Internet service providers prefer to measure connection speeds using this unit, because the numerical values are eight times larger than when the measurement was stated in megabytes per second. Caution: in print and especially in TV advertising, this unit is often presented as a misleading all-caps symbol MBPS.

megabyte (MB)

A unit of information, equivalent to 1 000 000 bytes. The megabyte is often used to mean $2^{20} = 1\ 048\ 576$ bytes and has occasionally been used to mean 1 024 000 bytes. These applications break the rules of the SI. The unit, equivalent to 2^{20} bytes, should be known as the **mebibyte** (see above).

megabytes per second (MB/s or MBps)

A unit of data transmission speed commonly used to measure the speed of file transfers. One megabyte per second is equivalent to one million bytes per second or 8 million bits per second.

megacycle (Mc)

1 million cycles, a term sometimes used as an informal name for the megahertz.

megacycle per second (Mc/s)

An older name for the megahertz.

megadalton (MDa)

A unit of mass equivalent to one million atomic mass units. See dalton.

megaflops (Mflops)

A unit of computing power, equivalent to one million floating point operations per second. See "flops".

megagallon (Mgal)

A unit of volume equivalent to one million gallons. It is frequently used in reservoir and water supply management in the U.S. One megagallon is equivalent to about 133 680.556 cubic feet, 3785.411 88 cubic meters, 3.068 883 acre-feet, or 0.378 541 188 hectare meters.

megagallon per day (Mgal/d or Mgd)

A unit of water flow. One megagallon per day is about 1.547 229 cubic feet per second or 43.812 638 liters per second.

megagram (Mg)

An SI unit of mass equivalent to one million grams or 1000 kilograms. This means that the megagramme is identical to the ton (metric ton). Large masses are almost always stated in tons in commercial applications, but megagrammes are often used in scientific contexts. One megagramme is equivalent to about 2204.623 pounds.

See also "ton" and "pound."

megahectare (Mha)

A unit of land area, equivalent to one million hectares. The kilohectare is also equivalent to exactly 10 billion (10^9) square meters, about 2 471 054 acres, or 3861.022 square miles. The symbol Mha is commonly used as a convenient abbreviation for "million hectares," even when the term megahectare is not applicable. "Megahectare" is not acceptable in the SI since it uses two prefixes: mega- and hecto-.

See also "hectare", and "acre."

egahertz (MHz)

A common unit of frequency, equivalent to one million per second. Frequencies of radio waves are commonly stated in megahertz.

megajoule (MJ)

A common metric unit of work or energy. The megajoule is equivalent to one million joules, which is approximately 737 562 foot-pounds, 947.8170 Btu, 238.846 (kilogram) Calories, or 0.277 778 kilowatt hours.

See also "Btu" and "calories."

MegaFonzie

Non-conventional unit that measures Coolness

A MegaFonzie is a fictional unit of measurement of an object's coolness invented by Professor Farnsworth in the *Futurama* episode "Bender Should Not Be Allowed on TV". A 'Fonzie' is about the amount of coolness inherent in the *Happy Days* character Fonzie.

megakelvin (MK)

A unit of temperature equivalent to one million kelvins. This unit is used in astrophysics. Temperatures in megakelvins are found in the interiors of stars or in highly excited plasmas. The reciprocal megakelvin (MK^{-1}) is used in colorimetry.

megalerg

A CGS unit of energy, equivalent to 10^6 ergs or 0.1 joules (0.073 756 foot-pounds). The "l" was added to "mega-erg" to make the unit pronounceable.

megaline

A metric unit of magnetic flux, equivalent to one million lines [2] or 0.01 webers.

megaliter (Ml or ML)

A metric unit of volume, equivalent to 1000 cubic meters. Commonly used in reservoir and water system management outside the U.S. The megaliter is equivalent to 264 172 U.S. gallons or 0.810 713 acre-feet.

megalithic yard

A unit of distance, equivalent to about 83 centimeters or 2.72 feet. It was defined in 1951 by the Scottish engineer Alexander Thom (1894-1985). Thom claimed this unit was used in the construction of many megalithic monuments, including Stonehenge. If this is true, then the unit was probably measured by the length of a workman's arm.

megametre (Mm)

A metric unit of distance, equivalent to 1000 kilometers or about 621.371 miles. Although this appears to be an appropriate unit for longer distances on the Earth, the megametre is seldom used.

megampere (MA)

A unit of electric current, equivalent to one million amperes. This unit is used in plasma physics and fusion research.

meganewton (MN)

A metric unit of force, equivalent to one million newtons. One meganewton is equivalent to about 101 972 kilograms of force or 224 809 pounds of force. The main engines of the U.S. space shuttle have a maximum thrust of about 2.28 meganewtons.

megaohm (megohm)

A common unit of electric resistance, equivalent to one million ohms. The spelling **megohm** is also used.

megaohm (megohm) centimeter

A unit of resistivity used for pure water and for other substances having relatively high resistivity. In the case of water, resistivity is a measure of purity. The higher the purity, the higher the resistivity. The resistivity of a conductor in megaohm centimeters is defined to be its resistance (in megaohms) multiplied by its cross-sectional area (in square centimeters) divided by its length (in centimeters). One megaohm centimeter is equivalent to 10 000 ohm meters.

megaparsec (Mpc)

A unit commonly used for the longest distance. The megaparsec is used by astronomers studying the most distant quasars and galaxies. One megaparsec is equivalent to one million parsecs, 3.2616 million light years or 30.857×10^{18} kilometers (30.857 zettametres).

megapascal (MPa, MP)

A common metric unit of pressure or stress, equivalent to one million pascals or one newton per square millimeter. One megapascal is equivalent to 10 Bars or approximately 145.038

pounds per square inch (lbf/in^2 or psi) or 20 885.5 pounds (10.443 U.S. tons) per square foot. The symbol MP is mistakenly used in engineering. However, MPa is the right unit for this specialization.

megapixel

A unit used to describe the size or resolution of an image or of a digital camera. One megapixel is one million pixels (picture elements, or "dots"). For example, a rectangular image 1000 pixels by 1000 pixels is comprised of one megapixel.

megapond (Mp)

A metric unit of force, equivalent to 1000 kilograms of force (kgf). The megapond is also equivalent to 9806.65 newtons, or 2204.6226 pounds of force, in the traditional English system. Although it is considered obsolete, the megapond is still used sometimes by engineers in Europe, especially in Germany.

megaton (Mton or Mt)

A unit of energy, used for measuring the energy of an explosion, especially a nuclear explosion. Supposed to be the amount of energy released by the explosion of one million (short) tons of TNT. The megaton is defined to be equivalent to 4.18 x 10^{15} joules (4.18 petajoules), 1.16 billion kilowatt hours, or roughly 4 trillion Btu.

megatonne (Mt)

A metric unit of mass or weight, equivalent to one million metric tons (tons), one teragramme (Tg), or about 2.2046 billion pounds.

megawatt (MW)

A common metric unit of power. One megawatt is equivalent to one million watts, about 1341.02 horsepower, or 947.817 Btu per second.

megawatt hour (MW·h)

Aa metric unit of energy, especially electrical energy. One megawatt hour is equivalent to exactly 3.6 gigajoules (GJ), about 3.412 million Btu, or about 2.655 billion foot-pounds.

megawatt day (MW·d or MWD)

A unit of energy used in the nuclear power and nuclear weapons industries. One megawatt day is equivalent to exactly 24 megawatt hours, 86.4 gigajoules (GJ), about 81.89 million Btu, or about 63.7 billion foot-pounds.

megayear (Myr or Ma)

A unit of time, equivalent to one million years.

megohm

A common unit of electric resistance, equivalent to one million ohms. This simplified spelling of **megaohm** was approved by the Institute of Electrical and Electronics Engineers (IEEE).

meile

A traditional distance unit in German speaking countries. The meile is much longer than the mile units of Western Europe. Typically, the meile is equivalent to 4000 klafers (fathoms) or 24 000 fuß (German feet). In Austria, it is 7586 meters (4.714 miles). In northern Germany, it is 4.6805 miles or 7532.5 meters. A version of the meile, known as the *geographische meile,* was defined to be equivalent to exactly 4 (Admiralty) nautical miles (24 320 feet, 4.6061 miles, or 7412.7 meters). The geographische meile was designed to be equivalent to $\frac{1}{15}$ degree [2] or 4/3 league. See also mil [4], the Scandinavian version of this unit.

mel

A unit of perceived musical pitch, originally defined by Stevens, Volkmann, and Newmann in 1937. Our perception of musical pitch is complex. Although tones of higher frequency are perceived as being higher in pitch, tones separated by equal intervals (frequency ratios), such as octaves, will not be perceived as being equally spaced in pitch. A pure tone of frequency 1000 hertz, at a sound level 40 decibels above the faintest sound a listener can hear, is defined to have a pitch of 1000 mels, and tones perceived as being equally spaced in pitch are separated by an equal number of mels. Because perceptions of pitch depend on a number of factors other than frequency, it is not possible to give a straightforward conversion between hertz and mels. For tones above 1000 hertz, the perceived pitch in mels is lower than the frequency in hertz. A 10-kilohertz tone is perceived at around 3000 mels. For tones lower than 1000 hertz, the perceived pitch is a little higher than the frequency in hertz.

mel (mel)

A unit of subjective pitch in all systems of units. It is equivalent to one-thousandth of a pitch of a simple ton, whose frequency is 1000 hertz and whose loudness is 40dB above a listener's threshold.

Note: The name of the unit is a shortened form of the word ***melody.***

Mercalli intensity scale

An empirical scale for rating the effects of an earthquake, as opposed to its strength (see magnitude [2] above). Mercalli estimates are stated as Roman numerals (I-XII) to avoid confusion with magnitude estimates on the Richter scale. The scale is named after an Italian geologist, Giuseppe Mercalli (1850-1914), who devised the first version of the scale in 1902. The modified version used in the U.S. and Canada was developed by Charles Francis Richter in 1956.

mercantile pound (lb merc)

A historic English unit of weight. The mercantile pound (*libra mercatoria*) was the commercial predecessor of the avoirdupois pound [1]. Used from about 1100 to 1300, the mercantile pound contained 15 troy ounces [2] or 7200 grains. This is equivalent to about 1.0286 avoirdupois pounds or 466.55 grams.

MERU (Milli Earth Rate Unit)

An informal unit of angular measure.

The **MERU**, or Milli Earth Rate Unit, is an angular velocity equal to $\frac{1}{1000}$ of Earth's rotation rate. It was introduced by MIT's Instrumentation Laboratories (now Draper Labs) to measure the performance of inertial navigation systems. One MERU = 7.292115×10^{-8} radians per second or about 0.2625 milliradians per hour

mesh

A traditional unit used to measure the fineness of woven products, such as fishing nets, fencing fabric, window screening, etc. It is equivalent to the number of strands per inch. For n mesh fabric, the distance between strands is $1/n$ inch or $25.4/n$ millimeters.

met

A unit of metabolism. Metabolism, a combination of all the processes happening in the body to sustain life, is measured in units of power expended per unit of body surface area.

One "met" is the metabolism of a seated, resting person, which is equivalent to about 58.15 watts per square meter (W/m^2) or 13.89 calories per second per square meter ($cal/m^2 \cdot s$), regardless of the person's size. Measurements of human metabolism generally range between 0.8-3.0 mets, although athletes can achieve 10 mets or more.

meter (m)

It is the base SI unit of length, exactly 1,650,763.73 wavelengths of the radiation in vacuum corresponding to the unperturbed transition between the levels $2p_{10}$ and $5d_5$ of the atom of krypton 86, the orange-red line. This definition was adopted by the 11CGPM of 1960.

On October 1984, during the General Conference of Weights and Measures, the meter was defined as the "length of the path traveled by light in a vacuum during a time interval of $\frac{1}{299\,792\,458}$ of a second".

The meter is also the SI unit of breadth, height, depth, thickness, radius, diameter, length of a path, wavelength, sound particle displacement, mean free path, stopping equivalent, mean linear range, the diffusion coefficient for neutron fluence, Burgers vector, displacement vector of ion, equilibrium position vector of ion, fundamental lattice vector, half-thickness, lattice vector and particle position vector.

Note: 1. The original definition of the meter was commissioned by the Paris Academy of Sciences in 1791 as: "One meter is one ten-millionth of the length of the meridional quadrant of the Earth's surface, passing through Dunkirk and a point close to Barcelona".

2. At the 7CGPM of 1927, the above definition was supplanted by the then official definition: The meter is the distance at $0^{\circ}C$ of the axes of two median lines drawn on the platinum-iridium bar. This bar was deposited at the International Bureau of Weights and Measures and was referred to as the prototype meter by the 1CGPM. This measure is subject to standard atmospheric pressure and supported by two rollers of at least one centimeter in diameter, symmetrically placed in the same horizontal plane and at a distance of 571 millimeters from one another. The prototype meter bar, of X-shaped cross-section, is made from an alloy of 90% platinum and 10% iridium.

3. Copies of the standard were safely stored with other countries, with the British copy being in the custody of the National Physical Laboratory. This latter copy was directly compared with the original copy in 1922 and indirectly compared with the original copy in 1949. These were found to agree within one part of 10^7.

4. The length of one meter is reproducible to part in 10^8. Standardization with a laser beam will probably increase the accuracy to 1 part in 10^{10}.

5. In U.K., the name of this unit is spelled as meter. The spelling in official translations of ISO Recommendations is always meter.

meter-atmosphere (m-atm)

Arbitrary unit of depth of equivalent atmosphere. X meter-atmosphere of gas is the depth (in meters) that an atmosphere would have if gas x were the only constituent and in the same amount as it exists in the actual atmosphere and reduced to standard temperature and pressure (s.t.p).

1 meter-atmosphere = 2.686 99 x 10^{25} molecules per square meter.

Note: 1. This unit is based on Dalton's law of partial pressure. As there are 2.686 99 x 10^{25} molecules in a unit volume of gas as s.t.p., the pressure exerted by these molecules is the same as that exerted by a column of gas, 1 meter high. If the partial pressures of two gases be x and y meter-atmosphere, then every cubic meter of the mixture will contain (2.686 99x) x 10^{25} and (2.686 99y) x 10^{25} molecules of each gas and their partial pressures will be in the ratio x:y.

*2. The unit has also been known as the **atmo-meter.***

meter- candle (mc)

The SI unit of the intensity of illumination. It is the illumination of one lumen uniformly over an area of one square meter.

1 mc = 1 lumen per square meter

Note: The recommended name of this unit is the **lux.**

meter cubed (m³)

The SI unit of section modulus.

Note: It is similar to the cubic meter.

See *"cubic meter"*.

meter-gram-wink system

System of units proposed in 1957. The base unit of length is the meter, that of mass is the gram and that of time is known as the wink, which is equivalent to ($\frac{1}{3000}$) microseconds. The unit of force is known as Samson, which is equivalent to 9×10^{13} newtons. The unit of work is an Einstein, which is equivalent to 9×10^{13} joules. Electrical units are also included with such names as the Simon for the unit of resistance.

See *"Samson"*, *"Simon,"* and *"wink"*.

meter kelvin (m K)

SI unit second radiation constant

meter kelvin per watt (m K W^{-1})

SI unit of thermal resistivity

meter per kilogram (m Kg^{-1})

SI unit of specific length

meter per second (m s^{-1})

SI unit of velocity, speed and mass transfer coefficient (diffusion rate constant)

meter per second cubed (m s^{-3})

SI unit of jerk

meter per second squared (m s^{-2})

SI unit of acceleration

Meter of water equivalent

A material-dependent unit, used in nuclear and particle physics and engineering to measure the thickness of shielding, for example, around a nuclear reactor, particle accelerator, or radiation or particle detector. 1 mwe of a material is the thickness of that material that provides the equivalent shielding of one meter ($\approx$39.4 inches) of water.

This unit is commonly used in underground science to express the extent to which the overburden (usually rock) shields an underground space or laboratory from cosmic rays. The actual thickness of the overburden through which cosmic rays must traverse to reach the underground space varies as a function of direction due to the shape of the overburden, which may be a mountain, a flat plain, or something more complex like a cliff side. To express the depth of an underground space in mwe (or kmwe for deep sites) as a single number, the convention is to use the depth beneath a flat overburden at sea level that gives the same overall cosmic ray muon flux in the underground location.

meter squared (m^2)

SI unit of slowing-down area, diffusion area and migration area.

Note:　The same as a square meter.

See *"square meter"*.

meter squared per hour ($m^2\ h^{-1}$)

Unit of kinematic viscosity used in the SI system

$1\ m^2\ h^{-1} = 2.77778 \times 10^{-4}$ meters squared per second.

See *"meter squared per second"*.

meter squared per second ($m^2\ s^{-1}$)

SI unit of kinematic viscosity.

Note:　It is also a unit of thermal diffusivity, diffusion and thermal diffusion coefficient.

meter to the fourth power (m^4)

SI unit of second moment of area.

Metonic cycle

A unit of time, equivalent to 19 years, used in astronomy in predicting the phases of the Moon. By coincidence, 19 years is equivalent to 6939.602 days. 235 lunar months is equivalent to 6939.689 days, just 125 minutes longer. As a result, the phases of the Moon repeat almost exactly after 19 years. (Since 19 years can contain either 3 or 4 leap days, the recurrence is not always exact as to the day of the month). Many lunar calendars, such as the Chinese and Jewish calendars, share this 19-year cycle. The cycle is named after the ancient Greek astronomer Meton (460 BC - Unknown), who first used it for predictions around 433 BC.

metric carat

The current internationally-recognized carat equivalent to exactly 200 milligrams.

Metretes

A **metretes** was an ancient Greek unit of liquid measurement equivalent to 39.3 liters.
See also "liter."

metric carat

Unit of mass. One-fifth of the gram.

1 metric carat = **0.2** grams = **2 x 10^{-4}** kilograms.

Note: 1. The unit was adopted by the 4th CGPM, 1907, for measuring of purity of diamonds, fine pearls and precious stones.

2. Not to be confused with the carat (karat) used as a measure of purity of gold.

See *"carat, metric"*.

metric feet

An informal unit of length.

A metric foot, defined as 300 millimeters (approximately 11.811 inches), has been used occasionally in the U.K. but has never been declared an official unit.

A Chinese foot is defined as around one-third of a meter, depending on the jurisdiction.
See also "inch", "millimeter."

metric grain

A unit of mass sometimes used by jewelers that is equivalent to 50 milligrams or ¼ carat. This unit is often used for pearls and is sometimes known as the **pearl grain**.

metric hundredweight

An informal unit of mass, equivalent to 50 kilograms or approximately 110.231 pounds, close to the traditional British hundredweight of 112 pounds. This unit is also known by its German name, the zentner, or (in English) the centner.

metric mile

An informal unit of distance used mostly in athletics. The metric mile is equivalent to 1500 meters or 1.5 kilometers (approximately 0.932 057 statute miles or 4921.26 feet). In U.S. high school competition, the term is sometimes used for a race of 1600 meters (0.994 194 miles or 5249.34 feet).

metric pound

An informal name for a mass of 500 grams (0.5 kilograms or 1.1023 pounds).

metric quintal

A unit of mass, equivalent to 1 decitonne, 100 kilograms or about 220.462 pounds. See quintal for a more complete description.

Metric ounce

An informal unit of volume.

A metric ounce is an approximation of the imperial ounce, U.S. dry ounce, or U.S. fluid ounce. These three customary units vary. However, the metric ounce is usually taken as 25 or 30 milliliters, when volume is being measured, or grams when mass is being measured.

The US Food and Drug Administration (FDA) defines the "food labeling ounce" as 30 milliliters, slightly larger than the 29.6 milliliter fluid ounces.

Several Dutch units of measurement have been replaced with informal metric equivalents, including the *ons* or ounce. It originally meant $\frac{1}{16}$ of a pound, or a little over 30 grams, depending on which definition of the pound was used, but was redefined as 100 grams, when the country metricated.

metric slug (metric slug)

Metric technical unit of mass. The metric slug is the mass that acquires an acceleration of one meter per second squared under the influence of a force of one kilogram-force.

1 metric slug = **9.806 65** kilograms

Note: The metric slug is not often used. It is generally simply referred to as the **metric-mechanical unit of mass.** It is also known as the **"hyl".** Alternative (but not used) names are the **"mug"** and the **"par".**

metric technical unit of mass

MkgfS unit of mass. The metric technical unit of mass is the mass that acquires an acceleration of one meter per second squared under the influence of a force of one kilogram-force.

1 metric technical unit of mass = **9.0806 65** kilograms.

Note: The unit is sometimes known as the **hyl** or **the metric slug.**

See *"hyl", "metric slug", "mug,"* and also *"tecma".*

metric ton unit (mtu)

A unit of mass used in mining to measure the mass of the valuable metal in an ore. Customarily, the metric ton unit is defined to be one metric ton of ore containing 1% metal, but it is the metal and not the ore that is being measured. Thus, this unit is a unit of mass equivalent to 10 kilograms (22.0462 pounds).

MeV

Unit of energy.

1 MeV = 10^6 electron volts.

MeV

Unit of energy.

$1\ MeV = 10^6$ electron volts

mho (mho)

SI unit of conductance, admittance and susceptance. One mho is defined as the conductance between two points of a conductor when a constant difference of potential of one volt that is applied between these two points produces a current of one ampere, with the conductor not being the source of any electromotive force.

1 mho = 1 A/V (1 Ampere/Volt).

Note: 1. The **siemens is preferred** instead of mho.

2. It is acceptable to refer to this unit as the **reciprocal mho**, though siemens is recommended.

3. The former name of this unit was the **absolute mho**.

4. The name mho was used for the first time by a British mathematician, William Thomson, 1st Baron Kelvin (1824-1907) in 1883.

See also *"Siemens"* and *"ohm, reciprocal"*.

MIC (mic)

Metric unit of inductance.

$1\ mic = 1\ microhenry = 10^{-6}$

Note: This name was used only by the Royal Navy.

Mickey

Informal unit of length in the "Humorous System of Units."

One mickey is the smallest resolvable unit of distance by a given computer mouse pointing device. It is named after Walt Disney's Mickey Mouse cartoon character. Mouse motion is reported in horizontal and vertical mickeys. Device sensitivity is usually specified in mickeys per inch. Typical resolution is 500 mickeys per inch (16 mickeys per millimeter), but resolutions up to 16,000 mickeys per inch (600 mickeys per millimeters) are available.

micri-erg (micri-erg)

Metric unit of energy, particularly molecular surface energy.

1 micri-erg = 10^{-21} joules.

Note: The name of the unit was proposed for the first time by an American physical chemist William Draper Harkins (1873-1951) in 1922. This unit has rarely been used.

micri (micri)

Metric unit of concentration. It is defined as one micri is a concentration of one milligram of solute in one liter of solvent.

1 micri = 0.001 kilograms per meter cubed

Note: This unit is also known as the "gammil" or "microgammil". It has rarely been used. See *"gammil"*

micro

SI prefic denoting x 10^{-6}. Examples include microampere, microbar, microcoulomb, microfarad, microgramme, microhenry, microjoule, microlumen, micrometer, micromole, microohm, micropascal, microsecond, microsiemens, microtesla, microvolt and microwatt.

Microcentury

Informal unit of time in the "Humorous System of Units."

According to Gian-Carlo Rota, the mathematician John von Neumann used the term microcentury to denote the maximum length of a lecture. One microcentury is 52 minutes and 35.7 seconds – one millionth of a century.

Microfortnight

An informal unit of time.

One unit derived from the FFF system of units is the microfortnight, one millionth of the fundamental time unit of FFF, which is equivalent to 1.2096 seconds. This is a fairly representative example of "hacker_humor" and is occasionally used in operating systems; for example, the OpenVMS TIMEPROMPTWAIT parameter is measured in microfortnights.

microkatal (µkat)

Unit of enzyme activity. One microkatal is equivalent to one micro mole of reaction product produced or consumed per second.

1 micokatal = 1 micromole per second.

micrometer (µm)

Unit of length used in the SI system.

1 micrometer = 10^{-6} meters.

Note: This unit was formerly known as the mircon.

See *"micron"*

micron (µ and now µm)

Metric unit of length. It is now known as the "micrometer."

1 **µm**= 10^{-6} meters.

Note: 1. The CIPM commissioned the use of this unit in 1879.

2. In 1968, the 13th CGPM decided to proscribe the use of the term micron and express 10^{-6} meters as the micrometer (µm).

micron (pressure) (µ mHg)

Metric unit of pressure. The micron is defined as the pressure that would support a column of mercury of length of one micrometer and density 13595.1 kilograms per cubic meter under the standard acceleration of free fall.

1 µ mHg = 10^{-3} micrometers of mercury = 0.133322387415 pascals.

Note: 1. This unit is usually known as the (conventional) micrometer of mercury.

2. The use of this unit is depreciated. It should be replaced by the millitorr.

mickey

> A unit used in computer science for programming computer mice and similar input devices. One mickey is the length of the smallest detectable movement of the mouse. This depends on the equipment. Typical values range between $\frac{1}{200}$ to $\frac{1}{300}$ inch or roughly 0.1 millimeters. Obviously, the name originates from the Disney cartoon character Mickey Mouse.

micro- (μ- or mc- or u-)

> A metric prefix meaning 10^{-6} (one millionth). The prefix originates from the Greek prefix *mikro-*, meaning small. In print, the prefix is sometimes abbreviated mc- or u- when the Greek letter mu (μ) is not available.

microampere (μA)

> A unit of electric current, equivalent to 10^{-6} amperes.

microarcsecond (μas)

> A unit of angle measurement sometimes used in astronomy. The microarcsecond is equivalent to 10^{-6} arcseconds or about 4.8481 picoradians.

microbar (μbar)

> A CGS unit of pressure, equivalent to 0.001 millibars, 0.1 pascals, 1 dyne per square centimeter (1 barye), or about 0.002 089 pounds per square foot. The microbar is used commonly in acoustics and sound engineering.
> See also "barye"

microcurie (μCi)

> A common unit of radioactivity. The microcurie is equivalent to 10^{-6} curies or 37 kilobecquerels. This corresponds to a radioactivity of 37,000 atomic disintegrations per second.

microdegree (μdeg) [1]

> A unit of angle measure, equivalent to a millionth of a degree or exactly 36 milliarcseconds.

microeinstein (µE)

A unit of light energy concentration used in measuring the flux or density of light or any form of electromagnetic radiation. The microeinstein is equivalent to 10^{-6} einsteins or one micromole of photons. The density of photosynthetically active radiation, for example, is reported in microeinsteins per second per square meter ($\mu E/s \cdot m^2$).
See also "Einsteins."

microequivalent (µEq or µeq)

A unit of relative amount of substance, equivalent to 10^{-6} equivalent weight. This unit is used, for example, in stating the concentrations of ions in drinking water.

microfarad (µF)

A common unit of electric capacitance, equivalent to 10^{-6} farads.

microflick (µf)

A unit of spectral radiance used in optical and communications engineering, equivalent to 10^{-6} flicks, or 1 microwatt per steradian per square centimeter of surface per micrometer of span in wavelength. This is mathematically equivalent to 10 milliwatts per steradian per cubic meter.
See also "flick."

microgramme (µg or mcg)

A metric unit of mass, equivalent to 0.001 milligrams (mg) or one millionth of a gram. Ingredients of drugs and vitamins are often stated in microgrammes.

microgray (µGy)

A unit of radiation dose, equivalent to a millionth of a gray or 0.1 millirads. Small doses of such size are often provided by natural sources in the environment.

microinch (µin)

A traditional unit of distance, equivalent to 10^{-6} inches, 0.001 mils, or 25.4 nanometres (nm). The microinch is used rather widely to state the roughness of optical surfaces, precise tolerances in machining, and for other industrial purposes.

microliter (µl, µL, mcl, or mcL)

A metric unit of volume, equivalent to 0.001 milliliters or 1 cubic millimeter (mm^3). Microliters are used in chemistry and medicine to measure very small quantities of liquid. This unit has also been known as the **lambda**.

micrometer (µm)

A common metric unit of distance, equivalent to 0.001 millimeters or about 0.039 370 mils. The name **micron** is also used for this unit.

micromicro- (µµ-)

An obsolete metric prefix denoting 10^{-12}. The prefix has been supplanted by pico- (p-).

micromicrofarad (µµF or mmfd)

An older name for the picofarad (10^{-12} farads). Though it is obsolete now, this name is still written on many capacitors.

micromicron (µµ)

A former name for a millionth of a micron, i.e., 10^{-12} meters. The name **bicron** was also used for this unit, which is now known as the picometre (pm).

micromole (µmol)

A unit of amount of substance, equivalent to a millionth of a mole (see below). This unit is used very commonly in biochemistry since a mole of a large organic molecule can be quite a large amount.

Micromort

A micromort is a unit of risk measuring a one-in-a million probability of death (from micro- and mortality). Micromorts can be used to measure the riskiness of various day-to-day activities. A micro probability is a one-in-a million chance of some event. Thus, a micromort is the micro probability of death. For example, smoking 1.4 cigarettes increases one's death risk by one micromort, as does traveling 370 kilometers (230 miles) by car.

micron (μ) [1]

A metric unit of distance, equivalent to one millionth of a meter. "Micron" is simply a shorter name for the micrometer. In 1968, the CGPM decided to drop the micron as an approved unit and recommend that micrometers be used instead. Microns, however, are still in common use.

micron (μ) [2]

An informal unit of pressure widely used in vacuum technology. In this context, a micron is a micron of mercury, i.e., 0.001 micrometers of mercury or approximately 1.333 microbars (μbar or μb) or 133.3 millipascals (mPa). For all practical applications, 1 micron is identical to 1 millitorr (mTorr).

See also "torr"

micronewton (μN)

A unit of force, equivalent to a millionth of a Newton or 0.1 dynes. The unit is often used in astronautical engineering to describe the tiny forces applied to spacecraft to adjust their attitudes in space.

See also "Newton", and "dyne."

micropascal (μPa)

An SI unit of pressure, equivalent to 10^{-6} pascals or 1 micronewton per square meter. This unit is used to measure the pressure of sound waves.

micropoize (μP, μPo, or μPs)

A unit of dynamic viscosity used primarily for describing the viscosities of gases. One micropoize is equivalent to 10^{-6} poises or 10^{-7} pascal seconds (Pa·s).

microrad (μrad)

A unit of radiation dose, equivalent to a millionth of a rad or 10 nanograys.

microradian (μrad)

A unit of angle measure, equivalent to 10^{-6} radians. The microradian is equivalent to about 0.208 533 milliarcseconds (mas).

microrem (μrem)

A unit of effective radiation dose, equivalent to a millionth of a rem or 10 nanosieverts. Doses in this range are much smaller than those provided by natural sources of radioactivity in the environment.

See also "rem."

icrosecond (μs or μsec)

A unit of time, equivalent to a millionth of a second.

microsievert (μSv)

A unit of radiation dose, equivalent to 10^{-6} sierverts or 0.1 millirems. The radiation doses resulting from exposure to natural sources such as radon gas in the atmosphere are often measured using this unit.

See also "Sievert"

microstrain (μstrain)

A common engineering unit measuring strain. An object under strain is typically deformed (extended or compressed) and the strain is measured by the amount of this deformation relative to the same object in an undeformed state. One microstrain is the strain producing a deformation of one part per million (10^{-6}).

microtesla (μT or mcT)

A common unit of magnetic field intensity, equivalent to 10^{-6} tesla. The unit is widely used to measure the strength of electromagnetic fields generated by powerlines or electronic equipment. By comparison, the strength of the Earth's own magnetic field at the surface is about 50 microtesla. One microtesla is equivalent to 0.01 gauss.

See also "tesla."

microvolt (μV or mcV)

A unit of electric potential, equivalent to 10^{-6} volts. This unit is used in cardiology and other medical fields to measure the small potentials within the nervous system.

middy

An informal unit of volume for beer used in many Australian pubs. A middy is generally 285 milliliters (or 10 British fluid ounces), larger than a pony but smaller than a schooner.

miglio

The traditional Italian mile. The miglio is equivalent to 1628 yards, which is 0.925 English miles or about 1488.6 meters. This is 32 yards (29.3 meters) shorter than the classical Roman mile.

mil (mil)

Metric unit of capacity, i.e., volume.

1 mil = 10^{-3} liters.

Note: 1. The name was given for the first time to the unit by J. Cocker in 1858.

2. The unit is also known as milli-inch or, alternatively, the **thou**.

See *"thou"*

mil [1]

A unit of distance, equivalent to 0.001 inches, which is a "milli-inch" in other words. Mils are used primarily in the U.S. to express small distances and tolerances in engineering works. One mil is exactly 25.4 microns, just as one inch is exactly 25.4 millimeters. This unit is also known as the **thou**. With the increasing use of metric units in the U.S., many machinists now avoid the use of "mil" because that term is also a handy slang for the millimeter.

mil, angular

A unit of plane angle, which, due to non-uniformity of usage, may equate to three values.

1. 1 angular mil = 0.001 radians or approximately 0.0572958°.
2. 1 angular mil = $\frac{1}{6400}$ of a full revolution or 0.525°.

3. 1 angular mil = $\frac{1}{1000}$ of a right angle or 0.09°.

Note: 1. The system of angular measure in which a right angle was divided into 1000 parts, known as mils, and was used for the first time by the U.S. during the World War II.

2. In Britain, the term **angular mil** generally refers to the milliradian. 1 milliradian corresponds to a target size of 10 millimeters at a range of 10 meters or 3.6 inches at 100 yards.

mil, circular

Imperial unit of area, equivalent to the area of a circle of diameter of one mil (10^{-3} inches)

1 circular mil = $(\pi/4)$ x 10^{-6} inches squared = 5.067 x 10^{-10} meters squared.

mile (mi)

Imperial unit of length. The mile is equivalent to 1760 yards.

1 mile = 1760 yards = 1609.344 meters.

Note: 1. In the U.K., the unit is legally termed as the **statute mile**.

2. The unit was commissioned in 1592.

In 1592, Parliament defined the **statute mile** to be 8 furlongs, 80 chains, 320 rods, 1760 yards or 5280 feet.

3. Using the international definition of the foot as exactly 30.48 centimeters, the international statute mile is exactly 1609.344 meters. (In technical U.S. usage, the statute mile is defined in terms of the survey foot, which is equivalent to about 1609.3472 meters. This unit is known as the **survey mile**).

4. In athletics, races of 1500 or 1600 meters are often known as **metric miles.**

5. The unit symbol (mi) is generally not recognized.

See also "furlong", "chain", "rod", "yard," and "feet."

mile (nautical)

Imperial and metric units of length. Generally, it is the average length of 1 minute of latitude.

1. *Imperial unit: (UKn m)i:*

The imperial nautical mile (UKn mi) is equivalent to 6080 feet, which is the length of a minute of arc at 48° latitude.

1 UKn mi = 6080 feet = 1853.184 meters.

Note: 1. The nautical mile is also known as a geographical mile.

2. The original definition is: one UKn mi is the mean of one minute longitude.

1 U.K. mi = 6080 feet = 1853.184 meters.

2. *Metric unit: (n m)i:*

One nautical mile (metric) is the length of a minute of arc at 45°, which is 1852 meters.

1 n mi = 1852 meters.

Note: This unit, also known as the **international nautical mile**, was adopted during the International Hydrographic Conference of 1929, with the U.K. and U.S. dissenting. In July 1954, the U.S. adopted the definition, leaving the U.K. as the only dissenter.

mile per gallon (U.K.) (mile/UKgal)

Unit of reciprocal fuel consumption.

1 mile per gallon (U.K.) = 3.540 06 x 10^{-1} kilometers per liter.

mile per gallon (U.S.) (mile/USgal)

Unit of reciprocal fuel consumption

1 mile per gallon (U.S.) = 4.251 44 x 10^{-1} kilometers per liter

mile per gallon (mi/gal or mpg) [2]

The unit formerly used in Britain, Canada, Australia, and other British Commonwealth nations to measure the fuel efficiency of motor vehicles, analogous to the U.S. unit but based on the imperial gallon [3]. Although still used sometimes, this unit has been officially supplanted by liters per 100 kilometers. x miles per imperial gallon is equivalent to $282.481/x$ liters per 100 kilometers. One mile per imperial gallon is equivalent to about 0.8327 miles per U.S. gallon.

mile per gallon equivalent (mpge or MPGe)

The unit customarily used in the United States to measure the energy efficiency of motor vehicles powered by sources other than gasoline. For each source, the U.S. Environmental Agency has identified a quantity of that source that nominally delivers 114,000 Btu of energy, which is the assumed energy content of one gallon of gasoline. This quantity is the gallon of gasoline equivalent (GGE) for that source. The efficiency of the vehicle is then the number of miles the vehicle travels on one GGE of energy.

mile per hour (mi/h or mph)

A traditional unit of velocity. One mile per hour is equivalent to exactly 22/15 feet per second, approximately 1.609 kilometers per hour (km/h), or exactly 0.447 04 meters per second (m/s).

mile, telegraph, nautical

Imperial unit of length. The telegraph nautical mile is 6087 feet, which is the length of a minute of arc at the equator.

1 telegraph nautical mile = 6087 feet = 1855.317 6 meters.

mille [1]

The traditional French mile equivalent to 1000 toises. This is equivalent to about 6394.4 feet, 1.211 statute miles, or 1949 meters. In modern France, the *mille* sometimes means the nautical mile (*mille marin*), which is equivalent to exactly 1852 meters.

mille [2]

In French-speaking part of Canada, the English statute mile of 5280 feet (1609.344 meters).

mille [3]

The Latin word for 1000 is sometimes used in English in very learned or literary contexts.

mil-foot

A mil-foot is a section of wire, one foot long and one mil in diameter. This would be a unit of volume equivalent to about 0.0377 cubic inches or 0.6178 cubic centimeters. However, the unit is used primarily in statements of resistivity in ohms per mil-foot or of density in pounds per mil-foot. The unit is also called the **circular mil-foot**.

milha

The traditional Portuguese mile one of the "longest miles" of Western Europe at 2282.75 yards (1.297 statute miles or 2087.3 meters).

military pace

Another name for a step. In the U.S. Army, the military pace is defined to be exactly 30 inches (76.2 centimeters) for ordinary "quick time" marching and 36 inches (91.44 centimeters) for double time marching. The same definitions are generally used by marching bands.

millenary

A unit of quantity (unit of court) equivalent to 1000.

millennium

A traditional unit of time, equivalent to 1000 years. The plural is **millennia** or sometimes **millenniums**.

milli. (m)

SI prefix denoting x 10^{-3}. Examples include milliampere (mA), millibar (mbar), millicandela (mcd), millicoulomb (mC), millifarad (mF), milligram (mg), millihenry (mH), millijoule (mJ), millikevin (mK), milliliter (ml or mL), millimeter (mm), millimole (mmol), millipascal (mP), millisecond (ms), millisiemens (mS), millitesla (mT), millivolt (mV), milliwatt (mW), milliweber (mWb).

milliampere-second (mA s)

Metric unit of radiation dose due to exposure to X-rays. It is defined as the product of the millimeter reading in milliamperes and the exposure time in seconds.

1 mA s = 0.001 A x 1 s

millicurie-destroyed (mcd)

An arbitrary unit of radiation dose due to exposure to X-rays.

It is equivalent to the amount of radiation emitted by a sample of a radioactive nuclide over a period during which its activity decreases by one millicurie.

Note: For radon 222 (for which this unit is most often used), it is approximately 133 milligram-hours.

millicurie-of-intensity-hour (Imch)

An arbitrary unit of radiation dose due to exposure to γ-rays. The experimentally determined value is:

1 millicurie-of-intensity-hour = 8.38 rontgens.

Note: The unit is known as the Sievert.

See *"Sievert"*.

millier (miller)

MTS unit of mass. This is the name that was used in the 1878 Weights and Measures Act to represent a million gram.

1 millier $=10^6$ grams = **1000** kilograms.

Note: It is better to call this unit the ton. It is also known as the metric ton.

milligal (mGal)

Unit of acceleration.

1 milligal = 10^{-5} meters per second square.

milligram-hour (mg h)

Arbitrary unit of radiation dose to γ-rays. One milligram-hour is the product of the equivalent radium content of the source in milligrams and the exposure in hours.

1 kilogram-hour = 0.001 grams x 1 hour.

millihg (millihg)

Metric unit of pressure. One millihg is the pressure that would support a column of mercury of length one millimeter and density 13595.1 kilograms per cubic meter under the standard acceleration of free fall.

1 millihg = 1 millimeter of mercury = 133.322387415 pascals.

Note: It is recommended to refer to this unit as the (conventional) millimeter of mercury. The unit is equivalent in size to the torr, or to one part in seven million.

milligram per liter (mg l⁻¹ l or mg L⁻¹)

Unit of mass density and concentration used in the SI system.

1 mg $L^{-1} = 10^{-3}$ kilograms per cubic meter.

millimass unit (mmu)

Arbitrary unit of mass. One mmu is $\frac{1}{16000}$ of the atomic unit (physical scale). The experimentally measured value is:

1 millimass unit = $1.037\ 38 \times 10^{-31}$ kilograms.

See *"atomic unit (physical scale)"*.

milliliter (ml or mL)

Unit of volume and capacity used in the SI system.

1 ml $= 10^{-6}$ meters cubed.

millimeter of mercury (conventional) (mmHg)

Metric unit of pressure. One (conventional) millimeter of mercury is the pressure that would support a column of mercury of length of one millimeter and density 13595.1 kilograms per cubic meter under the standard acceleration of free fall.

1 mmHg = 133.322387415 pascals.

Note: This unit is also known as the "millihg". It is equivalent in size to the torr or to one part in seven million.

See *"millihg"*.

millimeter of water (conventional) (mmH²O)

Metric unit of pressure. It is defined as one millimeter of pressure that would support a column of water of length of one millimeter and density of 1000 kilograms per cubic meter under the standard acceleration of free fall.

1 mmH²O = 9.80665 pascals

1 mmH^{2}O = 1 kilogram-force per meter squared.

millibar (mb)

A common metric unit of atmospheric pressure, equivalent to 0.001 bars, 100 pascals, 1000 dynes per centimeter squared, about 0.0295 inches (0.7501 millimeters) of mercury, or about 0.014 504 pounds per square inch. A millibar is the same thing as a **hectopascal** (hPa), and some weather agencies have replaced the millibar with the hectopascal in an effort to conform with the SI. However, many meteorologists do not support its use and continue to use millibars. In fact, an appropriate SI unit for atmospheric pressure would be the kilopascal (10 millibars or 0.145 038 pounds per square inch).

millicandela (mcd)

A unit of light intensity, equivalent to 0.001 candelass. The intensity of the light-emitting diodes (LEDs) used in electronics are stated in millicandelas.

See also "Candela."

millicurie (mCi)

A common unit of radioactivity. One millicurie represents radioactivity at the rate of 37 million atomic disintegrations per second, i.e., 37 megabequerels.

millidegree (mdeg) [1]

A unit of angle measure, equivalent to 0.001° or exactly 36 arcseconds.

millidegree (mdeg) [2]

A unit of temperature, equivalent to 0.001°, usually meaning 0.001 °C.

milliequivalent (mEq or meq)

a unit of relative amount of substance commonly used in chemistry. One mEq is equivalent to 0.001 equivalent weight.

millier

A former name for the tonne or metric ton. This name, obsolete now, was used in Britain to avoid confusion with the British long ton.

See also "tonne."

millifarad (mF)

A common unit of electric capacitance, equivalent to 0.001 farads.

See also "Farad."

milligal (mGal or mgal)

A unit of acceleration used in geology to measure subtle changes in gravitational acceleration. One milligal is equivalent to 10 micrometers per second per second or 10^{-5} meters per second per second. Ideally, the unit should be known as the millialileo.

See also "galileo."

milligauss (mG)

A unit of magnetic flux density, equivalent to 0.001 gauss, 0.1 microtesla, or 100 nanotesla. The magnetic fields generated by power lines and electronic equipment are often measured in milligauss.

milligram (mg)

A very common metric unit of mass, equivalent to 0.001 grams or 1000 microgrammes (µg or mcg). One milligram is equivalent to approximately 0.015432 grains or 35.274×10^{-6} ounces.

milligram per deciliter (mg/dl or mg/dL)

A conventional unit in medicine for measuring concentrations of cholesterol and many other substances in the blood. Internationally, the SI unit for data of this type is millimoles per liter (mmol/L). See the table of SI Units for Clinical Data for conversions of many common measurements.

milligray (mGy)

A common unit of radiation dose, equivalent to 0.001 grays, 0.1 rads, or 1 millijoule of energy per kilogram of matter. Because the gray itself is such a large unit, many practical radiation measurements are made in milligrays. In particular, the exposures caused by X-ray equipment are typically in the milligray range.

See also "gray."

millihenry (mH)

A common metric unit of electric inductance, equivalent to 0.001 Henry.

See also "henry."

millihg

An informal name (pronounced "millig") for the millimeter of mercury (see below).

millihorsepower (mhp)

A unit of power, equivalent to 0.55 foot-pound per second or 0.7457 watts. This unit is commonly used to state the power of small electric motors.

millijoule (mJ)

A common metric unit of work or energy, equivalent to 0.001 joules or 10^4 ergs.

milli-k

A unit used in nuclear engineering to describe the "reactivity" of a nuclear reactor. One milli-k is a reactivity of 0.001 or 0.1%. k is a common symbol for reactivity. This unit was introduced in the Canadian nuclear power industry. For a discussion of reactivity, see inhour.

millikelvin (mK)

A unit of temperature equivalent to 0.001 kelvins or 0.001 degrees Celsius (°C). This unit is used mostly by scientists investigating substances that are cooled very close to absolute zero.

millilambert (mLb)

A common metric unit of illumination, equivalent to 0.001 lamberts or 10 lux (lx).

See also "Lambert", "lux."

millilux (mlx)

A metric unit of illumination, equivalent to 0.001 lux. The natural illumination at night is measured in millilux.

milliliter (ml or mL)

A very common metric unit of volume. One milliliter is equivalent to 0.001 liters, exactly one cubic centimeter (cm^3 or cc), or approximately 0.061 023 7 cubic inches or 16.231 U.S. minims (see below). The milliliter is used almost entirely for measuring the volumes of liquids, with solids being measured in cubic centimeters. Note: until 1964, the milliliter was equivalent to 1.000 028 cubic centimeters.

millimass unit (mu or mmu)

A unit of mass, equivalent to 0.001 atomic mass units, used in physics and chemistry. This unit is also known as the millidalton (mDa). The millimass unit is an SI unit, but its proper SI symbol is **mu**, rather than the older symbol **mmu**.

millimeter (mm)

A very common metric unit of distance. One millimeter is equivalent to 0.001 meters, 0.1 centimeters, about 0.039 370 inches, or 39.370 mils.

millimeter of mercury (mm Hg)

A unit of pressure, equivalent to the pressure exerted at the Earth's surface by a column of mercury, 1 millimeter high. When a traditional mercury barometer is used, the pressure is read directly as the height of the mercury column in millimeters. One millimeter of pressure is equivalent to approximately 0.03937 inches of mercury, 0.01933 pound force per square inch, 1.333 millibars, or 133.3 pascals. In medicine, blood pressure is traditionally recorded in millimeters of mercury. In engineering, the millimeter of mercury is often supplanted by the torr, with each of these two units being equivalent to within 1 part per million. Hg, the chemical symbol for mercury, is taken from the Latin *hydrargyrum*, "water-silver," describing the silvery liquid metal.

millimeter of water (mmH$_2$O, mm WC, mm CE, mm WS)

A unit of pressure, equivalent to the pressure exerted at the Earth's surface by a column of water, 1 millimeter high. This is a small pressure, about 9.8067 pascals, 0.098 067 millibars, 0.03937 inches of water, or 0.204 pounds per square foot. The French symbol is mm CE (*colonne d'eau*), and the German symbol is mm WS (*Wassersäule*).

millimeter of water gauge (mm WG)

Another common name for the millimeter of water column. The word "gauge" (or "gage") after a pressure reading indicates that the pressure stated is actually the difference between the absolute or total pressure and the air pressure at the time of the reading.

millimicro- (mµ-)

An obsolete metric prefix denoting 10^{-9} or one billionth. This prefix has been replaced by nano- (n-).

millimicron (mµ)

A former metric unit of distance, equivalent to 0.001 microns or 10^{-9} meters. The millimicron has been replaced by its equivalent, the nanometre (nm).

millimole (mmol)

A very common unit of amount of substance, equivalent to 0.001 moles (see below).

millimole per liter (mmol/l or mmol/L)

The SL unit in medicine for measuring concentrations of cholesterol and many other substances in the blood. A table is provided for the conversion of conventional units, such as milligrams per deciliter (mg/dL), to SI units.

milline

A traditional unit of advertising. One milline is equivalent to the height of a line of "agate" type (5.5 points, or about 2 mm) times the width of a column times one million copies of the publication.

millinewton (mN)

A metric unit of force, equivalent to 0.001 newtons, 100 dynes, or about 0.101 972 grams of force (gf).

millinile

A unit used in British nuclear engineering to describe the "reactivity" of a nuclear reactor. One millinile is a reactivity of 10^{-5}. For a discussion of reactivity, see inhour.

millioctave (mO)

A unit used in music to describe the ratio in frequency between notes. The difference between two frequencies in millioctaves is equivalent to 1000 times the base-2 logarithm of the ratio between the two frequencies. One millioctave is equivalent to exactly 1.2 cents [3] or about 0.30103 savarts. If two notes differ by 1 millioctave, the ratio between their frequencies is $2^{1/1000}$ or approximately 1.000 6934.

millioersted (mOe)

A name sometimes used for the milligauss as a unit of magnetic flux density.

milliosmole (mOsm)

A unit of osmotic pressure, equivalent to 0.001 osmoles, commonly used in biology and medicine.

milliparsec (mpc)

A unit of distance in astronomy, equivalent to 0.001 parsecs. Used in studying crowded parts of the universe, such as globular clusters and galactic centers. The milliparsec is equivalent to about 206.265 astronomical units, 11.913 light days, or 30.8568 terametres (30.8568×10^9 kilometers or 19.1735 billion miles).

millipascal (mPa)

An SI unit of pressure, equivalent to 0.001 pascals or 1 millinewton per square meter. This very small unit is used to measure the pressure of sound waves.

millipascal second (mPa·s)

An SI unit of dynamic viscosity, equivalent to the centipoize (cP). This unit is gradually replacing the centipoize in many contexts.

milliphot (mph)

A unit of illuminance or illumination, equivalent to 0.001 phot or 10 lux.

millipoize (mP, mPs, or mPo)

A metric unit of dynamic viscosity, equivalent to 0.001 poises or 0.1 millipascal seconds (mPa·s).

millipound force

A unit of force, equivalent to 0.001 pound force or about 4.448 millinewtons. This unit is sometimes used in the U.S. space program in discussing the small attitude control thrusters of spacecraft.

millirad (mrad)

A unit of radiation dose, equivalent to 0.001 rads or 10 micrograys.

milliradian (mrad)

A unit of angle measure, equivalent to 0.001 radians. The milliradian is equivalent to about 0.057 296°, 3.437 75 arcminutes, or 3" 26.265'. In Britain, this unit is often known as the angular mil.

millirem (mrem)

A common unit of radiation dose, equivalent to 0.001 rem or 10 microsieverts (μSv). A millirem is roughly the radiation dose you would receive from wearing a luminous dial watch for a year.

millisecond (ms or msec)

A common unit of time, equivalent to 0.001 seconds.

millisiemens (mS)

A common unit of conductance, equivalent to 0.001 siemens or 1 milliampere of current per volt of potential difference. The millisiemens is often used to measure the salinity of seawater or brackish water since adding salt to water makes it much more conductive of electricity.

See also "siemens", "ampere", and "volt."

millisievert (mSv)

A unit commonly used to measure radiation dose. One millisievert is equivalent to 0.001 sieverts or 0.1 rem.

See also "Sievert", "rem."

millitesla (mT)

A common unit of magnetic field intensity, equivalent to 0.001 teslas or 10 gauss. Since the tesla is quite a large unit, many practical measurements are made in millitesla.

millivolt (mV)

A common unit of electric potential, equivalent to 0.001 volts.

milliwatt (mW)

A common unit of power, equivalent to 0.001 watts.

milliwatt hour (mW·h)

A common metric unit of work or energy, representing the energy delivered at a rate of one milliwatt for a period of one hour. This is equivalent to exactly 3.6 joules (J) of energy, or about 0.003 412 Btu, 0.859 846 (small) calories, or about 2.655 foot-pounds.

Mils, strecks

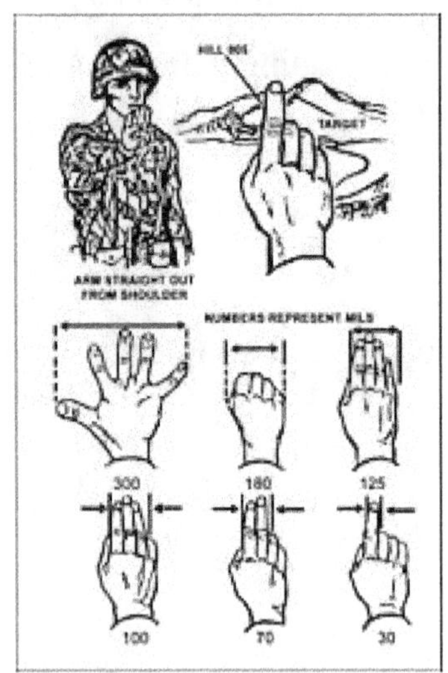

Estimating mils by hand

An informal unit of angular measure.

Mils and *strecks* are small units of angle used by various military organizations for range estimation and translating map coordinates used for directing artillery fire. The exact size varies between different organizations. There are 6400 NATO mils per turn (1 NATO mil = 0.982 milliradians), or 6000 Warsaw pact mils per turn (1 Warsaw pact mil = 1.047 milliradians). In the Swedish military, there are 6300 strecks per turn (1 streck = 0.997 milliradadians).

mina

A historic unit of weight, originating in Babylonia and used throughout the eastern Mediterranean. The mina is roughly comparable to the pound, but over the centuries, it varied quite a bit. In Babylonian times, it was a large unit, roughly 2 pounds, almost as much as a kilogram. The Hebrew mina, frequently mentioned in the Bible, is estimated at 499 grams (1.10 pounds). The Greek mina was equivalent to 100 drachmai or 431 grams (0.95 pounds). In Biblical times, the mina was equivalent to 60 shekels, and there were 60 minas in a talent.

miner's inch

A traditional unit of water flow in the western United States. The unit originally represented streamflow through an opening of one inch (25.4 millimeters) squared at a specified distance below the surface of the water. This distance varied from 4 to 6 inches. In Idaho, Kansas, Nebraska, New Mexico, North and South Dakota, Utah, and Washington, the miner's inch is legally defined to be equivalent to 9 gallons per minute or 1.2 cubic feet per minute (about 34.07 liters per minute). In Arizona, California, Montana, Nevada, and Oregon, the definition is 1.5 cubic feet per minute (42.48 liters per minute). In Colorado, the legal equivalent is 1.5625 cubic feet per minute (44.25 liters per minute).
See also "water inch".

-minex

A suffix used to create small numbers. The number n-minex is 10^{-n}, which is 0.000...0001 with a total of n-1 zeros between the decimal marker and the 1. Thus, one millionth (0.000001), for example, is 6-minex.
See also "dex" and –plex".

minim (m or min) [1]

A traditional unit of volume used for very small quantities of liquids. In pharmacy, the term drop traditionally meant the same thing as 1 minim. The minim is defined to be $\frac{1}{60}$ fluid dram or $\frac{1}{480}$ fluid ounce. The U.S. minim is equivalent to about 0.003 760 cubic inches or 61.610 microliters, while the British minim is equivalent to about 0.003 612 cubic inches or 59.194 microliters. As you might guess, the word originates from the Latin *minimus*, small.

minim [2]

A unit of relative time in music, equivalent to $\frac{1}{2}$ whole note (a half note) or $\frac{1}{4}$ breve
See also "breve".

minim (U.K.) (UKmin)

U.K. unit of volume (capacity). One minim (U.K.) is equivalent to $\frac{1}{480}$ U.K. fluid ounces.
1 UKmm = $\frac{1}{480}$ U.K. fluid ounces = 5.919 39 x 10^{-8} cubic meters.

Note: The U.K. minim is used for the measurement of liquid and solid substances.

minim (U.S.) (USmin)

U.K. unit of volume (capacity). One minim (U.K.) is equivalent to $\frac{1}{480}$ U.S. fluid ounces.

1 USmm = $\frac{1}{480}$ U.S. fluid ounces = 6.161 15 x 10^{-8} cubic meters.

Note: It is used only for the measurement of liquid substances.

minipin

An informal unit of volume for beer and other alcoholic beverages, used mostly in Britain. A minipin is ½ of a polypin. This is about 17 imperial pints or 10 liters (roughly 2.64 U.S. gallons).

See also "polypin."

minute (min)

Unit for time used in the SI system.

1 min = 60 seconds

minute (')

Unit of plane angle used in the SI unit.

1 minute = 2.90888 x 10^{-4} radians.

Note: The unit has also been known as the arcmin.

minute centesimal (ᶜ)

Unit of plane angle. One centesimal minute is equivalent to one hundredth of the grade.

1^c = 0.01 grades = $(\pi/2)$ x 10^{-4} radians.

Note: This unit has only been used in Europe.

See *"grade" and "gon"*.

mips

A unit of computing power equivalent to one million instructions per second. An "instruction" is a single program command to the computer's central processor. In a particular computer, there is a definite relationship between the rate at which instructions are processed, in mips, and the "clock speed" of the processor, measured in metgahertz (MHz). However, this relationship varies considerably between computers, so it is usually not meaningful to compare the mips rates of different machines. See also megaflops (above).

mired (mired)

Metric unit used to measure the reciprocal of color temperature. It is equivalent to the reciprocal color temperature of a body, which has a color temperature of one million kelvins

1 mired = 10^6 per kelvin

For example, a temperature of 2000 kelvins corresponds to a reciprocal of 500×10^{-6} and is equivalent to 500 mired, while a temperature of 50,000 kelvins is equivalent to 20 mired.

Note: The name of the unit (mired) is derived from **_mi_**cro-**_re_**ciprocal-**_d_**egree.

mite (mite)

Imperial unit of mass is equivalent to $\frac{1}{20}$ of a grain.

1 mite = ½ grain = $3.239\ 945 \times 10^{-6}$ kilograms.

mlb (2)

A traditional unit of mass for steam, equivalent to 1000 (not one million) pounds. This is one of many applications of the Roman numeral M used to represent a multiple of 1000. All these applications should be replaced by the metric prefix k- (kilo-).

-mo

A "unit" traditionally used in printing to describe the page size of a book or other publication. In traditional printing, large sheets are printed, folded, and then cut to manufacture the book. After the cut is made, the sheet has been divided into a certain number of "leaves". Each leaf folded at the spine of the book comprises two pages, front and back. When sheets were cut to form 4, 8, or 12 leaves, the resulting pages were described as quarto (4to), octavo (8vo) or duodecimo (12mo), respectively. Later, the suffix -mo, from duodecimo, was made into a suffix that can be attached to any number to indicate the number of leaves per sheet. Thus, 16mo indicates 16 leaves per sheet. **Link:** book sizes, from Bookbinding and the Conservation of Books, by Matt T. Roberts and Don Etherington, posted by Stanford University.

mohm (mohm)

CGS unit of mechanical mobility. It is the reciprocal of the mechanical ohm. One mohm is the ratio of a velocity of one centimeter per second to a force of one dyne.

1 mohm = 1 centimeter per dyne second = 1000 meters per Newton second.

Note: The name was suggested by Beranek, who derived it from ***Mo***bile ***ohm*** in 1954.

mohr cubic centimeter (Mohr cm³)

Arbitrary unit of volume used in saccharimetry. One Mohr cubic centimeter is the volume occupied by one gram of pure air-free water at a specified temperature, which is usually 17.5°C. At that temperature, the experimentally derived value of the unit is:

1 Mohr cubic centimeter = 1.00013 cubic centimeters.

Note: The unit is named after the pharmacist Karl Friedrich Mohr (1806-1879).

Mohs' scale

A scale of hardness primarily used for minerals. It was devised around *1812* by a German mineralogist Friedrich Mohs (*1773 — 1839*), and published in *1824*.

Mohs' scale consists of 10 common minerals in order of increasing hardness (shown in the second column below). An unknown mineral's position on the scale is determined by what it will scratch and what will scratch it. For example, the average fingernail will scratch gypsum and can be scratched by calcite. Therefore, a fingernail would be given a rating between 2 (gypsum) and 3 (calcite). Window glass is about 5.5, which shows ordinary quartz (7) will scratch it.

Although it is very convenient, there are many problems inherent with using scratching as a test for hardness. For example, many minerals scratch more easily in one direction than another due to their crystal structure.

Increasingly sophisticated methods for measuring hardness showed that the steps in Mohs scale are far from equal, especially at the high end. For example, on an equal-step scale, if a diamond is taken as 10, corundum would be 2.5 and topaz 1.6. Taking advantage of very hard synthetic materials that were not available to Mohs, the top end of the scale has been revised to provide finer (but not equal) gradations, as shown below.

	Original scale	**Revised scale**
1	Talc	Talc
2	Gypsum	gypsum
3	Calcite	Calcite
4	fluorite	Fluorite
5	Apatite	Apatite
6	orthoclase	Orthoclase
7	Quartz	vitreous pure silica
8	Topaz	Quartz
9	corundum	topaz
10	Diamond	garnet
11		fused zirconium oxide
12		fused alumina
13		silicon carbide
14		boron carbide
15		Diamond

molar mass of cellulose

In the pulp and paper industry, molar mass is traditionally measured with a method where the intrinsic viscosity (dL/g) of the pulp sample is measured in cupriethylenediamine (Cuen). The intrinsic viscosity $[\eta]$ is related to the weight-average molar mass (in <u>daltons</u>) by the Mark-Houwink equation:

$$[\eta] = 0.070 \, M_w^{0.70}.$$

 However, it is typical to cite $[\eta]$ values directly in dL/g as the "viscosity" of the cellulose, confusingly as it is not a viscosity.

See also "Dalton."

molar volume

A unit used by chemists and physicists to measure the volumes of gases. The behavior of gases under ordinary conditions (not at very high pressures or very low temperatures) is governed by the Ideal Gas Law. This law states that the volume V of a gas is related to its temperature T and pressure P by the formula $PV = nRT$, where n is the number of moles of gas present and the gas constant R is equivalent to 8.314 joules per mole per kelvin. The molar volume is the volume that one mole of gas occupies at standard temperature (273.16 kelvins, or 0 °C) and standard pressure (1 atmosphere, or 101.325 kilopascals). The molar volume is equivalent to 22.414 liters or 0.7915 cubic feet. (Occasionally, the term "molar volume" is used for the volume occupied by a mole of a substance which is not a gas. In such cases, the molar volume will be different for each substance).

mole (mol)

Base SI unit of an amount of substance. At the 14th CGPM in 1971, the mole was approved as the unit of quantity of matter and was declared to become one of the seven base units of the SI system. One mol of entities is the amount of substance that contains the same number of entities (6.022×10^{23}) as there are atoms in exactly 12 grams of carbon-12 (^{12}C). The elementary entity must be specified and may be an atom, a molecule, an ion, an electron etc., or a specified group of such entities.

Note: 1. In the above definition, it is clear that unbound atoms of carbon-12 at rest in their ground state are those referred to.

 2. The mole is an individual unit of mass, i.e., it relates only to a given substance.

 3. The unit was formerly known as the mol (mol) or the gram-molecule (gmol).

 4. The mole is also the unit of the extent of reaction.

5. The name mole first appeared in 1902, when it was used to express the gram molecular weight of a substance.

mole per cubic meter (mol m^{-3})

It is the SI unit of concentration (amount concentration).

Note: It is also the unit of solubility and ionic strength (concentration basis).

mole per cubic meter second (mol m^{-3} s^{-1})

It is the SI unit of rate of concentration and rate of reaction (based on the amount of concentration.

mole per kilogram (mol kg^{-1})

It is the SI unit of molality and ionic strength (molality basis) and mean ionic molality.

mole per liter (mol l^{-1} or mol L^{-1})

It is the unit for concentration used in the SI system.

1 mol L^{-1} = 10^{-3} moles per liter.

mole per second (mol s^{-1})

It is the SI unit of molar flow and rate of conversion.

mole per square meter (mol m^{-2})

It is the SI unit of surface concentration, surface excess concentration and total surface excess concentration.

Moment

An informal unit of time.

A moment was a medieval unit of time. The movement of a shadow on a sundial covered 40 moments in a solar hour. An hour, in this case, meant one twelfth of the period between sunrise and sunset. The length of a solar hour depended on the length of the day, which in turn varied with the season. Therefore, the length of a moment in modern seconds was not fixed, but on average, a moment corresponded to 90 seconds.

Mommes (mm)

A traditional unit of weight.

Mommes traditionally used to measure the weight of silk fabrics. Mommes is just one of many specialized units of measurements still used in the textile industry. 1 momme = 0.1280019 ounces per square yard (4.340 g/m^2). Heavier silks are more durable, more opaque and appear more "wooly". Here's some examples:

- 3-5 mm Gauze (open weave, needlepoint canvases, facings, linings)
- 4-6 mm Organza (bridal wear, evening wear, sheer curtains)
- 5-16 mm Habutai (simple plain weave, used for linings, light clothing, lingerie etc.)
- 6-8 mm Chiffon (translucent, lightweight, used for blouses, scarves, lingerie etc.)
- 12-16 mm Crepe de Chine (crisp, crimpled silk, hundreds of weaves and variations)
- 12-30 mm Charmeuse (weaved so the front has a sheen and the reverse is dull, tends to cling, used for drapes, bridal gowns, ties, linings etc.)
  - 35-40 mm Noil/Raw silk (rough texture, dull like cotton, often blended to make other materials. Silk over 30 mm is likely to be opaque)

mon (mon)

It is the unit of the flatness of rolled steel plates. A surface has a flatness of 1 mon, if no part of it is more than 25 micrometers above or below a straight line drawn between any two points, 1 meter apart on the surface.

Note: The unit was proposed for the first time in 1964.

month

Unit of time

1. The period of the revolution of the Moon around the Earth (sidereal month)

2. The period of phases of the Moon (synodic month)

3. The month of the calendar (calendar month)

month (mo or mon) [1]

A unit of time marked by the revolution of the Moon around the Earth. In many traditional societies, the appearance of the first tiny crescent Moon after the New Moon signaled the start of the month. This start of the month, based on the first appearance of the Moon, is still proclaimed in mosques in Islamic countries. Thus, the **lunar month** is defined as the average interval between two successive moments of the New Moon. Astronomers refer to this period as the **synodic month**. Its length is 29.530 59 days.

month (mo or mon) [2]

A civil unit of time, equivalent to approximately $\frac{1}{12}$ year but varying from 28 to 31 days [3]. The Sun and the Moon are our traditional timekeepers, but they are badly out of step with each other. A solar year is equivalent to approximately 12.368 lunar months. The large fraction in this number makes it difficult to design a calendar with a whole number of months in each year. There are at least three solutions to the problem:

[i] Use **leap months**. In the traditional Chinese and Jewish calendars, most years have 12 months, but some have a 13th month. In these **luni-solar** calendars, the length of the year varies between 354 and 384 days.

[ii] Define 12 synodic lunar months to be a year, not worrying about the length of the year. This is the solution of the Islamic calendar. Since the Islamic year has only 354 or 355 days, its length does not match the cycle of the seasons.

[iii] Observe the solar year and let the months be 12 arbitrary periods, not worrying about the Moon. This is the solution adopted by Julius Caesar, who established the civil calendar we use today. In this calendar, all months have 30 or 31 days except the second month, February. February has 28 days in ordinary years and 29 in leap years.

See also year [2].

moog

A proposed unit in synthetic music, equivalent to one volt per octave. The unit would honor Robert Moog (1934-2005), the inventor of the Moog synthesizer.

morgan (M)

A unit of genetic separation used in genetics and biotechnology. If two locations on a chromosome have a probability p of being separated during recombination in a single generation, then the distance between those locations is p morgans. In practice, measurements are made in centimorgans, each centimorgan representing a 1% probability. The unit honors the American geneticist Thomas Hunt Morgan (1866-1945), who received the Nobel Prize for Medicine in 1933 for his pioneering work in studying the genetics of the fruit fly *Drosophila*.

morgen

A traditional unit of land area in Northern Europe. "Morgen" means "morning," and most likely, the unit arose as the area a yoke of oxen could plow in one morning. The Dutch morgen, also used in Dutch colonies including old New York, is equivalent to about 2.10 acres or 0.850 hectares. In South Africa, this unit was defined to be equivalent to 10 246 square yards, which is 2.1169 acres or 0.8567 hectares. In Scandinavia and northern Germany, the morgen is a smaller unit, equivalent to about 0.63 acres or 0.25 hectares (2500 square meters). The Prussian morgen, standardized at 2553.22 square meters, was in common use during the nineteenth century. In Austria and southern Germany, the morgen was often the same as a joh, typically defined to be 0.5755 hectares or about 1.422 acres. **See also "acre", "hectare", and "yard."**

morgan (morgan)

It is the arbitrary unit of generic map distance (gene separation). One morgan is the distance along the chromosome in a gene that gives a recombination frequency of 1%.

Note: 1. Comparison with the physical dimensions of chromosome material leads to the conclusion that:

1 morgan = 3×10^6 angstroms.

2. The unit was named after the author of the gene theory, Thomas Hunt Morgan (1866-1945)

moszkowaki unit

It is a unit expressing the translation probability of nuclei from one state to another. It is used in nuclear physics.

Note: The unit was suggested for the first time in 1955

See also *"Weisskopf unit".*

mother cow index

Formerly used in real estate transactions in the American Southwest. It was the number of pregnant cows an acre of a given plot of land could support. It acted as a proxy for the agricultural quality, natural resource availability, and arability of a parcel of land.

motvos (E)

It is the metric unit of the horizontal gradient of gravitational acceleration. It is defined as the change in gravitational acceleration of 10^{-9} galileo over a horizontal distance of one centimeter.

$1 E = 10^{-9}$ Gal/horizontal centimeter.

mounce (mounce)

It is a metric unit of mass.

1 mounce = 25 grams = 0.025 kilograms.

This unit is also known as the "metric ounce", 1 mounce = 0.881850 ounces.

mouse unit (MU or U)

An unofficial unit of toxicity used in pharmacology. A mouse unit is the dose of a toxin that kills 50% of mice (i.e., it is the LD_{50} dose for mice). Typically, the mice are assumed to have a mass of 20 grams. The toxin is administered by intraperitoneal injection, and mortality is measured over a standard period that may vary according to the toxin. The size of the mouse unit (in milliliters or international units) depends on the specific toxin.

mug (mug)

It is a metric-technical unit of mass. It is the mass which is accelerated by 1 meter per second squared by a force of one kilogram weight.

1 mug = 9.806 65 kilograms.

Note: The unit is also known as the hyl, but is better referred to as the **metric technical unit of mass or metric slug**. In Germany, the unit is known as the Technische Mass Einheit (Engineering Mass Unit), which is abbreviated to TME.

See *"hyf", "metric slug" and "metric technical unit of mass"*.

mutchkin

A traditional Scottish unit of liquid volume. The mutchkin is about 15 British fluid ounces, which is about 426 milliliters or almost exactly 0.9 U.S. pints.

mwe

Abbreviation for meter of water equivalent. A unit used in nuclear physics to describe the shielding around a reactor, accelerator, or detector. 1 mwe of any material (such as rock, gravel, etc.) is a thickness of that material providing shielding equivalent to one meter of water.

myria (ma)

It is a depreciated prefix denoting x 10^4.

myriagramme (ma)

Unit of mass that is equivalent to 10^4 grams.

1 myriagramme = 10 kilograms.

See *"myria"*.

myriametre

Unit of length that is equivalent to 10 kilometers.

1 myriametre = 10^4 meters.

See *"myriad"*.

myria- (my-)

a metric prefix meaning 10 000. This prefix was part of the original metric system of 1795 and was used throughout the nineteenth and early twentieth centuries. It has been obsolete officially since 1960, when the CGPM adopted the standard list of SI prefixes. The ancient Greek word *myrios* means countless, without number. This was modified by later Greeks to form a word *myrioi* meaning ten thousand. The word **myriad**, generally used today to mean an indefinitely large number, originally meant the number 10 000.

myriad

Originally, a unit of quantity, equivalent to 10,000. A myriad is now any large number of items. In the Ordnance Survey mapping of the British Isles, a myriad is a square 100 kilometers on a side (thus covering 10,000 square kilometers).

myriagramme (myg)

A metric unit of mass, equivalent to 10 000 grams or 10 kilograms (about 22.046 pounds). Although it is considered obsolete now, the myriagramme was a useful unit comparable to the English quarter or Spanish arroba.

See also "pound", "quarter", "arroba

myriametre (mym)

An obsolete metric unit of distance, equivalent to 10 000 meters or 10 kilometers (about 6.2137 miles).

See also "mile"

N

N

A unit of reflective index sometimes used in atmospheric science. The index of reflection of the atmosphere is only slightly greater than 1. The value of the index N units is the number of millionths by which the index exceeds one. Thus, an index of reflection n is equivalent to $(n\text{-}1) \times 10^6$ N units.

nail (nail)

It is an imperial unit of length. It is equivalent to 2.25 inches.

1 nail = 2.25 inches = $\frac{1}{16}$ of a yard = 5.715×10^{-2} metres

Note: 1. In Britain, there are various units, all of which are $\frac{1}{16}$th of some larger measure. The ratio probably comes from the Roman digitus (literally, finger, and hence nail), having been $\frac{1}{16}$th of a pes.

2.   In Scotland, $\frac{1}{16}$th of the Scottish ell of 37 inches = $37/16 = 2\frac{5}{16}$ inches.

3.   In Orkney, Scotland, the distance from the knuckle to the tip of the middle finger is "given as eight to a yard, *i.e.* 4½ inches".

nail [1]

As a unit of mass:

- In Scotland, around the year *1400*, wool = 6 pounds, with the pound being the wool pound of Bruges. This is $\frac{1}{16}$th of the Bruges hundredweight of 96 pounds.

- In England, around the year *1500,* it began to be used as a synonym for the clove, 7 pounds, $\frac{1}{16}$th of a 112-pound hundredweight.

nail [2]

A unit of land area = $\frac{1}{16}$th of an acre.

See: *"acre", "digitus", "hundredweight", and "clove."*

nano (n)

It is a SI prefix denoting x10^{-9}. Examples include nanoampere (nA), nanocoulomb (nC), nanofarad (nF), nanohenry (nH), nanosecond (ns), nanosiemens (nS), nanotesla (nT), nanovolt (nV) and nanowatt (nW).

Nanoacre

Informal unit of area in the "Humorous System of Units."

The nanoacre is a unit of real estate on a Very Large Scale Integration (VLSI) chip, equivalent to 0.00627264 square inches (4.0468564224 millimetres squared) or the area of a square of side length 0.0792 inches (2.01168 millimetres). VLSI nanoacres have similar total costs to acres in Silicon Valley

Nanoacre is also a humorous unit of area of a computer chip, equivalent to one billionth of an acre or about 4.047 square millimetres.

See also "avre"

nanobar (nb or nbar)

A CGS unit of pressure, equivalent to 10^{-9} bars or 0.1 millipascals (mPa). The nanobar is frequently used in meteorology to express the partial pressure of atmospheric ozone.

See also "bar"

nanocurie (nCi)

A common unit of radioactivity. The nanocurie is equivalent to 10^{-9} curies or 37 becquerels. This corresponds to a radioactivity of 37 atomic disintegrations per second.

See also "curie"

nanofarad (nF)

A common metric unit of electric capacitance, equivalent to 10^{-9} farads. This unit was previously known as the **millimicrofarad (mμF)**.

See also "Farad."

nanogramme (ng)

A metric unit of mass, equivalent to 10^{-9} grammes, or one millionth of a milligramme.

nanogray (nGy)

A unit of radiation dose, equivalent to 10^{-9} grays or 0.1 microrads (μrad). This unit often occurs in the study of inhalation exposures.

nanoliter (nl or nL)

A metric unit of volume, equivalent to 10^{-9} liters or 0.001 cubic millimetres.

nanometre (nm)

A metric unit of distance, equivalent to 10^{-9} metres. Introduced in 1951, the nanometre replaced the **millimicron**. One nanometre is equivalent to 0.001 micrometres or 10 angstroms.

See also "Angstrom."

nanomole

A unit of amount of substance, equivalent to 10^{-9} moles. This unit is commonly used in biochemistry since a mole of a large organic molecule can be quite a large amount.

See also "mole."

nanonewton (nN)

A metric unit of force, equivalent to 10^{-9} newtons (see below) or 0.1 millidynes. Nanonewtons measure the force of solar radiation and the tiny forces exerted within living cells.

nanoradian (nrad)

A unit of angle measure equivalent to 10^{-9} radians. The nanoradian is equivalent to about 0.208 533 milliarcseconds (mas). Such tiny angles are observed in astronomy and geological measurements.

See also "radian."

nanosecond (ns)

A unit of time, equivalent to 10^{-9} seconds.

nanosievert (nSv)

A unit of radiation dose, equivalent to 10^{-9} sieverts or 0.1 microrems.

See also "Sievert."

nanostrain (nstrain)

An engineering unit measuring strain. An object under strain is typically deformed (extended or compressed), and the strain is measured by the amount of this deformation relative to the same object in an undeformed state. One nanostrain is the strain producing a deformation of one part per billion (10^{-9}). Strains in geological formations are often measured in this unit.

nanotesla (nT)

A unit of magnetic field strength, equivalent to 10^{-9} tesla or 10^{-5} gauss. The unit is used in geology to measure small changes in the Earth's magnetic field.

See also "tesla" and "gauss."

Nanocentury

Informal unit of time in the "Humorous System of Units."

A unit sometimes used in computing. The term is believed to have been coined by IBM in 1969 from the design objective "never to let the user wait more than a few nanocenturies for a response". A nanocentury is one-billionth of a century or approximately 3.156 seconds. Tom Duff is cited as saying that, to within half a percent, a nanocentury is π seconds.

See also "humorous system of units."

nanon (nanon)

It is a unit of length.

1 nanon = 10^{-9} metres

Note: The name is used by spectroscopists. The name is not recommended.

naubion

An ancient Egypt unit of volume.

As a unit of volume, it was used to describe an amount of earth.

In Ptolemaic times (*305 – 30 BCE*), it was a cube 2 *meh* (the royal cubit) on a side. Thereafter, in Roman times, a cube 3 *meh* on a side. Taking the *meh* at 52.5 centimetres, in Ptolemaic times, the *naubion* was about 1.16 cubic metres, and under the Romans, about 3.91 cubic metres.

See also "Cubit, royal."

nat or natural unit [1]

A unit of information content used in information and communications theory. The nat is similar to the Shannon but uses the natural logarithm (to the base e) instead of the logarithm to the base 2. If the probability of receiving a particular message is p, then the information content of the message is $-\log_e p$ nats. For example, suppose a message is a string of 5 letters or numerals, with all combinations being equally likely. In that case, a particular message has probability of $1/36^5$ and the information content of a message is $5(\log_e 36) = 17.9176$ nats. One nat is equivalent to $\log_2 e = 1.442\ 695$ shannons or $\log_{10} e = 0.434\ 294$ hartleys.

natural units or nat [2]

This is a system of units based on Gaussian or Heaviside-Lorentz units for electromagnetic quantities. These units are often used in particle physics in place of SI units.

In natural units, quantities that have dimensions of length, mass and time are given the dimensions of power or energy (usually expressed in electron volts), which effectively makes the rationalized Plank constant and speed of light both equal to unity.

nautical mile (nmi, naut mi, n mile, or NM)

It is a unit of distance used primarily at sea and in aviation.

The nautical mile is defined to be the average distance of the Earth's surface represented by one minute of latitude. This may seem odd to landlubbers but makes good sense at sea, where there are no mile markers. The latitude can, however, be measured. Because the earth is not a perfect sphere, it is not easy to measure the length of the nautical mile in terms of the statute mile used on land. For many years, the British set the nautical mile at 6080 feet (1853.18 metres), exactly 800 feet longer than a statute mile. This unit was known as the **Admiralty mile**. Until 1954, the **U.S. nautical mile** was equivalent to 6080.20 feet (1853.24 metres). In 1929, an international conference in Monaco redefined the nautical mile to be exactly 1852 metres or 6076.115 49 feet, a distance known as the **international nautical mile**. The international nautical mile is equivalent to about 1.1508 statute miles. There are usually 3 nautical miles in a league. The unit is designed to be equivalent to $\frac{1}{60}$ degree, although actual degrees of latitude vary from about 59.7 to 60.3 nautical miles. See also *"League"*.

nautical point

It is a unit of plane angle. 1 nautical point is equivalent to $\frac{1}{8}$ of a right angle.

1 nautical point = $(\frac{1}{8})$ x 90 degrees = 11.25 degrees.

Note: The unit is the same as the unit known as **points of compass**.

See *"points of compass"*.

neck (nk)

An informal unit of distance used to measure the distance one horse leads the other to finish of a race. The neck is usually interpreted to be $\frac{1}{4}$ <u>length</u> or a little less. This is roughly 2 feet or 0.6 metres.

neper (Np)

It is a unit of dimensionless quantities: amplitude level difference, power level difference and logarithmic decrement. The amplitude level N in nepers relates the two amplitudes Q_1 and Q_2 (expressed in the same units) by the formula:

N = 1n (Q_1/Q_2)

Thus, 1 neper is the amplitude level that corresponds to an amplitude ratio of *e*.

Note: 1. For power level differences, i.e., when Q_1 and Q_2 are power quantities, the above relation takes the form

$$N = 0.5 \, 1n \, (Q_1/Q_2)$$

2. In cases when the square of the amplitude of a vibration is proportional to the associated power, the neper and the decibel are related. The relation is:

$$1 \text{ neper} = 20 \log e = 8.685\ 89 \text{ decibels.}$$

3. The unit symbol N is generally used in telecommunication technology.

4. The unit was named after Scottish scholar John Naper (1550-1617). It was approved for the first time in 1928.

neper per second (Np/s or Np s^{-1})

It is a unit of damping coefficient.

nephelometric turbidity unit NTU, or ntu)

A unit measuring the lack of clarity of water. It is used by water and sewage treatment plants, in marine studies, and so on. Water containing 1 milligramme of finely divided silica per liter has a turbidity of 1 NTU. The NTU replaced the Jackson turbidity unit.

The NTU is measured with an electronic instrument known as a nephelometer. The water to be measured is placed in a standard container. A light beam passes through the water and strikes a sensor on the other side of the container. A second sensor is mounted at right angles to the beam, measuring light scattered by particles in the water. From the ratio between the light intensities at the two sensors, the turbidity in NTU can be calculated.

To calibrate the device, a standard solution is needed. An early approach was to suspend a measured mass of silica in a measured volume of distilled water. In another approach, defined quantities of reagents were mixed to produce a fine precipitate. The current technique employs microspheres of polymer, which led to a new turbidity unit, the Formazin Turbidity Unit (FTU). Measurements in NTU and FTU are roughly equivalent.

See also "Formazin turbidity unit FTU."

nepit

It is a unit of quantity of information. The quantity of information I in nepits is related to the probability P at the receiver after the message is received and the probability P_o before reception is expressed by the formula:

$$1 = \ln (P/P_o)$$

Note: The unit is also known as the **nit.**

See *"nit"*.

nent

In ancient Egypt, a unit of length = 4 *mahi*, about 82.04 to 83.04 inches.

net ton

It is the U.S. unit of mass, equivalent to 2000 pounds

1 net ton = 2000 pounds = 907.184 7 kilogrammes

Note: The unit is also known as the **short ton.**

neutron rontgen

It is the arbitrary unit of radiation dose due to neutrons. One neutron rontgen is the dose of fast neutrons, which is incident on a thimble ionization chamber of special characteristics and produces the same degree of ionization as would one rontgen of γ- or X-rays.

Note: 1. The unit is also known as **n-unit.**

2. A thimble ionization chamber is a chamber in which the outer electrode is thimble-shaped.

3. 1 neutron rontgen represents an absorbed dose in tissue of 2 to 2.5 rads approximately.

See *"n-unit"*.

new candle (cd)

It is a unit of luminous intensity. The official definition of this basic SI unit, given at the 9CGPM, is: The magnitude of the new candle is such that the luminance of a full radiator at the temperature of solidification of platinum (2045K) is 60 new candles per square centimetre.

Note: 1. The name of the unit is now the candela.

2. The name new candle was adopted by the CIE in 1937 for the CGS and MKS of light intensity

See *"candela"*, *"candle, new"* and *"bougie nouvelle"*.

New York Second

Informal unit of time in the "Humorous System of Units."

The New York Second ("the shortest unit of time in the multiverse") is defined as the period of time between the traffic lights turning green and the cab behind one honking. The idiomatic expression "in a **New York minute**", used in various contexts to mean an instant or a very short time, is of similar origin, referring to the busyness of New York and the impatience of its residents.

newton (N)

It is an SI unit of force. That force, which applied to a mass of 1 kilogramme, gives it an acceleration of 1 metre per square second.

1 N = 1 kilogramme metre per square second.

Note: 1. The unit was first proposed in 1900 and the name suggested was large dyne.

2. The name newton (after Isaac Newton (1642-1727)) was suggested for the first time in 1905. The name was commissioned by the IEC in 1938 and adopted by the 9th CGPM in 1948

newton metre (N m)

It is a SI unit of moment of force or torque. It is equivalent to the torque produced by the force of 1 newton acting at a perpendicular distance of 1 metre from an axis of rotation.

Note: 1 newton metre = 1 joule, but the joule is used mainly as a unit of energy.

See *"joule"*.

newton per coulomb (N/C)

The SI unit of electric field strength. An electric charge creates an electric field that attracts (or repels) other charges with a force proportional to the size of the charge. Since the volt is defined as a joule per coulomb, and the joule is equivalent to a newton metre, the newton per coulomb is equivalent to the **volt per metre**.

See also: "volt", "joule", "coulomb."

newton per metre (N m^{-1})

It is a SI unit of surface tension and surface pressure.

Note: It is also a unit of force per unit length and film tension.

newton second (N·s)

The SI unit of impulse is equivalent to the amount of momentum added to an object if a force of one newton is applied for one second. The newton second is equivalent to about 0.224 809 pound seconds (lbf·s) in traditional English units. Impulse and momentum have the same dimensions, but momentum is measured in kilogramme metres per second (kg·m/s) in the SI.

newton second per metre (N s m^{-1})

It is a SI unit of mechanical impendence.

newton square metre per kilogramme squared (N m^2 kg^{-2})

It is a SI unit of gravitational constant.

ngram

It is a unit of land area in Thailand. The ngram is equivalent to ¼ rai, 100 talangwah (tw), or exactly 400 square metres (478.396 square yards or just under 0.1 acres).

niacin equivalent (NE)

It is a unit used in nutrition. An essential nutrient, niacin is supplied in normal diets from tryptophan, an amino acid found in many foods. However, only a small fraction of tryptophan is converted into niacin in the body. Accordingly, 1 niacin is equivalent to 1 milligramme of actual niacin or to 60 miligrammes of tryptophan.

nibble

A unit of information used in computer science. A nibble is 4 bits or ½ byte. The cuter spelling **nybble**, suggested by byte, is sometimes used. In a different context, a group of 4 bits is sometimes known as a **quadbit** or a **hexit.**

See also *"bit"* and *"byte"*

nile (nile)

It is a unit of reactivity (dimensionless quantity that measures the departure of a nuclear reactor from its critical condition). The reactivity of the reactor in niles is equivalent to 100 (1-1/k), where k is the effective multiplication factor.

1 nile = the amount of reactivity, equivalent to 0.01

Note: The submultiple millinile (10^{-5} niles) is usually used.

nine [1]

A measure of "fineness" or purity of gold and other materials. For example, gold that is 99.99% pure, or 0.9999 <u>fine,</u> is known as "4 nines fine".

nine [2]

A measure of reliability or "availability" used in computer engineering. For example, a component has "3 nines" of reliability if it operates correctly 99.9% of the time or equivalently, if its failure rate is 0.1%. Thus, each nine represents a reduction of 90% in the failure rate. If the probability of correct operation is p, then the reliability, in nines, is equivalent to $-\log_{10}(1-p)$.

Nines

Numbers very close to, but below one (1) are often expressed in "nines" (N – not to be confused with the unit newton), i.e., the number of nines succeeding the decimal separator in writing the number in question. For example, "three nines" or "3N" indicates 0.999 or 99.9%, "four nines five" or "4N5" is the expression for the number 0.99995 or 99.995%.

Typical areas of usage are:

- The reliability of computer systems, i.e., the ratio of uptime to the sum of uptime and downtime. "Five nines" reliability in a continuously operated system implies an average downtime of no more than approximately five minutes per year (there is no relationship between the number of nines and minutes per year, it is pure coincidence that "five nines" relates to five minutes per year.)
- The purity of materials, such as gases and metals.

NIP

It is an informal unit of liquid volume. The term "nip" often means a "small amount" with no precise equivalent. In U.S. bartending, a nip is often taken to be 2 fluid ounces (about 59 milliliters). In Britain, a nip of spirits is considered to be ⅙ gill (about 22.95 milliliters or 0.776 fluid ounces). A nip of beer is ¼ pint (the same as a gill, 4 fluid ounces or about 117.7 milliliters) or sometimes ⅓ pint (189.4 milliliters).

See also *"gill"* and *"pint"*

nit (nt)

It is a SI unit for luminance, equivalent to 1 candela per square metre.

1 nt = 1 candela per square metre

Note: It is, however, recommended to use the candela per square metre.

nit (nt)

It is a unit of quantity of information. The quantity of information I in nit is related to the probability P at the receiver after the message is received and the probability P_o before reception by the formula:

$I = 1n\ (P/P_o)$

Note: The unit is also known as the **nepit.**

See *"nepit"*

noggin

It is an arbitrary unit of volume. The noggin is equivalent to a quarter of a pint

1 noggin = **0.25** pints = 142.065 23 x 10^{-6} cubic metres.

Note: 1. The value of the unit is similar to the U.K. gill.

2. The name noggin was originally applied to a small drinking cup but gradually became associated with the quantity of liquid (generally spirits) that such a cup could contain.

3. In North England, the large noggin is also known as 1 large noggin = **0.5** pints.

See *"gill, U.K."*

noise criterion (NC), noise rating (NR)

Units used in engineering to measure the acceptability of sound levels in enclosed spaces. The noise rating (NR) system was introduced by Kosten and van Os in 1962. Numerically, the NR rating is equivalent to the sound level, expressed in decibels at a frequency of 1000 hertz. The rating, however, requires lower levels at more objectionable higher frequencies. The noise criterion (NC) system, introduced by Beranek in 1957, is similar but is designed more toward preserving speech communication, requiring lower levels of both high and low frequencies. It was updated in 1971, and the updated system is known as PNC (Prefered Noise Criterion).

Non-conventional Units

These units describe dimensions that are not and cannot be covered by the International System of Units. Examples are measuring of Beauty, Bogosity, Coolness, Fame and data flow.

See "Helen", "Lenat", "Fame", "MegaFonzi"

nook

It is a traditional unit of land area in northern England. Originally, the nook was ½ virgate. A virgate, often known as a **yardland** in the north, was about 30 acres in southern England but tended to be closer to 40 acres in the north. A nook of land thus came to be 20 acres or about 8.094 hectares.

normal (N)

It is a term used in chemistry to describe a solution having a concentration of 1 gramme equivalent per liter. The normal concentration of an ion is effectively equivalent to the molar concentration divided by the valence (the number of free or missing electrons) of the ion.

normal cubic metre (Nm^3)

It is a unit mass for gasses, equivalent to mass of 1 cubic metre (35.3147 cubic feet) at a pressure of 1 atmosphere and at a standard temperature, often 0 °C (32 °F) or 20 °C (68 °F). The term **standard cubic metre** is also used. Sometimes, both are used with different temperatures. Because industry practice varies, these terms should always be defined wherever they occur. The symbol **Nm^3**, though common, is not permissible under the SI because this symbol means "newton cubic metre". An acceptable SI symbol would be "m normal".

normal liter (NL or Nl or Ndm^3)

It is a unit mass for gasses, equivalent to the mass of 1 liter (0.035 3147 cubic feet) at a pressure of 1 atmosphere and at a standard temperature, often 0 °C (32 °F) or 20 °C (68 °F). Airflow is often stated in normal liters per minute (Nl/min).

Normkubikemeter (Nm^3)

It is a German unit of volume, especially for gas. It represents one cubic metre of gas under standard reference conditions.

Note: The unit was also formally used in other Continental countries.

Normliter (l_n)

It is a German unit of volume, especially for gas. It represents one liter of gas under standard reference conditions.

nox (nox)

It is a metric unit of intensity of illumination, particularly low-level illumination.

1 nox = 10^{-3} lux

> *Note:* This unit was originally introduced in German for measuring illumination during the "black-out" in World War II.

noy (noy)

It is a unit of perceived noise. It is equivalent to the perceived noise of random noise, occupying the frequency band 910-1090 hertz at a sound pressure level of 40 decibels above 2 x10^{-5} pascals. A sound that is n times as noisy as this has a perceived noisiness of n noys, under the assumption that the perceived noisiness of a sound increases with physical intensity at the same rate as the loudness.

The noisiness N in noys is related to the perceived noise level in perceived noise decibels. (PNdB) and is expressed by the relation

$$N = 2^{(L-40)/10}$$

Note: This unit was proposed and named after Karl Kryter in 1959.

See *"decibel, perceived noise and sone."*

NTU

It is an abbreviation for **nephelometric turbidity unit**, a unit used in measuring water quality. Turbidity is an optical property, the scattering and absorption of light by solids suspended in water. In other words, water is turbid if it is not transparent. An instrument known as a nephelometer (from a Greek word meaning "cloudy") measures turbidity directly by comparing the amount of light transmitted straight through a water sample with the amount scattered at an angle of $90°$ to one side. This ratio determines the turbidity in NTU's. The instrument is calibrated using samples of a standard solution such as formazin, a synthetic polymer. Drinking water should not have a turbidity above 1 NTU, although values up to 5 NTU are usually considered safe. Outside the U.S., this unit is usually known as the FNU (Formazin Nephelometric Unit).

n-unit

It is an arbitrary unit of radiation dose due to neutrons. One n-unit is the dose of fast neutrons, which is incident on a thimble ionization chamber of special characteristics and produces the same degree of ionization as would one rontgen of γ- or X-rays.

Note: 1. The unit is also known as the **neutron-rontgen**.

2. A thimble ionization chamber is a chamber in which the outer electrode is thimble-shaped.

3. One n-unit represents an absorbed dose in tissue of approximately 2 to 2.5 rads.

See *"neutron-rontgen"*

O

obol, obolos, obolus

A historic unit of weight or mass. The obol is a very small weight that originated as the weight of a tiny Greek coin. In ancient Greece, the *obolos* was equivalent to ⅙ drachma, or roughly half a gramme (8 <u>grains</u>). In Rome, the *obolus* was equivalent to 1/48 Roman ounce (*uncia*) or about 0.57 grammes. In modern Greece, the *obolos* is an informal name for the decigramme (0.1 grammes).

See also "grain."

octane number or octane rating

A measure used to express the ability of gasoline to reduce engine knocking. Gasoline is a complex mixture of hydrocarbons (compounds containing hydrogen and carbon). Beginning chemistry, students learn that "octane" is the name of a hydrocarbon whose molecules contain 8 carbon atoms and 18 hydrogen atoms. The 8 carbons being arranged in a long chain. The hydrocarbons which cars need to prevent knocking is not octane but a different compound of 8 carbon atoms and 18 hydrogen atoms known as iso-octane or, in the more precise language of chemical nomenclature, 2,2,4-trimethylpentane. (In an iso-octane molecule, there are only 5 carbons in the chain. Carbons 6 and 7 are attached to the sides of the chain at the #2 position, and the last carbon is hooked onto the #4 position. Chemists call this a branched hydrocarbon). To determine the octane rating of gasoline, a sample of the gasoline is compared to a laboratory mixture of iso-octane and another hydrocarbon known as heptane (heptane has 7 carbons and 16 hydrogens, with the 7 carbons in a chain).

The mixture is adjusted until it has the same anti-knocking characteristics as the gasoline being tested. The octane rating is the percentage of iso-octane required in the laboratory mixture to produce this equivalence of knocking behavior. There are two ways to conduct the test, producing two ratings known as the research octane number (RON) and the motor octane number (MON). The MON is typically 8 or 10 points lower than the RON for the same batch of fuel. In the U.S., the number posted on the gas pump is the average of the RON and MON. This average is known as the pump octane number (PON). This number is a similar to the cetane number, which is used for rating diesel fuel. The octane rating is often misunderstood as a measure of the energy content of the fuel, but what it actually measures is the tendency of the fuel to burn rather than explode.

octant (octant)

It is a unit of plane angle used in all systems

1 octant = $\pi/4$ radian = 45°

octant [1]

A unit of angle measure equal to ⅛ circle, 45°, or pi/4 radians.

octant [2]

A unit of solid angle measure. One octant is ⅛ sphere, or pi/2 steradians, or about 5156.6 square degrees.

octarius

An obsolete name for the British Imperial pint (34.678 cubic inches or approximately 568.261 milliliters), used in British medicine and pharmacy during the nineteenth century. The octarius was equivalent to ⅛ congius (gallon).

octave (octave and sometimes o)

It is a unit of pitch interval used in all systems. The pitch interval I in octaves between two frequencies $f_1.f_2$, expressed in the same unit, is given by the relation:

$I = (1/\log2).\log\ (f_1/f_2) = 3.321\ 93 \log\ (f_1/f_2)$

Accordingly, the octave can be defined as the interval between two frequencies, $f_1\,f_2$ having a ratio $(f_1/f_2) = 2$.

Note: In the above expression, f_2 is greater than f_1.

See also *"savart" and "Cent."*

Octave [2]

Octave is a British unit of volume used for measuring whisky. It is approximately 16 gallons.

- 1 octave = 16 gallons

- 1 octave = 0.073 cubic metres.

During the *20th century* in England, an octave of whisky was 14 imperial gallons (about 64 liters) and an octave of sherry was 13¾ imperial gallons (about 62½ liters).

Octave [3]

Outside of music, the octave is also used to describe a group of 8 objects sequenced somewhat like musical notes. For example, in the Christian religious calendar, an octave is a period of 8 days beginning with a feast day and ending with the day one week after the feast day.

octavillo

A traditional Spanish unit of dry volume. The octavillo is equivalent to about 289 milliliters (a little more than a cup, in U.S. terminology). This is equivalent to about 17.64 cubic inches, 0.525 U.S. pints, or 0.5086 British imperial pints. Since octavillo means "eighth", one would expect the octavillo to be ⅛ of some other unit, but this is not the case. There are 4 octavillos in a cuartillo, 16 in an almude, and 48 in a fanega.

See also "cup" and "pint."

octennium

A unit of time, equivalent to 8 years.

octet (octet)

It is a term used by CCITT and other similar organizations denoting an addressable group of 8 bits.

1 octet = 8 bits

The convention for bit numbering within an octet is different from that used for a byte (which is an IBM term).

See *"byte"*.

oersted (Oe)

It is a CGSemu unit of magnetic field strength (magnetization force). In a magnetic field of strength of one oersted unit, magnetic moment experiences a couple of one dyne centimetre.

1 Oe = 10^3 /4π amperes per metre.

Note:　1. The unit was defined and named after a Danish physicist, Hans Christian Oersted (1777-1851), at the IEC in 1930.

2. Before 1930, the unit had been named the gauss.

3. The name Oersted was proposed by the American Institute of Electrical Engineers in 1894 for the CGS unit of magnetic reluctance but was not implemented.

ohm (ohm, Ω)

It is a SI unit of electric resistance, reactance, impendence and modulus of impendence. It represents the electric resistance between two points of a conductor, when a constant difference of potential of one volt, applied between these two points, produces in the conductor a current of one ampere, assuming that this conductor is not the source of any electromotive force.

1 Ω= 1 V/A

Note:　1. The standard ohm has been experimentally determined with a Lorentz machine, a development of Faraday's wheel at the National Physical Laboratory, to an accuracy of 12 parts per million.

2. The first known unit of resistance extends back to the year 1838 when Lenz produced a standard resistor, which consisted of a foot of No. 11 copper wire.

3. Maxwell, in 1868, defined the ohm as the resistance of a column of mercury of one metre in length and uniform cross-sectional area of one square millimetre. This definition makes the one ohm, equivalent to a mechanical unit of 10^7 metres per second.

4. The first International Electrical Congress (IEC) of 1881 defined the ohm as the resistance of a column of mercury held at a temperature of 0°C and with a length enough to fulfill the relation $1 \, \Omega = 10^9$ CGS-emu units of resistance

5. The first IEC resumed duties in 1884 and defined the length of the column to be 106 centimetres and 1 square millimetre cross section. However, this length did not quite make $1 \, \Omega = 10^9$ CGS-emu units of resistance.

6. The 4th International Electrical Congress of 1884 redefined the ohm to be the resistance of a column of mercury held at the temperature of the melting ice and has a length of 106.300 centimetres and mass of 14.4521 grammes and a uniform cross section. According to this definition, $1 \, \Omega = 10^9$ CGS-emu units of resistance up to six significant digits.

This definition became a law in the U.K. and U.S. in 1894. It was accepted by decree in France in 1896 and in Germany in 1898. This unit is known as international ohm $\Omega_{int.}$

7. The international ohm remained the standard until it was replaced by the absolute ohm in 1948. The change was agreed in 1935 when it was apparent that not only was the international ohm more difficult to produce accurately than the absolute ohm, but the international ohm was a very small unit.

8. The following multiples of the ohm are irregularly named:

10^3 ohm = 1 kilohm (not kilo-ohm)

10^6 ohm = 1 megohm (not mega-ohm)

10^{-6} ohm = 1 mircohm (not micro-ohm)

ohm, acoustical (Ω_a)

It is a CGS unit of acoustical resistance, reactance and impedance. It is defined as the ratio of the sound pressure level of one dyne per square centimetre to a source sound strength of one cubic centimetre per second.

$1 \, \Omega_a = 10^5$ pascal seconds per metre cubed

Note: 1. It is a name sometimes assigned to dyne second per centimetre to the fifth power.

2. The names **ram** and **ray** have been proposed as alternatives for this unit but never employed.

3. The idea of applying Kirchhoff's electrical circuit procedures to solve acoustical problems was suggested by Webster as early as 1919 but the acoustic ohm was first used by Stewart in 1926.

See *"acoustical ohm", "ram," and "ray."*

ohm, mechanical (Ωm)

It is a CGS unit of mechanical resistance and mechanical impedance. One mechanical ohm is the ratio of a force of one dyne to a velocity of one centimetre per second.

1 mechanical ohm = 1 dyne per centimetre second = 0.001 newton seconds per metre.

Note: 1. The **ram** and **ray** have been proposed as alternative names for this unit but never implemented.

2. The unit was proposed by Firestone in 1933 and he gave the dimensions of the unit as dyne per kine.

See *"ram", "ray," and "kine."*

ohm, reciprocal

It is a SI unit of conductance, admittance and susceptance. One reciprocal ohm is the conductance between two points of a conductor when a constant difference of potential of one volt applied between these two points produces in this conductor a current of one ampere, the conductor not being the source of any electromotive force.

1 reciprocal ohm = 1 A/V

Note: The recommended name of this unit is the **siemens**. An alternative name is the **mho.**

See *"siemens" and "mho."*

ohm, specific acoustical (Ω_s)

It is a CGS unit of specific acoustical resistance, reactance and impendence. One specific acoustical ohm is the ratio of a sound pressure level of one dyne per centimetre squared to a sound particle velocity of one centimetre per second.

$1\ \Omega_s = 1$ dyne/cm^2)/(cm/s) = 1 dyne second per cubic centimetre = 10 pascals second per metre.

Note: This unit is also known as the **rayl.** It was also known as the unit-area acoustical ohm (Ω_u).

See *"rayl"*

ohm, thermal (thermal ohm)

It is a SI unit of thermal resistance. It is defined as the thermal resistance for which a temperature difference of one kelvin causes an entropy flow of one watt per kelvin.

1 thermal ohm = 1 K^2/W

Note: This unit is also known as the **fourier.**

See *"fourier"*

ohm metre (Ω m)

It is a SI unit resistivity.

Note: It is also the unit of resistivity vector and residual resistivity.

ohma (ohma)

It is a MKSA unit of electrical potential, potential difference and electromotive force.

1 ohma = 1 international volt

Note: The name was first suggested by Bright and Clark in 1861 for the practical unit of potential.

ohmad (ohmad)

It is a MKSA unit of resistance, reactance and impedance.

1 ohmad = 1 international ohm.

Note: The name was suggested at first in 1865 as a practical unit of resistance, and then, it was supplanted by the name ohm in 1881.

oka or oke

A traditional unit of weight in Turkey and throughout the eastern Mediterranean. The oka is approximately 2.8 pounds or 1.28 kilogrammes, although its size varied somewhat over the large area formerly included in the Turkish empire. In Greece, the oka was standardized at 1282 grammes and remained in use until traditional units were prohibited in 1959. The Greek oka was divided into 400 dramja. In Cyprus, the oka was divided into 400 drachms and remained in use until the 1980s. In Turkey, the oka was redefined in 1931 to be equivalent to the kilogramme. The oka was also used sometimes as a unit of liquid volume, representing the volume (roughly 1.25 liters) occupied by an oka of water or wine.

okka

1. In Jordan, it is approximately 1.282 kilogrammes (approximately 2.826 pounds avoirdupois).
2. In Turkey, it is approximately 1.283 kilogrammes (approximately 2.828 pounds avoirdupois).

See also "oke."

okia

Various Middle Eastern units of mass which are remote descendants of the Roman *uncia*.

1. In Somalia, it is a unit of mass, approximately 28.0 grammes.
2. In Sudan, it is a unit of mass, approximately 37.44 grammes.
3. In Egypt, it is a unit of mass, = ¹⁄₁₂ *rotl* = 12 *dirhems*, after metrication in *1891*, = 37.5 grammes.

    Also romanized as okeah, wiqyya, uqiyya.
4. In Syria, it is a unit of mass, approximately 320.5 grammes in Aleppo and Homs and approximately 213.7 grammes in Damascus.

okta

A unit of proportion, equivalent to ⅛, used in meteorology to record the fraction of the sky covered by clouds. For example, if half of the sky is cloud-covered, the coverage is reported to be 4 oktas. The name of the unit originates from the Greek numeral 8, *okto*. It was coined to provide a word meaning "eighth" in all languages.

olf

An empirical unit of indoor odor intensity introduced by the Danish environmental scientist Povi Ole Fanger (1934-2006) in 1988. One olf is defined as the odor intensity produced by one 'standard' person (a standard person is also defined). The name originates from the Latin word *olfacere*, to smell. Ventilation reduces pollution and the resulting pollution in ventilated, enclosed spaces is measured in decipols.

olk

A traditional Iraqi unit of land area, now identified with the are the metric unit of area, equivalent to 100 square metres. Just like the area, the olk is approximately 1076.3910 square feet or 0.02471 acres. There are 25 olk in the Iraqi dunum, the common unit of agricultural land area in the country.

See also: "dunum"

olympiad

A unit of time, equivalent to four years. In ancient Greece, the Olympiad was referred to as the four-year interval between successive Olympic Games. The first Greek olympiad was in the period 776-773 BC. The Olympiad was revived in 1896 when the modern Olympics began. The period 2005-2008, known as the "28th Olympiad of the modern era," is the 696th Olympiad by the original Greek reckoning.

omer

The *omer* (Hebrew: עֹמֶר *'ōmer*) is an ancient Israelite unit of dry measure used in the era of the Temple in Jerusalem. It is used in the Bible as an ancient unit of volume for grains and dry commodities. The Torah mentions it as being equivalent to one tenth of an ephah. According to the *Jewish Encyclopedia* (1906), an ephah was defined as being 72 *logs*, and the *Log* was equivalent to the Sumerian *mina*, which was itself defined as one sixtieth of a *maris*. The *omer* was thus equivalent to about $^{12}/_{100}$ of a *maris*. The *maris* was defined as being the quantity of water equivalent in weight to a light royal talent and was thus equivalent to about 30.3 litres, making the *omer* equivalent to about 3.64 litres. The *Jewish Study Bible* (2014), however, places the *omer* at about 2.3 liters.

In traditional Jewish standards of measurement, the *omer* was equivalent to the capacity of 43.2 eggs, or what is also known as one-tenth of an ephah (three *seahs*). In dry weight, the *omer* weighed between 1.560 kilogrammes to 1.770 kilogrammes, this being the quantity of flour required to separate therefrom the dough offering.

The word *omer* is sometimes translated as *sheaf,* specifically an amount of grain large enough to require bundling. The biblical episode of the manna describes God as instructing the Israelites to collect *an omer for each person in a tent,* implying that each person could eat an omer of manna a day. In the Torah, the main significance of the *omer* is the traditional offering (during the Temple period) of an *omer* of barley on the day after the Sabbath or, according to the rabbinical view, on the second day of Passover during the feast of unleavened bread, as well as the tradition of the Counting of the Omer (*sefirat ha'omer*), the 49 days between this sacrifice and the two loaves of wheat offered on the holiday of Shavuot. During the Temple period, the offering of the *omer* was one of twenty-four priestly gifts and one of the ten which were offered to priests within the Temple precincts, when Jewish farmers would bring the first of that year's grain crop to Jerusalem.

Jews in Lancaster, Pennsylvania, used an *omer* board from about the year 1800 to keep track of harvest days between Passover and Shavuot. An example of such a board still exists at the Herbert D. Katz Center for Advanced Judaic Studies at the University of Pennsylvania.

Note: The unit occurs in the Bible (Exodus 16:16, 18, 22, 32, 33, 36) and is defined in Exodus 16:36.

See also "omer", "talent", "litre", and "mina."

omn. bih.

Traditional abbreviation for the Latin *omni bihorio* (once every two hours), a unit of frequency sometimes used in medical prescriptions. The abbreviation **alt. h.** (*alternis horis,* every other hour) is its alternative.

omn. hor.

Traditional abbreviation for the Latin *omni hora* (once every hour), a unit of frequency sometimes used in medical prescriptions. The abbreviation **q. h.** (*quaque hora*, each hour) is its equivalent.

onça, once, oncia, onza

Traditional names for the ounce unit in Romance languages. The Portuguese **onça** and Spanish **onza is** equivalent to $\frac{1}{16}$ libra or about 28.69 grammes (1.012 ounces). The French **once** is equivalent to $\frac{1}{16}$ livre or about 30.59 grammes (1.079 ounces). The Italian **oncia** or **onza** is no longer used but traditionally, it equaled $\frac{1}{12}$ libra or about 27.3 grammes (0.96 ounces).

See also "libra" and "livre."

Onosecond

Informal unit of time in the "Humorous System of Units."

An "onosecond" is the second after one makes a terrible mistake, such as deleting the wrong file or sending a text message to the wrong person, where the person in question can do nothing but say, "Oh no"

ons

A Dutch unit of weight or mass, now used as a metric unit, equivalent to the hectogramme (100 grammes, or about 3.5274 ounces).

open window unit (ow unit)

It is a FPS unit of an equivalent absorption area of a surface to a sound. One open window unit is equivalent to one square foot of a surface with a reverberation absorption coefficient of unit (perfect surface), which would absorb sound energy of a given frequency at the same rate as the surface under investigation.

1 ow unit = 1 square foot = 0.092 903 04 square metres.

Note: 1. This unit is also known as **sabin** or the (total) absorption unit.

2. The unit first used by an American physicist, Wallace Clement Sabine (1868-1919) in 1911. In 1937, it was renamed after him.

See *"sabin"* and *"absorption unit (total)"*.

osmole (Osm)

It is a unit of osmolality and osmolarity.

Note: 1. The osmolarity of a solution is the molality an ideal solution of a non-dissociating substance must possess in order to exert the same osmotic pressure as the solution under consideration. It is often used in biology and medicine.

2. The osmolarity of a solution is the molarity an ideal solution of a non-dissociating substance must possess in order to exert the same osmotic pressure as the solution under consideration. It is often used in biology and medicine.

ounce

It is a unit of mass in both the Troy and Avoirdupois systems

1. Avoirdupois systems: *Symbol:* oz

    1 oz = ($\frac{1}{16}$) pound = 0.028 349 5 kilogrammes.

2. Troy and apothecaries': *Symbol*: For *Troy ounce*: oz tr (in U.K.), oz t (in U.S.). For *apocaries ounce*: oz apoth (in U.K.) and o zap (in U.S.).

    1 oz tr = 1 oz apoth = 480 grains = 0.031 103 476 8 kilogrammes.

Note: 1. The Troy ounce is not lawful for trade in the U.K. except for the purpose of transactions in or in articles made from gold, silver or other precious metals, including transactions in gold or silver thread, lace or fringe.

2. The apothecaries' ounce is used mainly in the sale of drugs.

ounce (oz or oz av) [1]

A traditional unit of weight. The **avoirdupois ounce**, the unit commonly used in the United States, is $\frac{1}{16}$ pounds or about 28.3495 grammes. The avoirdupois ounce is also equivalent to 175/192 = about 0.911 457 troy ounces or 437.5 grains. The word ounce is from the Latin word *uncia*, meaning a $\frac{1}{12}$ part because the Roman pound was divided into 12 ounces. The word "inch", meaning $\frac{1}{12}$ foot, has the same root. The symbol oz is from the old Italian word *onza* (now spelled *oncia*) for an ounce. See avoirdupois weights for additional information.

See also "grain"

ounce (oz, oz t, toz, or oz ap) [2]

A second traditional unit of mass or weight. The **troy ounce**, traditionally used in pharmacy and jewelry, is $\frac{1}{12}$ troy pound, 480 grains, or about 31.1035 grammes. Thus, the troy ounce is equivalent to $192/175 = 1.09714$ avoirdupois ounces. This unit is the traditional measure for gold and other precious metals. In particular, the prices of gold and silver quoted in financial markets are the prices per troy ounce. The troy ounce is divided into 20 pennyweights or into 8 troy drams [2]. The troy ounce is sometimes abbreviated oz t or toz to distinguish it from the more common avoirdupois ounce. In traditional pharmacy, it was abbreviated as oz ap.

See also "grain", "dram", pennyweight."

ounce (oz or fl oz) [3]

A traditional unit of liquid volume, also known as the fluid ounce (fl oz).

ounce [4]

An old term for a $\frac{1}{12}$ part, the English equivalent of the Latin word *uncia* (see def. [1] above). In medieval times, the word was used sometimes for a unit of distance, equivalent to $\frac{1}{12}$ yards or 3 inches. It was also used for a unit of time, equivalent to $\frac{1}{12}$ moments or 7.5 seconds. In some settings, an ounce of time was divided into exactly 47 atoms.

ounce force (ozf or oz)

A traditional unit of force, equivalent to the force experienced at the earth's surface by a mass of one ounce. One ounce force is equivalent to $\frac{1}{16}$ pound foot or about 0.278 014 newtons.

ounce inch (oz·in)

A traditional unit of torque frequently used in regard to small devices such as wrenches. One ounce inch is equivalent to exactly $\frac{1}{192}$ pound foot or about 7.061 55 millinewton metres.

See also "pound-foot"

ounce mole (ozmol)

A unit of amount of substance. One ounce mole of a chemical compound is the same number of ounces as the molecular weight of a molecule of that compound measured in atomic mass units. Thus, the ounce mole is equivalent to 28.349 52 moles.

See also "mole" and "atomic mass unit."

ounce per gallon (oz/gal)

A traditional unit of mass concentration. One ounce per U.S. gallon is equivalent to 7.489 152 grammes per liter (g/L). In Britain, 1 ounce per imperial gallon is equivalent to 6.236 023 grammes per liter.

ounce per square foot (oz/ft^2)

A traditional unit of density still used widely in the U.S. for stating the density of coatings, the "weight" of leather, the rates of application for lawn chemicals, and many other applications. One ounce per square foot is equivalent to 0.305 152 kilogrammes per square metre (kg/m^2).

ounce weight (oz)

A traditional unit for measuring the density (incorrectly known as the "weight") of a fabric. In most cases, the stated ounce density of a fabric is its density in ounces per square yard (oz/yd^2). 1 ounce per square yard is equivalent to 33.9057 grammes per square metre (g/m^2 or gsm). However, when the fabric is shipped in rolls or bolts of a standard width, the ounce density is sometimes figured in ounces per linear yard, the width being understood (the standard width). For example, for a bolt of wool having a standard width of 60 inches (1.524 metres), a density of 1 ounce per linear yard corresponds to 31.0034 grammes per linear metre, or, taking the width into account, 20.3434 grammes per square metre.

ouncedal (ouncedal)

It is an imperial unit of force. One ouncedal is the force, which, when applied to a body of mass of one ounce, gives it an acceleration of one foot per second squared.

1 ouncedal = 0.008 640 934 648 newtons.

ounce, fluid (fl oz)

1. It is a unit of volume (capacity) used in U.S. for measurement of liquid substances. It is equivalent to $\frac{1}{16}$ U.S. of a liquid pint or 231/128 cubic inches.

1 U.S. fl oz (the standar d width)= $\frac{1}{16}$ fluid pint = 231/128 cubic inches = 2.95735295625 x 10^{-5} cubic metres.

2. It is a unit of volume used in U.K. for the measurement of liquid substances and occasionally of solid substances. It is equivalent to $\frac{1}{20}$ U.K. pint

1 U.K. fl oz = $\frac{1}{20}$ U.K. pint = 2.84130 x 10^{-3} cubic metres.

ounce, metric (metric ounce)

It is a metric unit of mass.

1 metric ounce = 25 grammes = 0.025 kilogrammes.

The name "mounce" is recommended for this unit. 1 metric ounce = 0.881850 ounces.

Oxgang

An obsolete unit of land area

An **oxgang** or **bovate** is   an   old   land   measurement   formerly   used in Scotland and England as early as the 16th century and sometimes referred to as an oxgait. It averaged around 20 English acres, but was based on land fertility and cultivation, and so could be as low as 15.

An oxgang is also known as a *bovate*, from *bovāta*, a Medieval Latinisation of the word, derived from the Latin word *bōs*, meaning "ox, bullock or cow".

In Scotland, *oxgang* occurs in Oxgangs, a southern suburb of Edinburgh, and in Oxgang, an area of the town of Kirkintilloch.

See also "acre."

P

pace

An arbitrary unit of length, equivalent to 2.5 feet.

1 pace = 2.5 feet = 0.762 metres

Note: 1. The pace is a traditional unit of distance, equivalent to the length of a person's "full" pace, i.e., the distance between two successive falls of the same foot. Thus, one pace is equivalent to two steps.

2. The Romans counted 1000 paces in a mile, with each pace being a little over 58 inches (or about 148 centimetres).

3. In English speaking countries, the pace is usually defined to be exactly 5 feet (01' 152.4 centimetres). This unit is also known as the **great pace** or **geometrical pace**.

Obviously, a good metric version of the pace is exactly 1.5 metres.

See also *"step."*

pace [2]

In the military, the term "pace" is often used as an alternate name for the step. See military pace.

pack (pack)

Arbitrary unit of mass, equivalent to 240 pounds. 1 pack = 240 pounds = 108. 862 168 8 kilogrammes. Note: This unit is used to measure wool.

The value of the pack changes from one place to another. See table.

Locality		pounds
Huntingdonshire		240
North Wales	lamb's wool	240

Yorkshire, Lancashire	lamb's wool	44
Clydesdale, Dumfrieshire, Selkirkshire	= 12 Scotch stones	
Kent	(BUT flax, not wool!)	240

Note: 1. In Germany, a unit of count is used for sheets of paper = 150,000 sheets.

2. In Great Britain, a unit of count is used for teazles, the thistle-like heads used in making wool cloth. Generally, 1 pack = 9000 heads of kings or = 20,000 heads of middlings

3. During *the 20th – 21st centuries* in the United States, a quantity of cigarettes in paper packaging = 20 cigarettes, a legal minimum. A few packs are made with 25 and are often for export to Canada or Australia.

pack year

A unit of quantity for cigarettes used in medicine to measure a patient's smoking history. One pack year is the equivalent of smoking one 20-cigarette pack per day for one year, i.e., a total of 7300 cigarettes.

packen

A traditional Russian unit of weight equivalent to 1200 funte, 30 pudi (see pud below), 1083 pounds, or 491.4 kilogrammes.

See also *"funte"*

packet (packet)

Unit of data. The packet is a relatively small unit of data, up to 8000 bits, transmitted over packet switching network as part of a message to be transferred from one user to another.

Note: 1. Each packet includes information as a header that identifies the destination address and the sequence of packet within the overall message

2. The packets travel independent of one another using different routes but are reassembled as a coherent message at the receiver.

3. There are different types of packets. Some carry user information, while others are used to request the network control to perform operations to establish or clear calls.

page (page)

1. A unit of information to be printed or displayed for a user of an information service. Also referred to as a Frame, but in the British system, it is known as the Prestel. Each page can consist of up to 26 frames, each containing 960 characters.

2. Unit of memory capacity. The value of the unit is usually 512 to 4096 bytes or words. It is also used when partitioning programmes into control sections.

3. Unit for the information displayed on the cathode-ray tube. It is a standard quantity of source programme coding, usually 8 to 64 lines.

pair (pr)

A unit of quantity, equivalent to 2. The word originates from the Latin word *paria*, meaning "equals". Originally, a pair was simply a group of similar objects, the number being unspecified. Eventually, this meaning was specialized to refer to a group of two.

pair royal

A unit of quantity, equivalent to 3. It is used in cribbage to describe three cards of the same rank. This usage recalls the original meaning of "pair" as a group of equivalent objects, not necessarily two in number. Four cards of the same rank form a "double pair royal".

Palermo scale

A scale used by astronomers to assess the risk of an impact on the earth by a comet or asteroid. The scale value is a logarithmic measure of the risk of an impact compared to the average risk of an impact by objects of the same size or larger over the years until the date of the potential impact by the newly discovered object. If the object in question has probability p of impact at a time T years in the future, the Palermo scale value is $PS = \log_{10} (p/0.03TE^{-4/5})$, where E is the projected energy of the impact in megatons of TNT. A possible impact is considered to be of concern if the Palermo scale value exceeds -2, i.e. if the impact is more than 1%, as likely as a random impact. The scale is used to prioritize the need for further observations of an object.

palm

[1] Arbitrary unit of length, equivalent to 0.25 feet or 3 inches.

1 palm = 0.25 feet = 0.0762 metres.

This unit was very commonly in medieval and early modern Britain. Similar units, all equivalent to ¼ the local "foot" unit, were used throughout northern Europe.

[2] Palm: A traditional unit of distance equivalent to the length of a person's hand from the wrist to the end of the middle finger.

In the English system, this unit is equivalent to 9 inches (22.86 centimetres) and is usually known as a span. The misunderstanding in the use of the two palm units is ancient. In Roman times, the longer unit was known as the *palmus major* and the shorter one as the *palmus minor*. In the nineteenth century, the 3-inches version was more common in Britain and the 9-inches version was more common in the U.S. This was probably because some Americans were familiar with the comparable Spanish *palmo* (see below).

[3] Palm is a name sometimes used in Dutch for the decimetre (10 centimetres, or about 3.937 inches).

palmo

A traditional unit of distance in Spain and Portugal.

The traditional Spanish palmo is equivalent to 9 pulgadas (see below) or ¼ vara. This is about 20.9 centimetres in Spain and a little more than that in Spanish Latin America.

In Texas, ¼ vara comes to 8⅓ inches (21.17 centimetres).

Under the metric system in Spain, the palmo is an informal unit equivalent to 20 centimetres.

The Portuguese palmo is equivalent to 0.1 braca or about 22.0 centimetres (8.66 inches).

These units are based on the width of a person's hand, stretched out from the tip of the thumb to the tip of the little finger, a definition identical to that of the English span.

Pao

The **pao** is an obsolete unit of dry measure (mass), which was used in South Asia. The name may have originated from the Punjabi ਪਾਉ *páo*, which was a traditional charge of one quarter of a seer per every maund of grain that was weighed, converted into a tax by Sawan Mal. Turner also cites a Sindhi word *pāu* (پاءُ), meaning a quarter of a seer.

The pao was recorded in the Bengal Presidency in 1850 but was not considered to be an integral part of the local system of weights. It was equivalent to four chitaks, which is equivalent to a quarter of a seer. The equivalent imperial weight at the time was given as 7 oz 10 dwt. Troy (233.3 grammes). The use of a quarter-seer weight in Ahmedabad had also been noted in a British East India Company survey of South Asian metrology conducted in 1821. The name of the unit was not recorded, but it would have been equivalent to 4 oz. 3 dr. 17 gr. Avoirdupois (119.8 grammes) based on the measurement of the Ahmedabad seer.

In Nepal, the pao was $\frac{1}{12}$ of a dharni, and equivalent to about 194.4 grammes in 1966. Convenient "pau" units of both 200 grammes and 250 grammes are currently used in retail sales in different parts of the country.

In Pakistan, the pao was slightly heavier, i.e., 233.3 grammes.

As to Afghanistan, it was reported in 1950 that 1 pao ≈ 1 pound (450 grammes) in Kabul, with four paos to one charak and sixteen paos to a seer

par (par):

Metric-technical unit of mass. It is a name suggested in 1940 for the metric slug. 1 par = 1 metric slug

Note: 1. Like the mug, the name par was proposed as an alternative to the metric slug or hyl but was never used.

2. The name is derived from the first three letters of the French word *paresseux.*

parasang

A historic unit of distance comparable to the European league.

The unit originated in Persia but was used throughout the ancient Middle East and Mediterranean. It was equivalent to roughly 3.5-4.0 miles or about 6 kilometres.

In Arabic, the unit is known as the **farasang**.

pari

An obsolete unit of area, equivalent to about 1 hectare

A **pari** was a customary unit of area, equivalent to 50×60 sana lamjel. In Manipur, India, it is approximately 1 hectare. A sana lamjel was defined by the ruler of the kingdom, Nongda Lairen_Pakhangpa, in 33 CE, as being equivalent to the distance from the floor to the tips of the fingers of his raised right hand while standing (a fathom) plus 4 finger width.

1 pari was equivalent to 2 lourak, 4 sangam, 8 loukhai, 16 loushal, or 32 tong

See also "fathom" "hectare."

parker (parker)

Arbitrary unit of absorbed ionizing radiation dose due to corpuscular radiation (i.e., $\acute{\alpha}$- and β rays). One parker is the dose of ionizing corpuscular radiation at which the energy absorbed by a substance is equivalent to the loss in energy during ionization caused by one roentgen of electromagnetic radiation. One parker of corpuscular radiation is equivalent to one roentgen of electromagnetic radiation.

Note: 1. The unit is named after an American medical physicist, Herbert M. Parker (1910-1984), who proposed it about 1950.

2. The unit is better known as the **rep (Roentgen equivalent physical).** The unit was at one time known as a **tissue roentgen.**

See *"rep"* and also *"rem"*.

parsec (pc):

Unit for length, used in the SI system, whose value is obtained experimentally. The parsec is the distance at which 1 astronomical unit subtends an angle of 1 second of arc.

1 pc = 3.258 light years = 2062648 astronomical units = 3.085 72x10^{16} metres.

The unit is used for astronomical measurements of distances of an order greater than those in the solar system.

Note: 1. The parsec is one of four units used in the SI system, whose values are obtained experimentally. The other three units are: *"electron volt," "astronomical unit," and "unified atomic mass unit."*

2. The parsec is formed by blending from a *"par*allax of one *seco*nd." Parallax is the change in the apparent relative orientations of objects when viewed from different positions.

3. Multiples formed by SI prefixes are used.

4. The unit was approved at the first meeting of the International Astronomical Union, which took place in 1922.

part per million (part/million)

Unit of (mass) density and concentration. One part per million is equivalent to a concentration of solvent of one milligramme per liter.

1 part/million = 1 milligramme per liter = 10^{-3} kilogrammes per cubic metre.

See "milligramme per liter".

particle flux unit (pfu)

A unit used to measure the rate at which energetic particles such as protons are received by spacecraft. These flux rates are a major component of the "space weather," the environment in which satellites and other spacecraft operate.

One pfu is a rate of one particle per square centimetre of detector area per steradian of solid angle scanned per second of time. (A steradian is about 79.6% of a sphere). In SI units, 1 pfu = 10^{-4} Per square metre per steradian per second.

pascal (Pa):

The SI unit of pressure and stress. It is the pressure resulting from the force of one newton acting uniformly over an area of one square metre.

1 Pa = 1 newton per square metre

Note: 1. Pressure is usually quoted as the root mean square pressure for a pure sinusoidal wave.

2. Pascal is also a unit of a bull, modulus, fugacity, modulus of elasticity, and shear modulus.

3. The unit is named after a French mathematician, Blaise Pascal (1623-1626), who was the first person to use a barometer for measuring altitude.

4. The unit was officially approved at the 14th CGPM in 1971.

pascal cubic metre (Pa m^3)

SI unit of quantity of gas.

pascal cubic metre per second (Pa m^3 s^{-1})

SI unit of throughput and leak rate.

pascal liter (Pa l or Pa L)

Unit for quantity of gas used in the SI system.

1 Pascal liter = 10^3 Pascal cubic metre.

pascal liter per second (Pa l s^{-1} or Pa L s^{-1})

Unit for throughput used in the SI system.

1 Pascal liter per second = 10^3 Pascal cubic metre per second.

pascal per kelvin (Pa K-1)

SI unit of pressure coefficient.

pascal per metre (Pa m^{-1})

SI unit of pressure gradient.

pascal second (Pa s)

S1 unit of dynamic viscosity.

Pascal second = 10 poise or 1000 centipoise.

Some scientists propose this unit to be referred to as the **poiseuille (Pl)**, but this name was rejected during the General Conference on Weights and Measures.

pascal second per metre (Pa s m^{-1})

SI unit of characteristic impedance of a medium and specific acoustic impedance.

pascal second per metre cubed (Pa s m^{-3})

SI unit of acoustic impedance.

passeree

An obsolete unit of mass.

A **passeree** is an obsolete unit of mass used in Bengal. It is approximately equivalent to 4.677 kilogrammes (10.3 pounds). Five seers is equivalent to one passeree. After metrication in the mid-20th century, the unit became obsolete.

Note: Some references define the unit as equivalent to about 4.6 kilogrammes (10.1412640605 pounds).

pastille dose

Arbitrary unit of radiation dose. One pastille dose is the dose of radiation required to change the color of a barium platinocyanide pastille from a specific apple-green color (tint 'A') to a specific red-brown (tint 'B').

Note: 1. It is equivalent to about 500 roentgens.

2. The unit was originally known as a B dose.

pasteurization unit (PU)

One pasteurization unit is the microorganism death that occurs in a product held at 60°C for 1 minute. It was defined in *1951* by Del Vecchio *et al,*. It is used in rating the effectiveness of pasteurization processes for beer and other products. The number of PU's required for a particular beverage depends on several factors, such as the microorganisms it contains, the type of packaging, etc. "Wild" yeasts, for example, such as occur in some types of Belgian ales, are more resistant to heat than domestic yeasts. A survey of large American breweries in *1955* found their processes averaged 14.8 PU's, with a range of 2.4 to 45.6 PU's. The success of pasteurization (i.e., what percentage of the microorganisms are killed) is affected by both temperature and by the length of time for which the product is held at that temperature. It is a tradeoff, high temperatures for short times or lower temperatures for longer times. Unfortunately, higher temperatures tend to affect the taste of the beverage. The total number of PU's for a particular pasteurization process for beer can be estimated from[*] :

$$PU = t \times 1.393^{(T - 60)}$$

where T is the temperature in degrees Celsius, and t is the time in minutes at which the beer is held at that particular temperature. In reality, the beverage does not instantaneously go to the desired temperature, nor does it cool down instantaneously.

Note: * Andrew Geoffrey Howard Lea and John R. Piggott, editors.

Fermented Beverage Production. 2nd edition.

Springer, 2003. Page 379.

pat

An individual serving of butter.

In the U.S. food industry, restaurant servings of butter were traditionally packaged at 48 pats per pound, making each pat ⅓ ounce (about 9.45 grammes). Less-generous portions such as 60, 64, or 72 pats per pound are also available (margarine is often supplied in these smaller portions). Outside the U.S., butter is traditionally packaged at 100 pats per kilogramme, making each pat equal to 10 grammes, but packages of 125 per kilogramme (8-gramme pats) or 150 per kilogramme (6.67-gramme pats) are also available. In U.S. recipes, a pat of butter is typically 2 teaspoons (⅓ fluid ounce, or about 10 milliliters).

See also *"teaspoon"*

Pau

A **pau** was a customary unit of capacity used in Brunei, Malaysia, Sabah, and Sarawak. A pau was 2 imperial gills (approximately 0.284 liters or 0.600 U.S. pints)

PBS

The Roman foot is equivalent to 29.67 centimetres (about 11.68 inches). The pes was divided into 12 unciae (inches). There were 5 pes (or *pedes*) in 1 passus (pace, see above), 10 in a decempeda, 625 in a stadium, and 5000 in the Roman mile.

pĕ

The traditional Portuguese foot, equivalent to 12 polegadas or about 33.324 centimetres (13.12 inches).

pearl grain

A unit of mass, equivalent to ¼ carat or 50 milligrammes;

See also *"carat"* and *"grain"*.

pebi- (Pi-)

A binary prefix meaning $2^{50} = 1\,125\,899\,906\,842\,624$.

This prefix, adopted by the International Electrotechnical Commission in 1998, is supposed to replace peta- for binary applications in computer science. The prefix is a contraction of "petabinary".

peck (peck)

U.K. arbitrary unit of volume (capacity), equivalent to 2 U.K. gallons.

1 peck = 2 U.K. gallons = 9.092 18 x 10^{-3} cubic metres.

Note: The U.K. peck is used for the measurement of solid and liquid substances.

peck (pk)

U.S. imperial unit of volume (capacity) for dry measure. One peck (U.S.) is equivalent to 16 U.S. dry pints.

1 pk = 16 U.S. dry pints = 8.809 767 542 x 10^{-3} cubic metres.

Note: The U.S. peck is used only for the measurement of solid substances.

In the British imperial system, a peck is a little larger, holding 554.84 cubic inches or approximately 9.0923 liters.

In Scotland, the traditional peck held about 9.1 liters for wheat, peas, or beans and about 12.1 liters for barley or oats.

The word "peck," originally spelled "pek," originates from the name of a similar old French unit. The origin of the French unit is, however, not known.

pencil hardness

A traditional measure of the hardness of the "leads" (actually made of graphite) in pencils. The hardness scale, from softer to harder, takes the form ..., 3B, 2B, B, HB, F, H, 2H, 3H, 4H, ... The letters stand for Black, Hard, and Firm. (There is no industry standard defining the scale therefore, there are some variations between manufacturers in how it is applied). In the U.S., many manufacturers use a numerical scale in which the grades B, HB, F, H, and 2H correspond approximately to numbers 1, 2, 2-1/2, 3, and 4, respectively. The pencil hardness scales are not just used for pencils only. They are used widely to state the durability of paints and other semi-soft coatings. The hardness rating of a coating is the hardness of the hardest pencil that does not penetrate and gouge the coating. This "scratch" hardness scale is analogous to the well-known Mohs hardness scale used in geology to measure the hardness of minerals.

-penny (-d)

An ending added to a number to indicate the size of a nail, as in "sixpenny (6d) nail" or "tenpenny nail". It is not clear how this terminology began, although the usual guess is that tenpenny nails originally cost ten pence per hundred. There is roughly a linear relation between the size designations and length. An n-penny nail is roughly $(\frac{1}{2}) + (\frac{1}{4})n$ inches long. This makes the tenpenny nail about 3 inches long, the eightpenny about 2.5 inches, and so on.

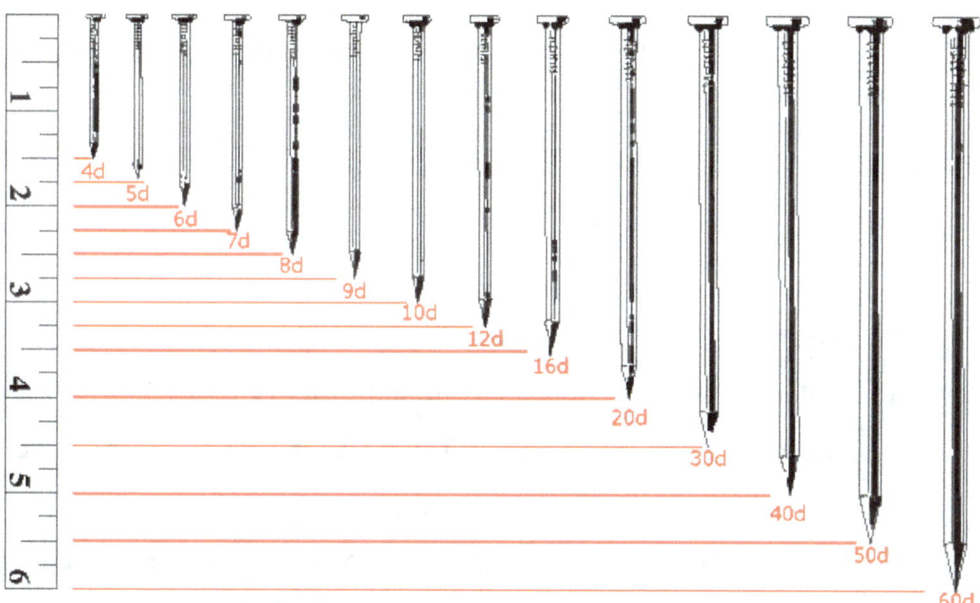

(American Electrician's Handbook, 12th ed.

pennyweight (dwt or pwt)

Imperial unit of mass. One pennyweight is equivalent to $\frac{1}{20}$ troy ounce.

1 pennyweight = 24 grains = $1.555\ 173\ 84 \times 10^{-3}$ kilogrammes.

$$= \tfrac{1}{20} \text{ Troy ounce}$$

$$= \tfrac{1}{240} \text{ Troy pound}$$

Note: The pennyweight is a unit of troy measure used specially with precious metals and precious stones.

The d in the traditional symbol "dwt" is from the Latin word *denarius* for the small coin, which was the Roman equivalent of a penny. (The letter d was also the symbol for the penny in the traditional English monetary system).

pentane candle

Unit of luminous intensity. It is equivalent to one-tenth of the luminous intensity of a standard pentane lamp and approximately equivalent to 1 candela.

percentile

A unit used in statistics to describe a portion of the individuals or events being studied. Suppose the data are arranged by numerical scores, from highest to lowest. A score belongs to the 78th percentile, for example, if it is greater than 78% of the scores but not greater than 79% of the scores. This procedure divides the scores into 100 percentiles, numbered 0th through 99th.

perch (perch)

Imperial unit of length.

1 perch = 16.5 feet = 5.5 yards = 5.029 2 metres.

Note: 1. This unit is also known as the **rod** or the **pole**

2. The unit has been in use in England from the time of Henry II (1154-1189)

3. In Ireland, the perch used to be 21 feet, which increased the Irish mile to 2240 yards.

4. The word perch (perche in French: see below) originates from the Latin word *pertica* (pole).

5. The Romans also had a distance unit known as the *pertica*, but it was shorter, 10 Roman feet (9-71 English feet or 2.96 metres).

6. The perch is also a traditional unit of distance in French North America. The perche is equivalent to 18 pieds (see below) or 3 toises. By legal definition in Canada, this is equivalent to 19.1835 English feet or 5.847 13 metres.

See *"rod"* and *"pole"*.

perch (masonry)

Unit of volume, equivalent to 24.75 cubic feet.

1 perch (masonry) = 24.75 cubic feet = 0.700 841 963 cubic metres.

perch (p)

Imperial unit of area.

1 perch = **30.25** square yards = 25.292 852 64 square metres.

Note: It is better to refer to this unit as the **square perch**. It is also known as **(square) rod** and **(square)**

perm

A traditional unit of water vapor permeability, i.e., the ability of a material to permit the passage of water vapor. If we want to keep things dry, we wrap them in something having low permeability. A material has a permeability of one perm if it allows transmission of one grain of water vapor per square foot of area per inch of mercury (inHg) of pressure difference per hour. The value depends somewhat on temperature. At 0 °C, one perm is equivalent to about 5.721×10^{-11} kilogrammes per square metre per pascal per second $(kg/(m^2 \cdot Pa \cdot s))$ or about 0.2060 milligrammes per square metre per pascal per hour $(mg/(m^2 \cdot Pa \cdot h))$. At room temperature, the equivalent is about 5.745×10^{-11} $kg/(m^2 \cdot Pa \cdot s)$. [The SI unit, $kg/(m^2 \cdot Pa \cdot s)$, simplifies to seconds per metre (s/m).] The lower the perm value, the better the vapor barrier.

per mensem

A traditional unit of frequency, equivalent to once a month.

per mill, per mil, or per mille

A unit of proportion, equivalent to 0.001 or 1 per thousand. Unlike percent, per mill is usually written as two words, although the one-word spellings **permill** and **permil** are also used. Its symbol, not available to most web browsers, is like the percent symbol, but with two zeroes in the denominator (roughly $^0/_{00}$). The spelling "per mill" seems to be more commonly used in the U.S., "per mil" being more common in Britain.

perm inch

A traditional unit of water vapor permeance. The perm value (see above) does not depend on the thickness of the material used as a water barrier. The permeance is the product of the perm value and the thickness, measured in inches. One perm inch is equivalent to about 1.453×10^{-12} $kg/(m \cdot Pa \cdot s)$ at 0 °C or about 1.459×10^{-12} $kg/(m \cdot Pa \cdot s)$ at room temperature. The SI unit $kg/(m \cdot Pa \cdot s)$ simplifies to seconds (s).

person hour

A gender-nonspecific version of **man hour**, a unit of labor equivalent to the work of one person for one hour.

perthousand

Another name for per mill (see above). In typography, "perthousand" is often used as the name of the per mill character.

perceived noise decibel (PN dB)

The sound pressure in decibels (above a datum level of 2×10^{-5} pascals root-mean square), as judged by an otologically normal binaural listener of a band of random noise of width, one-third to one octave centered on a frequency of 1000 hertz.

Note: Although the loudness of a note to an observer is related to the logarithm of its intensity, the decibel is not a measure of loudness since the sensitivity of the ear to changes of intensity varies with frequency. The equivalent loudness of a note is measured on the phone.

period

A unit of geologic time. The unit constitutes a subdivision of an era. The fundamental unit of the standard geological time scale.

perm (perm)

U.S. unit of water vapour permeability.

1 perm (0°C) = 57.213 5 $\times 10^{-12}$ kilogrammes per pascal second square metre,

1 prem (23°C) = 57.452 5 $\times 10^{-12}$ kilogrammes per pascal second square metre.

Note: Water vapor permeability is the ability of a material to permit the passage of water vapor. If we want to keep things dry, we wrap them in something having low permeability. A material has a permeability of one perm if it allows the transmission of one grain of water vapor per square foot of area per inch of mercury (inHg) of pressure difference per hour. The value depends somewhat on temperature. At 0 °C, one perm is equivalent to about 5.721×10^{-11} kilogrammes per square metre per pascal per second (kg/(m^2.Pa.s)) or about 0.2060 mg/(m^2.Pa.h). At room temperature, the equivalent is about 5.745×10^{-11} kg/(m^2.Pa.s). [The SI unit, kg/(m^2.Pa.s), simplifies to seconds per metre (s/m).] The lower the perm value, the better the vapor barrier. See also *"perm-inch."*

perm-inch (perm. in)

U.S. unit of water vapour permeance.

1 perm.inch (0°C) = 1.453 22 x 10^{-12} kilogrammes per pascal second metre

1 perm.inch (23°C) = 1.459 29 x 10^{-12} kilogrammes per pascal second metre.

Note: The perm value (see above) does not depend on the thickness of the material used as a water barrier. The permeance is the product of the perm value and the thickness, measured in inches. One perm inch is equivalent to about 1.453 x 10^{-12} kg/(m.Pa.s) at 0 °C or about 1.459 x 10^{-12} kg/(m.Pa.s) at room temperature. The SI unit kg/(m-Pa-s) simplifies to seconds (s).

permicron (permicron):

Metric unit of reciprocal length.

One permicron is the reciprocal length of a distance, which has a length of one micrometre.

1 permicron == l/micrometre = 10^6/metre.

Note: The unit was proposed for the first time in 1951 for the number of wavelengths in a micrometre (wave number). If the wavelength of a spectral line is 400 nanometres, its wave number would be equivalent to ($\frac{1}{400}$) x 103 = 2.5 permicrons.

pes

An ancient Roman unit of length, about 295.7 mm. The word also means a foot (the anatomical part, not the English unit of length). The basic unit of Roman linear measurement was the *pes* or **Roman foot** (plural: *pedes*). The **ancient Roman units of measurement** were primarily based on the Hellenic system, which in turn was influenced by the Egyptian system and the Mesopotamian system. The Roman units were comparatively consistent and well documented.

peta (P)

SI prefix denoting x10^{15}. Examples include: petabecquerel (qu), petahertz (th), petajoule (PJ), pentametre (Pm), and petawatt (PW).

The prefix was chosen to suggest the Greek *penta*, meaning 5, this being the fifth prefix (n = 5 in 10^{3n}) in the SI system of metric prefixes. The prefix is usually pronounced *pet-a*, with a short "e" sound rather than *pee-ta.*

petabecquerel (PBq)

A unit of radioactivity, equivalent to 10^{15} atomic disintegrations per second or 27.027 curies.

petabyte (PB)

A unit of information, equivalent to 10^{15} (one U.S. quadrillion) bytes. The petabyte is often used to mean $2^{50} = 1\ 125\ 899\ 906\ 842\ 624$ bytes, but this use breaks the rules of the SI. The unit, equivalent to 2^{50} bytes, should be known as the **pebibyte** (see pebi- above).

petaflops (Pflops)

A unit of computing power, equivalent to one quadrillion (10^{15}) floating point operations per second. Current computers cannot achieve this power. It is a goal for future generations of supercomputers.

See flop.

petagram (Pg)

A metric unit of mass, equivalent to 10^{15} grammes or 1 gigatonne (one billion metric tons). This unit is used in atmospheric science and other scientific contexts, where large masses are considered.

petahertz (PHz)

A unit of frequency, equivalent to 10^{15} hertz. The frequencies of infrared and visible light waves are expressed in petahertz.

petajoule (PJ)

A metric unit of energy. One petajoule is equivalent to 947.817 billion Btu, 277.7778 gigawatt hours, or about 9.48 megathems.

petametre (Pm)

A metric unit of distance, equivalent to 10^{12} kilometres. This is equivalent to about 621.371 billion miles or 0.1057 light years. The distance from the earth to the nearest star (other than the sun) is about 40 petametres.

petagram (Pg)

A metric unit of mass, equivalent to 1015 grammes or 1 gigatonne (one billion metric tons). This unit is used in atmospheric science and other scientific contexts, where large masses are considered.

petrograd standard (Petrograd standard)

Unit of volume used only to measure timber. It is equivalent to 165 cubic feet.

1 standard = **165** cubic feet = 4.762 28 cubic metres.

Note: The unit is also known as **standard.**

See *"standard"*.

pF

A unit formerly used in agricultural science to measure "soil suction" or soil moisture tension. Soil moisture tension is the pressure that must be applied to the moisture in the soil to bring it to hydraulic equilibrium with an external pool of water. This was measured in pF units as the logarithm of the pressure in centimetres of water. Currently, measurements are usually made directly in kilopascals (kPa).

pferdestiirke (ps)

The German word for horsepower, means the metric horsepower. The symbol ps is used for horsepower in both the Japanese and German automotive industries.

pfund (pfd)

A traditional German weight unit, corresponding to the English pound (see below). The pfund is equivalent to 16 unze or 32 lot.

Traditionally, the pfund varied in size from market to market and the various German states adopted different standards, ranging from something close to the English pound (454 grammes) to the Viennese pfund at about 1.2 pounds (560 grammes). When Germany was unified in the late nineteenth century, the pfund was redefined as a metric unit, equivalent to exactly 500 grammes (about 1.102 31 pounds). There is no change in the plural.

Pfund scale

A scale used in the honey industry to describe the color of honey. Measurements were originally made using the Pfund color grader, that consists of a wedge of amber-colored glass next to a wedge-shaped cell filled with honey. The instrument is read visually. The reading is the distance the wedge must be moved to make a match and is expressed in millimetres. Symbol, mm Pfund/

Honey Colors		
Color Name	Pfund Scale, millimetres	Optical Density
Water White	<9	0.0945
Extra White	9 – 17	0.189
White	18– 34	0.378
Extra Light Amber	35 – 50	0.595
Light Amber	51 – 85	1.389
Amber	86 – 114	3.008
Dark Amber	>114	—

A few examples of honey colors	
Honey Varietal	Average color as mm Pfund
Citrus	14
Eucalyptus	58
Heather	96

Color is not a factor in determining grades of honey in the United States, but a color designation usually accompanies the grade. The Pfund color grader "is not the officially approved device for determining color designation, when applying these United States grade standards for the color of honey." Instead, transmittance is measured at a wavelength of 560 nanometres, through 3.15 centimetres of a freshly-prepared caramel-glycerin solution that matches the color of the honey, as compared with the transmittance of pure glycerin. The optical density, as given in the last column in the table above, is log to the base 10 of 100 divided by the percent transmittance.

Note: 1. From Table 1. United States Standards for Grades of Extracted Honey. USDA, Agricultural Marketing Service. Effective May 23, 1985.

pH

A logarithmic measure used to state the acidity or alkalinity of a chemical solution. The properties of a liquid solution we call "acid" are caused by the presence of hydrogen ions (H^+). The pH of a solution is a measure of the concentration of these hydrogen ions. Technically, the pH of a solution is defined to be the negative logarithm of the concentration, measured in moles per liter. This unit is inverted in the sense that lower pH readings correspond to greater acidity and, therefore, more hydrogen ions. Lowering the pH by 1.0 implies multiplying the ion concentration by a factor of 10. Mathematically, the scale is open at both ends, but in practice, pH values usually fall in the range from 0 to 14. A neutral solution (neither acidic nor alkaline, like pure water) has a pH of 7.0. Numbers below 7 indicate increasing acidity, while numbers above 7 indicate increasing alkalinity. The pH ("potential of Hydrogen") scale was invented in 1909 by the Danish chemist Søren Peter Lauritz Sørensen (1868-1939)

Ph Eur unit

A unit used in the European Union to measure the potency of a vitamin or drug, i.e., its expected biological effects. For each substance to which this unit applies, the European Directorate for Quality of Medicines has determined the biological effect associated with a dose of 1 Ph Eur unit. Other quantities of the substance can then be expressed in terms of this standard unit. In many cases, the Ph Eur unit is equivalent to the international unit (1U).

phi unit

A logarithmic unit used to measure grain sizes for sand, grit, and gravel. The 0 point of the scale is a grain size of 1 millimetre, and each increase of 1 in the phi number corresponds to a decrease in grain size by a factor of ½. Thus, 1 phi unit is a grain size of 0.5 millimetres, 2 phi units is 0.25 millimetres, and so on. On the contrary, -1 phi unit corresponds to a grain size of 2 millimetres and -2 phi units to a size of 4 millimetres.

PHON (phon or P)

It is a unit of equivalent loudness of a sound, judged subjectively. It is a measure of the intensity level relative to a reference tone of defined intensity and frequency. The accepted reference tone has a rootmean-square sound pressure of 2×10^{-5} pascals and a frequency of 1000 hertz. Accordingly, the equivalent loudness in a phone is equivalent to the sound pressure level in decibels, above the accepted datum level (i.e., above $2 \times 10^{-}$pascal root-mean-square), as judged by an otologically normal binaural listener of a standard plane sinusoidally-progressive pure tone of frequency 1000 hertz coming from directly in front of the observer.

Note: The phone was one of two acoustical units defined at the first International Acoustical Conference held in Paris in 1937 and the other unit being the decibel. We have to note that the decibel and the phone scales are not similar since the sensitivity of the ear to changes in intensity varies with frequency. The two scales are nearly similar between 500 and 10000 hertz, but beyond this range, there is considerable variation. The phone scale is generally subjective, but when the actual sensation of loudness is logarithmically related to the intensity, the phone scale starts to give a true quantitative measure of loudness sensation.

See also *"sane".*

phot (ph or phot)

CGS unit of intensity of illumination. One phot is equivalent to the illumination of one lumen uniformly over an area of one square centimetre.

1 phot = 1 lumen per square centimetre = 10^4 lux

Note: 1. This unit is also known as a centimetre-candle.

2. The unit was legalized in France in 1919 and it was named phot by André Blondel (1863-1938).

See *"centimetre-candle."*

photo-second (ph.s or phot-s)

CGS unit of exposure.

1 phot-second = 10^4 lux seconds.

photon (1)

Metric unit for retinal illumination. One photon is the retinal luminance produced by a surface having a luminance of one nit (1 nit = 1 candela per square metre), when the area of the pupil of the eye is one square centimetre.

Note: This unit is also known as the **"luxon,"** and it is recommended to refer to it as **"troland."**

See also *"luxon," "troland' and "nit."*

photon (2)

The basic energy packet of electromagnetic radiation. The energy E in photons is related to the frequency f of radiation in hertz by the relation:

$E = hf$

where, h is the Planck's constant = 6.6249×10^{-34} joule seconds.

Note: 1. As an example, a photon of green light has an energy of 36×10^{-20}.

2. The unit is better known as quantum; it is also known as the ergon

See *"quantum"* and *"ergon"*.

pica (pica)

Unit of length used by printers,' to measure type size. One pica is 12 points.

1 pica = 12 points = (⅙) inch = 0.421 751 76 centimetres.

Note: The term pica is also used to describe type width, there being 6 picas to an inch.

See *"point (printers')," "brilliant," and "emerald."*

pico (p)

SI prefix denoting $\times 10^{-12}$. Examples include picoampere (pA), pico coulomb (pC), picofarad (pF), p1cohenry (pH), picometre (pm), picosecond (ps), picowatt (pW).

picul

A unit of weight, comparable to the European quintal, widely used in East Asia during the colonial period. The picul is equivalent to 100 catties, typically about 133.3 pounds or 60.5 kilogrammes. In recent years, the picul has been used as a metric unit, equivalent to 60 kilogrammes (132.28 pounds) in Thailand or 50 kilogrammes (110.23 pounds) in China. The unit is pronounced "pickle."

pie

The traditional foot of Spain.

The pie is equivalent to ⅓ vara or 12 pulgadas (see below)

The pie used in Spain is about 27.86 centimetres or 10.97 inches but in Spanish Latin America, the pie is generally longer.

The Argentine length is 28.89 centimetres or 11.37 inches. In Texas, ⅓ vara is 11⅑ inches or 28.22 centimetres.

piece (pc)

A unit of quantity, equivalent to 1.

This unit, like count (ct), is used to indicate that a measurement represents an exact count of items.

pied

The traditional French foot.

Pieds of various lengths were used in France, but the one best remembered now is the royal foot (**Pied de roi**), known as the Paris foot in English and the foot (**French measure**) in Canadian law. The pied de roi is equivalent to about 32.48 centimetres or 12.79 inches. The official Canadian definition is 12.789 inches (32.484 06 centimetres).

Today, the word *pied* is sometimes used informally in France as a metric unit, equivalent to 30 centimetres.

In French Canada, *pied* is generally used to refer to the English foot.

piede

The traditional foot of Italy.

This unit, no longer used, varied considerably from one region to another. One common length was about 29.8 centimetres, but lengths of 34.8 cm and 38 cm were traditional in Venice and Bologna, respectively.

pieze (pz)

MTS unit of pressure. It is the pressure resulting from a force of one sthene, acting uniformly over an area of one square metre or equivalent to 1000 pascals.

1 pz = 1 sthene per square metre = 1000 pascals.

Note: The unit was legalized in France in 1919.

one pièze =   1 kilopascal

| = | 10 millibars |

$$\approx 9.869 \times 10^{-3} \text{ standard atmospheres}$$

$$\approx \quad 7.501 \text{ Torrs}$$

$$\approx \quad 0.1450 \text{ pounds per square inch}$$

$$\approx \quad 0.2953 \text{ inches of mercury}$$

See *"sthene."*

pik or pic

A traditional unit of distance in the Eastern Mediterranean and Near East. The pik varied considerably, but a typical value is about 28 inches (71 centimetres). This is an "arm" unit, like the Italian braccio and the Russian arshin.

pin (pin)

Imperial unit of capacity (volume), equivalent to 4.5 gallons.
1 pin = 4.5 gallons.
Note: The unit is used to measure ale and beer.

pinch

An informal unit of volume used in food recipes. Historically, a pinch was defined as "an amount that can be taken between the thumb and forefinger" but without any definite equivalent in other units.
Recently, kitchen supply stores in the U.S. and other countries have begun selling sets of "mini spoons" in which the spoon labeled "pinch" is designed to hold exactly ½ dash or $\frac{1}{16}$ teaspoon, which is roughly 0.01 fluid ounces or 0.3 milliliters.
See also "teaspoon"

ping

A traditional unit of area in Taiwan, equivalent to about 3.305 square metres (3.953 square yards). This is the same unit known in Korea as the pyong (see below).

pint (U.K.) (UKpt)

Arbitrary unit of volume (capacity).

1 U.K. pint = (⅛) U.K. gallon = 0.568 261 x 10^{-3} cubic metres.

Note: 1. The U.K. pint is used for the measurement of liquid and solid substances.

2. Also known as **imperial pint**.

pint, dry (dry pt)

U.S. Imperial unit of volume, equivalent to (¹⁄₆₄) U.S. bushel.

1 U.S. dry pint = (¹⁄₆₄) U.S. bushel =0.550 610 x 10^{-3} cubic metres.

Note: The U.S. dry pint is used only for the measurement of solid substances.

pint, liquid (liq pt)

U.S. imperial unit of volume, equivalent to one eighth of the U.S. gallon.

1 U.S. liq pt = (⅛) U.S. gallon = 0.473 176 473 x 10^{-3} cubic metres.

Note: The U.S. liquid pint is used only for the measurement of liquid substances.

PIP

The smallest measured change in a currency conversion rate. This depends on the relative values of the two currency units. In converting euros to U.S. dollars, for example, a pip is 0.0001, but in converting U.S. dollars to Japanese yen, a pip is 0.01. This unit is also known as a tick.

pipa

A traditional Portuguese unit of liquid volume, originally very similar in size to the English pipe (see next entry).

The pipa has become a metric unit, equivalent to exactly 500 liters, which is 0.5 cubic metres, 132.085 U.S. gallons, or 109.996 British imperial gallons.

pipe

The pipe is a traditional unit of liquid volume, generally equivalent to 2 hogsheads. In the U.S., this means a pipe, which is equivalent to 126 U.S. gallons, about 16.844 cubic feet or 476.96 liters. In Britain, it is more complicated because traditional British hogsheads were of different sizes depending on what they contained. The British pipe was usually used as a wine measure, but even different types of wine had different size pipes.

See also *"butt" and "hogshead."*

Pirate-ninja

Informal unit of power in the "Humorous System of Units."

A pirate-ninja is defined as one kilowatt-hour (3.6 Mega joules) per Martian day or sol. It is equivalent to approximately 40.55 watts. Andy Weir, author of *The Martian*, revealed in a 2015 interview with Adam Savage that the Curiosity rover team at the Jet Propulsion Laboratory references milli-pirate-ninjas in their meetings.

pitch

Another name for "characters per inch," a unit used in printing.

pixel

A picture element.

Pixels do not have a fixed size. Their diameters are generally measured in micrometres (micron).

Although the pixel is not a unit of measurement itself, pixels are often used to measure the resolution (or sharpness) of images.

As a hypothetical example, a 600 x 1000 pixel image has 4 times the pixel density and is thus 4 times sharper than a 300 x 500 pixel image, assuming the two images have the same physical size.

planck (planck):

The SI unit of action. The planck is the action of energy of one joule over one second.

I planck = 1 joule second.

Note: 1. The unit was proposed in 1946 and is named after Max Planck (1858-1947). The unit has the dimensions of Planck's constant.

2. In 1972, there was a proposal to refer to the SI unit of angular momentum as a Planck, but it did not find support.

planck length

The length $(Gh/2\pi c^3)^{1/2}$ where h is the Planck constant, G is the gravitational constant and c is the speed of light. Its value is: Planck length = 1.615 99 x 10^{-35} metres.

planck mass

The mass $(hc/2\pi G)^{1/2}$ where h is the Planck constant, G is the gravitational constant, and c is the speed of light. Its value is:

Planck mass = 2.17684 x 10^{-8} kilogrammes.

It arises in theories relating quantum theory to gravitation.

planck time

The time $(Gh/2\pi^5)^{1/2}$ taken for a photon travelling at the speed of light c to travel a distance, equivalent to the Planck length (=1.615 99 x 10^{-35} metres), where h is Planck constant, and G the gravitational constant

Planck time = 1.70863 x 10^{-43} seconds.

See *"Planck length"*.

planck units

A system of units used in quantum theories of gravity based on the Planck length, Planck mass, and Planck time. The gravitational constant, the speed of light, and the rationalized Planck constant are all assigned the value of unity. Thus, all quantities that normally have dimensions involving mass, length, and time become dimensionless in this system.

See *"Planck length," "Planck mass," and "Planck time."*

platonic year

A unit of time used in astronomy.

The earth's axis of rotation is not fixed in space. The attraction of the moon causes it to slowly trace out a circle in the sky. This motion, known as precession, changes the orientation of the sky as seen from the earth's surface. The poles appear to shift their locations and the sun's point of crossing the equator slowly rotates through the constellations of the Zodiac.

The Platonic year is the length of time required for one complete precessional rotation, about 25 800 years. The unit is named for the ancient Greek philosopher Plato (ca. 428-348 BCE). It is sometimes known as the **great year**.

plethron

An ancient Greek unit of distance, equivalent to 100 Greek feet or ⅙ stadion.

The Greek foot was slightly longer than the English foot, and therefore, the plethron was approximately 100-105 English feet or 31-33 metres. Often represented as the length of a cord, the unit was frequently used for measuring land areas. The plural is **plethra.**

PLI (pli)

Imperial unit of line density. One pli is the line density of a material, which has a mass of one pound and a length of one inch and is of a uniform cross section.

1 pli = 1 pound per inch = 17.85 8 kilogrammes per metre.

plotter unit

A unit of distance used in typography, equivalent to $\frac{1}{40}$ millimetre or 25 micrometres. Thus, the smallest distance addressed by Hewlett Packard plotters has become a fairly familiar term in digital graphics design.

PN

A symbol for "nominal pressure," a measure used for rating piping, valves, fittings, etc. Nominal pressure is essentially the pressure rating of the piping system, measured in bars at a temperature of 20°C (68°F). (One bar is equivalent to 100 kilopascals or approximately 145.038 pounds per square inch in traditional English units). Industrial standards organizations, such as the American National Standards Institute (ANSI), set standards for pipes and fittings based on PN ratings. These standards specify in detail the size, composition, and strength of each component.

PNC

An abbreviation for **preferred noise criterion**, a unit used in engineering to measure the level of background noise in rooms or other enclosed spaces. Introduced in 1971, the unit is similar to the older noise criterion (NC), but a PNC rating requires lower levels of high and low frequencies than the corresponding NC rating. PNC ratings below 40 are generally required for residential or classroom spaces. PNC ratings are typically 10-15% lower than raw measurements of the sound level in decibels.

PNU

Abbreviation for protein nitrogen unit, a measure of the potency of the compounds used by doctors in allergy skin tests.

One PNU is defined as 0.01 microgrammes (µg) of phosphotungstic acid-precipitable protein nitrogen. Unfortunately, the potency measurements depend on the technique of measurement used. The results of one manufacturer are not comparable to those of another manufacturer. As a result, although PNU's are still used, they are being replaced by bioequivalent allergy units (BAU), which are measured by actual skin testing using reference preparations of standard potency.

point (point):

Metric unit for mass.

1 point = 0.01 metric carats = 2 x 10^{-6} kilogrammes.

Note: 1. This unit is only used for commercial transactions in diamonds, pearls and other precious stones.

2. The same name, "point," is used in the field of printing as a unit of length.

See *"point, printer's."*

point, printer's (point):

Unit of length used by printers to measure the depth of type face. One point is $\frac{1}{72}$ inch.

1 point (printer's) = ($\frac{1}{72}$) inch = 003514598 centimetres

Note: 1. Type sizes are also indicated by names, e.g., brilliant, emerald and pica.

2. "point" is used as a metric unit of mass, mainly with precious stones.

3. Eventually, the point was standardized in Britain and America as exactly $\frac{1}{72.27}$ = 0.013 837 inches, which is about 0.35 millimetres (351.46 micrometres). The value $\frac{1}{72}$ inch is used in continental Europe and known as a **Didot point** after the French typographer Firmin Didot (1764-1836).

4. In the U.S., Adobe software defines the point to be exactly $\frac{1}{72}$ inch (0.013 888 9 inches or 0.352 777 8 millimetres), a unit sometimes known as the big point (bp).

5. The German standards agency DIN has proposed that all these units be replaced by multiples of 0.25 millimetres ($\frac{1}{1016}$ inch).

See *"brilliant printers' "* and *"emerald printers' "*.

points of the compass

Unit of plane angle. One point of the compass is equivalent to $\frac{1}{32}$ of the circle (i.e., 360°)

1 point of the compass = ($\frac{1}{32}$) x 360 degrees = 11.25 degrees.

Note: 1. This unit was used when the seaman's horizon was divided into 32 parts known as the "rhumbs of the wind,"

2. The unit is also known as the **nautical point.**

See *"nautical point"*.

point (pt)

[1] A unit used to represent the smallest significant change in an arbitrary ratio. This usage is common in sports. Most sports "averages" are actually ratios of successful performances divided by attempted performances. Baseball's batting average is a good example. These ratios are computed to a fixed number of decimal places. Usually, three, and a point represents a change of 1 in the last decimal place. Thus, the batting averages .314 and .302 are said to differ by 12 points.

[2] Another name for a mil, a unit of distance, equivalent to 0.001 inches. Points are used with this meaning to measure the thickness, or **caliper**, of paper or card stock in the paper industry. One point is equivalent to 25.4 micrometres or microns.

[3] A measure of the specific gravity of a liquid typically used in brewing and winemaking. Specific gravity is the mass of a sample of the liquid divided by the mass of an equivalent volume of pure water. It is a dimensionless (unit-less) number, typically a little larger than 1. Each "point" represents an increase of 0.001 above 1. For example, a liquid of a specific gravity of 1.048 is described as 48 points.

poise (P, Ps, or Po)

CGS unit of dynamic viscosity. One poise is the dynamic viscosity that gives rise to a tangential stress of one dyne per square centimetre across two planes separated by one centimetre, when the velocity of streamlined flow is one centimetre per second.

1 poise = 0.1 newtons second per metre squared.

Note: 1. The unit is named after a French physician, Jean Louis Marie Poiseuille (1799-1869) and it was suggested for the first time in 1913.

2. In practice, the centipoise (cF) is of more used.

3. The British Standards Institution recommended that for calibrating viscometers, the dynamic viscosity of water at 20°C should be taken as 1.0020 centipoise.

poiseuille (Pl):

An SI unit for dynamic viscosity. One poiseuille is the dynamic viscosity that gives rise to a tangential stress of one newton per metre squared across two planes, separated by one metre, when the velocity of streamlined flow is one metre per second.

1 P1=1 newton per metre squared

Note: This unit was proposed by France and has only rarely been used outside France.

pol

An empirical unit of indoor air pollution was introduced by the Danish environmental scientist Povi Ole Fanger in 1988. One olf is defined as the air pollution produced by one "standard person," and one decipol is the perceived air pollution level in a space having a pollution source of strength one olf and ventilation with unpolluted air at the rate of 1 liter/second. In practice, nearly all measurements are made in decipols.

pole (1)

Imperial unit of area. One pole is equivalent to **30.25** square yards.

1 pole = **30.25** square yards = 25.292 852 64 metres squared.

Note: This unit is more strictly known as the **square pole**. It is also known as the **(square) rod** and the **(square) perch**.

See *"rod"* and *"perch"*.

pole (2)

Imperial unit of length, equivalent to 16.5 feet (5.5 yards).

1 pole = 5.5 yards = 5.029 2 metres.

Note: 1. The unit is also known as the **rod** or the **perch**.

2. In former times, there existed various local poles with lengths of between 3 and 7 yards.

See "rod" and "perch".

polypin

An informal unit of volume for beer and other alcoholic beverages, used mostly in Britain. A polypin of beer comes in a plastic container, often inside a rectangular cardboard box. It holds 32-36 imperial pints (18.2-20.5 liters) or, in the metric version, exactly 20 liters (5.28 U.S. gallons). The word polypin is a registered trademark of Biovision GmbH. It is the name of the polythene plastic used for the lining of the container.

The traditional British pin of beer is exactly 36 pints.

poncelet (P)

Metric-derived unit of power. One poncelet is the power available when a force of one hundred kilogrammes-force is displaced through a distance of one metre in the direction of the force within one second.

1 poncelet = 100 metres kilogramme force per second = **980.665** watts

Note: 1. The unit is named after a French engineer, Jean Victor Poncelet (1788-1867).

2. The unit was legalized in France in 1919.

pond (p)

MkpS unit of force, equivalent to one gramme weight.

1 pond = 10^{-3} kiloponds = 9.806 65 x 10^{-3} newtons.

See *"kilopond."*

pood

Pood (Russian: пуд, *pud*, IPA: plural: *pudi* or *pudy*) is a unit of mass, equivalent to 40 *funt* (фунт, Russian pound).

Since 1899 it is approximately set to 16.38 kilogrammes (36.11 pounds).

pot

[1] A traditional unit of volume in many countries of Europe, roughly comparable to the liter or to the English quart. In Switzerland, the pot is now a metric unit, equivalent to 1.5 liters. In Belgium, the pot is interpreted as 1.5 liters for dry quantities, but only 0.5 liters for liquids. The traditional pot is equivalent to 0.967 liters in Denmark and to 0.965 liters in Norway.

[2] A unit of volume used in Australian pubs. A pot of beer is 285 milliliters in Queensland and Victoria, and 575 milliliters in Western Australia.

[3] A traditional unit of volume in Jersey (Channel Islands). Still used to measure milk, the pot has always been roughly comparable to ½ gallon. In the current definition, one pot is equivalent to 69.5 Imperial fluid ounces (1.7375 quarts) or about 1.975 liters.

Potrzebie

A system of units belongs to a class known as "Humorous Units of Measurements."

In issue 33, *Mad* published a partial table of the "Potrzebie System of Weights and Measures" developed by 19-year-old Donald E. Knuth, later a famed computer scientist. According to Knuth, the basis of this new revolutionary system is the potrzebie, which is equivalent to the thickness of *Mad* issue 26, or 2.263348517438173216473 millimetres.

Volume was measured in ngogn (equivalent to 1000 cubic potrzebies), mass in blintz (equivalent to the mass of 1 ngogn of halva, which is "a form of pie [with] a specific gravity of 3.1416 and a specific heat of .31416"), and time in seven named units (decimal powers of the average earth rotation, equivalent to 1 "Clarke"). The system also features such units as *whatmeworry, cowznofski, vreeble, hoo,* and *hah.*

According to the "Date" system in Knuth's article, which substitutes a 10-clarke "mingo" for a month and a 100-clarke "cowznofski" for a year, the date of October 29, 2007, is rendered as "Cal 7, 201 C. M." (for Cowznofsko Madi, or "in the Cowznofski of our MAD"). The dates are calculated from October 1, 1952, the date MAD was first published. Dates before this point are referred to (perhaps tongue-in-cheek) as "B.M." ("Before MAD"). The ten "Mingoes" are Tales (Tal.) Calculated (Cal.) To (To) Drive (Dri.) You (You) Humor (Hum.) In (In) A (A) Jugular (Jug.) Vein (Vei.)

pottle

U.K. unit of volume (capacity), equivalent to half a U.K. gallon or 4 U.K. pints.

1 pottle = **0.5** U.K. gallons = 2.272 980 x 10^{-3} cubic metres.

Note: This unit is also known as a quartern.

See *"quartern"* and *"pint, U.K."*.

poumar

Imperial unit of line density. One poumar is the line density of a thread, which has a mass of one pound and a length of one million yards.

1 poumar = 10^{-6} pound per yards = 0.496 055 x 10^{-6} kilogrammes per metre.

Note: The unit is used in the textile industry as a measure of yarn count.

See also *"tex"*.

pound (Lb)

FSS and FlbfS unit of force and base unit of Stroud system of units.

1 Lb = 1 pound-force = 4.448 221 615 2605 newtons.

Note: 1. In case of using the unit as base unit of the Stroud system, it has to be spelled Pound with a capital letter.

2. It is better to call the unit **pound-force.**

pound (lb)

U.K. and U.S. unit, and FPS base unit of mass. Its size can vary from system to system. The most commonly used pound today is the international avoirdupois unit.

1 lb = 0.453 592 37 kilogrammes.

Note: 1. The defining relation between the pound and the kilogramme was deliberately chosen as a number divisible by seven to facilitate the conversion of grains to grammes, there being 7000 grains in a pound and hence 1 grain = 0.064 798 91 grammes.

2. The pound was so defined in the U.S. in the Federal Register of 1 July 1959 and thenceforth used by the National Bureau of Standards and the American Standard Association in the U.S. and by the National Physical Laboratory and the British Standards Institution in the U.K. It was legally adopted in the U.K. through the Weights and Measures Act of 1963.

3. The Imperial Standard Pound (the U.K. pound), as defined in the Weights and Measures Acts of 1855 and 1878, was, until 1963, the fundamental unit of mass in Great Britain. These Acts defined the Pound as follows: The weight in vacuo of the platinum weight (as mentioned in the First Schedule to the Act of 1878). In 1933, the UKIb, as defined by this Act, was compared experimentally with the kilogramme and the result was:

1 U.K. lb = 0.453 592 338 kilogrammes.

Weights and Measures Act 1963.

> *"The yard or the metre shall be the unit of measurement of length and the pound or the kilogramme shall be the unit of measurement of mass by reference to which any measurement involving a measurement of length or mass shall be made in the United Kingdom; and (a) the yard shall be 0.9144 metres exactly; (b) the pound shall be 0.453 592 37 kilogrammes exactly."*

4. Just as the kilogramme was once defined by reference to a cubic decimetre of water, so the pound was required (1824) to be restored, if lost, by reference to the weight of "a cubic inch of distilled water weighed in the air by brass weights at a temperature of 62° of Fahrenheit's thermometer, the barometer being at thirty inches".

5. The U.S. pound (USlb avdp) was originally derived from the international kilogramme, and authorized in the Mendenhall Order of 5 April 1893 as:

1 USlb advp = 0.453 529 427 7 kilogrammes.

6. An avoirdupois pound is equivalent to 16 avoirdupois ounce and to exactly 7,000 grains. The conversion factor between the kilogramme and the international pound was therefore chosen to be divisible by 7, and an (international) grain is, thus, equivalent to exactly 64.79891 milligrammes.

7. Equivalence to other units of mass

The table below sets out the relationships between the avoirdupois pound and:

- The troy pound (see troy pound).
- Three other historical pounds (see below): the Tower pound, the merchant pound and the London pound.
- the SOD-gramme metric pound used in some places for some time during metrication (see below), and
- an International System of Units (SI) unit of mass, the gramme.

English pounds											
	Pounds					Ounces					
Pound	avpd.	troy	Tower	merc.	London	metric	avpd.	troy	tower	Grains	Grammes
Avoidupois	1	$^{175}/_{144}$	$^{35}/_{27}$	$^{28}/_{27}$	$^{35}/_{36}$	$^{10}/_{11}$	**16**	$14^{7}/_{12}$	$15^{5}/_{9}$	7000	453.59
Troy/ap.	$^{144}/_{175}$	1	$^{16}/_{15}$	$^{64}/_{75}$	$^{5}/_{6}$	$^{3}/_{4}$	$13^{29}/_{175}$	**12**	$12^{4}/_{5}$	5760	373.24
Tower	$^{27}/_{35}$	$^{15}/_{16}$	1	$^{4}/_{5}$	$^{3}/_{4}$	$^{7}/_{10}$	$12^{12}/_{35}$	$11^{1}/_{4}$	**12**	5400	349.91

| Merchant | $^{27}/_{28}$ | $^{75}/_{64}$ | $^{5}/_{4}$ | 1 | $^{15}/_{16}$ | $^{7}/_{8}$ | $15^{3}/_{7}$ | $14^{1}/_{16}$ | 15 | 6750 | 437.39 |
| London | $^{36}/_{35}$ | $^{6}/_{5}$ | $^{4}/_{3}$ | $^{16}/_{15}$ | 1 | $^{14}/_{15}$ | $16\ ^{16}/_{35}$ | 15 | 16 | 7200 | 466.55 |

8. Some of the units related to the pound are given in the following table

Unit	Unit Symbol	Quantity measured	Corresponding SI unit	To convert to SI, multiply by:
Pound per foot second	Ib.ft/s	Momentum	Kilogramme metre per second (kg.m/s)	0.138 255
Pound foot squared	Ib.ft^2	Moment of inertia	Kilogramme per second (kg m^2)	42.140 1 x 10^{-3}
Pound foot squared per second	Ib.ft^2/s	Moment of momentum	Kilogramme metre squared per second (kg.m^2/s)	42.140 1 x 10^{-3}
Pound inch squared	Ib in^2	Moment of inertia	Kilogramme metre squared (kg.m^2)	0.292 640 x 10^{-3}
Pound per acre	Ib/acre	Surface density	Kilogramme per metre squared	0.112 085 x 10^{-3}
Pound per cubic foot	Ib.ft^3	Density (mass)	Kilogramme per cubic metre (kg/m^3)	16.018 5
Pound per cubic inch	Ib.in^3	Density (mass)	Kilogramme per cubic metre (kg/m^3)	27.679 9 x 10^{-3}
Pound per foot	Ib/ft	Linear density	Kilogramme per metre (kg/m)	1.488 16
Pound per gallon (U.K.)	Ib/UKgal	Density (mass)	Kilogramme per cubic metre (kg/m^3)	99.776 4
Pound per gallon (U.S.)	Ib/USgal	Density (mass)	Kilogramme per cubic metre (kg/m^3)	119.826

Pound per hour	Ib/h	Mass flow rate	Kilogramme per second (kg/s)	$0.125\ 998 \times 10^{-3}$
Pound per inch	Ib/in	Linear density	Kilogramme per metre (kg/m)	$17.858\ 0$
Pound per second	Ib/s	Mass flow rate	Kilogramme per second (kg/s)	$0.453\ 592$
Pound per square foot	Ib/ft^2	Surface density	Kilogramme per square metre (kg/m^2)	$4.882\ 43$
Pound per square inch	Ib.in^2	Surface density	Kilogramme per square metre (kg/m^2)	$0.703\ 070 \times 10^{3}$
Pound per square yard	Ib.yd^2	Surface density	Kilogramme per square metre (kg/m^2)	$0.542\ 492$
Pound per thousand square feet	Ib.1000 ft^2	Surface density	Kilogramme per square metre (kg/m^2)	$4.882\ 43 \times 10^{-3}$
Pound per yard	Ib.yd	Linear density	Kilogramme per metre (kg/m)	$0.496\ 055$

pound, troy (lb tr also Ib apoth)

U.K. and U.S. troy and apothecaries unit of mass.

1 Ib tr = 1 Ib apoth = 0.373 241 721 6 kilogrammes

Note: 1. The troy pound has legal standing in the U.S. but not in the U.K.

2. A troy pound is equivalent to 12 troy ounces and to 5,760 grains. Today, the grain is common to the avoirdupois and troy systems of units of mass, and an international troy pound is equivalent to 373.241 721 grammes.

3. The troy pound is no longer in general use. In Canada, Australia, the United Kingdom, and other places, the troy pound is no longer a legal unit for trade. In the United Kingdom, the use of the troy pound was abolished on 6 January 1879.

4. The troy pound is still used for measurements of precious metals such as gold, silver, and platinum and sometimes gems such as opals.

Most measurements of the mass of precious metals using pounds refer to troy pounds, even though it is not always explicitly stated that this is the case. Some notable exceptions are:

- Encyclopedia Britannica (a U.S. encyclopedia for about a century now), which uses either avoirdupois pounds or troy ounces, likely never both in the same article (which would make an awkward system with 14 7/12 ounces to a pound), and

- the mass of King Tut's sarcophagus lid. This is about 110 kilogrammes. It is often stated to have been 242 or 243 (avoirdupois) pounds, but sometimes, much less commonly. It is stated as 296 (troy) pounds.

See also *"troy units."*

pounds, Other pounds

Historically, in different parts of the world, at different points in time, and for different applications, the pound (or its translation) has referred to broadly similar but different standards of mass (weight). Some of these other pounds are described below.

a) French livre or pound

The livre (translated as the pound) is a French name for various units of mass since the Middle Ages. The name continues to be used today to refer to a metric pound (see below).

Notes: 1. The **livre esterlin** was equivalent to about 367.1 grammes and was used between the late 9th century and the mid-14th century.

2. The **livre poids** de marc or **livre de Paris** was equivalent to about 7,555 grains or about 489.5 grammes and was used between the 1350s and the late 18th century. It was introduced by the government of King John II of France.

3. The **livre métrique** was set to be equivalent to the kilogramme or 1,000 grammes, by the decree of *13 Brumaire an IX* between 1800 and 1812. This was a form of official metric pound (see below).

4 The **livre usuelle** was set to be equivalent to 500 grammes, by the decree of 28th March 1812. It was abolished as a unit of mass effective from 1st January 1840 by a decree of 4 July 1837.

b) Jersey pound

A **Jersey pound** is an obsolete unit of mass used on the island of Jersey from the 14th century to the 19th century. It was equivalent to about 7561 grains. It may have been derived from the French livre poids de marc (see above).

c) Roman libra or pound

A **Roman libra** or pound is an ancient unit of mass that was equivalent to approximately 327 grammes. It was divided into 12 *uncia* or ounces.

d) Tower pound

A **Tower pound** was equivalent to 5,400 grains. Prior to 1528, the British monetary unit, also known as the pound, was a Tower pound of silver (worth about £38 today). In 1528, the standard was changed to the Troy pound.

e) Libra mercatoria or mercantile, merchants' or commercial pound

A **mercantile pound or libra mercantoria**, also known as a **merchants' pound** or **commercial pound,** is an obsolete unit of mass used in England for most goods (other than money, spices and electuaries) until a point during the 14th century. It was equivalent to 9600 wheat grains (equivalent to 6750 grains). There were 12 tower ounces in a tower pound and a merchant pound was 15 tower ounces.

f) London or mercantile pound

A **London pound** was equivalent to 7200 grains. A London pound was 16 tower ounces or 15 troy ounces.

g) Wool pound

A **Wool pound** was equivalent to 6992 grains. It was a unit of mass used to measure the quantity of wool.

h) Scottish or trone pound

The **trone pound** is one of the obsolete Scottish units of measurement. It was equivalent to between 21 and 28 avoirdupois ounces.

poundal (pdl)

FPS unit of force. The poundal is the force, which, when applied to a body of mass of one pound, gives it an acceleration of one foot per second squared.

Note: 1. The name of the unit was suggested for the first time in 1876 by James Thomson (1822-1892).

2. The terms **ouncdal** and **tondal** were in use to represent the force required to accelerate 1 ounce, or 1 ton (respectively), by 1 foot per second squared.

3. Some of the FBS units related to the poundal are given in the following table.

Unit	Unit Symbol	Quantity measured	Corresponding SI unit	To convert to SI, multiply by:
Poundal foot	pdl. ft	Moment of force and torque	Newton metre (N.m)	$0.421\ 401 \times 10^{3}$
Poundal per square foot	pdl/ft2	Pressure	Pascal(Pa)	1.488 16
Poundal second per square foot	pdl.s/ft2	Viscosity (dynamic)	Pascal second (Pa.s)	2.488

4. Since the acceleration of gravity averages about 32.174 ft/sec^2 at the Earth's surface, one poundal is about 1/32.174 = 0.031 081 pound of force.

5. One poundal is also equal to approximately 0.138 255 newton, or 13 825.5 dynes.

pound cut (lb cut)

A traditional unit of concentration for shellac in the U.S. One pound cut implies that the shellac was manufactured by dissolving one pound of dry bleached schellac in one gallon of alcohol solvent (about 120 grammes of shellac per liter of solvent). The most common concentrations sold are 3, 4 and 5 lb cut, but diluted solutions of ¼ to 1 lb cut are sometimes used as sealers or polishes.

pound foot (lbf ft or lb-ft)

A traditional unit of torque. Torque is the tendency of a force to cause a rotation. It is the product of the force and the distance from the center of rotation to the point where the force is applied. Thus, it can be measured in pounds of force times feet of distance. One pound foot is equivalent to approximately 1.355 818 newton metres (N.m) in SI units. Algebraically, the torque has the same units as work or energy, but it is a different physical concept. To stress the difference, scientists and engineers traditionally measure torque in pound feet (or newton metres) and work or energy in foot pounds or (or joules).

pound-force (lbf)

FibfS base unit of force. One pound-force is the force, which when applied to a body of mass of one pound, gives it an acceleration equivalent to the standard acceleration of free fall.

1 pound-force = 4.448 221 615 2605 newtons.

Note: 1. It is important to distinguish this unit from the pound-weight, which is a none-coherent unit of force.

2. This unit is known as Pound (spelling with a capital letter) in the Stroud system.

3. Some of the units related to the pound-force are given in the following table.

Unit	Unit Symbol	Quantity measured	Corresponding SI unit	To convert to SI, multiply by:
Pound-force foot	Ibf. ft	Moment of force and torque	Newton metre (N.m)	1.355 82
Pound-force hour per square foot	Ibf. h/ft^2	Viscosity (dynamic)	Pascal second (Pa.s)	0.172 369x 10^6
Pound-force inch	Ibf. in	Moment of force and torque	Newton metre (N.m)	0.112 985
Pound-force per foot	Ibf/ft	Surface tension	Newton per metre (N/m)	14.593 9
Pound-force per inch	Ibf/in	Surface tension	Newton per metre (N/m)	0.175 127 x 10^3

Pound-force per square foot	Ibf/ft^2	Pressure	Pascal (Pa)	47.880 3
Pound-force per square inch	Ibf/in^2	Pressure	Pascal (Pa)	6.894 76 x 10^3
Pound-force second per square foot	Ibf.s/ft^2	Viscosity (dynamic)	Pascal second (Pa.s)	47.880 3

4. Equivalence to other units of force

	Newton (SI unit)	**Dyne**	**Kilogramme-force (kilopond)**	**Pound-force**	**Poundal**
1 N	$= 1$ kg.m/s^2	$= 10^{-5}$ dyn	≈ 0.10197 kp	≈ 0.22481 Ib$_f$	≈ 7.2330 pdl
1 dyn	$= 10^{-5}$ N	$= 1$ g.cm/s^2	$\approx 1.0197 \times 10^{-6}$ kp	$\approx 2.2481 \times 10^{-6}$ Ib$_f$	$\approx 7.2330 \times 10^{-5}$ pdl
1 kp	$= 9.80665$ N	$= 980665$ dyn	$= g_n .(1$ kg$)$	≈ 2.2046 Ib$_f$	≈ 70.932 pdl
1 Ib$_f$	≈ 4.448222 N	≈ 444822 dyn	≈ 0.45359 kp	$= g_n .(1$ lb$)$	≈ 32.174 pdl
1 pdl	≈ 0.138255 N	≈ 13825 dyn	≈ 0.014098 kp	≈ 0.031081 Ib$_f$	$= 1$ lb.ft/ s^2

The value of g_n, as used in the official definition of the kilogramme-force is used here for all gravitational units.

See *"pound-weight"* and *"Pound (Lb)"*.

pound mole (lbmol)

a unit of amount of substance. One pound mole of a chemical compound is the same number of pounds as the molecular weight of a molecule of that compound measured in <u>atomic mass units</u>. Thus the pound mole is equal to exactly 453.592 37 <u>moles</u>.

pound per square foot (lbf/ft^2 or psf)

a traditional unit of pressure. 1 psf equals about 47.880 <u>pascals</u> (Pa), 0.478 80 <u>millibars</u> (mb), or 0.192 79 inch of water (in WC).

pound per square inch (lbf/in^2 or psi)

a traditional unit of pressure. 1 psi equals 144 pounds per square foot (psf), 6.894 75 <u>kilopascals</u> (kPa), 68.9475 <u>millibars</u> (mb), 2.036 inches of mercury (in Hg), 27.7612 inches of water (in WC), or 70.5134 centimeters of water (cm H$_2$O). See below for related notations such as "psig."

pound-weight (ibwt)

Imperial unit of force. One pound-weight is the force, which, when applied to a body of mass of one pound, gives it an acceleration equivalent to the local value of the acceleration of free fall (g) expressed in feet per second square.

1 Ibwt = g poundal = 0.138 254 954 376 g newtons.

Note: The unit is a none-coherent unit and it is recommended to use the pound-force

See "pound-force".

pour cent mille (pcm)

It is a unit of reactivity (a dimensionless quantity that measures the departure of a nuclear reactor from its critical condition).

1 pcm = the amount of reactivity equivalent to 10^{-5}.

See *"nile"*.

pous

It is an ancient Greek foot. It is a unit of distance, equivalent to about 30.7 centimetres, a little longer than the modern English foot. The plural is **podes.**

The pous was divided into 16 daktylos (digits). There were 100 podes in a plethron and 600 in a stadion.

Pouter

Non-conventional unit that measures Obstruction

During World War II, scientists working for the British Department of Miscellaneous Weapons Development encountered a particularly obstructive Royal Navy officer known as Commander Pouter, for whom the unit of Obstruction was named due to his implacable opposition to any work being carried out in the field for which he was personally responsible.

Subsequently, the micropouter was used, as it was hoped that no individual of a similarly difficult disposition would be encountered. The pouter unit was too large for everyday use.

power (x)

[1] A unit expressing the magnifying power of an optical system. The power is defined to be the angular diameter of the image formed by the system divided by the angular diameter of the original object being observed. In simple telescopes, this is equivalent to the focal length of the primary objective (the big lens or mirror) divided by the focal length of the eyepiece lens. For binoculars, the power is customarily followed by the diameter of the objective lenses in millimetres. Therefore, "8x40" indicates binoculars with a magnifying power of 8 and lenses of diameter 40 millimetres.

[2] A measure of the focal power of a lens, which is equivalent to 40 times the focal length or 40 divided by the refractive power in diopters. For example, a 2.00 diopter lens in a pair of reading glasses is also described as 20 power.

[3] A term indicating that a measurement is a multiple of some standard quantity. For example, in computer technology, a 16x CDROM drive spins a disk 16 times faster than a "standard" speed drive.

pra-...

The names of units of rationalized magnetic quantities in the SI international system are obtained by prefixing the corresponding CGSemu unit names with pra- (representing the word "practical"). The idea was suggested at the 1930 meeting of the IEC but never taken up. The following table contains the four units involved.

See *"pragilbert"* and *"praoersted"*.

SI International Unit	Unit Symbol	Quantity measured	SI absolute unit is now used
Pragauss	praGs	Magnetic flux density	Tesla
Pragilbert	praGb	Magnetomotive force	Ampere-turn
Pramaxwell	praMx	Magnetic flux	Weber
praoersted	praOe	Magnetic field strength	Ampere-turn per metre

pragilbert (praGb)

The rationalized unit of magnetomotive force in the SI international system.

1 praGb = 4π ampere-turn

pramaxwell

A practical unit of magnetic flux = 10^8 maxwells or cgs magnetic units. From "practical" plus "maxwell." Recommended by Sub-Committee 2 of the Advisory Committee on Nomenclature of the International Electrotechnical Commission, meeting at Oslo in *1930*, but a number of national delegations objected to the term and it was not adopted.

praoersted (praOe)

The rationalized unit of magnetic field strength in the SI international system.

1 praOe = 4π ampere turns per metre.

practical units of electricity

These are a selection of electromagnetic units multiplied by a numerical factor to render them more useful for practical purposes. Examples are:

Volt	= 10^8 e.m.u.	Joule	= 10^7 e.m.u.
Ampere	= 10^{-1} e.m.u.	Watt	= 10^7 e.m.u.
Coulomb	= 10^{-1} e.m.u.	Henry	= 10^9 e.m.u.
Farad	= 10^{-9} e.m.u.	Oersted	= 1 e.m.u.
Ohm	= 10^9 e.m.u.	Gauss	= 1 e.m.u.

See also *"electromagnetic units of electricity"*.

preece (preece)

Metric unit of electrical resistivity, equivalent to 10^{13} times the product of 1 ohm and 1 metre.

1 preece = 10^{13} ohm metres.

Note: 1. The unit was named after Sir William Henry Preece (1834-1913) in 1900.

2. The name was suggested as unit of resistivity, which was equivalent to 1 megohm quadrant. It was the same numerically as the resistance measured in megohms of a cube with sides 10^7 metres in length.

prime

In France, *14ᵗʰ - 18ᵗʰ centuries*, an extremely small unit of mass was found to be equivalent to ¹⁄₂₄ grain, about 2.213 milligrammes. I was also known as a *carobe*.

1. In Prussia and other German-speaking areas, it is a unit of length used in mines, which is equivalent to ¹⁄₈₀₀ *Lachter* (also known as a *Berglachter* or *Bergwerklachter*). It is also equivalent to ¹⁄₁₀ *Lachterzoll* or 10 *Secondes*. It is also known as a *Peine*. In Prussia, about 2.615 millimetres. In Saxony, about 2.47 millimetres.

The *prime* was made obsolete by a purely decimal division of the *Lachter*.

In Luceme, it is used as unit of liquid capacity and dry capacity:

As of liquid capacity, it is equivalent to ¹⁄₄₀ *Mass*, about 43.2 milliliters

- As of dry capacity, it is equivalent to ¹⁄₁₀ *Becher*, about 217.2 milliliters.

prlsm dioptre (prism dioptre)

Unit of deviating power of a prism. The deviating power P of a prism in prism dioptres is related to the angle of deviation θ of a ray of light by the formula:

$P = 100 \tan \theta.$

Thus, one prism dioptre is the deviating power that corresponds to an angle of deviation of 0.009 999 67 radians.

Note: This unit is used mainly for narrow-angle prisms.

See also *"centrad"*.

promaxwell

CGS unit of magnetic flux.

1 promaxwell= 10^8 maxwells.

Note: The unit was proposed in 1930. It was later replaced by the weber.

This unit is similar to the pramaxwell

See *"maxwell"* and *"weber."*

Proof (alcohol concentration)

An informal unit used for measuring the alcohol concentration

Up to the 20th century, alcoholic spirits were assessed in the U.K. by mixing with gunpowder and testing the mixture to see whether it would still burn. The spirit that passed the test was said to be at 100° proof. The U.K. now uses percentage alcohol by volume at 20 °C (68 °F), where spirit at 100° proof is approximately 57.15% ABV. The U.S. uses a "proof number" of twice the ABV at 60 °F (15.5 °C).

prout (prout)

It is an arbitrary unit of nuclear binding energy. One prout is equivalent to one twelfth of the binding energy of the deuteron. Its experimentally derived value is:

1 prout = 185.7 $\pm$ 0.1 kiloelectronvolts = 195×10^{-6} atomic mass units. = $0.029\ 714 \times 10^{-12}$ joules.

Note: 1. The unit was suggested by Witmer in 1947 because the binding energies of most nuclei are frequently equivalent to some integral of this value (that is mentioned it the definition).

2. Heavy nuclei have binding energies of the order of 42 prouts. Lighter nuclei have binding energies greater than 42 prouts.

3. The name of the unit is after the Scottish physicist William Prout (1786-1850).

PSI (psi)

Imperial unit of pressure. One psi is the pressure resulting from a force of one pound-force, acting uniformly over an area of one square inch.

1 psi = 1 pound-force per square inch.

PSU or psu

An abbreviation for **practical salinity unit**. It is a standard measure of the salinity of seawater. The "unit" is a dimensionless (unitless) ratio obtained by measuring the conductivity of the water sample. Seawater of salinity 35 PSU has the same conductivity as a standard solution of potassium chloride (KCl) with a concentration of 3.243 56 % by mass. A sample of salinity, 1 PSU would have conductivity $\frac{1}{35}$ that of the standard solution. Based on this definition, measurements in PSU are nearly the same as direct measurements of salt ion concentration in parts per thousand.

pud or pood

a traditional unit of weight in Russia. The pud equals 40 funte or 1/30 packen; this is about 16.381 kilograms or 36.11 pounds. The plural is **pudi**.

Puddee

A **puddee** is an obsolete unit of dry volume used in Chennai (formerly Madras) in southern India. It was approximately equivalent to 2.89 imperial pints (1.591264 litres). Later, it was standardised to 100 cubic inches (1.64 litres) and referred to as the **Government puddee**.

After metrication in the mid-20th century, the unit became obsolete.

puff (puff):

Metric unit of capacitance.

1 puff = 1 picrofarad = 10^{-12} Farad

Pulse (p)

A unit of frequency, equivalent to the number of oscillations in 2π seconds, proposed by Sas and Pidduck in *1947*. The unit has never been used.

pulsatance

Unit of angular frequency. The angular frequency in pulsatance of frequency f hertz is $2\pi f$'.

Note: This name was suggested in 1947, but it is currently not used.

It is another name for the unit "pulse."

pulgada

The traditional Spanish inch is equivalent to $\frac{1}{12}$ pie (see above). The pulgada varies from about 23.2 to 21 millimetres (0.913 to 0.949 inches).

pull

A measure of the angular deflection in an overhead utility line at a pole, where the line changes direction. In the U.S., the measurement is defined by drawing an imaginary line between two points on the utility line, 100 feet from the corner pole, one point in each direction. The pull is then defined to be the minimum distance between this imaginary line and the corner pole (in feet). Pull p is related to the angle a of deflection by the formula $p = 100. \sin(a/2)$. This quantity is directly proportional to the sideways force exerted on the corner pole.

pump

In the United States, *the pump is* a unit of liquid capacity. It is the amount dispensed by a single depression of the pump fitted to a bottle, typically containing flavored syrup to be added to a coffee-based beverage.

Using the Monin pump, 1 pump is about 10 milliliters (about 2/3 of a U.S. tablespoon). A Torani pump dispenses slightly less, about 7.5 millilitres (about half of a U.S. tablespoon). The pump is also used for many other similarly-dispensed products with varying magnitudes.

puncheon

A traditional U.K. unit of liquid volume.

The puncheon is often reckoned as equal to 70 gallons. In the U. S. system, that would be about 9.358 cubic feet or 264.98 liters;

In the British Imperial system, it would be about 11.238 cubic feet or 308.34 liters.

There are other versions of the unit;

One puncheon is equivalent to 84 U.S. liquid gallons.

1 puncheon = 84 U.S. liquid gallons = 0.317 975 10 cubic metres;

In another, a puncheon of beer equals 72 gallons (roughly 272.5 liters).

pund

The Scandinavian pound, now reinterpreted as a metric unit, is equivalent to 500 grammes (1.1023 pounds). It is similar to the German pfund. The traditional Swedish (Stockholm) pund was equivalent to about 425.1 grammes (14.995 ounces).

punnet

A small square or sometimes rectangular container for fruit or vegetables, such as strawberries or bean sprouts. When used as a unit of measure, a punnet is generally the same thing as a dry pint in the U.S. or an Imperial pint in Britain. However, grocers use punnets of several sizes to package berries, fresh mushrooms, etc.

pyi

A unit of dry capacity and mass at Burma

- A unit of dry capacity, equivalent to 2¼ imperial quarts, approximately 2.557 liters.
- A unit of mass is approximately equivalent to 2.127 kilogrammes (about 4.69 pounds).

pyong

A traditional Korean unit of area equivalent to about 3.306 square metres or 3.954 square yards. The pyong is widely used in Korea to measure areas both inside and outside buildings. The Taiwanese ping (see above) corresponds closely to the pyong

Pyramid inch

An obsolete unit of length.

The **pyramid inch** is a unit of measure believed to have been used in ancient times by pyramidologists. Supposedly, it was one twenty-fifth of a "sacred cubit," 1.00106 imperial inches, or 2.5426924 centimetres.

pyron (pyron)

Arbitrary unit of power area-density. One pyron is the power area-density that results from a thermal power of one calorie per minute acting uniformly over an area of one square centimetre.

1 pyron = 1 calorie per square centimetre minute. = 697.8 watts per square metre.

Note: The unit was for some time known as a **langley.**

See *"langley"*.

Q

q- [1]

A symbol for the Latin *quaque*, "every," often used in medical prescriptions and orders. The symbol is used in combinations such as **q8h**, "every 8 hours," or **q2d**, "every other day."

q- [2]

A former German prefix meaning *quadrat-*, "square," seen in combinations such as **qm** (*Quadratmeter* or square meter) and **qkm** (*Quadratkilometer* or square kilometer). The SI does not allow the use of this symbol; it is rarely used in current works but is often seen in older documents.

q.d.

Abbreviation for the Latin *quaque die*, once a day, a unit of frequency traditionally used in medical prescriptions. This notation is sometimes modified for a lesser frequency by imbedding a number of days in the middle, as in **q.2d.**, every two days.

q.h.

Abbreviation for the Latin *quaque hora*, once an hour, a unit of frequency traditionally used in medical prescriptions. This notation is sometimes modified for a lesser frequency by imbedding a number of hours in the middle, as in **q.3h.**, every three hours.

Q

A metric unit of distance equal to exactly 0.25 millimeter (9.8425 mils) is used by typographers and page designers in Japan, in Germany, and in other countries in preference to the traditional point. One Q is equal to about 0.71 point, a little more or less depending on the exact definition of the point. This unit is also spelled **kyu**.

See also *"point."*

qadah

Informal unit for mass and capacity in some Arabic countries.

1.   In Aden: a unit of mass = 200 pounds (approximately 90.72 kilogrammes).

2.   In Sudan, a unit of dry capacity, approximately 2.0625 liters (about 1.87 U.S. dry quarts). Plural, akdah.

qadam

Informal unit of length is used in some Arab countries. It means foot.

1 qadam = 1 foot = 30.48 centimeters.

qama

A common Arabic unit of length. About 2 meters long.

In Aden, a unit of length = 5.5 feet (approximately 1.68 meters).

The unit belongs to the fathom family of units.

Qantar (also, kantar)

Various units of mass in the Middle East descended from the Islamic *kintar* or *qintar*, which in turn comes from the Roman *centarius*, the root meaning of both being 100 of a smaller unit.

1.   In Malta, a unit of mass = 100 rtal = 175 pounds (approximately 79.379 kilogrammes).

Like many Maltese units, the qantar shows traces of both the Arabic and British periods in the island's history. The value comes from assimilating British weights.

2.   In Egypt, a unit of mass = 45 kilogrammes.

In the *19th century,* = 100 *rtal* or *rottolo* = 45.35 kilogrammes. According to Doursther, in Alexandria, the *qantar* was already simply 45 kilogrammes and the same value was often used in Cairo as well.

See also "qintar"

qian

A traditional Chinese weight unit. In modern China, the qian is equal to 0.1 liang, or exactly 5 grams (0.1764 ounces).

See *"liang"*

q.i.d.

Abbreviation for the Latin *quater in die*, four times a day, a unit of frequency traditionally used in medical prescriptions.

qing

Informal unit of area.

In China, a unit of area = 100 *mu*, = 6²/₃ hectares (approximately 16.4737 acres).

qintar

A traditional Arabic unit of weight often called the cantar in English.

The qintar is the Arabic counterpart of the European quintal. The unit varied in size from market to market and over time.

In recent years, the qintar has been interpreted as an informal metric unit equal to 50 kilogrames (110.23 pounds); traditional qintars tended to be a few percent larger than this.

The qintar is equal to 100 rotls.

See *"quintal"* and *"rotls"*

qirat or qirat barsoum

In Egypt, a unit of length approximately 0.87 millimeters (approximately 0.034 inch).

quad

An imperial unit for energy.

1 quad $=10^{15}$ Btu.

This is approximately 1.055×10^{18} jouls

This unit is often used for national power supplies.

This unit is used for such purposes as reporting the total annual energy consumption in the American economy. One quad is roughly the amount of energy in:

- 44 million short tons of bituminous coal
- 172 million barrels of crude oil
- 980 billion standard cubic feet of dry natural gas
- 190 million barrels of motor gasoline
- 3.64 trillion standard cubic feet of hydrogen

Note: 1. USA's total energy consumption is about 80 quad per year.

2. It is also proposed as a large unit of length = ten million metres, or approximately the length of an earth quadrant."

quadbit

A unit of information equal to 4 bits or 1/2 byte. This unit is used in telecommunications, where data is frequently transmitted in quadbits. In other contexts, the same unit is called a tetrad, a nibble, or a hexit.

See also *"bit," "byte," and "nibble."*

quadra

A land area unit used in Brazil

Unit	Dimensions	Locale	Area in square meters
quadra gaúcha	60 *braças* × 60 *braças*	"widely used in Rio Grande do Sul"[1]	17,424

quadra de sesmaria	60 *braças* × 1 *légua*	"still common among ranchers in Rio Grande do Sul."[1]	871,200
quadra paraibana	50 *braças* × 50 *braças*		12,100

quadrant (quad)

Unit of plane angle in all systems of units.

1 quadrant = 90° = π/2 radian.

Note: 1. The unit is also called right angle.

2. In the MKSA system, "quadrant" is a unit of inductance. It was also sometimes used at the end of the nineteenth century as a unit of length

See *"right angle"*.

Quadrant, inductance (quad)

MKSA unit of inductance. One quadrant is the inductance of a closed circuit, which gives rise to a magnetic flux of one international Weber per international ampere.

1 quadrant = 1 international Weber per international ampere.

Note: 1. The 2nd International Electrical Congress of 1889 gave this name to the practical unit of coefficient of induction (a quantity now called inductance).

2. It is better to call the unit the **international Henry.**

3. The unit is also called the **secohm.**

4"quadrant" is used in all the systems of unit as a unit of angle:

1 quadrant = 90° = π/2 radian.

It was also sometimes used at the end of the nineteenth century as a unit of length.

See *"secohm"*.

quadrant (quad)

Metric unit of length.

1 quadrant = 10^7 meters

Note: 1. This unit was originally meant to be the length of the earth's meridional quadrant through Dunkirk and a point close to Barcelona.

2. "quadrant" is used in all the systems of units as a unit of plane angle:
l quadrant $\pi/2$ rad $= 90°$.

3. In the MKSA system, "quadrant" is a unit of inductance

quadrat- [q-]

A German prefix meaning "square." For example, the square kilometer is the quadratkilometer (qkm or km^2) in German.

quadrennium

A traditional unit of time equal to four years.

quadrimester

A unit of time equal to 4 months. Rare in the U.S., this unit is widely used elsewhere to describe an academic term of 4 months duration.

quadrumvirate

A unit of quantity equal to 4. The word was coined on the pattern of triumvirate.

quadruplet

a group of 4 items, especially 4 identical items; the word is also used for one member of the group.

quadword

A unit of information equal to 4 shortwords, 8 bytes, or 64 bits.

See also "byte" and "bit."

quantum

Arbitrary unit of energy associated with electromagnetic radiation. The energy E in quanta is related to the frequency f of the electromagnetic radiation in hertz by the formula:

$E = hf$

where h is Planck's constant $= 6.624\ 9$ x 10^{-34} joule second.

Note: 1. This unit was introduced by Planck in 1900.

2. In case of light energy, it is better to use the names **photon** or **ergon** instead of the name quantum.

See *"photon"* and *"ergon."*

quantum electrodynamics system of units

System of units used in the study of radiations (e.g., β- and γ- rays). The fundamental quantities in the system are the rest mass of an electron m, the action ($h/2\pi$, where h is Planck's constant), the velocity of light c and the electric constant (ε^o). The derived units are the length (λ_{ce} = the Compton wavelength of the electron), the charge [$(2\varepsilon_o hc)^{1/2}$], the time ($\lambda_{ce}/c$) and the energy ($mc^2$)

Note: The system is one of two systems of units form the Natural Systems of Units. The other system is the **Atomic System of Units (or Hartree System of Units),** which is often employed in the study of atomic structure.

See *"Atomic system of units".*

quarro

An obsolete Italian unit for length and mass

1.   In Lucca and Siena, Italy, in the *15th century*, a unit of length used for cloth, = ¼ *braccio*, about 146 centimeters.

2.   In Venice, *15th century*, a unit of mass for gold and precious stones = ¼ *oncia*. If the Venetian *grano* of the weight of the marc was ($\sim$238.5/4608 =) $\sim$0.052 grams, the *quarro* would be $\sim$1.24 grams.

quart, UK (UK qt)

UK arbitrary unit of volume (capacity). One UK quart equal to 2 UK pint or 1/4 gallon.

1 UK quart = **2** UK pints = **0.25** UK gallon = 0.001 136 52 cubic meter.

Note: 1. The UK quart is used for the measurement of liquid and solid substances.

2. There is a mention of a quart as a measure of ale in Chaucer's Miller's Tale (1390).

3. Until 1952, wines and spirits were measured in the UK in reputed quarts. Following the establishment of Imperial measure, the reputed quart was fixed at 2/3 imperial quart, which is equivalent to exactly 26 2/3 fluid ounces, about 46.24 cubic inches, or 757.682 milliliters.

4. In the U.S., wine was often measured by the champagne quart, which contains only 26 US fluid ounces instead of 32. This is equivalent to about 46.92 cubic inches or approximately 768.912 milliliters.

5. These measures have mostly disappeared in favor of the international wine bottle, which contains exactly 750 milliliters.

See *"quart, reputed', "pint, UK," "bottle,"* and *"gallon."*

quart, reputed

UK arbitrary unit of volume.

1 reputed quart = 26.67 fluid ounces = 0.761 x 10^{-3} cubic meter.

Note: Until the passing of the 1952 Customs and Excise Act, the reputed quart was used to measure the volume of wines and spirits. The UK quart is now in use.

See *"quart, UK"*.

QUART (US, DRY) (qt)

US imperial unit of volume (capacity) of solid substances. One US dry quart equal to 2 US dry pints or 1/32 bushel.

1 US dry quart = 2 US dry pints = 1.101 221 x 10^{-3} cubic meter

Note: The US dry quart is used only for the measurement of solid substances.

See *"bushel" and "pint."*

quart (US LIQUID) (qt)

US imperial unit of volume (capacity) of liquid substances. One US liquid quart equals 2 US liquid pints or 1/4 US gallon.

1 US liquid quart = 2 US liquid pints = 0.946 352 9 x 10^{-3} cubic meter.

Note: This unit is used only for the measurement of liquid substances.

See *"pint, liquid"* and *"gallon"*.

Quarta

An obsolete unit used in many countries

1. In the Cape Verde Islands, they are currently using it as two units:
   - One of the area = ¼ *alqueres*, approximately 4646.4 square meters (approximately 1.148 acres).

- One of dry capacity, = ¼ *alquiere*, approximately 10.398 liters (about 9.442 U.S. dry quarts).

2. In Florence and Venice, *16ᵗʰ century*, a unit of length = ¼ *braccio*, about 17.15 centimeters.

3. In Italy during the *16ᵗʰ century*, a unit of dry capacity = ¼ *moggio* or = ¼ *staio*.

4. In Venice, a unit of liquid capacity used for wine = ¼ *biconcia*.

See also "quart."

quarte

In France, a unit of dry capacity about 3.25 liters (about 2.95 U.S. dry quarts). In the Système Usuel (*1812 – 1839*), it was 3.125 liters.

quarter (qtr)

Arbitrary unit of volume (capacity). One quarter equal 8 UK bushels.

1 quarter = 8 UK bushel = 0.290 950 cubic meter.

Note: 1. This unit is in use in the UK for the measurement of liquid and solid substances.

2. The term "quarter" is used also as a unit of mass in UK and US.

3. The unit is also called seam.

See *"seam"*.

quarter (qtr or Q)

A unit of distance equal to 1/4 yards or 9 inches (22.86 centimeters). The quarter with this definition was frequently used in cloth measurement in medieval England, and it has continued to be used on occasion down to the present day. In particular, the English ell was often described as being equal to 5 quarters.

This unit is identical to the span.

See also *"span."*

quarter, UK avoirdupois (qr)

UK imperial unit of mass. One UK quarter equals one quarter of UK hundredweight.

1 qr = **0.25** UK hundredweight = 12.700 586 36 kilogramme.

quarter, US avoirdupois (quarter)

US imperial unit of mass. One US quarter equal one quarter of the US ton.

1 quarter = **0.25** US ton = 226.796 185 kilogramme.

quarter, troy (qr tr)

Imperial unit of mass. One troy quarter equal quarter of the troy hundredweight.

1 qr tr = **0.25** troy hundredweight = 9.331 043 O4 kilogramme.

quartern, UK dry

UK unit of volume (capacity) equal 1/4 UK peck or half UK gallon.

1 UK dry quartern = **0.25** UK peck = 0.5 UK gallon = 2.273 044 x 10^{-3} cubic meter.

See *"peck"*.

quartern, UK liquid

UK unit of volume (capacity)

1 UK liquid quartern = 0.142 065 2 x 10^{-3} cubic meter.

quartern loaf

A traditional English unit of weight for bread.

A quartern-loaf is made from a quartern of flour. The finished loaf usually weighs somewhere between 4 and 5 pounds (very roughly 2 kilogrammes).

quarter hour

In the United States, a unit of academic credit, obtained by satisfactorily completing a course that meets for one hour per week (or, typically, for three hours of lab work) over an academic quarter.

quarto

1. In Portugal, a unit of capacity is 3.46 liters (about 3.14 U.S. dry quarts).

2. In Brazil, a unit of dry capacity is 9.07 liters (about 8.23 U.S. dry quarts).

3. In Rome, 2.024 imperial bushels.

quarter tone

a unit used in music to describe the ratio in frequency between notes. The quarter tone, equal to 1/24 octave, is the basic interval in a 24-tone scale. Two notes differ by a quarter tone if the ratio in their frequencies is $2^{1/24} = 1.0293$.

See also "octave"

quartet

A unit of quantity equal to 4.

quartile

A statistical unit equal to 25 percentiles, or 1/4 of a ranked sample.

quarto [1]

A traditional Italian unit of volume equal to about 73.6 liters or 2.60 cubic feet.

quarto [2]

A traditional Portuguese unit of volume, not related to the Italian quarto nor to the English quart. The Portuguese quarto equals 2 oitavos, which is about 3.46 liters or 0.92 U.S. gallons. There are 16 quartos in a fanega, 124 in a pipa.

See also "gallon", "fanega" and "pipa"

quarto [3]

In English, a quarto is a page size.

quaver

a unit of relative time in music equal to 1/8 whole note or 1/16 breve.

Quibi

A unit of time equal to 10 minutes. First used in Quibi's own Super Bowel LIII advertising campaign, this word saw small amounts of ironic adoption.

Quibi (/ˈkwɪbi/ *KWIB-ee*) was an American short-form streaming platform that generated content for viewing on mobile devices and launched at the onset of the COVID-19 pandemic. It was founded in Los Angeles in August 2018 as **NewTV** by Jeffrey Katzenberg and was led by Meg Whitman, its CEO. The service raised $1.75 billion from investors.[1] It launched in April 2020 but shut down in December 2020 after falling short of its subscriber projections. In January 2021, Quibi's content library was sold to Roku, Inc. for less than $100 million.

quilate

An informal unit of mass

1. In Colombia, *in the 20th century*, a unit of mass = 200 milligrams, the metric carat.

2. In Portugal and Brazil (during the *19th century*), a unit of mass used for precious metal and stones about 199.1 milligrams. According to Doursther (*1840*), in Lisbon 205.8 mg and in Rio de Janeiro 199.2 mg. According to Klimpert (*1892*), 205.83 mg in both cities.

3. In Spain, a unit of mass for precious stones, *19th century*, = 4 Castillian *granos* = $\frac{1}{140}$ of a Castillian *onza* used for precious stones, about 199.7 milligrams. According to Klimpert, 199.693 mg.

Quinaria

A **quinaria** (plural: quinariae) is a Roman unit of area roughly equal to 4.2 square centimetres (0.65 in^2). Its primary use was to measure the cross-sectional area of pipes in Roman water distribution systems. A "one quinaria" pipe is 2.31 centimetres (0.91 in) in diameter.

Notes: 1. In Roman times, there was considerable ambiguity regarding the origin of the name and the actual value of a quinaria. According to Frontinus

1. Those who refer (the quinaria) to Vitruvius and the plumbers declare that it was so named from the fact that a flat sheet of lead 5 digits wide, made up into a round pipe, forms this ajutage. But this is indefinite because the plate, when made up into a round shape, will be extended on the exterior surface and contracted on the interior surface. The most probable explanation is that the quinaria received its name from having a diameter of 5/4 of a digit...

2. In other words, Vitruvius claimed that the name was derived from a pipe created from a flat sheet of lead "5 digits wide", roughly 9.25 centimetres (3.64 in), but Frontinus contested the definitiveness of this because the exterior circumference of the resulting pipe

would be larger than the interior circumference. According to Frontinus, the name and value is derived from a pipe having a diameter of "5/4 of a digit". Using Vitruvius' standard, the value of a quinaria is 6.81 square centimetres (1.056 sq in), and the resulting pipe would have a diameter of 2.94 centimetres (1.16 in).

The importance of this measure was that water taxes in ancient Rome were based on the size of the supply pipe.

quincena

A unit of time in Spanish-speaking countries generally considered equivalent to the English fortnight: two weeks or 14 days. However, the word is derived from *quince*, fifteen, indicating a period of two weeks that begins on one day and ends on the fifteenth day, two weeks later. Like fortnight, quincena is often used informally to refer to a period of approximately two weeks or half a month. The same unit is called the **quindicina** in Italian, the **quinzena** in Portuguese and the **quinzaine** in French.

quinquennium

A traditional unit of time equal to five years.

quint

An informal unit of dry capacity

On the island of Guernsey, during the *19th century*, it was a unit of dry capacity used for grain,

1 quint = 54.4 cubic inches.

quintal (q)

1. Metric unit of mass.

    1 quintal = **100** kilogramme.

    Note: This unit is also called the **metric centner**.

2. Imperial unit of mass.

    1 quintal = **100** pound = 45.359 237 kilogramme.

Note: 1. This unit is called **centner** and also **cental.** In US, this unit is called **short hundredweight.**

2. Quintal is a traditional unit of weight in France, Portugal, and Spain.

3. Quintal is also the generic name for a historic unit used in commerce throughout Europe and the Arab world for more than 2,000 years. The unit began as the Latin *centenarius*, meaning "comprised of 100" because it was equal to 100 Roman pounds. The centenarius passed into Arabic as the cantar or *qintar* and then returned to Europe through Arab traders in the form *quintal*.

4. The German zentner and English hundredweight are familiar forms of this same unit in northern Europe.

5. The traditional French quintal equaled 100 livres (48.95 kilogrammes or 107.9 pounds), but today the word "quintal" in France usually means a larger metric unit (see next entry). 6. The Spanish quintal is 100 libras (about 46 kilogrammes or 101 pounds).

7. The Portuguese quintal is larger; it is equal to 128 libras (about 129.5 pounds or 58.75 kilogrammes).

8. "Kwintal" is the English pronunciation given in Standard English dictionaries, but "kintal" (closer to the Spanish pronunciation) and "kantal" (closer to the French) are also used.

quintal (q) [1]

a traditional unit of weight in France, Portugal, and Spain. Quintal is also the generic name for a historic unit used in commerce throughout Europe and the Arab world for more than 2,000 years. The unit began as the Latin *centenarius*, meaning "comprised of 100" because it was equal to 100 Roman pounds. The centenarius passed into Arabic as the cantar or *qintar* and then returned to Europe through Arab traders in the form of a *quintal*. The German zentner and English hundredweight are familiar forms of this same unit in northern Europe. The traditional French quintal equaled 100 livres (48.95 kilogrammes or 107.9 pounds), but today the word "quintal" in France usually means a larger metric unit (see next entry). The Spanish quintal is 100 libras (about 46 kilogrammes or 101 pounds). The Portuguese quintal is larger; it is equal to 128 libras (about 129.5

pounds or 58.75 kilogrammes). "Kwintal" is the English pronunciation given in standard English dictionaries, but "kintal" (closer to the Spanish pronunciation) and "kantal" (closer to the French) are also used.

See also "cantar," "hundredweight," and "libra."

quintal (q) [2]

A common metric unit of mass equal to 100 kilogrammes or approximately 220.4623 pounds. Notice that the metric ton is roughly equal to its non-metric predecessors, but the metric quintal is about twice the size of the traditional quintal.

quire (qr)

A traditional unit of quantity used for counting sheets of paper. The word is from Latin, meaning "by fours." A quire was originally comprised of 24 sheets cut from four of the large sheets produced by the paper maker. In modern use, a quire is often reckoned as 25 sheets, so that a ream of 20 quires is now 500 sheets rather than the traditional 480.
See also "ream."

Q-unit (Q)

Arbitrary unit of potential heat energy of fuel reserves.
1 Q 2 10^{18} British thermal unit = 10^{21} joules.
Note: The unit was used originally by Sir John Cockroft in 1953 to express the world's fuel reserve.

qvinter [Danish]

In Denmark, a unit of length = $\frac{1}{144}$ *linie* = $\frac{1}{12}$ *skrupel*, about 0.01513 millimeters.

R

A commercial unit used to measure the effectiveness of thermal insulation.

A thermal insulator is a material manufactured in sheets that resists conducting heat energy. Its thermal conductance is measured, in traditional units, in Btu's of energy conducted times inches of thickness per hour of time per square foot of area per Fahrenheit degree of temperature difference between the two sides of the material. The **R-value** of the insulator is defined to be 1 divided by the thermal conductance per inch. This means R is an abbreviation for the complex unit combination hr.ft^2.°F/Btu. In SI units, an R-value of 1 equals 0.17611 square meter kelvins per watt (m^2.K/W). In clothing insulation units, this is about 1.136 do or 1.761 1 tog.

See also *"Btu"*

rabia

An informal unit of area.

In Morocco, a unit of area = 450 square meters (approximately 538.2 square yards).

racíon

An informal unit of capacity.

In Spain, a unit of capacity, about 0.29 liters (about 0.615 U.S. liquid pints)

rack unit

An informal unit of length. Symbol U.

1 *rack unit* (U) = 1.75 inches (44.45 mm)

It is used to measure rack-mountable audiovisual, computing and industrial equipment.

Rack units are typically denoted without a space between the number of units and the 'U.' Thus, a 4U server enclosure (case) is seven inches (177.8 mm) high, or more practically, built to occupy a vertical space seven inches high, with sufficient clearance to allow movement of adjacent hardware.

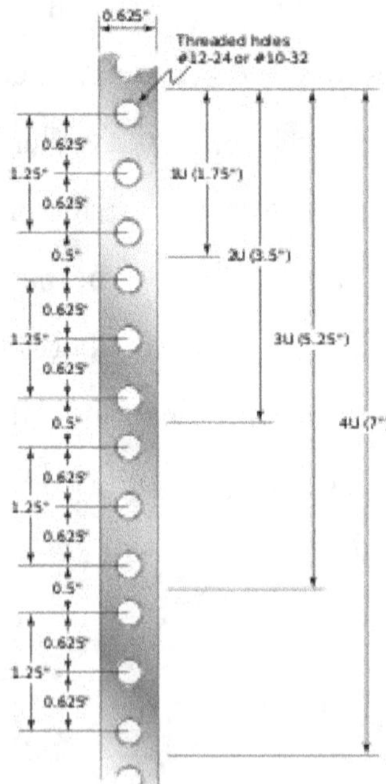

A typical section of rack rail, showing rack unit distribution

rad (rad, sometimes rd)

Arbitrary unit of absorbed ionizing radiation dose for the inorganic matter. One rad is equivalent to energy absorption per unit mass of 0.01 joules per kilogram of irradiated material.

1 rad = 0.01 joules per kilogram.

Note: 1. The rad was defined in CGS units by the International Commission of Radiology in 1953 and restated in the SI units (the above definition) in 1970.

2. In 1950, the rad replaced the roentgen for clinical work involving X-rays or radioactive sources. 1n air, an experiment has shown that 1 rad is equivalent to 1.15 roentgen. The numerical equivalent is different for other media. Unlike the roentgen, the rad is applicable to all types of radiation.

3. The symbol of this unit, "rad," is the same as the symbol of the unit radian. The symbol rd may be used to avoid confusion.

4. The rad has been replaced by the **gray**, equal to 100 rads.

See *"roentgen"* and *"gray."*

radar mile

The time required for a radar signal to travel a distance of one mile from the transmitter to an object and then return to the receiver. Both ordinary (statute) and nautical miles are used: the radar statute mile is about 10.8 microseconds (μs) and the **radar nautical mile** is about 12.4 microseconds. A radar kilometer would be about 6.7 microseconds.

radian (rad)

Supplementary SI unit of (plane) angle. One radian is the plane angle between two radii of a circle, which cut off on the circumference of an arc equal in length to the radius.

1 rad = 180/ π

Note: 1. It is also an SI unit of phase difference.

   2. A thousandth of a radian is sometimes called a **mil.**

   3. Use of the degree and its decimal submultiples is permissible when the radian is not a convenient unit. Use of minute and second is discouraged except for special fields such as cartography.

   4. The CIPM of 1980 specified that in the SI, the quantities plane angle and solid angle should be considered as dimensionless derived quantities. Therefore, the supplementary units' radian and steradian are to be regarded as dimensionless derived units, which may be used or omitted in the expressions for derived units.

See "mil".

radian per meter (rad m^{-1})

Unit of phase coefficient.

radian per minute (rad min^{-1})

Unit for angular velocity used with SI system.

1 radian per minute = 1.66667 x 10^{-2} radians per second.

radian per second (rad s^{-1})

SI unit of angular velocity and circular frequency.

radian per second squared (rad s^{-2})

SI unit of angular acceleration.

Radiation dose (Strontium unit)

The strontium unit, formerly known as the Sunshine Unit (symbol S.U.), is a unit of biological contamination by radioactive substances (specifically strontium-90). It is equal to one picocurie of Sr-90 per gram of body calcium. Since about 2% of the human body mass is calcium, and Sr-90 has a half-life of 28.78 years, releasing 6.697+2.282 MeV per disintegration, this works out to about 1.065×10^{-12} grays per second. The permissible body burden was established at 1,000 S.U.

radiation unit (ru)

Arbitrary unit of length in cosmic-ray studies.

1 radiation unit = ln 2 shower units.

Note: 1. This unit is also called **radiation length** or the **cascade unit.**

2. The radiation unit is an individual unit of length, i.e., its size depends on the conditions of a given set of circumstances.

See *"shower unit."*

radiocarbon year (^{14}C yr, yr BP)

A unit used in stating the nominal ages of plant or animal remains dated by radiocarbon testing. A very small proportion (roughly 1 part per trillion, or 10^{-12}) of the carbon in the ecosystem is radioactive carbon-14, which decays to nitrogen-14 with a half-life of about 5760 years. While a plant or animal is alive, the fraction of radioactive carbon in its body remains equal to the fraction in the atmosphere at that time. After a plant or animal dies, as the carbon-14 trapped in its body slowly decays, the age of the tissue can be measured by the fraction of radioactive carbon remaining. The age T of a sample, in radiocarbon years, is computed from the formula T = -8033 ln (R/A), where R is the measured ratio of carbon-14 to ordinary carbon-12 in the sample and A is a benchmark ratio measured in the atmosphere in 1950. Results are often stated as years before the present (yr BP), with 1950 representing the "present." The results are inaccurate for two reasons. One is that the formula assumes a half-life of 5568 years, which is now known to be too short. More importantly, the ratio of carbon-14 to ordinary carbon-12 in the atmosphere varies slightly over time. Much research has been done to determine the necessary corrections. As an example, a sample with a nominal age of 12,000 radiocarbon years has an actual age of about 14,000 ears. See the next table.

Age in Radiocarbon years	Age in Calendar years
9 600	11 000
10 200	12 000
11 000	13 000
12 000	14 000
12 700	15 000
13 300	16 000
14 200	17 000
15 000	18 000
15 900	19 000
16 800	20 000
17 600	21 000
18 500	22 000
19 300	23 000
20 000	24 000

rai

A traditional unit of land area in Thailand. The rai is now considered to equal exactly 1600 square meters, which is 0.16 hectares.

The rai is divided into 4 **ngan.** The unit is called the **hai** in northern Thailand and the **lai** in Laos. The word means "field," that is, an upland field rather than a rice paddy.

ram (ram)

CGS unit of acoustical or mechanical resistance, reactance and impedance.

1 ram = 1 acoustical or mechanical ohm.

Note: 1. The name of the unit was suggested by McLachlan in 1934 as an alternative for either the acoustical ohm or the mechanical ohm. The name ray was also suggested.

2. The names ram and ray were intended to commemorate the third Lord Rayleigh (1842-1919), a pioneer of acoustic measurement.

See *"ray", "Rayl'* and *"Rayleigh"*.

Rankine degree (degR)

Arbitrary unit of temperature interval or difference.

1 degR = 1 Fahrenheit degree = **(5/9)** kelvin.

Note: The original definition was: 1 Rankine degree equal **(1/180)** of the interval between the freezing and boiling points of pure air-free water, both under the pressure of one standard atmosphere.

ra -size

Metric unit of a size to which untrimmed paper is manufactured.

Rat Unit

1. (International Rat Unit) A unit of quantity of vitamin E, determined by the following biological assay. When a group of pregnant rats do not get enough vitamin E, they do not give birth; the fetuses are absorbed. One International Rat Unit is the minimum amount of *dl*-alpha-tocopherol acetate that must be given orally to tocopherol-deficient rats to prevent absorption of the fetuses in 50% of the rats.

2. A unit of mass for riboflavin = 4 micrograms of riboflavin

ray (ray)

CGS unit of acoustical or mechanical resistance, reactance and impedance.

1 ray = 1 acoustical or mechanical ohm.

Note: 1. The name of the unit was suggested by McLachlan in 1934 as an alternative for either the acoustical ohm or the mechanical ohm. The name ram was also suggested.

2. The names ram and ray were intended to commemorate the third Lord Rayleigh (1842-1919), a pioneer of acoustic measurement.

See *"ram," "Rayl,"* and *"Rayleigh"*.

rayl (rayl)

CGS unit of specific acoustical resistance, reactance and impedance. One rayl is the ratio of a sound pressure of one dyne per square centimeter to a sound particle velocity of one centimeter per second.

1 rayl = 10 pascals second per meter.

Note: 1. The unit is also called the **specific acoustical ohm**.

2. The unit is also equal to the product of the density of the gas and the velocity of sound in the gas. The air has, accordingly, a specific acoustic impedance of 40.7 rayl.

3. The name of the unit is after the third Lord Rayleigh (1842-1919).

rayleigh (R)

Arbitrary unit of brightness, especially of the night sky and of the aurora.

1 R = $10^{10}/4\pi$ quanta per meter squared second steradian.

Using the definition of the quantum in terms of the frequency f of the radiation in hertz,

1 R = 5 .272 O x 10^{12} f watt per meter squared steradian.

Note: The unit name is after the fourth Lord Rayleigh (1875-1947).

real

Informal unit of mass

In the Dutch East Indies and later Indonesia, *in-20ᵗʰ century*, a unit of mass used for precious metals equal to half a thail, approximately 27.045 grams. Also spelled reaal.

ream (rm) [1]

A traditional unit of quantity used for counting sheets of paper. The word is thought to be derived from the Arabic rizmah, meaning a bundle. A ream is equal to 20 quires, which would be 480 sheets, with the traditional definition of a quire as 24 sheets. In recent years, however, the ream has been redefined to equal 500 sheets. (Working backward, this changes the definition of a quire from 24 to 25 sheets.) The new definition reflects the current practice of marketing many kinds of paper in packages of 500 sheets. The older size of 480 sheets is now called a **short ream.**

ream (rm) (2)

A traditional unit of area equal to 3000 square feet (about 278.709 square meters). This unit represents the total area of a ream (1) of 500 full-size sheets of paper, each sheet being 3 feet by 2 feet. The "area ream" is commonly used in the U.S. paper industry for kraft paper, paperboard, and similar products, and it is also being used for non-paper products such as window films and other plastic films.

Reaumur degree (deg r)

Arbitrary unit of temperature interval or difference.

1 deg r = **1.25** kelvin.

Note: The original definition of the Reaumur degree was: one reaumur degree is one eightieth of the interval between the freezing and boiling points of pure air-free water, both under a pressure of one standard atmosphere.

rebah

An ancient Hebrew unit of weight or mass equal to 1/4 shekel.

The word means "quarter" in Hebrew.

reciprocal cubic meter (m^{-3})

SI unit of number density (Examples: acceptor number density, donor number density, electron number density, hole number density, intrinsic number density, neutron number density, number density of molecules or particles), and molecular concentration.

reciprocal cubic meter reciprocal second ($m^{-3}\ s^{-1}$)

SI unit of volume collision rate.

reciprocal electronvolt reciprocal cubic meter ($eV^{-1}\ m^{-3}$)

Unit for density of states used with SI system.

$1\ eV^{-1}\ m^{-3} = 6.24146 \times 10^{18}\ J^{-1}m^{-3}$

reciprocal Farad (F^{-1})

SI unit of elastance (reciprocal capacitance).

reciprocal Henry (H^{-1})

SI unit of reluctance.

reciprocal joule reciprocal cubic meter ($J^{-1}m^{-3}$)

SI unit of density of states.

reciprocal Kelvin (K^{-1})

SI unit of linear expansion coefficient.

Note: Also, unit of cubic expansion coefficient and relative pressure coefficient.

reciprocal megakelvin (MK^{-1})

A unit used in colorimetry and photography to measure the wavelength of light, especially for selecting filters to adjust the "color temperature." Light waves of a specific wavelength w meters can be assigned a temperature T using the theory of blackbody radiation. A blackbody is an ideal object that absorbs all the radiation it receives. If a blackbody is heated to temperature T, the radiation it gives off will have maximum intensity at wavelength w, where w and T are related by Wien's law, $wT = 2.90 \times 10^{-3}$ meter kelvins. The reciprocal of temperature, $1/T = w/(2.90 \times 10^{-3})$ K^{-1}, is thus a measure of wavelength. The wavelengths of visible light fall in the range 400 nanometers (extreme violet) to 700 nanometers (extreme red), corresponding to reciprocal temperatures in the range from roughly 130 MK^{-1} to 240 MK^{-1}. The reciprocal megakelvin has also been called the **mired.**

reciprocal meter (m^{-1})

SI unit of wavenumber and circular wavenumber.

Note: 1. Also, SI unit of attenuation coefficient, linear absorption coefficient, linear attenuation coefficient, linear ionization, macroscopic cross section, phase coefficient, power of lens, propagation coefficient and Rydberg constant.

2. In case of power of a lens, it is called diopter.

See *"diopter."*

reciprocal mole (mol^{-1})

SI unit of Avogadro constant.

reciprocal Pascal (Pa^{-1})

SI unit of compressibility.

reciprocal Pascal reciprocal second (Pa-1 s-1)

SI unit of dynamic fluidity.

reciprocal second (s^{-1})

SI unit of circular (angular, rotational) frequency.

Note: 1. Also, SI unit of collision rate, damping coefficient, decay constant, and velocity gradient.

called hertz,

See *"becquerel"*, *"curie,"* *"rutherford,"* and *"frequency".*

reciprocal second reciprocal cubic meter (s^{-1} m^{-3})

SI unit of slowing-down density and total neutron source density.

reciprocal second reciprocal square meter (s^{-1} m^{-2})

SI unit of molecule flow rate density and neutron fluence rate.

Note: See also reciprocal square meter reciprocal second.

reciprocal square meter (m^{-2})

SI unit of particle fluence.

reciprocal square meter reciprocal second (m^{-2} s^{-2})

SI unit of particle fluence rate, current density of particles and impingement rate.

Note: See also reciprocal second reciprocal square meter.

recommended dietary allowance (RDA)

units used in the U.S. to measure the amounts of certain nutrients found in foods or provided by supplements such as vitamin tablets. Each nutrient has its own RDA unit. **Link: Dietary Reference Intakes** from the University of Texas.

redshift (z)

A unit of relative distance used in astronomy. The universe is expanding, so distant galaxies are receding from the Earth. The faster the speed of recession, the farther the object is. Just as sound from a receding train is lowered in pitch, light from distant galaxies is shifted toward longer wavelengths, that is, toward the red end of the spectrum. The redshift equals 2 if the wavelength of light is z + 1 times the normal wavelength; thus, a redshift of 0.40 means that the wavelength of the light is 40% longer than normal. Using the Hubble space telescope, astronomers have measured redshifts greater than 5.0.

Redwood no.1

The English unit of kinematic viscosity determined by a viscometer and expressed as time in seconds taken by a given amount of liquid at a given temperature to flow by gravity through a specific length of the tube of a given bore. Corresponding units are **"engler"** in Germany and **"Saybolt universal second"** in USA.

Redwood second

an obsolete unit of kinematic viscosity given by readings on the Redwood viscometers commonly used in Britain and elsewhere. The reading is the time, in seconds, for 50 milliliters of a sample of a liquid to flow through the device. The viscosity in centistokes is given roughly by the formula 0.260 t - (0.0188 / t), where t is the flow time in seconds.

reel

A unit of running time used in the motion picture industry to describe the length of films, about 10 minutes. Early projectors used reels that held 1000 feet of 35mm film, which at 24 frames per second has a running time of 11.1 minutes. Later, 2000-feet reels became common, and finally, systems in which the film was fed from horizontal platters and reels were not used during projection, though they continued to be used to transport the print.

register ton (RT)

Unit of volume ("internal capacity" of a vessel). One register ton equal one hundred cubic feet.

1 register ton =**100** cubic feet = 2.831 685 cubic meters.

rehoboam

a large wine bottle holding about 4.5 liters, 6 times the volume of a regular bottle. Note: The "h" is silent in English pronunciation.

rel

A unit of magnetic reluctance proposed by Vladimir Karapetoff in *1911* but not adopted.

rem

Arbitrary unit of absorbed ionizing radiation dose (for organic matter), i.e., dose equivalent. The dose in rems is numerically equal to the product of the dose in rads and certain modifying factors.

Note: 1. The only modifying factor known with any certainty and therefore not automatically put equal to unity is the quality factor. It possesses the following values:

1 for β-rays with energies greater than 3×10^4 electronvolt, γ and X-rays;

1.7 for β-rays with energies less than 3×10^4 electronvolt;

10 for ά-rays and for neutrons of unknown energy;

20 for atomic nuclei and fission fragments.

2. The earlier definition was: 1 rem is the quantity of ionizing radiation such that the energy imparted to a biological system per gram of living tissue by the ionizing particles present in the locus of interest has the same biological effectiveness as one rad of 200 to 250 kilovolt X-ray.

3. The name of the unit stands for "**R**oentgen **E**quivalent **M**an (mammal)."

4. The unit was proposed and named by H.M. Parker in 1950. 5.

The unit is also called the **equivalent biological roentgen**.

remen

Old Egyptian unit of length and area.

1. In ancient Egypt, a unit of length about 37.5 centimeters. Also romanized as rmn.

2. An ancient Egypt, a unit of area, about 13.7 square meters. Notice that this is not a square remen.

ren

In China, a pre-Qin unit of length. In Zhou Dynasty, = 8 *chi*; in Han Dynasty, = 7 *chi*; about 5.6 *chi* at end of the Later Han.

The *ren* is perhaps unique among units based on the human body, as it is, in concept, the distance between the fingertips of the outstretched arms held vertically, that is, one up and one down.

rep

Arbitrary unit of absorbed ionizing radiation dose due to corpuscular radiation (i.e., ά- and β-rays). One rep is the dose of ionizing corpuscular radiation at which the energy absorbed by a substance is equal to the loss in energy during ionization caused by roentgen of electromagnetic radiation. 1 rep of corpuscular radiation is equivalent to 1 roentgen of electromagnetic radiation

Note: 1. The name of the unit stands for "**R**oentgen **E**quivalent **P**hysics".

2. The unit is also called the parker (after H.M. Parker, who proposed it for the first time in 1950) and the tissue roentgen.

RES or res

Symbol for "resolution," a unit defined to be the number of dots or pixels per millimeter in an image. The unit is often stated before the measurement. RES 1 is equal to 25.4 dots per inch (dpi).

retinol equivalent (RE)

A unit of dosage for retinol (vitamin A) and for related substances such as beta carotene. One RE is equivalent to 5 international units (1U), or 1.5 micrograms, of retinol. U.S. nutritional authorities recommend that an adult diet provide 1000 RE per day.

See also *"international unit"*.

revenue ton or tonne (RT)

A unit used for billing in the shipping industry.

The size of a shipment in revenue tons is the number of metric tons or the number of cubic meters in the shipment, whichever is larger.

See also *"ton."*

revolution (r, also rev)

Unit of plane angle. One revolution equals the angle at a point.

1 revolution = 360°

Note: The symbol tr is used in France and the symbol U is used in Germany.

revolution per minute (r/min)

Unit of rotational frequency.

1 revolution per minute = 0.104 720 radians per second.

Note: 1. The symbol tr/min is in use in France and U/min in Germany. Symbol tr/mn formerly used in France and rev/min in U.K. and U.S.

revolution per second (r/s)

Unit of rotational frequency.

1 revolution per second = 6.283 19 radians per second.

Note: 1. The symbol tr/s is in use in France and U/s in Germany. The symbol rev/s formerly used in U.K. and U.S.

reyn (reyn)

FBS unit of dynamic viscosity. It is equivalent to a force of one poundal per square foot (pdl/ft^2) acting on a fluid having a film or body one foot thick and producing a resultant shear rate of one foot per second.

1 reyn = 1 (pdl/ft^2) / [(ft/s)/ft] = 1 pdl/ft^2= 1.48815 newton seconds per meter squared (N.s/m^2).

Smaller microreyn unit is generally employed as being more practical.

Note: 1. The unit was suggested in 1961 and named after O.Reynolds (1842-1912).

2. The unit is used mainly in lubrication.

rhe (rhe):

Metric unit of fluidity, i.e., reciprocal viscosity.

(1) For dynamic fluidity: one rhe is the dynamic fluidity of a fluid which has a dynamic viscosity of one centipose (cP)

1 rhe = 1/cP = 1000 m^2/N s

(2) For kinematic fluidity: one rhe is the kinematic fluidity of a fluid which has a kinematic viscosity of one centistokes (cSt).

1 rhe = 1/cSt= 10^6 s/m^2

Note: 1. The name of the unit is derived from the Greek word rho, to flow. The unit, pronounced "ree".

2. The unit was introduced by the American chemist F.C. Bingham in 1928; he defined it as the reciprocal of the centipoize. However, it came to be used instead as the reciprocal of the poise itself, so the fluidity of a substance in rhes is 1 divided by its dynamic viscosity in poise.

rhm (rhm)

Arbitrary unit of effective strength of a gamma ray source. One rhm is the effective strength of a gamma ray source such that, at a distance of 1 meter in air, the gamma rays produce a dose of 1 roentgen per hour.

Note: 1. The name of the unit stands for **R**oentgen-per-**h**our-at-one-**m**eter.

2. The unit, with its name, was proposed in 1946 for the quantitative comparison of radioactive sources for which disintegration rates cannot easily be determined.

3. The rhm is of the same order of magnitude as the curie, i.e.

1 rhm = 1 curie (approximately).

See *"curie"*.

ri

A traditional Japanese unit of distance sometimes called the Japanese league because it is of similar length to the European league.

1 ri = 2160 ken or 12 960 shaku

(the shaku being the Japanese equivalent of the foot). This is about 3927 meters or 2.44 statute miles.

rice cup

a common name in English for the Japanese go, a unit of dry and liquid capacity equal to about 180 milliliters or 3/4 of a U.S. cup. Japanese rice cookers usually come with measuring cups having this capacity.

See also "cup."

Richter magnitude (M)

Unit of the dimensionless quantity; intensity of earthquakes. The magnitude of an earthquake M on the Richter scale is given by the formula:

$\log E = a + b M,$

Where E = total energy released and a and b are constants, the values of which are modified through observations. With E in joules, good working values of the constants are: a = -1.2, b =+ 2.4.

Note: The following table relates values of E to M from the formula and the constants given above.

M	E (in joules)
0	6.3×10^{-2}
4	2.5×10^{8}
8	1.0×10^{18}

1	1.6×10
2	4.0×10^3
3	1.0×10^6

5	6.3×10^{10}
6	1.6×10^{13}
7	4.0×10^{15}

9	2.5×10^{20}
10	6.3×10^{22}

rick

A traditional unit of volume for firewood.

A rick represents a stack of split firewood 4 feet high and 8 feet long, the logs being of a standard length, usually 16 inches. This is equivalent to 1/3 cord or 1.208 steres. However, because the size of a rick has been manipulated by vendors, it is illegal to sell firewood by the rick in several U.S. states. Arick is sometimes called a face cord or tier. The name of the unit comes from an old Norse word for a stack of wood.

See also *"cord"* and *"steres"*

Rictus scale

Non-conventional unit that measures Media Coverage of Earthquakes

Tom Weller suggests the Rictus scale for earthquake intensity (a takeoff of the conventional Richter scale), measuring media coverage of the event.

Rictus scale #	Richter scale equivalent	Media coverage
1	0–3	Small articles in local papers.
2	3–5	Lead story on local news; mentioned on network news.
3	5–6.5	Lead story on network news; wire-service photos appear in newspapers nationally; governor visits scene.
4	6.5–7.5	Network correspondents sent to scene; the president visits area; commemorative T-shirts appear.
5	7.5+	Covers of weekly news magazines, network specials; "instant books" appear.

ridge

A traditional Welsh unit of distance equal to 3 leaps or 20 feet 3 inches (6.1722 meters).

riga last

A traditional British unit of volume used for measuring timber.

The Riga last is named for the Latvian capital, Riga, which was a major port for the shipment of timber from Russian forests.

A Riga last is 80 cubic feet (2.265 cubic meters) of square-sawn timber or 65 cubic feet (1.841 cubic meters) of round timber.

See also *"last."*

right angle

Unit of plane angle used in all systems of units.

1 right angle = $\pi/2$ radians = 90°

Note: The unit is also called the quadrant.

See *"quadrant"*.

ring

A traditional English unit of quantity for boards and staves, which were shipped encircled by metal rings.

A ring equals 4 shocks or 240 boards.

ring size

A measure of the inside diameter or inside circumference of a ring.

A variety of ring sizing systems are used in various countries.

1. In the U.S., a ring of size n has an inside circumference of $1.43 + 0.102.n$ inches, or about $36.3 + 2.60.n$ millimeters. (There is some variation because U.S. ring sizes have never been standardized).

2. In Britain, traditional ring sizes are stated as letters A, B, etc.; if we replace the letters by numbers n (A = 1, B = 2, etc), then a ring of British size n has an inside circumference of $36.25 + 1.25.n$ millimeters, or about $1.43 + 0.049.n$ inches. A difference of 1 U.S. size thus corresponds rather closely to two letters in the British system.

3. In Japan, sizing is by the inside diameter in increments of 1/3 millimeter; a ring of Japanese size n has an inside diameter of $(n + 38)/3$ millimeters and an inside circumference of $39.8 + 1.047.n$ millimeters.

4. There is an international standard (ISO 8653) defining the ring size to be the inside circumference in millimeters, minus 40.

5. Rings are now sized by this standard in most of Europe, so a ring of European size *n* has an inside circumference of exactly 40 + *n* millimeters. (The British scale is aligned with the European scale, with British size C corresponding to European size 0 and a difference of four British letters corresponding to 5 European sizes.)

roc (roc)

CGS unit of electrical conductivity. This is a name proposed in 1964 for the CGS unit of electrical conductivity. The name stands for <u>r</u>eciprocal <u>o</u>hm per <u>c</u>entimeter.

1 roc = 100 Siemens per meter.

See also *"ram"*.

Rockwell hardness (RH-)

A measure of the hardness of a metal introduced by Rockwell in 1922. In a Rockwell hardness test, a penetrator makes an indentation in the metal under two constant loads, a "minor" load (generally 10 kilograms) and then a "major" load. The difference in penetration depth between the two loads provides the measure of the hardness, usually read from a gauge on the testing machine. There are several Rockwell scales for different ranges of hardness. The most common are the B scale **(RHB),** for which a steel ball is used as the penetrator, and the C scale **(RHC),** for which a cone-shaped diamond is used. The B scale is appropriate for soft metals, and the C scale for hard metals. Rockwell hardness numbers are not proportional to Brinell or Vickers or hardness readings.

See also *"Brinell number"* and *"Vicker number"*

rod (rd) (1)

Imperial unit of area. One rod equal to 30.25 square yards.

1 rod = **30.25** square yards = **25. 292 852 64** square meters.

Note:　This unit is more strictly called the square rod. It is also called the (square) **pole** and the square **perch**.

See *"pole (1)"* and *"perch."*

rod (rd) (2)

Imperial unit of length. One rod equal 5.5 yards.

1 rod = **5.5** yards = **5.029 2** meters.

Note: 1. This unit is also called pole and perch.

2. The name rod dates from about 1450.

See *"pole 2"* and *"perch."*

rod (rd) (3)

Imperial unit of volume. The (volume) rod equals to 1000 cubic feet.

1 (volume) rod = **1000** cubic feet = 28.316 847 cubic meters.

roede

A traditional Dutch unit of distance, reinterpreted in 1820 as a metric unit equal to exactly 10 meters (32.8084 feet). The roede has also been used as a unit of area equal to one square (linear) roede; this is equal to 100 square meters or 1 are.

See also *"rood"* and *"are"*

roentgen (R or r)

Arbitrary unit of radioactivity dose due to exposure to electromagnetic radiation (i.e., γ- and X-rays). One roentgen is the dose of electromagnetic radiation which will produce in the air a charge of 2.58 $\times 10^{-4}$ coulombs on all ions of one sign when all electrons of both signs liberated in a volume of air of mass one kilogram are stopped completely.

1 R = 2.58 $\times 10^{-4}$ coulombs per kilogram.

Note: 1. The former definition of the unit was: the dose of electromagnetic radiation which will produce ions carrying a charge of one frankline (of each sign) per 0.001 293 grams of dry air at standard temperature and pressure, i.e., per cubic centimeter of dry air. The unit, according to this definition, is identical to that given by the first definition.

2. The original definition of the unit was: the dose of electromagnetic radiation which, when the secondary electrons are fully utilized and the wall effect of the chamber is avoided, produces in one cubic centimeter of atmosphere air at a temperature of 0°C and 76 centimeters of mercury pressure such a degree of conductivity that one frankline of charge is measured at saturation current.

3. A dose of 1 roentgen corresponds to 2.082×10^{15} ion-pairs per cubic meter of dry air at standard pressure and temperature. It also corresponds to 8.69×10^{-3} joules absorbed per kilogram of air and 6.77×10^{10} MeV absorbed per cubic meter.

4. At one time, the roentgen was used in clinical work to describe both exposure and absorbed dose, but in 1956, it was decided to use the rad for dose and the roentgen for the unit of radiation exposure.

5. The unit name is also spelled rontgen.

6. The unit is named after W.C.Roentgen (1845-1923), the discoverer of X-rays.

See *"rad"*.

roentgen, equivalent biological (EBR)

Arbitrary unit of absorbed ionizing radiation dose (for organic matter), i.e., dose equivalent. One equivalent biological roentgen is the dose of radiation which, when absorbed by living tissue, produces a biological effect equivalent to the action of one roentgen of electromagnetic radiation. *Note:* The unit is now called the rem, and the definition has been modified.

See *"rem"* and *"roentgen"*.

roentgen equivalent man (or MAMMAL) (rem)

See *"rem"*.

roentgen equivalent physical (rep)

See *"rep"*.

roentgen meter squared per curie hour (R.m²/Ci.h)

Unit of specific gamma ray constant.

1 roentgen meter square per curie hour $= 1.936\ 94 \times 10^{-18}$ coulomb meters squared per kilogram.

roentgen-per-hour-at-one-meter (rhm)

See "rhm".

roentgen per second (R/s)

Unit of exposure rate.

1 roentgen per second $= \mathbf{0.258 \times 10^{-3}}$ Amperes per kilogram

roentgen, tissue

Arbitrary unit of absorbed ionizing radiation dose due to corpuscular radiation (i.e., ά- and β-rays) One tissue roentgen is the dose of ionizing corpuscular radiation at which the energy absorbed by a substance is equal to the loss in energy during ionization caused by one roentgen of electromagnetic radiation. One tissue roentgen of corpuscular radiation is equivalent to one roentgen of electromagnetic radiation.

Note: This unit is now called the **rep.** It was also known as the **parker.**

See *"rep".*

Roll

A U.K. unit of mass for butter and cheese equal to 24 oz (680 g)

rom (rom)

MKS unit of electrical conductivity. This is a name proposed in 1964 for the MKS unit of electrical conductivity. The name stands for <u>r</u>eciprocal <u>o</u>hm per <u>m</u>eter.

1 rom = 1 siemens per meter.

See also *"roc."*

Room

A U.K. unit of mass of coal equivalent to 15,680 lb (7,110 kg)

rood (rood) [1]

Imperial unit of area. One rood equal to one quarter of acre.

1 rood = 0.25 acres = 1011.714 105 6 square meters.

Note: The rood is a traditional unit of area used to measure land. A rood is the area of a narrow strip of land, one furlong (40 rods, or 660 feet) long and one rod (16.5 feet) wide. Thus, the rood is equal to 40 square rods (or perches), which equals 1210 square yards, or 10 890 square feet, or exactly 1/4 acre. That would be the area of a lot 22 yards wide and 55 yards deep, about the size of many suburban lots. One rood is approximately 101 1.714 square meters, or 0.101 171 4 hectares.

See also *'furlong", "rod," acre,"* and *"hectare."*

rood (2)

An old unit of distance, used in several ways. Rood (or roede) is an old Dutch word meaning a rod or pole. So the rood is, in some cases, another name for a rod. But in old England and Scotland, the rood was often longer than a "modern" rod of 16.5 feet; sometimes it was 20 feet, 21 feet, or even 24 feet. In Afrikaans-speaking South Africa, the rood was a standardized measure equal to 12 Cape feet, which is 12.396 English feet or 3.7783 meters.

room (room)

Imperial unit of mass equal 7 tons.

1 room = 7 tons = 7.112 328 356 x 10^3 kilograms

Note: The unit is used to measure coal.

See also *"chaldron"* and *"ship/load'.*

ropani

A unit of land area in Nepal, equal to about 508.7 square meters or 5475 square feet (0.05087 hectares or almost exactly 1/8 acre.

The ropani is divided into 16 annas.

rope (rope)

Imperial unit of length. One rope equals twenty foot.

1 rope = 20 feet = 6.096 meters.

rotl, rotel, rottle, ratel, or arratel

A traditional Arab unit of weight corresponding to the Roman libra, the French livre, and the English pound. There was considerable variation in the unit from time to time and from place to place, but usually, the rotl was about 0.9-1.15 pounds (450-530 grams). However, in some areas of the Near East, such as Syria and Palestine, larger rotls of 5.5 to 6 pounds (2.5-2.8 kilograms) were used. This unit has many spellings in European languages.

See also *"qintar "*

round

The basic unit of time in boxing, equal to 3 minutes.

rowland (rowland)

Arbitrary unit of wavelength. The experimentally derived value is:

1 rowland = 999.81/999.94 angstroms = 0.0998 7 x 10^{-9} meters.

Note: The unit was adopted by H.A. Rowland (1848-1901) because of a small error in the wavelength of the lines on Angstrom's map of the solar spectrum; this error was due to Angstrom's assumption that the Uppsala standard of length was 999.94 millimeters whereas it was 999.81 millimeters.

3. The unit has long been obsolete, having been replaced first by the angstrom and then by the nanometer.

rum (rum)

CGS unit of pressure.

1 rum = 1 barye = 0.1 pascals

Note: The name was suggested in 1934 as an alternative for the barye. It was formerly called the **barad.**

run

A unit of density for woolen yarn used in the U.S. Yarn is described as *n* run if there are *n* 1600-yard hanks of the wool per pound. Actual yam ranges from about 0.5 run to 8 run. The unit is also called the **American run.**

rundlet

A traditional measure of liquid volume, dating back to the Middle Ages. A rundlet is a small barrel usually holding 18 wine (U.S.) gallons (roughly 68.1 liters).

running foot

Another name for a linear foot. Terms such as running meter and running yard are used similarly. See also *"foot."*

rute

A traditional German unit of distance corresponding to the English rod. In fact, "rute" is the German word for rod. The rute had varying lengths, as short as 10 fuss (German feet) and as long as 16 fuss. This could be anywhere from about 3 meters to 4.5 meters.

R-unit, Solomon

Arbitrary unit of radiation dose rate (i.e. radiation intensity) due to X-ray. One Solomon R-unit is the intensity of X-radiation from a source equal to that from one gram of radium placed two centimeter's from an ionization chamber, there being a platinum screen one-half a millimeter thick between the radium and the chamber. The unit is now standardized as:

1 Solomon R-unit = 2100 roentgens per hour.

See also *"R-unit, German"*.

R-unit, German

Arbitrary unit of radiation dose rate (i.e., radiation intensity) due to X-ray.

1 German R-unit = 2.5 Solomon R-units = 5250 roentgens per hour.

See *"R-um't, Solomon."*

rutherford (rd):

Metric unit of radioactive disintegration rate, i.e. activity. One rutherford is the quantity of a radioactive nuclide required to produce one million disintegrating atoms per second, or, simply, one million disintegrations per second.

1 rd = 2.70270 x 10^{-5} curies.

Note: 1. The unit was named after Lord Rutherford (1871-1937). The name was proposed in 1946 and it was approved by the American Research Council in 1949.

2. It is recommended to use curie instead of rutherford.

rydberg (rydberg)

Derived unit of energy, particularly in atomic studies, of the Hartree system of units. It is defined as one half of the potential energy of an electron in the first orbit in Bohr's theory of the hydrogen atom.

It is given by:

1 rydberg $= e^2/2a_o$

where e is the atomic unit of charge and a_o is the atomic unit of length. Hence,

1 rydberg = 2.425 2 x 10^{-18} joules.

Note: The unit is also called **atomic unit of energy.**

See *"atomic unit of length"* and *"atomic unit of energy"*.

rydberg (I) (rydberg)

CGS unit of reciprocal length and wave number. One rydberg is the reciprocal length of a distance, which has a length of one centimeter.

1 rydberg = 1/cm = 100/meter.

Note: 1. The name of the unit was suggested by Candler in 1951 and is named after J.R. Rydberg (1854-1919), who was a scientist in the field of atomic spectra.

2. This unit is known as **kayser** and **balmer.**

See *"balmer"* and *"kayser"*.

S

sabin

FPS unit of sound absorption for a surface. It is equivalent to one square foot of perfectly absorbing surface.

1 sabin = 1 square foot = 009290304 meter square.

Note: 1. Also known as (total**) absorption unit, open window unit** (ow unit), and **square-foot unit of absorption.**

2. The name of the unit is after W.C. Sabine, who is a pioneer of architectural acoustics. The name was given to the unit by the American Acoustical Society in 1937.

3. Wallace C. Sabine was the first scientist who used an open window as a perfect absorber.

4. The absorption a in sabin is related to the volume v (in cubic feet) and the reverberation time T (in seconds) required for the intensity of the sound to decay by 60 dB, by the relation: $a = 0.161 \ v/T$.

See also *"absorption unit (total)"* and *"open window unit."*

sack [1]

A traditional unit of volume. Sacks of different commodities are of different sizes, but a typical measure is 3 bushels (about 105.7 liters based on the U.S. bushel or 109.1 liters based on the British Imperial bushel).

See also *"bushel".*

sack [2]

A traditional unit of weight, varying for different commodities shipped in sacks.

In Britain, for example, the sack was a traditional measure for wool, fixed by Edward 11 at 364 pounds (26 stone) in 1340.

In the U.S., a sack of salt is traditionally equal to 215 pounds, a sack of cotton 140 pounds, and a sack of flour 100 pounds. A sack of concrete is traditionally 94 pounds in the U.S., 87.5 pounds in Canada.

sadzhen or sagene

> A traditional Russian unit of distance corresponding roughly to the English fathom and French toise.
>
> Early in the 1700s, Czar Peter the Great fixed the length of the sadzhen at exactly 7 English feet. This equals 3 arshin or 2.1336 meters.
>
> **Sagene** is an older transliteration of the Russian word.

Saffir-Simpson category

> A ranking of the strength of a hurricane, introduced by two American meteorologists and used by the U.S. National Weather Service to rank storms in the Atlantic and northeastern Pacific Oceans.

S.A.G. foot

> The South African geodetic foot.

sailmaker ounce (smoz)

> A traditional unit measuring the weight (per unit area) of sailcloth. The weight in sailmaker ounces is the weight in ordinary (avoirdupois) ounces of a piece of cloth 36 inches by 28.5 inches. Thus 1 smoz is equal to 1.263 ounces per square yard (oz/yd^2) or 42.828 grams per square meter (g/m^2 or gsm). However, spinnakers (the large triangular foresails of yachts) are traditionally named by the fabric weight before it is finished, so these names do not correspond exactly to the sailmaker-ounce weights. A "half-ounce" spinnaker, for example, has a weight of about 0.85 smoz or 37 gsm, and a "three-quarter-ounce" spinnaker has a weight of about 1 smoz.

salmanazar

> A large wine bottle holding about 9 liters, 12 times the volume of a regular bottle.
>
> See also *"bottle."*

saltspoon (ssp)

> A unit of volume formerly used in U.S. food recipes.
>
> The saltspoon equals 1/4 teaspoon or about 1.2 milliliters.
>
> See also *"teaspoon"*.

samson (samson)

Unit of force in a system of units called meter-gram wink.

1 samson = 9×10^{13} newton.

Note: In this system of units, the unit of time is equal to (1/3000) microsecond and is called wink. The unit of work is called Einstein and equal to 9×10^{13} joules.

Sana lamjel

An obsolete unit of length.

Sana lamjel was a customary unit of length used in the erstwhile kingdom of Manipur, now a state of India. The unit of length, defined by the ruler of the kingdom, Nongda Lairen Pakhangpa, in 33 CE, being equal to the distance from the floor to the tips of the fingers of his raised right hand while standing (a fathom), plus 4 finger-widths.

The unit became a standard for land measurement. An area of 50×60 sana lamjel was equal to 1 pari. 1, pari was 2 lourak, 4 sangam, 8 loukhai, 16 loushal, or 32 tong.

The value was later redefined by King Khagemba (1597–1652) to be defined by the distance between the fingertips of his outstretched arms, plus 4 finger-widths.

After metrication in India in the mid-20th century, the unit became obsolete.

sao

A traditional unit of land area in Vietnam. The sao varies somewhat from province to province. It is equal to 360 square meters (430.6 square yards) in many places, but as much as 500 square meters (598.0 square yards) in others.

saros

A unit of time used in astronomy, mostly in predicting solar and lunar eclipses.

The saros is equal to 6585.32 days (6585 days 7 hours 23 minutes), which is exactly 223 lunar months. (This is either 10 or 11 days more than 18 years, depending on the number of leap years during the period.) Astronomers in ancient times discovered that the saros is very nearly equal to 19 eclipse years (6585.78 days). This means that one saros after an eclipse the Sun, Moon, and Earth return almost exactly to the same position and another, very similar eclipse occurs. However, because of the 7 hours 23 minutes included, the Earth has turned about one third of a revolution and the new eclipse occurs about 116° of longitude west of the preceding one. After 3 saros, the eclipse returns nearly to its original location. Thus eclipses at a particular location tend to repeat with a period of 3 saros or 54 years 1 month. Thus the last total solar eclipse in North Carolina, on 1970 March 7, will repeat on 2024 April 8 and again on 2078 May 11.

Sarpler

Sarpler, **Sarplier**, or (in Scotland) **Serplathe** was a U.K. weight for wool.

The *Oxford English Dictionary* defines a sarpler as 80 tods, where a tod is usually 28lbs thus usually 80 x 28 lbs, or 160 stone, = 2,240 pounds (1,020 kg)

Another definition, half the quantity, is given by Cowell's 1607 book (fourscore=80, 80 stone = 80 x 14lbs = 1,120 pounds (510 kg)

One sarpler of wool is three sacks. In every sack, 26 stone at 14 pound the stone, which makes 264 lbs., so as there is in a sarpler of wool 78 stone and 792 lbs.

- In the late 19th century, the sarpler begins to be defined as a long ton (2240 pounds of wool). This value may also be an error, in this case arising from a mistaken substitution of the tod for the stone.

saunder's theatre cushion

Unit of absorption for a surface. It is the absorption of a cushion taken from the Saunders theater at Harvard and which is now preserved by the Acoustical Society of America.
Note: This unit was the standard used by Wallace C. Sabine in his work on the acoustics of buildings in 1896.
Note: The sabin is used now.
See *"sabin"*.

savart (s)

Unit of the dimensionless quantity, frequency (pitch) interval. It is the interval between two frequencies f_1, f_2, having a ratio:
$f_1, f_2, = 10^{1/1000} = 1.00231$.
Alternatively, the pitch interval l_s in savarts between two frequencies, f_1 *and* f_2, is given by:
$l_s = 1000 \log(f_1, f_2,)$ savart $(f_1, > f_2)$.

Note: The savart is related to the octave by the relation:

$$1 \text{ savart} = 10^{-3} / \log 2 = 3.32193 \times 10^{-3} \text{ octaves.}$$

See also *"savart, modified"*.

savart modified

Unit of the frequency (pitch) interval. The pitch interval l_{ms} in modified savarts between two frequencies f_1, f_2, $(f_1, > f_2)$ is given by the relation:

$$l_{ms} = (300/ \log 2) \log (f_1,/f_2), = 996.594 \log(f_1,/f_2)$$

Note: l_{ms} is related to the corresponding pitch intervals l_o in octaves and l_s in savarts by:

$$l_{ms} = 300 \, l_o = 0.996594 \, l_s$$

Saybolt Universal second (SUS) and Saybolt Furol second (SSF or SFS)

Units of kinematic viscosity given by readings on Saybolt viscometers. The Saybolt Universal viscometer is used for liquids having viscosities below 1000 centistokes (or 10 stokes, see entry for stokes below). The Saybolt Furol viscometer is used for more viscous road and fuel oils ("furol" is an acronym for fuel and road oils). In both cases, the reading is the time, in seconds, for 60 milliliters of a sample to flow through the device. The Furol viscosity readings are roughly 1/10 the Universal readings. For liquids whose viscosity exceeds 50 centistokes at 37.8 °C (100 °F), one SSU is approximately 0.2158 centistokes or 0.2158 mm^2/s. For very viscous liquids (viscosity exceeding 500 centistokes) at 50 °C (122 °F), one SSF is approximately 2.120 centistokes or 2.120 mm^2/s. Exact equations were published in 1996 by the American Society for Testing and Materials (ASTM practice D2161). The Saybolt seconds are considered obsolete, but they have been used traditionally in the petroleum industry and are common in technical articles.

scale

A measure describing the resolution of a map, architectural plan, or some similar document. A map, for example, might be described as "1:250 000 scale". In general, 1:n scale means that 1 unit of distance on the map or plan represents n of the same units in fact. It doesn't matter what unit of distance is used as long as it is the same in both cases. On a 1:250 000 scale map, 1 centimeter on the map represents 250 000 centimeters (exactly 2.5 kilometers) on the ground. On the same map, one inch on the map represents 250,000 inches (about 3.9457 miles) on the ground. The use of the terms "larger" and "smaller" referring to scale is often confusing. A l:*m* scale map has a larger scale than a 1:11 scale map if *m* is less than *n*. For example, a 1:100 000 scale map has a larger scale than a 1:250 000 scale map, and the same place or object will appear larger on the larger scale map. Mathematically, the notation l:*n* is simply another way of writing the ratio 1/*n*.

Scaramucci

Informal unit of time in the "Humorous System of Units."

A Scaramucci is 11 (sometimes 10) days and is named after the length of White House Communications Director Anthony Scaramucci's tenure under President Trump. A Scaramucci is shortened to a Mooch.

scheffel or schepel

Traditional units of dry volume. The German scheffel and Dutch schepel have both been redefined within the metric system, but in very different ways: the scheffel equals 50 liters (1.4189 U.S. bushels) and the schepel 10 liters (0.2838 U.S. bushels). Both words are usually translated as "bushel" in English, and both units were originally closer to the English bushel; the schepel was roughly 0.75 bushels or about 26 liters.
See also *"skep"*.

schock

A traditional German unit of quantity equal to 60.
See also *"shock"*.

Schoenus

Informal unit of area or length

Schoenus (Latin: *schœnus*; Greek: σχοίνος, *schoinos*, lit. "rush rope"; Ancient Egyptian: *itrw*, lit. "river-measure") was an ancient Egyptian, Greek and Roman unit of length and area based on the knotted cords first used in Egyptian surveying.

schooner

An informal unit of liquid volume. A schooner is a large tumbler or drinking glass holding about 400 milliliters or 13.5 U.S. fluid ounces.

Similarly, in Queensland, New South Wales, and the Northern Territory (Australia) a schooner of beer holds 425 milliliters.

In South Australia, however, a schooner is only 285 milliliters.

schoppen

A traditional German unit of liquid volume for wine, now interpreted most often as 250 milliliters (1/4 liter or about 8.45 U.S. fluid ounces).

schtoff

A traditional Russian unit of volume equal to 10 charki. This is equivalent to about 1.23 liters or 1.30 U.S. liquid quarts.

score

A traditional unit of quantity equal to 20.

The score, like the dozen, helps us describe a moderate number of objects. This is one of the many cases in which English has two words for similar concepts, one word from the Old French spoken in 1066 by the Norman conquerors of England and one from the old English spoken by the Anglo-Saxon people they conquered. In this case, dozen is the French word and score is the old English word, derived from the Norse word *skor,* meaning a notch cut in a stick as a tally mark. The suffix -score can be added to a number, as in threescore (60) or fivescore (100).

Scots foot, Scots mile

Traditional distance units in Scotland.

The Scots foot equals 1.005 405 4 English feet (about 12.065 English inches or 30.645 centimeters).

The Scots mile equals 320 falls or 5920 Scots feet, which is about 5952 English feet (1.127 English miles or 1814.2 meters).

The English foot and statute mile, of course, are now official in Scotland.

Scoville unit

A unit measuring the concentration of capsaicin, the "hot" ingredient in chile peppers. A measurement of, say, 50 000 Scoville units means that an extract from the pepper can be diluted 50 000 to 1 with sugared water and the "'burn" of the capsaicin will still be barely detectable by the human tongue. (In practice, the measurements are now made with liquid chromatography.) The unit was invented in 1912 by the American pharmacologist Wilbur L. Scoville, who was working on the use of capsaicin in the muscle pain-relieving ointment Heet. Actual chile peppers have capsaicin concentrations from 5000 to 500,000 Scoville units.

Scoville heat unit

An informal unit to measure the Pepper Heat

The Scoville scale is a measure of the hotness of a chili pepper. It is the degree of dilution in sugar water of a specific chili pepper extract when a panel of 5 tasters can no longer detect its "heat." Pure capsaicin (the chemical responsible for the "heat") has 16 million Scoville heat units.

scruple (scruple)

Imperial unit of mass equal to 20 grains.

1 scruple = 20 grains = 1.295 978 2 kilograms.

Note: The unit is one of three imperial units used in sale of drugs. The other two are **drachm** and **apothecaries ounce.**

See *"drachm"* and *"ounce, apothecaries."*

Scrupulum

A unit of area, mass, or time.

Scrupulum, meaning a tiny stone (from *scrupus* sharp stone), indicates a weight of 1/24 of an ounce or, by extension, of other measures. Metaphorically, the stone is thought to be sharp and pricking, like a thorn.

- As a weight or a coin, 1/24 of an *uncia* or 1/288 of an as
- As a measure of land, 1/288 of a *jugerum*
- As a measure of time, 1/24 part of an hour, or 2.5 minutes.

The forms *scripulum, scriptulum, scriplus* and *scriptulus* can be found, *scriptulum* being also associated with the lines on a draughtboard.

seah

An ancient Hebrew measure of both liquid and dry volume.

The seah was equal to about 13.44 liters (about 3.55 U.S. liquid gallons or 2.96 British Imperial gallons).

The *se'ah* or *seah*, plural *se'im*, is a unit of dry measure of ancient origin found in the Bible and in Halakha (Jewish law), which equals one third of an *ephah*, or *bath*. In layman's terms, it is equal to the capacity of 144 medium-sized eggs, or what is equal in volume to about 9 U.S. quarts (8.5 liters). Its size in modern units varies widely according to the criteria used for defining it.

The seah is found in Genesis 18:6, where Abraham orders Sarah to prepare three se'im of flour into loaves:

According to Herbert G. May, chief editor of two Bible-related reference books, the bath may be archaeologically determined to have been about 5.75 U.S. gallons (22 liters) from a study of jar remains marked 'bath' and 'royal bath' from Tell Beit Mirsim. Using the standard of a *bath* unit, which has been established to be about 22 liters, 1 *se'ah* would equal about 7.3 liters or 7.3dm^3.

The *Jewish Study Bible* estimates the biblical seah at 7.7 liters (2.0 U.S. gal).[3

seam (seam)

1. Imperial unit of capacity (volume) equal to 8 U.K. bushel.

1 seam = 8 U.K. bushels = 0.290 950 cubic meters.

Note: 1. The unit is also called **quarter.**

2. The unit is used mainly to measure grains.

See "quarter".

2. Imperial unit of mass, equal 120 pound.

1 seam = **120** pounds = 54.431 084 4 kilograms.

Note: The unit is used to measure the glass.

sea mile

in most cases, another name for the nautical mile.

Season

a portion of a year. The word "season," derived from a Latin word meaning the time for sowing, originally meant one of the periods of the agricultural year. It has come to be used informally to mean the period of time characterized by any activity (such as the "football season") or, more specifically, as an informal unit of time equal to roughly 1/4 year. Ideas of what constitutes a season in this latter sense vary from country to country. In North America, the astronomical seasons begin at the instants of equinox (for spring and fall) or solstice (for summer and winter), on or near the 21st days of March, June, September, and December. In meteorology, however, the seasons begin on the 1st days of March, June, September, and December.

secohm (secohm)

MKSA unit of inductance. One secohm is the inductance of a closed circuit, which gives rise to a magnetic flux of one international weber per international ampere.

1 secohm = 1 international weber per international ampere = 1.000 490 053 3 henrys.

Note:　1. The unit is also called **international henry**. It has also been called the **quadrant.**

　　　　2. The name of the unit was proposed for the first time by Ayrton and Perry in 1887.

See *"quadrant"*.

second (s)

Base SI unit of time. The definition adopted at October 13, 1967, meeting of the 13th General Conference on Weights and Measures is:

"The second is the duration of 9,192,631,770 periods of the radiation corresponding to the transition between the two hyperfine levels of the fundamental state of the atom of caesium 133." The frequency 9,192,631,770 Hz was carefully chosen to make it impossible, by any existing experimental evidence, to distinguish the new second from the ephemeris second based on the Earth's motion.

Note:　1. The standard second is experimentally reproducible using an Essen-ring quartz clock to an accuracy of 1 part in 10^{12}.

　　　　2. The second is also the SI unit of duration, period, time interval and time constant, half-life, mean life and specific impulse.

See also *"second, sidereal," "second ephemeris."*

second (...")

Unit of plane angle used with SI system equal 1/360 of the degree.

1 " = (1/360)° = π/648000 rad = 4.84814 x 10^{-6} rad.

Note: 1. The second can be subdivided decimally.

2. When using decimal fractions of the second, the unit symbol is placed after the figures, e.g., 6.2". In astronomical work, it generally precedes the decimal point, e.g., 6".5.

second, centesimal (..^{cc})

Unit of plane angle equal to one-tenth of the grade.

1^{cc} =0.1 grades = (π/2) x 10^{-6} radians.

See *"grade"*.

second, ephemeris (s):

Unit of time. It is exactly 1/31,556,925.9747 of the tropical year of 1900, January, 0 days, and 12-hour ephemeris time.

Note: 1. In the above definition, one tropical year means the time interval between consecutive passages, in the same direction, of the Sun through the Earth's equatorial plane.

2. The above definition was accepted by the ICWM in 1954.

3. The original definition of the second was: 1 second is the fraction 1/86400 of a mean solar day. One mean solar day is the time interval between consecutive passages of the Sun across the meridian, averaged over one year. The second, according to this definition, is called **"mean solar second"**.

The difference between the two definitions is, at present, about 2 parts in 10^8.

second, sidereal

Unit of time. It is defined as the fraction 1/86400 of the time for one complete rotation of the Earth on its axis.

The experimentally observed size is:

1 sidereal second = 86164.09892/86400 = 0.997270 s.

second per cubic meter (s m^{-3})

SI unit of resistance (fluid flow).

second per liter (s l⁻¹or s L⁻¹)

Unit for resistance (fluid flow) used with SI system.

second per meter squared (s m⁻²)

SI unit of kinematic fluidity.

section

A unit of land area in the United States and Canada.

1 section = 1 square mile = 640 acres (approximately 259 hectares).

In the USA, the section was first defined by an act of *20 May 1785* and subsequently in the Land Act of 1796.

sed

A symbol for **standard erythemal dose**, a unit used to measure the amount of skin-reddening ultraviolet radiation received by a person in the Sun or in a tanning salon. One SED is equal to a dose of 100 joules per square meter (J/m^2) of skin surface. The radiation producing skin reddening is confined to a narrow range of wavelengths around 300 nanometers, so the energy is measured only in these wavelengths using a standardized procedure. A tanning rate of one SED per hour is equivalent to 27. 778 milliwatts per square meter (mW/m^2) of skin surface.

seemeile

The German name for the nautical mile.

See also "nautical mile"

seer [1]

A traditional weight unit in India and South Asia.

The seer equals 1/40 maund, and, like the maund, it varied considerably from one area to another. The official size in British India was 2.057 15 pounds or 0.9331 kilograms. In Pakistan, the seer is now considered equal to the kilogram. The unit is sometimes spelled **ser.**

seer [2]

A traditional unit of dry volume in northern India, equal to a little more than a liter. This is roughly the volume of a seer of grain.

SEER

an abbreviation for **seasonal energy efficiency rating**, a U.S. and Canadian measure of the efficiency of an air conditioner. The rating is equal to the total output of the air conditioner over an entire cooling season, in Btu, divided by the total electrical energy consumed, in watt hours. Since this is a ratio of two energy units, the result is a dimensionless (unitless) number. In 2005 the required SEER for home central air conditioning systems was raised from 10 to 13.

seidel

A traditional unit of liquid volume in Austria.

The traditional seidel was equal to about 354 milliliters; this is about 12.0 U.S. fluid ounces or about 12.5 British fluid ounces. Today, a seidel of beer in southern Germany and Austria is a small mug holding 300-500 milliliters, frequently the latter (1/2 liter or about 16.91 U.S. fluid ounces).

semester (sem)

An informal unit of time. The word semester comes from the Latin words for "six months," and originally, a semester was understood to equal 6 months or 1/2 year. However, the word is now used chiefly to mean half the academic year at a school or college, a period of time that can vary from 15 to 21 weeks.

semester hour (sem hr)

A unit of academic credit, supposedly equal to one semester's study for a period of one hour per week. However, "academic hours" are slightly shorter than regular hours (often 50 or 55 minutes per class) are typically used in these calculations.

semi-

A common English prefix meaning 1/2. In statements of frequency, *bi-* and *semi-* have become confused and it isn't always clear what a word like "semimonthly" means. This is how it's supposed to work: in adverbs of frequency, semi- means "twice every" or "every half." Bells on a ship ring **semi-hourly** (every half hour) and the tides usually occur

semidiurnally (twice a day); a **semiweekly** newspaper is published twice in a week; a semimonthly payroll is paid twice every month; and days and nights have the same length semiannually (twice a year). For something that happens once every two time units, use bi-

semibreve

A unit of relative time in music equal to 1 whole note or 1/2 breve.

See also *"breve"*.

semiquaver

A unit of relative time in music equal to 1/16 whole note or 1/32 breve.

See also *"breve"*.

semitone

A unit used in music to describe the ratio in frequency between notes. The unit is actually used in two slightly different ways. In one use, two notes are said to differ by one semitone if the higher note has frequency exactly $16/15 = 1.0667$ times the frequency of the lower one. Also, the semitone is used as a synonym for the half step in the standard chromatic scale; in this use, two notes differ by a semitone if the higher note has frequency exactly $2^{1/12} = 1.0595$ times the frequency of the lower one.

sennight

An old English name for a week formed as a contraction of seven nights. The word is pronounced like "senate."

sensation unit

Unit of loudness. For sound of pressure P, the loudness S in the sensation unit is $S = 20 \log_{10}(P/P_o)$, where P_o is the sound pressure level, which can just be detected by the ear.

Note: 1. The unit, as defined, is based on one-for-one relationship between sound pressure and loudness, which is a false assumption.

2. The unit was suggested in 1925.

septennium

A unit of time equal to 7 years.

septet

A unit of quantity equal to 7.

Ser

A **ser** is an obsolete unit of dry volume in India. In 1871, it was defined as being exactly 1 litre. After metrication in the mid-20th century, the unit became obsolete. It was the unit in pre-modern India which was so close to the metric values of volume approx. equal to a liter.

See also "liter."

seven

a unit of volume for beer in New South Wales and some other sections of Australia. A seven of beer is a glass holding 200 milliliters (about 7 Imperial fluid ounces). This volume is called a butcher in South Australia and a glass many other parts of Australia.

seventh.

A unit used in music to describe the ratio in frequency between notes. Two notes differ by one seventh if the higher note has frequency exactly 15/8 times the frequency of the lower one. On the standard 12-tone scale, the seventh is approximated as 11 half step, corresponding to a frequency ratio of $2^{11/12} = 1.8877$.

sextant (sextant)

Unit of plane angle.

1 sextant = $\pi/3$ radian = 60°.

sextarius

A Roman unit of liquid volume. The word means "sixth," and the unit was equal to 1/6 congius. The sextarius held about 530 milliliters, very close to the capacity of the British and U.S. pint.

shackle (shackle)

Unit of length used for measuring the length of cable and equal to 15 fathoms.

1 shackle = 15 fathoms = 27.432 06 meter.

Note: The mentioned value of the shackle was given in 1949 by the British Navy to replace the old value of 12.5 fathoms.

shade number

A unit of light transmission for the protective glasses used in welding. If T is the fraction of visible light transmitted, the shade number is $1 + 7(-\log_{10} T)/3$. For example, if 1% of the light is transmitted, the shade number is 4.

shaftment

An old English unit of distance equal to 2 palms.

A shaftment is the distance from the tip of the outstretched thumb to the opposite side of the palm of the hand. The ending "-ment" is from the old English word *mund*, hand. The shaftment was an important unit in Saxon England, where it was equal to about 16.5 centimeters (6.5 inches). After the modern foot came into use in the twelfth century, the shaftment was reinterpreted as exactly 1/2 foot or 6 inches (15.24 centimeters). The shaftment continued in common use through at least the fifteenth century, but it is now obsolete.

shake (shake)

Unit of time equal to 10^{-8} seconds.

1 shake = 10^{-8} seconds

shaku

A Japanese word meaning "measure" or "scale," also used for several traditional units in Japan:

[1] As a unit of distance, the shaku is the Japanese foot, equal to about 30.30 centimeters or 1 1.93 inches;

[2] As a unit of area, the shaku equals 330.6 square centimeters (51.24 square inches);

[3] As a unit of volume, the shaku equals about 18.04 milliliters (0.61 U.S. fluid ounces).

shannon (Sh)

A unit of information content used in information and communications theory. The definition is based on the idea that less-likely messages are more informative than more-likely ones (for example, if a volcano rarely erupts, then a message that it is erupting is more informative than a message it is not erupting). If a message has; probability p of being received, then its information content is $-\log_2 p$ shannons. For example, if the message consists of 10 letters and all strings of 10 letters are equally likely, then the probability of a particular message is 1/26'0 and the information content of the message is 10(log$_2$ 26) = 47.004 shannons. This unit was originally called the bit [2] because when the message is a bit string and all strings are equally likely, then the information content turns out to equal the number of bits. One Shannon equals log$_{10}$ 2 = 0.301 030 hartley or log$_e$ 2 = 0.693 147 nat. The unit is named for the American mathematician Claude Shannon (1916-2001), the founder of information theory.

shed (shed):

Metric unit of area, especially the cross-sectional area of an atomic nucleus.

1 shed = 10^{-21} barn = 10^{-52} square meters.

shekel

An ancient Hebrew unit of weight (and also a coin having that weight). The shekel was the Hebrew version of a Babylonian unit used throughout the Middle East. Accounts differ on its size. A frequently quoted equivalent is 252 grains, which is equal to 0.5760 ounces (avoirdupois) or about 16.33 grams, but other sources quote a value of 8.4 grams or various values between these two extremes.

sheng

A traditional unit of liquid volume in China. Like the Indian seer (see above), the sheng is a little more than a liter; 1.035 liters (1.094 U.S. quaerts) is one quoted equivalent.

shetland

A unit of volume for beer in Western Australia equal to 115 milliliters (4 Imperial fluid ounces). This quantity is a smaller version of the 5-ounce pony; its name refers to Shetland ponies, small horses from the Shetland Islands north of Scotland.

Sheppey

Informal unit of length in the "Humorous System of Units"

A measure of distance equal to about $\frac{7}{8}$ of a mile (1.4 km) defined as the closest distance at which sheep remain picturesque. The Sheppey is the creation of Douglas Adams and John Lloyd, included in *The Meaning of Liff*, their dictionary of putative meanings for words that are actually just place names. It is named after the Isle of Sheppey in the U.K.

shift

a unit of time equal to the scheduled period of work at a factory or other place of business. Businesses operating on a 24-hour basis typically organize the day into three daily shifts of 8 hours each. This usage is consistent with the old English meaning of "shift" as an arrangement or division.

shipload (shipload)

Arbitrary unit of mass equal to 242 tons.

1 shipload = 242 tons = 245.883 352 x10^3 kilograms

Note: The unit is used to measure the coal.

See also *"chaldron"* and *"room."* q2a1

shipping ton (shipping ton)

Unit of volume used for ship cargo. It represents a volume of forty cubic foot.

1 shipping ton = **40** cubic feet = 1.132 674 cubic meters.

Note: This unit is called **measurement ton** and also **freight ton**.

sho

A traditional Japanese unit of liquid volume. The sho equals 1.8039 liters, which is 1.9061 U.S. quarts or 1.5872 British Imperial quarts.

shoe size

All shoe sizes express in some way the approximate length of the shoe, or at least the length of the last, the form on which the shoe is made. In the U.S., a difference of one full shoe size represents a length difference of 1/3 inch (8.47 mm), so shoe size n represents a length of $Z + n/3$, where Z is the length of a size 0 shoe (if there were such a thing). The value of Z is 3-11/12 inches (99.5 mm) for infants' and boys' shoes, 3-7/12 inches (91.0 mm) for girls' shoes, 7-11/12 inches (201.1 mm) for women's shoes, and 8-1/4 inches (209.6 mm) for men's shoes. The size number for a woman's shoe is 1 larger than for a man's shoe of the same length (for example, a man's 7-1/2 is the same length as a woman's 8-1/2). In Europe, shoe sizes are measured in Paris points, a unit equal to 2/3 centimeter. Ski boots and hiking boots worldwide are measured in mondo points, which are simply millimeters.

short hundredweight (sh cwt)

U.S. unit of mass equal 100 pound.

1 short hundredweight = **100** pound = 45.359 24 kilograms.

short ton (sh tn and also sh ton)

U.S. imperial unit of mass. One short ton equals to 2000 pounds.

1 short ton = **2000** pounds a 907.184 74 kilograms.

Note: 1. This is a U.S. unit (symbol is sh tn) and there is no corresponding U.K. unit.

2. In the U.S., the unit is also called **net ton** or just **ton**.

3. The unit is the basic unit in all terms involving the "ton refrigeration."

See *"ton refrigeration."*

shot

[1] A traditional unit of liquid volume. The term "shot" is often used informally to mean "a small serving." In the U.S., a shot is legally equal to one fluid ounce or 29.574 milliliters. However, many bartenders use larger shot glasses holding 1.25 fluid ounces (37.0 milliliters), and some shot glasses hold the same as a jigger: 1.5 fluid ounces or 44.4 milliliters.

[2] Another name for a shackle as unit of length for anchor chains. In this use, common in the U.S., a shot equals 15 fathoms, 90 feet or 27.432 meters. The origin of this name for a length of chain is not certain. It may be a corruption of "shut" since anchor chains are formed by shutting clasps or shackles to join shorter lengths of chain.

Shortz

Non-conventional unit that measures Fame

This is a unit of fame, hype, or infamy, named for the American puzzle creator and editor Will Shortz. The measure is the number of times one's name has appeared in The New York Times Crossword Puzzle as either a clue or solution. Arguably, this number should only be calculated for the Shortz Era (1993–). Shortz himself is 1 Shortz famous.

See also "Warhol."

Shot

An informal unit of volume.

The shot is a liquid volume measure that varies from country to country and state to state, depending on legislation. It is routinely used for measuring strong liquor or spirits when the amount served and consumed is smaller than the more common measures of alcoholic "drink" and "pint." There is a legally defined maximum size of a serving in some jurisdictions.

The size of a "single" shot is 20–60 ml (0.70–2.11 imp fl oz; 0.68–2.03 U.S. fl oz). The smaller "pony" shot is 20–30 ml (0.70–1.06 imp fl oz; 0.68–1.01 U.S. fl oz). According to Encyclopedia Britannica Almanac 2009, a pony is 0.75 fluid ounces[l] of liquor. According to Wolfram Alpha, one pony is 1 U.S. fluid ounce. "Double" shots (surprisingly not always the size of two single shots, even in the same place) are 40–100 ml (1.4–3.5 imp fl oz; 1.4–3.4 U.S. fl oz). In the U.K., spirits are sold in shots of either 25 ml (approximating the old fluid ounce) or 35 ml.

shovel

An informal unit of volume. In U.S. building trades, a common rule of thumb is that a cubic yard contains about 150 standard (no. 2) shovels of material. This means that a shovel contains about 5 liters and a cubic meter is about 200 shovels.

shower unit (s)

Arbitrary unit of length in cosmic-ray studies. One shower unit is the mean path length required to reduce the energy of a charged particle by one-half.

Note: The shower unit is an individual unit of length, i.e., its size depends on the conditions of a given set of circumstances. The value of s in air is 230 meters; in water is 300 millimeters, and 35 millimeters in lead.

See also *"cascade unit."*

SI unit of exposure (SI unit)

Unnamed unit expressed in coulomb per kilogram.

1 SI unit = 3876 roentgens.

sidereal day (sidereal day)

Unit of time.

A unit of time used in astronomy, equal to the period of time in which the earth makes one rotation relative to the stars. If we could view the earth from outside the Solar System, we would see that it actually completes 366.242 rotations during one year (one revolution around the sun). We only count 365.242 because one rotation is cancelled out for us by our tour around the sun. Thus the sidereal day, the average interval between two successive risings of the same star, is shorter than the mean solar day (see <u>day</u>) by 1/366.242. The sidereal day equals 23 hours 56 minutes 4.090 54 seconds, or 86 164.090 54 seconds. Like the regular day it is divided into 24 **sidereal hours**, each sidereal hour being divided into 60 **sidereal minutes** and each sidereal minute into 60 **sidereal seconds**. The sidereal hour equals 59 minutes 50.17 seconds; the sidereal minute equals 59.8362 seconds, and the sidereal second equals 0.997 270 second. Traditionally, observatories had clocks set to this sidereal cycle, and astronomers still use sidereal time in making telescope settings.

See *"day, sidereal."*

sidereal year

Unit of time. It is the time period during which the Earth returns to the same point in its orbit with reference to the stars. It is equal to **365.256 365 56** days in the year 1900, increasing at the rate of 0.11×10^{-6} days per century.

1 sidereal year = 365 days 6 hours 9 minutes and 9.984 seconds = $3.155\ 814\ 998\ 4 \times 10^{7}$ seconds.

See *"year"*.

Siegbahn unit (X or XU)

Arbitrary unit of length, particularly wavelength in X-ray spectra. The experimentally derived value of the unit is:

1 x = (1.002 02 $\pm$ 0.000 03) x 10^{-13} meters.

This value is formalized by assigning the value 3 029.45 X to the spacing of the (200) planes of calcite at 18°C.

Note: 1. The unit is also called **X-unit** or **X-ray unit.**

2. It is better to use the nanometer as a unit.

See *"nanometer".*

siemens (S)

Derived SI unit of conductance, admittance, modulus of admittance and susceptance. It is the reciprocal of the ohm. One siemens is defined as the conductance between two points of a conductor when a constant difference of potential of one volt applied between these two points produces in this conductor a current of one ampere, the conductor not being the source of any electromotive force.

1 siemens = 1 A/V.

Note: 1. This unit is also called **mho**, but it is recommended to use siemens.

2. This unit was formerly called **absolute siemens** (S_{abs}).

3. The unit was approved by IEC in 1933 and adopted by the CGPM in 1971.

4. The name Siemens was used in Germany up to 1930 for the unit of resistance; its size was approximately equal to that of the international ohm.

5. The name is after E.W. Siemens (1816-1892).

See *"mho"* and *"aim, reciprocal."*

Siemens per meter (S m^{-1})

SI unit of conductivity.

Siemens square meter per mole (S m^2 mol^{-1})

SI unit of molar conductivity.

sieve

A traditional measure of the fineness of a wire screen (such as the screening used in a sieve). Higher sieve numbers correspond to finer screens.

In the U.S., 10 sieve fabric has openings of 2 millimeters; 100 sieve has openings of 0.15 millimeters. A similar but slightly different scale was used in Britain.

In the metric system, sieve fineness is specified by the diameter of the openings, in millimeters or micrometers.

sievert (Sv)

Derived SI unit of dose equivalent. The sievert is the dose equivalent when the absorbed dose of ionizing radiation multiplied by the dimensionless factors Q (quality factor) and N (product of any other multiplying factors) stipulated by the International Commission on Radiological Protection is one joule per kilogram. It equals 100 rems exactly.

Note: 1. The sievert is used specially as an arbitrary unit of the radiation dose due to γ-rays. It is defined as the dose of γ-rays delivered in one hour at a distance of one centimeter from a point source of one milligram of radium enclosed in a platinum container with walls of thickness half a millimeter. The experimentally determined value is 1 sievert = 8.38 roentgens approximately.

2. It was originally called the millicurie-of-intensity-hour.

See *"millicurie-of-intensity-hour"* and *"rem."*

sign (sign)

Unit of plane angle equal 30°.

1 sign = 30° = $\pi/6$.

Note: The unit represents the mean angular extent of one sign of the zodiac.

simon (simon)

Unit of resistance in a system of units called meter-gram.

1 simon = 30 ohms

Note: In this system of units, the unit of time is called **wink** and equal to (1/3000) microsecond, the unit of force is equal to 9×10^{13} newtons and is called samson. The unit of work is called Einstein and equal to 9×10^{13} joules.

siriometer (siriometer)

Arbitrary unit of length, mainly astronomical distances of an order greater than those in the solar system.

1. One siriometer equal to 10^6 astronomical units.

    1 sirioineter = 10^6 astronomical units = 149.600×10^{15} meters.

2. One siriometer equal 5 parsecs.

    1 siriometer = 5 parsecs = 154.286×10^{15} meters.

Note: When first proposed, the siriometer was meant to represent the distance of the star Sirius. Sirius is now known to be at a distance of 2.7 parsecs.

See *"parsec"* and *"astronomical unit."*

siriusweit (siriusweit)

Unit of length mainly astronomical distances and equals 5 parsecs.

1 siriusweit = 5 parsecs = 154.286 x 10^{15} meters.

Note: The unit used mainly by the German astronomer M.H. Seeliger (1849-1924).

See *"parsec".*

sixth

A unit used in music to describe the ratio in frequency between notes. Two notes differ by one minor sixth if the higher note has frequency exactly 8/5 times the frequency of the lower one or by a major sixth if the higher note has frequency exactly 5/3 times the frequency of the lower one. On the standard 12-tone scale, the minor sixth is approximated (roughly) by 8 half steps, corresponding to a frequency ratio of $2^{2/3} = 1.5874$; the major sixth is approximated by 9 half steps, corresponding to a frequency ratio of $2^{3/4} = 1.6818$.

skein (skein)

Arbitrary unit of length, equal to 360 feet.

1 skein = 360 feet = 109.728 meters.

Note: The unit is used mainly to measure cotton yarn.

skin erythema dose (SED)

Arbitrary unit of radioactive dose due to exposure to electromagnetic radiation (i.e., γ- and X-rays). One skin erythema dose is the dose of electromagnetic radiation, which, in eighty percent of the cases, slightly reddens or browns the skin within three weeks after exposure. The experimentally derived value is 1 skin erythema dose = 1000 roentgens approximately (for γ- rays); 600 roentgens approximately (for X-rays).

skot (skot)

Metric unit of luminance, particularly low-level lummance.

1 skot = 10^{-3} apostilb.

Note: 1. The unit was introduced in Germany for measuring "black-out" lighting during World War II.

2. It is better to use **millinit** instead of this unit.

See "nit".

slinch

A unit of mass invented by the U.S. National Aeronautics and Space Administration (NASA). The unit is part of a system based on the pound of force and the inch. One slinch is the mass accelerated at one inch per second per second by a force of one pound; thus, the slinch equals exactly 12 slugs (see below) or about 386.088 pounds (175.1268 kilograms). The word is a contraction of **slug-inch.** In the U.S. military aircraft industry, this unit is sometimes called a **mug**. It has also been called a **snail**.

slug (slug)

FSS unit of mass and also the British technical unit of mass. One slug is the mass that acquires an acceleration of one foot per second square under the influence of a force of one pound-force.

1 slug = 9.806 65/0.304 8 pounds = 14.593 9 kilograms.

Note: The unit is also called **gee pound.**

See *"gee pound."*

slug, metric (metric slug)

Metric-technical unit of mass. The metric slug is the mass that acquires an acceleration of one meter per second squared under the influence of a force of one kilogram-force.

1 metric slug = 9.80665 kg.

Note: The name metric slug is not often used; it is generally simply referred to as **the metric-technical unit of mass**. It is also called the **"hyl".** Alternative proposed (but not used) names are the **"mug"** and the **"par."**

See *"hyl,"* *"mug,"* and *"metric technical unit of mass."*

smoot

A humorous unit of distance invented in 1958 by a fraternity at the Massachusetts Institute of Technology. The fraternity pledges of Lambda Chi Alpha measured the length of Harvard Bridge using pledge Oliver R. Smoot ('62). According to Smoot himself, the bridge turned out to be 364.4 smoots long "plus epsilon," but this has been recorded as 364.4 smoots "plus an ear." The bridge is still marked in smoots. Proposals to change the definition of the unit by remeasuring it with Smoot's son Steve (MIT '89) or daughter Sherry ('99) were rebuffed. One smoot equals 67 inches (170.18 centimeters). Oliver Smoot became an attorney but continued his interest in standards and measurement. He is a past Chairman of the Board of Directors of ANSI, the American National Standards Institute, and currently, he is the President of the International Organization for Standardization (ISO).

snellen (snellen)

Unit of the visual power of the eye.

Note: The unit is named after the Dutch ophthalmogist Herman Snellen (1834-1908).

Snellen fraction

a ratio (such as 20/20 or 20/100) measuring the acuity (sharpness) of a person's eyesight for objects at a distance. The denominator (number after the slash) is the distance at which the detail of a letter on a standard test chart would subtend an angle of one arcminute, and the numerator (number before the slash) is the testing distance, the distance at which the person correctly identifies the letter. By custom, the ratio is often stated with a standard testing distance such as 20 feet or 6 meters; thus 20/100 (or 6/30) means that the person located 20 feet (or 6 meters, respectively) from the chart can identify a letter subtending an angle of one arcminute at a distance of 100 feet (30 meters). The fraction is also stated as a percentage, for example "20% vision" rather than 20/100. The unit is named for the Dutch ophthalmologist Herman Snellen (1834-1908), who developed the first standard methods for measuring visual acuity.

soendre

A traditional unit of land area in Bhutan, equal to roughly 1/20 acre or about 200 square meters.

sol (sol)

Unit of time equals 24 hours 36 minutes.

1 sol = 24 hours 36 minutes.

Note: The unit represents a **Martian day.**

Sol

An informal unit of time.

The United States-based NASA, when conducting missions to the planet Mars, has typically used a time of day system calibrated to the mean solar day on that planet (known as a "sol"), training those involved on those missions to acclimate to that length of day, which is 88,775 SI seconds, or 2,375 seconds (about 39 minutes) longer than the mean solar day on Earth. NASA's Martian timekeeping system (instead of breaking down the sol into 25×53×67 or 25×67×53 SI second divisions) slows down clocks so that the 24-hour day is stretched to the length of that on Mars; Martian hours, minutes and seconds are thus 2.75% longer than their SI-compatible counterparts.

The Darian calendar is an arrangement of sols into a Martian year. It maintains a seven-sol week (retaining Sunday through Saturday naming customs), with four weeks to a month and 24 months to a Martian year, which contains 668 or 669 sols depending on leap years. The last Saturday of every six months is skipped over in the Darian calendar.

solar day mean

The duration of one rotation of the Earth on its axis, with respect to the mean Sun; the length of the mean solar day is 24 hours of mean solar time or 24 hours, 03 minutes and 56.555 seconds of mean sidereal time.

solar mass ($M_\odot$)

a standard unit of mass in astronomy equal to the mass of the Sun: this is a convenient yardstick for measuring the masses of other stars, clusters, nebulae, and galaxies. The best estimate for the solar mass is $(1.98847 \pm 0.00007) \times 10^{30}$ kilograms. Since the masses of remote objects cannot be measured with precision the solar mass can be approximated as 2×10^{30} kilograms (2 nonillion kilograms in the U.S. system of naming large numbers).

solar neutrino unit (sun)

A unit used by astrophysicists to measure the rate at which neutrinos from the Sun are detected on Earth. Neutrinos are elementary particles with no charge and little or no mass (in 1999, it was reported that neutrinos do have a small mass). Scientists want to detect neutrinos because they carry crucial information about processes deep inside the Sun, but neutrinos are very hard to catch: most of them pass right through the Earth without interacting with anything. The solar neutrino unit, therefore, is extremely small: it is defined to be 10^{-36} neutrino capture per target atom per second.

solar second, mean

A unit equal to 1/86400 of a mean solar day.

solar time, mean

Time that has the mean solar second as its unit and is based on the mean Sun's motion.

sone (sone)

Unit of loudness. The loudness S in sones is related to the equivalent loudness P in phons by the formula: $S = 2^{(P-40)/10}$. Thus, 1 sone is the loudness that corresponds to an equivalent loudness of 40 phons.

Note: 1. The unit is defined so as to give scale values approximately proportional to the observed loudness of the sound.

2. The unit is analogous to the **noy.**

3. The unit was proposed by Stevens and Davis in 1938 and is recognized by the American Standards Association.

See *"phon"* and *"noy"*.

sotka

A Russian name for the are a metric unit of area equal to 100 square meters. This unit is commonly used to state the areas of small tracts of land. One sotka is approximately 1076.4 square feet, 1 19.60 square yards, or 0.02471 acres. The unit is sometimes transliterated from the Cyrillic as **cotka.**

See also *"are"* and *"acre"*.

South African geodetic foot (S.A.G. ft)

A unit of distance used for surveying and geodetic measurement throughout southern Africa. The S.A.G. foot is slightly shorter than the standard British or American foot; it equals 30.479 726 54 centimeters or 0.999 991 898 49 feet.

space (entire)

Arbitrary unit of solid angle. One space is the solid angle corresponding to the entire space at the center of a sphere.

1 space (entire) = 12.566 370 61 steradians

See *"steradian"* and also *"hemisphere"* and *"spherical right angle."*

span (Span)

Arbitrary unit of length, equal 9 inches.

1 span = **9** inch = **0.2286** meters.

This distance represents the span of a man's hand with fingers stretched out as far as possible. The old English word *spann* meant precisely this unit of measure; all the other uses of the word "span" came later.

spherical right angle

Arbitrary unit of solid angle equal to the solid angle corresponding to the one eighth of the entire space surrounding the center of a sphere.

1 spherical right angle = 0.125 spaces (entire) = 1.570 796 3 steradians.

See *"space {entire),"* *"steradian,"* and also *"hemisphere."*

spat (s)

Metric unit of length, particularly for astronomical measurement of distance.

1 S = 10^{12} meters

1 S = 6.68449 astronomical units.

Note: 1. The unit was suggested by Callou in 1944 to remove the necessity of using large numbers for describing distances- the Sun is 0.15 spat from the Earth.

2. The name of the unit is used also as unit of solid angle.

See *"spat (sp)"*

spat (sp)

Unit of solid angle equal the solid angle of the sphere.

1 sp = 4π steradians = 12.566 4 steradians.

Note: The name of the unit is used also as unit of length.

See *"spat (S)"*.

spindle

A traditional measure of length used for yarn. The length varied with the material; a spindle of cotton yarn, for example, was 15 120 yards (13.826 km), and a spindle of jute was 14 400 yards (13.167 km). The cotton spindle was also equal to 18 hanks.

Square

An informal unit of area.

1 square = 100 square feet (9.29 m^2)

The *square* is an Imperial unit of area that is used in the construction industry in North America and was historically used in Australia by real estate agents.

A roof's area may be calculated in square feet and then converted to squares.

square (of flooring)

Arbitrary unit of area equals 100 square feet.

1 square = **100** square feet = 9.290 304 square meters

Note: Used mainly to measure the area of the building.

square degree ($\square^{\circ}$) or (($^{\circ}$)^2)

Unit of solid angle equal to $(\pi/180)^2$ steradians.

1 square degree = $(\pi/180)^2$ steradians.

square grade (g)^2

Unit of solid angle equal to $(\pi/200)^2$ steradians.

1 square grade = $(\pi/200)^2$ steradians.

square inch (in^2)

U.K. and U.S. unit of area.

1 square inch = **0.645 16 x 10^{-3}** square meters.

square inch per tone-force (in^2/tonf).

U.K. unit of compressibility.

1 square inch per ton-force = 64.749 0 x 10^{-9} per pascal.

square meter (m^2)

SI unit of area.

square meter kelvin per watt (m² K W⁻¹)

SI unit of thermal insulance.

square meter per joule (m² J⁻¹)

SI unit of spectral cross section.

square meter per kilogram (m² Kg⁻¹)

SI unit of mass attenuation coefficient, mass energy transfer coefficient, mass absorption coefficient, mass energy absorption coefficient and specific surface.

square meter per kilogram-force second (m²/kgf.s)

MKFS unit of fluidity.

1 m²/kgf.s = 0.101 972 per pascal second (Pa-¹.s⁻¹).

square meter per mole (m² mol⁻¹)

SI unit of molar absorption coefficient and molar attenuation coefficient.

square meter per second (m² s⁻¹)

SI unit of diffusion coefficient, thermal diffusion coefficient and thermal diffusivity.

square meter per steradian (m² sr⁻¹)

SI unit of angular cross section.

square meter per steradian joule (m² sr⁻¹ J⁻¹)

SI unit of spectral angular cross section.

square meter per volt second (m² V⁻¹ s⁻¹)

SI unit of mobility.

square mile (mile²)

U.K. and U.S. unit of area.

1 square mile = **2.589 988 11 x 10⁶** meters squared.

Note: The symbol mi² is used in U.S.

square mile per ton (mile^2/UKton)

U.K. unit of the specific surface.

1 square mile per ton = 2.549 08 x 10^3 square meters per kilogram.

square yard (yd^2)

UK and U.S. unit of area.

1 square yard = **0.836 127 36** square meters.

square yard per ton (yd^2/ton)

U.K. unit of specific surface.

1 square yard per ton = 0.822 922 x 10^{-3} square meters per kilogram.

stab (stab)

SI unit of length equals one meter.

1 stab = 1 meter.

Note: The name stab was proposed to replace the meter but was never employed.

stack (stack)

Unit of volume (capacity) used mainly for the measure of fuel and timber equal to 108 cubic feet. 1 stack = 108 cubic feet = 3.058 219 476 cubic meters.

stade, stadion or stadium

A historic unit of distance originating in ancient Greece. Greek athletic fields were all of roughly the same size, and the **stadion**, equal to 600 podes (feet), was the traditional length of the field. Archaeological measurements show that the stadion was a little more than 200 yards or a little less than 200 meters. The stadion at Olympia, where the original Olympic Games were held, measures 630.8 feet or 192.3 meters; at Athens, the stadion was 606.9 feet or 185.0 meters. **Stadium** is the Latin spelling; in the Roman world, the stadium was equal to 625 Roman feet (*pes*) or 1/8 Roman mile. This is equivalent to 606.95 feet, 202.32 yards, or 185.00 meters. The plural is **stadia**.

stadia (stadia)

Unit of length used in ancient Egypt equal (925/5000) kilometers.

1 stadia = 185 meters.

Note: This unit goes back to 200 B.C. when Eratosthenes made the first reliable measurement of the circumference of the Earth by observing that the Sun was directly overhead at Syene at noon at the summer solstice and was about 7° from the vertical at Alexandria, a distance of 5000 stadia (925 kilometers) to the north. From this, he calculated the circumference of the Earth was about 26000 miles.

stadion

An obsolete unit of length

The **stadion** (plural **stadia**, Greek: στάδιον; latinized as stadium), also anglicized as **stade**, was an ancient Greek unit of length, consisting of 600 feet.

standard (standard)

Unit of volume used only to measure timber, equal to 165 cubic feet.

1 standard = 165 cubic feet = 4.762 28 cubic meters.

Note: The unit is also called **Petrograd Standard**.

See *"Pelrograd standard"* and also *"stere"*.

standard atmosphere (atm)

Unit of pressure. According to the International Civil Aviation Organization (ICAO), the standard atmosphere is equivalent to a pressure of 1.013250×10^5 Newtons per square meter, 760 torrs, or 1013.250 millibars.

1 standard atmosphere = **1.013 25** bars = **760** tons = **0.101 325 x 10^6** pascals.

Note: The ICAO standard atmosphere was introduced about 1940 and has been used internationally since 1954.

3. In 1922, the National Advisory Committee on Aeronautics (NACA) introduced a definition for the standard atmosphere and in 1924, the International Commission for Air Navigation (ICAN) introduced a similar definition which is" the pressure of a column of mercury 760 millimeters high at specific temperature". The main difference between the two standard atmospheres is that in NACA atmosphere, the acceleration due to gravity is taken to be 9.806 6 meters per square second, whereas it is 9.806 2 meters per square second in the ICAN atmosphere.

standard cable

Unit of attenuation. The unit compared the attenuation produced in the circuit under test with that in a standard cable, which was defined as a theoretical cable 1 mile in length, resistance 88 ohms, capacitance 0.054 microfarads, inductance 1 millihenry and leakance 500×10^3 mho.

Note: The unit was adopted in 1905 by the National Telegraph Company in the USA and by the Post Office in Great Britain. It was replaced by the transmission unit (TU) in 1922 and then it was superseded by the bel in 1923.

See *"transmission unit"* and *"bel"*.

standard cubic foot (SCF)

A once-common volume measure for gas in the gas industry. It is the amount of gas in a cubic foot when the gas is under one atmosphere pressure and at 20°C.

standard deviation (sd)

A mathematical unit used to describe the "spread" or dispersion of a set of data. Each item in the data set has a deviation from the mean (the ordinary average) of the data. The standard deviation is computed by taking the squares of these individual deviations, averaging these squares, and then taking the square root. If the data set conforms to a known distribution, such as the normal ("bell curve") distribution, then one can compute the percentage of the data which will fall within a certain distance of the mean, as measured in standard deviations, for example, if the data set conforms to the normal distribution, 68.3% of the data will fall within one standard deviation of the mean and only about 4.5% will fall outside 2 standard deviations from the mean.

standard drink

a measure of alcohol consumption used for various legal and statistical purposes. The amount of alcohol in a standard drink varies by country; in the U.S. a standard drink includes exactly 14 grams of alcohol. The standard is 10 grams in many European countries, 8 grams in the United Kingdom, and 13.6 grams in Canada.

standard gravity

Unit of acceleration due to gravity. It was agreed at the 1968 CGPM that for metrological work, the value of the acceleration due to gravity at Potsdam was to be taken as standard value.

Standard gravity = The acceleration due to gravity at Potsdam = 9.812 60 meters per squared second.

Note: The above value is also used as the reference base for the international gravimetric system of units.

standard volume

Unit of volume used with gas. It is the volume occupied by 1 kilogram molecule of a gas at 0°C and at a pressure of 1 standard atmosphere.

1 standard volume = 22.414 cubic meters.

stanine

A statistical unit used in educational testing. Test scores are normalized (mathematically transformed) so that they have a mean ("average") of 5 and a standard deviation of 2. This transformation naturally divides the ranked scores into 9 classes called stanines 1-9. The percentage of scores in each stanine is 4, 7, 12, 17, 20, 17, 12, 7, and 4, respectively. The technique originated in the U.S. military during World War 11, and the word is a contraction of "standard of nine."

stapp

A unit used to express the effects of acceleration or deceleration on the human body. One stapp represents an acceleration of 1 g for a period of 1 second, or 9.80665 meters per second per second for 1 second. The unit is named for the U.S. Air Force physician John P. Stapp (1910-1999), a pioneer in research on the human effects of acceleration during the 1940s and 1950s.

stat (St).

Arbitrary unit of radioactive disintegration rate, i.e. activity. One stat is the quantity of radon ` that, due to its being situated in air, gives rise in one second to a charge of one franklin in air.

1 stat = 3.63 x 10^{-27} curies.

stat-.... (s---)

A prefix denoting a CGSe unit (used in the U.S.). Some of the CGSe units and the equivalent SI units are given in the following table.

CGSe UNIT	Quantity	Corresponding SI unit	To Covert from CGSe to SI, multiply by:
Statampere (sA)	Electric current	Ampere (A)	$0.333\ 564 \times 10^{-9}$
Statampere centimeter squared (sA.cm^2)	Electromagnetic moment	Ampere meter squared (A m^2)	$33.356\ 4 \times 10^{-15}$
Statampere per square centimeter (sA.cm^2)	Current density	Ampere per square meter (A/m^2)	$3.335\ 64 \times 10^{-6}$
Statcoulomb (sC)	Electric charge	Coulomb	$0.333\ 564 \times 10^{-9}$
Statcoulomb (sC.cm)	Electric dipole moment	Coulomb meter (C.m)	$3.335\ 64 \times 10^{-12}$
Statcoulomb per cubic centimeter (sC.cm^3)	Volume density of charge	Coulomb per cubic meter (C/m^3)	$0.333\ 564 \times 10^{-3}$
Statcoulomb per square centimeter (sC.cm^2)	Electric polarization; Electric flux density	Coulomb per square meter (C/m^2)	$-3.335\ 64 \times 10^{-6}$ $^-0.265\ 442 \times 10^{-6}$
Statfarad (sF)	Capacitance	Farad (F)	$1.112\ 65 \times 10^{-12}$
Stathenry (sH)	Inductance	Henry (H)	$0.898\ 755 \times 10^{-12}$
Statohm (sΩ)	Resistance	Ohm (Ω)	$0.898\ 755 \times 10^{-12}$
Statohm centimeter (sΩ.cm)	Resistivity	Ohm meter (Ω.m)	$8.987\ 55 \times 10^{9}$
Statsiemens (sS)	Conductance	Siemens (S)	$1.112\ 65 \times 10^{-12}$
Statsiemens per centimeter (sS/cm)	Conductivity	Siemens per meter (S/m)	$0.111\ 265 \times 10^{-9}$
Statvolt (sV)	Electric potential	Volt (V)	$0.299\ 792 \times 10^{3}$

Statvolt per centimeter (sV/cm)	Electric field strength	Volt per meter (V/m)	29.979 2 x 10^3

stathm (stathm)

CGS unit of mass. It is equal to one gram.

1 stathm = 1 gram.

Note: This name, as other names, was proposed as an alternative for the gram, but never employed.

See also, *"bes"* and *"brieze"*.

step

[1] **A** traditional unit of distance, equal to 1/2 pace. The step is traditionally equal to 30 inches or 76.2 centimeters. However, U.S. marching bands often use a shorter step of 22.5 inches (57.15 centimeters), so until steps are made every 5 yards; this works well on American football fields, which have a chalkline every 5 yards. Using this shorter step is called marching "8 by 5."

[2] **A** unit used in music to describe the ratio in frequency between notes. Two notes differ by a step if the higher note has a frequency exactly $2^{1/6} = 1.12246$ times the frequency of the lower one. This unit is often called the **full step** to distinguish it from the half step.

See also *"pace."*

steradian (sr also sterad)

Supplementary SI unit of solid angle. It is the solid angle which, having its vertex in the center of a sphere, cuts off an area of the surface of the sphere equal to that of a square having sides of length equal to the radius of the sphere.

Note: The CIPM of 1980 specified that in the S1, the quantities plane angle and solid angle should be considered as dimensionless derived quantities. Therefore, the supplementary units radian and steradian are to be regarded as dimensionless derived units, which may be used or omitted in the expressions for derived units.

stere (st)

SI unit of volume used especially for measuring timber volumes. It is equal to one cubic meter.

1 st = 1 cubic meter.

Note: The unit was extensively used in France for measuring bundles of firewood.

See also *"standard"*.

sthene (sn)

MTS unit of force. It is equal to the force which, when applied to a body of mass one ton, gives it an acceleration of one meter per second squared.

1 sn = 1 ton meter per square second = 1000 newtons.

Note: 1. The unit was originally proposed by the British Association in 1876.

2. The unit was formerly called the *funal*.

See *"funal"*.

Sthène

An obsolete unit of force

- The **sthène** (French: [stɛn]; symbol **sn**), sometimes spelled (or misspelled) **sthéne**[1] or **sthene** (from Ancient Greek: σθένος, romanized: *sthénos*, lit. 'force'), is an obsolete unit of force or thrust in the metre–tonne–second system of units (mts) introduced in France in 1919. When proposed by the British Association in 1876, it was called the **funal**, but the name was changed by 1914. The mts system was abandoned in favor of the mks system and has now been superseded by the Système International (SI).

1 sthène = 1 kilonewton

$\approx$ 101.9716 kilogram-force

$\approx$ 224.8089 pound-force

$\approx$ 7,233.014 poundals

stigma (σ):

Metric unit of length, particularly nuclear lengths.

1 σ = 10^{-12} meters.

Note: 1. The unit was proposed by Callou in 1944 to give reasonable numbers for atomic measurements.

2. This unit has also been called the **bicron**.

See *"bicron"*.

sthene (sn)

A metric unit of force, part of the "meter-ton-second" system sometimes used by European engineers. One sthene is the force required to accelerate a mass of one ton at a rate of 1 m/s^2. Thus, the sthene is equal to the kilonewton, so 1 sthene is equivalent to 10^8 dynes, 224.809 pounds of force, or 7233.01 pounds. The name comes from the Greek word *sthenos*, strength.

stick (stk)

[1] an. Informal unit used to measure butter. 1n the United States, butter is usually sold in 1-pound packages containing 4 sticks; thus, 1 stick equals 1/4 pounds (roughly 113 grams). On the other hand, 1 stick is also considered equal to 1/2 cup (roughly 118 milliliters). Thus, the unit is used both as a weight measure and as a volume measure.

[2] an informal unit of distance used in electrical work in the U.S. One stick is equal to 10 feet (3.048 meters) because electrical conduit of various kinds is traditionally supplied in 10-foot lengths called sticks.

stilb (sb)

CGS unit of luminance. It is equal to one candela per square centimeter,

1 stilb = 1 candela per square centimeter = 10^4 nits

Note: The name of the unit was proposed by the French physicist A Blondel (1 863-193 8) in 1921.

See *"candela per square centimeter"* and *"nit."*

stokes (St)

CGS unit of kinematic viscosity. One stokes is the kinematic viscosity of a fluid with a dynamic viscosity of one poise and a density of one gram per centimeter cubed.

1 stokes = 1 poise cubic centimeter per gram = 0.1×10^{-3} meter square per second.

Note: 1. The name of the unit is after the mathematician Sir George G. Stokes (1819-1903), who was a Professor at Cambridge.

2. The unit has also been called the **stoke**. It was formerly called the **lentor.**

3. The British Standards Institution recommends that, for the calibration of viscometers, the kinematic viscosity of water should be taken as 1.003 8 centistokes at 20° C.

See *"poise"* and *"lentor"*.

stone (stone)

U.K. imperial unit of mass equals 14 pounds.

1 stone = 14 pounds = 6.350 293 18 kilograms.

Note: There is no corresponding U.S. unit.

stop

A unit of relative exposure used in photography. In optics, a "stop" is a ring-shaped baffle or shield used to reduce the aperture (the diameter of the opening) of a lens. In photography, the amount of light used to expose the film can be controlled either by varying the aperture, by varying the length of time the shutter is open to admit light, or by some combination of these two methods. Two exposures differ by one stop if one is made with twice the light of the other; similarly, they differ by n stops if one is made with 2^n times the light of the other.

storey or story

An informal unit of distance equal to the average distance between floors of a building. In British English the spelling is "storey," and the plural is "storeys"; Americans write "story" and "stories." Typically, a story equals 10 to 12 feet (3.0-3.6 meters). The origin of this use of the word "story" is not entirely clear, but in medieval times 3, tier of sculptures or stained glass windows on the front of a cathedral was called a stor(e)y because it usually told a story, and the number of stories was a measure of the size of the building.

streck

A unit of angle measurement used in the Swedish military, equal to 1/17.5 degree. This is equivalent to 3.429 minutes of arc (moa), 1.0159 mil (in NATO terminology), or 0.9973 milliradians.

stremma

A traditional Greek unit of area now redefined to equal exactly 1000 square meters or 0.1 hectares (0.24710 acres).

strich (strich)

Unit of length equal to 1 millimeter.

1 strich = 1 millimeter = 10^{-3} meters.

Note: The name is sometimes used to replace the millimeter.

strob

A metric unit of angular velocity. The strob represents a rotation rate of one radian per second or 9.54930 rpm. The name comes from the Greek *strobos,* meaning "rotating."

strontium unit (SU)

Arbitrary unit of concentration of strontium-9O in an organic medium (e.g., soil, milk, bone) relative to the concentration of calcium in the same medium.

1 SU = 10^{-9} curies of strontium-90 per kilogram of calcium.

Note: This unit is also called the **sunshine unit.**

See "Sunshine Unit."

Stuck

An obsolete unit of volume

Stuck was a form occasionally found in English writing as a corruption of the German "Stück" itself, an abbreviation of *Stückfass* (formerly written *Stückfaß*), referring to the volume of a wine cask of around 1000-1200 liters. It was normally used in reference to German wine production.

sturgeon (sturgeon)

MKSA unit of magnetic reluctance equal to the reciprocal of international henry..

1 sturgeon 1/international henry

Note: 1. The name was suggested by Sir Oliver Lodge in 1892,

2. The name of the unit is after W. Sturgeon (1783-1850), one of the inventors of the galvanometer.

Sumner unit (sumner unit)

Unit of enzyme activity referred to urease. Sumner unit is the amount of enzyme that will liberate 1 milligram of ammonia-nitrogen at 20°C in 5 minutes.

1 Sumner unit = 14.25 International Union of Biochemistry activity unit.

Note: The name of the unit is after J.B. Sumner (1877-1955), the biochemist who was the first to isolate enzymes and who was awarded the Nobel Prize for chemistry in 1946.

Sun

A unit of mass used in astronomy to express the masses of stars. Stars are so massive that it's difficult to grasp their relative sizes. Using the Sun's mass as a unit helps us visualize them relative to something familiar. The best current estimate of the mass of the Sun is 1.9891×10^{30} kilograms or 1.9891×10^{27} tons.

Sun

An informal unit of mass.

Solar mass ($M_\odot = 2.0 \times 10^{30}$ kg) is also often used in astronomy when talking about masses of stars or galaxies; for example, Alpha Centauri A has the mass of 1.1 suns, and the Milky Way has a mass of approximately 6×10^{11} $M_\odot$.

Solar mass also has a special use when estimating orbital periods and distances of 2 bodies using Kepler's laws: $a^3 = M_{total}T^2$, where a is length of the semi-major axis in AU, T is an orbital period in years and M_{total} is the combined mass of objects in $M_\odot$. In the case of planet orbiting a star, M_{total} can be approximated to mean the mass of the central object. More specifically, in the case of Sun and Earth, the numbers reduce to $M_{total} \sim 1$, $a \sim 1$ and $T \sim 1$.

sunshine unit (SU)

Arbitrary unite of concentration of strontium-90 in an organic medium (e.g., soil, milk, bone) relative to the concentration of calcium in the same medium.

1 SU = 10^{-9} curie of strontium-90 per kilogram of calcium.

Note: This unit is also called strontium unit.

See *"strontium unit"*.

survey foot (U.S.) (U.S. survey foot)

U.S. unit of length. It is defined as (1200/3937) of the meter.

1 U.S. survey foot = (1200/3937) meter = 0.304 800 6 meters.

Note: This unit is used for Coast and Geodetic surveys within the U.S.

See also *"foot"*.

svedberg (S)

Unit of sedimentation coefficient, i.e., time. The sedimentation coefficient S in svedbergs is related to a: velocity v of the boundary between the solution containing the molecules and solvent (in meter per second), distance x from the boundary to the axis of rotation (in meters) and the angular velocity ω of the centrifuge: causing sedimentation (in radian per second) by the formula: $S = 10^{-13} \, v/\omega^2 x$.

1 svedberg $= 10^{-13}$ seconds.

Note: The unit name is after T. Svedberg (1884-1971), the Swedish pioneer in the use of the ultracentrifuge.

Sverdrup (Sverdrup)

Unit of rate flow equal to a flow of one million cubic meter per second.

1 Sverdrup $= 1 \times 10^6$ cubic meters per second

Note: 1. The unit is used mainly to measure the flow of ocean currents.

2. The name of the unit is after H.U. Sverdrup (1888-1957), director of the Norwegian Polar Institute.

swing

An informal unit of time describing the length in days of one work cycle. For example, a worker who works 7 days in a row and then gets 3 days off is said to have a swing of 10 days. This usage doesn't seem to be related to the "swing shift," which is a shift that begins in the afternoon and ends at night.

SWU

Symbol for the **separative work unit,** a unit used in the nuclear power industry to describe the work required to enrich uranium (that is, to increase the fraction of uranium 235, the isotope which undergoes fission to produce energy). The details are quite complex but roughly speaking, about 4.5 SWU are needed to enrich 1 kilogram of uranium, more or less depending on the degree of enrichment needed for a particular reactor.

symbol per second (sym/s)

A unit of transmission rate for radio signals, especially for the transmissions between satellites and ground stations. In the simplest form of transmission, data can be sent in bits, which have only two states (on or off). To increase data transmission rates as much as possible, information is sent in units called "symbols," which have a number of states so that each symbol can include several bits of information. In practice, transmission rates are usually stated in Ksym/s (thousands of symbols per second) or Msym/s (millions of symbols per second).

T

ta

In Vietnam is a unit of mass, approximately 60.450 kilogrammes (approximately 133.3 pounds).

In the south of Vietnam, it had various values depending on the commodity measured: charcoal, manioc, potatoes and lime, 60 kilogrammes; live hogs or rice, 100 kilogrammes; paddy, 68 kilogrammes.

tablespoon or tablespoonful (tbsp, tblsp, Tsp or T) [1]

a unit of volume used in food recipes. In the U.S., the tablespoon is equal to 1/2 fluid ounce; this is about 14.8 milliliters. In Canada, the traditional tablespoon is 1/2 Imperial fluid ounce (14.2 milliliters). In Britain, traditional tablespoons varied somewhat in size, and various older references give sizes in the range from 1/2 to 5/8 Imperial fluid ounce (14.2-17.6 milliliters). Under the metric system, the tablespoon has become more or less standardized at 15 milliliters in Britain, Canada, and New Zealand and 20 milliliters in Australia. The U.S. tablespoon equals 3 teaspoons or 1/16 cup; the traditional British tablespoonful was often equal to 4 teaspoonfuls or 1/10 teacupful. The metric tablespoon equals 3 teaspoons (4 in Australia).

See "fluid ounce" "cup."

tablespoon or tablespoonful (tbsp, tblsp, Tsp, or T) [2]

a unit of volume used in bartending. U.S. bartenders use a tablespoon of 3/8 fluid ounce or 1/4 jigger; this is equivalent to about 11.1 milliliters.

tắc

In Vietnam, it is unit of length and of area:

- for length, officially = 4 centimeters, but sometimes 4.7 centimeters
- for area, = 2.40 square meters, but in the central area, 3.3135 square meters. Also called a *thốn*.

tael or tahil

a traditional unit of weight used throughout eastern Asia. During the colonial period, the tael was more or less standardized throughout the region at 4/3 ounce avoirdupois (1/16 catty, 1/12 pound, or about 37.8 grams). In Japan, however, the tael was identified with a slightly smaller traditional unit and is considered equal to 1.323 ounces (37.51 grams). The tael is usually considered equal to the Chinese liang.

See also "ounce", "pound."

Tagwerk,

In Germany, a unit of agricultural land area, literally translated, "daywork." Like many early units of land area, it represents the area that could be plowed in one day.

- in Bavaria = 40,000 square *Fuss*, approximately 3407.27 square meters (approximately 0.84 acre).
- in Hannover about 2602 square meters.

talanto

Informal unit of mass

1   talanto = 100 pound.

The value of the talanto was defined at the United States of the Ionian Islands, by an Act of Parliament dated *24 May 1828*

talbot (talbot)

SI unit of luminous energy. One talbot is the luminous energy corresponding to one joule of radiant energy having a luminous efficiency of one lumen per watt.

1 talbot = 1 joule lumen per watt = 1 lumen second

Note: 1. The unit is equal in size to the **lumberg**.

2. The unit is an MKS unit and first used in 1937.

3. The name of the unit is after W.H.Fox Talbot (1800-1877) who discovered the principle of the flicker photometer in 1834.

See *"lumen "watt", "joule"* and also *"lumberg"*.

talent

a historic unit of weight, used in various forms throughout the eastern Mediterranean. The Hebrew sacred talent, mentioned in the Bible, was equal to 60 minas or about 30 kilogrammes (66 pounds). The Greek talent, also equal to 60 minas, was smaller, 25.8 kilogrammes or about 57 pounds.

See also "minas"

tamna

In Morocco, a unit of land area, approximately 225 square meters (approximately 269.1 square yards).

tan [1]

a traditional Chinese weight unit, now spelled **dan** in English transliteration. During the European colonial era the tan was equal to 100 cattys or 1600 taels. This is equivalent to 133.333 pounds, making the tan comparable to the European quintal as a commercial weight unit. In modern China the tan, or rather the dan, is equal to 100 jin, which is exactly 50 kilogrammes (110.231 pounds).

See also "catty"' "pound", "quintal"

tan [2]

a traditional unit of land area in Japan equal to 10 se or about 991.7 square meters (0.099 hectare or 0.245 acre).

See also "acre"

Tank

- A **tank** is an obsolete unit of mass in India approximately equal to 4.4 g.

  After metrication in the mid-20th century, the unit became obsolete.

- In Mumbai (formerly Bombay), the tank equalled 17 1/72 grains (about 1.1 grams), and 72 tanks equalled 30 pice. In the 16th century, the tank was reported to be 20.96 g (323.46 grain).

tappet hen

An informal unit of volume.

- A size of drinking vessel, containing 2 Scottish pints.
- A size of bottle used for port, equivalent to three ordinary bottles, = 2.273 liters.

tarea

A traditional unit of land area in the Dominican Republic and some parts of Central America. The tarea is generally equal to 900 square varas, so it is the area of a square 30 varas (about 25.05 meters) on a side. In the Dominican Republic, the tarea equals about 628 square meters or 751 square yards; this is 0.0628 hectare or 0.155 acre. The Spanish word *tarea* means a task or job, so this unit, like many land area units, originated as the area which could be "worked" in a given time.
See also "yaras", "hectare", "acre"

tarefa

a traditional unit of land area in Brazil, varying in size from one locality to another but generally at least 3000 square meters (0.3 hectare or 0.741 acre). In the states of Alagoas, Rio Grande do Norte, and Sergipe the tarefa equals 3025 square meters (0.3025 hectare or 0.748 acre); in Ceará the unit equals 3630 square meters (0.363 hectare or 0.897 acre); and in Bahia the tarefa is 4356 square meters (0.4356 hectare or 1.076 acre). The Portuguese word *tarefa*, like the Spanish *tarea*, means a task or job.
See also "hectare", "acre"

tatami

a Japanese unit of area equal to the area of a traditional tatami mat, 0.5 ken by 1 ken or about 90 centimeters by 180 centimeters (roughly 1.62 square meters or 17.5 square feet). This unit, used especially for measuring the area of rooms in houses and apartments, is also called the **jo**.
See also "ken"

Tathe

A **tathe** or **tate** is a unit of area which was used in Fermanagh and Monaghan, equivalent to 60 Irish acres.

Four tathes make a *quarter* of land, four quarters make a *ballibetagh* and, in Fermanagh, seven ballibetaghs make a *barony*, of which there were seven. However, the measure of a ballibetagh is far larger in Fermanagh than in Monaghan. In total at this period in time (1609), it was estimated that Fermanagh which had 51 ballibetaghs and a half of "chargeable lands" contained the same area as Monaghan which had 100 ballibetaghs.

A quick survey of 1608 found the Tathe to be only half the extent assigned to it by the Irish which was 60 native Irish acres.

See also "acre"

tartous

In Syria, a unit of area, also called the *denum*.

Mohazafat or Latakia	800 square meters (approximately 957 square yards).
Damascus	919 square meters (approximately 1,099 square yards).
Homs and Aleppo	919.3 square meters (approximately 1099.5 square yards).

tatami

In Japan, a traditional unit measuring the area of a domestic room. The tatami is a woven straw mat used as floor covering. Its size became standardized in the Muromachi Period (*1338 – 1573*) at one ken long and half a ken wide. The ken, however, has varied. It is approximately 1.82 meters (1.97 in the Kansai area, including the cities of Kyoto, Osaka, and Kobe). Thus 1 tatami is approximately 1.66 square meters.

Tatum

Informal unit of time in the "Humorous System of Units"

A tatum is the "lowest regular pulse train that a listener intuitively infers from the timing of perceived musical events." It is named after the jazz pianist Art Tatum, who was notable for his high-speed playing

teacupful

a unit of liquid volume used in British food recipes. The teacupful is the same volume as an Imperial gill: 5 fluid ounces, 8.670 cubic inches, or about 137.7 milliliters.
See also "gill"

teaspoon or teaspoonful (tsp or t) [1]

a unit of volume used in food recipes. The U.S. teaspoon is equal to 1/3 tablespoon or 1/48 cup; this is equivalent to 1/6 fluid ounce, about 0.30 cubic inches, or approximately 4.9 milliliters. In Canada, the traditional teaspoon is 1/6 Imperial fluid ounce or about 4.74 milliliters. In Britain, a traditional **teaspoonful** in the kitchen was equal to 1/8 Imperial fluid ounce or approximately 3.55 milliliters, but the medical teaspoonful was usually 5 milliliters. In metric kitchens in Britain, Canada, Australia, and New Zealand, a teaspoonful is exactly 5 milliliters.
See also "fluid ounce", "cup"

teaspoon or teaspoonful (tsp or t) [2]

a unit of volume used in bartending. U.S. bartenders use a teaspoon equal to 1/8 fluid ounce or 1/12 jigger; this is equivalent to about 3.7 milliliters.

technical atmosphere (at)

a metric unit of pressure equal to one kilogramme of force per square centimeter. The technical atmosphere equals about 980.665 millibars (mb), 98.0665 kilopascal (kPa), approximately 28.96 inches of mercury (in Hg), or 14.223 pounds of force per square inch (lbf/in^2). This is about 97% of the average pressure of the earth's atmosphere at sea level.

Technical unit of mass (called kilohyl)

The unit of mass in the meter—kilogramme force—second system of units, approximately 9.80665 kilogrammes. Sometimes called the metric technical unit of mass (symbol, TME), the metric slug, the mug, or the par. It is also called the hyl! The Russian physicist M. F. Malikov proposed it be called the inerta, symbol i, but this name was never used.

See also "hyl"

tebi- (Ti-)

a binary prefix meaning 2^{40} = 1 099 511 627 776. This prefix was adopted by the International Electrotechnical Commission in 1998 to replace tera- for binary applications in computer science. In particular a **tebibyte (TiB)** is 2^{40} = 1 099 511 627 776 bytes. The prefix is a contraction of "terabinary."

TECHMA (techma)

German abbreviated name for ***technische Masseneinheit***, which 15 the German name of the **metric technique unit of mass**.

See *"metric technical unit of mass"*.

TECHNICAL ATMOSPHERE (at)

Arbitrary unit of pressure. One technical atmosphere is the pressure resulting from a force of one kilogramme force acting uniformly over an area of one square centimeter.

1 technical atmosphere = 1 kilogramme-force per square centimeter = **9.806 635x 10^4** pascal.

teener

In North America, *late 20th – 21st centuries*, a unit of mass used in retail trade in cocaine, in theory = $\frac{1}{16}$ of an avoirdupois ounce (1.77 grams), but in practice often 1.5 g. Also called a "half ball", because two teens is an "eightball" (⅛ avoirdupois ounce), which is usually 3.5 grams. Other terms for the eightball include "ball", "pool", "an 8", "skate", "bitch" and "full guy".

It is interesting to note that while the buyers and sellers usually measure in grams, the names of the units of mass refer to the avoirdupois ounce. Continuing the series above:

- 7 grams (a quarter-ounce): "q balls", "quatches", "quarters
- 14 grams (half an ounce): "half", "h bomb", "half z", "half zip", "half zone", "half zipper"
- 28 grams (an ounce): "o", "zip", "zone", "zipper"

For greater weights the names are based on grams, based on the "key" (kilogramme).

TELEGRAPH NAUTICAL MILE (telegraph nautical mile)

Unit of length equals 6087 feet.

1 telegraph nautical mile = **6.087 x 10^3** feet = 1.855 32 x 10^3 meter.

telegraph units of electrical resistance

Prior to the introduction and standardization of the ohm, engineers building telegraph systems had an acute need for a unit of resistance, and they devised a number of short-lived, often local, units to meet that need.

- A French unit, attributed to Digney: the resistance of 1 kilometer of iron wire 4 mm in diameter. About 9.266 B.A. ohms[1], about 9.142 true ohms. In *1867*, redefined as 10 Siemen's units, about 9.534 ohms.
- A unit attributed to Brèguet. About 9.760 B.A. ohms[1], about 9.629 true ohms.
- A Swiss unit, following Hipp. About 10.42 B.A. ohms[1], about 10.28 true ohms. In *1867*, redefined as 10 Siemen's units, about 9.534 ohms.

- A German unit by *1848*, 1 German Meile (7532.83 meters) of copper wire ¹⁄₁₂ of an inch (2.1 millimeters) in diameter at 20° centigrade. About 57.44 B.A. ohms[1], about 56.67 true ohms. Superceded by the Siemen's unit.

- An American unit, the resistance of one statute mile of No. 9 iron wire. The American Telegraph Company had standards wound to support use of this unit. Superceded by the B. A. ohm.

In addition the Varley unit and the Mathiessen unit (both based on an English statute mile of wire) were telegraph units.

TENTHMETRE (tenthmetre)

Metric unit of length, especially the wavelength of visible and near-visible radiation.

1 tenthmetre = 10^{-10} meter

Note: It is better to call this unit the **"angstrom"**.

See *"angstrom"*.

TERA-..... (T)

SI prefix denoting $x10^{12}$. Examples are: terabecquerel (Tbq), terahertz (Thz), terajoule (TJ), terametre (Tm), teraohm (tΩ) and terawatt (TW).

terabecquerel (TBq)

a unit of radioactivity equal to 10^{12} atomic disintegrations per second or 27.027 curie.

terabyte (TB)

a unit of information equal to 10^{12} (one trillion) bytes. The terabyte is often used to mean 2^{40} = 1 099 511 627 776 bytes but this use breaks the rules of the SI. The unit equal to 2^{40} bytes should be called the **tebibyte** (see above).

teraflops (Tflops)

a unit of computing power equal to one trillion (10^{12}) floating point operations per second. See flop.

teragram (Tg)

a metric unit of mass equal to 10^{12} grams or 1 megatonne (one million metric tons). This unit is frequently used in atmospheric science and other scientific contexts where large masses are considered.

terahertz (THz)

a unit of frequency equal to 10^{12} per second or 1 per picosecond. Infrared and visible light waves have frequencies measured in terahertz.

terajoule (TJ)

a metric unit of energy commonly used in the energy industry, equal to 10^{12} joules. One terajoule equals 947.817 million Btu, 277.7778 megawatt hours (MW·h), or about 9480 therms (see below). See also "joule", "Btu."

terameter (Tm)

a metric unit of distance equal to 10^{12} meters or 10^9 kilometers. This is about 6.6846 astronomical units. The distance from Saturn to the Sun is about 1.43 terameters.

terannual

an adjective meaning 3 times per year or once every 4 months. Not to be confused with triennial (once every 3 years).

terawatt (TW)

a metric unit of power equal to one trillion (10^{12}) watts or about 1.341 billion horsepower.
See also "horsepower"

terawatt hour (TW·h)

a metric unit of energy equal to one billion kilowatt hours (kW·h), 3.6 petajoules (PJ), or about 3.412 trillion Btu.
See also "Btu"

tertian

a traditional unit of volume for liquids. The tertian, like the tierce (see below) takes its name from the Latin for 1/3. It equals 1/3 tun, which is 2 tierces or 84 U.S. gallons (about 318 liters).
See also "gallon"

tesla (T)

The SI unit of the magnetic flux density and magnetic polarization. It equals to the magnetic flux density given by a magnetic flux of one weber per square meter.
$1\ T = 1\ Wb/m^2$.

Note: 1. This unit was formerly called **absolute tesla** (T_{abs}). It must be distinguished from the international tesla (T_{int}) formally abandoned in 1948.

2. The name was approved by the IEC in 1954 and used by the SUN Committee for the unit of magnetic flux density in the MKS system of units in 1961.

3. The name of the unit is after N.Tesla (1857-1943) who invented the Tesla coil in 1892.

TEU

a unit of cargo capacity, especially for container ships. These ships carry cargo in standard metal boxes, called containers, which can be transferred easily to trains or trucks. TEU is an abbreviation for "twenty-foot equivalent unit." One TEU represents the cargo capacity of a standard container 20 feet long, 8 feet wide, and (usually) a little over 8 feet high, or half the capacity of a similar container 40 feet long. One TEU equals about 12 register tons (see ton [3] below) or 34 cubic meters.

See also "feet"

tex (tex)

Metric unit of line density (mass per unit length). One tex is the line density of a thread which has a mass of one gramme and a length of one kilometer.

1 tex = **1** gramme per kilometer = 10^{-6} kilogramme per meter.

Note: This unit is used in the textile industry as a measure of yarn count.

equals 10 drex or 9 denier.

See also "drex", "denier"

therblig

a unit of physical activity used in time-and-motion studies in industrial engineering. A therblig represents one of 18 standardized activities identified by the American industrial psychologists Frank B. Gilbreth (1868-1924) and Lillian Moller Gilbreth (1878-1972): search, find, select, grasp, hold, position, assemble, use, disassemble, inspect, transport loaded, transport unloaded, pre-position for next operation, release load, unavoidable delay, avoidable delay, plan, and rest for overcoming fatigue. The word is Gilbreth spelled backwards (considering "th" as one letter).

therm

UK unit of heat energy. One therm is the heat required to raise 1000 pounds of water through 100°F.

1 therm = 10^5 (International Table) British thermal unit (Btu) = 1.05505585262 x 10^8 joules.

Note: The British Association, at their Bath Meeting in 1888, decided to use the name therm for the heat required to raise 1 gramme of water through 1 degree Celsius but eight years later the calorie was adopted as the name of the unit and the therm went into a state of suspended animation until it was given its current definition by the Gas Act of 1920.

therm (European Community)

The therm (European Community) is legally defined in the council of the European Communities Directive 80/ 181/EC of December 20, 1979. The therm (US) is legally defined in the Federal Register, vol33, No.146, pp.10756, of July 27, 1968. Although the European therm, which is based on the International Table Btu, is frequently used by engineers in the US, the therm (US) is the legal unit used by the US natural gas industry.

1 therm (European Community) = 1.05506 E+08 joule

1 therm (US) = **1.054804 E+08** joule

therm per gallon (therm/UKgal)

UK unit of calorific value volume basis.

1 therm per gallon = 2.32080 x 10^{10} joule per cubic meter.

thermal...

This adjective was in use with units of electricity (ampere, coulomb, farad, henry, ohm) to obtain analogical units of heat. This is deprecated now.

thermal ampere

The SI unit of thermal current. One thermal ampere corresponds to an entropy flow of one watt per kelvin (W K^{-1}). Formerly it was defined as the heat flow rate of one watt.

thermal coulomb

The SI unit of the thermal charge. One thermal coulomb corresponds to an increase in entropy of one joule per kelvin (J/K).

Note: The former definition of this unit was such that it corresponded to a quantity of heat of one joule.

thermal farad

The SI unit of thermal capacitance. One thermal farad is the thermal capacitance for which an amount of entropy of one joule per kelvin added to a body raises its temperature by one kelvin.

1 thermal farad = 1 joule per square kelvin.

Formerly this unit was defined as: the thermal farad is corresponding to a quantity of heat of one joule resulting in a temperature increase of one kelvin.

1 thermal farad = 1 joule per kelvin.

thermal henry

The SI unit of thermal inductance. It is the thermal inductance for which an entropy flow of one wall per kelvin is associated with a kinetic energy of one joule.

1 thermal henry = 1 J K^2/W^2.

The former definition of this unit was such that it corresponded to a heat flow rate of one watt associated with a kinetic energy of one joule. 1 thermal henry = 1 J/W^2

thermal ohm

The S1 unit of thermal resistance. It is defined as the thermal resistance for which a temperature difference of one kelvin causes an entropy flow of one watt per kelvin.

1 thermal ohm = 1 K^2/W.

Note: The unit is also called **fourier.**

See "*fourier*".

thermal volt

Unit of thermal potential difference in all the systems of units. One thermal volt across a conductor of heat corresponds to a temperature difference of one kelvin.

1 thermal volt = 1 kelvin.

See *"thermal."*

thermie (th) . . .

Basic unit of heat energy in the meter tonne second system. It is the quantity of heat required to raise the temperature of one tonne of air-free water from 14.5°C to 15.5°C at a constant pressure of one Standard atmosphere. It is equal to 10^6 fifteen-degree calorie. Its value is experimentally defined as:

1 th = 10^6 fifteen degree calorie = 4.1855 x 10^6 joule.

Note: The unit was legalized in France in 1919.

See *"calorie, fifteen degree"*.

thimbleful

an informal unit of volume, often used as a prototypical small amount in statements such as "a thimbleful of matter from a neutron star would weigh 100 million tons." A thimble holds just about one cubic centimeter (or one milliliter).

third [1]

a unit used in music to describe the ratio in frequency between notes. Two notes differ by a **minor third** if the higher note has a frequency exactly 6/5 times the frequency of the lower one or by a

major third if the higher note has a frequency exactly 5/4 times the frequency of the lower one. On the standard 12-tone scale, the minor third is approximated by 3 half steps, corresponding to a frequency ratio of $2^{1/4} = 1.1892$; the major third is approximated by 4 half steps, corresponding to a frequency ratio of $2^{1/3} = 1.2599$.

third (') [2]

a unit of time equal to 1/60 second. The symbol for this rarely-used unit is a triple prime, suggesting a natural progression from the minute ') through the second ") to the third").

third-octave

A unit of frequency interval describing a band of frequencies such that the highest frequency is $2^{1/3}$ = 1.260 times the lowest. This unit is commonly used in noise control and abatement.

Thirds, fourths

An informal unit of time.

The term "minute" usually means $\frac{1}{60}$ of an hour, coming from "a minute division of an hour". The term "second" comes from "the second-minute division of an hour", as it is $\frac{1}{60}$ of a minute or $\frac{1}{60}$ of $\frac{1}{60}$ of an hour. While usually sub-second units are represented with SI prefixes on the second (e.g., milliseconds), this system can be extrapolated further, such that a "Third" would mean $\frac{1}{60}$ of a second, and a "Fourth" would mean $\frac{1}{60}$ of a third, etc. These units are occasionally used in astronomy to denote angles.

See also "minute", "second", and "hour."

Tod

This was an English weight for wool. It has the alternative spelling forms of *tode*, *todd*, *todde*, *toad*, and *tood*. It was usually 28 pounds or two stone. The tod, however, was not a national standard and could vary by English shire, ranging from 28 to 32 pounds. In addition to the traditional definition in terms of pounds, the tod has historically also been considered to be $\frac{1}{13}$ of a sack, $\frac{1}{26}$ of a sarpler, or $\frac{1}{9}$ of a wey.

See also "stone", "sack", and "pound."

Toise

A unit of area, length, or volume

A **toise** (French pronunciation: [twaz]; symbol: **T**) is a unit of measure for length, area and volume originating in pre-revolutionary France. In North America, it was used in colonial French establishments in early New France, French Louisiana (*Louisiane*), Acadia (*Acadie*) and Quebec. The related *toesa* (Portuguese pronunciation: [tuˈezɐ]) was used in Portugal, Brazil, and other parts of the Portuguese Empire until the adoption of the metric system.

A. Unit of length]

- 1 toise was divided into 6 feet (French: *pieds*) or 72 inches (*pouces*) or 864 lines (*lignes*) in France until 1812.

In 1799 the metre was defined to be exactly 443.296 *lignes* or $^{13,853}/_{27,000}$ toise, with the intention that the metre should equal $^{1}/_{10,000,000}$ of the distance from the pole to the equator. This had the effect of making the toise approximately 1949.03631 mm.

According to an article written in 1866, during measurement of various standard length artefacts from several countries, the toise was measured as 1,949.03632 mm.

- 1 toise was exactly 2 metres in France between 1812 and 1 January 1840 (mesures usuelles).
- 1 toise = 1.8 metres in Switzerland.
- 1 *toesa* = 6 feet (Portuguese: *pés*) = 1.98 m in Portugal.

B. Unit of area

- 1 toise was about 3.799 square metres or, of course, a square French toise, as a measure for land and masonry area in France before 10 December 1799.

C. Unit of volume

- 1 toise = 8.0 cubic metres (20th century Haiti)

thou

Imperial unit of length. One thou is equal to one-thousandth of an inch.

1 thou = 10^3 inch = **25.4 x 10^6** meter.

Note: 1. This unit is in use in UK since Victorian times.

2. The unit is also known as **mil.**

See *"mil"*.

thousandth mass unit (TMU)

Arbitrary unit of energy. One thousandth mass unit is the energy equivalent of the mass of a hypothetical molecule with a relative molecular mass of 0.001 gramme per mole (physical scale). Using Einstein's equation

$E = mc^2,$

with m = 1 atomic mass unit (physical) and c = velocity of electromagnetic radiation, the experimentally derived value of the unit is:

1 thousandth mass unit = 0.149 176 x 0^{-12} joule.

thread

Arbitrary unit of length equals 1.5 yard.

1 thread = 1.5 yard = 1.371 6 meter.

Note: Used mainly to measure cotton yarn.

thumb

another name for an inch.

See also "inch."

tical

a traditional unit of weight in southeast Asia, originating as the weight of a coin of the same name. In Myanmar (Burma), where the unit is still in use for measuring the weights of precious metals and drugs, the tical is equivalent to 16.4 grams.

tick [1]

an informal unit of time equal to the length of one cycle of a clock. A tick of a computer's system clock also called a jiffy, is usually 0.01 seconds. A tick in athletics is the smallest increment of time measured in a timed competition, usually 0.1 second or 0.01 second.

tick [2]

a unit used in finance and investing to express the smallest measured change in a price or index. For example, at the Chicago Board of Trade in the U.S., a tick in the price of many agricultural commodities is equal to 1/4 cent ($0.0025) per bushel [3].

See also "Bushel."

Ticks

The "tick" is the amount of time between timer interrupts generated by the timer circuit of a CPU. The amount of time is processor-dependent

360° YEAR

Unit of time. It is the time period for a 360° revolution of the mean sun, measured from a fixed equinox. It is equal to **365.255 189 7** days in the year 1900.

1 sidereal year = 365 days 6 hours 7 minutes and 28.39 seconds = 3.155 804 839x107 seconds See *"year"*.

tidal day

a unit of time equal to the average period between two successive passages of the moon through the meridian (the imaginary line across the sky from due north to due south). High and low tides repeat with this period (on average), so the unit is fundamental to predictions of these tides. The tidal day, also called the **lunar day**, is equal to approximately 24 hours 50.272 minutes (1490.272 minutes).

tierce

an old English unit of volume, equal to 1/3 butt or 42 United States gallons. The tierce is almost exactly 159 liters. The name of the unit is French; it is derived from the Latin *tertius,* meaning 1/3. The tierce is identical to the petroleum barrel [2].

See also "butt", and "barrel."

timber

a traditional unit of quantity for furs equal to 2 score or 40 bundles. This unit, which persisted at least into the nineteenth century, originated because furs were shipped in bundles of 40 pressed between two boards or timbers.

See also "score."

time

statements of the time of day are made in various ways in different countries. To avoid confusion in international communications, the International Organization for Standardization (ISO) established (in 1986) International Standard 8601 for the representation of dates and times. The

ISO 8601 format for time statements is HH: MM, or HH:MM: SS, where HH is the hour number (00 to 23), MM is the minute number (00 to 59), and SS is the second number (00 to 59, except on those very rare occasions where a "leap second" 60 has been introduced as described under day [2]). Decimal fractions of the second can be added, as in 07:14:23.625. Colons are specified as the separators in the representation (if separators are used at all, HHMMSS is also acceptable). The times called 1:23 am and 1:23 pm in U.S. practice are represented as 01:23 and 13:23, respectively. Midnight can be represented as 00:00 of the new day or as 24:00 of the day ending. For additional information, see ISO's Date and Time Format FAQ.

See also "day."

time zone [1]

a unit representing the difference in time between a given location and Universal Time. Under ISO 8601 (see previous entry), the difference is positive if the local time is later than Universal Time and negative if it is earlier; this means that time zones are generally positive in the Eastern Hemisphere and negative in the Western Hemisphere. U.S. Eastern Standard Time is time zone -05, while Pacific Standard Time is time zone -08. For some areas, the difference between local time and Universal Time is not an exact number of hours; these time zones are specified by giving the time difference in hours and minutes. For example, Newfoundland Standard Time is time zone -03:30 or -0330. The time zone is added after a time: for example, 13:23-08 represents 1:23 pm U.S. Pacific Standard Time and is equivalent to 21:23 Universal Time. The same instant is 22:23 in Central European Time, represented by 22:23+01. The traditional acronyms for time zones, such as EST for Eastern Standard Time, may be confusing or meaningless, especially outside their country of origin, so they should not be used in international communications. Worldtimezone.com and thetimenow.com have up-to-the-moment time and time zone information for the entire world.

time zone [2]

an informal unit used to express differences in longitude between two places on the Earth. On the average, a time zone spans 15° of longitude. Of course, actual time zones have irregular boundaries, so this is only approximate. At the latitudes of the continental U.S., time zones average about 800 miles wide.

tin

an informal unit of volume equal to approximately 8 Imperial fluid ounces (227 milliliters, or roughly the same as a U.S. cup). This is the volume of an English 50-cigarette tin, formerly common as a kitchen unit in North Africa and the Middle East. It is still seen in books of recipes from that area.

See also "fluid ounce," and "cup."

tithe

a traditional unit of proportion equal to 1/10. The word "tithe" is an old one, drawn directly from the Anglo-Saxon word for a tenth.

tithing

an old English unit of land area equal to 1/10 hundred or 10 hides. Very roughly, the tithing was about 12 acres or a little less than 5 hectares.

See also "acre" and "hide."

TMC ft

an abbreviation for "thousand million cubic feet," commonly used in water management in India. One TMC ft is equivalent to about 28.317 million cubic meters or 22 956.8 acre-feet. One TMC ft/day is about 11 574 cubic feet per second or 327.74 cubic meters per second.

TME

MkgfS unit of mass. It is the German symbol of the metric technical unit of mass *(Technische Masseneinheit)*.

See *"metric technical unit of mass."*

tod

Arbitrary unit of mass, equal 28 pounds.

I tod = 28 pound = 12.700 586 36 kilogrammes.

Note: Used mainly to measure wool.

toe

a symbol for a **tonne of oil equivalent**, a unit of energy used in the international energy industry. 1 toe represents the energy available from burning approximately one tonne (metric ton) of crude oil; this is defined by the International Energy Agency to be exactly 10^7 kilocalories, equivalent to approximately 7.4 barrels of oil, 1270 cubic meters of natural gas, or 1.4 tonnes of coal. 1 toe is also equivalent to 41.868 gigajoules (GJ), 39.683 million Btu (MM Btu) or dekatherms, or 11.630 megawatt hours (MWh).

See also "Btu", "barrel", "joule."

tog

Unit of the insulation of clothing.

1 tog = 0.100 degree Celsius meter square per watt ($^{\circ}Cm^2W^{-1}$)

Note: This unit was suggested for the first time in 1946.

toise

Unit of length used for geodetic measurement.

1 toise = 1.949 meters.

Note: The unit was introduced by Charlemagne in 790 and was in France until replaced by the meter at the end of the 18th century.

tolerance unit

Unit of engineering tolerance (tolerance allowed for fitting cylinders into cylindrical holes. If D is the geometrical mean of the diameter steps involved, the size of the tolerance unit I is given by:

$i = 0.45\, D^{1/3} + 0.001\, D$ (D in millimeters, i in micrometers);

$i = 0.052\, D^{1/3} + 0.001\, D$ (D in inches, i in milli-inches).

Note: 1. Sixteen grades of tolerance are allowed and these are designated IT.1 to IT.16. These grades are called fundamental tolerances.

2. The unit is approved by the International Organization for Standardization.

ton (of TNT)

Arbitrary unit of explosive power of a nuclear weapon. A nuclear weapon of power one ton has an energy equivalent of one ton of trinitrotoluene.

1 ton = 5 x 10^9 joule.

Note: The units normally employed are the kiloton (=10^3 ton) and the megaton (=10^6 ton).

ton

Imperial unit of mass equal 20 hundredweights.

1. Avoirdupois measure:

1 ton = **20** hundredweights = **2240** pounds = 1 016.046 908 8 kilogrammes.

Note: 1. This is the UK name of the unit. In the US, where it is almost obsolete, it is called the **long ton** or the **gross ton**. The US unit called the ton is more properly called the **short ton** or the **net ton**.

2. The name displacement ton is employed when referring to the tonnage of ships.

3. The ton, as a unit of mass, was in use in the late fifteenth century and is mentioned in an act of Henry V (1422) in which the measurement of coal from Newcastle is defined.

See also *"ton, short"*.

2. Troy measure (ton tr)

1 ton troy = **20** troy hundredweights = **2000** troy pounds = 746.483 443 2 kilogrammes.

Note: Some of the UK units derived from the ton is given in the following table.

UK unit	Unit Symbol	Quantity Measured	SI Unit	To convert UK unit to SI, multiply by:
Ton per cubic yard	UKton/yd^3	Mass density	Kilogramme per cubic meter (kg/m^3)	1.328 94 x 10^3
Ton per hour	UKton/h	Mass flow rate	Kilogramme per second (kg/s)	0.282 235
Ton per mile	UKton/mile	Linear density	Kilogramme per meter (kg/m)	0.631 342
Ton per square mile	UKton/mile^2	Surface density	Kilogramme per square meter (kg/m^2)	0.392 298 x 10^{-3}
Ton per thousand-yard	UKton/1000yd	Linear density	Kilogramme per meter (kg/m)	1.111 16

ton, assay (assay ton)

Metric unit of mass.

(1) UK assay ton: One UK assay ton contains as many milligrammes as (long) ton contains troy ounces.

1 UK assay ton == (2240x7000)/480 milligrammes = 0.0326667 kilogrammes.

(2) US assay ton: One US assay ton contains as many milligrammes as a short ton contains troy ounces. It is sometimes called the short assay ton.

1 US assay ton = (2000x7000)/480 milligram = 0.0291667 kilogramme.

ton, fluid

A unit of volume. It is equal to 32 cubic feet.

1 fluid ton = **32** cubic feet = 9.0614 x 10^{-2} cubic meters.

Note: This unit is used for many hydrometallurgical, hydraulic and other industrial purposes.

ton, freight

See *"freight ton"*.

ton, gross

Other name for ton (Avoirdupois measure)

See *"ton"*.

ton, long

Other name for ton (Avoirdupois measure).

See *"ton"*.

ton, measurement

See *"measurement ton"* and also *"height ton"*.

ton, metric

Obsolete name for **tonne.**

See *"tonne"*.

ton, net

See *"net ton"* and also *"short ton"*.

ton of refrigeration

The rate at which heat is removed by melting one short ton (910 kg) of ice in 24 hours is called a ton of refrigeration or even a ton of cooling. This unit of refrigeration capacity came from the days when large blocks of ice were used for cooling and is still used to describe the heat-removal capabilities of refrigerators and chillers today. One ton of refrigeration is exactly equal to 12,000 BTU/h, or 3.517 kW.

ton, register

See *"register ton."*

ton, shipping

See *"shipping ton"* and also *"freight ton"*.

ton, short

See *"short ton"*.

ton mile

UK unit of traffic factor, i.e., mass carried x distance.

1 ton mile = 1.635 17 tonne kilometer.

See *"tonne-kilometer,*

ton-mile per gallon (UK) (UK ton. mile/UKgal)

UK unit of traffic factor, i.e., mass carried x distance/volume.

1 ton mile per gallon (UK) = 0.359 687 tonne kilometer per liter.

See *"tonne kilometer per liter"*.

tondal

Imperial unit of force. One tondal is the force which, when applied to a body of mass one ton, gives it an acceleration of one foot per second squared.

1 tondal = 1 ton foot per second squared = 309.691 097 802 24 newtons.

ton-force (tonf)

Imperial unit of force. One ton-force is the force which, when applied to a body of mass one ton, gives it acceleration equal to the standard acceleration of free fall.

1 ton-force = 9 964.016 418 183 52 newtons.

See *"standard gravity."*

Note: Some of the UK units derived from the ton-force are given in the following table.

UK unit	Unit Symbol	Quantity Measured	SI Unit	To convert UK unit to SI, multiply by:
Ton-force foot	tonf ft	Moment of force and torque	Newton meter (N.m)	$3.037\ 03 \times 10^3$

Ton-force per foot	tonf/ft	Force per unit length	Newton per meter (N/m)	32.690 3 x 10^3
Ton-force per square foot	tonf/ft^2	Pressure	Pascal (Pa)	0.107 252 x 10^6
Ton-force per square foot	tonf/in^2	Pressure	Pascal (Pa)	15.444 3 x 10^6

ton of refrigeration

Imperial unit of refrigerating capacity, i.e., heat flow rate. One ton of refrigeration is the rate of extraction of heat when one short ton of ice of specific latent heat 144 international table British thermal units per pound is produced in 24 hours from water at the same temperature.

1 ton of refrigeration = 3 516.85 watt.

Note: 1. The unit is of American origin and is recognized by the American Society of Mechanical Engineers.

2. In British Standards, there is a definition for a ton of refrigeration in which the long ton (2240 pounds) is employed, but it is little used. The kilocalorie per second is the preferred unit for British refrigeration engineers.

3. In continental Europe, the unit of refrigeration was, until recently, known as the **frigorie.**

See *"frigorie"*.

tonne (t)

a metric unit of mass equal to 1000 kilogrammes or approximately 2204.623 pounds avoirdupois. The SI uses this French spelling for the metric ton (see ton [2] above) to distinguish it clearly from the long and short tons of customary English usage. Large masses are often stated as multiples of the tonne, although technically, the SI requires that masses be stated as multiples of the gram. Thus, a mass of 10^3 tonnes = 10^6 kg = 10^9 g is often called 1 kilotonne (kt) instead of 1 gigagram. In the United States, the Department of Commerce recommends that the tonne be called the **metric ton.**

tonne kilometer (t·km or tkm)

The metric unit of freight transportation, equal to the transportation of one tonne (metric ton) for a distance of one kilometer. The tonne kilometer is equal to almost exactly 0.685-ton miles (0.684 944 ton-miles, to be more exact.

tonneau

the traditional French ton, equal to 2000 livres or about 979 kilogrammes (1.079 U.S. ton). The tonneau was also used as a measure of volume equal to 42 cubic pieds (50.84 cubic feet, or about 1440 liters). In the wine trade, the tonneau was a shipment of 100 cases, or 1200 bottles (about 900 liters of wine).

See also "livre", "feet", and "bottle."

tonne kilometer per liter (t km l^{-1} or t km L^{-1})

Unit for mass carried x distance/volume (traffic factor).

tonne per cubic meter (t m^3)

Unit of (mass) density used with SI system.

1 tonne per cubic meter = 10^3 kilogramme per cubic meter.

tonnes per hectare (t/ha)

A common metric unit measuring crop yields. One tonne per hectare is equal to about 0.446 090 U.S. (short) tons per acre.

ton-weight (tonwt)

Imperial unit of force. One ton-weight is the force which, when applied to a body of mass one ton, gives it an acceleration equal to the local value of the acceleration of free fall expressed in feet per second squared.

1 ton-weight = 309.691 097 802 24 g newton

Note: This is an inconsistent unit and its use is deprecated. The ton-force should always be used in its place.

See *"ton-force"*.

TOR (tor)

An SI unit for pressure. It is defined as the pressure resulting from a force of one newton acting uniformly over an area of one square meter.

1 tor = 1 N/m^2.

Note: 1. 1t is recommended to use the new name of this unit, i.e., "Pascal".

2. The unit is named after E.Torricelli (1608-1647), the Florentine scientist who, in 1643, discovered the properties of the barometer.

Torino number

an arbitrary scale adopted in 1999 to express the likelihood that an asteroid or comet might collide with the Earth causing damage. Named for Torino (Turin), Italy, site of a June 1999 conference on near-Earth objects, the scale is intended to convey accurately the appropriate level of concern caused by newly-discovered objects, thus discouraging sensational press reports. The scale ranges from 0 (object certain to miss the Earth or too small to cause significant damage) to 10 (object certain to hit the Earth and large enough to cause catastrophic damage and global climate disruption).

torr (Torr)

Non-metric unit denoting degree of vacuum (pressure). From the definition of the standard atmosphere as a pressure of 750 torr, the torr is equivalent to a pressure of one millimeter of mercury within one part in 7×10^6.

l torr = (1/760) atmosphere (exact value) = ($101325/760$) pascals (exact) = 133.322 pascals (approximate)

Note: 1. The torr is equal in size to the (conventional) millimeter of mercury to one part in seven million.

2. The torr was adopted by the British Standards Institution in 1958 but was in use in Germany long before that.

3. The unit is named after E.Torricelli (1608-1647), the Florentine scientist who, in 1643, discovered the properties of the barometer.

torr litre per second (Torr.L/s)

Unit of leak rate used in vacuum technology equal one thousandth of a lusec.

l torr liter per second = **1.0 x 10^{-3}** lusec = 133.322x10^{-3} pascal meter cubic per second.

See *"lusec"*.

tot

a unit of volume for liquor. Generally, the term is used informally, with no fixed definition. However, in British pubs, the usual understanding is that a tot is 1/6 gill; this is equivalent to 5/6 Imperial fluid ounce or about 23.7 milliliters.

See also "fluid once", "gill."

tother

Arbitrary unit of mass equals 2400 pounds.

1 tother = 2400 pound = 1088. 621 688 kilogrammes.

Note: 1. Used mainly to measure the lead.

2. Also called **fodder.**

tower weights

the weight system used as the basis for English coinage during the medieval era; it is named for the Tower of London, where the Royal Mint was located. The system was based on the tower pound of 5400 grains (about 0.7714 avoirdupois pounds or 349.91 grams). The pound was divided into 12 ounces, and each ounce contained 20 pennyweight, making the pound equal to 240 penny weight. (This structure was later echoed, in a reversed way, by the traditional English monetary system, in which the pound was divided into 20 shillings and each shilling into 12 pence.) In 1527, Henry VIII abolished the tower pound in favor of the slightly larger troy pound (see troy weights below).

See also "grain"

Township (twp) (US)

US unit of area equals 36 square miles.

1 township (US) = 36 square mile = 93.239 571 6 $\times 10^6$ square meters.

Note: The unit is divided into 36 sections. The section has a size of one square mile.

townsend

CGS unit of electrical breakdown in a gas, i.e., the field strength *(E)* divided by the gas number *(N)*.

1 townsend = 10^{-17} volts per centimeter square.

Note: The unit is named after Sir John Townsend (1866-1957), who initiated the kinetic theory of ions and electrons in gases.

transmission unit (T.U.)

The unit of intensity level used in all systems is equal to 1 decibel.

1 transmission unit = 1 decibel.

Note: This was one of several names proposed as alternatives for decibels.

traffic unit (TU)

an alternate name for the erlang.

See also "Erlang."

tray

> an informal unit of volume used for berries in U.S. retail produce markets. Berries are typically stocked in corrugated cardboard trays holding six containers of one (dry) quart each, a total volume of about 6.6 liters.
>
> See also "quqrt."

trey

> an old English word for three, derived from the old French *treis* (now spelled *trois*). The word survives as the name for a three-spot showing in dice or a three card in card games.

trilliard

> a unit of quantity equal to 10^{21}, which is one sextillion in American terminology or 1000 trillion in traditional British terminology. The name is coined to parallel *Milliard*, which has long been a name for 1000 million.

trimester

> a unit of time equal to 3 months or 1/4 year; another name for the quarter [2]. At certain U.S. colleges, a trimester is an academic term roughly 14 weeks long. In reckoning the length of human pregnancies, a trimester is a unit of 14 weeks, with the first-trimester beginning on the first day of the last menstrual period.

troland (Td)

> Metric unit of retinal illumination. One troland is the retinal illumination produced by a surface having a luminance of one nit when the area of the pupil of the eye is one square millimeter.
>
> *Note:*   1. The unit is named after L.T.Troland (1889-1932). Troland proposed this unit in 1916 under the name of photon
>
>   2. The unit has also been called the **Luxon.**
>
> See *"photon"* and *"luxon"*.

tropical year (a; a$_{\text{trop}}$)

> Unit of time. This is the year on which the calendar is based. It is the time between two consecutive passages in the same direction of the sun through the Earth's equatorial plane. It is equal to **365.242 198 78** days in the year 19000, decreasing at the rate of 0.000 006 14 days per century.
>
> 1 tropical year = 365 day 5 hours 48 minutes 45-9747 seconds = $3.155\ 692\ 597\ 47 \times 10^7$ seconds.
>
> See *"year."*

troy units

This system of weights was at one time the legal system for the weighing of precious meters in the UK. The fundamental unit is the Troy pound, which is equal to 5760 grains. The system includes the following:

l troy pound (lb tr) =	**12** troy ounces
l troy ounce (oz tr) =	**20** pennyweights
1 pennyweight (dwt) =	**24** grains

1 grain (gr) (no symbol in US) = **1/480** troy ounce

Note: 1. The Troy weights were introduced in England in the early fifteenth century and it was officially legalized in 1824.

2. The Troy pound was abolished in 1878 but the Troy ounce of 480 rains is still a legal unit of mass.

3. Troy units are no longer legal in the UK but they are still legal in the US.

4. Tradition maintains the name Troy is derived from Troyes, the French town famous for its great medieval fairs.

See *"grain"*, *"ounce, troy"*, and *"pennyweight"*.

truss

a traditional weight unit, generally equal to 4 stone or 56 pounds (about 25.4 kilogrammes). The truss was used primarily for measuring hay. In 1795, Parliament specified that a truss of hay should equal 56 pounds for old hay or 60 pounds (about 27.2 kilogrammes) for new hay.

See also "stone" and "pound."

TSI (tsi)

Imperial unit of pressure. One tsi is the pressure resulting from a force of one ton-force acting uniformly over an area of one square inch.

l tsi = 1 ton-force per square inch = $15.444\ 3 \times 10^6$ pascal.

tub

Arbitrary unit of mass equals 84 pounds.

l tub = 84 pound = 38.101 _759 08 kilogramme.

Note: Used mainly to measure the butter.

The tub has different values for different commodities. The *Oxford English Dictionary* has quotations illustrating other values of a "tub" as a unit:

- Tea (1706): "about 60 pounds"
- "Camphire" (1706): "from 56 to 86 pounds"
- Vermilion (1706): "3 to 4 hundredweight" (i.e., 336-448 pounds)
- Camphor (1858): "130 Dutch lbs"

In Newfoundland, Canada, a tub of coal was defined as 100 pounds, while a tub of herrings was 16 Imperial gallons and a tub of salt was 18 Imperial gallons.

tun

Unit of volume (capacity) equals 4 hogsheads.

1 tun = 4 hogsheads = 252 US gallon (liq.) = 0.953 923 73 cubic meters

Notes: 1. It was a unit of volume used for wine and other liquids.

2. "Tun" is an old French word for a large cask used in shipping wine.

3. Tuns of various sizes were used throughout the Middle Ages. More recently, the tun has been regarded as equal to 2 butts or 252 U. S. gallons; this is equivalent to 33.6875 cubic feet or about 953.93 liters.

tunnland

a traditional unit of land area in Sweden. The tunnland is equal to 56,000 square Stockholm feet (*kvadratfot*); this is equivalent to 4936.4 square meters, 0.493 64 hectares, or about 1.220 English acres. The tunnland was divided into 32 kappland. Like the Danish tønde land (see above), this unit originated as an area that could be planted with one *tunna* (barrel) of seed.

See also "hectare", "acre"

turn (T)

Unit of plane angle.

1 turn = 2π radian == 360°.

Note: The unit is also called the **circle.**

twelfth

a unit used in music to describe the ratio in frequency between notes. Two notes differ by a twelfth if the higher note has a frequency exactly 3 times the frequency of the lower one. On the standard 12-tone scale, the perfect twelfth is approximated as 19 half steps, corresponding to a frequency ratio of $2^{19/12} = 2.9966$.

Twenty-foot equivalent unit (TEU)

The **twenty-foot equivalent unit** (abbreviated **TEU** or **teu**) is an inexact unit of cargo capacity, often used for container ships and container ports. It is based on the volume of a 20-foot-long (6.1 m) intermodal container, a standard-sized metal box which can be easily transferred between different modes of transportation, such as ships, trains, and trucks.

The container is defined by its length, although the height is not standardized and ranges between 4 feet 3 inches (1.30 m) and 9 feet 6 inches (2.90 m), with the most common height being 8 feet 6 inches (2.59 m). It is common to designate a 45-foot (13.7 m) container as 2 TEU rather than 2.25 TEU.

A 20-foot-long (6.1 m) ISO container equals 1 TEU.

twip

a unit of distance used in computer graphics for high-resolution control of the elements of an image. One twip is equal to 1/1440 inch, about 17.639 micrometers, or 0.070 556 kyu. "Twip" is an acronym for "twentieth of a point," which is accurate if the point [2] is interpreted as being exactly 1/72 inch.

typp

Imperial unit of reciprocal line density. One typp is the reciprocal line density of a thread which has a length of one thousand yards and a mass of one pound.

1 typp = 1000 yard per pound = 2 015.91 meter per kilogramme.

Note: This unit is used in the textile industry as an indirect measure of yarn count. The direct unit of yarn count is used in preference to the typp.

U

U

[I] a commercial unit of thermal conductance (heat flow).

The **U factor**, as it is also called, is the conductance through an insulator as measured in Btu's of energy conducted times inches of thickness per hour of time per square foot of area per °F of the temperature difference between the two sides of the material.

The U factor is numerically equal to 1 divided by the R-value.

[2] a unit of distance used to measure the height of the standard racks in which audio, video, or computer components are mounted. 1U is equal to 1.75 inches (44.45 millimeters), so that, for example, a 2U component is 3.5 inches high, and a 22U rack houses a stack of components 38.5 inches high.

[3] German symbol for a turn or revolution *(Umdrehung)*, usually seen in combinations such as **U/min**, the German equivalent of the English symbol rpm for revolutions per minute.

UI

An alternate symbol for the international unit (IU).

In many languages, the two words of the phrase "international unit" are reversed. In French, for example, the phrase is *unite' international*.

uld, ulp

Units of data precision used in computer science. The symbol ulp stands for "unit in the last place," the smallest increment in a variable that can be recorded internally by the machine. Similarly, uld stands for "unit in the last digit," a change by 1 in the last (right-most) digit of data represented decimally.

um, ums

Symbols are sometimes used for the micrometer (micron).

The symbol **um** is acceptable in situations where the Greek letter mu (μ) is not available to make the proper symbol um. However, the "plural" symbol **ums** is never acceptable because the SI prohibits adding -s to a symbol to form a plural.

uncia [1]

A Latin name for the fraction 1/12 is subsequently used in many ways to represent a twelfth part. The Romans had no mathematical notation for fractions. When they needed to refer to a fractional part of anything, they would often state its nearest equivalent in *unciae.*

uncia [2]

The Roman ounce equal to about 27.2875 grams of 0.9625 ounce avoirdupois. There were 12 ounces in a Roman pound, and the word *uncia* means a 12th part; its name gives us the ounce, of course, and also the inch.

Unglie

A **unglie** ("finger") is an obsolete unit of length equal to three-fourths of an inch (1.905 cm) that was used in India and Pakistan. After metrification in both countries, the unit became obsolete.

unified atomic mass unit (u)

Unit of mass, which can be used in addition to SI units as a unit of (unified) atomic mass constant. One atomic mass unit (modified) is equal to one-twelfth of the rest mass of a neutral carbon-12 atom.

$1 \text{ u} = 1.660\ 565\ 5 \times 10^{-27}$ kilogramme.

Note: 1. This unit is also a unit of (rest) mass of particles, mass excess and mass defect.

2. This unit is also called **atomic mass unit (international scale)** and also **Dalton.**

3. Atomic mass unit (unified) is one of four units used with the SI system, whose values are obtained experimentally. The other three are: "electronvolt", "astronomical unit," and "parsec".

4. Use of the old atomic mass unit (amu), defined by reference to oxygen, is deprecated.

unit

[1]unit (of blood)

a unit of volume for human blood and various blood components or products. A unit of whole blood is 450 milliliters, which is about 0.9510 u.s. pint. For components of blood, one unit is the amount of substance that would normally be found in one unit of whole blood. The adult human body contains roughly 12 units of whole blood.

[2] unit (of heroin)

a unit of mass or weight for heroin equal to exactly 700 grams (0.7 kilogramme or about 1.543 pounds). This unit, standard in the Southeast Asian drug trade, is also called the **Asian unit** in us. Drug enforcement.

[3] unit (of alcohol)

a unit of the alcohol content of beverages used primarily in Britain. One unit of alcohol represents an alcohol content of 10 milliliters or, by weight, 8 grams. The alcohol content of a liter of a beverage is numerically equal to the percentage of alcohol by volume, so that, for example, a wine that is 12% by volume contains 12 units per liter or 9 units in a standard 750 ml (3/4 liter) bottle.

[4] unit (of energy)

in Britain, another name for the kilowatt hour, which was formerly called the Board of Trade Unit.

unit call (UC)

A measure of telecommunications traffic density.

The unit call is a dimensionless "unit" representing a traffic density of 100 call-seconds per hour, or 1/36 erlang

See also *"Erlang."*

unit case

A conventional unit of sales volume in the US soft drink industry. A unit case consists of soft drinks, syrup, powder, or whatever equivalent to 24 eight-ounce servings (6 quarts or about 5.678 liters).

unit pole

CGS unit of magnetic pole strength. Unit pole is the magnetic pole that, when placed 1 centimetre from an equal pole in a vacuum, is repelled with the force of one dyne.

1 unit pole = 0.125 663 7 x 10^{-6} weber

Universal Time (UT or Z)

The correct name for the time system previously called Greenwich Mean Time (GMT): the standard time at longitude 0°. Universal Time is five hours later than Eastern Standard Time in the US. It is always stated on the 24-hour clock; thus, an event occurring at 1:26:15 pm Eastern Standard Time occurs at 18:26:15 UT (five hours after 13:26:15). Technically, the time shown on clocks is figured from Coordinated Universal Time (UTC), an international system of time measurement regulated by very precise atomic clocks. From time to time (either on June 30 or December 31), UTC is adjusted by the addition of a "leap second". This event, widely reported in the press but poorly understood by the public, keeps UTC within 0.9 seconds of mean solar time at longitude 0° as measured by the Earth's slightly uneven rotation.

unze

A traditional German weight unit corresponding to the English ounce.

The unze equals 1/16 pfund.

Although the pfund has been assimilated into the metric system (as 500 grams), the unze is effectively obsolete. It varied in size from about 28 to 35 grams. The word comes directly from the Latin *uncia*; the plural is **unzen.**

urna

A Roman unit of volume equal to 4 congii, 24 sextarii, or 1/2 amphora.

This is equivalent to about 12.75 liters (3.37 US liquid gallons or 2.80 British Imperial gallons). The Latin word *urna* was also used more broadly to mean a jug, giving rise to the English word *urn.*

See also *"congii"* and *"sextraii."*

USP unit

A unit used in the US to measure the potency of a vitamin or drug, that is, its expected biological effects.

For each substance to which this unit applies, the U. S. Food and Drug Administration has determined the biological effect associated with a dose of 1 USP unit. Other quantities of the substance can then be expressed in terms of this standard unit. In most cases, the USP unit is equal to the international unit (IU). "USP" is a registered trademark of the US Phatmacopeial Convention, Inc., a private standards organization that establishes standards for the pharmaceutical industry.

V

The metric unit of pressure equals 10^3 dynes per centimeter square.

1 vac = 10^3 dyne per centimeter square = 100 pascal.

Note: 1. The unit equals in size to the millibar. It 1s better to use the millibar.

2. The unit was proposed by Florescu in 1960.

vagon

a traditional unit of mass or weight in countries of the former Yugoslavia. Originally considered to be the weight that could be carried by a wagon, the unit has been "metricized" and is now defined to be equal to the dekatonne, that is, 10 metric tons or 22 046.23 pounds avoirdupois.

See also "tonne" and "pound."

var

The SI unit of the reactive power of an alternating current.

1 var = 1 V A = 1 W

Note: The word *"var"* is made up from Volt-Ampere-Reactive.

vara

An important Spanish and Portuguese unit of length. One meaning of the word is rod or pole. It is sometimes spelled *bara* or *bar*.

In *1568*, Phillip II declared the prototype of the *vara* kept in Burgos to be the official standard for Spain and all its possessions. To distinguish this *vara* from the many others, it is often referred to as the *vara* of Burgos.

The square *vara* was an important land measure, and in some areas, the *vara* itself became a unit of area.

The *vara* as a unit of length is as follows:

Argentina

1 *vara* ≈ 86.6 centimeters (about 34.09 inches)

Brazil

1 *vara* ≈ 1.10 meter (about 43.31 inches)

Chile

1 *vara* ≈ 83.59 centimeters (about 32.91 inches)

Colombia

1 *vara* = 80 centimeters (about 31.5 inches)

Varley unit

A unit of electrical resistance, *19th century*, standardized at the Electric Telegraph Company in Great Britain, and in concept, equal to the resistance of 1 mile of copper telegraph wire. In the *1870's* Fleeming Jenkin measured at 25.61 B.A. ohms.[1]

The unit was named for C. F. Varley, an engineer working for the company who devised a method of locating faults in underground wires by comparing their resistance to that of good wires.[2]

One Varley unit (or Varley's unit) was later taken as equal to 25 Siemens units (definition 2), about 23.5 ohms.

Vat

Informal unit of capacity

1. In the Netherlands, a legal measure of capacity = 100 liters. One *vat* = 100 litrons or kannen = 1000 *matjes* or *verres*. It had the same value in Belgium.

2.   In Holland and Belgium, various units are used in the freighting of ships:

Locale	Equivalents	Commodities	liters
		milk	29
Amsterdam	= 717 *mengels*	olive oil	Doursther: 853.4 Simmonds: 1024.9
	= 4 *barriques*	wine	Doursther: 914.4 Simmonds: 1098.2
	a type of ship ton based on volume		= 40 cubic feet
	a type of Shipton based on weight		

3. In Brussels, a unit of dry capacity used for cinders, about 50.89 liters, equal to the unit called the measure used for cinders in Louvain and Diest.

4. In England, a unit of dry capacity used for coal about 415.15 liters. Also spelled *vatt*. "The London chaldron was usually defined as four *vatts* 'ringed and heaped'."

Vedic

A Vedic measure of distance was used in ancient India. Its value was about 10 km (6.2 mi), although the exact value is disputed among scholars (between 8 and 13 km or 5 and 8 mi)

vedro

A traditional Russian unit of volume equal to 100 charki. The vedro is about 12.30 liters (3.249 U.S. liquid gallons or 2.706 British Imperial gallons). In Bulgaria, the vedro has also been used informally as a name for the dekaliter (exactly 10 liters or 2.642 U.S. liquid gallons). The word vedro means a bucket.

velte

Informal unit of capacity

1. In France, a pre-metric unit of liquid capacity used in gauging the size and content of barrels,

2. In Colombo, Sri Lanka, a unit of liquid capacity = 2 English wine gallons = 5 *canades* or *Canadas* = 10 quarts = 150 drams = 462 cubic inches, about 7.57 liters. Also called a *welt*.

3. In Mauritius and in the Seychelles, a unit of capacity, the colonial velte or velt, 7.4505 liters. It is 1/30th of a cask.

verge

An old name for the yard, taken from the Latin word *virga* for a twig or stick. In modern French, *verge* is the customary word for the English yard.

vergée

A traditional unit of land area in the Channel Islands, British crown dependencies just off the northwest coast of France. The unit varied from one bailiwick to another. In Jersey, the vergee is equal to 19 360 square feet or exactly 4/9 acre (0.179 861 hectares). In Guernsey, it is smaller at

17 640 square feet (1960 square yards, about 0.404 96 acre, or about 0.163 882 hectare). The name of the unit is a old Norman word meaning an orchard.

vershok or verchok

A traditional Russian unit of distance equal to 1/16 arshin, 1.75 inches or 4.445 centimeters. The plural is **vershki**.

verst, versta, vehrsta

A traditional Russian unit of distance, formerly used throughout Eastern Europe. The verst equals 1500 arshin, which is 3500 feet, 0.662 88 miless, or 1066.8 meters. Although **vehrsta** is the best transliteration of the Russian, the spelling **verst** is common in English. The German spelling **werst** is also used sometimes. In Finnish, the unit is called the **virsta**. The Russian plural is **vehrsty**.

velocity of light (c)

Light waves travel at 300,000 kilometers per second (approximately). Also, the velocity of radio waves.

velocity of sound

Sound waves travel at 332 meters per second (approximately) in air at sea level.

verber

Unit of charge has the same size as the coulomb.

1 verber = 1 coulomb.

Note: The name was in use in the early 1860s.

vibration (vib)

Unit of frequency used in all the systems of units. One vibration is the frequency of a periodic occurrence, which has a period of one second.

1 vib = l/second

Note:　　1. The unit, as defined, is better called the **hertz.**

2. The unit is also called cycle (per second)

3. In France, the vibration is used with the following meaning:

1 vibration (French) = 0.5 vib = 0.5 hertz.

viertel [1]

A traditional unit of volume in several European countries. Oddly, although the name means "quarter" in German, the traditional viertel is not really 1/4 of any other unit. The Danish viertel equals 8 pots or about 7.74 liters (2.04 U.S. liquid gallons or 1.70 British Imperial gallons). In Switzerland, the viertel is 40 schoppen, which is exactly 15 liters (3.9626 U.S. liquid gallons or 3.3000 British Imperial gallons).

See also, "pot", gallon", schoppen"

viertel [2]

A unit of volume for wine in Austria is equal to exactly 1/4 liter (250 milliliters) or about 8.45 U.S. fluid ounces.

See also "fluid ounce."

violle

An obsolete unit of light intensity equal to 20.17 candela. One violle is the intensity of a square centimeter of platinum, glowing at its melting temperature of 1769 °C (3216 °F). The unit is named for the French physicist Jules Violle (1841-1923), who proposed it in 1881; it was the first unit of light intensity that did not depend on the properties of a particular lamp.

See also candela."

virgate

an old English unit of land area equal to 1/4 hide. This is roughly 30 acres or 12 hectares. The virgate was also called the **yardland** or **yard of land**.

See also "hide", "acre", and "hectare."

violle

Metric unit of luminous intensity. One violle is the luminous intensity of one square centimeter of platinum at its temperature of solidification (2045 K).

1 violle = 20.17 candelas

Note: The name of the unit is after J.L.Viollee (1841-1923), who, in 1884, proposed that luminous intensity should be defined in terms of black body radiation.

Virgate

The **virgate, yardland,** or **yard of land** (Latin: *virgāta* [*terrae*]) was an English unit of land. Primarily a measure of tax assessment rather than area, the virgate was usually (but not always) reckoned as ¼ hide and notionally (but seldom exactly) equal to 30 acres. It was equivalent to two of the Danelaw's oxgangs.

See also "hide", and "acre."

viss, vis, vise

a traditional unit of mass or weight in southern India and southeast Asia, equal to 100 ticals. The name is derived from the Tamil *visai*. The traditional size of the viss is about 1640 grams (about 3.62 pounds), but it is currently used in the Southeast Asian drug trade as a metric unit equal to exactly 1600 grams (1.6 kilograms or 3.527 pounds). This metric unit is called the **choi** or **joi** in Laos and Thailand.

voegtlin

Unit of activity for pituitary extract.

volcanic explosivity index (VEI)

A measure of the severity of a volcanic eruption. The VEI scale is from 0 to 8; an index value of v corresponds to an output of at least 10^{3+v} cubic meters of magma. The Mt. St. Helens eruption of 1980 was a 5 on this scale, and the largest eruption of historic times (the Tambora eruption of 1815) rated a 7.

volt (V)

The SI unit of electric potential, electric potential difference, electromotive force, thermoelectromotive force and Peltier coefficient. It is the difference of electric potential between two points of a conducting wire carrying a constant current of one ampere when the power dissipated between these points is equal to one watt.

$1 \text{ V} = 1 \text{ W/A}$

Note: The following definitions of the volt were formerly used:

1. In 1860, Lord Kelvin used the definition: One volt is (approximately) the electromotive force of a Daniell cell. This definition was recorded by the British Association for the Advancement of Science in 1873. The electromotive force of a Daniell cell is 1.08 V.

2. In 1893, the International Electrical Congress defined the international volt (V_{int}) as One international volt 1000/1434 of the electromotive force of a Latimer-Clark cell. In 1894, this definition became law in the UK and the US. In 1896, by decree, France started to use it and in 1898, in Germany. The relation between the electromotive force of the Latimer-Clark cell and the volt depends on the temperature. The accepted relation is:

$E\theta \text{ (L-C)} = 1.4333 - 0.00119(\theta - 15)7 \times 10^{-6}(\theta - 15)^2,$

Where:

E_θ *(L-C)* is the electromotive force of Latimer -Clark cell at θ^oC.

3. Later, the Latimer-Clark cell was replaced by the Weston (cadmium) cell at 20^oC. The electrolyte is a saturated solution and has excess $CdSO_4$. (8/3)HZO crystals are always present; decinormal sulphuric acid is used. The accepted relation between the electromotive force of the Weston cell and the volt is:

$E_\theta(W) = 1.01858 - 4.06 \times 10^{-5}(\theta\text{-}20) - 9.5 \times 10^{-7} (\theta\text{-}20)^2 + 1 \times 10^{-8}(\theta\text{-}20)^3$

Where:

$E_\theta(W)$ is the electromotive force of the Weston cell at θ^oC.

4. The name of the unit is after the Italian scientist A. Volta (1745-1827), who did pioneer work on electrical cells.

volt-ampere (VA):

The SI unit of apparent power of alternating current. The product of the root-mean-square volts and the root-mean-square amperes.

1 VA = 1 V A

volt, equivalent

Arbitrary unit of energy, particularly in atomic studies, equal to one electronvolt.

1 equivalent volt = 1 electronvolt

Note: Equivalent volt is the former name of the electronvolt.

See *"electronvolt"*.

volt, thermal (thermal volt)

Unit of thermal potential difference in all the systems of units. One thermal volt across a conductor of heat corresponds to a temperature difference of one kelvin.

L thermal volt = 1 kelvin.

See *"thermal.."*.

volt per kelvin (V K^{-1})

The SI unit of Seebeck coefficient and Thomson coefficient.

volt per meter (V m^{-1})

SI unit of electric field strength.

volt squared per kelvin squared (V^2 K^{-2})

SI unit of Lorenz coefficient.

volume unit (vu)

Unit of magnitude of a complex electric wave, e.g., corresponding to speech or music, used in all systems of units. One volume unit is equal to the number of decibels by which the wave differs from a reference magnitude. This level is the power produced by a sinusoidal wave developing one milliwatt in an impedance of 600 ohms.

Note: The unit was formally recognized by the Institute of Radio Engineers in 1938 in an attempt to have a standard system for measuring volume in telephony and allied sciences. It was recognized by the American Standards Association in 1951.

volumetric unit (vu)

a unit of volume equal to 200 cubic feet (5.663 cubic meters), used in the U.S. forest products industry for wood chips and other by-products of lumber production.

volumetric weight

a measure of the size of a package used for billing purposes in the airline industry. The volumetric weight of a package, in kilogrammes, is equal to $lwh/6000$, where l, w, and h are the maximum length, width, and height measurements of the package in centimeters. Shippers are billed for the larger of the volumetric weight and the actual weight of the package. Since the calculation assumes a density of only 1/6 gram per cubic centimeter (1/6 the density of water), the volumetric weight is used only for rather light packages that take up a lot of space on the aircraft.

W

Waffle House Index

The Waffle House Index is used by the Federal Emergency Management Agency (FEMA) to determine the impact of a storm and the likely scale of assistance required for disaster recovery. The measure is based on the reputation of the Waffle House restaurant chain for staying open during extreme weather. This term was coined by FEMA Administrator Craig Fugate.

wagon

Informal unit of mass.

In Yugoslavia, a unit of mass used for sunflower seed, tobacco, and so on = 10,000 kilogrammes.

wah

A traditional unit of distance in Thailand, now aligned with the metric system as exactly 2 meters (6.562 feet). This unit is the Thai version of the fathom. It is seen mostly in connection with the talangwah or square wah (4 square meters or 4.784 square yards), a common unit of area in Thailand.

Wales

In Britain, Wales has long served as an informal unit of area, much as Rhode Island has been used in the US. Wales has an area of about 8015 square miles or 20 760 square kilometers; it is 7.67 times the size of Rhode Island.

wall

A unit of count throughout Germany, Denmark, and Sweden = 80.

In Wales, a unit of length applied to Welsh flannel = 12 feet 10 inches. There are about 40 walls to a piece.

wan

A unit of quantity in China equal to 10 000.

In Chinese, the wan is used much as the thousand is used in the West as a basic unit for large quantities. Thus, 100 000 is 10 wan, and 1 000 000 is 100 wan. However, as in the case of the Greek word *myrios* (myriad), the word *wan* is also used in Chinese to mean an indefinitely large number.

wang

Informal unit of mass.

In the Dutch East Indies, and later Indonesia, a unit of mass used for precious metals, equal to $^1/_{48}$th of a thail, approximately 1.127 grams.

Warhol (Warhol Unit)

Non-conventional unit that measures Fame

This is a unit of fame or hype, derived from the dictum attributed to Andy Warhol that "everyone will be world-famous for fifteen minutes". It represents fifteen minutes of fame. Some multiples are:

- 1 kilowarhol – famous for 15,000 minutes, or 10.42 days. A sort of metric "nine-day wonder".
- 1 megawarhol – famous for 15 million minutes, or 28.5 years.

First used by Cullen Murphy in 1997.

Also used simply as meaning 15 minutes, as the Warhol worm, which could infect all vulnerable machines on the entire Internet within 15 minutes.

See also "Shortz."

watch [1]

A traditional unit of time defined as the time a sentry stands watch or a ship's crew is on duty. On both land and sea, one watch is usually equal to 4 hours.

At sea, the evening watch (16-20 hours, or 4-8 pm) is often divided into two shorter watches called "dog watches." When dog watches are in effect, sailors will have watch assignments that rotate through the day instead of falling at the same hours every day. Watches at sea are divided into 8 bells (4 bells for dog watches). The word *watch* is derived from an old English word *wæccan,* which means "stay awake."

watch [2]

Another name for a shift. This use is being popularized in the US by CNN Headline News and by the NBC television series *Third Watch.*

water column (WC)

A notation seen in pressure measurements.

See also *"inch of water"*, *"centimeter of water"*, *and "millimeter of water"*.

water horsepower (whp or Whp)

A unit of power used in the US primarily in rating pumps.

If a pump has a capacity of Q gallon per minute and develops a pressure ("head") of P feet of head, then its power rating is $QP/3956$ water horsepower. This calculation assumes the density of water to be 8-1/3 pounds per US gallon, which is approximately correct but not exact. As a result, the water horsepower equals 746.043 watts (550.253 foot pounds per second), slightly more than the ordinary mechanical horsepower.

See also *"horsepower"* and *"gallon."*

water inch

A traditional unit of water flow is supposed to equal the flow through a circular opening one inch in diameter, assuming the flow is caused only by gravity. However, this flow rate also depends on the pressure of the water above the opening. One estimate is 14 pints per minute or 2520 gallons per day (this is equivalent to 6.530 liters per minute); this estimate assumes the water level is constantly 1/12 inch (1 line) above the top of the opening Another is 500 cubic feet per day, which is much larger: 3740 gallons per day or about 9.832 liters per minute The latter estimate may depend on a mid-nineteenth century British engineering definition which required the hole to be centered 1 inch and 1 line below the water surface, placing the top of the opening 7/12 inch (7 lines) below the water level.

water measure

In England, *at least as early as the 15ᵗʰ – 19ᵗʰ century*, a system of capacity measures was used for goods sold from shipboard, separate from the ordinary system used on land. It survived longest as a measure for coal, still at around 5 pecks to the bushel (including the heap).

watt (W)

The SI unit of power. It is the power that gives rise to the production of energy at the rate of 1 joule per second. Volts times amperes equals watts.

1 Watt = 1 joule per second

Note: 1. The unit was formally called "absolute watt" (W_{abs}).

2. The **var** and the **voltampere** are units identical with the watt but used for special kinds of electrical power. The former definition of the thermal ampere made it equal to the watt

3. The watt is also the unit of heat flow rate and sound energy flux.

4. The unit was proposed for the first time by C.W.Siemens in 1882. It is named after the Scottish engineer James Watt (1736-1819). The difficulty of using the letter W in the French language held up its international recognition until 1889.

See *"var"* and *"voltampere"*.

watt equivalent

An informal unit of luminous flux

With the phaseout of the incandescent lamp in the United States and European Union in the early 21st century, manufacturers and sellers of more energy-efficient lamps have compared the visible light output of their lamps to commonly used incandescent lamp sizes with the *watt equivalent* or *watt incandescent replacement* (usually with a lowercase was a unit symbol, as opposed to capital W for the actual wattage). 1 watt incandescent replacement corresponds to 15 lumens. Thus, a 72-watt halogen lamp, a 23-watt compact fluorescent lamp and a 14-watt light-emitting diode lamp, all of which emit 1500 lumens of visible light, are all marketed as "100-watt incandescent replacement" (100w).

watt-hour (W h)

Unit for energy used with SI system. It is the energy expended when a power of one watt is available for one hour.

1 watt per hour = 3.6×10^3 joule

See "kilowatt-hour".

watt per cubic meter (W m^{-3})

SI unit of heat release rate.

watt per kelvin (W K^{-1})

SI unit of thermal conductance.

watt per kilogramme (W Kg^{-1})

SI unit of absorbed dose rate and kerrna rate.

watt per meter kelvin (W m^{-1} K^{-1})

SI unit of thermal conductivity.

watt per square meter (W m^{-1})

SI unit of density of heat flow rate.

watt per square meter kelvin (W m^{-2} K^{-1})

SI unit of coefficient of heat transfer.

watt per square meter kelvin to the fourth power (W m^{-2} K^{-4})

SI unit of Stefan-Boltzmann constant.

watt per steradian (W sr^{-1})

SI unit of radiant intensity.

watt per steradian square meter (W sr^{-1} m^{-2})

SI unit of radiance.

watt square meter (W m^{2})

SI unit of first radiation constant.

wave or wavelength

A unit of relative distance equal to the length of a wave: this could be a light wave, a radio wave, or even an ordinary water wave. In communications engineering, the length of an antenna is often stated in waves. In optics, the surfaces of lenses and mirrors are sometimes required to be polished to within a very small fraction of a wavelength of green light (546 nanometers).

wave number

CGS unit of reciprocal length, especially reciprocal wavelength. It is the number of wavelengths per centimeter.

Note: 1. The name wave number was adopted by the British Association in 1872 to replace reciprocal wavelength in spectroscopy.

2. The name was proposed by G.J. Stoney and IE. Reynolds in 1871.

See also *"kayser"*.

weber (Wb)

The SI unit of magnetic flux and fluxoid quantum. It is the magnetic flux that, linking a circuit of one turn, produces in it an electromotive force of one volt as it is reduced to zero at a uniform rate in one second.

Note: 1. The unit was formerly called *"absolute weber"* (Wb$_{abs}$) and must be distinguished from the international weber (Wb$_{int}$), formally abandoned in 1948.

2. The unit was first mentioned by name by C.W.Siemens in his presidential address to the British Association in 1882. It is named after W.E. Weber (1804-1891), one of the promoters of the absolute system of units.

3. The unit was approved by the British Association in 1895 and by the ICE in 1933. In 1948, the unit received recognition by the General Conference of Weights and Measures.

4. The weber, at one time, was used as the international unit of current; it was soon replaced by the international ampere.

weber (Wb) (pole strength)

CGSemu unit of magnetic pole strength equal to one dyne per oersted.

1 weber = 1 dyne per oersted.

Note: This unit has no SI equivalent because pole strength is not an SI quantity.

weber meter (Wb m)

SI unit of magnetic dipole moment

weber per meter (Wb m^{-1})

SI unit of magnetic vector potential.

week (mean calendar)

Unit of time equal to 7 days (mean solar)

1 week = 7 days = 604 800 seconds.

Note: 1. The custom of the seven-day week, with one day set aside for rest and religious observance, goes back more than 3000 years to the ancient civilizations of the Middle East. The seven days originally had an astrological significance; there is one day for each of the five visible planets and one each for the sun and the moon. Christians and Moslems inherited the seven-day cycle from the Jewish religion. The Romans picked up the idea from the Persians and were using the week as early as the first century. When the Emperor Constantine legalized Christianity in the Roman Empire, early in the fourth century CE, the Christian version of the week, with Sunday as the day of religious observance, became official throughout the Empire. Since none of the units of Roman date-keeping (the month, the quarter, and the year) equal a whole number of weeks, this made it necessary for the first time to have tables (we call them calendars!) showing the ever-changing relationship between the days of the week and the dates of the month.

2. There are different traditions as to which day of the week is the first. In the US, most calendars show Sunday as the first day of the week, but the International Organization for

Standardization (ISO) specifies that the week begins with Monday. There are also different ideas about how to number the weeks of the year, which is sometimes necessary for business purposes. The official solution to this question is that week 1 of the year is the week (beginning with Monday) that contains January 4. By this convention, week 1 of 2005 will be the week of January 4-10, 2005.

weisskope unit

A unit expressing the transition probability of nuclei from one state to another.

Note: The unit was first used by V.F. Weisskopf in 1951 and was given his name in 1958.

wet ton, dry ton

units used to measure sludge, slurries, compost, and similar mixtures in which solid material is soaked with or suspended in water. A wet ton is an ordinary ton [1] of the material in its natural, wet state; a dry ton is a larger quantity of the slurry, containing a ton of the solid material plus a variable amount of water.

See also *"ton [1]."*

wey

British units of mass equal 252 pounds (avoirdupois).

1 wey = 252 pound = 114.305 277 2 kilogrammeS.

Wheaton

Non-conventional unit that measures Twitter followers

The Wheaton is a measurement of Twitter followers relative to celebrity Wil Wheaton, equal to 500,000 followers.

The unit was invented by John Kovalic in the May 21, 2009, edition of his webcomic *Dork Tower*. The comic includes references to units named for other celebrities, such as Neil Gaiman, John Hodgman, Jonathan Coulton, and Felicia Day.

Whey

A unit of mass used for butter and cheese

Whey is a unit of weight for butter and cheese.

Whey (Essex) is exactly equal to 236 pounds (107 kg).

1 Whey (Essex) $\equiv$ 59/56 Barrel

1 Whey (Essex) ≡ 236 pounds

1 Whey (Essex) ≡ 107.04779932 kg

Wiffle

Informal unit of length in the "Humorous System of Units"

A wiffle also referred to as a WAM for Wiffle (ball) Assisted Measurement, is equal to a sphere 89 millimetres (3.5 inches) in diameter – the size of a Wiffle ball, a perforated, light-weight plastic ball frequently used by marine biologists as a size reference in photos to measure corals and other objects. The spherical shape makes it omnidirectional and perfect for taking speedy measurements, and the open design also allows it to avoid being crushed by water pressure. Wiffle balls are a much cheaper alternative to using two reference lasers, which often pass straight through gaps in thin corals.

A scientist on the research vessel EV *Nautilus* is credited with pioneering the technique.

Winchester measure

A system of volume measurement.

Winchester measure is a set of legal standards of volume instituted in the late 15th century (1495) by King Henry VII of England and in use, with some modifications, until the present day. It consists of the Winchester bushel and its dependent quantities, the peck, (dry) gallon and (dry) quart. They would later become known as the Winchester Standards, named because the examples were kept in the city of Winchester.

Winchester measure may also refer to:

- The systems of weights and measures used in the Kingdom of Wessex during the Anglo-Saxon period, later adopted as the national standards of England, as well as the physical standards (prototypes) associated with these systems of units
- a set of avoirdupois weight standards dating to the mid-14th century, in particular, the 56-pound standard commissioned by King Edward III, which served as the prototype for Queen Elizabeth I's reform of the avoirdupois weight system in 1588
- a type of glass bottle, usually amber, used in the drug and chemical industry, known variously as the Boston round, Winchester bottle, or Winchester quart bottle

Winchester quart

an informal British unit of volume used for certain chemicals shipped in cylindrical, narrow-necked bottles. A Winchester quart originally held 2 British Imperial quarts (about 2.273 liters); now, it generally holds exactly 2.5 liters. This unit is not related to the Winchester bushel, and the origin of its name is not known.

See also *"quarts."*

wind chill temperature index (WCTI)

A measurement of the combined cooling effect of low air temperature and wind on the human body. The index was first defined by the American Antarctic explorer Paul Siple in 1939. As originally used by US meteorologists, the wind chill index (WCI) was computed from the temperature T (in °F) and wind speed V (in mi/hr) using the formula:

$WCI = 0.0817(3.71 \text{ sqrt}(V) + 5.81 - 0.25V)(T-91.4) + 91.4$.

In 2001, US and Canadian meteorologists agreed on a revised definition of the wind chill temperature index (WCTI). The US version, with the temperature in °F and wind speed in miles per hour, is

$WCTI = 35.74 + 0.6215T - 35.75V^{0.16} + 0.4275T \, V^{0.16}$.

The Canadian formula, with temperatures in °C and wind speed in km/h, is

$WCTI = 13.12 + 0.6215T - 11.37V^{0.16} + 0.3965TV^{0.16}$.

wink

The base unit of time in a system of units called meter-gramme-wink.

1 wink = $(1/3000) \times 10^{-6}$ seconds.

Note: In this system of units, the unit of force is equal to 9×10^{13} newton and is called Samson. The unit of work is called Einstein and equal to 9×10^{13} joule.

wine gallon

A former English unit of volume equal to 231 cubic inches.

The wine gallon was adopted as the official gallon for liquid measurement in the United States, so now it is usually called the US liquid gallon.

wineglass

An informal unit of volume used in US bartending equal to 4 (U.S.) fluid ounces or about 118.3 milliliters. This unit is the same as the traditional gill.

See also *"gill"*.

wineglassful

A unit of volume used in British food recipes. The wineglass holds 2.5 (British imperial) fluid ounces, 5 tablespoonfuls, 1/2 gill, or about 71.0 milliliters. One wineglassful is equal to 0.60 US cups.

See also *"gill"* and *"cup."*

Wobbe number

The Wobbe number, or Wobbe index, is a description of a fuel gas (or mixture of gases) used in deciding whether that gas can be substituted for another in a particular burner. For example, can propane be used in a kitchen range made to burn natural gas? The Wobbe Index is sometimes called the Interchangeability Factor. Symbol, WN or WI.

The Wobbe number is named for the Italian engineer Goffredo Wobbe, who in *1926* published a paper defining a measure of fuel gas "quality" with the idea that fuels of the same quality would be interchangeable.

word [1]

A unit of information in typing. Typing speed is usually expressed in words per minute (wpm). For this purpose, a "word" is considered to be exactly 5 characters (spaces included). For example, a typing speed of 30 wpm is equivalent to 150 characters per minute or a keystroke rate of 2.5 hertz.

word [2]

A unit of information in computer science, often representing the amount of data processed by a computer in a single instruction. The size of a word varies with the computer system; it was usually 32 bits (4 bytes) or 64 bits (8 bytes) on mainframe computers but is usually 16 bits (2 bytes) in modern microprocessors. Sometimes, a **shortword** is 2 bytes, a **longword** (or **double word**) is 4 bytes (32 bits), and a **quadword** is 8 bytes.

See also *"bit"*, *"byte"*

working level (WL)

A unit of radiation exposure used for measuring exposure to radon gas in the US. One working level represents a concentration of short-lived radon decay products in one liter of air, resulting in the ultimate emission of 1.3×10^5 MeV or 20.8 nanojouls (nJ) of energy. Exposures are measured in working level months (WLM). Cumulative exposure of workers is measured in **working level months (WLM)**, representing exposure to one working level for 170 hours. In undergoing mining,

US law says miners must not be exposed to levels exceeding 1 WL and cumulative exposure must not exceed 4 WLM per year. In other industries, exposures are limited to 0.3 WL. In homes, the US Environmental Protection Agency recommends exposure levels not exceeding 4 pCi/L, or 0.04 WL.

workweek or work week [1]

A unit of time equal to the length of time a person "normally" works in a week. In many countries and in many industries, a specific number of hours, such as 35 or 40, constitutes a workweek either by law, by contract, or by custom, and workers who work more than that during a calendar week are entitled to be paid overtime wages.

workweek or work week [2]

A unit of time equal to the number of working or business days in a week (see above). During the nineteenth century, the workweek was usually 6 days but it is now 5 or 4 in most countries. Of course, individual workweeks are shorter if civil or religious holidays occur during the week.

wrench sixes

Fixed wrenches in the US are sized in fractions of an inch or in multiples of ¼ inch, while metric wrenches are sized in millimeters.

wyde

a unit of information in computer science equal to 2 bytes or 16 bites. This name for the "double-byte" was proposed by the American computer scientist Donald Knuth. It has achieved at least use, but it is not well-established.

See also *"bit" and "byte"*

X

× or x or X

The usual symbol for power is a unit of magnification. More generally, × or x is used with its mathematical meaning, "times," to indicate that a measurement is a multiple of some standard or reference measurement. For example, an image marked 200× is shown at 200 times the actual size (that is, distances are 200 times the actual size), and a 10x CD-ROM drive is one capable of transferring data 10 times faster than the "normal" or standard speed.

X-unit (X and also XU)

Arbitrary unit of length, particularly wavelength in X-ray spectra. The experimentally derived value was subsequently formalized by assigning the value 3 029.45 X to the spacmg of the (200) planes of calcite at 18 °C. This gives:

$1 \text{ X} = (1.002\ 02 \pm 0.000\ 03) \times 10^{-13}$ meters.

Note: The unit is also called the X-ray unit; alternatively, it is called the Siegbahn unit. It was abandoned in 1948 in favor of the angstrom, which was itself subsequently abandoned in favor of the nanometer.

See *"Siegbahn"* and *"angstrom"*.

Y

yard (yd)

Imperial unit of length.

1 yard = **0.914 4** meter.

Note: 1. The definition of the yard has been given legal enforcement in the UK in the Weights and Measures Act of 1963 and in the US in Document 59-5442 of the US Department of Commerce, National Bureau of Standards, 1959.

2. The UK yard was originally defined in the Weights and Measures Act of 1878 as follows: The straight line or distance between the centers of the two gold plugs or pins in the bronze bar by this Act declared to be the imperial standard for determining the imperial standard yard measured when the bar is at the temperature of sixty-two degrees of Fahrenheit's thermometer, and when it is supported on bronze rollers placed under it in such a manner as best to avoid flexure of the bar and to facilitate its free expansion and contraction from variations of temperature, shall be the legal standard measure of length, and shall be called the imperial standard yard, and shall be the only unit or standard measure of extension from which all other measures of extensions, whether linear, superficial or solid, shall be ascertained. In 1922, the UK yard, as defined by this Act, was compared experimentally with the meter; the result was:

1 UK yard = 36/39.370 147 meter = 0.914 398 41 meter.

In 1960, the bronze bar was found to be contracting at a rate of approximately 10^{-6} inches per annum.

3. The US yard was originally defined in the US law of 1866 and made definitive in the Mendenhall Order of 5 April 1893. Its size was given by:

1 US yard = 36/39.37 meter = 0.914 401 83 meter.

yard of ale

a traditional Scottish measure of volume. A yard of ale is roughly 2.5 pints (1.4 liters) served in a slender glass one yard tall.

See also "pint."

yard of land

Unit of area equal to 30 acres.

1 yard of land = 30 acres = 121.405 692 672 square meters

See *"acre"*.

yarım

Informal unit of land area.

In Ankara, Turkey, a unit of land area, about 516.753 square meters, = 4 şinik.

year (y or a)

Arbitrary unit of time. There are several types of years derived from the orbital movement of the Earth. The values for their lengths in days have been experimentally determined. The length of the different types of years are given in the following table.

Type of year	Days	D H M S	10^7 Second
Anomalistic	$365.259\ 641\ 34 + 3.04 \times 10^{-6}T$	365 06 13 53.012	3.155 843 301 2
Eclipse	$346.620\ 031 + 3.2 \times 10^{-5}T$	346 14 52 50.7	2.994 797 07
Gaussian	365.256 898	365 06 09 55.8	3.155 819 58
Gregorian	365.242 5	365 05 49 12	3.155 695 2
Julian	356.25	365 06	3.155 76
Sidereal	$365.256\ 365\ 56 + 1.1 \times 10^{-7}T$	365 06 09 09.984	3.155 814 998 4
Tropical	$365.242\ 198\ 781 - 6.14 \times 10^{-6}T$	365 05 48 45.9747	3.155 692 597 47
360°	365.255 189 7	365 06 07 28.39	3.155 804 839

Note: 1. All times are related to the ephemeris second. 1900 January 0 day is taken as reference.

2. The change in the length of the year is given in the column of the days. In this column, T is the number of Julian centuries after 1900 January 0 at 12 h ephemeris time.

3. The year was known to the Egyptians and Babylonians over five thousand years ago. Its approximate value of 365.25 days was taken. The Egyptians divided the year into 13 months, twelve of 30 days each and the length of the 13th month they used it to adjust the length of the year.

See also *"anomalistic year", eclipse year", "Gaussian year", "Gregorian year", "sidereal year", "tropical year", "360° year'* and also *"second ephemeris".*

yearhundred

An old and rarely used name for the century (100 years). This unit is the English counterpart of the word for a century in other Northern European languages such as German (*Jahrhundert*) and Swedish (*århundrade*).

yearthousand

An old and rarely used name for a millennium (1000 years).

yi

A unit of quantity in Chinese equal to 100 000 000. The yi is used with the wan (10 000) in expressing large numbers, one yi being the same as one wan wan (ten thousand ten-thousands).

yin

Informal unit of length in China

1 yin = 33⅓ meters.

Yocto- (y-)

A metric prefix denoting 10^{-24} (one septillionth) Adopted by the CGPM in 1990, the prefix is derived from the Latin *octo* and Greek *okto*, meaning 8 because this is the eighth prefix ($n = 8$ in 10^{-3n}) in the SI system of metric prefixes. The y was added arbitrarily to provide a non-confusing letter for abbreviations

yoke

Another name for a pair.

The yoke is used in describing teams of animals, especially oxen used to pull plows or wagons.

Yojana

A **yojana** is a measure of distance that was used in ancient India, Thailand and Myanmar. A yojana is about 12–15 km.

Yosemite Decimal System

A scale for rating the difficulty of outings ranging from day hikes to extreme mountaineering.

It was first devised by the Sierra Club in the *1930s* when it ran from 1 to 6, but today it runs from 1 to 5. The 5 category is the only one subdivided decimally, and it is open-ended: new numbers are added as climbers accomplish ever more difficult climbs. In principle, the rating of a climb is based on its most difficult portion, called the "crux."

1: Hiking on a clear, well-maintained trail. Could do it on a bike.

2: Hiking that requires route-finding skills through thick brush, over fallen trees or rough talus.

3: So rough you must use your hands to keep from falling.

4: Steep terrain, rope often required.

5: Technical climbing.

Yotta- (Y-)

A metric prefix denoting 10^{24} (one septillion). The prefix was coined to the parallel the prefix yocto-

yottameter (Ym)

A metric unit of distance equal to 10^{24} meters or 10^{21} kilometers. One yottameter equals 32.408 megaparsecs (Mpc) or 105.7 million light years. We out not to need longer distance units than this because the radius of the observable universe is not more than about 200 yottameters.

young

A proposed unit of luminous flux for the Y stimulus in the trichromatic color system.

yrneh

A unit of reluctance suggested by Vladimir Karapetoff[1] in *1911*, Henry spelled backwards (it is a reciprocal Henry). The term was not taken up.

Z

Z

A common symbol for Universal Time. This symbol is often used with a 4-digit statement of the time in hours and minutes; thus, 8:43 UT is written 0843 Z. The symbol is often pronounced "zulu," the name of the letter Z in the international radio alphabet.

z

The symbol for redshift, a unit of relative distance used in astronomy.

zak

A Dutch unit of volume is now interpreted as a metric unit equal to the hectoliter (100 liters). The hectoliter is equivalent to 26.417 U.S. gallons, 21.999 British imperial gallons, or 3.5315 cubic feet.

This is a metric version of the British sack.

See also *"sack"*

zentner (Ztr)

A traditional German unit of weight or mass, comparable to the traditional quintal and to the English hundredweight. Similar units were used in Scandinavia.

Originally the zentner was equal to 100 pfund, or German pounds. 100 pfund varied from 110 to as much as 120 pounds avoirdupois (49.9-54.4 kilogrammes), depending on the market. After the introduction of the metric system in Germany, the zentner was redefined to equal to exactly 50 kilogrammes, which is about 110.231 pounds. In English, the zentner is commonly spelled **centner**.

zepto- (z-)

A metric prefix denoting 10^{21} (one sextillionth).

Adopted by the CGPM in 1990, the prefix is derived from the Latin *septem*, meaning 7, because this is the seventh prefix ($n = 7$ in 10^{-3n}) in the SI system of metric prefixes. The *s* was replaced by a *z* to avoid confusion with the abbreviation for the second, which is an SI base unit.

zetta (z-)

A metric prefix denoting 10^{21} (one sextillion). The prefix was coined to parallel the prefix zepto.

zettameter (Zm)

A metric unit of distance equal to 10^{21} meters or 10^{18} kilometers. One zettameter equals about 32.408 kiloparsecs (kpc) or 105 702 light years. This is a little more than the diameter of the Milky Way galaxy in which we live.

zhubov scale

A scale for reporting ice coverage of polar seas.

See also *"ball"*.

zoll

The traditional German inch equal to 1/12 fuss.

Originally, the zoll was equal to 1.037 inches (about 2.634 centimeters).

In Switzerland, it is now considered a metric unit equal to exactly 3 centimeters (1.1811 inches).

There's no change in the plural.

Zolotnik

A **zolotnik** was a small Russian unit of weight, equal to 0.1505 avoirdupois ounces, or 4.2658 grams (about 65.83 grains). Used from the 10th to 20th centuries, its name is derived from the Russian word *zoloto*, meaning gold. As a unit, the zolotnik was the standard for silver manufacture, much as the troy ounce is currently used for gold and other precious metals.

This unit was originally based on a coin of the same name. The zolotnik circulated in the Kievan Rus until the 11th century; it was equal in weight to the Byzantine Empire's solidus.

See also "gram", and "ounce."

zuzu

Ancient Babylonian unit of mass, about 4.09 grams.

www.ingramcontent.com/pod-product-compliance
Lightning Source LLC
Chambersburg PA
CBHW081105300726
48976CB00010B/2659